PRESENTED GRATIS, WITH No. 246, OF

"LLOYD'S PENNY SUNDAY TIMES."

LONDON :

PUBLISHED BY E. LLOYD, AT THE OFFICE OF "LLOYD'S WEEKLY
LONDON NEWSPAPER," 12, SALISBURY-SQUARE, FLEET-STREET.

DON CÆSAR DE BAZAN.

A Romance of Spain.

BY THE AUTHOR OF "THE BLACK MANTLE," "MABEL," "ADA, THE BETRAYED," "JANE SHORE,'
ETC. ETC. ETC.

BY

MALCOLM J. ERRYM.

The soul of honour, yet so full of strangest fancies,
The world and he could not get on together,
Till love of gentle woman charmed him from his wayward spirit.

SHAKSPERE.

LONDON:

PUBLISHED BY E. LLOYD, AT THE OFFICE OF "LLOYD'S WEEKLY LONDON NEWS-
PAPER," 12, SALISBURY-SQUARE, FLEET-STREET.

1845.

PREFACE.

THE great popularity of the drama of DON CÆSAR DE BAZAN induced the Publisher to consider that the novel would not be unacceptable to the public. In a novel, a vast variety of details and nicer shades of character can be set before the reader, which the stage has neither time nor capability of doing. There the more prominent scenes only can be seized and presented to an audience, who must, for themselves, fill up any hiatus, and imagine a connexion frequently between events which, in the more discursive pages of a volume, can be fully entered into, and minutely explained with due reference to the plot.

That the Publisher, in presenting this work to the public, has exercised a sound discretion, and not miscalculated, has been abundantly proved by the result, which has shown itself in the shape of a very heavy demand, indeed, for the work—so heavy, that the Author is here requested to apologise for some disappointments which unavoidably occurred in the execution of some orders.

If the surest indication of merit be success, the Author of DON CÆSAR DE BAZAN may hope that he has succeeded in catching and fully carrying out the spirit of the character; for, although the main features of the plot are the same as those which gave so much life and animation to the drama on the stage, the readers of this work will not have failed to perceive what a large amount of careful filling was required to make that very sketchy production into the shape and consistency of a romance.

The Author of Don Cæsar de Bazan has been, during the progress of that work, at such intervals as his various literary labours permitted him, actively engaged upon an English Romance of Modern Life, which will be immediately published by Mr. Lloyd, and which he hopes to find has merited and received the kindest consideration of his numerous readers.

With most grateful thanks for the many highly flattering press notices this work has received, as well as for private commendation of a character most gratifying to him, the Author takes his leave of the noble, chivalric Don Cæsar de Bazan, and hopes, to use an old Spanish proverb, that not *literally*, but *"literaturally,"* he may "live a thousand years."

London, July, 1845.

DON CÆSAR DE BAZAN.

A Romance of Spain.

BY THE AUTHOR OF "ADA, THE BETRAYED;" "JANE BRIGHTWELL;" "GRACE RIVERS;" "LOVE," &c.

A soul of honour, yet so full of strangest fancies,
The world and he could not get on together.—SHAKSPERE.

CHAPTER I.

THE CARNIVAL AT MADRID.—THE BROTHER AND
SISTER. — THE MYSTERIOUS STRANGER. — THE
ASSASSIN.

IT is carnival time, and what city so joyous as
Madrid? Where is now the sombre seriousness of the
Spaniard?—wreathed in smiles, where all his suspicions?—dissipated by the laughter-loving throng that
haunt street, square, and walk. The habitually merry
are mad with joyous excitement—the serious laugh—
even the sternest gravity relaxes into smiles, while it
shakes its head in apparent disapprobation of the masquerading frivolity of the gay carnival. Laughter,
music, jests, songs, shrieks of merriment, dances—all
conspire to give the streets of Madrid an appearance
of wild, rollicking, roaring hilarity—which, were a

stranger, who knew not the occasion, suddenly to see,
would induce in him a belief that the whole population had gone mad, and were indulging in a wild
saturnalia of insanity. The streets are thronged till
one wonders where the hosts of people have come
from, and it would almost seem not a very outrageous
belief that all the merry, droll spirits of Madrid hid
themselves during the dull interval between one carnival and another, and then rushed out full of such
wild glee that they knew not how to contain themselves. Then, again, the climate is so favourable to
such an out-of-door fete. The bright glorious sunshine
beams down upon the city and its inhabitants with
such resplendant beauty—scarcely the slightest cloud
for one brief moment dims the lustre of the brightest
of skies. There is in the very air a delicious feeling
of hilarity—a lightness—a buoyancy of elasticity; and
more especially at the carnival time, when surely some
of the well-known laughing gas must be mingled with
the air of Madrid, just then, in sufficient quantities to
give a fillip to the spirits of its inhabitants and a madness to their mirth.

All the restraints of society appear to be forgotten—
the marked difference of rank, so zealously maintained usually in Spain, vanishes. Their depressing
religion, which, although one of shew exteriorly, is one
of gloom and tyranny within—their habitual reserve of
character—all is changed, as if by the touch of some
enchanter's wand. The carnival has come, and the
grave Spaniard becomes a Merry Andrew! The
street are thronged from an early hour—for Spaniards
are not late risers—for a good reason, too, inasmuch as
young and old, rich and poor, enjoy a sleep, or *siesta*,
during the mid-day heat, for some hours. It is, there-

fore, from early morning till about half an hour before noon, that the streets have an appearance about them of bustle. Then the noise, the clatter, and excitement gradually subside, until, by one o'clock, the city is as quiet as some place in which the inhabitants had all been swept off by dire pestilence. This state of repose lasts till the sun begins to dip down towards the west, and there are grateful shadows cast from the tall houses over the streets, and squares, and gardens. Then Madrid awakes—throngs of persons stream along the streets,—and all is life, bustle, excitement, and activity.

It is carnival time. The sun has passed its meridian more than two hours—the fiercest mid-day has subsided. The *siesta* is over, and young and old have hastened out from their dwellings to make merry. And what a sparkling, picturesque-looking crowd throngs the city—what gay costumes of all climes and all nations, interspersed with grotesque buffoonery, that the most reserved mind cannot choose but unbend a little, and enjoy at the carnival time a laugh. The twang of hundreds of musical instruments fills the air; sometimes a hundred voices will join in the same popular chorus—sometimes a throng will gather round some well-known minstrel, and, after hearing his song, disperse to gather food for fun and hilarity in some other quarter. Not only to the middle and lower classes of Madrid is this wild riot of the carnival confined; the license to mingle in the motley throng, masked, induces many of the wealthy and noble to embrace the opportunity of being a little natural and enjoy themselves.

Then the windows, too, are crowded with spectators. Every balcony has it burthen, and thousands of flashing eyes from beautiful faces look with delight upon the scene below; while such musical laughter rings upon the ear, that no arranged melody is necessary to make the sunny air full of song. Yes; it is the carnival time! and love, joy, mirth, and gladness abound. Practical jokes are abundant; but none are taken but in good humour. From the balconies the maskers below are pelted with all sorts of harmless matters— sugar plums being one of the most ordinary missiles. Lovers in masks linger beneath the balconies of the fair ones who hold their hearts enchained—now and then there may be a fierce glow, as the jealous eye detects, even beneath all disguise, a rival. The merry, happy crowd would soon teach any troublesome spirits that the season of hilarity was not to be marred by them.

Toil is a thing unthought of during that joyous period: universal hilarity reigns throughout the entire city—all the sternness of rule is laid aside—and the poorest, the meanest heart in Madrid, at that time, rejoices, and lays up stores of grateful pleasant remembrances of the happy, mirth-moving carnival of one year, to last it till time shall bring round that of another.

There are some parts of the city which, from their size and the manner in which they are shaded by tall, beautiful trees, are more especially frequented by the merry revellers. The gardens adjoining the palace are thrown open to the people, and there the carnival maskers congregate in dense masses. Dances are got up, and pursued with reckless hilarity—groups form themselves round itinerant musicians—shouting, laughing, swearing, huzzaing: such a scene of wild delight never could take place in any country but one in which there is usually much restraint. The population of Madrid resemble boisterous children, on the occasion of their carnival, just let loose from school.

The soft, delicious climate, as we have remarked, affords every facility for out-door amusements, as well as permitting of a gay and gorgeous taste in clothing, which more northern regions, from the necessity of guarding against the fluctuations of the weather, cannot pretend to. Such a gaily-apparelled mass of human beings scarcely any other capital could hope to produce.

But it is when the first dim shade of the coming night steals over the city, that the very essence of the carnival of Madrid may be said to shew itself. Then thousands of maskers, who shrink from the boisterous revelry in broad daylight, issue forth into the streets to enjoy for some hours the scene of wild excitement, and to contribute their ample share to the general gala, by their splendid costumes and munificence—for these persons are among the wealthy, and large sums are given away at the carnival, if it be but for the pleasure of seeing a scramble among the motley crowd for the money. Then, too, the sweet cool air which gently fans the heated houses of Madrid, at evening time, comes over the spirits of the multitude with an exhilarating effect. Those dance now who never dance at any other time, and the whole capital is until midnight one scene of uproarious festivity. The temperate habits of the people prevent any excesses, such as would take place in our own country, if such unbridled license were given to all classes. Iced lemonade, sherbet, coffee, and thin wines of an acid flavour, are almost the only drinks. True, there are some who cannot in any country, or under any circumstances, be both merry and wise—so, during the carnival at Madrid, there will be a shout and a roar of laughter occasionally, after some rollicking dare-devil spirit, who had sacrificed too fully at the shrine of Bacchus, and staggers through the crowd in all the bewilderment of incipient intoxication—a butt for all sorts of witticisms and practical jokes; and it is well if the unlucky drunkard escapes with his clothes on his back from the hands of the amused multitude.

Such an one appeared to have afforded food for the minds of the carnival maskers, just as the golden rays of the sun were beginning to fade a little in their grandeur and glory, for there was a loud and uproarious shout of derision, as a tall man, attired in the faded garb of a once gay and sparkling gallant, crossed one of the principal squares, and dived into a wine-shop to escape his tormentors.

Two men in masks and cloaks appeared to take a more than particular notice of the intoxicated, faded looking gallant we have mentioned, and they pointed after him, as they conversed together, with significant gestures.

" Indeed!" said one to the other. " Do you not recognise?"

" On my faith, no! I cannot say that my acquaintance extends quite to so low a grade as a drunken idle, with as ragged a suit upon his back as one could well imagine to hold together at all."

The last speaker was a stout robust man. He was plainly attired; but the fashion of his garments was of the first quality; and, although he was masked, his general air and manner sufficiently proclaimed him as one of those haughty grandees, who had stolen out, now that the sunset was near at hand, to become a spectator of the carnival sports,—perchance to pick up materials for political speculations, from any stray expressions which might fall from the lips of the people.

His companion, from the deference he shewed to him, and from the manner in which he calmly put up with the sneering, insulting tone in which he was answered, seemed one of those mean sycophantic spirits, who prowl after great men, satisfied with anything but neglect.

They both stood apart under the portico of the church of our Lady of Loretto, so that, although they were themselves rather enveloped in the gloom cast by the shadows of the massive building, they had a clear view of the merry revellers in the open space in front of the sacred edifice, the contiguity of which in Madrid by no means puts any bounds to popular amusements. The priesthood of catholic countries, unlike the evangelical gentry of our own, think it good policy to amuse the people.

For a few moments there was silence between those two men, until they gazed after the swaggering figure of him who had become, from his dress and the state of inebriety he was in, such tempting food for the merriment of the people.

"And yet, although your lordship knows him not now," said the sycophantic speaker, "his name was once familiar to you, as it is now to all Madrid."

"Who is he?" was the careless question.

"The celebrated, and once wealthy, witty, and gallant, Don Cæsar de Bazan, Count of Orfilla, a Chevalier of the Holy Order of Jerusalem, and Heaven only knows what beside."

"Don Cæsar de Bazan! Oh, I remember. Has he come so low?"

"Ay, and lower; for now and then you may see him in a kennel. Yet does he keep about him a strange pride, which is sadly ludicrous and at variance with the fallen state of his fortunes. He has squandered all his estate; he is dreadfully in debt. He drinks continually, he says, to drown his cares: and yet he is jealous of what he calls his honour—as if a man, worth nothing, could be honourable. It is only for such as yourself, Don Jose ——"

"Hush! I do not wish my name mentioned even in a whisper in the streets of Madrid. Be more careful, Don Moress.—What were you about to say?"

"It may seem that I was about to congratulate myself upon having the distinguished honour of such a patron as your illustrious self; but such was not my thought, when I was about to add that it was only for such as yourself, if there could ever be such another, to talk of honour! You, who have the very soul of the king in your keeping, and who have fascinated her, towards whose beauty your heart leaps high with hope ——"

"Hush, hush! That I have hopes, I may not deny; but steep and difficult still is the path to my high ambition. Be secret and discreet, and be assured that you shall climb with me to power and consequence. Already, as the minister and favourite of the king, I stand upon a dizzy height; but I must be more!—The queen is beautiful."

"An angel!"

"Hush, hush! Have you properly instructed the assassins I required you to procure me?"

"I have. And the Marquis de Tranguera will assuredly to-night expiate the folly of attempting to cross your path, by his life. Moreover, I have no doubt but the carnival crowd will get hold of the bravos, and probably take their lives, for the people hold it as a heavy crime indeed for any brawling of so serious a character to take place in the streets at such a time. Then ——"

"Enough—enough!"

At this moment, there was an unusual stir and pressure among the people, who were diverting themselves in the immediate vicinity of the church. Hundreds of persons made their way on to the marble steps, and loud cries "Viva! viva!" accompanied by the clapping of hands, appeared to announce the recognition of some popular favourite. In a space, which was soon cleared for her reception, stood a young girl, attired in the fanciful toilet of a street dancer. In her hand she carried a guitar, and loud cries of "The gitano—the gitano!" from the multitude, would appear to stamp her as a well-known member of that strange and mysterious race of people who make temporary homes in any country and clime.

A second glance at her fair features and delicate complexion would be amply sufficient to convince any one that she was by no means a member of that fraternity, although probably her companionship at times with them, and an adoption to some extent of their costume, had caused her popularly to be considered as one of the race of them.

That she was a general and especial favourite with the people might easily be perceived, for numberless friendly greetings were addressed to her, and several small coins were thrown at her feet, which she picked up and acknowledged by smiles, while she struck occasionally a few wandering but melodious notes on her guitar.

The age of this young girl did not appear to be above seventeen, or eighteen at the utmost. She was very beautiful; and, from her commanding stature, there was an air of dignity mingled with the sweet simplicity of her face, which gained her the involuntary respect of all who saw her, at the same time that they gazed with unalloyed admiration at her sparkling eyes and beautifully expressive features. She had been but a very short time in Madrid, and her beauty, her skill on the guitar, as well as her unrivalled dancing, had gained her a reputation, which promised her a golden harvest. Whenever she appeared she was welcomed warmly, and those who spoke to her were wonderfully charmed with her gentleness and amiable discourse. Truly, she was the idol of the people of Madrid, and the festivities of the carnival would have gone off languidly, without the soul-inspiring presence of the lovely and gifted Maritana.

There was a mystery, too, about her birth, and who she was, which greatly tended to raise the interest felt in her. Moreover, she gave, of the surplus alms which were bestowed upon her, much to the poor, who had not her charms to move the compassion of the wealthy. No wonder, then, that she was so great a favourite;—and, when she now appeared, looking, as all thought, more radiantly beautiful than ever, with a gay carnival costume, she made more sensation, and received far more grateful homage than would Charles the Second, the then gloomy, morose, and greatly-feared king of Spain, whose prime minister and great favourite was the wily and rascally Don Jose, who now stood with his confidant beneath the church portico, most rudely hustled by the rabble, as Maritana made her appearance.

By the space which was in a few moments cleared round her, it would seem that the populace took it for granted she would favour them with one of her exquisitely beautiful dances, and they were not disappointed, for, slinging the guitar round her shoulders by the ribbon to which it hung, she executed a *pas seul* with such grace, firmness, decision, and beautiful poetry of movement, that when she had finished, and glanced around her with the soft, bewitching smile she knew so well how to assume—and yet it could hardly be called an assumption, for it came fresh from her heart—the applause was clamorous and general, and numerous bouquets of flowers and coins were thrown towards her.

Some young cavaliers, too, came forward to bestow their alms more freely, in order to exchange a word and a smile with the lovely Maritana, which to them was an ample reward for enduring the half-serious, half-playful shout of the multitude at them. There was an old man, too, who hobbled from the throng to look in the sweet eyes of the dancer, and the people patted him on the back, and laughed and shouted again, when they saw him draw forth a purse, and expected to see a pistole at least handed to Maritana, who stood with such a wicked, playful, sunny smile, waiting for the old man's trembling largess, that she made a conquest of every heart.

"Eugh, eugh!" coughed the old man. "There, my dear; I never give anything to anybody; but you—eugh, eugh!—are an angel—eugh!—quite an angel! There, there; don't be extravagant. There, there, there!"

He placed in her hand a coin, and, with a ringing laugh, she held it up, exclaiming,—

"A maravedie—a maravedie!" [A small copper coin, of about the value of two-thirds of a farthing.]

A shout from the multitude testified to their derisive appreciation of the munificence of the old man, who looked about him in mute astonishment, for he really fancied himself quite a liberal-minded man.

"Why, you old sinner!" cried a young, dare-devil looking, handsome fellow, stepping forward. "So you think a glance from the bright eyes of Maritana is to be paid for with a maravedie? Oh, you generous old rogue! I shouldn't wonder now if some day you were to find yourself on fire with your over generosity!—Ha! ha! ha!"

The lad, it would appear, had not ventured upon such a prophecy without good cause for knowing that it was about to occur—for, before the words "What do you mean by that, Lazarillo?" could come well from the lips of the beautiful Maritana, a small cracker or squib, in common use at the carnival, called cavelleros, which had no doubt been tied to the old man's short cloak, began spluttering and exploding behind him, to the great amusement of the bystanders.

"These rogues enjoy themselves," said Don Jose, in a whisper, to his companion.

"Ay, truly said. And yon boy—I have seen him before—is bold and forward; witty and intelligent beyond his years!"

"And the dancer—although she is no gitano—is most beautiful. By our Lady, I never saw her equal! If, now ——"

"Eh, signior?"

"Nothing—nothing."

"How are you, Maritana?" cried the boy, whose name was Lazarillo; "I have been hunting for you all over the city. Why, you never dance now before our door, Maritana; how is that? It was so cheerful and so delightful to hear you of an evening."

"Oh, Lazarillo, your master, the old armourer, told me I turned your head, and he could get no work done by you, on my account; so, out of good nature to you, Lazarillo, I avoid the street."

"Now, confound my old master, the armourer! I have often thought of running away from him for no excuse at all, but now I have a good one. Maritana, I will come with you."

"With me?"

"Yes; and I will keep the crowd off you, and pick up for you the quartils, rials, dollars, and pistoles that are showered upon you."

"And the maravedies?"

"Ay, and the maravedies; though I suspect you get but few of such churl's coin, beautiful Maritana."

"Ah, now, Lazarillo, you have settled all my doubts; you shall not go with me."

"Not go! because I called you beautiful! Why, why, Maritana, all the city calls you beautiful."

"But I don't take all the city with me as a consequence, Lazarillo; so, once for all, you must stay with your old master, and look after the arms of the guard that I always see you scrubbing at in his shop."

"The arms of the guard, indeed! They are fine soldiers, and send their muskets and swords to the armourers every day to be cleaned. But now I swear—yes, I swear——"

"No, don't, Lazarillo."

"Yes, I will, that from this day none of their arms shall be cleaned by me; I will turn a vagabond, a complete——"

"Little ——" added Maritana.

"Vagabond," continued the boy; "and for once his majesty's guard, when their arms are sent for, shall find them as they sent them, untouched. I won't be an armourer's boy any longer. I don't know what I'll do exactly; but I'll run away, and then think, and if you won't let me follow you ——"

"Which I assuredly will not."

"Then I will—I don't know what."

"A song—a song, Maritana," cried the people, "a song—a song."

"There, you hear," said Maritana. "Now, get out of my way, will you? I must sing to my best patrons after all—the people, for they are always kind to me. Go to your work, Lazarillo; do go to your work."

"If I do ——"

"A song—a song—a song."

The boy was hustled away, and Maritana found herself now so strenuously called upon, that she brought forward her guitar from across her shoulders, and, striking a lively prelude, she at once reduced the dense multitude around her to silence, after which, in a rich, sweet, natural voice, she sang a melody then very popular at Madrid.

"The sunlight is breaking,
    Madrid is awaking,
        Joy sparkles in lovers' eyes;
    The day god is coming,
    Guitar strings are humming,
        And sweetly the night blossom dies.
            Tirala—tirala—ti—rala.

"O'er forest, o'er river,
    And the dear Guadalquiver,
        The light of the morn cometh clear;
    Young hearts are beating,
    Shy lovers retreating,
        'Tis carnival time of the year.
            Tirala—tirala—ti—rala."

The melody was exquisite, and trifling as was the song, yet coming as it did from the lips of Maritana in such soul-enchanting accents, it pleased all hearts, and such bravos rent the air when she had finished as might well have added to the generally amply sufficient pride of every proud *prima donna* in the world. She curtseyed gracefully, and then slinging the guitar again over her shoulders, she was about to leave, when a young man pressed forward, saying,—

"Oh! gitano, tell my fortune for a rial."

"Tell him he's a fool, and take the rial," whispered Lazarillo.

But Maritana, perhaps, had a fortune-telling reputation to lose, so she shook her head at Lazarillo, and taking the young man's hand in her's, she attentively examined the palm, saying,—

"Your name is Pedrone. You love a young wife. You have an uncle."

"That's me," said the old man, who had given the maravedie, pressing forward.

"I know it. And you have a young wife."

"Eh?"

"'Tis a tale for yourselves."

The crowd laughed uproariously; and while the old man took his nephew by the arm to ask him what the gitano could possibly mean, she was preparing to depart, and had waved an adieu to the armourer's boy, when Don Jose, more closely enveloped in his cloak than he had been before, advanced and intercepted her progress, saying,—

"You tell fortunes, my pretty wench, do you."

"Sometimes," she replied, as if she did not very well like her customer.

"And so do I," he added, as he seized her hand. "You are born to greatness, and before seven days have elapsed you will find yourself in a situation of envy."

Before she could make any reply to him, he had mingled among the motley group of carnival merry-makers who were around, and disappeared. For an instant she lingered, as if the words of the stranger had made really some impression on her. Then she laughed at the folly of paying any attention to them, and tripped lightly away, to carry her charms and fascinations to some of the other crowded parts of the city.

A man, richly apparelled, at this moment ascended the steps of the church, as if to obtain a good view of the people in their showy costumes. There was upon his face, which was not masked, an expression of great good humour, and although his attire and general appearance bespoke the man of rank, yet the *bonhommie* of his face showed that he had none, if any, of the prejudices of his station.

He had not been there a minute, and was laughing at the strange antics of a buffoon, when two men stole softly behind him, and before any one could guess their murderous intentions, they had buried two poniards up to the hilt in his back.

With a faint scream he turned upon the assassins; but his strength failed him, and he fell backwards down the marble steps among the crowd below, while the cowardly, dastardly assassins fled immediately into the church, where they claimed sanctuary.

CHAPTER II.

DON CÆSAR AND HIS TORMENTORS. — THE ARMOURER'S BOY'S INDISCRETION.—THE MINISTER AND HIS OLD ACQUAINTANCE.

SUCH an assassination as that which had just taken place upon the steps of the church of our Lady of Loretto, if it had occurred at any other than the carnival time, would scarcely have excited the indignation it then did among the populace, thousands of whom may be said to have witnessed the deed. Unhappily in Spain the dagger of the hired bravo was too familiar a weapon, especially in the conduction of court intrigues, to excite any violent degree of wonder; for, from the monarch downwards, it became a favourite, because an easy mode of getting rid of obnoxious persons.

Hence the sight in the streets of Madrid of a murdered body was by no means a very rare occurrence; but at the carnival time, when all sorts of business was suspended, they saw no reason why that of assassination should be tolerated and allowed to go on. Accordingly, a yell from the multitude announced its disapprobation of the act, and for some minutes all the pleasurable sounds of the carnival were suspended, while a rush was made to the steps of the church to raise the wounded man.

He was quite dead, and they laid him down again against one of the massive pillars, while loud shouts and angry execrations burst from many mouths on account of the atrocious deed.

"Drag them out of the church," cried Lazarillo, the armourer's boy—"drag them out, and give them a taste of carnival law."

A rush was made towards the door of the sacred edifice; but the foremost among its invaders was met by a monk, who said nothing, but holding up a small ebony cross, he stood in the way of that immense throng, which fell back as if it had been opposed by a thousand armed men. Those who were in the front took off their caps and fell on their knees, while from the interior of the church came the deep, solemn tones of the priests chanting mass. A rapt stillness pervaded the multitude, and the old monk said, solemnly,

"Sanctuary!"

The people crept down the steps in awe and fear; they, as if by one accord, moved away from before the sacred edifice, which exercised so slavish a fear over their minds as to contravene the laws of inevitable justice, and the tone of their carnival hilarity scarcely recovered itself for many minutes. But then again the din and the pleasant uproar commenced. The laugh, the dance, the song, and the murdered man and his murderers were alike forgotten.

It was well, too, for Lazarillo that he was not seen by any ecclesiastic to have spoken the words which for a moment had induced the multitude to forget themselves so far as to invade the sanctuary of the church, as, if he had, the consequences would have been most fatal to him; but luckily he escaped; and now, with all the thoughtless elasticity of youth, he was the gayest among the gay, singing, dancing, laughing, and leaving his old master to look after the work himself, and the arms of the royal guard to remain unclean, for all he cared, till the day of judgment.

It would seem, however, that the very spirit of the carnival maskers was under some restraint now in the immediate neighbourhood of the church, for the great mass of them moved off to a neighbouring square, and as they did so, they made such a bustle, that from out the wine shop in which he had taken refuge, and no doubt found much comfort in the discussion of divers deep potations, came the ragged, faded-looking, but still handsome gallant who had been named by the confidant of Don Jose the minister, as Don Cæsar de Bazan, the most dissolute nobleman of Spain, and one of the most reckless, dare-devil characters that the whole country could produce. He was, as we have said, of a good stature, and he bore about him all the traces of having been a man of the most prepossessing appearance; indeed still, despite all the disadvantages of a most unhappy wardrobe, he looked something of the gentleman. There was a grand air and carriage about him which dignified his rags—for rags they were, literally, in which he was attired. His age might have been about seven or eight-and-thirty, and dissipation alone had succeeded in leaving any traces of wear and tear upon his face and figure.

The clothing he had on was worse far than poor or mean apparel, for, alas! it was faded, dilapidated finery. The gold and silver embroidery was black; the lace hung in threads, and the once magnificent cloak would have puzzled a conjuror to tell how to get it on, or, once on, how to get it off. Indeed, how Don Cæsar managed ever to get into or out of his strange apparel was a miracle and a mystery. His cap, once possessed of a nodding, graceful plume, now only boasted of a long draggled-looking feather, which looked as if it had made acquaintance at different times with all the kennels of Madrid. His moustache had grown out of all reasonable bounds. On one boot he had a spur, on the other foot a shoe down at the heel.

But Don Cæsar de Bazan was a gentleman and a Spanish nobleman, so he wore a sword, which he would not have parted with except with his life, and he knew how to use it, too, although it was in want of a scabbard, and the naked blade stuck very oddly through a hole in his tattered cloak, giving anybody who came too near to him the chance of a very ugly poke indeed.

Nobody very well liked to quarrel with him, for there was a something dangerous in his wrath. As for the commonalty generally, they adored him, because he was a nobleman who condescended to come among them, drink with them, laugh and joke with them, and on many occasions he had shown so much courage in defending them from oppression, that no wonder he was a general favourite, although now at the carnival time human nature could not forbear making a jest of him. Besides, he had taken an enemy into his mouth to steal his brains; not that Don Cæsar was absolutely so drunk as not to know what he was about, but he had had enough wine to feel amazingly comfortable, and very ready for anything in the shape of an adventure which might present itself to him.

He, therefore, upon hearing the tumult outside the wine shop, and the rush of people, sallied out, and leaning against the door-post, he demanded to know what was amiss.

"A poor devil," cried Lazarillo, who chanced to be passing at the moment, "has had a couple of stilettos put into his back on the church steps."

"Ha! An assassination! Hang me now if I haven't seen two ill-looking chaps about this afternoon; and, by Jove! there they are."

"Nay, Don Cæsar, that is not them. The rascals have taken sanctuary."

"Say you so? Arrant knaves, no doubt."

"Ay, truly. One of them had a ragged cloak, such a ragged cloak!"

"Oh!"

"And such a naked sword, rusty and old, poking through a hole in it; and such a feather! His moustache, too, had not been trimmed for a week. In short, he just looked like such a care-for-nought, odd-fish as—as—as —— "

"As who, boy?"

"Don Cæsar de Bazan."

"Now, by the mass! —— "

The boy was out of his way, with a shrill laugh, before the incensed Don Cæsar could lay hold of him; but he pursued him, nevertheless, although the chase did not last long, for the sword getting between his legs, threw him down, and when he rose, by the assistance of some one, he found it to be one of the ill-looking men in cloaks whom he had pointed out to Lazarillo. In fact, it was no other than Don Jose, who, for reasons of his own, wished to have some conversation with the once gay and wealthy Don Cæsar, who was now in such a decayed state of fortune in consequence of his numerous extravagancies.

The state of Don Cæsar's mental faculties prevented him, for some moments, from getting anything like a distinct view of the features of the man who had helped him to rise, and even when he did, he was not at all clear-headed enough to recognise him, although they had, in point of fact, been old acquaintances, at a time when Don Jose was not the courtly favourite he now was, and fortune wore a very different aspect to Don Cæsar than it now did.

"Well, Don Cæsar," said Jose, "do you not know me?"

The dissipated nobleman stood as upright as he could, and strove to call to mind who his questioner was, for the sound of his voice was familiar, and there was a something, too, about his countenance, which came across his memory with a dim recollection of having known him somewhere.

"Do you not know me, Don Cæsar?" repeated Don Jose.

"I cannot say I do," was the reply. "I suppose I owe you something?"

"Indeed! What makes you imagine that?"

"Simply because you claim my acquaintance. Are you a tailor or embroiderer? Do you vend ruffles and collars, or follow you the more noble calling of an armourer? By the mass! in my time I have employed scores of such fellows."

"You are wrong," said Don Jose. "I am a gentleman, and knew you when you were in better trim than you are now."

"Then you are a most extraordinary fellow, for the very last person I should have expected to accost me me in the streets of Madrid, is any one who knew me

when I was in better trim. Why, man, I have a malignant fever on me."

Don Jose started back a pace or two, as he exclaimed,—

"Indeed! Good God! why did you not say so before?"

"Because I thought it was so well known that no old friend would come near me. The malignant disorder I smart under is poverty, and if that is not enough in this world to warn off all acquaintances, I don't know what is. My good sir, whoever you are, you may go to the devil. 'Tis true, I am Don Cæsar de Bazan, Count of Orfilla; but fortune has played me some scurvy tricks, and reduced my possessions to a tattered cloak and a scabbardless sword. Now you not only know me, but you know what I am now. My good sir, take pattern by others, and get out of my way when you see me coming. I have now no splendid mansions in which to welcome splendidly splendid guests. My liveried lackies are all gone. My gold and silver plate has all found its way to the jeweller's from whence it came. My costly furniture, my pictures, my rare works of art of every description, my horses, my equipages, have all vanished. Ha! ha! They left me my sword, because it was an awkward job to take it away from me, I suppose. There is not a poorer devil in Madrid than I, and yet am I, as you say, Don Cæsar de Bazan; and who cares? I don't weep for my own fallen fortunes, so I cannot well complain that the world laughs with me as well as at me. Now you know all about it, my good sir, so go your way and moralize, if you will."

"What you say," replied Don Jose, "brings clearly back to my mind some occasions on which you entertained the grandees of Spain most royally in your mansion. But still I can scarcely imagine any kind of circumstances that could have so far diminished your once splendid fortune, as to leave you in such a condition as you are now in."

"Diminished, did you say? By St. Jago! I wish my once splendid fortune was only diminished. It has disappeared altogether; and as for your not being able to imagine how it came about, I can only pity your lack of fancy, and bid you a fair morning. Talking makes me thirsty. Adieu, sir, adieu."

"But, Don Cæsar, tell me how it was?"

"Why all the world knows there are two great temptations which make war upon a man's purse. Bright eyes for one; bright, sparkling wine for the other. Talk of splendid fortunes, where are they that will stand against such modes of getting rid of them? and then, if any plethora of wealth should occur, there are dice. Now you are as wise as your neighbours; and, by-the-bye, who the devil are you?"

"My name is Don Jose."

"Oh, the king's favourite. I marvel I did not know you. Excuse me, Don Jose, but you have the same look you used to have when men called you Crawling Jose."

The don bit his lips, and a flush of anger came across his face. He seemed for a moment about to make some angry reply to Don Cæsar; but he took wit in his passion and held his tongue, turning away, without a word, in another direction; while Don Cæsar, making an effort to strike the hilt of his sword, by which he poked the point of it into somebody's stomach behind him, cried,—

"To the Prado—to the Prado, if you feel offended. Come on Don Crawling Jose, favourite of a king; I will give you satisfaction. I have not had much practise in fence lately, but yet I think sufficient of the old habit remains to enable me to cope with you. Ha! he flies. A cowardly rascal, on my soul! What does he mean by talking to me? Don Crawling Jose. Ha! ah! ha!"

" Sir, sir, you have got your awkward long rapier through a hole in your cloak," cried a little man ; " and, as you turn about, it pokes into people's faces and throats, sir."

" Very likely," said Don Cæsar, and he strode across the road, humming some air of Old Castile, such as once his own brilliant saloons had oftimes rung with, when he was the gayest nobleman in Madrid.

Scarcely had he got half way to the other side of the square in which his little dialogue with Don Jose had taken place, when a movement in the crowd announced some commotion, and there advanced a detachment of the king's guard, which was proceeding to change the sentinels at the winter palace. The soldiery came on but slowly, for the dense mass of people made it difficult for them to proceed, and the officer at their head, with a vexed look, was sometimes compelled almost to come to a halt, in consequence of the great pressure around him.

Shuffling along by his side, was a man who, by his gestures, appeared to be engaged vehemently in making some excuses about something, while the officer listened to him sternly, as if far from being satisfied with what he said, in explanation of something wrong.

" Most worthy and brave captain," said the man, " you say you will complain of me to the commandant, and so I shall be ruined ; for the arms of the guard will be taken elsewhere to repair and make, and to clean. Now, worthy and mighty sir, allow me to swear to you that it is no fault of mine, honourable sir. You must know, brave captain, that I have a scapegrace, a rascal, an idle young vagabond of an apprentice, named Lazarillo, beneficent sir, ——"

" Peace, peace—I will hear no more."

" But, gracious sir, one moment mitigate your extremely just wrath. This Lazarillo—you may have seen him, great sir—a likely lad enough to look at, but fearfully fond of light and frivolous amusements. His duty was to clean the arms of which your mightiness so justly complains ; but, instead of doing so, great sir, he puts on his best doublet and hose, puts a feather in his cap, and out he goes to enjoy himself at the carnival, brave and noble sir, leaving the arms to clean themselves, for all he cared. I thought them done, of course, wonderful sir, and, until your complaint reached my ears, I had no suspicion but they were all right—not the least suspicion. I swear by St. Jerome, St. Jago, St. Peter, our Lady of the Rock, the Apostle of Berne ; by the relics of St. ——"

" Pshaw ! what care I for your protestations. If it be the lad's fault you mention, you must bring him to the guard-room, and the guard shall lay their leather belts across his shoulders to make him more mindful for the future."

" Yes, worthy and generous sir—oh, yes. Scourge him well, an idle, dissolute, care-for-nothing, troublesome young knave. I assure you his name is Lazarillo ; all over Madrid is he known on account of his mischievous pranks. You will cure him, noble sir, and you will excuse me."

" Produce the lad, and I will consider."

" Merciful Providence ! here he is. You rascal ! oh, you villain ! you scoundrel, Lazarillo ! Now, sir —now we shall have some old scores paid off on your back. I have him, noble captain. Here he is, sir. Oh, I have him fast enough now. Take him away to the guard-room, good sir, and strap him well ; an arrant young rascal as ever lived. Here he is, sir— here he is."

The armourer had made a dart forward, and seized upon Lazarillo, whose cruel destiny would make him be upon that spot at so unfortunate a moment for himself. At an order from the captain of the guard, he was seized by one of the soldiers, and held fast, not-

withstanding all his twisting and twining to get away. However, he succeeded in making it so difficult to hold him, that the guard came to a complete stop, and so many of the carnival maskers thronged around to see what was the matter, that the captain scarcely knew how to force his way forward, although he was most anxious so to do.

At any other time than the height of the carnival, he would have had very few scruples as to forcing his way with his troop through the crowd ; but well he knew that at such a time it was neither politic nor safe to anger the multitude, and that he would not be backed by his superiors in any rough usage of the carnival jesters ; so he endeavoured by fair words to secure a passage with his young prisoner ; but the latter would not be so easily consigned to the tender mercies of the soldiers, and called out, lustily,—

" Friends, are you going to see a poor boy taken prisoner because he loves the carnival ? Shame on you all if you do. What a great thing it is for his majesty's guard to capture me, because I have laughed, sung, and danced at the carnival !"

" Shame, shame, shame !" shouted the mob. " Let the boy go. Rescue, rescue ! Shame, shame !"

" My good sir, " said the armourer, " take him away. Lash him well ; he ——"

Some one at this moment gave the armourer such a crack on one side of the head, that he reeled again, and when he turned round to see who it was, he found himself confronted by Don Cæsar de Bazan, who, pushing himself forward, stood full in the way of the guards, as he said,—

" Now, what is this, at the merry carnival time, sirs ? Who have you a prisoner ?"

" Oh, Don Cæsar, say a word for me," cried Lazarillo."

" Oh, it's you, you young rascal, is it, who flouted at me some time since ? You are a wicked young rascal."

" Oh, but, Don Cæsar, forgive me."

" Very good. Now, sir captain of his majesty's guard, let the boy go ; for 'tis but a boy, indeed, scarcely more than a child."

" Hurrah !" cried the mob—" hurrah ! Let him go."

" Not with my life," said the captain. " March— march !"

" Halt !" cried Don Cæsar, as he still maintained, not without some difficulty, his place in front of the troop, for he was not quite so steady upon his legs as he might have been, had he abstained from his last flask of wine. " Halt ! We will have no quarrelling at the carnival. Give up the boy with a good grace, and then go on to the devil, if you like."

" Bravo, bravo, Don Cæsar !" cried the people ; " make him give up the boy."

" Drunken fool !" cried the officer of the guard ; " you know not what you are saying, or what you are doing. Stand aside ; 'tis treason to stop the king's guard. Stand aside, I say, and save yourself from the consequences of this folly, if it be persevered in."

Don Cæsar pulled forward his dilapidated cap, till the long, straggling, dirty feather hung nearly over his face, and then advancing a step or two nearer to the officer, he said, in firm tones,—

" Sir captain, do you know who I am ?"

" No, nor care. Stand aside, and allow the troop to pass, or you shall be arrested."

" Sir captain, I am Don Cæsar de Bazan, Count of Orfilla. It appears, from what I hear, that this affair is quite a personal matter between you and this young boy, and therefore it is quite in your power to forego any revenge against him, or any punishment you may think he deserves. I pray you let him go."

" I shall do no such thing."

" Recollect, it is the carnival time, when the people

have more than usual license, and for that reason, sir, I ask you to excuse him."

"This is insolence. He is my prisoner, and shall go when some well-dealt stripes have taught him his duty, and not before."

Still Don Cæsar spoke in the same calm, unruffled tone, saying,—

"Sir, I, a noble of Spain, request the personal favour of you, that you will forgive this boy. My name is Don Cæsar de Bazan, Count of Orfilla, although you see me now in but poor plight. As a personal favour, will you be pleased to let him go?"

"Certainly not. March—march!"

The troop made an effort to press forward, but it was so hemmed in by the crowd, that a movement beyond a few inches became impossible, and the soldiers were afraid, for their very lives' sake, to come in violent collision with a carnival mob.

"So," added Don Cæsar, "you will not do me this little favour, sir captain?"

"I will not."

"Why, then, you shall fight me for it. I will honour you so far as to cross swords with you; and if you fancy, or would allege that you have not sufficient cause to give me a meeting, that may suffice."

As he spoke, Don Cæsar took from his hand a miserable, tattered glove, and threw it in the captain's face; after which he drew his sword from his side, and flourishing it in the air, he cried,—

"Come on—come on. There is the private garden of the ancient Capuchin convent at hand. If you have any pretensions to the uniform you wear, you will follow me, sir captain."

The captain of the guard hesitated, and the mob shouted and hurraed. All the sports of the carnival now sunk into complete insignificance in comparison with what was promised by the duel between Don Cæsar de Bazan and the captain.

The throng increased in density every moment, and before the alarmed soldiers could determine upon any line of conduct, or receive any instructions from their leader, the boy Lazarillo was taken from them, and conveyed some distance among the mob in triumph. Don Cæsar still beckoned the officer to follow him. Hisses burst from the crowd, as they supposed the captain hesitated from cowardice. He found himself in imminent danger of some very rough usage, and whilst his face was flushed with the wildest passion and excitement, he tore his sword from its sheath, and, in a hoarse voice, he cried,—

"Lead on—lead on, Don Cæsar, or Don Devil. Your blood be upon your own head. Lead on; I will fight you, since you will have it so, and I take all to witness that you alone are answerable for the issue of the contest."

So saying, with ferocious gestures, he rushed after Don Cæsar, followed by the dense throng of maskers in all their strange, many-coloured, fanciful and glittering costumes, to the place which had been mentioned as fit for the fight, by the dissipated nobleman who had so generously stepped forward to the rescue of the boy.

CHAPTER III.

THE GARDEN OF THE CAPUCHINS.—THE DUEL.— THE VICTORY AND THE DEATH.—THE ARREST OF DON CÆSAR.

OF course the mob felt a degree of especial satisfaction at all these proceedings, such as might fairly be expected of any mob, and the shouts, the hurras, and the vehement gesticulations, as they argued the question, some against, but by far the majority in favour of Don Cæsar, were of the most animated description. A Spaniard is, in his general character, grave and re-

served, but once succeed in arousing him from the apparent lethargic influence of his disposition, and you have as animated a man as a Frenchman, without the French flippancy and pettiness which makes one always so ready to laugh.

The chivalrous manner in which Don Cæsar had taken part with the boy, was extremely likely to win him golden opinions among the people, who, right or wrong, are ever willing to take part with any one who shows a disposition to resist the ruling powers. But in this instance no wonder their partizanship grew strong and earnest, for they happened to be, what mobs very rarely are, quite in the right, inasmuch as the attempted conduct of the captain of the palace guard was really of a most arbitrary and outrageous character, and, particularly at the carnival time, should never have been thought of. The real person to blame was the armourer himself, who entrusted his own duties to the volatile boy, who, at such a period of idleness and licence, preferred the gay, thronged streets, to polishing up arquebuses.

But subordinates always suffer, and had it not been for Don Cæsar's interference, the punishment hinted at by the captain would, no doubt, have been duly inflicted upon poor Lazarillo. As it was, however, the matter had now assumed a far more serious turn, by urging the captain of the guard into a quarrel with the well-known Don Cæsar, whose reputation as a swordsman outlived all his other reputations, and kept him out of many a scrape; because people, when they would otherwise have fought with him, took wit in their anger, and preferred a whole skin to a delicate puncture from the long Toledo of the Don.

There were two persons who followed Don Cæsar as closely as did the irascible captain of the guard, and these were Maritana and Lazarillo; both of whom were as intent upon stopping the fight as he was upon taking it up.

The boy outstripped every one, and just as his generous friend had set foot in the gardens of the Capuchin convent, he caught him by the cloak, and might possibly have detained him, had not a long strip of that dilapidated garment come away in his hands.

Notwithstanding the serious turn which the whole affair was now taking, the mob could not forbear a shout of laughter at this incident, and even Don Cæsar smiled, as he said,—

"Now, boy, this is too bad. Do you want to expose the rather threadbare condition of my doublet, that you tear away my cloak?"

"No, no—but, Don Cæsar, hear me—do hear me, Don Cæsar. It is for me you are going into this quarrel. Nay, now, don't shake your head at me. Let them take me to prison if they will; but I implore you, Don Cæsar, not to fight."

"Now, Lazarillo, you mistake altogether," said the don. "'Tis true, I first addressed this captain on your account; but he insulted me personally, and I fight him on my own account, you see; so dry your eyes, you foolish boy, and stand by to see the fight."

"No," cried Maritana—"no, you shall not fight. Remember the time—remember, too, where you are. Don Cæsar—Don Cæsar—if such be your name—let me implore you but to think of the danger you encounter."

"Danger!"

"Yes, such danger as should make you shrink."

"I am a Spanish nobleman; but I tell you, fair one, I will consent to believe that my danger is most imminent, provided you will repay me for passing through it, by a smile and a kiss."

Maritana shrunk back, as a tear started in her eye.

"Oh, sir," she said, "you treat this matter too lightly. You may vanquish your opponent; but do you not know that a duel during the carnival time will

be visited upon the conqueror with the severest consequences? You may, too, be killed."

"I am already slaughtered by those bright eyes. They have more power to kill me than a thousand swords, fair one."

"But, Don Cæsar," sobbed Lazarillo, as he clung to his arm,—"Don Cæsar, if you are killed, I shall drown myself."

"Pho, pho! boy; you will live yet to be a bold fellow, and wear a sword of your own."

"But will you forgive me?"

"Forgive you, boy—I have nothing to forgive. If I fall, though, you shall be my executor. The task will give you no trouble, my lad. I have nothing but my sword, and nobody has thought proper to take that from me, because it was a dangerous plaything."

"Now, sir," cried the officer of the guard—"now, sir, I am here to meet you. Draw, and defend yourself."

"Nay, my good friend, don't you see I was talking to a lady? Have you no gallantry, because you have no civility?"

"Bravo! bravo!" shouted the mob. "Bravo! bravo!"

At this moment the guard made a desperate effort, under the command of the lieutenant, to reach the gardens, and put an end to the intended combat; but the carnival maskers were not so easily to be baulked of the rarest piece of sport they could possibly expect, and they closed round the soldiery, hustling and push-

ing them about until they were defeated and totally powerless; so it seemed the strange duel was likely enough to proceed without interruption, except from the cheers and plaudits of the surrounding throng, which was each moment becoming more and more excited.

"Once more I implore you, Don Cæsar, not to fight," said Maritana. "Wait until the carnival is over."

"Yes, wait," said Lazarillo.

The don merely smiled, and drawing from his side his scabbardless rapier, he glanced at its shining blade, as he said,—

"My good sword, you have never yet been used but in defence of innocence, or in asserting a righteous cause. Now, play well thy part, for mercy's sake. Sir captani, come on, unless cowardice, that general accompaniment of cruelty, paralyses your arm. Room, my friends—room!"

Don Cæsar made a large circle in a moment, by several sweeps of his sword, which no one seemed to like coming in the way of; and then the captain of the guard, trembling with passion and excitement, flew forward to commence the encounter, with a vehemence which looked as if it would be a very short one.

The swords rung together with a tremendous clash, and, for a moment, every sound else was hushed, as all around watched the rapid play of the weapons, which in their gyrations looked like flashes of light moving rapidly round each other. Then, suddenly, there was a still louder clash, as the blades met, and the sword of the captain of the guard went spinning up in the air, leaving him totally unguarded, and at the mercy of his adversary.

The fight, however, and its attendant circumstances, appeared completely to have overpowered all the effects of the wine which Don Cæsar had taken, and he was as sober, calm, and collected as he had ever been in his life before.

Instead of, as an angry man would have done, taking immediate advantage of the defenceless state of his adversary, he instantly lowered the point of his own sword, and said,—

"Sir, are you satisfied? Will you now pardon the poor boy for his very venial offence? I again ask it of you as a personal favour to Don Cæsar de Bazan?"

The cheer that burst from the crowd at this signal

act of generosity in Don Cæsar, who was so decidedly the victor in the conflict, was heard from one end of Madrid to the other, and penetrated the walls even of the palaces, the convents, and the splendid mansions of the nobility, filling many minds with wonder as to what extraordinary circumstance had so excited the popular lungs.

But all the generosity of his adversary seemed only the more to inflame the wild, ungovernable passions of the officer of the guard. He stamped, swore, and became almost purple in the face with rage, as he cried,—

" My sword—give me my sword ! and I will punish yet this brawling street ruffian. Where is my sword ?"

" Duck him," said a voice.

" Hurrah !" shouted the mob, and a hundred hands were stretched out to seize the captain ; and had not Don Cæsar, who just then was the most popular and powerful man in Madrid, interposed to save him, he would, most probably, have met with some terrible rough usage from the mob ; but the don threw his sword before him, saying,—

" No, no, friends—no. He is an officer and a gentleman, albeit he may be a fool."

These words converted the popular wrath into a roar of laughter, and perhaps put the finishing stroke to the captain's mad rage, for he nearly danced with passion, as he shrieked,—

" My sword—my sword—my sword !"

" Give him his sword," said Don Cæsar.

" Confound his sword ; here it is," said a burly fellow. " It fell on my head. Look here ; here's a cracked crown, all through his infernal sword."

The mob were perfectly electrified with the outrageous fun, as they considered it, of this incident, and when the burly fellow showed where there was some blood upon his head, the amusement became actually terrific.

" Give him his sword again," cried Don Cæsar. " If he will fight, the consequences now be upon his own head."

" I hope they may," said the man upon whom the sword had fallen ; " for as far as you have gone at present, the consequences have been all upon my head."

" Come on—come on," said the captain, stamping furiously, and regarding the loud laughter of the mob only as so many additional insults heaped upon him.

" Have a moment's patience," said Don Cæsar. " Lazarillo, come hither."

The boy flew to his side.

" Did you not say something about the lieutenant of the guard having interceded for you ?'

" Yes ; he urged the captain to let me go, as I was such a mere boy, and it was the carnival time."

" Good. The commissions in the royal guard go by seniority and regular rotation. That lieutenant deserves to be a captain, so I will provide a vacancy for him. Now, Sir Orlando Furioso, come on when you will, I am ready for you."

The captain turned now ghastly pale, and possibly, if, without indelible disgrace, he could have avoided the conflict, at that moment he would have done so ; but he had let go the only opportunity he had, with a good grace, and without a stain upon his honour, of doing so, and he felt compelled to stand the issue of a combat which he began to feel was very far from being at all a doubtful one. He knew that he must fall, and he again crossed swords with Don Cæsar with a conviction that his moments were numbered.

He fought with more skill, because he fought with not so much heat of temper, and he confined himself for some minutes more to defence than to attack, showing himself to be a far better swordsman than any one would have supposed, considering how quickly Don Cæsar had disarmed him in the first flush of the affair.

The combat now became deeply interesting, for it was really an exquisite trial of skill, and both appeared to fight with admirable coolness and precision. The countenance of the captain of the guard was as pale as death, and those who were nearest to him could see the drops of perspiration standing upon it in heavy beads. He was in mental fear, that man ; for he knew that his end was come, and that he was but for a few brief moments protracting an existence which was now horrible.

He could have saved his life by throwing down his sword and abandoning the contest ; but what, then, would life have been to him but one scene of misery, degradation, and disgrace ? Never again could he have shown his face among gentlemen. He would have become an outcast among men, a wretch to be shunned, a bully, who shrunk at last, in conscious cowardice, from the danger his own bad passions had led him into.

He must die ! he must die ! He felt that he must die, and he fought, as some despairing man swims in the fathomless ocean, where he knows that a thousand miles of waters lie between him and any shore.

The mob was noiseless. Every breath was suppressed, and the only perceptible movement among the people was when they swayed to and fro, with a strange sympathetic movement in unison with the variations in the attitudes of the combatants.

Suddenly, then, there was a cry of pain and terror, and the sword of the captain of the guard dropped from his nerveless hand. Don Cæsar had run him through the body, and in another moment, with a sullen sort of dash, the lifeless corpse fell to the ground.

For a few moments the same rapt stillness prevailed among the multitude of persons assembled as had characterised it during the fight, and then Don Cæsar spoke, as he carefully wiped the blade of his sword with a corner of his tattered and remarkable-looking cloak.

" Lazarillo," he said, " your friend the lieutenant will be a captain."

" But you—you !" cried the boy. " What will become of you ?"

" Never mind me."

" Unhappy man," said Maritana, as tears flowed from her eyes, " you will be sacrificed to your noble generosity."

" Not at all ; I have nothing to lose. The most cunning person in the world would get nothing from me, and, if they clap me in prison for a while, why I shall at least have the comfort of finding myself thoroughly out of reach of my creditors."

The sound of military music at this moment came plainly to every ear, and many voices cried aloud,—

" Fly, Don Cæsar, fly ! The guard—the guard !"

" Seek sanctuary," said Lazarillo. " The church protects an assassin, and it surely must an honourable gentleman, who has slain his adversary in fair fight. For my sake, dear Don Cæsar, seek sanctuary."

" No, my young friend, no. I don't like the gloom of a church always. Besides, I have fought fairly, God knows, and have a thousand witnesses to the fact. Who shall touch the honour of Don Cæsar de Bazan, on account of this duel ?"

Nearer and nearer came the sound of the martial music, and some persons pressing forward from the outskirts of the mob, announced that a large force, which could not be resisted, was approaching rapidly, under the command of some officers of distinction.

" Let them come," said Don Cæsar. " The higher in rank the officers the better they will know what sort of respect they owe to a Spanish nobleman."

The boy clung to him wildly, weeping bitterly, and now there was a great movement among the crowd, and the head of a large body of troops appeared slowly, but surely, pressing forward and taking prisoners those who in any way showed a disposition to impede their progress. Some mounted officers came first, and in a very few moments the few persons who remained between the advancing soldiery and Don Cæsar were scattered, and he stood, along with the boy, in the open space where he had fought the duel which had just ended so fatally to the passionate captain of the royal guard.

"Seize that man," said a mounted officer, pointing to Don Cæsar with his sword.

"Who summons me to surrender?" said Don Cæsar. "Because, if I like not the party issuing the mandate, it will be dangerous work for the first three or four of you who may venture to lay hands on me."

"We summon you to surrender," said the mounted officer, "in the name of Charles the Second, King of Spain."

"Then, sir, there is my sword."

As he spoke, Don Cæsar advanced carelessly and handed his sword to the officer, who seemed somewhat struck with the manner of his prisoner, for he had come out, as he thought, to quell a street riot merely.

"Who are you?" he said, in a tone which had a tinge of involuntary respect mingled with it.

"I am Don Cæsar de Bazan, Count of Orfilla, and I claim the privilege of being accused before my king."

The officer touched his helmet, as he said,—

"Don Cæsar, I am really sorry to see you so situated. I have heard of you."

"And of my numerous creditors, no doubt."

"Why—a—yes; but you have been very unfortunate."

"Somehow the Bazans are an imprudent family."

"Are you, however, thoroughly aware of the situation in which you have placed yourself? A fatal duel never occurred but once before at the carnival time, during his present majesty's reign, and then the survivor was hanged, and the king would not be moved to mercy."

"Hanged was he?"

"Yes, most surely."

"That's awkward, very."

"Well, I should say it was, Don Cæsar. If there be anything that it is difficult for a gentleman to do with a good grace, I should say it would be to be hung."

"But the king must recollect I am a Spanish nobleman, and that my opponent fell in fair fight."

The officer shook his head, as he said,—

"I much fear for you. You are my prisoner. Soldiers, see to Don Cæsar de Bazan—march."

"This is pleasant," said Don Cæsar, as he drew his tattered cloak around, and pulled his dreadfully cut and tarnished hat over his brows—"this is pleasant. Confound the carnival time. How can people help fighting at any time, I should like to know? Hanged—hanged—humph! no—that won't do—not at all—unless, to be sure, they made the gallows so high that it was out of reach of my creditors. Then, indeed, there would be something to be said in favour of the proposition. Lazarillo."

"Yes, yes."

"Good bye to you. I'm going to be hung, they say."

"Oh no—no! Seigniors, save him—save him!"

"Hush, boy, hush! and don't make a riot. When by chance you come across any of my creditors, and they consist of everybody who ever gave credit to anybody in Madrid, you will have the goodness to tell them they may scratch my name out of their books, for they must accept of my death as payment in full."

"I will not leave you. Oh, Don Cæsar—Don Cæsar! this is all owing to me."

"Pshaw! nonsense, boy; you take a wrong view of the subject completely. But if these troopers will let you walk along with me, I have no objection."

"I will stay by you; no one shall force me from your side. If they take you to prison, they shall take me too; if they hang you, they shall hang me."

There was a slight tremor, indicative of emotion, in Don Cæsar's voice, as he said,—

"My boy, I wish I had known you when fortune wore a different aspect to me. But, no matter, I have had a merry life till lately, and then, somehow, I think, my creditors multiplied themselves by ten, and made the law believe it. Confound the greasy rogues, they left me nothing but my sword, Lazarillo. Hilloa! what shout is that?"

"It is the people. They are not so cowardly as to let you be taken. They have run round the Grand Place, and will rescue you. Hark, hark!"

"Rescue! rescue! rescue!" was shouted by a thousand throats, and the mounted officer, in a loud voice, as the soldiery turned a corner, and found themselves met by an imposing armed mass, cried,—"Halt."

"Rescue! rescue!" again shouted the mob; "rescue for Don Cæsar. Down with them! rescue for the brave Don Cæsar."

"You hear, you hear," cried the delighted boy; "you hear they are not such cowards as to let you be taken. You will be saved yet. Hurrah! hurrah!"

"Hush, boy, hush; this will not do."

"Not do, Don Cæsar? Hark to them. Now I will be bound Maritana has spoken to the people, and told them how cowardly it would be to let you be taken away in such a style. Hurrah! rescue! rescue!"

"You will get yourself into trouble, Lazarillo, if you don't be quiet," said Don Cæsar.

The mounted officer now rode to the front of the troop, and addressing the people, he said,—

"Are you mad, that you place yourselves in the way of death? We must take our prisoner, and, if resisted, we must fire upon you. Make way—make way."

"Rescue for Don Cæsar! a rescue—a rescue!" was the only reply from the mob.

Then came a shower of missiles from among the crowd, which exasperated some of the soldiers, who began to get their arquebuses ready for action; and Heaven only knows what the result might have been, had not Don Cæsar pressed forward, despite his guard, and said,—

"For my sake, and for the sake of all, who are in any way dear to you, I beg you will offer no opposition to the guard—they must do their duty, and I declare, on my honour, that I will not accept of liberty at the price of bloodshed in the streets of Madrid. Soldiers, march."

The troop marched on, and the crowd, slowly, but most reluctantly, fell back, to allow it to pass, while the officer rode close to Don Cæsar, saying,—

"Your whole conduct, so honourable to yourself as it is, shall reach, through me, the ears of the king, and I will make it a personal request to procure your pardon. If anything can move his majesty to look over the affair, the generous manner in which you have prevented a popular riot, of the most serious character, ought to do so."

"Sir," said Don Cæsar, "I am much beholden to you; and can you do me, of your own power, the favour of allowing this boy to come with me for a time?"

"Certainly. If you do have to die it will be this evening."

"Short work that," ejaculated Don Cæsar. "Well, well, it cannot be helped. How my creditors will mourn."

CHAPTER IV.

THE RIOT IN THE STREETS.—THE VENGEANCE OF THE MOB.—THE CONFLICT.—THE MYSTERIOUS MASK, AND THE RECOGNITION.

DON CÆSAR DE BAZAN was now, to all intents and purposes, the popular idol of the carnival. There was not one now among the vast crowd that followed, instead of obstructing the soldiery, who did not, by voice or gesture, imply his sympathy with the prisoner. But most of all did the women declaim loudly in his favour, accusing the men around them of cowardice, for not saving him, and making more disturbance about him than treble the number of male population could have done, had they tried their utmost.

Indeed, had not Don Cæsar and his guard very soon arrived at the gates of the principal prison of Madrid, and disappeared from public view within its gloomy walls, the don himself might have found his generous wishes disregarded, and there would have been, perchance, a popular tumult in his favour, in spite of himself.

Don Cæsar de Bazan was just the sort of person in every respect qualified to become a great favourite with the people. He was, firstly, a man of rank, who had come down from his own high estate, to mingle among them ; then he was liberal to a fault, for he never took care of anything, and if, by any chance, he was the possessor of a couple of pistoles, any tolerably well concocted tale of distress would, in a few moments, suffice to get one of them from him.

Then, again, he was careless, and he drank, and he was drowned in debt—all popular vices, which act as almost popular recommendations to hundreds and thousands of people, who, finding haughty austerity too frequently the companion of good outward conduct, cannot think of the possibility of sobriety and careful living being pleasant, instead of austere. The fact is, that in all communities, your fine cautious people, who never, by any accident, are off the stilts of propriety, are generally the most disagreeable members of society, and seem as if they would strive to make good conduct wear as ugly an aspect as they could. Hence, thousands of the gay and thoughtless are hurried into all sorts of excesses, because they find all that is agreeable, gay, and generous, arrayed on that side of the question ; and all that is morose, cold, haughty, and unsocial on the other, and such wild, harum-scarum, racketty, devil-may-care fellows as Don Cæsar de Bazon, shine wonderfully, when contrasted with some canting hypocritical brute, who, as Shakspere has it, "because he is virtuous, would allow no cakes and ale."

It is by making truth, good conduct, and virtue disagreeable, that vice ranges so many thousands under its banner, and we shall invariably find that popular feeling will assuredly go with the gay, the generous, thoughtless libertine, in preference to the man who is virtuous and prudent ; because, in real truth, he seems not to have the courage to do otherwise.

If people who are religious and moral would but at the same time condescend to be a little agreeable, they would make many converts ; but nothing will convince the vast majority of such persons that Heaven can be propitiated without a sombre and groaning aspect, or the scales of virtue kept evenly balanced, without all sorts of little persecutions, and a gloomy demeanour, as if a smile would be destruction.

Don Cæsar, then, was an eminent favourite, for he was brave, generous, and noble. His faults were spots in the sunshine, certainly, but by no means sufficient to dim the brilliancy of his general character. All knew he had been extravagant—all knew he had gamed, drank, rioted, and led a life of roaring pleasure, until he had not a maravedie left, and that was all that could be said against him ; he had never done a dishonourable action, although he never did a wise one. No wonder, then, that Don Cæsar de Bazan was the popular idol of Madrid, especially when he now was in such serious trouble, solely in consequence of a generous desire to save a poor boy from angry punishment. The women—oh, the women would have pummelled

the soldiers to death, if they could have had their way, for there was everything in the whole affair to excite their warmest sympathies.

"Poor fellow," cried an amazonian-looking female, who certainly did not belong to the *softer* sex. " Poor, dear fellow ! So they took him to prison because he wouldn't have the poor boy beat. Oh, the wretches ! it's very clear they never had any children of their own, or they'd as soon have bit off their own noses. I'd like to have the dealing with some of them. Don Cæsar is worth them all put together. Poor, dear man."

"And he's handsome, too," sighed a young creature, in a fancy dancing costume. " What a shame to put a very handsome fellow in prison for anything."

"I tell you what it is," said the man, upon whose head the sword of the captain of the guard had fallen, and who, in consequence, felt very much hurt, both corporeally and mentally, at the whole transaction. "I'll tell you what is—it's all owing to that old armourer, Mendoza Ferara—it's all owing to him—he accused the boy ; and the captain, who is now dead, rest his soul, said he'd have the boy lashed with the soldiers' belts, and Don Cæsar said he shouldn't, and then the consequences came on my head, and poor Don Cæsar will ne'er drink another cup of wine."

"Never ?" cried the women.

"No, never."

"Why, you don't mean to say—eh—eh ?"

"Yes, I do though. They'll hang him."

"What ! hang Don Cæsar ?"

"Such a handsome fellow !" sighed the young girl.

"Yes, they will though ; I heard the mounted officer of the guard tell him so."

"Lor ! holy virgins, protect us. You don't mean such a thing, surely ? Well, if I was a man ——"

"You'd be a dragoon, I suppose."

"Take that for your impertinence, will you ! I'd burn down the armourer's shop."

"Would you go the armourer's ?"

"Yes, I would."

"A good thought, a good thought," cried a man, who had just heard the last words. " Friends, let's go to the armourer's, for 'twas he who made all the mischief. To the armourer's—to the armourer's."

The dense mob was just in that state, that it was ready to embrace any suggestion that promised any degree of excitement or amusement. An ominous sort of calm had come over the people, and each man had been looking in his neighbour's face, with that sort of expression, which, if translated, might well mean, " What shall we do now ?"

The suggestion, therefore, to go to the armourer's, and inflict upon him a condign punishment, was most acceptable, and a thousand throats called out immediately,—

" To the armourer's—to the armourer's !"

This cry was echoed and re-echoed by the mob, in a thousand different voices ; the mob being masked, none feared to utter his thoughts openly, as his neighbour could not distinguish him, had he feared such was his desire.

At a time like this, during the carnival, the streets are filled with various masks, dressed in all kinds of costume—some of them are really handsome and beautiful, besides being costly, while others are as simple and poor ; but all exhibit signs that would tell a stranger it was a carnival.

The costumes were dictated only by the taste of the wearer, and masks were dressed in all kinds of dresses —in all the extravagance that the whims and absurdities of the individual is capable of perpetrating.

Merriment and joviality were the chief characteristics of such occasions—care was left far behind—mask passed and repassed mask, and each one in his turn had something new to say to the next mask he met, and so on throughout; and the confusion that existed in the motley throng need be seen to be thoroughly and duly appreciated.

Daylight had departed, leaving the inhabitants to their illuminations, torches, and various other kinds of light—they really made the city appear very beautiful and strange. Fireworks were added to the scene, and attracted vast crowds of spectators, and the different lights thrown by them on the assembled multitude, caused many to look picturesque in their costumes, while a larger class appeared absurd, and many hideous.

Presently there came imperceptibly a change o'er the spirit of the scene—there were still the same figures, and they were occupied as before; but there was an air of uneasiness about the majority, that caused a considerable alteration to take place, and some few words were uttered to some masks by others as they passed, and this again was carried on by others; the gambols yet went on, but with more ostentation than spirit.

This lasted for some time, until a general movement was about being made, and then they were hurrying to and fro, till they collected in a mass round the door of the armourer.

Cries and shouts were heard, and the door was assailed by many hands at once, but no notice was taken from within.

Men were now seen rushing from all parts, and verging towards a common centre; the armourer's shop being the point of attraction where they all met. Many hurried on to the scene of action, thrusting their masks into their pockets, and altering their dress, so as to be more convenient in case any struggle was about to take place, that they might be ready for action; others, on the contrary, kept their masks on, and disposed their disguises so that they might not be known again—so, indeed, that they might not serve as marks to recognise them again.

The hammering and knocking at the armourer's door continued without intermission, but it produced no effect; shouts and calls to him were uttered, but the inhabitants were deaf to them. Impatience and anger now took possession of them, and they seized hold of any and everything that could be turned into a weapon of offence, and with it they endeavoured to burst in the door, at the same time they uttered threats and cries of an alarming character.

In a short time, however, a whisper ran through the crowd, anxious glances were cast first up one way and then down another. The rumour was, that the guard was coming, and about to make an attack upon them—that, indeed, they were at that moment collecting at various points, uniting the various bodies that were posted at different places; but this reinforcement was made to enable them to make a sudden and successful descent among the rioters, and capture the most active.

For a moment, there was a pause among the multitude—no one appeared to lead at that moment, or be capable of doing so; there appeared no prospect of forcing the armourer's door, for there was a singular want of means; but suddenly some one called out in a loud voice,—

"There is no time to lose. Fire the house—throw a brand in at the window!"

The words, "Fire the house—throw a brand in at the window," and "bravo," ran through the mob like wildfire, and an instant attack was made upon the windows; stones were hurled, and sticks were thrown, until the whole of the windows were entirely knocked in, and a clear breach made that way.

"The guard is coming—the guard is coming!" ran from mouth to mouth, and then another shout arose from the multitude, for simultaneous with the cry of "The guard is coming," a blazing torch was thrown into the armourer's house through one of the windows.

This was followed by another and another, until a dozen blazing brands were thrown in, and then all was hushed, and a dead silence ensued. Every voice was dumb with expectation; each man gazed intently on the house, as they expected the forked flames to arise and burst out in extreme violence.

In this they were not mistaken; for but a few moments had elapsed ere a dense smoke issued out of the windows, which was hailed by a loud "bravo," that was again re-echoed when the first forked flame had burst out, and in a few moments more the armourer's shop was in flames.

Loud shouts rent the air, while the roaring and cracking of the flames resounded far and near, and in the midst of all the hurrahs of the mob, formed a scene at once grand, terrific, and striking.

The lurid glare of the flames threw an unearthly hue upon the surrounding multitude, exhibiting on their countenances all the various passions that animate such a mass of men, urged on to deeds of violence on the impulse of the moment.

The populace were collected close round the armourer's house, and as the fire increased, they got further back; but the mass of human beings that were behind forced those in front yet nearer to the fire, until a slight explosion or two of fire-arms, that appeared to have been loaded, caused the mob to stand a little further back than before.

There was much commotion among the populace, who thus turned the festivities of the carnival into a riot, in which much mischief was done, and some danger incurred. Each moment, as the flames burst out afresh, there arose a cry of exultation from the angry and revengeful multitude.

Again there was a sudden pause among the mass of men who had thus promiscuously banded themselves together for a certain object, and to preserve the completion of it.

"The guard—the guard!" was cried out by a stentorian voice; it was echoed by a thousand others, and, in the next moment, the guard appeared, and made a desperate rush towards the armourer's house, as if to seize upon those who were nearest to the scene of conflagration.

All was confusion in an instant; a scene of the wildest disorder prevailed; some attempted to escape, and some were for making a stand; but between one and the other they could not readily escape, and the guard had to force a passage by the weight of their own bodies, and the hard blows they unsparingly dealt around them. In such a state of indicision the military has always a great advantage, and with the damage which had already been done to the old armourer's house, he might have escaped, only that he had the imprudence to hilloa before he was out of the wood, contrary to the wise practical injunction of the peasant, and that he accomplished by coming to his door suddenly, from whence no one knew or cared, and crying out in as loud a voice as he could,—

"Seize the knaves—seize the knaves!"

No sooner had the words escaped his lips, than the Amazonian woman, who had been the first to suggest the propriety of paying the armourer a visit, made a dart forward, and seizing him by the cloak as he strove to escape, dragged him back among the people, who laid hold of him in an instant, and before the soldiery knew very well, in the confusion, what was going on, he was carried away towards one of the public fountains, where he was ducked to everybody's heart's content, except his own.

"Take that," said the Amazonian woman, "and

don't get poor boys into trouble again, you old sinner."

"He's dreadfully ugly," remarked the young dancer, "and so a good ducking serves him quite right."

The armourer sat down half dead, and looking as like a gigantic drowned rat as possible, on the steps of a neighbouring church, and there he began swearing vengeance by all the saints in the calendar, and cursing his evil stars that day, while various little skirmishes were taking place among the people and with the soldiery, who were making some prisoners, for the sake of doing something, although they could not well tell who was guilty and who innocent.

After a while, being contented with six prisoners, the guard, finding that the fire at the armourer's was put out, and the people beginning again in some quarters the carnival games, would have retired, but the prisoners were by no means so scrupulous as Don Cæsar about what means might be employed to rescue them, and they called loudly to the mob not to suffer them to be taken at the carnival time.

This appeal was not made in vain, for a rush was made by some stout fellows, which effected such confusion temporarily among the guard, that the prisoners made their escape in all directions, which so aggravated the officer in command, that he gave immediate orders to secure as many of the ringleaders of the tumult as possible, in lieu of the prisoners who had made so sudden an escape, an order which it was now quite clear could not possibly be obeyed without some very serious consequences ensuing, inasmuch as many of the populace were now armed with weapons they had snatched from different persons and places.

There was great fear that more mischief might happen in the streets of Madrid, as no one can count on the mischief a mob may feel inclined to commit when once it is set in motion; the soldiery were sent to quell the disturbance.

Soldiers are no favourites with mobs, nor are mobs any favourites of the military; far from it, especially when any of either side have fallen; and, on this occasion, the knowledge that a captain of the guard had fallen, somewhat ruffled the temper of the soldiers, and they felt well satisfied with their duty, and disposed to use anything but gentleness.

As the soldiers advanced upon the mob, there was a dead silence for a minute or two, during which you could distinctly hear the heavy, regular tramp of the soldiers, and then the fury of the mob gave vent to itself in one deep groan, and then oaths and curses of all kinds were uttered in plenty.

Many of the mob, no doubt, wished themselves out of it, but there was no escape, and "Do as Rome does," appears the natural feeling upon such occasions, and the hindermost support the foremost in an efficient manner, by not letting them run away.

Excitement and angry feelings had got then to their height, and the mob immediately began to defend itself and repel the aggression of the soldiers; and when ordered to retire, a shout of defiance arose, accompanied by vollies of stones and missiles of all kinds.

The order was given to charge the mob and disperse them, especially as there were several of the soldiers hurt by the stones.

In another instant the rushing sound of a mass of men pressing forward, in deadly encounter, met the ears of all those whose keen eyes watched the motions of the guard as they came on.

The mob were resolute and excited to madness, and opposed the guard with their bodies. Some persons wore swords and fire-arms; the bulk had but such weapons as chance enable them to seize Shots were fired; some of the mob staggered and fell.

Oaths, curses, and groans mingled together while they rushed in their turn upon the soldiery, and a fierce contention ensued between them. The discipline and arms of the military, however, enabled them to beat the people back, not before, however, they had lost an officer, who fell wounded, and he would have been dragged away by them but the soldiers rushed forward to save him from their hands.

In doing this, they were compelled to charge through a mass of people with their bayonets, but they succeeded in saving him.

Apparently there was a new reinforcement of the mob, for they made a desperate attack upon the military, which they only repelled by firing; and the mob, feeling the effect of this, were driven nearly to frenzy, for several had been killed, and many wounded; and as the mob continued to make attacks, the soldiers now kept up a discharge of fire-arms, which was answered from several quarters by some few small arms by the mob; but these did not do much mischief. Several soldiers were wounded.

Suddenly there was a great shout among the populace, and a female figure rushed forward and placed herself between the soldiers and the mob, so that the former could not fire at them without her becoming a victim.

"Maritana—Maritana!" was shouted from the lips of the mob, as she stood thus before them.

For the moment there was a cessation of hostilities. The mob held back, and the military ceased to fire.

Her appearance turned the tide of affairs, as if by magic. Neither party felt at all disposed to renew the conflict, and in a very few moments she was left alone in the open space where so serious an affair had began.

Both parties had carried away all who were hurt, except the body of one man, and that lay within a few paces of where Maritana stood.

CHAPTER V.

THE PROPHECY TO MARITANA. — THE AMBITIOUS FEELINGS OF A YOUNG HEART. — THE ILLUSTRIOUS STRANGER.

MARITANA stood for some moments in silence, herself much surprised at the effect she had been able to produce, and which she could only explain to her own mind by supposing what we have hinted to be the fact —namely, that each party was extremely desirous of putting an end to a fight from which there was to be gained neither honour nor any degree of profit.

She was startled by hearing a low groan near her, and then her eyes fell upon what appeared to be a lifeless body; but as she had heard a sound, she knelt down by his side, saying,—

"Do you live? speak if you live, and I will fetch you assistance. Speak or move."

The mortally wounded man rolled over on his back, and fixed his glazed eyes upon her face, as he said, in faint, wandering accents,—

"A priest—a priest!"

"Yes, yes," said Maritana; "I will fetch you one."

Then there was a faint sigh, and the body became perfectly motionless. The man was dead.

"Alas!" she said, "no priest can avail you now, poor lump of clay. This is a dreadful night; horror fills my brain, and I tremble. Oh, God! oh, God! when will all this end?"

"It is over," said a voice close to her; and suddenly rising, she saw by her side the man in the cloak, who had before spoken to her so mysteriously. "It is over now," he repeated. "The soldiery are withdrawn by order of Don Jose, the king's favourite minister. He is a great friend to the people."

"Indeed! I have heard him spoken of as cruel and crafty, and is a friend to no one but to himself. Perhaps the king himself ordered the withdrawal of the troops, and not the wicked minister, whom all men so much condemn."

"Indeed, lovely Maritana, you are hasty in your condemnation of a man you can know nothing really of."

"I have heard enough; but he is nothing to me, nor I to him. Signior, I bid you a good evening."

"Nay, do not go so hurriedly. I have a something to say to you of vast importance. You must know I can read the stars, pretty Maritana."

"If I mistake not your voice, you are one who has already made such protestations to me."

"You have a good memory. I am the same person. You are born to be great."

"Great!"

"Ay; have you no ambition?"

"Ambition!"

"Why do you echo my words? I wish to hear what your own opinions and feelings may be upon such a theme as this ambition, which is at once the blessing and the bane of so many men."

"The blessing and the bane?"

"Yes, both. The blessing when it stirs men to deeds which be within the compass of ordinary probability, because from no other feeling could we gather sufficient impulsive energy to dare the dangers and overcome the numerous obstacles which must visit the career of every one who would make himself higher than he is."

"But how the bane?"

"Because ambition knows no bounds, and having leaped high, to probability, and made good its footing, it takes another bound to impossibility, and falls for ever."

Maritana sighed as she replied,—

"You are a stranger; but you have touched upon a theme which, since my earliest childhood, has been to me a dream of romance and pleasure. I am ambitious. Yes, I, the poor street-singer, would fain mount even higher than any but one who ever offered me a recompense for the wild notes of my guitar, or the untutored cadences of a voice I fain would make heard in the palaces instead of the streets of this fair city—yes, I am ambitious. I long for rank, for power, the power to make others as happy as I think, ay, as I am sure, I should be myself. I like to dream that a day may come when I may not always be the the poor, lowly Maritana."

"Indeed!"

"Yes—oh, yes. When I was a child it was foretold by one who had strangely the gift of prophecy that I should be a countess. Since then the thought has grown with my growth, and through all the viscissitudes of varying fortune the bright idea has ever clung to my imagination, and I have seen it as afar off, like some glittering object I yet had a faint hope ultimately to reach."

"Maritana, you are indeed ambitious. The language you use, and your manner of using it, convinces me that you have the very romance of ambition in your temperament. That prediction which you say was made of you in early life has indeed clung to you through many years, and I can well see how deep an impression it has made upon your imagination."

"It has indeed. But I do not like to think of it. Those wild dreams of the fancy will not bear the sober light of reason. I would not destroy that which makes up the whole romance of my existence. Do not talk to me of my ambition, signior. Let me cherish it in my own breast if I can; and, perchance, I shall find, as I have heard some aver, who are wiser in the world's way than myself, that there is as much joy in hope and expectation, if not more, than in the actual fulfilment of our daring schemes or dreams of future greatness. It is a theme I wish not to converse further on. Once more, signior, I wish you a good even. I know not

why I have been moved to say so much to you. It is contrary to my habit."

"Stay, Maritana, and I will tell you why you have said so much to me. You have done so because it is your destiny. I am one of those who must and will figure in your history. You have arrived at a crisis in your fortunes, and you could no more prevent yourself from telling me you were ambitious, and wherefore you were so, than I could oppose a barrier to your future greatness."

"My greatness! You mock me."

"No, on my soul, I do not. I repeat the words—your future greatness, Maritana."

"I had forgotten, this is carnival time, and you are amusing yourself with the poor dancer."

"No, Maritana, no. But there is one thing you must explain to me. Some minutes since you talked of your ambition reaching so high that it excepted only one with whom you thought not of being on a level; who is that one?"

"The queen."

"Humph! You do except her majesty."

"I do, and bless her too. Oh, she has smiled upon me as none but she can smile."

"Indeed!"

"Yes, signior, and if anything could add to the strange notion that has perhaps so foolishly possessed me of future greatness, the smiles of the queen might well have such an intoxicating effect upon the poor street-singer. Yes, she has smiled upon me."

"Where was that?"

"Oh, more than once. I am not noticed here in Madrid; but I have long enough played my guitar in this city of palaces to know the queen. She has a smile for all; but as she has passed, as often she does, nearly unattended through the streets, I have always fancied that the smile she had for me was gentler and more gracious than that she bestowed on any one else."

"Indeed this is very strange, and yet, yet ——"

"Yet what, signior?"

"I ought not to wonder at it. When saw you the queen last, fair one?"

"Yesterday, as she went to the church by the fountain. She sent me a pistole, and the gentleman she sent it by said to me, in the queen's name,—

"'Her majesty hopes you will lead a just life, and she will be good to you.'"

The cloaked courtier, in whom the reader recognises again Don Jose, the favourite minister of the king, was silent for some moments, during which he seemed to be buried in such deep thought, that Maritana had walked some distance away before he became aware that she had at all removed herself from the spot. Suddenly, however, looking up, he discovered her at some distance, and walking quickly after her, he said,—

"Maritana, pause a moment."

She turned and looked at him inquiringly, and he added,—

"The fortune-teller who in your childhood told you you should be a countess was right."

"Right!"

"Yes, you shall be a countess; I am certain of it. Keep my words in your remembrance, and meet me at this spot an hour hence."

"A countess—a countess! Oh, Heaven! can my dreams be true? No, no. This is some mockery—some carnival freak, merely to deservedly punish my absurd ambition. I, the poor street-singer, a countess! and yet—I know—that is, people tell me I am —am ——"

"Beautiful, you would say," whispered Don Jose; "and they are right. It is your rare beauty which shall raise you to the height you long to reach. Be punctual here one hour from this time, and now adieu."

He rapidly turned away from the spot; but he had not proceeded many paces before he slunk into an entry until a man had passed, who was attired in coarse, common garments, but who trod the street with a lordly air, and who muttered, as he passed Don Jose, " She is an angel—she is an angel."

When he had gone a few paces past the entry, he seemed to have espied Maritana, and, by the sudden animation he displayed in his movements, it would seem as if his words must have referred to her, for he rapidly made up to her; and, although she flew from him the moment she observed him, he seemed determined to overtake her, and he ran very quickly in the same direction until both were out of sight.

Then Don Jose emerged from his hiding-place, and, glancing after the man who had made use of the energetic expression concerning his admiration for Maritana, he laughed aloud, and muttered,—

" 'Tis well—'tis very well. How well everything works for me! That is the king, and he loves this girl, Maritana. He is like most royal wooers, not over fond of difficulties in the way of his passion; and I, as his majesty's prime minister and favourite councillor, must see what difficulties there are shall be surmounted as easily as may be, and the more particularly as certain little schemes of my own most admirably fit in with this amour in which the king wishes to be engaged."

For some minutes he leaned against the column which supported the veranda of a house, and appeared in deep reflection. Then, suddenly wrapping his cloak about him, he muttered, as he walked slowly in the same direction which had been taken by Maritana and her royal lover,—

" If anything could possibly move the lovely Queen of Spain to listen to my daring suit, it would be an abundant proof of her husband's infidelity, and she shall have it. Yes; by Heaven and by hell she shall have it. I love her—I adore her; but yet have I hitherto kept my passion concealed like a slumbering volcano, because I have had certain well-founded fears for the safety of my head, if I so much as breathed one word which could bear such a meaning to her ears. Now, though, I do begin to think my time has come, and that fortune is smiling propitiously upon me. I shall, I must succeed; I am sure to succeed. Who shall now stay me in my onward career? I began with being less than the least about the court; but there shall be no virtue in intrigue, in lying, in assassination, or in all sorts of chicanery, if I do not leave off in being greater than the greatest, —and that, to my mind, means favourite of the king, and lover of the queen; so I shall hold sovereign sway in Spain, and be its virtual head. Who dare then say me nay? Truly, I begin to think I was born for great things! All goes well with me; I am already rich beyond all comparison with any of the grandees, and I am thriving in my designs I have set heart upon. Now for an attentive consideration of the ways and means of future proceeding."

So saying, he walked rapidly away, nor did he for some time notice that he was followed closely by his satellite Moress, who had been dodging him as close as he could, in the hope of overhearing some of his master's villanous cogitations.

Don Jose was by far too well acquainted with the personal appearance of the King of Spain to entertain any doubt whatever as to the person who was pursuing Maritana being that monarch in disguise, and he was quite right, for it was, indeed, no other than Charles the Second, who had, unknown to any one, thus stolen out into the streets, with the hope of being rewarded for his trouble by some intrigue, which should, by its novelty, beguile the tedium of a royal existence.

Charles had some good qualities, but they were seldom seen, even when they did not interfere with the gratification of his passion; when they did happen to do so, the most microscopic eyes could not have discovered one of them. His queen, of whom Maritana had spoken in such eulogistic terms, was fully deserving of anything that could be said in her praise. She was young, beautiful, and accomplished; but, alas!

" Familiar charms will fail to please,"

and the dissolute, irascible being behaved towards her with the greatest possible indifference, and openly avowed that he cared nothing for her, giving her ample reason to believe that he was concerned in criminal intrigues. All this she bore without a murmur; if she wept, it was in secret. True, she became paler each day, but that silent reproach was the only one that Charles the Second could ever have said—if, indeed, he had noticed it at all—she had given him for his brutality.

He was just such a man to have just such a minister and confederate as the infamous Don Jose.

He had seen Maritana more than once, and he had, after some struggle with his pride in even addressing a word of admiration to one in so lowly a station of life, made up his mind to follow her, and tender her his gracious notice and protection, never for a moment dreaming that there could be anything like virtuous feeling in the mind of a dancing girl. The very idea was absurd; why, he knew well that there was extremely little among the highest and, by courtesy, noblest members of the court.

Charles the Second of Spain, something like our Charles the Second of England, was too proud for a great many things, but not in the least degree too proud to be vicious.

He succeeded in keeping Maritana in view through several streets, until she, fancying that he was not following her further, paused for breath, remarking to herself, as she panted, and held by some railings for support,—

" How I dread that strange, dark-looking man who has now twice to-night endeavoured to procure some conversation with me. I have a most singular horror of him."

Scarcely were the words out of her mouth, when the object which had produced them suddenly darted forward; and, before she could remove from the spot, and trust again to her fleetness for escape, he seized her by the arm, saying, in a passionate voice,—

" Lovely creature, why do you fly from one who loves you?"

" Help! help! Unhand me, signior, or my cries will raise me many defenders."

" Indeed! who dares to lift a hand against ——" He paused, and, in a lower tone, added,—" But your alarm is needless, beautiful being. I love you; let that at once suffice."

" I say once more, signior, unhand me," cried Maritana, " or your singular assumption shall meet with its just reward! What have I done that you should thus persecute me? I am not so friendless as you suppose."

" Persecute you?"

" Ay, signior, persecute me. You look surprised! If ever you harboured in your breast the outrageous fancy that your addresses could be agreeable to me, dismiss it once, and leave me."

" Why this cool disdain?"

" 'Tis not disdain. Call it, signior, by another name, and you will nearer hit the feeling."

" What name, fair one?"

" Hatred!"

" Pshaw! this is coquetry; part of the arts by which you, and such as you are, enhance your favours. Once more, I tell you plainly and explicitly, I love you; and, what I apprehend is more to the purpose, I am very rich."

"Is this language to an unprotected girl manly, sir? Is it becoming the lowest in Madrid?"

"Perhaps not, but it may better become——"

"You pause for a word; I will supply it. You would have said, it would better become a ruffian, such as your appearance at once bespeaks you."

"My appearance? Humph! I am scarcely used to so harsh a judgment on my looks."

"Then you are used to being much flattered, signor, for Nature must have been sadly in want of materials of beauty when she fashioned you."

"Hem! Ah, hem! We, that is I—a-hem!"

Maritana walked away; but the king was not to be so easily foiled, and once more he pursued her, but she did not this time fly as before, but called loudly for help, and the royal lover precipitately fled in an opposite direction, when the first person he met was Don Jose, who would not have ventured to accost him, had not the king himself first spoken.

Night was now rapidly approaching, and, perhaps, the exciting events of the day had somewhat contributed to thin the streets of the carnival maskers It was only now and then that some peal of laughter would come upon the ear, or a troop of merry blades would sweep onwards with torches and masks, and, in some cases, with drawn swords, not caring if their fun took rather a mischievous turn.

These, however, gradually decreased, for nearly all who had been out for the last six or seven hours had become thoroughly tired and exhausted, so that they were glad to seek some place of rest, where they could sleep off the fatigues of one day to prepare themselves for the coming festivities and wild gaieties of that which was so soon to come. On crept the night, until the churches pealed forth the hour of twelve.

The silence that reigns in Madrid at the hour of midnight is complete and striking. No sounds meet the ear; you listen in vain for a footstep, and you cannot catch even the sounds of the retreating footsteps of some itinerant friar or monk.

The buildings look like formidable masses of stone that never sheltered human beings; the few lights glimmer far apart, and are so solitary that they appear to be useless. Death-like silence prevails; not any sign of life can be traced; not the howl of a dog even breaks in upon the solitude of the night.

The starry hosts above look quietly down upon the blackened earth, and, sparkling, throw a sweet, but subdued lustre over the heavens—in themselves not more silent than the city itself.

Palace and humble dwelling all are closed, and no light gleams from any stray window; stragglers are no longer abroad, and sleep has settled upon the eyelids of the inhabitants of that ancient and populous city.

The old palaces, the large palaces of the nobility, that are the pride and beauty of Madrid, are not well viewed at such an hour; but their dark frowning structures stand up boldly in the night-air and mock the senses to the belief that they were the work of men's hands, but men who had been swept away from the earth.

The moon rose, and threw a quiet and chaste light over the whole city, which appeared like an enchanted one—for the silvery rays fell upon the white walls, and caused them to appear so distinctly, and so beautiful. Sudden and clearly-defined were the lights and shades.

The quiet streets were illumined on one side by the rays of the moon, while the other was thrown in a deep shade by the houses that intercepted the moonlight, ay, a deeper shade still—from the very contrast the two sides exhibited.

Grotesque and strange forms were thrown upon the opposite walls, that the imagination might well pursue, and give life to, calling from the depths of memory things that have long lain forgotten; but now, at this still hour of the night, when all is as motionless and silent as the grave, they rise, and we once again, though unexpectedly, and perhaps unknown, revisit the scenes, and enter into new combinations, serving the poet and the painter with new and apt imagery, and then deemed efforts of thought, the scintillations of a great mind, and not the hidden spark that requires but circumstances to call it into light and existence.

The sounds of the watch making their rounds through the city indeed disturb this deep stillness; the measured tramp of men, their approach, their presence, and their gradual disappearance, the retreating footstep, all—all tend to awaken in the mind a full sense of loneliness, and the solitariness that can be felt even in a large city.

Insensibly the sounds die away, and are no longer heard. We listen in vain; was it a dream—a vision, that flits away as the mind regains its empire, and becomes a thing of nought? How much like visions are past events, and how unlike future ones?

How still the earth, how still the heavens; not a sound save the beating of the observer's own heart, and the sound of his own breathing, calm and quiet, serene and beautiful. What a moment for contemplation! the mind lifts itself above the sphere in which it exists, and turns to thoughts of dark futurity.

In the sunny climate of Spain the morning's dawn rapidly succeeds the midnight hour, and before the city had lain so wrapt in deep repose three hours, the signs of life and animation began slowly to arise, and a faint gleam of light showed itself sweetly upon the highest spires and house-tops.

CHAPTER VI.

THE CONFERENCE OF THE KING AND THE MINISTER. — THE HUMILIATING PENANCE.—A ROYAL PERSONAGE OUT OF TEMPER, AND THE RESULTS.

WE have said that Don Jose would not have ventured upon a recognition of his royal master had not the latter spoken to him first, for kings, however jealous they may be of their prerogatives, do not invariably wish to be known when they have thought proper to throw off the state of majesty, and mix with the common people, who are not anything by the grace of anything, and only useful when the taxes are required to be paid.

But Charles the Second of Spain had few if any scruples in allowing his minister, Don Jose, to be aware that the royal inclination prompted him to come into the streets of Madrid in disguise, and he accordingly accosted the fawning sycophant, who was far more the minister of the king's pleasures than a statesman.

"Jose," said the king, "you are out late."

"Your majesty's example," replied the minister, "should influence all loyal subjects."

"Pshaw! I want no jesting now. Have you seen in the streets a—a kind of dancing or singing girl?"

"Young and beautiful?"

"Yes—yes."

"Her name is ——"

"Maritana, as I have heard the people say. By St. Jerome, she is young and beautiful, indeed. She is a perfect divinity! Such eyes—such lips—a voice of music; she is perfection itself. You have seen her, Jose?"

"I have, your majesty; and when I did see her my thought was—if I may be excused for stating it—that she was a fit mate for a king."

"A good thought, too, Jose; but she carries her coquetry to great lengths."

"Indeed, your majesty!"

"Yes. I followed and spoke to her—I told her I was rich, and proffered my love; but, from some strange caprice, she said me nay, and called even for assistance, when I further pressed my suit."

"Arrant coquetry, your majesty; she plays her part well, sire. But, if she did but know that it was the Lord's anointed who sought her, we should soon see a rapid change in her manner."

"But that, Jose, she must not know. I cannot allow the name of majesty to be mixed up with such intrigues."

"Most certainly not; such would be most impolitic. Were I your majesty, I would on such occasions take the name of some member of your majesty's court—some name that would be a guarantee for wealth and power, while, at the same time, your kingly dignity could not suffer by coming in contact with the bourgeois."

"Not a bad thought, Jose; but then, the grandees of Spain are as jealous of their honour as even the king can be of his."

"But who dare complain of any assumption of your majesty?"

"Ah, truly. I will, for the future, in all intrigues among the people, call myself Don Jose."

"Don Jose?"

"Aye; surely your advice is good."

"But, your majesty, by assuming my name, I fear ——"

"You fear what? How dare you complain?"

"I fear your majesty, at least in this affair, would suffer, because I have reason to believe I am in bad odour with this lovely dancer."

"Ah! Have you, then, followed her?"

"On your majesty's account, I have—not on my own; but she by some means found out who I was, and treated me to some hard names. So, by assuming my name, I fear your royal attractions would suffer."

"Well, well, Jose, we will think of it; perhaps on some other occasion I may honour you so far as to assume your name. But, mark me, that girl must be mine, by force or by fraud. You understand me, Jose?"

"Perfectly. But there is a curious circumstance connected with her, that I am endeavouring to elucidate."

"What is it?"

"This. It appears, by the manner and the language of this girl, that she is not of the lowly origin her present appearance would lead one to suppose. I have been making some inquiries, and my belief that she would turn out to be a personage of some consequence, is strengthened by the answers I have received."

"Indeed! You surprise me."

"Not more, your majesty, than I was myself surprised. My belief is, in brief, that she has been in very early life stolen by the gitanos, and that she is the daughter of some noble family."

"This may be possible, Jose."

"It is probable, sire, she is no gitano, although the people name her such, and she has, in part, the costume of that strange race. But if your majesty feels sufficiently interested in her to command me to pursue my inquiries, I shall do so most diligently."

"Sufficiently interested!" exclaimed the king; "I tell you, Jose, I am deeply interested. Pursue your inquiries by all possible means. I shall not love her the less that she should turn out to be by birth worthy of the attentions of a monarch."

"Your majesty's orders shall be obeyed."

The king now walked on for some distance, while at about a pace behind him came Don Jose, who kept a profound silence, until he should be again addressed by the royal voluptuary, whose odd temper and habits no one knew better how to adapt himself to than Don Jose.

After they had proceeded thus for some distance the king said, suddenly,—

"Has there got been some disturbance in the streets to-night, Jose?"

"There has, sire."

"I heard firing."

"Oh, it was only a few of the rabble shot—no one of any sort of consequence. The guard apprehended one Don Cæsar, whom your majesty remembers at one time as making quite a sensation in Madrid by his extravagancies, before your majesty came to the throne."

"I have some faint recollection. Why was he arrested?"

"He is a wild, dissolute, wine-drinking fellow, with more wit than judgment, and he must needs have a duel with a captain of the guard. The captain fell, for this Don Cæsar is an unequalled swordsman, so the guard arrested him."

"Humph!"

"And the people, with whom he was a special favourite, would fain have rescued him, and in the accompanying squabbling, some few of them were shot."

"Ah!"

Here the conversation concerning Don Cæsar stopped, and again for a time the king walked on in silence, until suddenly the sound of a guitar came upon his ear, and he paused as he said,—

"Jose, that is Maritana's guitar. I have listened before to her brilliant execution."

"In faith, your majesty has a fine ear."

"Go on, and see if I be right. I will tarry here for you, beneath this portico."

Don Jose walked on, in obedience to the orders he had received, and upon cautiously slinking round a corner, he observed about seven or eight gay young cavaliers, who were listening to a song of Maritana, which she was herself accompanying upon the guitar. They were loud and vehement in their plaudits when she had finished, and one of them said,—

"Bravo, bravo, pretty Maritana. Here is payment for you, and may you never lose your beauty or your skill on the guitar, for when you do, Madrid will lose one of its principal charms."

"Oh, signor," she replied, "you are too good."

"Farewell, Maritana; farewell."

"Adieu, signiors; adieu."

The merry party walked away, and when they had got a little distance off, Jose returned to the king, saying,—

"She is alone, and your majesty, if it so please you, may again urge your suit; but I should advise you to speak to her quietly, rather trying to remove any impression against you she may have already conceived, than pressing your suit."

The king made a gesture of impatience, and walked towards Maritana, who uttered a slight scream when she saw him, which induced him to think that, as before, she contemplated flight, and he flung his arms round her, crying,—

"Lovely Maritana, you shall—you must be mine!"

Alarmed beyond measure at this outrage, she called loudly for help, and, unfortunately for the royal lover, her cries were heard by the young cavaliers who had so lately parted from her, and, before the king was aware of their presence, they had returned and surrounded him and Maritana.

"Why, what is this, Maritana?" cried one.

"This man," she gasped, "this man ——"

"What did he do?"

"He has followed and insulted me the whole of this evening. Let him go, signiors, let him go; and if you will see me as far as the Place Jerome, I shall be much beholden to you."

"We don't feel disposed to let him go quite so easily," said one. "Who are you, scoundrel?"

"Villain!" said the king, and he laid his hand upon his sword, "let me pass!"

"Not yet—not yet," cried the cavaliers, as they drew their swords and surrounded him.

Fury flashed from his eyes, and he half drew his sword from its sheath, but prudence told him how useless was any resistance against so many, and he returned it again, saying,—

"Gentlemen, this is only a jest. Good evening."

"Oh, but it's no joke," said one.

"This is carnival time," added the king; "and surely a gentleman need not be called to account for speaking to a pretty woman."

"Certainly not; but no gentleman ought to persecute a pretty woman. You say, Maritana, that this fellow, who is ill-looking enough to be the devil in disguise, has followed you about contrary to your wishes. You don't like him?"

"Like him—I abhor him!"

"What shall we do with him, gentlemen?"

"Make him ask pardon on his knees," said one.

"Duck him in the fountain, near at hand," suggested another. "There has been one ducking match there already, and there may as well be another."

"Signiors," said the king, "I am a gentleman; here's my sword, I will maintain my honour against any one of you in combat."

"Well, there's something in that," said one; "but we don't think the matter worth killing you for; so you shall be let off easy. What say you, gentlemen, to making this ugly fellow show us a little how he can jump?"

"Bravo! bravo!—a good thought," cried the others, and two of them immediately laid their swords across at a distance of about four feet from the ground, crying,—

"Jump over that, and we will let you go."

"Gentlemen," said the king, looking in vain about him for assistance, and much wondering what could have become of Don Jose, "gentlemen, this is folly."

"Folly or not, you shall jump."

"Besides, it's the carnival time," said another. "when folly rules paramount. Make him jump."

The king bit his lips, and stamped with fury as he cried,—

"Help! help! Here, guard! guard!"

"It's of no use your calling, jump you shall, so you had better do so with a good grace as with a bad one. Come now, over—over."

"Idiots! you know not whom you are insulting."

"Nor do we care. Over—over."

"I am ——"

"A good jumper, no doubt. Give him a goad, Juan—give him a goad."

The young cavalier who was addressed as Juan, drew his sword, and applied its point so smartly to the hinder portion of the king's person, that with a roar of dismay, which was irresistibly amusing, he cleared the swords in a moment, and then ran off as fast as his legs would carry him in such a storm of passion, that he scarcely knew whither he was going, and instinct alone led him to the garden-gate of his palace, where was always a page in readiness to admit him privately at any hour of the day or night.

Never had that page seen his royal master in such a perfect frenzy of rage as on that night, or rather early morning, and he shrunk back perfectly aghast, as he saw the pale face, knitted brows, and distended eyes of the infuriated king.

"How now, sirrah," he cried; "you kept me waiting."

"I humbly beg your majesty's pardon."

"How dare you humbly beg my pardon—ha!"

The page stammered and stuttered something that was perfectly unintelligible, and much rejoiced was he when the king dashed past him without further parley, and made his way into the state apartments.

"Well," he said, as he drew a long breath of relief, "something has gone all wrong with the king, I never saw him in such a rage in all my life. He is not the best tempered man in the world at any time, but to-night he is perfectly furious. It's a mercy he didn't run me through."

And so indeed it was, for his most gracious majesty was just in the royal humour to do mischief to somebody, and he was not very particular as to whom it might be.

Before, however, he could reach his private apartments, he had an opportunity of being ill-tempered, such as he did not expect, and he was a little soothed by it, since it gave him the satisfaction of being revenged upon somebody, and as he was angry with all the world, it answered very well indeed.

He was hastily crossing an ante-chamber adjoining another apartment in which was the usual palace guard that remained on duty all night, when an officer came up to him, and respectfully saluting him, said,—

"Will your majesty be pleased to grant me a moment's audience?"

"Well, sir, what is it?"

"Sire, last night there was a duel fought in the streets."

"Yes, yes—go on, sir."

"A captain of your majesty's guard was slain by one Don Cæsar; it was in fair open fight, and Don Cæsar, at the conflict as well as after it, behaved with much generosity and chivalrous courage."

"And what then?"

"I have to humbly sue to your majesty for Don Cæsar's pardon. I have served your majesty faithfully eighteen years, and never yet asked a favour."

"Indeed! Give me writing materials."

"They are here, sire. Heaven bless you for your clemency to a brave but unfortunate man. Don Cæsar is a man of much indiscretion, but of much honour, and I still have hopes he may be an ornament to your majesty's court. But for him, there would have been a very serious collision between the guard and the people, who wanted to rescue him, but he would not permit them."

While the officer was speaking, the king stood by a table writing, and when he had done, he said,—

"There, take that order to the keeper of the prison, and see that it be obeyed."

"I humbly thank your majesty. Long may you live, sire. This act of clemency fills my mind with more gratitude than I have power to express. I promised Don Cæsar that I would intercede for him, and I, from my heart, thank your majesty for this great condescension and mercy."

The king gave a ghastly sort of smile, and then passed on, satisfied thoroughly with himself, and not at all abashed to hear the grateful tones of the officer's voice ringing in his ears. That officer, the reader will recollect, was the same who had promised Don Cæsar that the generous manner in which he had behaved, when the mob would have produced a scene of bloodshed, by attempting to rescue him, should be reported to the king.

When Charles had passed out of the room, the officer continued to gaze after him for some moments in silence, and then he said,—

"Well, they say that he is cold-hearted and vicious, and that he delights in cruelty, but he has now shown that he can do a generous action in spite of all that people say of him. Henceforth he will find me a better servant than ever. I long to be enabled now to do something in requital of this kindness."

With such grateful feelings dwelling at his heart, the officer took up the paper which he never entertained a doubt was the pardon of Don Cæsar. He held it close to the window in order to read it. There were but few words, and they were written not very intelligibly, but the officer's face grew red and pale by turns as he read them, and then the paper dropped from his hands as he uttered the exclamation of—

"Gracious Heaven!"

The words on the sheet of paper which gave the officer such a pang of disappointment and alarm were these,—

"*Don Cæsar de Bazan to be hanged at seven o'clock.*"
"CHARLES."

Well might that generous-minded man shudder as he again took up the document which he had supposed had been of so very different a tendency. He was silent for some minutes, and then with a burst of indignation which he could not suppress, he said,—

"The callous, cold-hearted villain! Now I swear that if Don Cæsar de Bazan be executed in this cruel, shameful manner, that I will seek some honourable employment in another clime, and never call myself again a Spaniard. Shame! shame on the cruel act. And to calmly receive my thanks and praises for his clemency. Oh! Charles, Charles, you are indeed as bad as any one can possibly say. You are cruel, crafty, cholic, and unjust—sacrificing to passion those whom justice should have spared. What can I do for you, poor Don Cæsar—brave, but doomed man? You are lost—you are lost!"

At this moment, an equerry of the palace came into the outer room, and approaching the officer, he said,—

"I am sent by the king to command that a written order he has given to you, be taken to the place of confinement of the person to whom it refers."

The officer turned sharply, and was on the point of making some imprudent answer, but he knew that the person who was speaking to him was one of those court favourites who would repeat anything he heard to the great danger and disadvantage of any one—so he repressed his honest indignation, and merely said,—

"His majesty's orders shall be obeyed, sir."

The equerry bowed and withdrew, while the officer with a heavy heart, repaired to the guard-room and ordered his horse.

While these things were going on at the palace, Don Jose was not idle, for although he had hidden himself and was quite resolved to incur no personal risk by taking the part of his beloved sovereign, whose involuntary humiliation he saw and very much enjoyed; he was fully alive to the commission that had been given him concerning the beautiful but disdainful Maritana.

The hour at which he had asked her to meet him was already passed, and when the young men had again left her, he slunk out of his hiding-place, and followed her. He was, however, far more prudent than his master, for he took care that she should be completely out of hearing of her late defenders before he spoke to her, and then quickening his pace, he called to her.

"Maritana—Maritana!"

She paused, and turning to him, exclaimed,—

"Oh! I had forgotten my appointment."

"So I feared," said Don Jose, "for you are walking in a directly opposite direction, and the hour is already passed. I have something to say to you of vast importance to your interests, and shall I say your ambition, which reaches so high?"

"My ambition! Sir, I have seen almost enough to-night to make me wish to leave Madrid and wander once again, as some time since I was accustomed to do, among the wilds of nature."

"What! and bury that lovely face and form among hinds? Oh! execrable thought. You might as well make a prisoner of yourself to the tomb."

"I have had thoughts of a convent."

"Ah, there I am perfectly easy. The convents like to see penitents very much, but they must bring something with them more substantial than piety. There is no fear of your going into a convent."

"Is it indeed so?"

"It is; but this is idle talking. I have something to tell you which should give you much satisfaction, and far from making you wish to leave life or Madrid, should present both with new and varied charms to you."

"What can that be?"

"Tell me again, truly, that you are ambitious."

"Oh! signor, you know how to touch a chord that vibrates to my heart. I am ambitious!"

"You say the queen has smiled on you?"

"Twice or thrice."

"'Tis well. She has spoken to me of you."

"To you of me?"

"Ay, truly; and to convince you that I do not deceive you, I have the liberty of using her majesty's name in declaring to you that she has resolved upon making you a countess."

"A countess?"

"Yes; the dream of your young ambition will be verified. The prophecy of early life shall be fulfilled to you, and whoever it was who told you you would come to such a dignity, should be henceforward honoured by you as a true prophet. You shall be a countess, Maritana."

The eyes of the beautiful girl flashed with a new brilliancy, as she said,—

"Can it be real? Oh! signor, do not deceive me. Do not raise proud, ambitious hopes which may again be quenched for ever. La Countess! I, the poor street singer? Oh! 'tis madness."

"Not if the queen wills it."

"No, no, not if the queen wills it. But what assurance can I have that she does so will it?"

"Did you never hear of Don Jose?"

"The king's favourite?"

"Why, people do say he is; but be that how it may, I am he, and let that knowledge, which I desire you to keep secret, be an assurance to you that I have the queen's orders to make you the promise you have heard pass my lips."

"Don Jose! Men call you crafty."

"Humph! do they?"

"And cruel."

"That is their confounded malevolence. When you have lived a little longer in the world, you will find that the most virtuous characters are always the most misrepresented."

"But to make me a countess appears so very improbable, I cannot believe it."

"Nor will you until to-morrow."

"To-morrow—say you to-morrow? So soon? Oh! how my heart beats with excitement. A countess and to-morrow! Don Jose, if you are trifling with me, or if this be but some plan to deceive me to dishonour, the vengeance of a blighted heart will not sue to Heaven in vain."

"I am not deceiving you."

"I am not a gitana, but yet they have taught me how to revenge myself on my betrayers."

"I swear to you, Maritana, that I am not deceiving you. A countess you shall be, and that to-morrow, provided you will implicitly abide by the directions I shall give you."

"Your directions?"

"No; I should have said the queen's, because I act wholly for her in this business."

"The good queen."

"Ay, and the beautiful queen. You must to-morrow morning, by an early hour, present yourself at my hotel, and by showing this ring to the porter, you will be admitted, when I will fully explain to you the part you have to act."

"To-morrow morning?"

"Yes, at an early hour. I should say, indeed, this morning, for already the city is light with the rising sun. Come to me at eight o'clock—speak of this interview to no one, or you will mar your own good fortune; and remember it is the queen who speaks these words to you through me, who am but her messenger. You will be punctual?"

"Yes—yes."

"'Tis well; you will be a countess ere noon to-morrow. Farewell, now—you will be a countess. Dream of state and grandeur, for most assuredly they will be yours."

CHAPTER VII.

THE ROYAL CLOSET.—THE MINISTER'S EXCUSES.—A SOLILOQUY OF A VILLAIN.—THE DAYLIGHT.

It was about four o'clock in the morning when Don Jose arrived at the palace, which he entered by the same means that Charles himself had, through the private gardens, and a staircase that led to the room in which the page was waiting the arrival of Don Jose.

It was not without some feelings of an unpleasant character that Don Jose came near the royal apartments; for again the recollection of what occurred in Madrid returned to his mind; but, then, Don Jose was a courtier, and believed that he could well excuse himself for what had happened, and, at the same time, he would endeavour to impress upon his royal master what he himself had suffered in aiding him in his pleasures.

Some such thoughts as these passed through his mind as he went through the different parts of the palace, on his way to the ante-chamber, where the page and officer of the guard were waiting, and who had both met with such astonishing intimations of the royal displeasure, that could not, it would appear, be exhibited elsewhere.

Entering the ante-chamber, the door of which he carefully closed after him, he observed the page, with a thoughtful and no very pleased brow, was standing gazing at some of the tapestry and hangings that almost surrounded the apartment, as though he were either intent upon examining them, or he was absorbed in thought, which latter was the most probable.

Don Jose walked quietly up to the page, and, placing his hand upon his shoulder, exclaimed,—

"So, Sir Page, are you sleeping? Has watching so overcome you, that you do not see who enters the king's ante-chamber?"

"Oh, signior," replied the page, "I wish I could escape the knowledge sometimes; but they leave such causes of recollection behind, that I can't forget."

"Humph! I do not understand you," replied Don Jose; "but, tell me, has our gracious sovereign passed this way to his chamber?"

"Yes, signior, the king has been past, and is in there," replied the page, pointing significantly to the chamber, "and well I know the king has returned."

"Indeed, he has given you some good and substantial reason for knowing it, I'll be bound. Well, well, he's a generous master to his servants."

"I'd rather be free from his gratuities, signior," said the page, shrugging his shoulders.

"Why, boy?" inquired Don Jose.

"Because they came this morning in the shape of blows, and he appeared to be in such a humour that I never recollect to have seen him in before. 'Twas no use to be right, unless you were out of reach, for it didn't prevent one from being soundly boxed. Oh! he is in a most terrible humour, I assure you, signior."

"Ah, well, I can easily imagine all that; the fact is, he has met with some little incidents that have led to this, and I am not surprised at it. However, I will in and see his gracious majesty."

Don Jose was about doing as he had said, when the officer who had been so singularly unsuccessful in his intercession with Charles for the pardon of Don Cæsar, stepped forward, saying,—

"Pardon me for delaying you one moment, Don Jose; but I would have a word or two with you, and beg your intercession with the king, who really is in a singular state of mind this morning."

"Indeed," replied Don Jose; "pray what would you wish me to do?—and for whom am I to intercede?"

"For Don Cæsar de Bazan," replied the officer.

"Oh, I understand."

"See here," continued the officer, holding out the piece of paper; "see here, I took this gentleman, who had a duel with an officer of the guard, who certainly deserved the punishment inflicted on him. Don Cæsar killed the officer of the guard——"

"Of course," replied Don Jose; "proceed."

"After giving him a second chance of his life, and was taken prisoner by some of the guard; and he would have been rescued, but for his own conduct, which was such as did honour to a gentleman and a nobleman. He repressed a popular tumult, and saved the guard from, probably, massacre, refusing to accept of his liberty at the expense of a single drop of blood shed in the streets of Madrid."

"Well," replied Don Jose, "has his majesty been made acquainted with the affair?"

"Yes, I have informed him of what has occurred, and of Don Cæsar's behaviour; I promised, on my word, as a gentleman and a soldier, I would inform his majesty, and I thought it probable I should obtain his pardon."

"And what said the king?"

"As I told him all, he requested writing materials and wrote this paper, which I believed to be Don Cæsar's pardon, and which I thanked him for as he passed into his closet; but look, Don Jose, and see what he has written."

"Ah! I see," replied Don Jose, reading; "'tis his execution at seven o'clock this morning. His majesty is *not*, then, in very good humour."

"Very far from it," replied the officer; "but what is to be done? Time flies rapidly, and Don Cæsar's hour for execution will quickly arrive, and he will be expecting his pardon; instead of which, here is his death-warrant."

"No agreeable substitute, certainly. I know Don Cæsar well enough; he is a wild, dissolute man—a good fencer, and one more likely to commit some mischief from a sudden ebullition of temper, than any cool, deliberate, or predetermined crime."

"Exactly; but such was not the case now, for he was rashly hurried on by the man who fell mortally wounded. Don Cæsar behaved with unexampled generosity, and saved Madrid from a popular tumult, and the guard from disgrace and defeat. Surely, it is a disgraceful occurrence as to execute such a man as this—a nobleman and gentleman, too; surely that cannot be allowed to take place. Will you, Don Jose, intercede with the king for pardon; or, at least, a respite, and then his pardon will surely follow."

"I will endeavour to obtain a pardon. The king is somewhat indisposed and angered at these tumults, no doubt; but I will intercede for Don Cæsar."

"Thanks, signior, thanks; but, in the meantime, how am I to act? I scarcely know what way to proceed; whether to wait the issue of your intercession, or proceed to Don Cæsar with this unpleasant and unlooked-for piece of intelligence."

"Proceed at once to Don Cæsar," replied the minister, "and at once unfold to him all that has happened, and, at the same time, bid him prepare for death, for who can confidently predict the issue?"

"No, no, certainly, no one. I have been so deceived to-day, that I will not believe a thing till it is more than done, or proven; till, indeed, it be a matter of history," replied the officer, despondingly.

"Well, well, signior," replied Don Jose, "do, do; but, at the same time, tell him he has a friend in the person of Don Jose, who will intercede with the king for his pardon, and hopes to get it; but, Heaven knows if our worthy monarch be in some moods, it will be hard to make him do any act at all; but my part shall not be wanting in this affair."

"Thanks, Don Jose, thanks," replied the officer; "I will at once to my unfortunate prisoner, and inform him of all that has happened since I saw him."

"Do so," replied Don Jose; "farewell!"

The officer quitted the waiting-room, leaving Don Jose at the door of the king's private closet, where he paused ere he turned the handle of the door, as if he were considering in his own mind the most likely nature of attack he should meet with from Charles, and the best mode of meeting and defending himself from it by inventions and falsehoods of the most outrageous character he could call to his aid.

Having apparently settled this in his mind, he quietly opened the door, and then pushing aside some drapery, stood in the royal closet.

For a moment or two Don Jose was not aware whether the king was present or not, so entire a stillness reigned in the apartment. A motion of Charles's brought him the intelligence that he was there.

Charles was seated in a chair, the high back of which was turned towards the door, which prevented Don Jose from seeing him, and he advanced cautiously till he brought himself on a line with the king's chair, and then he waited in silence till his majesty should deign to notice his presence.

The king was immediately aware of his minister's approach, and when he halted, he turned his face full upon him, and quietly regarded him with a stern look, but without deigning to speak to him. Don Jose saw the monarch's humour was not such a one as would be easily assuaged, far from it; but he had great confidence in himself and his own powers, but yet he deemed it better to allow a pause to ensue rather than be the breaker of it himself; and the king still continued to look hard at him.

It was curious to see the steady, angry glance of Charles the Second as he regarded his minister, and the cool assurance, yet deprecatory look, with which it was returned for several seconds.

"So, then, now all is safe, and we are duly housed in our palace, our worthy and politic minister can seek us, and possibly offer his aid; but there is neither danger nor lawless mobs here, and Don Jose can be courageous."

"Your majesty surely can but jest, or some great misapprehension has ——"

"Misapprehension!" exclaimed Charles, hastily; "what misapprehension can possibly exist, when facts are as plain as the noon-tide sun?"

"Pardon me, your majesty; but facts are most to be suspected when they speak so very plain."

"How?"

"I repeat, your majesty, that when a fact appears so very clear and plain as to be deemed unmistakeable, at that moment have the greatest doubts; for, as certain as you give way to such false signs, error will be the inevitable consequence."

"Don Jose," replied Charles, "I am in no jesting humour, and the absurdities you have just uttered are not such as you should greet the ear of your king with."

"Pardon me, your majesty," replied Don Jose

with apparent warmth and earnestness, "but I do not jest; what I have said I am ready to prove, and rest my life upon the result. I jest with your majesty ——"

"Silence, sir, and hear me!" cried Charles, stamping with his foot, and striking the arm of his chair with his clenched fist. Don Jose bowed low, and Charles proceeded.

"Where did you leave me?"

"In the streets of Madrid, your majesty," replied Don Jose, again bowing low.

"Yes, you did," replied the king between his teeth; "you did—you left your king at the moment of danger, when he needed help, when he was surrounded by armed ruffians, whose swords were drawn against him—he had to seek safety in flight, for there was not even one Spaniard who stood by his side to aid or defend him. Was it not so, Don Jose?"

"It was, your majesty," replied Don Jose, with another genuflection.

"You knew my extremity, Don Jose—you knew my extremity, did you not?"

"I certainly suspected, nay, believed it."

"You suspected and believed it! is that the way two Spanish gentlemen would have behaved to each other had they met with a like interruption—is it the way a minister ought to treat his king—did you render me the aid I needed, Don Jose?"

"I did not, as your majesty knows full well," again replied Don Jose, bowing low.

"Then, in the fiend's name, man," exclaimed Charles, in a fit of almost ungovernable fury, "what have you to allege by way of answer to such an accusation, so patiently listened to—are these the facts you would have me doubt?"

"I pray your majesty to grant me a patient hearing. I, as your majesty well knows, was in the streets of Madrid ——" said Don Jose.

"Oh, you were?" replied Charles, with silent mockery and contempt in his manner.

"And I," returned Don Jose, "met with the same party by whom your majesty was assaulted."

"Yes, yes, you did, and ran away, leaving me in the midst of them," replied Charles, quickly.

"Gracious sire, permit me to say no to that ——"

"How—will you tell me you did aid me?" exclaimed Charles, with a start.

"No, I did not aid your majesty," replied Don Jose, with admirable coolness; "but I strenuously endeavoured to do so, but, unfortunately—I should say, fortunately—I was not so well disguised as your majesty, and I was mistaken for your majesty, and immediately set upon by those men in the most murderous and cowardly manner; my life, or your majesty's, as I am convinced they believed, was their object, and had I not exerted my utmost skill and strength, I must have been slain."

"Humph!"

"Could I, your majesty, have flown to the succour of another—could my life have been available to your majesty, I would have rushed on them; but it could not, and to make a successful stand against so many was out of the power of any man, and I was becoming each moment more and more surrounded; I could not return a single thrust—all I could do was to parry and avoid the murderous thrusts made at me; finding I was unequal to such a contest, for the odds were not equal, I turned and fled, and fortunately found refuge within the church of Santa Maria, or I should have been borne away a mangled and bloody corpse."

"Indeed," said Charles, who began to listen with less contempt, but with an angry brow.

"Nay, more, your majesty; my blood had poured out on the very marble that paved the sanctuary, but for the interposition of a grey-beard priest, who threw himself between me and the bloodthirsty villains, who stood with their naked weapons, scarce awed by the place they were in, or the words of the good priest, who exhorted them to put up their weapons and quit the sanctuary. Fortunately some of the guard came up, and I then escaped under their escort; and here I am, your majesty's most patient servant."

Charles mused for some moments upon the excuses of his minister, and his anger gave way; but he had been too deeply offended to pass it off without feeling some vexation, though the occurrence was unavoidable, and Don Jose probably imagined the course of his thoughts, and believing that he had done all he needed, he adroitly turned the conversation, and mentioned the name of Maritana.

"What of the gitana?" he inquired, hastily.

"I have heard much, but I cannot just now tell your majesty more than the account of it; and that is, Maritana is no gipsy—she is connected by blood to a noble house. This I have learned from careful inquiries which are yet in course of being made."

"Are you sure of your intelligence?" inquired the king.

"Certain, your majesty; and expect to be confirmed in all my anticipations. She is the niece of a noble house, and was stolen, when young, by the gipsies, out of revenge for some real or fancied injury. This is being developed, and your majesty may yet succeed in all you desire."

"This is strange news!"

"But not more strange than true. But, to perfect my plans, I desire more authority from your majesty. This girl is ambitious, and I have made certain promises, and I want but your majesty's approval and permission to act as the case may require."

"I want rest, Don Jose, and shall retire; but you have my royal word that you are permitted to do aught you think requisite for the furtherance of the scheme." As the king spoke, he rose and quitted the closet, leaving Don Jose alone.

"So," communed the crafty, designing Don Jose, "so I am not a bad hand at excuses. My old craft has not at all forsaken me, and I can fool the king as usual. Ha! ha! Well, well, some are born to cheat, and some to be cheated. I flatter myself I belong to the former category. Poor Charles, he believes me; and after all it is for his own advantage, for where could he get a minister so useful to him as myself? And now let me consider what progress I am making in my daring scheme of ambition—a scheme which would appal any one but myself. I love the queen—yes, and she must be mine. If anything will accomplish such a result, it will be by awakening all the jealousy which surely exists in every woman's nature. She shall be convinced of the king's infidelity to her, and having so royal an example, perchance she may be induced to follow it. I can but try. In order, then, that such an occurrence as the king having a mistress should be brought fully under the queen's eyes, this girl, Maritana, shall be placed in a position about the court which shall make the king's intrigue with her notorious. Moreover, his own feelings will be better consulted by making him believe her noble, than a mere dancing girl. She shall become the wife of this Don Cæsar de Bazan, and I think I can offer him some inducements to leave her his name as a legacy; for die he must, and shall, or he would be much in the way. If, too, I manage this affair well, I can materially serve the king as regards his intrigue with her, for she shall not know who she marries at the time she marries; and she shall be made to believe that the Don Cæsar she knew was not the real one, but a mere adventurer assuming the title. I will to the prison shortly and perfect this business, which, if it place the queen in my arms, places Spain at my disposal along with the greatest loveliness it can boast of possessing. 'Tis a rare and politic scheme, and would sadly puzzle a less subtle head than mine. Now for the meeting with this girl, who is to play so odd a part in the drama I am preparing as a stepping-stone to my own ambition.''

Thus soliloquized Don Jose as he stood alone in the royal closet, a cool, designing villain, who could make men's vices and their lives the means by which he climbed the giddy ladder of fortune.

He paused, and, after a few moments' reflection, he seated himself in the chair in which Charles had himself had been sitting but a few moments before, and looking around him he said,—

"Well, this is indeed a right royal closet, and one that well befits the majesty of Spain."

It was indeed as Don Jose had said, a right royal closet, for such it was called; yet it might have deserved a much higher name than this.

The closet, as it was called, was a large room, in which the king spent much of his time and saw many of his statesmen and some foreigners. It was splendidly furnished, both as regards the extreme comfort and elegance of the apartment, and the richness and costliness of its furniture.

The hangings were of the finest texture and pattern, loaded with ornaments, while the rich gilding that ran round the ceiling and sides of the room gave it the appearance of a piece of rich and curiously-wrought mosaic work, adorned by every device that fancy could devise, or art execute; no cost or pains had been spared in the adornment of this room.

The carpets, too, were thick and soft to the tread, while the lively and delicate tints gave a life and animation difficult to be conceived. The foot felt the elasticity of the carpet in the tread; the soft, down-like feeling, and the utter silence of the step as it was walked over, had a peculiar and beautiful effect.

The heavy curtains were drawn close before the windows, and excluded the light from the closet most effectually. But Don Jose suddenly arose, as if he had just thought of something, and walking to the window, he drew the curtains on one side, and admitted the sun beams into the royal closet, exclaiming as he did so,—

"'Tis day, and I, too, need repose; but I have too much employment, and I have no confidants, and none aid me save those who do it unwillingly, and those I thank not."

CHAPTER VIII.

THE PRISON.—THE EXPULSION OF LAZARILLO.—THE OFFICER'S ARRIVAL. — THE GAOLER. — THE CONVERSATION.—THE GRIEF OF LAZARILLO.

DON JOSE was right, for the bright sun was shining sweetly on Madrid; alike on palace or prison did its rays fall, and as little heeded the gilding of the one or the sombre poverty of the other—the pleasures of one or the misery and pains suffered in the other.

This was the most beautiful time of the whole four-and-twenty hours, when the air was yet cool and grateful to the senses, yet warm enough to animate all living creatures, and bright enough to make everything in nature look happy and cheerful; but there were many hearts in Madrid that were sad enough, and though the walls of a prison contain much misery, yet they sometimes hold the stoutest and merriest hearts that beat in the city.

The prison itself was certainly strong and spacious enough for its purpose. The architect had not spent too much pains or time in devising or executing ornaments; it was composed of plain walls and gates, and a number of cells and guards, all for the accommodation of the prisoners, who were not usually grateful for this attention, and that in which Don Cæsar de Bazan was secured was one of the many, and differed but little from the others.

The old gaoler, a man whose age must have been great, for he was nearly bald, and what hair did remain was white, with tottering gait, and querulous voice, was busying himself about from one place to another, mumbling in his speech, and declared that it was many a day since he had a prisoner there,—it was really a pleasure.

Lazarillo had followed the unfortunate Don Cæsar and officer, and entered the prison; but he had been rudely thrust out, and the gaoler would by no means hear of his being in attendance upon Don Cæsar, as being out of all character—a thing that would interfere with his own pleasures by far too much.

Cuffed about from one to the other, he was thrust out among the soldiery, who seeing him, at once recollected the cause of the quarrel between their captain and Don Cæsar arose originally respecting him, and immediately proceeded to inflict summary chastisement upon the poor youth, who begged hard to be allowed to remain in prison with his benefactor, the only one who had ever taken an interest in his fate.

Little heeded were the boy's remonstrances; he was looked on with an evil eye by the soldiers, who had most of them suffered, some from blows and others from missiles, so that they were fully equal to the task of punishing a boy who could not resist them, and who was too much distressed by the misfortunes of his benefactor to make the attempt, and even unwilling to seek safety in flight.

Just as he gave himself up for lost, a tumult took place, and a bustle ensued at the gate. Some one had demanded admittance, and in another moment the officer of the guard, who had promised to intercede for Don Cæsar, arrived, and stepped into the court-yard, where Lazarillo stood at the mercy of the soldiery.

Lazarillo no sooner beheld him, than he called out to him, and escaping from the hands of the soldiers, he ran to him and begged he would protect him.

"Did I not see you last evening," he said, "by the side of Don Cæsar de Bazan?"

"You did, you did," exclaimed the boy, sobbing—"you did; and—and these men will not let me remain here, but turn me out from the presence of him whom I have brought into this trouble."

"What is the meaning of all this, men? Can you find no other way of venting your anger than in ill-treating a boy? For shame—for shame! Back to your quarters, and let me see no more of this. And you, Lazarillo, return with me to the dungeon of Don Cæsar."

Lazarillo followed the officer in silence, but his looks evinced how grateful he felt for the permission thus given him to attend upon Don Cæsar.

In the meantime the officer, calling for the gaoler, desired to be conducted to the cell of the prisoner.

Of all the irksome duties that he had ever been called upon to perform, the one which now claimed his attention was decidedly the most irksome to that officer, who was so brave, and so generous, and humane a man. He had not made the promise to Don Cæsar lightly that he would interest himself in his behalf, for, as he truly stated to the king, he had served him long and zealously, and now, for the first time, asked for a favour which should not have been a difficult one for any monarch to grant, inasmuch as it only called upon him for the exercise of that prerogative which has been justly termed the brightest jewel in a crown.

And, indeed, but for the untoward circumstances which had ruffled the temper of his majesty so much, there

is no reasonable doubt but that the officer would have been successful in his application to procure a pardon for Don Cæsar, whose offence, after all, in a chivalrous and military nation, was but a venial one, and rendered far more excusable on account of the manner in which it had been committed.

But the king was angry; and, therefore, (?) Don Cæsar must be hung. Royal wrath must be appeased, and if, in our country, we are told that—

"Wretches hang that jurymen may dine,"

we can readily believe that in despotic Spain, at the period of which we write, some tremendous peace-offering to the wounded dignity of the king would be highly requisite; and, consequently, the first person who came under the royal cognisance as an offender was sure to suffer.

The few words which had been spoken to the officer by Don Jose had not awakened in his mind any very sanguine hope of a pardon for Don Cæsar, for he reasoned correctly enough, when he told himself that such an act of clemency was not likely to be instigated by the crafty cruel minister for mercy's sake alone, and Don Cæsar, in the eyes of his gallant new friend, was a doomed man, whom nothing short of a miracle could save.

The cell, or strong room, in which our don was confined, was one of small dimensions, and by no means agreeable aspect, for the gaoler had heard of his prisoner before, and doubted not that he possessed fully

sufficient daring to attempt any scheme for his own liberation, be it attended with danger to himself, or to any other, of any kind or amount. Therefore had he deemed it highly necessary to make assurance doubly sure by the security of the place into which he had put his new prisoner.

But, like sunshine, the mind of Don Cæsar de Bazan shone as brightly in the cell of a prison as it would have done in the gilded saloons of a palace. Nothing seemed to have power sufficient to depress him below the reckless harum-scarum tone which usually characterised him. Ah! what might not such a man have been, if, in addition to his many brilliant social qualities, he had but been in possession of a little of that prudence which comes to the aid of meaner minds, and raises them, while the really gifted, the generous, the devoted, fail never to rise again, because they are so liberal they cannot condescend to be honest.

Poor Don Cæsar was drowned in debt without the real intention of cheating any one of a maravedie. He had brought ruin upon many whom he would gladly have served; but, then, he never made a calculation in his life; and then he was in a prison, and with a prospect of death before him, the same wild, careless, generous, odd character that he was when he first found himself in possession of an ancient honourable title, and an income which even he was some years in getting rid of, with all his genius for every kind of extravagance.

"There," said the gaoler, as he opened the rusty-locked door of Don Cæsar's cell for the officer; "there you'll find him. He's the oddest fellow ever I had here. Whenever I have passed the door I have heard him singing some song about women and wine, and all that kind of thing, as if he were on the Prado on a moonlight night, and had nothing in the world to do but to enjoy himself."

"But why place him in such a dungeon as this?"

"Oh, you don't know what desperate stories I have heard of him. If he were to give me the slip now, what do you suppose my place would be worth? Now, young jackanapes, what can you want here?"

"Not you, you may depend," said Lazarillo. "My friend, that portrait of you on the great knocker outside is extremely like."

"Now, confound your impudence, you shall troop this minute out of the prison."

" Nay, nay," said the officer. " Let the boy stay. His devotion to his friend, Don Cæsar, does him honour ; and you must recollect, Mr. Gaoler, you have provoked the retort he has given to you."

" Yes," mumbled the old gaoler, " it takes a deal of provocation, truly, to get an impertinent answer from such a young monkey. I'm sure he needn't be so anxious to stay in a prison, for he'll be in every one in Spain yet before he dies."

" Ah !" said Lazarillo, " I shall try and get made a gaoler before then ; but I'm afraid I shall not be considered ugly enough. Why don't you wear some amiable mask, old boy. You would look all the better for it."

" Hold your tongue, you ape. If you say another word I shall not be myself."

" Then whatever you turn to you will gain by the exchange."

The irascible gaoler lifted his keys to strike Lazarillo, but the officer saved the blow by pulling him after him into Don Cæsar's dungeon, saying,—

" Come, come, boy, do not let your tongue wag so fast, or it will be continually bringing you into trouble. Come along—come along."

" Hilloa !" cried Don Cæsar, " whom have we here ? A creditor, or not ; say at once."

" It's I," said Lazarillo ; " and I'm a debtor."

" And I, likewise," said the officer. " Do you recollect me ?"

" I do. Your hand, brave sir. This visit is friendly, and I much rejoice that I am at home. I cannot ask you to be seated, because they have such scant courtesy in this prison that they have not, as yet, paid me the compliment of accommodating me with a chair."

" I will have that changed before I leave ; but I come now on a most melancholy errand."

" The devil you have !"

" Yes, Don Cæsar ; I have a painful announcement to make to you."

" A meeting of my creditors has taken place, I suppose."

" No. According to my promise, I petitioned the king for your pardon, but the moment was unpropitious ; and, therefore, I fear I did you more harm than good. I was desired to give you the sad news, which you will find contained in this paper. Don Cæsar, if I could save you I would freely renounce all I possess in this world."

The officer spoke in a tone of deep emotion, and he handed to the prisoner the formidable scrap of paper which contained the fatal words that had been written on it by the king. There was barely sufficient light to read by in that dismal, dungeon-like room, but Don Cæsar's eyes had got accustomed to it, and he read the paper, while Lazarillo stood on tiptoe, and got a sufficient glimpse of its contents to know the fatal purport of them.

The boy seemed completely stunned for a moment with grief, and bursting into a passion of tears, he clung to Don Cæsar, exclaiming,—

" Oh, no, no, no ! They shall take me instead. It was all owing to me, and why should you suffer ? If they had lashed me to death, what would it have been in comparison to this ?"

" Now, Lazarillo," said Don Cæsar, calmly, as he returned the paper to the hands of the officer, " what a strange, foolish boy you are. Crying ! why, Lazarillo, I thought you quite a soldier."

The boy sobbed as if his heart would break, and Don Cæsar, finding he could not disengage himself from the frantic embrace of the good-hearted lad, who, in so many respects, resembled himself, turned to the officer, saying,—

" Sir, I am a poor one at thanks, but such words of

good feeling as I ought say to you for what you have done for me, pray imagine. For once in the way, I have a creditor whom I can speak gratefully to."

" Alas ! I have done nothing."

" The intention, sir, is to me the deed. As for this boy, if you can let him stay with me the few hours I have yet to live, I shall esteem it a favour ; for you see what a foolish fellow he is, and I must reason him out of such nonsense as he is now indulging in."

Lazarillo suddenly turned from Don Cæsar, as if actuated by a momentary impulse, and throwing himself at the feet of the officer, he cried,—

" Oh, sir, is there no way to save him ? It is all my fault, and none of his. But for me, he would have never seen the inside of this dreary prison. If by any representations the king could be induced to hang me instead of Don Cæsar, only think, sir, what a good thing it would be. Try to persuade him, sir. Tell him I don't mind it a bit ; but save this kind, generous man. If he dies, I will die too. Oh, save him ! save him !"

The officer turned aside to hide the emotion which began to be visible in his countenance. He made no answer to the boy's wild appeal, for he could say nothing of a satisfactory nature, and he was not a man who liked to dilate upon his own griefs and feelings. Don Cæsar alone of the three appeared capable of conversing in his ordinary manner ; and it was strange to hear him, the condemned man, offering consolation to those whose hearts were heaving with grief on his account.

" Now, really," he said, " you do not consider either of you what numberless persecutions I escape by this sudden death that awaits me. My creditors are all men of family ; I mean as to numbers. Creditors do always, somehow, have a lot of children ; and in a few years I should find myself persecuted by a young fry of tailors and cravat-makers, sueing for debts which they had inherited from their fathers along with the ledgers. Come, now, Lazarillo, you shall stay with me, and we will make the most of the time I have left to me. Did you say seven o'clock ?"

" Seven o'clock," replied the officer. " You have scarcely two hours to live."

" Humph ! and the carnival time, too. It is not quite correct ; but let it pass. My life is my last possession ; and if the king will have that, no one can say him nay."

" I cannot ask you to hope," said the officer, " but, believe me, if I leave you now, it is to make the most strenuous efforts yet to entreat some one in your behalf. The queen, perchance, may have some influence ; she shall be applied to, and during the brief space there is for execution, all shall be done that can be done."

" Blessings on you," cried Lazarillo. " Hasten, sir, hasten."

The officer in another moment left the dungeon ; and poor Lazarillo again clung to Don Cæsar's arm as he looked in his face imploringly, saying,—

" You do not fear death ?"

" Fear ! No, Lazarillo. None of my name ever knew what fear was. I have not led the best of lives ; but, bad as it is, I would, if my own choice had been permitted me, yet awhile have lived beneath the sunny skies of Spain. Besides, you and I, you young rascal, would have been such great friends henceforward, and you could have come about with me, and given me notice when any of my creditors were near at hand ; but it's of no use talking, and least of all is it of any use crying. So, Lazarillo, don't make a girl of yourself, but remain with me, and be a little rational. I wonder, now, if there is any intention of giving us anything to eat or drink."

" Can you think of such things ?"

"Aye, to be sure. If I don't, I have an inward monitor in the shape of a stomach, which says, very intelligibly, 'Don Cæsar—Don Cæsar, it's remarkably near breakfast time.' "

The boy wrung his hands as he cried,—

"Alas! alas! to think that each moment so much advances that fatal one when you will be murdered. 'Twas a fair fight. Oh, it will be shameful to kill you for it. I will tell them so—I will shame them from the deed. They surely cannot—will not—dare not take your life on such a ground."

"Why, Lazarillo, when you come to consider it, there are two or three disagreeable circumstances connected with the affair. First of all, it was the carnival time, when, by old custom, no swords should be drawn; but, somehow, the Bazans, where they have a cause of quarrel, are apt to forget everything but the carrying it out at once. Then, again, when I come to recollect, we fought in the Garden of the Capuchins, and last, though not least, you hear from our friend the officer that the king was out of temper."

"Alas! alas!"

"Ah! so you see, Lazarillo, there is not much chance for us—for me, I mean; and now, my boy, tell me what will become of you, for I am afraid you have done yourself no good by becoming the friend of Don Cæsar de Bazan. I wish I had known you, Lazarillo, when fortune smiled on me. Then you should have ruffled it with the best of them, and never wanted a friend; but now, I fear, my good word is no good at all."

"Yes, yes; it is indeed to me—I shall think of it as long as I live. Don Cæsar, I shall never, never forget you. I shall not expect to be the happy, careless boy I ever was, because I shall always lay your death at my door; but I will pray for you, and if ever I should have the means, there shall be no end of masses for your soul."

"Why, as to that, my boy," replied Don Cæsar, "don't trouble yourself; I have not that amount of faith in masses which makes me think them worth paying for; so keep your money, if ever you should have any. If you should, however, Lazarillo, be so fortunate in life, and I hope to Heaven you may, as to have money to spare, and you still, as I am sure you will, think kindly of your old friend, the wild, dissolute Don Cæsar de Bazan, just give in my name to some poor devil what you can spare, and I shall believe, if my soul is not past doing good to, it will be of more avail than feeding fat monks to say masses for me."

"Think you so?"

"I am sure of it, Lazarillo. 'Tis flat heresy to say so, but between you and I, my boy, the priesthood are a set of greasy rogues, who fatten upon the credulity of foolish people. They are self-elected to the office they hold, and I will have nothing whatever to do with them."

"My father had not a good opinion of priests and monks."

"Then he was a sensible man, Lazarillo. How goes the time, boy? Hast any idea?"

"None whatever, but I dread to think. Don Cæsar, Don Cæsar, look about. Think you there is any chance of an escape from this place?"

"Why, to tell the truth, Lazarillo, I have been looking about me with some such idea, for if I saw anything in the shape of an opportunity, I would just as soon be outside this gloomy place as not, but I feel quite clear that there is no chance of escape. The walls are thick, the door strong, and as for window, there is none, unless yon grating, which is so far beyond our reach, be called one, from excessive courtesy towards it."

"Alas, alas!" exclaimed the boy, "it seems to me all like a dream."

"If it is, Lazarillo, I wish part of the vision would be in the shape of a breakfast; for although a man is condemned to die, it is quite a needless piece of aggravation to famish him first."

"Can you, indeed, think of eating?"

"Think of eating! Indeed I can, and of drinking too. I've been very seriously thinking of both for some time. There is a war within me, which breakfast only can allay, and I don't see why we should not have some. I will owe for it, as I do for everything else. It will be but another item to carry forward, so here goes for an attempt to get a little credit, if it be the last one I shall find it necessary to make."

The only available means of making a disturbance in the prison, was with the aid of a wooden bench, on which Don Cæsar sat. There was certainly a table likewise, but that was too heavy to move conveniently, so the don contented himself with the bench, which he banged against the door of his dungeon so vigorously, that the whole prison in a few moments echoed with the sound.

The noise had the desired effect of bringing some one to the door, which was, however, not opened, for there was was a small square piece in it that opened, and allowed the gaoler from without to survey his prisoners. With a countenance not at all expressive· of amiable feelings, he appeared, saying,—

"What now? What's all this riot about?"

"My sweet sentimental-looking friend," said Don Cæsar, "have you breakfasted?"

"What if I have?"

"Why, then, you will please to remember we have not."

"Oh, have you got any money?"

"Not exactly."

"Not a maravedie," said Lazarillo.

"Then how can you have the d—d impudence to expect any breakfast?"

"You can put it down to my account."

"Bah! your account indeed. All your accounts will very soon be settled, I'm thinking. Bah!"

So saying, the amiable gaoler at once withdrew from the door.

CHAPTER IX.

THE MINISTER AND THE DANCER.—THE CONSENT TO AMBITION.—THE ARRANGEMENT WITH MARITANA.

At the very time that the humane and gallant officer of the guard was with Don Cæsar in his prison, the wily Don Jose was conversing with the beautiful Maritana, in a room of his own mansion, in the immediate neighbourhood of the palace. It was an apartment which was in every respect calculated to produce a strong impression on the fancy of Maritana. A higher and purer taste than ever Don Jose de Santerem possessed had presided over its furnishing and decorations. Everything was in the most exquisite good keeping, and he had allowed Maritana to be some time alone in the place, in order that she might have thorough leisure to admire the costly and beautiful objects that thronged that magnificent room, and made her for a time almost afraid to move, lest she should dispel the charm that came over her romantic imagination, when first such a blaze of splendour met her enraptured gaze.

"Oh," she murmured, "could I ever hope to dwell always amid such scenes as these, what a halo of joy would surround my heart, and what a life of everlasting delight would mine be. Surely my destiny speaks to me, through the beauty of all these glittering objects around me, telling me that I was born for them, and that the time will indeed come when I shall be so blessed as to become their much envied possessor

What a fate is mine, condemned to wander in the public streets, and, at the bidding of any one who may reward my endeavours with a beggar's pittance, to sing those strains which I would gladly hear echo in such a place as this. Ambition, ambition—what a home it has found in my heart! I cannot be contented with my humble station. Dare I trust to the words which have raised such fond hopes in my breast? Alas! I feel that if all should prove a delusion, if no one of the glorious reveries of my ambitious soul be gratified, I am no longer fit for the life I have been leading, but must die, or be something widely different from the street minstrel I have been."

" The dreams of ambition shall be all realised—more than realised," said a voice behind her, and, turning with a half-suppressed scream, she beheld Don Jose, who, unknown to her, had, with his usual slinking, cat-like movement, glided into the apartment.

" You here ?" she exclaimed.

" Yes; did you not expect me, lovely Maritana ?" he said.

" I—I did, but not so suddenly; I was alarmed for the moment."

" Look around you, and recover your feelings, by regarding those objects of magnificence, which will fade into the most common-place matters, in comparison with what you will possess."

" Dare I believe my eyes and ears ?"

" Both; I speak no word to you but shall be carried out by proof to the very letter. I have promised you wealth and rank."

" You—you have."

" And both shall be yours, Maritana, provided you will allow yourself to be implicitly guided by me in the mode taken to obtain them."

" I will listen to you."

" Do so; the queen ——"

" Aye, the queen—the queen! it is from her that all this power comes? Assure me of that, and I accept all without a tinge of suspicion—no feeling but gratitude shall find a home in my heart. The queen is so good, so kind, so noble; she has stooped from her high estate to smile upon the poor street singer. Yes; twice has she noticed me. The queen! And now she would raise me to such a soaring height, that, while while my heart pants for its attainment, I tremble at the thoughts of my coming happiness."

" You are convinced of my sincerity ?"

" I am; for the queen's is a name you dare not to trifle with."

" True; and now for my instructions to you. The manner in which you are to be ennobled must be by marriage; but various political reasons render it necessary that your marriage should be conducted in a very secret and peculiar manner."

" Indeed !"

" Yes; you will wed one to whom your heart is already attached—one whose name sounds musically in your ears. You will be the Countess de Bazan, by a marriage with Don Cæsar. The queen will see that his future fortunes are well adapted to the support of his ancient and honourable name, and you, as his countess, will enjoy rank and privileges equal to those of the haughtiest grandees of Spain. What say you, Maritana, are you prepared to become the Countess de Bazan ?"

" Prepared ! Oh, it's a dream, a dream of joy !"

" You are willing ?"

" I know it cannot be but a dream; I shall awaken, and find some sad reality. It cannot be real; it must be all a dream."

" It is no dream, Maritana; the Queen of Spain is your friend, and with it, therefore, there needs nothing whatever but your own concurrence in the arrangements that shall be proposed to you, to carry out all her wishes for your welfare, and place you at a height of dazzling splendour."

" Do with me what you will; I accede to all and every condition. Let the result be what you promise, and my eternal gratitude will be due to you."

" You view this matter, Maritana, in so judicious a light, you have so true and just an appreciation of the circumstances which surround you, and you show so noble a confidence in the queen's arrangements, that, doubt not, her majesty will take an opportunity of expressing to you how much you have pleased her by the manner in which you bear your change of fortune."

" Oh, tell her how my heart beats with grateful feelings towards her ! Tell her I would die to serve her; that my whole life would be too short to allow me to express one half my gratitude; tell her that if ever one in her exalted state had a true, fond heart attached to her, it is she. For her I would brave any peril; tell her, sir, that, next to Heaven, I love her; that her name shall be ever mingled with my prayers; and that with my last breath her image will ever live in my heart. I cannot find language in which to couch all my ardent gratitude."

" You have said enough, Maritana; the queen will be well pleased with the report which I shall have the honour of taking to her concerning the matter."

" But, tell me now, what is to be done ?"

" You must be guided by me implicitly, Maritana; and, when you are married, you must be veiled so closely, that your future husband shall obtain no glimpse of your features ——"

" But ——"

" Hear me out. Nor you of his."

" But ——"

" It is the queen's pleasure."

" Then I, of course, submit at once. There cannot be any imposition."

" You yourself can guard against that, by listening to the priest as he mentions the name and title of your husband; and, if you hear other than Don Cæsar de Bazan named, do you at once tear off your veil, and see the person who is attempting to impose upon you. These doubts, Maritana, I must say, are unworthy of you, and I should much regret, indeed, to have to report them to the queen."

" No, no; I have banished them, and consent to be veiled."

" 'Tis well; you must promise solemnly not to make any attempt to see your future husband, and you must likewise promise an inviolable silence, beyond the few words that it is absolutely necessary you should utter during the performance of the marriage ceremony."

" I promise."

" 'Tis well; nothing now can stand in the way of your future greatness, Maritana, and I shall soon have the honour, as well as the pleasure, of hailing you as a countess. You will remain here for a few moments, during which refreshments will be brought to you, and then a carriage will be ready to convey you at once to where your nuptials will be performed."

" What—so soon ?"

" At once, lady."

" But ——"

" Oh, her majesty will brook no delays."

" Then, of course, I submit to her gracious pleasure in all things."

" You do right. This free giving in to all her majesty's feelings and wishes prepares you for a glorious career in the court. Your husband first ennobles you, but, from the great favour you will undoubtedly enjoy, he will stand indebted to you for many an honourable and lucrative employment, so that the weight of gratitude will soon be taken entirely from your heart, and you will feel that in all respects you are worthy of the fate that has awaited you."

"Then, Don Cæsar, of course, is pardoned for the duel which took place in the Gardens of the Capuchins, and which terminated so sadly in the death of the captain of the guard."

"Oh, most certainly. At first, the king was angry—very angry, indeed, far beyond his usual custom, and he ordered Don Cæsar for instant execution; but I interposed, because I not only pitied the noble signior, but I likewise knew the kind intentions of the king. The result was that I obtained his pardon. But beware; remember the conditions on which you are to wed him. Not a word of recognition—not a word in signification that you know any of the circumstances connected with him."

"I have promised."

"Nay, you have almost sworn."

"And I will keep my oath."

"Then all will be well, Maritana, and I shall be the first to hail you as the Countess de Bazan—an ancient and honourable title, and one that has been ever in the hands of brave men. Indeed, such have been the great services rendered from time to time to the Spanish monarchy, by the illustrious house of Bazan, that many privileges have been granted to it by different kings. One of those is the right to be covered even in the presence of majesty—a right only enjoyed by two other grandees of Spain."

"Indeed!"

"Aye; and you, as Countess de Bazan, will have the right of having your train borne by four pages, while no other lady of the court dare appear with more than three."

"Oh, can I, indeed, aspire to so much rank?"

"You have it in your grasp; all is in your hands, and no one but yourself could now baulk you of the glorious prize you have drawn in the lottery of fate. You will be much envied."

"Yes, yes, I shall, indeed. I, the poor Maritana—the street minstrel, to approach so near the very throne of Spain. 'Tis like some fairy tale, and transcends all sober belief, while the entranced imagination drinks in with delight the sweet words that promise so much happiness. But yet, in thought, I have often dwelt upon what joy it would be to become that which I soon shall be. I ever scorned the humble life I was leading, and when titled wealth has placed great largess in my hands, I have received it with a bursting heart, as if it came from one with whom I should be equal. Oh, surely, when destiny designs any of its creatures for high fortunes, the mind, even long before the glorious vision is realized, leaps proudly to the goal of its fond hopes, and ever has some dim foreknowledge of that glory and that happiness, which, in the fulness of time, is to be."

"You are quite right, Maritana. I much admire your philosophy, and your words convince me how well calculated you are to give more lustre to the title which will be yours than ever it can bestow upon you."

"Already I feel myself no longer the wandering minstrel of the streets of Madrid."

"Most certainly; you are quite another character."

"My heart tells me I am a countess."

"Every inch a countess! By the mass," said Don Jose, aside, "here is pride and ambition enough to supply the whole court with those commodities."

"But," added Maritana, after a pause, as she glanced at herself in one of the magnificent mirrors that adorned the gorgeous apartment, "is this a fitting costume for my new condition?"

"Most certainly not; but the queen has given orders concerning it. She has remarked that you are about her height, and she has desired me to place at your disposal one of her own court costumes. In the next chamber to this you will find all that you can require. Make your toilet as rapidly as you can, and in the interim a carriage will arrive to convey you to your intended husband."

Maritana's heart beat quickly as she walked towards the door leading to the inner chamber. At the moment a female attendant opened it, and with a profound bow to his victim, Don Jose said,—

"Countess, this attendant will assist you at your toilet."

The attendant curtsied to the very ground, and with pride, love, and exultation flashing from her eyes, the beautiful Maritana returned the supercilious bow of the minister, and entered the inner apartment, which had been duly prepared for her reception, and which abounded with luxuries of which she had not the slightest conception, and which were to her as delightful as they were new.

When Don Jose was alone, and the door was closed between the two apartments, he folded his arms across his breast and stood for a few moments perfectly motionless and silent. Then a slight movement of his whole frame would have let those who knew him intimately into the secret that he was enjoying a very hearty laugh for him. He had acquired the knack of laughing silently. There was no mirth whatever in it, but a wonderful quantity of self-congratulatory villany. The suppressed laugh of such a man was far more dangerous than his open frowns.

After a few moments then, he walked up to a time-piece which stood upon a silver bracket, and attentively examined it as if his thoughts were at the same time busy with something else, in the midst of which he wished to note how the time was passing.

"More than half-past five," he muttered. "Time creeps on slowly, but everything works well for my schemes. How most men, situated as I am, would tremble at their own successes, and shrink from looking up to the giddy height which I aspire to reach, and which I will reach, or all my old craft has deserted me, or some special miracle shall interfere to foil me, and that would be scarcely fair, sent here as we all are into this teeming world to do our best, according to the various powers we possess. But the age of miracles is past, if ever it came, and I have nothing to fear so long as I preserve this head-piece, which can concoct enough schemes to circumvent the whole world.

"What am I, and what was I? Those are questions the answers to which speak largely of what the future shall be to me.

"I was a poor friendless scholar, with scarce a rial to call my own, and that not very long ago. I am the minister and the favourite of the King of Spain. Wealthy beyond precedent, for I have made all suitors for favours pay well ere they obtained that which they sought. Having done so much, who shall say to me, 'Now, Don Jose, pause?' No one—no one. I have embarked on a career the destinies of which are but half accomplished; if, indeed, half the more brilliant and delightful portion is not yet to come. Let me consider."

He walked slowly to and fro several times, and then he spoke in a lower tone, indicative that his dark, subtle mind was making its arrangements as he proceeded.

"The court of Philip is divided into two powerful sections. The one holds to the king, despite all his profligacies, and the other to the queen, who is as virtuous as gentle, and as full of rare and noble qualities as she is fair. Fair! by Heavens, she is beautiful—a divinity, and yet the king neglects her. He is satiated with her charms, or she is too intellectual for his gross tastes, and he feels himself subdued in her presence. Hence he seeks in intrigue for means of pleasantly passing his leisure hours, making me the minister of his pleasures as well as his minister of state. Well, well, it matters not much to me which path I tread, so that it lead to the objects of my high reaching ambition. Not a whit—not a whit.

" I love the queen, I adore her! Besides, I am the king's favourite, and, therefore, am the head and chief of the court party, who flatter all his vices ; but the queen has ever held me at arm's length, repelling my humble offers of service, so that with those who crowd around her—and there are some among them of the highest and noblest—I hold no sway. They openly defy me, and treat me with a contempt which, if it were politic—which it is not—to own I see, I would amply revenge.

" Well, I hold half a reign here. Could I win the queen, I should govern all Spain. All honours, all profits would be wholly at my disposal. The favourite of the king, the minister of state, and the lover of the queen. Well done, Don Jose, well done. Who would thus dare to bend other than a glance of reverential respect on thee ? I should indeed then have reached a height unequalled. My proudest dreams of ambition would be fulfilled. In all but the name, I should be absolute king of Spain."

Don Jose was so elated with this picture that he had thus vividly presented to himself, that he drew up his not unhandsome figure to its full height, and surveyed himself with a proud, exulting expression in the same mirror which had reflected but a short time since the beauties of the bewildered Maritana, who, in her way, was as intoxicated with ambition as Don Jose.

Suddenly, then, his whole aspect changed, and he said,—

" But hold. This exultation is ill-timed, and most unlike me. Much has yet to be done ere I can hope to place myself in the position imagination paints to me in such glowing colours. I must reflect — reflect deeply upon the means to be employed. Nothing must be overlooked—nothing forgotten—nothing forgotten.

" The king's intrigues no one dare mention to the queen, and if they did, all evidence of them is out of the question, unless they took place within the immediate circle of the court. I think I know woman well. If anything will move the purest, best, and noblest to sin, it is the one grand master feeling of all their hearts—jealousy ! Yes, if I can once rouse the queen to a thorough sense of how the king deserts her for low amours, she is mine—mine irrevocably. She is pure and beautiful; but if she were otherwise, what would her conquest be worth to me ? It is because she seems so far above all temptation I would tempt her ; because she seems to stand on such an inaccessible rock of virtue that I would make her fall. The value of a conquest ever depends upon the strength of the enemy that is overcome. I want no barren temples.

" Well, all is in good train. The king has become enamoured of this street-singer ; but he shrinks from stooping so low. She shall be ennobled by a marriage with Don Cæsar de Bazan, and I have a means of inducing him to consent to the match which cannot fail. Maritana shall be told that the Don Cæsar de Bazan she knew in the streets was an impostor, and that the real nobleman possessing that title to whom she has been married belongs to the court, and claims her as his wife. The king shall personate that character, while Don Cæsar himself dies at seven o'clock this morning. Then when the king's intrigue with Maritana is at its height, I will to the queen, and throwing myself at her feet, tell her how she is dishonoured, and hint to her, if that I can but raise her passion sufficiently, how she may be revenged. It shall be done, and it must succeed. When too late, the king shall sign a pardon for Don Cæsar, which will appease the popular ferment in his favour, as well as

make me stand well with Maritana, who still will pity the supposed impostor."

At this moment the sound of carriage wheels came upon the minister's ears, and a page appeared at the door of the room, to announce the splendid carriage he had ordered to carry himself and Maritana to the prison of Don Cæsar de Bazan, where he intended to have the nuptials celebrated, which should confer upon Maritana the title that would make her high enough in the king's estimation to become his mistress.

The page, after respectfully speaking his errand, retired ; and Don Jose approached the door of the inner chamber to summons Maritana, as, indeed, there was now but little time to lose if he meant to carry his deep and artful scheme into execution without protracting the period of Don Cæsar's existence.

CHAPTER X.

THE INTERVIEW IN THE PRISON.—THE PROPOSAL AND ITS RESULTS.—THE PARDON.—THE QUEEN'S MESSENGER.

DON JOSE tapped gently at the door of the inner chamber, where Maritana had gone to attire herself in garments more befitting the rank she was so very shortly to assume, and as he did so, he banished from his features all the look of guilty exultation and cunning they had worn while he had been conversing with himself, and settling the particulars of his dark and villanous scheming.

The response to his knock was the immediate opening of the door and the appearance of Maritana, so changed—so very different a being to what she had been when last he saw her, that, involuntarily, and it was seldom Don Jose was taken by surprise, he stepped back several paces, and for the moment could scarcely believe that the brilliant, beautiful being before him was the street-singer, who so recently had obtained a living in the streets of Madrid by her beauty and her own talents.

Maritana, by the slight smile that curled her cherub-like lips, seemed much to enjoy the surprise of the minister. The dress she wore was a superb one, and set off her beautiful figure to the greatest possible advantage ; so that she felt herself quite a different creature to what she had been, and that now there could be no longer any cause for doubt that her splendid and noble career had indeed begun.

" It is needless, lady," said Don Jose, " for me to congratulate you upon your appearance. The silent compliments of your glass must have told you how beautiful you are."

" I am ready," said Maritana ; and there was that in her tone which proclaimed the pride that was swelling at her full heart.

" We have no time to lose, lady. My carriage waits ; but, permit me to add, that if I were not Don Jose de Santerem, the minister and the favourite of my king, I would fain be, this day, Don Cæsar de Bazan."

With these words, Don Jose, who had lived quite long enough in a court to have become an adept in the art of flattery, took the hand of Maritana in his own, and gallantly led her down the grand staircase of his splendid mansion to the carriage which had been commanded to be in waiting.

Half bewildered by the enchantment of everything around, she stepped into the carriage. Don Jose gave a whispered instruction to the servants, and away they dashed at great speed through the streets of Madrid.

" Remember," said Don Jose, as the carriage dashed into a large court-yard, and drew up, " remember, Maritana, you will be closely veiled, so that you will not see your husband, nor he you, and you are to say nothing but the necessary words in the marriage ceremonial. Break these injunctions, and all the magnificence that surrounds you shall fade away like the chimera of a dream."

"I remember," she said, "and will obey. It is the queen's wish, and that is law to me."

"Yes, yes. It is the queen's wish."

Maritana knew not where she was, for, although the exterior appearance of the prison was familiar to her in consequence of her wanderings about the streets of Madrid, she was prevented from seeing it on account of the blinds of the carriage having been already drawn by Don Jose, and the interior she was completely ignorant of.

She was handed out of the vehicle very ceremoniously, and into a room from which Don Jose desired her not to stir on any account whatever, and then he left her, just as the prison clock struck the hour of six, and Lazarillo was weeping bitterly in the dungeon of Don Cæsar, as every fleeting minute brought the hour of his sad fate nearer, and decreased the hopes of pardon which the boy had at first entertained and clung to, but which now had almost entirely faded away.

Little did either he or Don Cæsar imagine how important a part the latter was playing, although immured in a dungeon, and with a sentence of death hanging over his head, in the intrigues of the wily minister of Spain.

"Oh, Don Cæsar," cried Lazarillo, "the hour is drawing near. Can you think of no means of saving your life?"

"No, boy, none; but don't make such a fuss."

"Can I help it? What can be done? Can I do anything?"

"Yes, you can."

"What—what? Oh, tell me what.

"Why, let go the cuff of my coat; it's very frail, and, if you go on tugging at it in that kind of way, it will most assuredly come off."

"But, Don Cæsar——"

"But, Lazarillo——"

"I—I know not what to say."

"Nor I either. What would you do now, Lazarillo, to pass away the time, if you had only an hour or so to live in this world?"

"I should confess my sins first."

"Ah, you might, and leave yourself some time; but, bless you, boy, it would take me a month, so that won't do, you see. I couldn't think of beginning such a long job."

"Then, try to think of some friend who, perhaps, at the last moment, might have influence enough to save you. Surely there is some one who would move in your behalf; you cannot be utterly friendless, Don Cæsar."

"Yes, I am."

"No, no."

"But I say yes, yes. Just do you have a splendid fortune, and spend it to all the last maravedie, and then see how many friends you have got. My good boy, you know nothing of the world at all, and I know too much."

"But, in all your period of prosperity, did you never succeed in attaching one honest heart to you?"

"Not one."

"That is very sad."

"It is, Lazarillo, and most sad things are amazingly true things. Yet, stay, I am speaking too fast; when I was arrested, there was one who interceded for me with a pathos and a grief that no other could have used."

"There was one. Oh, I thought surely there would be one."

"Yes; did you not see him? An old man threw himself before the commandant, almost under his horse's feet. He knew the penalty of what I had done, and he held up his withered hands, while the tangled locks of his whitened hair shivered in the breeze, and

the tears flowed down his cheeks. He would scarcely take denial; but, with accents which should have reached all hearts, he wept as he cried,—

"Mercy—mercy—oh! mercy for Don Cæsar de Bazan. Spare him—spare him yet!"

The boy threw himself on Don Cæsar's breast, as he cried,—

"I was sure there would be one. It was ——"

"Who, Lazarillo?"

"Your father."

"Oh, dear, no, it was my tailor; you see, he didn't like to lose all chance of his debt. Some piece of good luck might come over me yet, if I lived, in the shape of a legacy."

"No hope—no hope!" cried the boy, and he wrung his hands, while his bitter sobs resounded through the dungeon.

"None—none!"

"No friends; alas! no friends."

"Not one. Don't make such a noise, Lazarillo; it makes me ten times hungrier than before to hear you."

At this moment the door of the dungeon was opened, and the gaoler stood in the entrance, saying,—

"This way, Don Cæsar; there is one come to see you."

"Is there, indeed? Well, miracles will never, I suppose, cease. Come on, Lazarillo, we will not part just yet, boy, come who may."

The gaoler led his prisoner along a spacious corridor, and thence into a far more comfortable apartment, in which were some tables and chairs; and, as an imposing-looking object, and one which could not fail in an instant to strike the eye of every one who might enter the room, was a clock placed in the centre of one of the walls, and which told the hour of ten minutes past six.

"You see, Lazarillo," said Don Cæsar, as he pointed to it, "there is not much time now to spare."

The boy only wept; and Don Cæsar, turning to the gaoler, as he was leaving the apartment, said,—

"And where is this person who has come to see me in the last hour so graciously? Mind, if it's one of my creditors, you had better tell him it's of no use whatever."

"It is a friend," said a voice from the recess of one of the deeply-set windows, and Don Jose at the same moment stepped out into the middle of the room, forming a remarkable contrast by the richness of his attire, and the numerous jewels that glittered upon him, with the squalid apparel and faded finery of the poor doomed Don Cæsar.

"Lazarillo," said the prisoner, "I told you the age of miracles had not virtually ceased, for here is a minister of state come to see a man without a coin, and condemned to death."

"You judge harshly of human nature, Don Cæsar," said Jose. "I came here as your friend."

"Indeed."

"Yes. Look at that clock."

"It's a very good clock, I dare say, in its way, and it's very friendly of you to tell me to look at it."

"By it you perceive you have but three quarters of an hour to live."

"Don't cheat me—a minute more, if you please. A minute may not be much to you; but, situated as I am, it comes to a great thing."

"Alas! Don Cæsar, I sincerely and, from the bottom of my heart, pity your unfortunate condition."

"Do you?"

"Indeed, I do. Sit down; I have something of very great importance to say to you."

"I hope it won't take long, for time, you know, with me is rather precious."

"You are condemned to die at seven o'clock."

"Thank you."

" I have flown hither to you on the wings of friendship. You know I have some influence with the king. I cannot forget that we have spent many happy hours together, and although you are condemned to death, your honour is untouched. My heart bleeds for you, Don Cæsar. Is there anything I can do for you ?"

" Get my pardon."

" Ah ! that I cannot. The king has taken a vow, and resisted all my prayers and entreaties. Anything but that."

" Well, that's awkward, as it happens to be one of those kind of things that act as a *sine qua non*. It seems to me that in a little while I shall require no favours."

" Ah, me ! I am deeply hurt at your fate. Anything in the world but your life."

" Which is what I want most."

" I cannot grant it to you ; but, alas ! Don Cæsar, it's unmanly to weep. I cannot—cannot save you."

" God help him !" cried Lazarillo. " Oh, sir, go to the king and try again. Don Cæsar slew the officer of the guard in fair fight. Tell him it will be a blot upon the honour of his name to take the life of a noble, brave, and honourable gentleman upon such paltry grounds."

" Who is this ?" said Don Jose, looking at Lazarillo with a face indicative of surprise.

" An apt question," said Don Cæsar, " for it at once puts me in mind that I can ask a favour of you."

" Name it."

" You see this boy, Don Jose. He is a brave, noble-hearted lad. If you be serious in your offers of service to me, you will prove it by giving me your word of honour, that when I am gone you will take care of his fortunes."

" I solemnly promise. He shall be attached to my household, and if I find him apt and clever, he shall not lack patronage and ample promotion."

" Don Jose, I thank you from my heart. What say you, Lazarillo ?"

The boy could scarcely speak for tears, and he said, falteringly,—

" While Don Cæsar lives, sir, I cannot leave him. After he has left me, I will be to you a faithful servant."

" That will do, boy, I esteem you the more for your devotion to your friend, Don Cæsar ; and now tell me, Bazan, is there anything else I can do for you ?"

" No, no. Nothing."

" But think again ; you have but three quarters of an hour to live, recollect."

" I beg your pardon, it's not much more than thirty-five minutes. Look at the clock."

" I see. Well, well, bethink you what else can I do to pleasure you, Don Cæsar."

" Oh, nothing. I am really obliged to you, Jose, on this young lad's account ; more obliged to you than I can well express. If you should ever meet any of my creditors, you can tell them to score my name out of their books, for, most certainly, they will never get anything now. At seven o'clock the name and title of the Count de Bazan of Orfilla will be extinct. In half-an-hour—I mean, in thirty-five minutes—all my debts will be paid along with the last one, which nobody likes to pay, however honest he may be—the debt of nature. By-the-bye, is that clock quite right ?"

" They go by it here, fast or slow."

" Oh, do they ? Then it's all the same, and quite as pleasant."

" Quite, as you observe ; but you will permit me to say, Don Cæsar, that notwithstanding all the pleasure I feel in acceding to the request you have made, it is not the one which I fully and entirely expected would have come from your lips."

" Indeed."

" No, Don Cæsar. It appears to me marvellous, that in spite of all your courage, all your cool defiance of death, and all your pride, may I add, as a Spanish nobleman, you have never yet considered one thing."

" And what, in the name of all that's wonderful, is that one thing, Don Jose ?"

" The manner of your death."

" Don Cæsar sprung to his feet, as he exclaimed,—

" By Heavens, you are right. I have not given that a thought."

" I knew you had not."

" But—but I am a nobleman. The manner of my death cannot, will not be derogatory to my rank. The king surely will not dream of carrying his insane fury so far as to degrade, as well as kill me."

" Ah !" said Don Jose, " it wants less than the half-hour now by several minutes, and, as I have remarked, they go by that clock here most religiously."

" Confound their faith. But tell me, Jose, what is to be the manner of my death, now you have suggested the inquiry to me so urgently ?"

" You will be hanged."

" Hanged ?"

" I said hanged."

" By the neck ?"

" Precisely. Dingle-dangle."

" Like a dog."

" Or any other animal you please."

Don Cæsar sat down again, and passed his hand across his brow, as he said, in a lower tone,—

" Too bad, too bad. I dreamed not of this. Why should I die the death of a felon, instead of that of a soldier and a gentleman ? What have I done, that this needless aggravation of the most extreme punishment my supposed offence could be visited with, should be heaped upon me ?"

" It is monstrous," cried Lazarillo. " Why don't they hang me instead ? Oh, it is most monstrous."

" Perhaps they will, if you wag your tongue so very freely, my boy," remarked Don Jose. " You must have sufficient discretion not always to say exactly what you think, or you will never do for any employment about the court."

" Bah, Don Jose !" exclaimed Cæsar ; " you have not come here to bring me this piece of news without its antidote. You expected me to ask the favour of you, that I might die the death of a gentleman ?"

" I did."

" And you said you could grant me anything but my life ?"

" I certainly said so "

" Then grant that I may escape this death you say is prepared for me. Give me any other ; but to come into the hands of the common hangman, eugh ! my blood turns at the very thought. Don Jose, let me be shot by a file of soldiers—it were a death more worthy of me, for I have done nothing dishonourable, and wherefore should my end be dishonoured ? Can you grant me that request ?"

" I can."

" And you will, Don Jose. Say you will rob death of half its bitterness, by robbing it of all its humiliating, degrading circumstances."

" I will, but ——"

" Ah, you have a condition. Now I see it all. Lazarillo, my boy, I don't know but the age of miracles may have passed away, for although the minister has come to see the poor prisoner, he has some purpose of his own to answer by the visit. Say on, Don Jose. Tell me at once what you expect of me in return for the favours you can grant me ? Heaven only knows what it can be, for I am not in a situation to do any one a service. Speak freely, for time is getting rather short with me."

" I will speak freely to you, Don Cæsar. You shall be shot by a party of the royal guard now in the pri-

son, instead of being hung, and I will provide for this boy most handsomely, on condition that you do me a very trifling service in return."

" Name it, name it."

" I want you to marry."

" To what ?"

" To marry a lady whom I will present to you."

" Marry under my present circumstances ? Marry —oh! it's no use. There ain't time—because ——''

" There is ample time, if no unnecessary delays are interposed. My condition of service to you is that you marry a lady who is now in this building."

" You don't say so? Marry or be hung—marry and be shot! What an odd combination of evils altogether. But what use can it be for me to marry? Why I am little better than a dead man—I have nothing to leave."

" You have ——"

" Oh! so I have. Now I see it—my name. You want me to bestow my name upon some one ?"

" I do."

" I thought as much. I understand it all now—oh, dear, yes. Some untitled lady—some—some horrid old witch wants to be a countess."

" No, she is young and beautiful."

" Well, don't tell me. You should consider my feelings, with only, let me see, twenty-five minutes to live."

" Your feelings will be spared, for the lady will be closely and thickly veiled, and you must give me your word of honour that you will not seek to break her incognito."

" Then I know she is old and ugly."

" Fancy what you like. Do you consent?"

" Yes; it's all one to me. It will pass the time away—married and shot within twenty-five—three minutes I mean. Was there ever anything so interesting ? Lazarillo, make a play of me some day, will you? I have not time myself, as you see, my hands are full of business. These though are strange clothes to be married in. If the lady were a prudent, economical wife now, what a world of rents she would find in my garments to darn. I'm afraid she will be rather shocked at so ragged a bridegroom."

" She will not see you, so closely veiled will she be; but still I have, thinking that your consent would be easily given to such a small matter, provided for you a dress fully befitting your rank."

" A small matter, indeed; but the clothes—the clothes, my friend Jose."

" Are in the adjoining apartment, where Lazarillo can act as your valet."

" I breathe again—so far so good, but let me in all honesty assure you, Don Jose, that a hungrier bridegroom was never yet attended by a hungrier valet. To speak most expressively, we have had no breakfast, to say nothing at all about no supper last night."

" A banquet shall be prepared for you."

" A banquet ?"

" Yes; everything that you can desire shall be placed before you. The richest wines shall flow from golden cups while you live. Don Cæsar de Bazan, you shall live as a Spanish nobleman of boundless wealth."

" My dear fellow, you enchant me. A banquet— rich wines—golden goblets—new apparel—a wife— what's o'clock? Oh! hang that clock. Well, well— it can't be helped I suppose, I have heard of a short life and a merry one. If mine be merry, it will be amazingly short. Come, Lazarillo, dry your eyes, boy. You see fortune, fickle as she is, is resolved to light me from the world with one of her blandest smiles. You shall drink and be merry, you young dog."

" I cannot—I cannot."

" But you must, and hark you, Don Jose, I like company, and I will have my banquet along with the very file of the royal guard that will have the honour of putting me out of the world. They are jolly fellows, doubtless, and while I go and dress, be so good as to give them my express compliments and an invitation. Pray apologise for the shortness of the notice by telling them that I am rather pressed for time just now. Come along, Lazarillo, come along, and help me to dress."

So saying, Don Cæsar took Lazarillo by the arm, and led him away with him through a door which had been pointed out by Don Jose.

The latter when he was left alone, stood for a moment gazing after Bazan with looks of astonishment. Then he suddenly said, as he moved towards the other door of the apartment in which this truly singular conference had taken place,

"Was ever so strange and hair-brained a fellow? He looks upon death as calmly as any other man would upon one of the most common and ordinary courses of life. But I have no time to lose. Of my own authority I can commute his punishment from hanging to shooting, only it shall be announced to him in due form. Humph! I have his free pardon in my pocket, but it is far more convenient to me that he should be shot than saved.

"I hold it as a political maxim that all people are either useful to me or very much in the way, and those who have been once useful are sure to be in the way afterwards, so it becomes one of the duties I owe to myself to put them out of it as quickly as possible."

With these sentiments of political and social reality, Don Jose was on the point of leaving the room, when he was stopped by a person in rich liveried costume, who, bowing low, presented him with a packet.

He changed colour as he took it in his hand, and said,—

"You are from the queen, as I guess by your dress?"

"I am, signior."

"Do you wait an answer?"

"Such are my orders."

Don Jose retired with the note to the recess of one of the windows and read these words,—

"FOR DON JOSE DE SANTAREM,

"We desire much the pardon of Don Cæsar de Bazan, to which we have been solicited by a brave officer. His majesty cannot be found by my messengers. We, therefore, charge you to stay the execution of Don Cæsar until we can procure from the king a pardon in full form for that unhappy gentleman.
"ISABEL R.

"From our palace at Anjueras."

Don Jose read the document twice, and then placing it carefully in his pocket, he turned to the messenger, saying,—

"With my humble duty to her majesty, favour me by stating that her orders shall be fulfilled. Off with you at once, for no doubt her majesty is anxious for an answer. Say that the execution shall be stayed for a week."

The messenger bowed and turned from the room.

"Indeed," muttered Don Jose, "indeed! So, Isabel cannot find the king, and condescends to appeal to the minister. Now what meddling fellow has been to her on Don Cæsar's behalf? That officer of the guard, I'll be sworn; but they shall be disappointed, for by heaven, earth, and hell, I swear he dies at seven o'clock."

Don Jose then hurried from the room, and, having made all his previous arrangements to the great wonderment of the officials of the prison, all he had to do was to give immediate orders that the banquet should be laid upon the tables and everything got ready for the instant nuptials of the Count de Bazan with the lovely Maritana, who we may well suppose was waiting with no small degree of impatience for the fulfilment of the great promises of Don Jose.

All became bustle and animation within the prison. The banquet, which had been sent from Don Jose's mansion, was spread in the same apartment where was the clock, so that Don Cæsar could have no difficulty in knowing to a moment how long he should have to enjoy himself with the good things of this life, to which he had now been so long a stranger.

So singular a thing as a rich banquet spread for one at the point of death never had before occurred within the walls of that building, and the wondering officials could scarcely be made to believe that the prisoner was at all to suffer; or, if so, most certainly not at the hour which had been appointed, and to which it wanted so very short a period of time.

CHAPTER XI.

THE APPEAL TO THE QUEEN.—THE MARRIAGE IN THE PRISON.—THE DESPAIR OF THE PAGE.—THE LAST BANQUET.

IT was the officer of the guard who had appealed to the queen in favour of Don Cæsar. Although ostensibly attached to the suit of the king, that generous-minded man had succeeded, despite all obstacles, in making his way to the presence of Isabella of Spain, with the hope of being successful in inducing her to use what influence she might possess in order to save the gallant, chivalrous, but indiscreet Bazan from the fate that awaited him; a fate so little in accordance with his fault, and which Phillip would never have dreamt for one moment, under the circumstances, of adjudging him to, had it not been as we have before explained, that the royal mind was in a state of unwonted agitation, and required vehemently some sacrifice to appease its royal acrimony.

But even Phillip the Second of Spain, crafty and cruel as he was, had moments of reflection, when he felt he might go a little too far with the haughty grandees who surrounded his throne. One of these moments came after he had given the order for the execution of Don Cæsar, and when the first flush of his gratification was over at having found some one upon whose devoted head he could wreak his vengeance, he almost trembled at what effect it would produce upon the minds of the ancient nobility of his court to sacrifice one of their number as he was about to do Don Cæsar.

The members of that nobility would not have stirred an inch to save Don Cæsar from starvation or from perdition, but when it came to his being hanged for a duel it was quite another matter, and they would be extremely likely to feel that their aristocratic privileges were grievously violated.

All this struck the king forcibly, and, when he had a little recovered from his indignation, to sign an order for the unconditional pardon of Don Cæsar de Bazan was almost a natural result of his cogitations.

With this order, as we have seen, Don Jose was provided, but it suited not his crafty views to use it, and, as we have seen, he expressed a determination not to do so until it should be too late to save his life.

What was a human life compared to the crafty designs of Don Jose de Santarem, or the achievement of one iota of his wild and desperate ambition?

The officer, however, could not know of this relenting on the part of Phillip, and hence he considered that the queen, probably, was the only person who could hope to obtain the pardon of the unhappy prisoner.

We have said that he experienced difficulty in getting access to the presence of Isabella, for her own particular attendants knew well that, if any one came from that portion of the court more immediately connected with the king, to seek an interview with her, the intelligence brought was seldom of a pleasant or satisfactory character, and hence there was an endeavour on the part of the confidential attendants around the queen to spare her the news from the messenger's own lips, and to extract it themselves from him, in order that, if compelled to carry it to her ears, they might do so as softly and as gently as possible, consistent with truth.

When the officer of the guard, therefore, arrived at the palace of Anjueras where was the queen, which he did as quickly as the distance between the prison and that place could be traversed, he found that she was not easily accessible, and it was not until he said to her principal attendant,—

"Tell her majesty that the errand I come upon is one of mercy—one of my own seeking, and one in which I am deeply interested individually," that Isabella consented to receive him in a small chamber, where she usually saw the most distinguished and highly favoured of her guests.

The moment he was admitted to her presence, he threw himself at her feet, and in a voice of much manly emotion, he cried,—

"Madam, I need make no apology for thus intruding upon you. I came on an errand of mercy, and that I know is ever welcome to you."

He then briefly, but distinctly. revealed to the queen the whole particulars connected with Don Cæsar's arrest, and the manner in which the king, because he was evidently fretted by other circumstances, had condemned him to death so hurriedly.

When he had concluded, the queen sighed deeply, saying,—

"Alas, sir, my influence, I grieve to say it, is very small indeed with his majesty. I am here, in this place, living a life of sadness and seclusion, because I know that my presence amid the gaieties and festivities of the court is unwelcome."

"Then have I no hope."

"Nay, sir, do not despair. The feelings which have brought you hither do you infinite honour, and if it were in my power at once by a word to save him whom you have interested yourself for, it should be done; but, alas! that I cannot do. But still, the Queen of Spain ought not to be powerless in a matter which merely concerns the exercise of a merciful prerogative. I will myself write a missive to the king, praying for the pardon of this Don Cæsar. You shall be the bearer of it, and, while you are gone, my best prayers shall not be wanting for your success."

"Oh, your majesty, how can I sufficiently thank you? My heart is full, and I have no words in which to tell you how truly grateful I am. But the execution of this most unhappy but virtually innocent nobleman is fixed for an early hour."

"Ah, you have ascertained that."

"I have. By seven o'clock, the sentence which condemns him to death will be carried into effect;—what can I do if denied admittance to the king, which is more than probable, until past that hour?"

"I know not—I am powerless. Yet stay—Don Jose de Santarem is the only one who would dare, in defiance of the king's orders, to postpone the execution. He is a man whom I suspect of much craft and villany, and I would fain have no sort of communication with him; but this is a case in which all scruples must give way. You shall have another note from me, addressed to Don Jose, requesting what I surely ought to command, that the execution of Don Cæsar shall be postponed until I can see the king myself."

"Thanks, thanks, your majesty; a grateful heart thanks you. God bless you, and grant you happiness."

"I am afraid there is no more happiness for me in this world. But, be that as it may, I will do all that can be done for this unhappy nobleman; and, in order that you may feel quite at ease, I will send one of my own suite with you to present my note to Don Jose, the minister, in case, from your failure in seeing the king, it should become necessary to use it."

"That, indeed, will surely save him. What language can I assume to assure your majesty how deeply I feel this condescension?"

"Say no more. Surely it is but a duty in persons situated as I am now, to the unfortunate, to save them, if possible, from too excessive rigour. I do not —cannot see why this Don Cæsar should not be spared."

The queen then wrote a note to the king, which the officer, as he shrewdly suspected, found it impossible to deliver, and one to Don Jose, which, we are already aware, reached his hands in the prison; and the reception it obtained from him, crowned with the gross falsehood he sent back to the queen by her messenger, we are likewise aware of. Little he cared for justice, thus slighting, in reality, the commands of Isabella, although, in his own mind, he was determined that, by dint of lies, the occurrence should redound to his credit with her even, notwithstanding Don Cæsar should perish.

The officer was partially satisfied, but not wholly so. He would have gladly made his way himself to the prison, to be assured that the queen's note to Don Jose had been properly attended to, but his duty at the palace forbade him to do so, unless, by neglecting it, he placed himself in a worse situation even than that from which he sought to rescue Don Cæsar; so, although on the tenter hooks of impatience, he was compelled to wait until chance should throw some one in his way who would be able to afford him some information on the subject, which he now felt so warmly interested in.

The queen was satisfied with the reply sent to her by Don Jose, and never for a moment dreamed that, villain as he was, he would dare to deceive her in the manner he really contemplated; but, believing that Don Cæsar was for the time saved, she made arrangements to endeavour to see the king during the day, and procure his pardon in due form.

Return we now to the events which were occurring in such rapid succession in the person of the ill-fated but accomplished Don Cæsar.

Before he had finished attiring himself in the costly apparel which had been provided for him by the crafty Jose, every preparation had been made for that banquet which had been promised him, and which he, as well as the minister, fully believed would be the last he would partake of in this world, which he was so soon to leave.

A large table was brought into the apartment of the prison, and upon it were placed, in glittering profusion, the various articles which had been brought from the mansion of Don Jose, in order to carry out his schemes.

There were plates and dishes of silver—cups of burnished gold, and choice confections—wines of the richest and rarest qualities of which Spain could boast. Indeed, Jose reckoned upon the influence of the wine as an inducing reason for Don Cæsar to agree to the proposal which he had to make to him, provided he should not be able to ensure his compliance by any other means. As we have seen, however, he was successful, without much difficulty, and the banquet came in only as a means of intoxicating the senses of Don Cæsar, and keeping him fully up to the mark, as regarded the intended marriage which he had consented to.

All was arranged there before he again made his appearance; so that, when he did issue from the inner chamber, he found a transformation that looked little short of magical in the one he had left.

The personal appearance of Don Cæsar de Bazan, now that he was, as he believed, for the last time in his life, attired in the splendid apparel befitting his rank, was striking and commanding in the extreme. He looked the very beau ideal of a nobleman and a gentleman, characters that do not always go together in any country. His step appeared lighter and more elastic; his brow more elevated; and there was a fire and brilliancy in his eyes which showed how great an effect old associations were having upon him, and how much more at home he found himself in the costly apparel which now adorned him, than in the faded rags he had cast off so recently.

The boy Lazarillo was weeping; but no such womanish weakness came across the soul of Don Cæsar, and he strode into the apartment where the banquet was prepared with all the easy grace that would have characterised his movements, had he been in his once superb mansion, about to feast the nobility of Spain, as he had very frequently done to his cost.

"Ha! ha!" he exclaimed, as he entered the room, and saw the preparations for feasting which had been so rapidly completed; "this is as it should be; I never thought again to look on such a sight as this, except in a dream; sparkling wine from sparkling cups. Don Jose, I thank you. These things smooth the path between this world and another. This is most rare and pleasant! Oh, beautiful, spirit-stirring wine; thou bane and blessing—my greatest enemy, and yet my only friend! What would life be without thee? The very mischief that you do is doubtful, and more joy comes from it than despair. Now I will envy no one; and, when you tell the tale of Don Cæsar's death, say that he fought his man fairly, and slew him; that he was condemned harshly to die for the act, and that he died as a soldier and a gentleman should die, with a brave heart, and the light of dancing joy in his eyes, and the taste of rich, glorious wine on his lips."

"Gracious goodness!" said the gaoler, who was in the room, "don't you want a priest?"

"Aye, if he be a jolly fellow, and will pledge me deep in the wine-cup; but, if he wishes to pray, and tell me of that which I shall soon know for a certainty, while his is all guess-work, I humbly decline his services. The canting, greasy rogues, I know them well! No priest for me."

"What an odd fellow!" ejaculated the gaoler; "of all the wild devils that ever I came near, he beats them."

"Hark ye, Don Jose!" said Cæsar; "I requested that the guard should partake of the banquet with me. They are, no doubt, brave, frank-hearted fellows— soldiers mostly are. I invite them in my name, and, for the next——By-the-by, what's o'clock? The diable! I have not much time to spare. Send for them. There is but time sufficient for a few bumpers. Hurrah! wine, wine, wine and good company for ever—I mean for about a quarter of an hour."

"And do you really wish for such company, Don Cæsar, and at such a time?" said Jose.

"Do I really wish it, Don Jose! Most certainly. Let them come; they are brave fellows all, no doubt; and I would fain they knew beforehand that I cannot entertain any ill-will to those who do but their duty, even presuming that that duty is not to me the most agreeable thing in the world."

"Oh, Don Cæsar," cried Lazarillo, "do not have them here; I shall look upon them as your murderers."

"Tush, boy, tush! Do not say so. A soldier is bound to obey orders, and they who will, in obedience to their officer's command, have to take my life, I consider no more answerable or blameable for the act than the arquebuses they fire at my breast."

"As you please," said Don Jose. "Your will shall be law here, and no wish you can utter shall be ungratified, with the exception of——"

"A wish to live," said Cæsar—"I understand you. Quick, quick—let me have the jolly fellows here at once. I am no hermit; I like good cheer, and I like company. If I cannot get it extremely select, why, then I take it as it comes, and from the low as well as from the high I extract amusement."

Don Jose gave the order for the guards to enter, which the soldiers obeyed rather dubiously, as if they had a suspicion that their reception from the man they were so shortly to shoot might not be of the most friendly character; but such apprehensions, if they at all existed, were very quickly dispelled by Don Cæsar, who cried out,—

"Come on, my lads, come on—drink and be merry. Nay, never hang back, men. Come on, I say. Here is glorious, sparkling, soul-inspiring wine. Do not fancy that because it will be your duty to shoot me that I think the worse of you, or intend that the short time I have yet to live shall be passed unpleasantly. No; the shorter the time the more need is there to make much of it; so here's a bumper to you all. Hurrah—hurrah!"

Thus encouraged, the guards joined in the spirit-stirring shout of Don Cæsar, and crowding round the table, after piling their arquebuses against the wall, they filled for themselves cups of the generous wine, and seemed completely to forget the very disagreeable piece of duty that was so near at hand.

Don Jose left the room, for he had some of his politic arrangements to make, while Lazarillo retired as far as he could from the boisterous revelry of the soldiers, who, as the executioners of Don Cæsar, however much they might be compelled to act from orders they dared not resist, he could not and would not mingle in any way with.

"Come, boy, come," cried Don Cæsar; "drink a cup with us."

But the boy only shook his head, and tears stood in his large handsome eyes.

"Well, well," added the reckless Cæsar, "the boy is wayward and weak at heart on my account. Drink away and drown all care, my brave fellows. Life is short at the best, and we ought to seize every enjoyment we can as it flits by us. The only difference to me is, that it will be uncommonly short; but still it's long enough for a song, I'll warrant; so here goes. You must give me a jolly, rattling chorus. Hurrah!"

He then, in a melodious voice, struck up the following popular refrain, which Madrid at the time was ringing with, to the delight of all the young, wild, rollicking blades of the city:—

"To the vine, to the vine,
    As in beauty it grows;
Like the fair hair of beauty
    It gracefully flows.
Let us sing, ha, ha, ha!—ha, ha, ha!
To fellows of blood 'tis a duty
To sing to the vine and to beauty!

"The blushes, the blushes,
    That bloom on the fair,
Like the sunny west sky,
    So gorgeous, so rare.
Let us sing, ha, ha, ha!—ha, ha, ha!
To fellows of blood 'tis a duty
To sing to the vine and to beauty."

"Hurrah! hurrah!"

"A maiden's fond lips,
    When they lisp soft of love,
Breathe strains to the soul
    As from ———"

At this moment, while every glass was charged, the door of the prison opened, and an official personage habited in black appeared. There was an instantaneous cessation of the song, and all its wild accompaniment, while the boy darted forward with despair in his countenance, for he thought that the time had arrived when Don Cæsar was to be taken out to death.

"Don Cæsar de Bazan, Count of Orfilla, and Chevalier of the order of our Lady of Loretto," said the new comer; upon which Don Cæsar laid down the full goblet he had in his hand, and with more dignity than one could have thought, at such a wild moment, he could have thrown into his manner and bearing, he bowed to the speaker, who, after acknowledging the salute, continued to read from a parchment document he held in his hands, as follows :—

"We, Phillip II., King of Spain, taking into our gracious consideration the rank, as a grandee of our kingdom, of Don Cæsar de Bazan, Count of Orfilla, now condemned to death, and that the crime was one committed in the heat of blood, do here advisedly decree ——"

"He is saved! he is saved!" cried Lazarillo; "oh, thank Heaven! He is saved! he is saved!"

"Decree," continued the messenger, in the same tone, "that he shall not be hanged according to our original sentence."

"Yes, yes," shouted the boy; "my friend—my preserver—my kindest, best, noblest friend. He is saved!"

"But," added the reader, "that he shall be shot by twelve of the Royal Guard."

"Oh, God!" cried Lazarillo, and but for the timely support of Don Cæsar he must have fallen to the floor, such a death-like faintness came over him, as he now found all his hopes extinguished, and that the messenger had only come formally to announce the change in the sentence from the civil form of punishment to one more congenial to the feelings of the prisoner.

The messenger then folded up the paper, and made a bow to Don Cæsar, who returned it with another, such as would have attracted the attention of some of the court of the haughty monarch, who was made such a puppet of by Don Jose, for the furtherance and the carrying out of his own ambitious and criminal projects.

The moment the messenger was gone, Don Cæsar again seized his wine-cup, as if nothing had happened to disturb the hilarity of the scene, and, with a voice which rang again through the chamber, he shouted,—

"—————— Heaven above,
Let us sing—Ha, ha, ha! ha, ha, ha!
To fellows of blood 'tis a duty
To sing to the vine and to beauty.
Hurrah—hurrah!"

"Bravo! bravo! well done, my lads; but really some of you are not looking so cheerful as you ought. What's life but a dream, from which, perchance, death is the awakening? I shall be roused from my slumbers, if such a theory be correct, by the loud thunder of your arquebuses."

Thus encouraged, the soldiers again drank freely, and the spirits of the whole party rose rapidly, while Lazarillo stood apart, with his head resting on his hands, plunged in the most profound grief. But what singular transformation suddenly takes place in the manner and appearance of the boy? No one is looking at him, and now he stands erect, and a half dubious smile crosses his face—he glances towards the guard, still busily engaged in their carousal, and then, with trembling eagerness, he fumbles in his pockets, muttering to himself, as he did so,—

"Thank the Holy Virgin I am an armourer's boy, and have had charge of the muskets of the guard—who so quick as I in unloading them, when brought to master's shop? I have the screw here. Oh! blessed chance. Now, if they will give me but two or three minutes, I may yet save him."

With such trembling eagerness, that he could scarcely steady his hand to the work, he took one of the ramrods from the arquebuses, and fixed to its extremity a small metal screw which would draw the charge. Then, one by one, he succeeded in extracting the bullets from the powder. One of the guard saw him handling the arquebuses; but he had no suspicion of what he was about, and did not interfere with him. The work was done—the bullets were all in Lazarillo's pocket—it seemed to him like a dream. He sat down upon the floor of the dungeon, and burst into tears of joy.

Don Cæsar heard him weeping, and half turning towards him, he said, reproachfully,—

"Lazarillo, Lazarillo, this is not kind of you, boy. If my life is a short one, let it be merry. Come and join us. A cup of wine will help to chase away those tears."

Before the boy could make any reply, the door of the apartment was thrown open, and Don Jose, entering hastily, said,—

"Don Cæsar, your bride comes."

"The devil!" cried the prisoner; and laying down the cup of wine that he had been in the act of carrying to his lips, he glanced towards the door, adding, —"Now for the two most important affairs of my life, my marriage and my execution. Quite a choice of evils, if I had to choose between them; and I don't know that the fact of them both coming together will aggravate either."

In another moment, Don Jose stepped to the door, and met Maritana, who was slowly approaching, led by the gaoler, for she was so closely and impenetrably veiled that it was quite impossible she could see anything. The darkness in which her beautiful eyes were shrouded was most profound.

Don Cæsar, at the first glimpse of the rich garments in which his bride elect was attired, made a wry face, as if he would say, "Oh, here is some old crabbed court spinster, who endeavours, by bravery of apparel, to hide the wrinkles time has made on her cheeks;" but a second glance, notwithstanding the lady was veiled, staggered him in his opinion; for there was no concealing the native grace and dignity of the figure he saw approaching him. The gliding beautiful walk of Maritana could not be concealed, any more than it could be assumed by one not possessed of her marvellous beauty and grace.

As she advanced, led by the hand by Don Jose, he met her, and involuntarily paying her the homage of a bow, although she could not see it, he took from the minister the fair, delicate hand of Maritana, and gazed upon it with a sudden love for its owner such as he had never yet felt for woman.

"This is your bride," said Don Jose.

"Ah!" replied Don Cæsar, "you are now striving to make life valuable to me indeed! This fair hand must surely belong to a fair face. Lady ——"

"Remember your solemn promise," whispered Don Jose.

"All I wish is just one glance at the features which ——"

"You will be hung instead of shot, if you make the attempt."

"I must refrain then; but it's rather hard. How fair a hand—! a young one, who can doubt?—childlike in its beauty—the soft dimpled knuckles—the taper fingers. Don Jose, a word with you, if you please."

"What is it?"

"Could not you give me another half hour?"

"Impossible!"

"A quarter?"

"I cannot—I dare not."

"Well, that is hard. Not one ten minutes, I suppose. What's the use of my marrying? Heigho!—well—well. There's a fate, I have heard, in these things, and mine is an odd one. You tremble, lady."

"She dare not answer you," said Jose. "She has sworn solemnly to exchange no words with you. Do not seek to induce her to break her oath."

"The priest waits," announced the gaoler.

Don Jose pointed to the door significantly. The guard took their muskets, and marched from the room; Don Cæsar gave one glance around him, and then again turning to his unknown bride, he said,—

"Lady, I devote to you the remainder of my existence. All I ask in return, is one kiss."

She shook her head.

"Nay, I will shut my eyes, if necessary, while I take it—or one eye."

She shook her head, and he thought he heard her sigh, or make some sound between a sigh and a sob.

CHAPTER XII.

THE PAGE'S REQUEST—THE EXECUTION—THE BODY
IN THE COURT-YARD—THE MARQUIS AND MAR-
CHIONESS DE ROLANDO.

DON CÆSAR was about to make some remark which might have been considered, in some degree, not wholly in accordance with the promise of discretion he had made to Don Jose, when the latter in a louder voice, cried—

"To the chapel—to the chapel, Don Cæsar; in one minute it will be seven o'clock."

"I am ready," said Cæsar—"I am ready."

"One word," whispered the page, as he clung to Don Cæsar's cloak—"one word, my generous defender, ere you go. Have you no farewell for me?"

"I have, my boy; God bless you. Be a brave fellow—serve your new master faithfully—drink deep, and make your life as merry a one as you can. Don't say in after years you didn't get some good moral advice from me."

"I won't."

"Love the girls, too, bless their hearts! They make a man more amiable than would fifty homilies."

"I will."

"That'll do, then. Good bye, Lazarillo, good bye."

"But, Don Cæsar, turn your head this way, I want to whisper something to you."

"Well—I attend."

"After your marriage you will be taken into the court-yard and shot."

"I believe I shall. A quick method of obtaining a divorce—is it not, my boy?"

"Yes, yes; but grant me one request."

"I swear it."

"When you hear the report of the arquebuses please to fall flat down."

"I rather think I shall."

"You promise me?"

"Without a single reservation. You might have relied upon me doing so without any promises at all, Lazarillo. Really, you seem to have taken leave of your senses within these few minutes."

"No, no; I have not. On the contrary, I have found some of my wits. You will be sure to fall down?"

"Rely upon it."

"God bless you, Don Cæsar—God bless you."

"The same to you, boy—farewell. I'm glad to see you put a better heart on the matter now. You look quite resigned."

"I have taken a second thought of it."

"Very good."

Don Cæsar, seizing the boy's hand, and then turning to Don Jose and to Maritana, said—

"I beg to apologise for this delay. I am quite ready now for the two little incidents which, I suppose, the next quarter of an hour will see concluded."

"Lead on," cried Jose, as the gaoler and the singular bridal procession made its way towards the small chapel which was attached to the prison.

The priest was waiting, and a very few minutes sufficed to bestow upon the veiled bride the title of Countess de Bazan.

Some sudden faintness came over her, either from joy at finding her ambitious anticipations fulfilled, or at the novelty of her situation, and she had to be accommodated with a chair. Don Jose then whispered to the captain of the guard, who, thereupon, took Cæsar by the arm, and significantly pointed towards the court-yard. At that moment seven o'clock sounded from the neighbouring steeples,—the hour of execution had arrived, and, evidently in a state of bewilderment, Don Cæsar followed the captain to the court-yard of the prison.

What were his thoughts and feelings at that moment it was impossible to say: perhaps they wandered back to early scenes of love and happiness; perchance there was a heartfelt pang for a life misspent in riot and extravagance; or, perhaps, he was thinking that he was never less inclined to die than now that he was the husband of one whom he loved, although he had not seen her face, nor knew if she entertained the least feeling of attachment towards himself.

"Is she ignorant of the doom that awaits me?" he asked himself; "or can she be so heartless as to connive at it, looking only to the poor vanity of being called a countess."

Little time, however, had Don Cæsar for reflections painful or otherwise. It was not two dozen paces from the chapel to the court-yard, and there were the soldiers drawn up ready to fire the fatal volley, which he fully believed would hurry him to eternity.

The window, too, in the apartment where the strange banquet had been held, and where Lazarillo still remained, looked into the court-yard, and strange enough to appearance did Lazarillo look, as he rather carelessly leant upon the window-sill to see the execution, which he, and only he, knew would be a complete failure. Oh, how often he put his hand in his pocket again and again, to assure himself that he had made no mistake, but really had the twelve bullets there, which else would have found a home in the defenceless heart of Don Cæsar. At last he kept his hand in his pocket altogether, which saved him a deal of trouble, and he almost laughed as he saw the soldiers look carefully to the priming of their arquebuses.

"You are a nice article," said the gaoler to him; "pretending to be so sorry one minute, and now taking it so easy."

"What an ugly devil you are," said the boy; "have you got such a thing as a looking-glass in your house?"

*   *   *   *   *

The moment Don Cæsar was conveyed from the chapel to execution, Jose became anxious to get Maritana out of the prison; but her indisposition seemed momentarily to increase rather than to diminish, and the thick veil which had shrouded her face from all observation was forced to be removed to allow her to taste of some wine which was brought to her in the same cup that Don Cæsar, her husband, had so recently pressed to his own lips.

Jose had meant to get her away from the prison at once, so that none even of the officials of that place should have an opportunity of recognising her again, in consequence of having seen that beautiful face, which never could be forgotten. He was foiled, however, in this, and now he found that she was too weak to be instantly hurried to the carriage, and that, perforce, she would hear the fatal discharge of fire-arms which would prove the death of her husband.

Upon recovering from her faintness, she looked around her with an anxiety which the wily Jose easily translated into a wish to see him to whom she had been so recently united.

" Where is he ?" she said in a faint voice ; " where is he ?"

" Remember your promise," whispered Jose. " Ask no questions. Are you strong enough now to come away ?"

" My husband ?"

" Psha, Maritana—I beg your pardon, Countess de Bazan. You have no consideration for the queen's wishes."

" The queen ? Does she wish ——"

" That you leave this place with me immediately. Such are her majesty's commands."

" I am ready—I am ready. The queen's wishes are laws to me. How much I owe her—the good queen who smiled upon me when I was a street singer, and now has made me a countess. I am ready."

She rose and accepted of Don Jose's supporting arm, while he led her rapidly from the chapel, followed by the attendants, who desired to do honour to the minister from fear rather than from affection. The nearest route to the gate was through the chamber where the banquet had taken place, and where Lazarillo still was watching with intense eagerness, from the open window, the preparations for the execution. Don Jose well knew what a spectacle attracted the boy's attention, and he attempted to hurry Maritana through the room, lest she should obtain a glance of the awful scene in the court-yard, which was transfixing Lazarillo's attention.

" On, on, lady !" he whispered. " You are expected at court—on, on. Quicker if you can."

An involuntary cry burst from the lips of the boy, although he knew that all was safe, and a stern voice was heard from the court-yard, calling,—

" Present—fire !"

In an instant a tremendous report followed, and a volume of blue smoke curled in at the open window of the apartment. A loud scream burst from Maritana's lips, and Don Jose, with a stamp of his foot, uttered a tremendous oath.

" Gracious Heaven, what was that ?" said Maritana ; " what was that ?"

" An execution, madam," replied Jose. " A great criminal has suffered for his crimes."

" God have mercy upon his soul !"

" Amen."

She trembled violently, and clung closer to Don Jose, who hurried her onward, congratulating himself that her suspicions had not been awakened to the fact that the great criminal he spoke of was the man to whom she had so recently given her hand at the altar, and sworn to love, an easy oath for her to take, since his image was already enshrined in her heart.

* * * * *

Don Cæsar, although with no shadow of a hope that he could possibly escape the death that was prepared for him, had faced the deadly weapons of destruction that were levelled at his heart most bravely. The court-yard was one at the back of the prison, and occasionally used for private executions. It was rather attached than belonging to the edifice, for it was only inclosed with low walls, and not at all guarded, since there was but one door from the prison to it, and that was never opened except on such occasions as the present. Whether, in consequence of being stunned by the report of the fire-arms, or with a recollection of the singular request of Lazarillo, certain it is that at the moment of the discharge down went Don Cæsar as flat as if he had received the whole twelve bullets in his heart.

The officer of the guard then turned away his head from what he considered the sickening sight of the corpse, and gave the word for the soldiers to leave the place, so that in a few moments Don Cæsar was alone, and, had he chosen to avail himself of the facilities he now had of escape, he might soon have placed himself out of danger. The authorities of the prison had received no orders concerning the disposal of what they considered the body, so they let it lie where it was till some one should come, and the whole affair, with all its harshness, all its secrecy, and all its mysteries, was considered to be at an end.

Indeed, Lazarillo began to be a little alarmed when he saw Don Cæsar never stirred, and when he was at length told he must leave the prison, his alarm grew strong, that, after all, perhaps, Cæsar had received some serious hurt ; but he could find no excuse for going into the court-yard alone, or unwatched.

" Come," cried the gaoler, " be off with you. We don't want boys here. Be off with you."

" But Don Jose said I might stay."

" Yes, with Don Cæsar ; but there's no Don Cæsar to stay with now, so don't make that an excuse. Why, you are as anxious to remain in prison as other people are to get out of it."

" But, good sir ——"

" Come, come, be off with you ; we are going to breakfast, and don't want your company."

So poor Lazarillo was ejected from the prison, notwithstanding all his urgent remonstrances to the contrary.

" Well," ejaculated Lazarillo, when he found himself fairly in the street ; " I never could have supposed I should have cried at being turned out of a prison. What shall I do ? I am the page of Don Jose now, and can go to his house if I like ; but, about Don Cæsar. How shall I rescue him. He did not move. Can he be hurt ? Is it possible that some grievous accident has befallen him ? How can I ascertain ? Alas ! alas ! I am very miserable."

Having arrived at this very unsatisfactory conclusion, Lazarillo sat down on a door-step, and wept until another boy passed, and began laughing at him, upon which he jumped up, and ran after him to give him a thrashing, in which he fully succeeded ; and it would appear that the exercise and the little excitement had done him some good, and sharpened his wits a little, for, clapping his hands together, he cried,—

" I will go round to the back of the prison, and try if I cannot get a peep at him."

This resolution was no sooner come to than it was acted on, and off set Lazarillo as fast as he could, making a very considerable detour round a number of houses in order to get to the back of the prison, which looked towards the open country, and so far was easy of access.

He was not a long time in reaching the low wall which inclosed the court-yard, and after taking a long and anxious glance at the windows of the prison to ascertain if any one was watching, he with some trouble scrambled on to the wall and obtained a view of the court-yard. It gave him an exquisite pang of grief to see Don Cæsar still lying as he had fallen, when the report of the arquebuses of the guard had struck upon his ears.

"He is dead!—oh, he is dead!" moaned the boy, and then, heedless wholly of his own danger in so intruding, he jumped down from the summit of the low wall into the court-yard.

Still no one appeared to observe or intercept him, and, with a feeling of awe lest he should really be in company with the dead, he approached the still form of Don Cæsar. The tears struggled to his eyes, and bitter sobs came from his heart as he said to himself, "How could this have happened? there were but twelve arquebuses, and I have twelve bullets in my pocket? Can one of these have been loaded again, and so taken his life? Oh, unhappy chance!—oh, miserable chance!"

He had now approached quite close to the body, and, kneeling down beside it, he wrung his hands, crying aloud, in the bitterness of his heart,—

"Oh, my poor Don Cæsar! who has been so good to me although I have often flouted at him in the streets when he was not quite steady! My best, dearest friend, Don Cæsar! They have killed him—they have killed him, though I did take all the bullets out of the arquebuses of the guard! Oh!—oh!"

"The devil you did!" cried Don Cæsar.

A cry of joy burst from Lazarillo, and, throwing himself upon the earth, he said,—

"You are not dead—you are not dead!"

"I really can't say," was the reply.

"But you speak."

"Ah, very true."

"Then you know you are not shot?"

"Indeed I don't though; I know—I believe I know, that I think I am, I believe, shot."

"You are saved—you are saved to me!"

"Am I?"

"Yes, yes, thank Heaven! Oh, what I have suffered on your account!"

"Well, you are balancing the account now; for just now, when you came with such a dab across my stomach, you knocked all the breath out of me, and now you are laying upon me, and won't let any more come in."

"But you are not hurt? There are no bullets in your breast?"

"I think not; but really I can't say. You seem to know best, Lazarillo. Was I dreaming, or did I hear you say you had taken the bullets out of the arquebuses?"

"I did, Don Cæsar. Here they are; you can count them. You will find twelve, so you cannot be shot."

Don Cæsar gave one of his legs a vigorous shake, and then the other, after which he said,—

"Well, my boy, I do begin to think that only one of my calamities have happened."

"One! What do you mean?"

"Why, that I am not executed and married both. It would have been too much in one day."

"You are not hurt at all then?"

"I really think not."

"And you feel well?"

"Tolerably well, I thank you."

"But what made you lie down so still?"

"Because a man has no business to move about after he is shot."

"But you were not."

"But I thought I was, which is all the same thing. You wouldn't have a man with a dozen bullets in his chest think of getting up and walking about would you?"

"Oh, I am so thankful—so delighted! You know, Don Cæsar, while you were drinking with the guard, I extracted the bullets from the muskets."

"But how?"

"Don't you know I am an armourer's boy?—only that was what first got me into trouble, and then got you into trouble. You know, the muskets of the guard are loaded every day, but they are not fired off, and my master's duty was to clean and load them fresh every morning. That duty he always left with me; but the carnival came, and—and ——"

"You didn't do it?"

"No, I didn't. Well, that got me into trouble, you remember; but I had in my pouch the implements of my trade, and I did unload the arquebuses while the guard was engaged with you and the wine, so that you see, Don Cæsar, all that they fired at you was a quantity of powder."

"Very satisfactory, indeed."

"Oh, yes; and you see that's how you were saved, and God be thanked for it. Oh, I am so well pleased I should like a dance."

"Oh, you ain't married. I didn't think much of that part of the business a little time ago; but it has become serious now that I really am not dead. It's not to be laughed at now, and as for dancing, I always had an objection to dance at any one else's wedding, and to leave my own as completely out of the question as possible."

"But you are saved, and that's all I care for."

"Mind what you say, Lazarillo. It will come round to dinner time soon; and, besides, I don't know that I am quite safe yet. I cannot take upon myself to say whether I am dead or not in law. I wonder whether this affair will act as a discharge in full to all my debts. Humph! when I come to think of it, I should say not, for the arquebuses were not a discharge in full. I'm afraid, Lazarillo, my creditors will be giving you a dinner and a piece of plate, or something of that sort."

"Never mind me. Get up."

"And what then?"

"Run away."

"Judicious advice, I dare say. Think of the feelings of a husband, Lazarillo."

"But if you are sure they may still endeavour to kill you, for my sake, as well as for your own, make your escape. The wall here is very low. You can jump over it, I am sure. Seek the open country, and rely upon me to bring you food and necessaries. I implore you not to remain here, Don Cæsar, another moment."

"They certainly have used me rather scurvily here," said the don, as he sat up; but scarcely had the words passed his lips, when Lazarillo said,—

"Down, down; be dead again!"

"What for?"

"There's somebody coming."

"The deuce there is! Just tell him, whoever he is, that I'm stone married—I mean dead!"

CHAPTER XIII.

THE QUEEN'S REFLECTIONS.—THE MINISTER'S PASSION.—THE RING.—GUILTY EXULTATION.

How poorly does the mind ill at ease assort with the splendour of a palace—even with the most beautiful and the choicest portion of that palace; and how little can the greatest ease and abundance of all that can make life valuable, cause the sad heart to rejoice at the riches of art and nature that abound on all sides. Such were the unhappy feelings of the lovely and amiable Queen of Spain, who sat weeping in her boudoir, surrounded by all that could be desired.

The boudoir was a choice specimen of what art could create—the beauties that were not in nature, but produced by combinations purely of mental origin; the painter and architect had not striven in vain to produce a scene scarce surpassed by any age or country. It was of Moorish character, and so successfully was the design carried out, that while sitting in it, one

curious design, and the richness, softness, and beauty of the whole was extraordinary ; it looked like a scene of enchantment, and a picture of some fairy palace.

The furniture, too, was the rarest and most costly, such, indeed, as well befitted such an apartment. The most curious woods—and there were few that did not grow in some portion of the Spanish dominions, extending as they did over the two worlds—the richness of the drapery was such that it can scarcely be imagined—the richest silks and velvets that could be procured from far-famed Venice, the queen of the Adriatic, were called in aid of the general effect : there was nothing but what was soft and luxurious.

Such a place would have been one in which happiness might be found, if happiness were at all to be found in Madrid ; but yet expectation would have been disappointed, for here unhappiness dwelt amidst beauty and luxury ; for there was many a heart to be found in a humble cottage that experienced more pure delight and happiness than the amiable Queen of Spain.

Her bosom heaved with deep sighs, and the rapt stillness of the apartment was broken but by the sound of her own sobs—sounds so ill in accordance with the place, that they created double sorrow and respect for the unfortunate who could sit alone in the midst of so much magnificence and yet become a prey to grief.

Such was the situation in which the Queen of Spain found herself. She was seated on a sofa, and leaning her face upon her hand, while the tears chased each other slowly down her face, and her eyes were mournfully directed towards the beautifully painted window, through which the sun's rays penetrated with a yet warmer and more beautiful, because subdued tone.

The colours of the window were thrown on the rich carpet, which received an additional beauty from the reflection, while the curtain was drawn nearly across the window, leaving but a small portion of it to be seen, and to allow the sun's rays to enter the boudoir.

The queen herself appeared to be unconscious of all around her. Melancholy sat on her brow. Alas! that majesty itself should not be free from sorrow ; but what station in life can be exempt from that which is almost a consequence of our very nature ? We are born to feel sorrow and grief as well as joy, and he is the happiest amongst us who has the least cause for grief, and not he who is wholly free, for there are none such.

could easily call to mind the days of their domination, and believe all the richness and splendour of those times had returned.

The illusion was by no means unnatural, for the beauty of the ornamental workmanship was so unlike what is produced in northern Europe, that we should be carried away by the extreme magnificence. The arabesque that ran over the whole ceiling, was formed of some splendid carving, and gilded with all the care and accuracy of which art is capable.

Soft carpets were spread beneath the feet, so the footstep could not be heard ; long and beautiful curtains hung before the windows, to exclude the sun, and keep cool the air within the apartment, and, indeed, soften any strong sound that might, by accident, reach the royal boudoir.

The sides of the room were also richly ornamented ; not a vacant spot could be seen ; all was occupied by some piece of device that added to the general effect —indeed, it would have been very difficult to have separated one piece of ornament from the whole, or to have followed with the eye the various convolutions of any one piece of carving, and then determine where it began and where it terminated ; the whole was so interminably blended together, that, in fact, no one part could be separated from the other.

One thing, however, could not escape notice, and that was the painted window, not one of the separate panes of which but formed part of some beautiful and

"How transient the sudden gush of sweet feelings, raised by the conduct of my dear but wayward husband!" sighed the queen. "I thought, indeed, it would scarce have lasted so short a time, and my new-born hopes are crushed and withered, like the early flower, whose blossom is cut off by the cold winds and biting frosts.

"He was angered when I first saw him in the forest, when I heedlessly threw myself in his way, and I believed him in danger. Perhaps he might have had cause, and yet 'twas unkind to do so—very unkind to upbraid me, not for doing what I did, but for that which I did not do.

"Surely—surely there must be some cause for this —some secret that I can but guess at. Ah! who would be a queen, and have the object of her best love but half her own, and scarce that? I know not on whom to fix any suspicion. 'Tis hard to say of this one she is too forward, or of that she listens complacently, or of another she is too beautiful. He is the king, and the subject can but feel happy when the royal tongue stoops to flatter.

"Ah! did he but know the pangs I feel, he would scarcely act so, I think; but beauty has its influence upon the heart of Charles, I fear, and perhaps unduly so; and yet, I would not judge too rashly, or too hardly—no—no—and yet, what else can cause such coldness from one whom I love so dearly? He was kind, very kind, in the forest, and all the way home too; but yet, he left me suddenly—ay, 'twas on business—but ought business to have called him away at a moment when returning affection was apparent? 'Twas cruel, and so sudden, and yet he did not leave me as though he regretted doing so.

"There was a re-kindling of unkindness about the hasty manner, and a harshness in the tone of voice, that ill accorded with those in which he had been speaking but a few moments before. Indeed, how suddenly men can change from one mood to another, and what business could he have that was so urgent that it could not bide awhile, but drag even royalty from its privacy. I fear there was more good will towards its dispatch than there ought to be. Ah! I fear—I fear—and yet, I almost fear to say what most oppresses my mind. Surely the king must have had some assignation that drew him from my side. Yes, yes—unhappy queen—queen but in regal mockery: a queen that does not possess the heart of her king."

Here the beautiful and amiable lady burst into a fresh flow of grief, and her tears fell fast, and her bosom heaved with deep and sorrowful sighs. In a little time her grief became less poignant, and she spoke in those low, soft accents that characterised her tones before.

"I recollect now," she began, "'twas Don Jose who touched the king, and whispered something to him; it cannot, surely, be that that minister can pander to the unchaste desires of even Charles; no, no, surely not. And yet—and yet, I have always something like a suspicion of Don Jose.

"There is something strange about that man, and yet I am loth to suspect any one without a cause; and yet, the face will sometimes tell of the heart to those who look carefully; and why should I have any suspicion of the man if his general demeanour or his features do not breed distrust in my mind? I am sure I do not willingly permit my mind to be biassed against him, far from it; he is courteous, civil,—but ought he to be otherwise?

"Then, he is constantly in the company of the king, and if ought should happen, he cannot be ignorant. I pray Heaven that Charles has not too complaisant a counsellor—protect him, indeed, from flatterers, and from such men as would commit any act, however despicable, that had the request of a king to gild its exe-cution. For Don Jose—but, I go too far; he may be innocent of all, I pray Heaven, he may.

"Don Jose certainly was the cause of his quitting me; he did not think of the affair till Don Jose mentioned it, and then with a hasty and scarcely courteous excuse, he abruptly turned from me, though he had one foot on the steps that led up to the palace; and then, too, he quitted in the company of Don Jose. What am I to think of this? 'tis passing strange. Don Jose, it would appear, is at the bottom of all this."

She paused, and she thought she heard a noise at the door of the boudoir; she turned her head, and beheld one of the ladies in waiting, standing, as if she desired to approach, and immediately she perceived that the queen was aware of her presence, she advanced, saying,—

"Pardon, gracious lady, for this intrusion upon your majesty's privacy; but we feared you had been so long alone that sadness and melancholy had oppressed you."

"I am sad and melancholy, too," replied the queen; "I hope it may be without a cause, Inez."

"The hope is not more fervent in your majesty's breast than in those of your attendants," replied the lady.

"I believe it, Inez. And you have come, perhaps, at an opportune moment, and have interrupted sorrowful reflections, that, however impossible it may be at all times to resist indulging in, yet they lead but to little good, and certainly render one unhappy."

"Heaven forbid that such unhappiness should overtake your majesty," replied the lady. "Say, your majesty, is there nothing we can do to dissipate the clouds that hang on your brow? will you permit your attendants to intrude themselves, and try what may be done by conversation towards such an end?"

"You may; but I fear I shall be an unsatisfactory patient," replied the queen, with a smile.

"Nay; your majesty is visibly improving already," replied the lady, as she quitted the presence of the queen, and soon after returning, accompanied by several ladies, who were the personal attendants and friends of the queen. Their conversation was lively and diverting for a time, and then it flagged, which was soon perceived by the Lady Inez, who immediately said,—

"Would your majesty not like a little music? you are usually diverted with sweet sounds."

"Yes, I am," replied the queen; "and yet, I care not for that to-day,—'tis barely in unison with my feelings; and yet, I think I could listen with pleasure to the song of Roderique, the page: he has a singularly fine voice, and sings well."

"He does, your majesty; he is quite a marvel, and he can play no less."

"Let him appear, and we will listen to the sounds of his voice and his guitar."

The Lady Inez quitted the apartment in search of the page, congratulating herself upon having devised something that would relieve the queen from some portion of her melancholy for, at least, a time. She was not long in her search, for she discovered the page, who had escaped from his attendance upon the queen, as he was wont, to bury himself in his musical studies, and, ere long, she drew him into the boudoir.

"Come, Roderique," said the queen, "are you in the vein to-day to sing the song I have often desired you to sing?"

"I can never be otherwise when your majesty desires it," replied the youth, boldly.

"So young, and yet so courtly," replied the queen.

"Nay, your majesty; kindness as well as beauty can win the hearts of those who serve you."

"Indeed, the boy speaks well, your majesty; and I think, sincerely, too," interrupted the Lady Inez.

"Well, we hope so," said the queen. "Let him begin."

Roderique seated himself on a stool, and accompanying himself on his guitar, sung the following,—

"Weep not, fairest, best, and dearest,
　　You are loved full well;
Hearts beat for you, and fond eyes glisten
　　More than tongue can tell.

"Minstrels, though they sing their bravest,
　　Cannot paint to thee
The joy that fires the heart with rapture,
　　At thy smile so free.

"Then, weep not, fairest, best, and dearest,
　　You are loved full well;
Hearts beat for you, and fond eyes glisten
　　More than tongue can tell."

The sounds had ceased some moments ere the queen again spoke, and the page sat mute, looking on the ground, as though he awaited the accustomed expressions of approbation, or some new comment.

"You have done well, Roderique," said the queen; "your music has charmed away some of the melancholy by which I was oppressed. The relief will be, however, I fear, of short duration."

"I would I could as easily charm away the cause as I have appeared to remove for a time the effect."

"I would you could, boy," replied the queen; "but that is far beyond your art to cure."

At that moment an attendant entered the boudoir, and, advancing towards the queen, said,—

"Don Jose waits, may it please your majesty."

"Don Jose!" exclaimed the queen, with a start.

"Yes, your majesty," replied the attendant, "and begs permission to see your majesty."

"I don't know how to answer that message, and yet I know no particular reason why I should refuse that man an interview. The king may have sent him, and then I should be refusing to receive the king's message, and if not, have I not a right to command here, and need not fear intrusion a moment longer than I am disposed. Besides, I may hear something from this crafty man that may assure me of my future happiness. Yes, yes, he shall be admitted."

"Will your majesty permit that Don Jose should approach your presence?" inquired the attendant.

"Yes," replied the queen, "he may be admitted. Stay," continued the queen; "I scarce think I will—and yet desire him to enter at once. And you, ladies, can retire, but not so far as to be without hearing when I call."

The attendants retired, and Don Jose was heard as he walked along until he entered the royal boudoir.

"Well, Don Jose, you have honoured us with a visit, for which we thank you. But tell me, where is your master?"

"The king, gracious lady ——"

"Yes, the king," replied the queen, watching narrowly the countenance of Don Jose.

"His majesty is nowhere ——"

"Nowhere, Don Jose; surely that cannot be intended as an answer to my question."

"I beg your majesty's pardon. I was at the moment endeavouring to recollect where his majesty really was, or would be at this precise moment."

"Ah, well, we'll not tax your memory or knowledge to such an extent as that; but where was he when you left him the last time you saw him?"

"He had but just returned to the royal closet, there to enjoy a few short moments in solitude, until he should be recalled from his privacy by stress of public business."

"I fear the stress of public business comes very heavily on the king," said the queen.

"It does, indeed, your majesty."

"Yes, it allows him no time to indulge in any of the little pleasures of private life."

"There is doubtless a heavy sacrifice on that head, gracious lady, I am disposed to believe; but his majesty makes them without effort or regret."

"Indeed; without effort or regret?" repeated the queen, slowly. "Ah! does he, indeed? He has no love for his queen—he must be cold and passionless."

"Indeed, his majesty, fortunately for himself, can extract a pleasure from many of the bitters of his life—mixes with his subjects most graciously, and thus knows what other monarchs can but imagine."

"His majesty, doubtless, does not confine himself merely to one class of his subjects?"

"No, no, your majesty; he has no bias—he would do justice to all, and hence his impartiality in this respect," replied Don Jose.

"I mean, that business, or perhaps pleasure, may often entice his majesty into the society of the beauties with which Madrid and the court doubtless abound."

"Gracious lady ——"

"Nay, Don Jose, you cannot misunderstand me—the gallantries of his majesty cannot have escaped so clear and discerning an eye as yours."

"Your majesty may believe me."

"Nay, nay, I do not wish you to descend to particulars, but as his minister, and being in his confidence, you must be well aware of the fact."

"Your majesty presses very hard on me, by presuming it already an ascertained fact that the king is gallant, and that I have some knowledge of it."

"Yes, Don Jose, we do so, exactly," replied the queen.

"It is scarcely fair to put the question thus, but I dare not tell your majesty an untruth; the king, it is true, is a gallant and courteous gentleman, and much admired by—by ——"

"By those who care not, perhaps, to conceal the fact that they are for a time the favourite of a king."

"There are many, no doubt, your majesty, who would do so," replied Don Jose; "and yet, it is an ungrateful theme to speak of, the gallantries and weaknesses of an amiable and generous monarch."

"Nay, Don Jose, you will not lose his esteem for what you may say on this score."

"Your majesty is gracious. I cannot but admit there may be much that would even strengthen your majesty's suspicions on that score, and yet, there is nothing that puts the matter beyond a doubt."

The queen paused, and it was some moments ere the conversation was renewed. She was much affected, and Don Jose appeared to be equally so.

"I feared that something of this kind must be the cause of his majesty's absence from our side. He was wont to pay more attention, and graciously pleased to pass more days in our society than he does now hours."

"His majesty's infidelity, if unfaithful he be, is the less excusable that he must abandon so much beauty and worth for objects not possessing those qualities in anything like the extent that your majesty does."

"Don Jose!" exclaimed the queen, reproachfully.

"Your majesty may be angry with an honest heart for speaking the truths that he believes are perceptible to all; but the amiability of your disposition much enhances the sin of his majesty."

"I trust, Don Jose, that you, the king's minister, do not abet the follies of even such a master for the purpose of retaining his favour."

"Can your majesty think it possible I could do such a thing?" said Don Jose, with a tear in his eye. "No, your majesty, for great as the distance there is between us, I could not look on such a form, such loveliness, and so much kindness and condescension without feeling the utmost love and admiration. No, madam, my heart bleeds for you, but I could not increase your woes—I would rather offer any consolation in my power."

"What mean you, Don Jose?" exclaimed the queen.

"Gracious lady, had your station not been so exalted above me, I had said more, but the acute feelings of the subject must be lost and never reach the ear of royalty; the heart may burst with emotion, but the tongue dare not utter them; the eyes may devour the ravishing beauty, but the subject dares not to approach even to the hem of the garment."

"Don Jose," said the queen, interposing, "this is language you dared not repeat before a master who, whatever his faults may be, has been a kind and generous master to you; this language to your queen is such that were I to repeat it to him, would cost you your honours—this is more than ingratitude."

"Pardon me, gracious lady," said Don Jose, and he knelt on one knee; "if I have used warmer language than I ought, it was but the strength of feeling that hurried me away; I meant not to wound your feelings, or encounter your anger; believe me, you mistake me altogether. I did but mourn for one so good and beautiful, and so neglected, as though you had been a sister; my presumption was great, but may I hope you will forgive my transgression?"

"Arise, Don Jose," replied the queen, coldly; "I accept your explanation, and hope it is sincere, and that we shall not be again called upon to repress such displays of feeling."

"Your majesty's rebuke shall not pass unheeded," exclaimed Don Jose, in an apparently sincere tone.

"If his majesty forgets his queen in the company of his courtiers, it shall never be said the same forgetfulness extended to his queen, and she either forgot herself or her station."

"No less could be expected from your majesty," said Don Jose, in a cringing tone; "but has your majesty no commands that I can execute this carnival time?"

"None," replied the queen; "and yet, now I recollect, I think there is one; it is a mission of mercy, and will come well from the minister of the king."

"Name it, your majesty, and if it depend on me or my exertions, depend upon its being done," said the wily minister.

"But first tell me, is it true, as I have heard say, that you have in prison a noble though thoughtless gentleman, who was unhappy enough to be engaged in a quarrel yesterday during the carnival?"

"There was something of the sort, your majesty; the deed was committed in a place and at a time when these things should be most strenuously avoided—of this your majesty is well aware, I presume."

"Truly we are, and hence we would interpose between stern justice and the unfortunate culprit; especially as he is a nobleman and a gentleman—his fortune's reduced we hear?"

"That is truly the case, your majesty," replied Don Jose; "for he was possessed of but his own wardrobe, and that of the scantiest and the most ragged; indeed 'twas a wonder how such things held together."

"And that is one reason," replied the queen, "why he would have but few friends."

"Indeed, your majesty is pretty correct there, and yet the populace were his friends; but that might be on account of his rags being so much like their own."

"The populace, Don Jose, is but a bad friend at any time, and will scarce last true for a great while."

"Your majesty is quite right there," replied Don Jose.

"Therefore it is we wish to interpose our poor influence in his favour, inasmuch as he is represented to be a man of high honour and integrity, and the cause of quarrel was one that robbed the act of much of its criminality."

"Oh, yes, your majesty," replied Don Jose, "there are some circumstances about it that cause the whole affair not to look so black as the mere statement would lead us to believe."

"Most true," replied the queen; "we wish this man's life may be spared—indeed, that he may be pardoned—and believing his life in much danger we desire that you would interfere with all possible dispatch."

As the queen spoke, Don Jose felt somewhat puzzled as to the nature of the boon the queen was about to demand at his hands, and, when it did come, he was for some moments at a loss to conceive how he could answer it.

At last, he thought, she does not know of his death, for however accurate her knowledge may be of his capture and the cause, yet she does not appear to have heard of that; but I will not be hasty—I may make something out of it, and yet work to advantage.

"Your majesty may be correct as to the imminence of the danger, for the deed done is one that will demand a heavy retribution at his hand, though the quarrel that led to it was one that he had generously taken up in protection of a poor boy whose punishment was greater than his deserts, and he fled to escape the infliction."

"That is what we have heard, Don Jose," replied the queen; "am I to ask you a second time for this favour?"

"Certainly not, your majesty. To be your agent in such an affair would give me greater pleasure than I have words to describe; but your majesty is aware that though I can do much, yet there are things I cannot do, and to attempt some others would be destruction."

"Surely, this is not one of them?" said the queen.

"Not if I have a token from your majesty to signify it is your wish he should be saved; then I will undertake to do what I can for Don Cæsar—without it, though I would attempt all your majesty desired ——"

"No; 'twould be no mercy to destroy one to save another," replied the queen. "Take this ring, 'twill be a sufficient sign that I have asked this of you."

As the queen spoke she took from her finger a diamond ring of great value, and held it towards Don Jose, who immediately took it, saying—

"Thanks to your majesty. The token is a valuable one, and I will preserve it, not only in remembrance of your majesty, but also of the purpose for which it was given."

"Then if you save this gentleman you will earn my thanks, Don Jose," said the queen.

"And such a reward will be well worth Jose's earning," replied Don Jose, exultingly, and then, he added, "I take my leave of you, gracious lady, to execute your mission."

"And take with you my good wishes for your success," replied the queen, and Don Jose quitted the apartment.

"She is ignorant what she wished to prevent has already happened, and the token she has given me will not be used for any such purpose; but yet 'twill be better employed, to my thinking, by some future use I may have for it. Much may yet be done, and one repulse may be followed by another, but success may at length terminate my endeavours."

The interview had lasted some time, and now the shades of night had thrown the city of Madrid into darkness, and the queen advanced towards the window, which she opened, and looked out upon the scene below and above. She paused as she gazed upon the scenery around; her view was limited; the late buildings in the neighbourhood of the palace threw a sombre hue around, and their tall, dark walls, formed a barrier, through which the eye could not pierce.

But above there was another scene of boundless extent—the heavens were sparkling with millions of stars, that shone like diamonds set in jet.

"Beautiful! most beautiful!" exclaimed the queen, as she gazed upon the scene. "Lo! what a sight for a mere mortal. The power to contemplate such a scene ought to confer happiness; thought is lost in the immensity of the view, and yet that is but a small portion to that which we cannot see. I would that my Charles were here to view the tiny lights shine forth from Heaven; but he, alas! is in the arms of some wanton."

A sigh escaped the breast of the beautiful lady, as she thought of the temptation that rank and power placed in the way of the king. She sighed, too, as she thought that man would fall before the force of beauty, and that she had no cause to think the king less liable to such weakness than others.

In this moody and melancholy strain ran her thoughts, while she gazed upon the starry heavens above her. The thousands of sparkling gems that studded the wide range of space before her drew from her repeated bursts of rapture and wonder, and yet she continued to gaze out of that window, as though she had never beheld such a scene before. The scene, indeed, was not new, yet it never lost the attractive power it possessed the first time she gazed upon it. Unlike a mere view of a limited spot or space, the immensity of the heavens filled the mind with astonishment, and prevented her dwelling on one spot, and again the fact that all connected with it was dark, doubtful, and conjectural, gave it a charm that few earthly things themselves possess.

CHAPTER XIV.

THE UNEXPECTED RECOVERY.—THE JAILOR'S FLIGHT. —THE FOREST OF AVANGUE.—REFLECTIONS OF DON CÆSAR.

THE person who was approaching from the prison to the spot where lay Don Cæsar de Bazan (for he had laid down again with great quickness upon the alarm being given to him by Lazarillo), was an under turnkey, who, in passing a staircase window, had chanced to notice Lazarillo, as he thought, attempting either to rob or to remove altogether the body that lay in the court-yard.

This man did not stop to give himself time to see that Don Cæsar was recovering likewise. How could he suspect anything half so outrageous? But he bustled down the staircase as quickly as he could, and said nothing to any one; for he wished not only to have all the glory of having made the discovery that some one was in the court-yard, but to have the merit of seizing the intruder unheeded.

Like very many clever people, it will be seen how, by such means, he defeated his own object, and by grasping at too much, like the dog in the fable, he lost everything. Hurrying, then, down the staircase like a madman, he made for the court-yard, and that so precipitately and hurriedly, that the page heard him the moment he opened the door leading to it. We call Lazarillo the page, because he now, by the word of Don Jose, actually stood in that station to him.

It did not take long for the energetic jailor to reach the spot where was Don Cæsar and his young friend. He immediately laid violent hands on Lazarillo, exclaiming,—

"You are my prisoner, you young rascal! You shall smart for this. Come along, you young villain."

"Oh, let me go, sir," said the boy; "I only came here to see my dead friend Don Cæsar."

"I let you go! I think I see myself letting you go. Come away; you shall be locked up for this."

"Will you have no mercy, sir?"

"None whatever."

"Then I must interfere," said Don Cæsar, suddenly starting up.

To describe the effect of his appearance upon the jailor transcends the power of language. For a moment he was petrified with astonishment, and then, with a shout of terror, he made a rush from the place as if a legion of devils had been at his heels.

"Come on now!" cried Don Cæsar; "come on!" and, in a moment, both he and Lazarillo vaulted over the low wall. They sped on to the nearest church for refuge, and there Don Cæsar intended to wait until he was satisfied there was no pursuit after him, in which event he intended getting clear of the city, and concealing himself for a time, according to the advice of Lazarillo.

They both waited in the church till mid-day, when few persons were abroad.

The extreme repose and quiet that reigns in the city of Madrid at the hour of noon is such, that it might be called the city of the dead, for scarce at that hour will a beggar be seen to crawl through the streets and bye-ways.

The heat is excessive—all here is in extremes, and nothing moderate—there is no shadow. The sun appears vertical, and illumines both sides of the way at once, and the heating rays find their way to every inch of the city, so that heat from above and radiated heat from below, form a state of things almost unbearable to a foreigner coming from the north.

In addition to this stillness, there are no signs of life; you by chance perceive some lazy beggar, of whom there are enough, who has by some chance left his place of repose, perhaps to seek one that is more shady and luxuriant than the one he had quitted; but not for long will you see him, for up the first arch or gateway that he meets, he there sits down drawing his legs out of the way of the sun, and then leaning his form against some wall or door, he dozes away the hours in blissful heedlessness of the past, present, or future.

Here and there indeed, you might see the form of some lean and sallow complexioned monk, whose ascetic disposition would lead him to court the praise of the world or his superior, by his disregarding the hour of noon, which is passed in siesta, when, indeed, it might be truly said all Madrid sleeps, and walking abroad upon some charitable mission, and exposing himself to the heavy heating rays of a scorching sun, from whose beams there is no protection whatever.

The city looks like one vast mass of uninhabited dwellings, and no inhabitants, for there is not a blind that is not drawn down so as to exclude the rays of the sun, and not a human being will stir upon business from his shaded nook; indeed, business is only attended to early and late, for towards the evening when the heat of the day has abated, and the promenades become cooled by the light breeze that springs up towards sun-set, then, indeed, Madrid springs into new life, and her streets become full; but during the noon-tide hour Madrid is as the city of the dead, where, indeed, the houses are standing, but the inhabitants carried off by some cause of destruction not apparent.

The silence was most complete; the sound of a foot-fall is of rare, very rare occurrence, and the sound of a human voice a still rarer sound, and look where you would, up or down, on this side or that, nothing would meet your eye save the heating rays of the sun, that almost blinded you by its brightness and painful glare, and almost suffocated you by the extreme warmth of the air you breathe, that has almost a suffocating feel with it.

The repose and quietude of a scene like this is great, and even startling to a stranger, to the inhabitants of more temperate climes, who are accustomed to exert themselves throughout the day, and cease toward the evening from all avocations whatever; but here solitude reigns in the midst of a populous city for many hours in the day.

It was at this time, then, that Don Cæsar, after wrapping his cloak as carefully round him as possible, to conceal the glittering bravery of his apparel, sallied out from the church with his young and now well pleased friend, Lazarillo, to seek some more effectual place of concealment, or, at all events, one in which he, Don Cæsar, would feel more freedom of action, and better pleased in, than with the gloom of the dim church aisles, for which he had certainly no particular affection for; wild and unguarded as he was, he had an intellect that enabled him to see, in the midst of all his frivolity and extravagance, the disgraceful state of superstition in which the priesthood kept the ignorant poor, and the ignorant rich likewise, who allowed themselves to be ridden over by the self-interested professors of religious bigotry.

"Lazarillo," he said, "did you hear mid-day strike?"

"I did."

"Then what think you of moving away from here? I do not like this place."

"Nor I much. We have not been perceived, and I am not quite sure that you would be safe here, since you had actually been condemned to death."

"Oh, but I would plead that in the eye of the law I must be dead, since I have been executed."

"Which might not avail you."

"Where, now, would you advise me to go?"

"Out of the city. What say you to Aranjues?—it is not very far from Madrid, and yet far enough to make your meeting with any one who might recognise you an extremely doubtful case."

"'Tis a sweet spot that same Aranjues," said Don Cæsar, "and I should like it far better than any other you could name."

"Then let us leave here at once."

"But you forget, my boy, that it is too far to walk. Seven leagues would be a weary march beneath a midday sun."

"At the portal of St. Matin there are always mules to let on hire. You can take one of them."

"And enrol a new creditor in my list, which certainly does not boast of a mule driver."

"You have no money?"

"Need I reply? When did I ever have any money?"

"Then you must sell your cloak, or, indeed, I should advise that you went to one of the Jew's shops by the Grand Pallazo and sold this entire suit, buying a plainer one, and pocketing the difference in cash, which, I should say, ought to be a good handful of pistoles."

"A handful of pistoles?"

"Aye, surely."

"I will do it. When have I had or seen a handful of pistoles? It shall be done. Come on, my boy—come on; and here we are, by the bye, within a hundred yards of a shop of the kind. I have often heard that at the siesta time in Madrid the Jews are the only portion of the population that are wide awake."

A shop of the description mentioned by Lazarillo was soon found, and after the Jew had depreciated every article that composed the really gorgeous and rich suit of apparel that Don Jose had gave to Don Cæsar, a bargain was struck, which placed on Don Cæsar's back a good-looking plain suit of grey cloth,

without ornament, and five pistoles in one of the pockets of it.

"Now, Lazarillo," he said, "we will be off to the forest of Aranjues."

"You can," said the boy, "but you forget that I am in a situation which you procured me."

"Truly, with Don Jose."

"Yes—and I think for your sake I had better go to him alone, and endeavour to do you some good."

"You can do me some good, Lazarillo. Despite all my jests at matrimony, and all the danger I have gone through, I love that fair young creature—for fair and young I am convinced she is—to whom I was so strangely united in the prison. Go to Don Jose's, and be it your care, Lazarillo, for the sake of my future happiness in this world, to find out who she is."

"I will—you may depend upon me; but do not be indiscreet in coming to Madrid without letting me know first where to find you, or communicate with you."

"I will not. Adieu, my boy, and God bless you."

Don Cæsar was not long in suiting himself with a mule, and in the course of the afternoon he reached the delightful locality of Aranjues, a district abounding in the varied splendours of vegetation.

It is scarcely possible for those who have not seen the luxuriance and beauty of Spanish vegetation, to form any conception of it. The environs of Madrid abound with every beauty with which a rich and splendid country can exhibit.

Villas of the most imposing appearance are dotted about, and built in such a style of magnificence and grandeur, that they become a matter of wonder and admiration. No one can gaze upon them, and think Spaniards poor, for there appears a vast number of palaces. Then each is surrounded by its own grounds —long rows of the stately chesnut trees adorn the walls, while the cork tree is at once distinguished by its peculiarities, as are many others, among which we must not forget the orange.

Scenes like these are rare, north of the Pyrenees; indeed, they are not to be found; but in Spain they are abundant enough. The groves are truly majestic; they extend to a great length, and the foliage so thick, as to be perfectly impervious to light—so beautiful, and so various, that it delights the eye, that never tires in gazing upon such loveliness.

Here, too, is the palace—a palace that has often been the favourite residence of Spanish kings—where many a jovial hunt has been held, and the delightful groves have re-echoed to the sound of the horn, and the deep baying of the hounds.

Nothing could exceed the exultation and pleasure of such a scene. It must have been truly delightful to have seen the royal hunt—the huntsmen riding through the green groves of a large forest, and the gigantic trees occasionally hiding them from view; and then, again, appearing more and more indistinct each time, till only the sound of them, as they cheer each other on, comes faintly on the ear, until it ceases altogether.

It is beautiful, indeed, when the sun is passing his meridian, to sit beneath the cool shade of some gigantic inhabitant of the forest, and expose the form to the light zephyr that plays through the trees of the forest, the foliage exhibiting a rich variety of colour and disposition.

Such a siesta is delicious, and such as the meanest peasant in Spain can enjoy—warmth, shade, and coolness may be had at the same moment—a dreamy state of existence, in which the happier time of the day of life often passes away, without any drawback on future consequence.

Sometimes it would happen that a shepherd would seat himself beneath the broad branches of the majestic chesnut-tree, and by the side of the shepherdess of his heart he would play upon the pipes, giving out melodious tones that appear to be the effects of enchantment, especially if, as often happens, the performer is hidden from your view.

Then, the very flocks that he tends are disposed to seek the shade, and listen to the sweet dulcet notes of the shepherd's pipe.

Now and then a rarer animal might be seen gazing at a distance upon this scene of peace and beauty, but with watchfulness; for, ever suspicious, they will not abide the approach of man, be he ever so harmlessly disposed.

Then, when the noontide heat has somewhat cooled, when the sun is descending to the western horizon, then indeed the beauties of a Spanish sunset may be seen and appreciated. Strange it is, that such a country should be given up to anarchy and bloodshed, when each man's hand is at his brother's throat—that each hill and dale, mountain and plain, have been so watered with Spanish blood, shed by Spaniards. 'Tis a sad reflection, but one that never can be entirely absent from the mind of the foreigner when he visits such favoured spots.

The sun gradually tints the foliage with his brightest hues; long and deep shadows are cast that form strong contrasts with the cloudless skies above. Down in the west are all the glowing colours that grace the rainbow—a world of beauties meet the eye at every glance—the scene is worth a voyage on purpose to view it.

The sun's rays glancing among the luxuriant foliage, defines the dark line of trees that forms the horizon, and presents such a contrast to the æther-like appearance of the heavens.

Then the time has arrived for the herdsman to gather his flock together, and seek the cover that shelters them more from man and beast than from the weather. The lofty mountains, that may be seen from some situations, are slightly tinged with a heavenly blue, that gradually deepens, until the setting sun throws them entirely in the shade, and leaves but a deep black mass, standing abruptly in the heavens, and then sinking gradually from the sight, until it becomes invisible as the light decreases.

Such is the scenery in the neighbourhood of Madrid, of which much more could be said; indeed a volume might be written, but it will suffice for our purpose. Let the reader imagine all that is rich and beautiful, all that is luxuriant and striking, and he may have some idea of the environs. The trees alone are a study, and the delightful groves of chesnut, orange, and cork trees, form a combination of beauties once seen will never be forgotten.

Don Cæsar, although he had looked at this scene often in days of prosperity, when he was the courted and admired centre of a glittering throng, never perhaps gazed around him with so much real delight as now, when, in the decay of his fortunes, a strange chance had brought him to that spot once again.

He dismounted from his mule, and having satisfied the demands of the owner of the beast, who had come behind it all the way, he leaned against an aged, gigantic tree, and gazed around him with unmingled pleasure.

" This, indeed," he said, " is a scene of enchantment, and worth the living for. Somehow, several circumstances have occurred within these two days now to bind me closer to existence than ever I was bound before. I, who went to death with scarce a thought, now tremble at the risk I ran, and that can only be because there have arisen new ties to bind me to life. First there is that boy, whom I regard with affection; then there is my—wife—wife—what an odd sound—my wife—my countess. I love her—I know she's handsome—I adore her—she is kind-hearted—

I heard her sigh. Her hand—can I ever forget that hand? I think I see it now, in all its delicate beauty, resting in my own—and she is my wife—ay, truly—my countess—and I will know who she is, and I will see her and have her, were ten thousand Don Joses and a million of court intrigues to say me nay."

" A bold resolution," said a voice near him, and, upon turning hastily round, Don Cæsar saw a plainly dressed, grave-looking man a few paces from him.

Observing that there was a something of displeasure in Don Cæsar's glance, the stranger added,—

" I listened to you unintentionally, sir. This, you know, is nature's drawing-room, and if any one will make soliloquies in it, he should not grumble that he is overheard."

" My friend," said Don Cæsar, " I am not of a grumbling disposition. Who are you? where do you live? and where do you come from?"

" My name is Sancta Varez. I live at the goatherd's cottage you may see between the trees. I am an author. I come from Madrid. Pray who are you?"

" Don Cæsar de Bazan."

" What! the dissolute scapegrace of a wild harumscarum ——"

" That'll do—I am he. You know me, I see, quite well, so you need not proceed in your catalogue of my discretions and virtues."

The stranger laughed, and then said, good humouredly,—

" You shall dine with me, and sleep to-night in the same house, if you will. Come on; I have heard of you; some good and some bad, but none so very bad but it might be worse."

" Or so very good, I suppose, but it might be better?"

" Exactly."

The stranger led him to the cottage, where he made him most welcome; indeed, so much so, that more than once Don Cæsar was on the point of making a confidant of him, and, as far as himself was concerned, he would have done so, but he feared to compromise Lazarillo in any way.

The day wore on very pleasantly indeed, and when night came, the stranger placed in Don Cæsar's hands some papers, saying,—

" I go to rest early, but these may amuse you till your own hour of repose."

The papers contained a short and interesting narrative, which, from authentic resources, we here present to the reader.

————

Among the mountains of the Alhambra, in the South of Spain, lived a herdsman, known by the name of El Sorda; he was a strange and singular being—solitary and wandering in his habits, he had turned herdsman from choice, as it led him from the society of men, with whom he associated as little as possible.

It was known to the peasantry that El Sorda had a cottage among the mountains; it had been seen, but never entered by any human being, and once a female form had been seen beside him in the eventide by some peasant, who had rambled further than usual, or some other herdsman, who had been in search for some stray member of his flock; all reported the beauty of the female whom they had seen, but whom they were unable either to describe as El Sorda's wife or daughter; they one and all, indeed, bore testimony to her beauty, so far as it could be correctly judged from the distance at which it was seen, but then there was an air of mystery about her, and this might add considerably to the supposed charms of this unknown maiden.

El Sorda was tall, handsome, but aged, though his eye had not lost any of the fire of youth; he was yet active and hardy, and possessed more strength than even his appearance warranted, and that bespoke a hardy frame and resolute mind. His complexion was dark, even for a Spaniard; indeed it was often said that he was of Moorish descent, and of this there was every probability, for neither the heat of the climate nor constant exposure could well account for the peculiar complexion of his skin; even of the daughter—for all who had seen her gave the preference to that designation—they declared that, notwithstanding the care that appeared to be taken of her, yet her complexion was scarcely truly unmixed Spanish.

Year after year rolled on, and El Sorda was looked upon as one they were used to see and not understand; he now and then was the subject of conversation between young and old, but none could give any information concerning him; no one knew more than that the strange being who inhabited the mountains was El Sorda the herdsman, and that was all; any other question that might be made was always unanswered, for none knew more.

El Sorda's cottage was in an out-of-the-way nook; few had ever occasion to go that way, nor had the traveller need to stop unless he had lost his way, and then El Sorda would direct him, but never offered him the hospitality of his own cottage. It was delightfully situated; the vegetation of the surrounding parts was indeed all that could be imagined of the most beautiful and fruitful portion of the most beautiful and fruitful country in Europe—perhaps in the world. The Alhambra had long been known for its beauty and historic recollections, and, perhaps, there was not a choicer spot than that in which dwelt El Sorda, the herdsman.

At the usual times of the year, El Sorda proceeded to a distant town, where he sold his flocks, and purchased the necessaries of life, and such things as he chose for his own and his daughter's use; on those occasions, he was usually gone more than one day, and during his absence his daughter tended the flocks; but then they were left in security, and required but little care, and all access to his house was cut off, save to such as were determined to intrude themselves upon his privacy, and such an occurrence had never happened, and no one had ever contemplated such a circumstance; indeed, few would have been adventurous enough to have attempted such a deed, for there was something about El Sorda that made him appear a most dangerous and disagreeable enemy, and, therefore, he was respected.

It so happened that during one of El Sorda's half-yearly visits to the markets, a stranger was wounded after resisting some robbers, who attempted and succeeded in taking from him a considerable booty, and left him for dead on the road. He was not discovered until some time after, and there yet being signs of life about him, they placed him upon a kind of litter, and were about to convey him to the next monastry, but the stranger appeared in such extremity, that they stopped by the way, and carried him to El Sorda's cottage.

For the first time did any of the peasantry see the interior of his hut. It was clean and well furnished, that is for a peasant's hut in Spain; nay, there were some luxuries that they never dreamt of; but the view they had was very transient, for the stranger was laid on a couch and there left.

There was one thing, however, they did see, and that was the surpassing beauty of El Sorda's daughter, which they failed not to report, and it became known among the inhabitants of the adjacent parts for many miles, that there was a beautiful maiden imprisoned in the mountains of the Alhambra.

The return of El Sorda was hourly expected, when the stranger was left in his cottage, and when he did so, he was not a little displeased to find that his privacy had been invaded by even a wounded man.

"Isabel," said El Sorda to his daughter, "was there no help for this intrusion? Could you not have said I was from home, and you could render no assistance to the wounded man; thou shouldst have sent them to the monks of St. Francis, who would have attended at once to his bodily ailments and his spiritual welfare."

"They said, father," replied the daughter, with a tear in her eye, "that he would die if carried further, and I could not let him die for want of aid, while it was in my power to afford it; indeed I had scarce power to say nay to them, for they appeared to consider that hospitality under such circumstances could not be refused, and they entered, merely informing me of what had happened, and there placed him, where he has been asleep ever since."

El Sorda's brows were bent, and he paused for some minutes ere he spoke again, and, when he did so, he said—

"You well know, daughter, that it is from no churlish disposition that I refuse to mix with, and afford every right that can be demanded of me, and more; but I will not herd with those who are beneath me, neither will I follow in the shadow of those who were once my equals; but I would, as I will, hold myself aloof from all mankind. If you cannot abide my determination the world is open to you—you need not stay with me. I do not desire you to shut yourself up with an old man in his mountain home."

"Dearest father," she exclaimed, "how can you speak thus of your own Isabel. You know I love no earthly being save you, and know none other protector, nor will I. I have forgotten all to come with you."

"I do not doubt you, my dear child," exclaimed El Sorda, "but you are young and inexperienced in the ways of the world, and your father is too stern to submit to an indignity. But no more of this. We will see what can be done for our guest, since we must have one."

So saying he arose and examined his wounds, which he declared, though severe and dangerous, were of that character that with careful treatment he would, without doubt, recover.

For some days the young stranger lay in such a state of weakness that he could scarce be said to be sensible of what was going on around him.

During this time El Sorda tended his herds and flocks as usual, coming home in the evening and carefully examining the state of his guest, which, though slowly, improved.

The report of the beauty of El Sorda's daughter had spread far and wide, and had not failed to reach the ears of many noble families, and among them Don Sebastian de Seveille, a dissolute nobleman, who had neither honour nor remorse, and cared not what deed he committed, so long as it served as the stepping-stone to some object he had in view; and being satiated with all the pleasures the world afforded him in a legitimate way, he cared not what he did; and the very idea of a mountain beauty, difficult to be got at, was a fillip to his passions, and he determined to engage in an adventure that should promise him anything in the shape of agreeable novelty.

He could not undertake the expedition without the precaution of taking with him a trusty confidant, whose only qualification consisted in his being a strong, ruffianly, and unscrupulous man, ready to second his patron in any deed of barbarity, provided he was to reap any advantage from it.

Don Sebastian, accompanied by his satellite, proceeded to the mountains of Alhambra, and frequented the neighbourhood of El Sorda, hoping to obtain a view of the beauty he had heard so much of; but they were unable to effect their object for some days,

owing to the unapproachable character of the place, save to those who turned from the ordinary road, and this at first they were loth to do; but this difficulty they soon overcame, since their nature was not of a very diffident character.

One day, as Isabella was tending to a little garden in which grew many of the rarest plants and flowers, besides herbs of all kinds,—for she delighted in this amusement, having scarce any other, save such as her household duties required, besides embroidery and music, which she used to indulge in in secret—Don Sebastian and his companion neared the spot, and requested she would help them to some refreshment, and allow them to rest awhile.

"I cannot offer you more than the fruits of the garden, and a seat beneath yonder orange tree," she replied, pointing to the spot she spoke of.

They were somewhat disappointed, expecting to obtain access to the house, which was evidently denied them. Though somewhat offended, yet he could not well resent it. He endeavoured to enter into conversation with her; but this she declined, by answering in as few words as she could, and as the sun was verging towards the horizon, El Sorda returned home, and eyed the two strangers with disdain and suspicion.

On their parts, they as ill liked him, and informed him of the cause of their visit, and begged he would direct them on their road.

"If your road be unknown to you," he said, "the sooner you seek it the better; 'tis reckoned dangerous of late, and I have heard of some accidents lately on it, and the robbers are unscrupulous. It lies before you, and if you can use speed, you will yet be safe before dark."

"We do not fear them much," smiled the strangers; and they parted without saying more.

St. Sebastian and his companion moved onwards, and did escape being robbed; but he was by no means disposed to give up the pursuit, on the contrary, he was more than ever determined to obtain the prize he sought, and it would appear that her beauty had inflamed his passions to the utmost, and he vowed, by fair or foul means, she should be his.

He determined that he and his accomplice, and another whom he would also employ, should attack the cottage, and secure the person of this strange man's daughter, and carry her off to his own castle, and there retain her a prisoner till she consented to his wishes, and if she would not, a man like Don Sebastian would not hesitate at using force. * * *

The days passed pleasantly enough at the cottage of El Sorda with the stranger who had been so near destruction, and only saved by the kind treatment of the beautiful Isabella. Rest and quiet did much for the wounded man, who began to grow daily stronger, and it is very probable that at any other place he would have been longer ere he had been cured, for here there was so much repose, pure air, and simple diet, that he had not one of those many obstacles to a cure that, ordinarily, are as difficult to overcome as the disease.

There was another source of happiness to the stranger, and that was, the extraordinary beauty and propriety of the nurse that tended him. He looked at her by day, and thought on her by night. She was the sole object of his imagination, until, at length, he became madly in love with her, and yet he felt an objection to declare the passion that consumed him.

At length, unable to forbear any longer, he confessed the love he bore her, and conjured her to say who and what she and her father were.

"I am Don Alvarez de Segovia," he said, in conclusion. "I am sure that one so gentle and so beautiful cannot but belong to another class, and not what you seem. I love you to distraction, and would make you a bride, and mistress of a large fortune, if you can return the love I bear you."

" For Heaven's sake, forbear, signor," replied the fair Isabella. " If my father were to hear this he would deem you had violated the rights of hospitality in the declaration you have made ; believe me, 'tis misplaced."

" Misplaced it cannot be," replied the stranger, "when you are the object ; for one so beautiful in person, so faultless and amiable in mind, cannot be deficient in the only other requisite to make up the sum of female perfection, virtue ; neither can I have violated any rights of hospitality, for man cannot do more to woman than honestly offer his hand and heart to the woman he loves."

" Yes, signor, I admit all you say to be true ; but yet my father has, during his life, met with so many instances of ingratitude and injustice, that he has forsworn ever to—Merciful Heaven! what was I about to say ?"

" Nay, never falter. I am no seeker into other men's affairs, much less am I likely to divulge what I do know ; therefore, speak freely."

Isabella hesitated, and her colour fled, and the stranger said, in earnest tones,—

" If you fear aught, confide in me, and I will protect you, and my offer is yet yours."

" Nay, nay, you misunderstand me ; 'tis I who was about to break the confidence of my father, but 'tis necessary, since you look upon it in the light you do. My father has forsworn the rank he once bore, when his lands were violently wrested from him."

" He too has suffered misfortunes, then ?" said Don Alvarez.

" Yes ; he has, indeed, signor."

" And does he intend to immure you in this cottage from the gaieties of life, the blessings and pleasures, too? they all make up the sum and substance of existence."

" I am very happy with my father, signor, and have no wish to leave him," replied Isabella.

" I would not wish you ; my lands are broad enough and rich enough to support us all in splendour. Surely, as a father, he would rejoice to see you at least placed above the mean condition that he must leave you in here."

" 'Tis contentment that makes all things sweet."

" And you may be content, too, with a much better lot, Isabella, and much happier ; but he must leave you unprotected, an evil of great magnitude, for you know not the baseness of the world, and how they would seek your ruin, and neither parent nor brother to protect you."

" The world will not be so unjust as to injure the helpless, nor seek to destroy the orphan,"

" Look at your father's case," replied Alvarez ; " he, at least, has met with deep ingratitude and heavy misfortune."

Isabella paused, and then said,—

" Forgive me, signor, if I cannot argue with you ; you have silenced, not convinced me."

" I would not press you unduly, sweet Isabella," he cried, " but love urges me on ; tell me, may I hope for your consent if I obtain your father's ? I owe a deep debt of gratitude to you, and, let me add, one of love."

" Seek not to increase your obligations, signor," said El Sorda, entering the cottage with a clouded brow ; " had not your proposals bore the appearance of honour, my knife had drunk your heart's blood."

" Honour is not the only shield I wear," replied Don Alvarez, proudly ; " my hand never yet failed in its defence against one, and even though an invalid, I could use it."

" Well said," replied El Sorda ; " you will be well enough to travel by to-morrow, and I will obtain mules for you to enable you to do so."

" I understand, sir," said Don Alvarez. " Hospitality, however coldly given, when accepted of, deserves thanks ; you have mine. You have, doubtless, heard what passed between me and your daughter ?"

" I did ; and decline your relationship. We are strangers, and why cannot we continue so ?"

The stranger retired to his apartment, a small bedroom, where he passed the remainder of the day, and came not out to his meals, but sat there, solitary and alone.

Night shrouded the earth, and while one side of the verdure-clad mountains was bathed in moonlight, the other was steeped in darkness, and this was the side on which El Sorda's cottage was built, towards which three men crept stealthily. They were the base creature, Don Sebastian, his companion, and a hired ruffian ; their object was the abduction of the beautiful Isabella. They gain the garden, and enter the house, and a scream is heard, and on the instant clashing of swords ensues.

" Help ! help !" screamed Isabella.

The cry was no sooner uttered, than Don Alvarez rushed from his chamber, and with a light saw two men lying extended on the ground ; one was El Sorda, the other the ruffian, and Isabella in the arms of two others, struggling. Alvarez instantly plunged his sword into the body of one ; he staggered, and fell, mortally wounded ; the other turned and fled.

He who had fallen was Don Sebastian. El Sorda lifted up his head, and smiling, said, pointing to the body of Don Sebastian,—

" My old enemy, the cause of all my miseries and misfortunes. I die now in peace with all men ; be a husband to my Isabella, and recollect she is an orphan. You will find in Madrid deeds belonging to me that will give her an ample dowry now he is dead. Come here, Isabella, my child, the partner of your father's exile, receive my last blessing. Don Alvarez, promise a dying man you'll be true to her."

" I will, as I hope for mercy hereafter. She shall be mine before to-morrow's sundown at the nearest monastery."

" Thank Heaven !" exclaimed El Sorda, and he fell back a corpse.

* * * * * *

Don Alvarez was as good as his word, and never had reason to repent taking to wife the beautiful orphan ; and they lived many years of happiness. As El Sorda said, there was a large dowry which Sebastian had unjustly possessed himself of, and which came to her. So she was not a portionless bride to Don Alvarez.

" Now to bed," said Don Cæsar.

CHAPTER XV.

THE COMMUNICATION TO THE KING THAT MARITANA IS NOBLY BORN.—THE INTERVIEW OF A ROYAL LOVER. — THE FETE AT THE MARQUIS DE RO-TONDO'S.

THE page made what haste he could to the magnificent hall of Don Jose de Santarem, his new master, for he was most anxious, if he could, to gather some intelligence for Don Cæsar, who, however he might be paid or entertained by any one else, he continued to consider as his great friend and patron.

With a sagacity, too, far beyond his years, he had come to the conclusion that there was so much scheming going on, on the part of Don Jose, that it was more than probable, could he, Lazarillo, find out any clue to his designs, he might use it as a means of rendering Don Cæsar's safety quite certain.

Hence was it that, in preference to remaining with Don Cæsar in the forest of Aranjues, which, if he had merely consulted his inclinations, he would have done, he made haste to reach the mansion of the flattering, unscrupulous minister, with a great anxiety, as soon as possible, to form one of his household, and with a determination, if it could be done, to win his entire confidence.

The new page knew not how much Don Jose's own reflections were tending towards such a result. But it was the case; for, with a tact at reading character, which his greatest enemies could not deny that he possessed, Jose had made up his mind that Lazarillo was a bold, daring, acute, and enterprising boy, and if he could win him over to his service, would be just the sort of agent he wanted in many of the court-intrigues by which he sought to attain the perilous objects of his ambition.

"Such a boy," he reasoned, "as yon lad, who stuck by Cæsar so gallantly in his prison, is just the one I want as a confidential servant. As a boy he will not be suspected, and if I mistake not greatly, he has far more tact and discretion than falls to the lot of many a man. His handsome appearance, too, will make him a favourite in the palace, whither I shall take him often; and if he will but be faithful to me, and unscrupulous in my service, he will be able to discover for me many a secret, which an older agent would attempt in vain to overhear or to get related to him. A boy is unsuspected; and such a boy as this young armourer will be of immense value to me."

There was but one error in Don Jose's reasonings, and that was one into which such men always fall, and is founded upon the infamous diction of, we believe, Talleyrand, who said, that every man had his price. Don Jose thought that the acuteness, the sagacity, the fidelity, and the depth of attachment which he saw in Lazarillo's character, could all be purchased. He had not the least idea that, in addition to these qualities, which he so much admired, his new page had some others, which, far from admiring, he, Don Jose, was more likely to look upon as inconvenient incumbrances, namely, a high sense of honour, a feeling heart, and a liberality of disposition, which set all bribery at defiance; and if we add to this, his attachment, sudden, but strong and enduring as life itself, to Don Cæsar, we shall readily see that he was not likely to become the useful agent which Don Jose calculated upon making him.

The mansions of the grandees of Spain are never closed night or day; but the magnificent paved halls are always full of pages and lacqueys, whose business it is to prevent intrusion, so that the privacy of the inner apartments cannot be very easily invaded by any one.

Don Jose's mansion, one of the most superb in the city, was no exception to the general rule, and when Lazarillo, in his not over fine or nice apparel, knocked about as it had been, too, during his recent carnival adventures, arrived at it, he began to entertain serious doubts if he should be lucky enough to obtain an audience of the great man by merely asking for him; but he was not one to hesitate long, and thinking possibly that Don Jose might have left some message appertaining to him, he walked boldly into the hall.

A lad about his own age, in the gorgeous apparel of a state page, called to him in an insolent tone, saying,—

"Be off, beggar, be off—no beggar's brats here. Lay a stick across that fellow's shoulders, Carlos."

"In an hour or two I wouldn't mind," said another, who, like the first speaker, was stretched at full length upon a bench; "but just now the exertion would be something like suicide—it would kill me. Wait till the sun has got below the church steeple of Santa Anna, and then I am ready for anything."

"Then I suppose I must execute my own sentence," said the first youngster, in an affected tone, as he made a languid movement to rise from his recumbent position.

"Perhaps it would not be prudent to try," said Lazarillo.

"What do you mutter, knave?"

"Oh, you are dull of comprehension, are you?" added Lazarillo. "It strikes me you are not half awake."

Stepping up to him, as he uttered these words, he gave him such a twitch of the nose before he was aware of it, that the page roared again, and a general confusion ensued in the hall, during which Lazarillo darted up a marble staircase, hotly pursued by one of the men servants, whose unwieldy bulk, however, put it beyond a matter of doubt that the young agile boy could have raced him for hours without a chance of capture.

"Stop, you villain, stop!" cried the servant; "where are you going? Stop—stop—how dare you pass me?"

"Then why don't you pass me?" cried Lazarillo. "I want to see Don Jose, and I will see him."

"You see Don Jose! Was there ever such impudence! Why, dukes and counts wait his leisure!"

"But I am neither a duke nor a count, so have not time to wait anybody's leisure. Where is he?"

"You infernal young assassin!"

A door at the head of the staircase was suddenly opened, and Don Jose himself appeared.

"What is all this disturbance?" he cried, angrily.

"This boy, your excellency—drunk, or mad, or an assassin—has forced his way through the hall up the grand staircase, even to where you see him."

"Do you mean to tell me that a boy can, if he please, force his way through all the idle knaves I keep below to guard me from intrusion?"

"No, your excellency—yes—that is—no—yes—oh, dear. He wouldn't tell what he wanted, and pulled Pedro's nose."

The slightest indication of a smile crossed Don Jose's face as, turning to Lazarillo, he said,—

"Is this true?"

"Partly so," replied the boy. "As to pulling Pedro's nose, if Pedro be his name, I admit it; but as to not telling what I wanted, that I deny. On my first appearance I was abused, and that same Pedro requested some one else as idle as himself to lay a stick across my back, and so I walked up stairs without troubling them any further."

"You were right."

"But, please your excellency ——"

"Silence, sir. Suppose this lad had come to me on some special business of vast importance, and suppose he had been a timid lad, as thank Heaven he is not, in that case, meeting with nothing but insult in my hall, he would have gone away again, perchance to the detriment of the state."

"But look at his ragged jerkin, your excellency."

"Take care, my friend, that in a short time yours is not as ragged in consequence of losing the good situation you now enjoy. Lazarillo, follow me."

So saying, Don Jose held open the door for Lazarillo, who followed him into the private apartments, while the man who considered the ragged jerkin such an unanswerable argument stood aghast upon the landing.

"The Virgin protect me!" he muttered. "What's the world coming to? Who would have thought it? He really knows him. I'm a ruined man. I—I—don't know what to say or what to do. I'll hang myself—I—no, I won't, I'll go and have my dinner—yes, my dinner. I'll eat upon it; I always eat upon anything of grave importance. I'll certainly eat upon it, and consider what I had better say and what I had better not say—what I had better do and what I had better not do. Oh, what a world we live in!"

Don Jose led Lazarillo through one apartment into

another which lay beyond it, and which was smaller and less likely to be interrupted. He then sat down with his own back to the light, and directed Lazarillo to stand in such a manner that he, Don Jose, could obtain a full view of his countenance. Then he said to him, in a tone of assumed carelessness, which did not, however, impose upon the boy,—

"Have you long known Don Cæsar de Bazan?"

"I have not, sir."

"But you knew him by sight, in common with all Madrid, in the public streets?"

"I did, and have done so now for more than a year."

"Your actual acquaintance with him, then, is recent?"

"We never exchanged a friendly word till he got himself so seriously into trouble by taking my part, when the cruel captain of the guard, instigated by my old master, the armourer, would have punished me."

"And you were so grateful for that interference that you followed him to prison?"

"I was most grateful."

"Then now that he is no more, do you think you can serve me faithfully if I bind you to me by benefits?"

"I am sure I can."

"'Tis well; you shall be my private and confidential page, and you shall receive such liberal allowance and treatment as shall make it well worth your while to be faithful and discreet."

"I am much beholden to you, sir."

"You shall be; and now tell what you know of the street-singer, Maritana?"

"Maritana! the beautiful Maritana! Oh, she is a charm of beauty! I could follow her all day long, and never tire of gazing at her."

"Indeed! You seem enraptured with her."

"I am—I am."

"Then mark me, boy; the first test of your discretion in my service will be to see this Maritana and not to know her."

"See her and not know her—not seem to know her?"

"Exactly. You will see her in a far different position of life to that in which you have been accustomed to regard her, but by no word or look must you venture to recognise her; should she even know you again, which she may do, despite the great change which will soon be effected in your appearance, you must deny your identity. On no account must you speak to her of the past. You understand me, boy?"

"I do, sir, and will obey you."

"You shall have your reward for so doing. From this moment, remember, you are in my service. I will give orders that you have proper apparel, and that you receive good treatment from my household."

"I thank you, sir. I don't think Pedro will be otherwise than civil now."

"Nor I. But you must avoid brawling with Pedro, or any one else, for I set my face against it most especially. Take this note to the hall. Ask for Ambrosio, who is my major-domo; in it I have informed him what to do as regards you, and what position you are to hold in my household. He, too, will provide you with costume befitting your own confidential situation and my rank."

"Oh, sir," said Lazarillo, "how happy should I be if poor Don Cæsar had not suffered!"

"I made every effort to save him."

"A thousand thanks, sir."

"But the king was inexorable, and would not be moved. Had he consented, which I most earnestly prayed him to do, to put off the execution for a day or two, I doubt not but that Don Cæsar, whose premature death I much regret, would have been saved."

"He would have been pardoned?"

"He no doubt would; but that is too late now."

"Shall I tell him?" thought Lazarillo, and at the moment almost of the mental question he decided in the negative; for, despite all Don Jose's fair speaking, there was an air of hypocrisy about him which convinced the page of the devilish duplicity and insincerity of the man.

"Now, Lazarillo," he added, "you can go. Be discreet, vigilant, and faithful, and your fortune is made."

Lazarillo bowed and left the room.

"He will suit me most admirably," said Don Jose. "And now for another part of my plan, which is to place Maritana in such a position about the court, that she shall be a recognised member of it, and as such, without the trouble of secresy, can be brought into the presence of the king; when, if her young, ambitious spirit be not dazzled and bewildered by the rank and magnificence around her, she is something surely more than woman."

He took some rapid strides to and fro in the apartment, which, though a small one, was fitted in a style of the most gorgeous magnificence. A slight smile curled his lips, and then pausing, he took his plumed hat from a side table as he muttered,—

"Yes, the Marquis de Rotondo is the man who will answer my purpose. Weak, vain, and foolish, he has not moral courage sufficient to deny anything I may choose to assert. His real rank gives him a certain standing at court, which no ephemeral nobility could acquire; and yet he is the most abject creature I have. He and his marchioness, renowned for folly as they both are, have still been useful to me, and in this affair they shall be eminently so."

Don Jose descended the grand staircase of his mansion, and all became obsequious attention in his hall. By his order the carriage was brought immediately to the grand entrance, and he was upon the point of stepping into it, when the major-domo, with a low obeisance, stayed his progress.

"What now?" cried Don Jose.

"Your excellency, the Countess de Bazan says—she—she ——"

"She what?"

"Will not remain here."

"Indeed! Tell the countess—yet, stay; let the carriage wait. I will myself see her. There is some mistake."

With a frown upon his brow, for Don Jose was not the sort of man to allow himself to be interrupted in any of his plans good-temperedly, he again ascended the marble staircase of his splendid mansion, and hastily striding across a corridor, he made for the door of an apartment, into which, when they had arrived from the prison after the supposed execution of Don Cæsar, he had ordered Maritana, announcing her at the same time to his servants as the Countess de Bazan, to be shown.

"Confound her impatience!" he muttered. "I must say something to quiet her. Perhaps I had better at once take her with me, or Heaven only knows what extravagance she may be guilty of next. However, I will explain to her what I wish her to believe—namely, that she is a relation of these Rotondos, and has been stolen by gipsies in her infancy. They will back the story, for what I assert is to them law, and so will Maritana be secured a creditable home until the king shall choose to make an attempt to see her, and induce her to become his. That object once attained, and surely I can sufficiently awaken the jealousy of the queen to induce her to take the only revenge in her power—namely, to have a lover herself, and that lover no other than Don Jose de Santarem, the favourite minister."

Thus muttering to himself the secret aspirations of

his soul, he tapped at the door of the room where was Maritana, and, in compliance with her permission, he entered the apartment, which was none of the least showy in the mansion, for he wished to subdue reason and reflection by glitter and display.

Maritana seemed to have been weeping, and Don Jose on the moment assuming an air of surprise, exclaimed,—

"What! in tears, Countess de Bazan, on such a day as this! You do indeed surprise me."

"I am sad at heart, Don Jose," she replied. "Where is my husband? Why is all this strange mystery kept up now? Have I not married according to the queen's commands? Surely she has no wish that I should be left in the harassing state of mental disquietude I am now in."

"Most certainly not. But permit me to inform you that reasons of state and matters of very great importance to his honour compel your husband to be absent from you for some few days."

"'Twere better, sir, such information had come from his own lips."

"Ah, true; that was an omission of his; but one cannot think of everything."

"And where is he?"

"Absent at present from Madrid. I hope, however, that a very few days will restore him to you; and in the meantime I have something to tell you which will excite, I think, your liveliest feelings of surprise and joy."

"Indeed!" said Maritana, languidly.

"Yes. A noble family now represented by the Marquis and Marchioness de Rotondo, have satisfactorily discovered that you are their niece."

"Their niece!—I their niece?"

"Yes. You were stolen when young, and an orphan, by gipsies; but now they long to embrace you as a near and dear relative."

"This is incredible!"

"The queen vouches for its truth. It was by her orders that long and laborious inquiries were instituted, until, finally, she found that such was the fact, and then she was resolved upon raising you to the rank you now hold, as a compensation for the long time you have lingered in a situation of life so far below your right and your deserts."

"The queen?"

"Yes, the queen, who is the authoress of all the good that has befallen you. My carriage even now waits at the door to carry you to your illustrious relatives, whose reception of you will at once convince you of the accuracy of what I have stated now to you."

Maritana looked bewildered, as indeed she well might, at this most singular communication. So many events had come so thickly upon her within the last eight-and-forty hours, that she might well have doubted if all were not the uneasy visions of sleep. Don Jose saw her surprise, and taking her by the hand, he said at once,—

"The carriage waits, countess; will you allow me the honour of leading you to it?"

She rose from the splendid ottoman on which she had been seated, and passively followed him across the corridor and down the grand staircase. The pages lined the hall. The major-domo, with his white wand of office, headed them. She was handed to the carriage, and she heard Don Jose in an audible voice give the order—

"To the Marquis de Rotondo's."

She sunk back in the carriage, and covering her face with her hands, she strove, now that she had shut out external objects, to arrange in her own mind the order in which all the strange events had happened to her, which filled her mind with such a sense of confusion, and kept her imagination in such a continual whirl.

Don Jose watched her with keen and anxious eyes. He guessed the state of her mind, and he smiled, as he thought to himself,—

"She is endeavouring thoroughly to understand her position; but she will find it impossible. Her thoughts will contain the forms of a thousand disjointed images, which she will not be able to arrange. I have spread over her the meshes of my subtle policy, and she cannot escape me. There is no chance for her, no hope that she should; she is necessary in my plans, and if she be sacrificed to them, what care I? She is not the first victim, neither will she be the last."

"Tell me again," she said, suddenly, "how it is that I am related to these people to whom you are taking me?"

"There is not time now—here we are at the Marquis de Rotondo's hotel. You will meet with a kind and a courteous reception, for the marquis and marchioness are quite convinced of your relationship, although they have not yet had all the particulars from the queen of how she found it out. You understand me, countess?"

"I am endeavouring."

"Exactly. Here we are now, and I shall have the distinguished happiness of introducing you to your illustrious relatives."

The carriage now stopped at the entrance to a most magnificent mansion; for, on the principle that fools have fortune, the Marquis de Rotondo was immensely rich, and kept the most distinguished company in Madrid.

Several servants in gorgeous liveries received the guests, and the names of Don Jose de Santarem and the Countess de Bazan, were echoed from mouth to mouth, as they were announced to the Marquis and Marchioness de Rotondo.

They were escorted into a magnificent hall, where they had not been many moments ere they were joined by the marquis; and if ever Maritana thought there was in the world an undignified looking marquis, it was surely this of Rotondo. He beat even our Marquis of Londonderry, who is perhaps as great an idiot as ever had a title prefixed to his name, and that is saying a great deal indeed. He rather resembled a cook than anything else. There was about as much intelligence in his face as an active imagination might discover in a cod's head, and, take him altogether, he looked most sadly out of place in his own truly gorgeous house.

He came into the room with a sort of waddling walk, and the moment he saw the minister, he said,—

"My dear Don Jose, is it you indeed? How can I sufficiently thank you for the honour you have conferred upon me? The marchioness—lovely creature, though I say it—will be here immediately. Pray be seated."

CHAPTER XVI.

MARITANA'S QUESTION.—THE PROMISE OF DON JOSE TO INTRODUCE HER TO HER HUSBAND AFTER THE ROYAL HUNT.—THE PAGE'S JOY AT SEEING DON CÆSAR.

"MARQUIS," said Don Jose, taking the Marquis de Rotondo a few paces apart, "my principal errand here was to inform you that the situation of comptroller of the royal pug dogs was vacant."

"Good God! you don't say so?"

"I do; and what is more, the grand keeper of the gold fish is in a very ailing condition."

"No—no."

"I—I assure you."

" Really ?"

" It is the fact. Now, marquis, the man who in the Spanish court could fill both these high, important, and much sought after offices ———"

" Both ?"

" Yes, both ; must be a man of no common mind—no common energy—no common character, altogether, marquis."

" Gracious me, I should think not indeed !"

" I know of but one."

" Is there one ?"

" Yes ; and he is ———"

" Who—who ?"

" You."

The Marquis de Rotondo very nearly fell down, he was so amazed at these words.

" Allow me to be seated," he faltered ; " you are too good, Don Jose. Is it possible—can it be possible, that in your great wisdom, and in your great influence with his majesty, you have really thought proper to name me as the person who was qualified to fill those offices."

" I have not yet named you to the king, but I shall do so upon receiving your consent."

" My consent ! Oh, gracious, what can I say to thank you for so much honour ? Comptroller of the royal pug dogs, and grand keeper of the gold fish, to be concentrated in one humble individual ! What will the marchioness say — oh, what jealousies will arise among the grandees ? And, already I am considered as an extra stick in waiting. Come this way into the saloon—come along—come along. You must have some refreshment."

The marquis led the way into a brilliant saloon, which, as a fair specimen of such rooms in Madrid, deserves a description.

This apartment was one of great magnificence and grandeur ; all that could dazzle the mind, enchant the senses, was certainly to be met with here. There is so much of Moorish elaboration of ornament abounding in the large mansions, castles, and palaces of Spain, that it would be difficult to enumerate more than the general appearances.

The Moors were so long masters of the greater part of Spain, that they gave a tone to the tastes of the inhabitants, and few places form so interesting a spectacle to the stranger as a Moorish palace or fortress ; and the Spaniards boast themselves of their richness in this respect. Indeed, there are some who would boast of Moorish blood in their veins ; the northern nobility, however, look upon these with no great favour, and they boast themselves uncontaminated by such mixture.

The Moors, however, left many memorials of their long stay in the kingdom, and none more beautiful than their buildings, which are so well known for the profuseness and richness of their ornaments, and their workmanship, which is of the most exquisite character.

The apartment was long and spacious ; lighted by windows at each end, which were in themselves specimens of art, being worked into various devices by means of stained glass ; and so beautiful was the effect that the light that entered these windows gave a tone and character to the whole place, so different to what we are acquainted with in Europe, that our minds at once revert to the descriptions given of eastern palaces, and the tales of the genii.

The floors were all so carefully laid down that not a sound answered to the tread, and not the smallest inequality could be felt ; the sides of the apartment were divided by pillars into a variety of sections, richly ornamented by wreaths of flowers, and a variety of symbols in gilt, and colours forming a *coup d'œil* that at once struck the mind of any one who first entered such a place, and who was a stranger to such scenes.

There were also many beautiful designs spread over the whole apartment, for it was spacious and lofty, and the ceiling was most elaborately ornamented by numerous scrolls, and some fine carvings that were richly gilt, and mixed with other colours that ran with and so intermixed themselves that it was difficult to separate them in the mind, and imagine how any one part would have done without the presence of the other.

These apartments are by no means rare along the shores of the Mediterranean, but in Northern Europe never seen ; and few, indeed, of the inhabitants of that portion of the globe can even imagine the gorgeous magnificence of the Moorish palaces. They have not been exaggerated by the most vivid works of purely an imaginative character.

Such was the apartment of which we have in vain endeavoured to convey an idea to the reader ; and what an addition to its real character must it have been to see the dark-featured Moors themselves quietly reposing upon their ottomans during the noontide heats ; the turban, scimetar, and other portions of the Moorish costumes being all in strict keeping, must greatly have enhanced its character.

All that was glittering, gorgeous, and magnificent was there seen, but nothing heavy or inelegant. The richness and elaboration of ornament never ran to the opposite extreme, and became either heavy or inelegant ; far from it ; beauty, proportion, and lightness appeared to prevail everywhere in spite of the excess of ornament.

Seated in this place was the Marchioness de Rotondo ; and how shall we attempt to describe her ? Tall and scraggy beyond all ordinary tallness and scragginess ; a nose, the tip of which seemed in a perpetual state of conflagration ; a voice, compared to which, the creaking of a door on ill oiled hinges was melody itself—but our readers, after thus much, can imagine all that we could say of the Marchioness de Rotondo, whom the marquis thought the perfection of loveliness, and youthful withal, although decidedly on the shady side of forty.

" My dear marchioness," cried the marquis, " here is Don Jose has done us the honour of a visit with—a—lady."

" We are too much honoured," said the marchioness, who, by the-bye, squinted a little—but, no matter.

" It is my pleasing duty," said Don Jose, raising his voice, and introducing Maritana as he spoke, " to introduce you, for the first time, Marquis and Marchioness de Rotondo, to your niece, who, when an infant, was stolen by gipsies, and brought up by them until lately, when it was discovered that she was your niece."

" Good gracious !" said the marquis.

" We—we have no niece," faltered the marchioness.

" Think again," said Don Jose. " I say, Marquis de Rotondo, this lady is your niece."

" Then, if you say it, she is."

" Your long-lost niece."

" My long-lost niece !"

" Ah, now you recollect. Your brother, you know, had a daughter who was taken by gipsies. He died of grief—her mother followed him in a year after his death to the grave. The child was sought for in vain until now, and here she is."

The marquis rubbed his eyes, and looked at the marchioness, and the marchioness rubbed her eyes, and looked at the marquis. They then both looked at Don Jose, and from Don Jose to Maritana, and, at length, made a faint effort to say, " very good," but the words stuck in his throat, and he found great difficulty in giving utterance to them.

" Are you not very much pleased," said Don Jose, " and very much surprised ?"

" Oh, very—very."

" Tell your niece how welcome she is."

"Niece what's your name, we are very glad to see you."

"Your niece here is a countess. Ah, marchioness, I can see a very strong family resemblance to you in her face."

This was a decided compliment, and the marchioness bowed to it, saying,—

"Your excellency is too good. The countess has a little the advantage of me in point of youth; but, now you mention it, I do see a great family likeness."

"I thought you would. The countess is now a little fatigued, and will, no doubt, feel glad of a little repose. Will you order a chamber to be prepared for her, and permit me to take my leave, as I may be wanted at the palace?"

"Oh, yes, yes; but do be prevailed upon to take some refreshment. What shall we order?"

"Nothing for me, I pray you. Farewell. Marquis— marquis."

"Yes, yes."

"I shall not forget the pug dogs, nor the gold fish, you may depend."

"Your excellency is too good. If you will call his majesty's attention, too, to the fact that I have been a stick in waiting now for nearly five years, it may facilitate the matter."

"It will do so, you may rest assured. Imagine both the appointments yours, marquis; and believe me sincere, when I assure you, that I know of no one throughout the whole court so eminently qualified as yourself to be a stick in waiting, as well as to fill the two highly honourable posts which will soon be yours."

"Oh, your excellency!—you overpower me."

"Adieu—adieu. Marchioness, I kiss your hands. Countess de Bazan, adieu."

And so Don Jose, having thus provided Maritana with a home, and at some one else's expense, left the mansion of the Marquis de Rotondo, quite satisfied that neither he nor his marchioness would dare to deny the relationship to Maritana which he had foisted upon them.

"So far, so good," he said, as he threw himself back luxuriously in the carriage. "All works well. Maritana can now be introduced at court. The king is quite sufficiently smitten with her to pay her the most marked attentions, and the court gossips will soon talk of nothing else but the attachment of the king to the young and beautiful Countess de Bazan. That such rumours shall meet the ears of the queen shall be my especial task; and then, I flatter myself I have a chance of success. What a pleasant thing, too, it is, in the midst of all this, to have got rid of Don Cæsar so comfortably and easily. What a terrible stumbling-block he would now have been in the way of all my projects."

How very pleasant and delightful a reflection this was to the wily and cunning minister any one could easily have seen, had they but enjoyed the privilege of a glance at his face, which, however, now that he was a little natural in his feelings and appearances, he took especial care should not be the case. Not that Don Jose de Santarem made a point of being inaccessible to people—far from it; but he did take care that those who came near him should not be able to gather from his physiognomical expression what was passing in his politic brain.

It shewed, too, a minute and intimate acquaintance with human nature, that to those who he knew were not intriguantes, Don Jose satisfied himself by assuming an appearance of cheerfulness when he was sad—of sadness when he was cheerful—of a mind fully at ease and free from care when he was most racked by anxieties—and of an aspect of care and anxious thought when nothing in particular was pressing upon his consideration; while, to the old court flatterers, the practised hands at deceit, and any kind of chicanery which flourished so luxuriously at the court of Spain, he adapted a very different course—one which he found strikingly successful in throwing them completely out as regarded his intentions, his motives, or his feelings. That plan was to make no disguises at all, but to allow his countenance and manner to express always actually what he meant, a degree of sincerity which they never dreamed of giving him credit for; so, when Don Jose looked to some of these court crocodiles excellent and cheerful, they, with a depth of wisdom peculiarly their own, had no faith in it, but puzzled themselves wonderfully to guess what was going wrong with him that he was striving to hide beneath the cloak of so pleasant an exterior. That he was deceiving them by candour and simplicity they never for a moment imagined.

Now in his carriage, which proceeded at a very rapid pace, he smiled in the blandest manner, and now and then very nearly laughed as he thought how craftily, and yet how easily he seemed to be bending the destinies of all around him to an accordance with his own views.

"How fortunate," he muttered, "that the queen, too, is virtually—in consequence of the bad understanding between her and the king—banished from the court; else would she long ere this have been well aware of the death of Don Cæsar, for whom she still dreams of interesting herself with the king. I must keep her in such ignorance for a time; she will see me, and be civil to me, while such a point has to be gained by her as the redemption of a criminal from death. Now I have all my future proceedings well arranged."

He was silent for some few moments, after which he drew up in his own mind a sort of programme of his future proceedings, muttering their results and order as he did so, and counting off the different occurrences upon his fingers, as if he were Omnipotence itself, and had the ordaining of the fates of human beings even as he pleased.

"This girl, Maritana, will become the mistress of the king; her ambition will blind her to all else. Yes; Maritana, I have decided, is to become the mistress of the king, while I exercise over her mind a vast control, in consequence of being—as I shall take ample occasion to prove to her—the architect of her brilliant fortunes. The queen can hold no conversation with her; therefore, she need never know the misrepresentations in which it has suited me to indulge. By the king thus publicly keeping a mistress, the gulf which already separates him from his queen will be for ever rendered impassable; and surely her woman's nature will aid me in my own designs. I love her—that is, I love her in my way, and she shall be mine, not only because she is a lovely woman, but because she is Queen of Spain. Humph! I cannot help thinking, again, what an amazingly lucky thing it is that Don Cæsar is dead, so agreeably and comfortably, just at a time when his living would be of such troublesome consequence."

By this time Don Jose reached his mansion, and he strode through the hall, between the ranks of respectful domestics, with a haughty air; nor was there any appearance but that of the most dutiful homage on the faces of those who were fed and clothed at his expense, until he had ascended the grand staircase, and disappeared into the superb suite of apartments where he usually sat; then it was quite another thing, and the domestics of the minister became again the lazy, supercilious, insolent set of varlets they really were.

Some lolled upon chairs, others leaned lazily against the marble columns, and the laugh and gibe commenced going merrily round, for it was the time of day when they knew, or thought they knew, that Don Jose always remained at home; but for once they were grievously disappointed, for the hour had come when the minister had to meet the king by special appointment, and he had only driven home in order to make some necessary and urgent alterations in his dress, before he could venture to appear before the monarch.

He had ordered the carriage to move on, and return only at such time when he considered he should be ready for it. He never liked his carriage to be in waiting at his door; it was, if so, an indication that he himself would soon appear, and if any one wished to see him, it would give them an opportunity; perchance it might have guided the dagger of some assassin.

To the consternation of all the idle herd in his magnificent hall, he again suddenly made his appearance, and casting upon them a glance of displeasure, which they quailed under, he reached the street, and meeting the chariot a few paces from his own door, he directed that he should be immediately driven to the palace.

The king was waiting anxiously the arrival of the infamous man who was far more the panderer to his pleasures than the minister of his government; and, at length, when Don Jose's name was announced by one of the royal pages, he ordered that he should be instantly admitted.

Jose bowed low when in the presence of the monarch, who, with a wave of his hand, which seemed to signify, "Never mind etiquette now," said,—

"Well, Jose, what news?"

"I have been indefatigable in your majesty's service. All is arranged, I hope, to your royal wishes."

"What of Maritana?"

"She is the Countess de Bazan."

"Aye, truly; the Countess de Bazan—more fitting for the arms of a king than could have been the street-singer, Maritana. *He* is dead, of course?"

"As your majesty says, *he* is dead, of course."

"'Tis well. I have a fancy, Don Jose, that this same Bazan would have been very troublesome to us, if allowed to live."

"Extremely so, sire."

"Ah, I thought so much; and Maritana—how does she take her new dignity? Does nobility sit gracefully upon her?"

"As if she were born to it, your majesty. The loveliness you before were pleased to admire will bear no comparison to the charms you will now discover, and which seem to have been developed by the enchantment of her new situation."

"Indeed!"

"It is as I say, your majesty. Of course, your majesty's gracious pardon for Don Cæsar came too late, and so Don Cæsar left this world, let us sincerely hope, for a better; in which case, neither I nor your majesty can be said to have done him any injury."

"Pshaw!"

"And, besides, kings can do no wrong."

"Cease this mummery, Jose, and tell me where you have bestowed the lovely Maritana."

"She is now at the house of the Marquis de Rotondo, who has had the good fortune fully to discover his relationship to her; and, therefore, has the greatest pleasure in granting her an asylum."

"Ha! we will go there."

"If I might humbly advise your majesty, I should say wait till to-morrow."

"We are occupied to-morrow, Jose—we have arranged a royal hunt in our forest of Aranjues. We wish to let our queen hear, by the joyous notes of our horns, as they ring through the forest glades, that even her withdrawal from our court has not quenched all its mirth and vitality."

"After the hunt, if your majesty will, I can charge myself to take such measures as shall assure you an interview with the new Countess de Bazan, without the danger of spies or interruption."

The king considered for a few moments, and then he said,—

"Let it be so arranged. We will to the hunt to-morrow, and, at its termination, you and I, without servants or retinue, can ride to Madrid, and proceed to the house of the Marquis de Rotondo. All the minor details of the affair I leave to you."

The king slightly inclined his head, as a signal of dismissal to Don Jose, and the minister immediately retired; but, before he left the palace, he wrote the following note to Maritana:—

"To the Countess de Bazan, from Don Jose de Santarem.

"MADAM, — As your most humble servant and friend, permit me to announce to you, that to-morrow I shall do myself the honour of visiting you, and of bringing one with me who possesses a near and a dear title to your affections.

"Believe me to be, madam, with all possible sincerity,   "JOSE SANTAREM."

This billet he despatched by a special messenger, and then he considered he had done enough for the day. There was only one other trifling piece of business which occupied him for a few moments, and that was to see a man who kept assassins in his pay, and who, on more than one occasion, had, for a consideration, removed troublesome persons from the minister's way, by the use of the stiletto. The next morning the royal hunt took place.

CHAPTER XVII.

THE HUNT IN THE FOREST. — THE STORM. — THE NAME OF THE CHARMER.—SUNSET.—THE PALACE AND THE WAITING MARITANA.

THE scene that was now about enacting was one in which considerable excitement and interest was exhibited. A royal hunt is always a matter of some importance, however unimportant the object of it may be. Dogs, huntsmen, and steeds form a medley that gratifies the commoner, who looks on the wild scene with delight.

The Forest of Aranjues has been a royal chase from the time it can be first found to be mentioned in the records of history. Its extent and beauty, too, greatly enhance the pleasures of a hunt, and has this recommendation to it, that, besides the natural inducements to a chase, it has all the beauties of perhaps one of the most beautiful countries in the world. Here the sylvan scenery was of the most enchanting description; hill and dale; thickly-wooded places, and others of a more open character: but the trees were of such growth and grandeur, that the eye in gazing on them conveyed notions to the mind of the most sublime and exalted character.

Such was the spot where Charles was about to give a splendid hunt, and in which he himself was to take his own pleasure; for Charles was by no means insensible to the love that is almost innate within men to seek for sport and pastime where there was danger and difficulty. At such times the boldest and bravest rushed forward and exposed themselves to any danger.

Beneath the spreading boughs of the lordly denizens of the forest browsed the stately stag, whose antlered head presented a formidable weapon, if used for offence or defence; but the animal usually depends more upon speed for its safety than any power with which it might be gifted of doing mischief; indeed, had some animals been thus gifted, their power being equalled by their will, great danger would often be the result.

But the beautiful and noble animal is timid, and

never turns, save when there is no longer any chance of escape left; then, indeed, its gentle nature seems changed, and it boldly turns upon its pursuer, and woe betide the man or beast who comes within the reach of its antlers, for he will surely be gored, and, from the nature of the wound, it is very dangerous, and difficult in healing.

The scene was one of great splendour. The huntsmen in their royal liveries, their attendants, and the splendid dresses and arms of the courtiers who waited upon Charles; while the officers of the guard, and a select body of that corps, were at hand in case of need at any one moment.

The hounds had been laid on the track of a fine buck, one that had been noticed for several days previous to have wandered about these precincts. He had been discovered this day browsing under the large branches of a cork-tree, and he no sooner beheld the hounds, and heard their cry, than, throwing his head up, he snuffed the air, and led gallantly away, and was soon lost to view, ere the king had, in fact, mounted.

The dogs, however, were quickly laid on, and led away with a sure scent, and they came, by hard riding, in the course of time, in full view of the animal. He stood on the banks of a small rivulet, and looked back on the coming host, and then quietly and gently plunged into the stream and swam across to the other side.

The king had seen the animal take water, and well knowing there was a spot above which he could cross,

and perhaps intercept the animal, he turned his horse's head towards that spot, and thus separated himself from his retinue.

Charles soon crossed the stream, while many of the attendants swam, as the buck had done; but they had lost sight of the animal, and were merely following the dogs that still kept up the chase by the scent that they had regained after they had lost it through the water. The king caught a glimpse of the animal through the trees, and being full heated by the sport, he urged his horse onwards, in hopes of turning the creature and holding him at bay until his retinue had time to come up.

Little heeded Charles of the danger of the attempt, nor was he aware of the distance his retinue were from him. His whole ardour was in the chase, and he spurred his Andalusian courser on after the flying stag.

He came in sight of it at length; the animal was panting and wearied, but still it rushed on with great swiftness, and Charles as eagerly followed it. At length the animal evidently decreased its speed, and Charles checked the headlong career of his own steed; and then the stag, as if unwilling to go any further, or thinking that he had but one enemy to contend with, turned and boldly faced the king.

This was an unexpected occurrence, and Charles was certainly nonplused; but he checked his steed, and for a moment stood in doubt what to do, and the next he was lying on the earth nearly senseless. The stag, the instant the king hesitated, charged him with great force. The horse was thrown over, and, fortunately for Charles, fell another way; and in another moment he would have been dreadfully gored, most probably to death; but fortunately one of the officers of the guard galloped up and interposed himself and horse between the king and the stag, receiving its charge at the same moment; he was overthrown, but contrived to wound the irritated animal, and, before the king could rise, he sprung to his feet and rushed bodily at the stag, and transfixed it with his sword through the heart.

The beast reeled and staggered, and then fell to the earth, kicking and plunging violently.

The officer then turned to the king, who had been almost stunned, and unable to rise from the effects of the fall, and immediately helped him to regain his feet.

"Thanks," said the king, when he had somewhat recovered himself, and stood leaning against the trunk of a cork-tree, "thanks; you have done good service to-day, when it was most needed, and shall not go unrewarded."

"My duty, sire, prompted me to do what I have done; it was no more than any subject would have done to save his sovereign," replied the officer.

"Say no more—Charles cannot be ungrateful; our word is past, and it is enough. By what name are you known?"

"Juan de Biscay," replied the officer, bowing.

"Then, Don Juan de Biscay, you shall be retained about our person in some honourable employment, such as shall be significant of our appreciation of your conduct."

At this moment the hounds appeared in sight, and soon rushed in upon the noble animal that had been slain, and which was in its last throes, and soon put an end to it. A few minutes more, and several of the courtiers came up, and began to congratulate the king upon the death of so fine a creature; among them, too, was Don Jose.

"You may congratulate this brave gentleman for having not only slain the stag, but saved our life at the same moment, but not without danger of his own."

A general inquiry took place, and the whole of the affair was easily surmised, and Charles was helped to an attendant's horse, and they soon after began to return to the palace, through a very circuitous route; in fact, the king had come a very long way, though in the ardour of the chase he had not noticed it.

The news that the king's life had been endangered spread like wildfire; it was instantly carried round from mouth to mouth, and long before the king arrived at the palace, the queen had been made acquainted with it.

Utterly unable to comprehend the precise nature of the danger, and how far it had been escaped, she was seized by the most lively alarm; and, hastily arraying herself lightly, she quitted the palace to meet her royal consort as he came towards it.

Charles was walking with his courtiers, who were a little way in the rear, when he perceived the approach of the queen. This was a sight which gave him much annoyance and vexation; it was inopportune, for Charles had been at that moment conversing with his minister, Don Jose, and Maritana formed the principal topic in it. When, therefore, the king saw the queen, he was much angered, and looked coldly on her.

The queen came up to Charles with a look of alarm, and tears stood in her eyes, and, throwing herself on his bosom, uttered some scarcely audible words of joy at being thus assured of his safety.

"Thank Heaven," she said, "that it has spared your majesty, and may danger never again encircle your majesty's person."

"Lady," replied Charles, "this is too open—too—"

"But has not your majesty been in great danger? At least, I heard so, and flew hither to see if ——"

"Nay, moderate your transports, they," replied Charles, imperiously, "are more fitted for the chamber than the public eye; I like not the public embraces."

"Surely, surely your majesty will forgive a loving and dutiful wife if she has exceeded the etiquette in a matter where life and death has been the cause. I could not hear your majesty was in danger and present peril, and yet not fly to the spot to ascertain if you were hurt."

"You see that I am not—I am saved, and it ill becomes the Queen of Spain to exhibit such passion before the eyes of the whole court."

"Your majesty misconstrues all I have said or done," replied the queen, meekly; "I meant not to be officious nor intrusive; I know not in what I have offended. Will your majesty tell me in what I have done amiss?"

"You are too much in public, my gracious lady," replied the king, in angry tones; "too much in public."

"I will go where your majesty lists."

"I should more admire any queen in her own retirement; her chamber is a more proper place than the public forest."

"Your majesty's wishes are commands, and yet I know not that I have offended. I know not which of these things you wish done that I have not already done. Can your majesty tell me aught in which I have done amiss?"

"I hate to see women," cried Charles, getting angry,—"to see women popularity-hunting in Madrid; to seek to gain sympathy from this one and that one, and get up a reputation for purity. I tell you, madam, you are too much in public."

"Does your majesty fear that I shall become acquainted with your intrigues? — that you fear my presence will retard some new affair you have in hand?"

"This insolence, madam, must be repressed; if you know not your obedience to your lord, you must be taught it to your sovereign."

"I would I were met by the same clear conscience I myself possess by your majesty, for I can say I never wronged you in deed or in thought."

During this conversation the sky became overcast, unnoticed by any of the party. A sudden flash of lightning shot across the sky, and a few heavy drops of rain fell as a warning to the party to take the nearest shelter that offered itself; but none was to be had but such as the boughs of a gigantic cork-tree afforded them. To this they immediately repaired, while the king's suite betook themselves to the nearest shelter that they could reach, save Don Jose, who sought shelter under the same tree with the king and queen.

They had not long sought shelter ere the storm increased most rapidly; the very face of Nature seemed altered, and the bright, sunny landscape was changed to an angry and stormy scene; the wind howled through the forest, and the rain fell heavily—in plashing torrents, that swelled the little brooks to foaming torrents, the larger ones to overflowing.

The tree which the king and queen had sheltered themselves under now showed signs of having been thoroughly saturated, and the heavy collected drops of moisture fell upon the royal pair.

The queen, seeing this, and that the king had but a light hunting suit on, took off her cloak, and offered it to him, saying,—

"I pray your majesty take this cloak, and save yourself from the effect of the rain that now begins to fall through the tree, or the consequences of getting wet may be injurious."

"No," replied Charles, "I heed it not."

"Do not refuse it because I offered it; I am sure it will be useful, and even necessary."

"Nay, nay, I heed it not," replied Charles, somewhat moved by this proof of affection; "keep it on; you have much greater need of it than I have; you are frail, and I am strong, and more capable of resisting hardships than you, lady. Be advised, and put it on; I shall not hurt. See, the clouds clear off, and we shall have the bright sun out in a few moments."

The king's prognostics of the weather were correct; for, before many minutes were over, they were enabled to quit their shelter and proceed, followed by their court, towards the palace of Aranjues.

Don Jose, who had been an attentive listener during this scene, felt well pleased enough with the earlier portion of it; but he was by no means so well pleased with its termination, and determined in his mind that he would prevent Charles and the queen from entering the palace together; and, just as he arrived, in company with her, at the grand entrance, Don Jose stepped up to Charles, and pulled his cloak; and, when the king turned his head, he whispered the word "Maritana" in his ear.

This had its effect with the king, whose whole demeanour immediately changed from the pacified and pleased air he had assumed, to a colder and more ceremonious one; and, turning to the queen, he said,—

"I must leave your majesty."

"So soon!" said the queen, in surprise; "I had hoped your majesty would have deigned to enter the palace with me."

"And so I would; but I have just this moment bethought me of some affairs of importance that will be necessary that they be immediately attended to."

So saying, Charles hastily quitted the queen, accompanied by Don Jose.

"Your majesty had nigh forgotten," whispered the minister.

"By Heavens I had!" replied the king; "my horse! my horse! What, ho! my horse there!"

In the course of a few moments he and Don Jose were mounted. The horses' heads were turned towards Madrid, and at a very rapid pace, which forbade the interchange of much conversation, they made for that capital, and the costly residence of the weak and imbecile Marquis de Rotondo.

CHAPTER XVIII.

DON CÆSAR IN THE FOREST—THE DETERMINATION —MADRID—THE WINE HOUSE AND THE FRIGHT OF THE TOPERS—THE CREDITORS.

THE sun declines towards the west—beautifully serene and mild is the air—the sky without a cloud, not even a floating vapour that could rob the sun of some golden ray, and so gild his departure from this most beautiful of all European countries.

The heavens were cloudless—nothing but the pure ether shone around on every side—the intense blue was gradually losing that intensity, and a pale colour took its place, but so gradually and so imperceptibly that it could scarce be noticed, but the fact was evident. Little by little did the pure deep blue of the heavens fade, and, as the spectator gazed towards the setting sun the scene was changed, for then a halo surrounded the sinking luminary, throwing upwards glorious beams of light, tinting the heavens with its own bright rays, and imperceptibly mingling them with the darkness of space.

There was no gorgeous colouring—no tinted clouds —no gilding of spires and mock mountains in the heavens — nothing but the chastest scene met the eye, and with the last warm beam a gradual shade overspread the heavens, and in a moment more the edge of the horizon shot along its whole length a momentary streak of fire, and then, in a short space, but a subdued and white light was all that remained to point out the spot where the sun had sunk.

The forest trees, ere the sun had sunk beneath the horizon, gave forth lengthened shadows—the landscape was beautiful, and of the most sylvan character—perfectfully beautiful—and such as can be found nowhere save in Spain. Their tall and graceful stems shot up high into the air; their richness and luxuriance of foliage—their size, and, above all, the rich lawns that appeared as though laid out at their feet, gave the whole view such a character that once seen can never be effaced from the memory of man.

The appearance of the shepherd with his sheep is a pleasing contemplation, for here the flock follow the shepherd as obedient as his dog. There can be nothing more beautiful than the complete understanding that exists between man and brute. The dog, when he takes one, is not to assist in driving the herd, but to assist in its defence, should it be required.

A general dimness now overspreads the face of nature—the view is more limited, but scarcely so as to render the contemplative character of the scene the less interesting, for, as you near the tall denizens of the forest, a deeper gloom yet pervades the dark shades beneath their branches.

At such a moment as this it is sweet to wander among the lovely groves and enjoy the coolest and most delicious hour of the day,—a moment when the evening breeze springs up and fans the heated frame of man, and revives the energies of his almost enervated frame.

The silence—the fragrance of the delicious herbage and trees—the gentle gale—the soft and subdued sounds that reach the ear, all combine to render the evening hour one of enchantment and of soul-subduing emotions.

Such an eve as this had crept over the forest of Aranjues after the royal hunt, which, from various leafy coverts, had been seen by the delighted and yet dreadfully tantalized Don Cæsar, who, while he entered fully into the spirit of the chase, and felt delighted to catch such a glimpse of what he had once been qualified, by his station and wealth, to enjoy, could not fail likewise to feel how sadly changed were his position and prospects now.

The din of the chase was over—night had nearly come, and Don Cæsar stood beneath the shade of a gigantic cork tree, in a, for him, strange mood of serious thought.

A thousand times he felt inclined to rush forward, even at any risk, and take part in the glorious excitement of the chase, with which the old forest had rung so merrily, and which struck so many answering chords of memory in his imagination—now awakening keen sensations of regret for his misspent life, and then filling his whole soul with visions of the future, which he began to think he might still make worthy of the ancient, honourable name he bore.

"I have been thoughtless," he said to himself—"I have been most indiscreet—I have allowed myself to become the dupe of those who flattered me in prosperity, but who, like vermin, deserted the falling house of my once brilliant fortunes. I have led the wildest, gayest, meteoric life of all the nobles of the court, and the result is poverty and a reputation for a recklessness that knew no bounds, and yet my worst enemies, if I really have any bad enemies, cannot say that the honour of the name I bear has ever suffered in my keeping. If I have erred, it has been on the side of thoughtless extravagance, and even my creditors, who think themselves so hardly used, are not so— the knaves, while I did pay them, they fattened on me, making me the scape-goat for the debts of a hundred others, and yet they grumble now because their avarice could not succeed in carrying out fully the kind intentions of their ledger."

The night was fast coming while Don Cæsar was indulging in these sad meditations — meditations which, alas! came too late, like most feelings of reformation, which scarcely ever find a home in the breast until they come hand in hand with a feeling that it would have been well had they come sooner, and not delayed until they could only add an additional pang to the present, by pointing out what might have been, but which, alas! now can never be.

Cæsar sighed deeply—he was not accustomed to sighs—it was the first he had breathed for a long time, and, in a moment afterwards, he said,—

"This will not do. I am getting sad and melancholy. Perhaps it's the influence of that odd, lonely sort of hut; where, to tell the truth, I have been made more welcome than I could have hoped for. It may be that there is a sobering, melancholy aspect about these gigantic old trees, that makes me feel in such bad spirits. Whatever it is, it won't do—most emphatically it won't—or—stay—egad, I have it! No wonder—by the mass! now I recollect all about it—no wonder my spirits sink below zero—no wonder I feel my brain languid and a weight at my heart. Oh, of course, I have heard of such things as quite natural and incidental to my condition. How could I possibly cast about for any other reason, when I have so very good and satisfactory an one at hand? Am I not a married man?"

Having arrived at this conclusion, Don Cæsar gathered the remnants of his tattered cloak about him, and walked slowly through the sweet, romantic forest glade, which had been the scene of his musings.

"A married man!" he repeated to himself. "Yes, I, Don Cæsar, the sworn foe to Hymen, the great worshipper of Venus, to be a married man at last! There is a Countess de Bazan, and here am I, a lonely, melancholy wanderer, with all the weight and responsibility of matrimony, without any of its satisfaction. A married man—a married man! I feel already as if a large family was following me about, conferring upon me the euphonious appellation of father, along with strong demands for four meals a day, and a wonderful lot of wearing apparel. I sincerely wish they may get all they require. Humph! this cloak, my old and constant companion; the last gift of the most confiding tailors in Madrid, will have to be made up into jerkins and trunks for the young Bazans. Yes, I am a married man—a—a married—but where the deuce is my wife? If I had been shot by those fierce fellows of the Royal Guard, all would have been well, and I need not have troubled myself; but as it is, affairs are different, and as I have, in a moment of indiscretion, given my name to a lady, it behoves me that I see what use she makes of it."

There was, for a moment, an attitude and an aspect of pride about Don Cæsar, which showed that the chivalric and haughty feeling of a Spanish grandee was far, very far, from being dead within him, and then, with another such sigh as had attracted his own attention a short time before, he added, in a lower tone,—

"It seems to me that she must be beautiful. Her hand was soft and white. I marked the child-like, dimpled knuckles, and the long tapered fingers. She must be young and beautiful. Who is she? that is the question—or, rather, who was she? for, if the truth must be spoken, she is my wife. Who can she have been? How strange—how very strange! Don Jose, too, at the beginning of it all. He, a man who never does anything without some motive of self-interest. What—what might not my imagination surmise? One of two propositions is certain; either she who now has a right to call herself the Countess de Bazan, willingly traffics with my honour, believing me dead, or she is the victim of some of Don Jose's evil plots and plans, and requires my protection."

He stopped, and folding his arms across his breast, remained for some minutes in silent thought. Then suddenly, with a start, he exclaimed,—

"To Madrid—to Madrid! Why do I linger here? I might as well be immured within the walls of the sanctuary, to avoid which I sought the seclusion of these leafy groves. I will dare all, and proceed at once to Madrid. This tattered cloak, which has indifferently well preserved my new suit I took in exchange for that Don Jose gave me from the thorns and briars of the forest, would betray me in Madrid. I will leave it here, and, trusting to good fortune, my own sword, and a stout heart, I will to the city. Be-

ing married, I will seek my wife. She is my countess; and woe be to him who breathes but upon the unsullied lustre of my name. If I find her worthy, they shall reach her honour through my heart; if she be unworthy—no—no—she cannot be unworthy—I will not believe her unworthy. That hand—she trembled too —I thought, likewise, I heard her sigh, and once she leant half-caressingly upon my arm—she is not unworthy! I will to Madrid and find her, be she whom she may. Not a hundred Don Joses shall keep me from her. To Madrid—to Madrid!"

At this moment, when Don Cæsar had so thoroughly made up his mind to the long walk to Madrid, and the mere chances of meeting with any vehicle of which he could avail himself to lighten the toilsome journey, the low tinkling sound of the bells that adorned the heads of some mules that were advancing, struck upon his ears, and, almost at the same instant, he heard the muleteers chanting some rude melody, such as they were wont to cheer their weary way with when returning towards the capital after some long journey.

"Now," said Don Cæsar, "are these mules coming from, or going to the city? If the former, it is a rare and lucky chance for me."

He listened attentively for some minutes, until he became convinced of the agreeable fact, that the train of mules was not only very numerous, but that it was coming through the forest of Aranjues towards Madrid.

It was common for journies into the provinces to be performed either in the night time, or at an early period of the morning, in order to escape the extreme heat of the day, when the animals were scarcely equal to any exertion, either of strength or speed, and the return was arranged in the same manner, so that, in the suburbs of Madrid, after dusk, the soft tinkle of the mules' bells, and the rather monotonous, but still not unpleasing song of the muleteer, are far from unusual sounds.

Don Cæsar, being impatient, made rapid progress to meet the advancing cavalcade, which very slowly emerged from among the trees into the open glade of the forest, presenting a collection of some dozen of mules, gaily caparisoned, with two or three men, whose duty it was to keep them from straggling. It required no very great persuasion to induce them to allow Don Cæsar to mount one of the animals. The promise of a cup of wine when they should reach the city amply sufficed, and, at a tolerably rapid pace, Cæsar found himself, to his great satisfaction, once more on his route to Madrid.

It did not strike him that Lazarillo would be much disappointed upon coming to the forest and not finding him; but he made up his mind that he would take an immediate opportunity of letting the page know of his arrival in Madrid, and so possibly spare him the journey to Aranjues altogether, which to undertake, considering his new duties as an attendant upon Don Jose, must be inconvenient.

What with one delay and another, the night, or, rather, the morning, was advanced before Don Cæsar saw in the distance the spires of Madrid, and heard the hum of life in the city. His impatience much increased, although he had no fixed rule of action when he got to Madrid, nor had he made up his mind as to what course he should first adopt when he once more found himself in those streets which were so familiar to him. He was one, however, who always preferred acting upon the chances of the moment, rather than upon any fixed scheme, and, although he thought over what he had best do, he only came at last to the conclusion he might have come to at first—namely, that he must be guided by circumstances, and the inquiries he might be able to make of any one whom he should by chance encounter in Madrid, with the means of giving him any intelligence.

Soon, however, a new difficulty presented itself, for when the muleteers put Don Cæsar in mind of his promise concerning the wine, he found that, with his usual carelessness, he had left all that remained of the money he had obtained from the clothes-dealer at the hut in the forest, and that, as usual, he found himself in the streets of Madrid without a maravedie.

But a man who is accustomed to be without money is by no means a novice in expedients, and Don Cæsar, turning to the muleteers, said,—

" My friends, do you know Jeronimo, the wine dealer in the Place de Thomas ?"

" Well, signor, well," cried one of the men. " He keeps the best wine in Madrid."

" Ah! that's the very reason why we became acquainted. Now you will go to him and order just what you like, telling him that a noble gentleman will call in half an hour and pay for it."

The muleteers looked at each other with doubtful expressions; but Don Cæsar placed his hand upon his heart and said,—

" I will come to Jeronimo's in the course of half an hour, on my honour."

This was irresistible, and, with many thanks, the men made the best of their way to the wine-shop, while Don Cæsar, quite delighted to find himself again in Madrid, took a turn before the church of San Lorenzo, and another thought as to what he should do.

" I wonder now," he said to himself, " if my creditors have heard of my execution. I warrant had I fallen into a large fortune I should soon have had them all around me. Now if I could but ascertain if Jeronimo thought me dead. I wonder, really, if, at last, they have erased my name from their ledgers, and fairly given up the debts. Surely my execution must have made food for gossip in Madrid. It may not be safe for me to convince people that I am alive; but it may be very convenient to appear now and then as one's own ghost. Now, there's Vasquez, the little tailor, lives close at hand; I see no very particular reason why I should not call upon him and resolve my doubts. If he knows of my execution I am quite sure all my creditors do, for he has made a point of following me up more than any of them, and running from one to the other continually, to plot and plan how any stray real I might become possessed of could be taken from me. Yes, I will call upon Master Vasquez and ask the news."

Acting upon this mad-brained resolve, Don Cæsar walked on rapidly till he came to a house, the lower part of which was occupied by the little tailor, whose ledger could have borne ample testimony to the extreme liberality with which Don Cæsar was wont to give his orders, and how he always desired everything to be of the best, regardless of expense. Truly he was quite regardless of what the brave apparel might come to, and well he might.

It was an odd and an unusual hour for the little tailor to have a visitor, and the shop was closed; but that did not deter Don Cæsar, for he hammered at the door with great determination, and when, at length, the little tailor's wife made him get up, and look out at the window to see who it was, and he did so, Don Cæsar stood so close to the door that he was completely hidden from sight, and he would answer none of the interrogatives put from the window, lest his voice should betray him.

" My dear," said the tailor to his wife, after he had cried " Who's there?" from the window till he was tired, " it's nobody. " Some rascal has had too much wine, and made all that knocking just to alarm us, and now he has run away."

But Cæsar soon showed that he had not ran away, for no sooner had the tailor got snugly into bed again, than he commenced such a thundering appeal at the door, that Master Vasquez, with one spring, was out on the floor in a moment, as he ejaculated,—

" Gracious Providence! who can it be ?"

" Go and see, you chicken-hearted fool," said his wife. " Go down stairs and see, directly, will you ? Am I, perhaps, to be burnt in my bed, all through your idleness ? But I deserve it all, for ever consenting to become the wife of such a narrow-minded wretch."

" But, my dear——"

" Don't my dear me. I'm an undone woman. If I had had Juan Banchardi, the courier, I shouldn't have been the wretched female I am now. Oh, he is a model of a man; taller than the big trumpeter of the guard, and stouter a great deal than Master Flantini, the handsome Italian. Ah, me, what a wretch I am !"

" That's true," muttered the little tailor, as he pulled on a portion of his apparel, and prepared go down stairs.

" What do you say, you monster ?"

" My dear, I only said all the world knew you were a fine woman."

" Oh."

" Oh, indeed," muttered Vasquez, as he shuffled down the stairs. " I shall just keep a sharp eye on Master Flantini; he's here much oftener than I like."

By this time Don Cæsar had got out of all patience, and was hammering away at the door as if he were quite determined to break it in; nor would he speak, though the little tailor, from the inner side implored him to do so; therefore, he was at length compelled to open the door, and Don Cæsar, stepping into the passage, lifted his cap from his head, and said, in a solemn voice,—

" I am Don Cæsar de Bazan."

The tailor uttered a shriek, as he cried,—

" Murder! Saints protect me—a ghost! Oh—oh! murder—go away! You were ex—e—cu—cuted! Murder !"

" You know of my melancholy end ?"

" Oh, gracious, yes ; but mine's worse, to be haunted by a ghost."

" Listen. I am compelled, for my sins, to haunt all to whom I owe money in Madrid."

" Lord have mercy upon me! Go away! It's serving me out worse than you. I forgive the debt. Oh, dear sir—go away. Good ghost, don't mind what you owe me."

" The debt is recorded on your books."

" I'll—I'll scratch it out. Have mercy upon me. If you must visit here, come to my wife when I am not at home; people do so who I wish were ghosts, so you who are one may as well; but don't make me nervous. I forgive you all the debt freely. God bless you, Mr. Ghost; do go away."

" I was shot to death."

" I know it."

" Here's one of the bullets. Take it as a keepsake from me. It went into my brain through my eye,—this one."

" Murder—oh! don't—murder! I'm nearly dead. I tell you I forgive you the debt in full."

" Throw a receipt out at the window."

" I will; oh! dear, yes, I will indeed—anything you please, good ghost—oh! dear—oh! dear."

The little tailor, with trembling hand, wrote a receipt in full, and threw it from the window to Don Cæsar, who having secured it, walked quickly off to the wine-merchant's, saying, as he went,—

" Well, my ghost, it appears, can satisfy my creditors, if I could not, who say there is no such thing as retributive justice in the world. My creditors have been haunting me for some years past, and now I have it in my power to return the compliment."

When Don Cæsar reached Jeronimo's, the wine-merchant, he heard the muleteers drinking merrily, and just as he reached the door, they came out, followed by the merchant himself, who said,—

" But where is this signor who, on his honour, was to pay for you all ? He don't come."

Don Cæsar stepped behind a column, and one of the muleteers replied,—

" He will come. There was no mistaking him ; he is a gentleman, and if I mistake not, some great Don. I have seen too many of them not to know one ; let him be where he will, he will call and pay you, good Master Jeronimo."

" But what sort of a man was he—tell me his name ?"

" That we cannot—farewell."

" Knaves, do you think to go away thus ? I'll teach you to play your tricks upon me."

The wine-merchant walked a few paces from his door after the muleteers, and then he turned round to call his man to his assistance, when his eyes fell upon Don Cæsar, who stood on the threshhold of his house.

" Put it down to my account," said Don Cæsar, solemnly.

The wine-merchant tumbled backwards, as if he had been shot, and then scrambling to his feet, he shouted,—

" A ghost—a ghost !" and made the best of his way to the nearest church, into which he rushed with tremendous vehemence, thinking himself safe nowhere else from the visitations of Don Cæsar's apparition.

CHAPTER XIX.

THE DREADFUL INTERVIEW.—THE REPULSE OF THE KING.—THE AWFUL DISCLOSURE TO MARITANA.— THE APPOINTMENT FOR THE MORROW.

IT was late in the evening when Don Jose and the king reached the superb mansion of the Marquis de Rotondo.

They entered the mansion unchallenged by any of the numerous attendants, for Don Jose was too well known, and the respect the marquis had for him was as well known, so that his appearance excited no wonder or question ; indeed, every facility was given him, and they proceeded at once to that part of the mansion they most desired.

Don Jose was well acquainted with the localities, and the king himself was not ignorant of them ; and Jose entered an ante, or small room, that led into another of larger dimensions, saying, at the same time, in a low tone,—

" If your majesty will be graciously pleased to remain here, I will prepare Maritana for the interview."

" I am impatient, Don Jose, of delays," replied Charles. " Shorten the time as much as may be."

" Your majesty may depend upon me," replied Don Jose ; " but your majesty must recollect that we have an uncommonly tender game to play, and a substitution to effect."

" Which, methinks would scarce be so very undesirable a one, Don Jose."

" Certainly not ; but your majesty forgets you have an assumed character to take."

" True. Speed on your errand, then," said the king ; " and remember I wait."

Don Jose could scarce forget it, and he had not the inclination to do so, since an impatient monarch is scarcely an animal to be played with without much risk.

Don Jose immediately sought for Maritana, and him she was anxiously expecting ; for he had promised her some satisfaction respecting him she had so mysteriously become united with.

" Ah, Maritana—I should have said Countess de Ba-
zan—I have come hither as you requested ; the time is near at hand when ——"

" When I shall see my husband, Don Cæsar de Bazan," she exclaimed, joyfully. " It will be a moment for which I shall ever be grateful for."

" Oh," said Don Jose, smiling, " you must not forget your gratitude is also due elsewhere, Mari—Countess de Bazan."

" The queen, you would say ?"

" Yes."

" Can I ever forget her ? Has not her goodness been greater than gratitude can ever sufficiently repay ? Could I ever forget her sweet voice and kindly smile ? Oh, no, no, Don Jose, never !"

" She is indeed kind and gentle," said Don Jose ; " and I hope that in these qualities you will endeavour to imitate her, and let your life be one of obedience and gratitude, not only to her, but to the man who has thus raised you to the rank of Countess de Bazan."

" Surely—surely, I will ; could you doubt it ?—but yet there is some strange mystery respecting all this, which I hope will shortly be set at rest by his appearance."

" Precisely ; that will be done as far as it is possible, Maritana. But you have not yet informed me how you pass your time—is your happiness as great as it used to be ?"

" Oh, yes ; save in one particular. I am alone, and seek only for the time you say is so near at hand ; that is the only one point upon which I feel any doubt or fear. All else is joy—all else is sunshine of the soul ; but when—when will this one anxiety cease ?"

" You yourself shall, ere long, be the judge," replied Don Jose ; " but let me ask you, have you no further wish that remains ungratified, nothing you would wish done ?"

" No, no, nothing else."

" Nothing ! think again, Countess de Bazan," said Don Jose.

" Yes, yes ; there is one thing I wish," replied Maritana, with vivacity, " and I have wished for it ever since I received this title, and what I hope will not be denied me."

" Speak," replied Don Jose, " and your wish shall be gratified."

" Oh, say you so before you know it ? Well, you are a bold promiser."

" I have been rather a fortunate one, have I not ? and I have hitherto kept my word."

" You have—you have."

" Then, say what you wish ; and if it be within my power, and it's pretty extensive, your wish shall not be ungratified."

" Then I would wish to see the queen."

" The queen !"

" Yes ; the queen. I would throw myself at her feet, and pour out my whole heart in gratitude to her for her great kindness to the poor street-singer of Madrid."

" Well, well ; so you shall. The wish is a worthy one, and it shall be gratified."

" But when, Don Jose ? You have told me before that I should do so ; and yet, I have not seen her beautiful face. I have not heard her sweet, yet thrilling tones. I have not seen her sparkling eye. Oh, Don Jose, I long much to see the good and kind queen who has done so much for me."

" And so you shall, Maritana ; but you must yet restrain your impatience. There are things that I can't do, and many that I can ; and many of these latter are influenced by time and circumstances, you know. We are not infallible, though we have greater powers than many."

" Then you can't do what I ask you ?" said Maritana, sadly.

" Yes, I can, but not yet ; there are some few things

that intervene between this and then. You are yet young to the ceremonies of a court, and now you have become one of the titled, you must be guided by the same ceremonies that they are guided. Thus much is expected of you; but, be assured of this, your gratitude shall come to the ears of her majesty. I myself will inform her of your grateful feelings, and that you will endeavour to merit the boon she has conferred on you."

"Yes, yes, I will," replied Maritana. "I will endeavour to deserve the kindness and goodness she has shwon me."

"And now," said Don Jose, "you are satisfied, I suppose, that all that has been promised has been done, nay, more. You are now a countess."

"I am, Don Jose; thanks to the queen."

"I have also not been idle, you must admit, Maritana."

"You have not, Don Jose; and my gratitude will not be less to you than you deserve. I can never sufficiently thank you for what has been done; and should it ever be in my poor power to return such favours, it shall be done."

"'Tis well, Countess de Bazan; and I yet predict a higher destiny for you."

"A higher! but my ambition reaches no higher."

"No higher! Where's your ambition, Maritana—where's your ambition?"

"It is mine no longer. When I became another's, I lost it all, aud his wishes shall be mine. I am his, and wait but his coming."

At this moment Charles crossed the threshold, and stood within the room. He motioned to Don Jose, and the latter retired a few paces towards the other door, when the king exclaimed,—

"He is here—Maritana, he is here!"

The sound of his voice acted like magic, and with a sudden start Maritana turned fearfully around, and no sooner beheld Charles than she uttered a loud scream.

"Hush, Maritana, for Heaven's sake, hush!" exclaimed Don Jose, advancing,—

"God bless my shoe-buckles," exclaimed the Marquis de Rotondo, who, at that juncture, was attracted by the scream, and popped his bald head in at the door, and stared with amazement on the whole group that stood like a picture.

"Begone!" exclaimed Don Jose, hastily and angrily, to the marquis, and the bald head was immediately withdrawn, like magic.

Don Jose then advanced to Charles; and, laying his hand on his arm, said, softly,—

"Not yet—not yet—this is not the moment."

Charles hesitated, but left the apartment the same way he had entered it.

"Who—who was that man?" exclaimed Maritana, much agitated.

"It is a mistake, Maritana, an inexplicable mistake."

"A mistake?"

"Yes, and one that I cannot explain to you now. Meet me here to-morrow, and I will then explain it."

"A mistake!—cannot explain. What can all this mean, Don Jose?"

"You shall know, Countess de Bazan; but let me first know that you will meet me here to-morrow."

"Yes; I shall be here."

"Be it so; I will then explain what has occurred."

CHAPTER XX.

THE INTRIGUE ARRANGED FOR THE KING.—THE COURT FETE.—MARITANA'S STRANGE OPINION OF THE MARQUIS DE ROTONDO.—THE PAGE'S JOURNEY TO ARANJUES, AND MEETING WITH THE QUEEN.

DON JOSE well knew that his imperious master was not the man likely to be satisfied with these proceedings that had taken place at the house of the Marquis de Rotondo; and, therefore, after he had, as we have seen, succeeded, to a certain extent, in quieting Maritana, he hastened to the palace, where the king had betaken himself, in great dudgeon, in order to attempt convincing him that what had been done was for the best.

As he surmised, he found Philip anxiously expecting him; and, upon entering the monarch's cabinet, he was met by a frown, and an instant indignant remark of,—

"So, Don Jose, what am I to think of what has occurred? By heavens! has all your finesse and judgment come to this, that, at the very sight of me, she whom, but a short time since, you flattered me was willing to throw herself into my arms, should utter a scream of terror."

"Pardon me, your majesty; I never in my life so far presumed as to flatter the King of Spain."

"What mean you?"

"Most humbly, your majesty, that all I promised shall be performed. Your majesty is aware that this girl, who has been honoured by your majesty's regard, knew not of the high destiny that awaited her. That she should feel some surprise at finding the man who was introduced to her as her husband not the one she expected, might well be looked for; but that first feeling of surprise—perchance, mingled with a little degree of consternation—cannot occur again; and I humbly solicit your majesty's attention to the fact, that one step has already been made in this delightful business."

"One step—what step?"

"Maritana has had her scream at first sight of your majesty."

"A most flattering step, truly."

"I humbly presume it to be an important one; she cannot, in any conscience, pretend to be either alarmed or surprised when she sees you again, so that there can be no trouble or hesitation about inviting her to the palace. Whatever she may say, there can be no scene which will attract the public attention of the court."

"Indeed!"

"Yes, your majesty. Far better is it for you to have an interview with her in some private apartment of your palace, than in the house of the Marquis de Rotondo, who, however much he may be your majesty's and everybody else's humble servant who has ought to give, still has scarcely discretion sufficient to keep his tongue from wagging."

"Then why, in the name of all the saints, take me there at all," said the king angrily.

"Ah, your majesty, I wanted that first scream over elsewhere than in your own palace."

"On my soul, Jose, you have a tortuous mode of proceeding in this business. Is it to be believed that the King of Spain is to have all this difficulty in suing to his arms a street dancer?"

"The difficulty, your majesty, enhances the victory."

"It does; and yet it seems incredible."

"Your majesty must not take your court as a standard of morals."

"Pshaw! Jose. You must tell this girl who and what she is intended to become. However much difficulty may add a piquancy to triumph, the triumph should not be so long delayed, or it loses all its value. I am not accustomed to sue in vain."

"Perhaps, if your majesty chose to announce at once who you really are, you might dazzle her imagination."

"No, Jose, no. My queen—but no matter—no matter. Since you speak as if what had already occurred was but in the due order of your politic and crafty scheming, pray enlighten me regarding the next step which has to be pursued in this business."

"Your majesty understands the minutiæ of the plan?"

"On my faith, no."

"It is simply this—and, upon consideration, you will perceive how well we have forwarded it by what has already been done. Maratina fancies she has wedded the Don Cæsar de Bazan, whom she had en-tertained a tender feeling for ——"

"Curse her tender feelings."

"Precisely, your majesty—whom she had enter-tained a tender feeling for in the streets. She shall be duly informed that the wild, reckless character she fancied to be Don Cæsar, was an imposter, and has met his death; but that she has really, at the com-mand of the queen, been united to the nobleman bear-ing that title, who is her husband, and, as such, claims her love and affection. This Don Cæsar your majesty can personify, and she is now, by what has occurred, fully prepared to receive some revelation of a nature contrary to her expectations."

"And how, think you, she will take the news?"

"Well, of course. The title, the wealth, the death of him she might have preferred, the queen's presumed wishes, all will combine to induce her readily to receive your majesty in a befitting manner. There can be no doubt of complete success; but I would have wagered my head, that under any other terms than supposing herself your wife, even your majesty might have sighed in vain for the lovely and really accomplished girl."

"On my soul, I do believe so. I have set myself heart and soul upon this matter, and I would rather lose the best province of my kingdom, than this girl who is so difficult to woo."

"Your majesty may be well assured of success. If I might humbly advise your majesty, there should be given one of those court entertainments which your majesty has been accustomed to give, and to lend a charm to by your own gracious presence."

"Yes, yes; it shall be done."

"The Marquis and the Marchioness de Rotondo can be, of course, among the guests, and they will bring Maritana. I will, in the interim, see her, and, in answer to the eager inquiries she is sure to make, I will make to her a solemn promise that in the course of that court fete she shall be introduced to her hus-band, Don Cæsar de Bazan. Whether or not he be the Don Cæsar of her fancy, or another, I will not say to her; but your majesty, at the fete, can be intro-duced to her in some apartment where no one dares interrupt you, and can plead your own cause, and should you find her obdurate, claim her as your wife, a title she cannot deny, and she must be yours."

"It shall be done, Jose, as you advise. We will give directions for such a fete as that you mention, and, in the meantime, be it your duty to prepare Maratina, as far as prudence will admit, for the surprise that awaits her."

Don Jose having thus succeeded in pacifying the king, thought it high time to leave while he could, and he accordingly bowed himself out of the royal cabinet, with no very exalted opinion of his royal master's discernment.

As for poor Maritana she was left at the Marquis de Rotondo's in a state of mind of the most painful description. She knew not what to make of the scene she had recently passed through; but from the glance she had of the man who had been so suddenly intro-duced to her, and so suddenly withdrawn, she knew that he was not the gay, handsome, careless cavalier, whom she loved, even for his very faults, more than she would have loved any one else for their virtues.

The puzzled Marquis and Marchioness de Rotondo

had, since Maritana's residence with them, prudently avoided, as much as possible, any confidential conver-sation with her, for so short had been the time that the poor marquis had not been able to get anything like full instructions from Don Jose as to what he should say to Maritana, or how back up the story of his supposed relationship to her.

Now, however, Maritana was resolved that the marquis should not avoid some close questioning, and, accord-ingly, upon the departure of Jose, she desired to see him, and he could not, as he was in the house, very well fuse her request.

When he made his appearance, she said—

"Marquis, allow me to ask some particular ques-tions. They must be easy ones for you to answer, and it is not hoping too much when I implore explicit an-swers from you."

The marquis looked very fidgetty, but begged to know the purport of the questions.

"In the first place, marquis, how did I become re-lated to you?"

"To the best of my belief, madam, I really don't know."

"You don't know?"

"Certainly not; but Don Jose, who is my very par-ticular friend, does, and to him I beg to refer you."

"This is very strange."

"Very—ahem!"

"Do you know Don Cæsar?"

"I cannot say I do. It is quite sufficient for me to have the honour of knowing his countess. (She don't seem to be aware that her husband has been shot) added the marquis aside (what a very extraordinary female.")

"Then, in fact, marquis, you know nothing about me or my husband?"

"Nothing whatever, madam."

"But, you can tell me what man was that who made his sudden appearance here some time since."

The marquis shook his head.

"Enough," said Maritana. "There is some dread-ful secret, I feel convinced, connected with my pre-sent position, and no one has the heart to tell it to me."

So saying, she burst into tears, and the Marquis de Rotondo, after fidgetting about the apartment for a little time, and saying, "Bless my heart—really—dear me," &c., made his exit, about as much puzzled as Maritana to account for what was going on.

That was the same night as that on which Don Cæsar returned to Madrid, and it so happened that Don Jose thought it extremely politic to pay a visit to the queen, who still resided in the palace in the forest of Aranjues, for, since he had obtained of her her ring, as a warrant for him to interest himself in stay-ing the execution of Don Cæsar, he thought he might take great advantage of that circumstance to ingratiate himself into her favour, by an affectation of what exer-tions he had made; and as, sooner or later, she must know that Cæsar had been executed, he deemed it far better the news should come from his own lips than any one else's, as he could give what colour he pleased to the transaction—a very great consideration to such a man as Don Jose.

After, then, he had got rid of all his numerous en-gagements for the day, he took some sleep, and then ordering horses, he started for Aranjues during the night, intending to arrive at early dawn, see the queen, and get back again before the business of the day should have far commenced.

To his great joy, he ordered Lazarillo to accompany him, who thereby hoped to be able to see Don Cæsar, which he had not had the remotest opportunity of at-tempting, since they had parted in the forest. La-zarillo had not the most remote notion that Cæsar

would be so reckless as to show himself again in Madrid so soon after his supposed execution.

The journey was rapidly performed, so that, before the morning had shown its faintest hues, Don Jose and his retinue arrived at the outskirts of the forest.

CHAPTER XX.

THE ASSASSINATION OF THE QUEEN'S MESSENGER.— THE VIOLENT INTERVIEW OF DON JOSE WITH MARITANA.—THE PROMISE.

THE shadows of night were upon the wane, and day was near breaking. The dimness of night became, perhaps, dimmer for a time, and few objects could well be distinguished beyond the immediate vicinity. The dews had been heavy, and the grass was laden with moisture.

It was a still and silent hour, no noise, even of some stray animal, was heard. A deathlike silence reigned everywhere, and solitude appeared unnaturally solitary; no being stirred or moved; a wilderness could not be more silent, and more devoid of even motion.

The grey dawn of morning was perceivable in the east, and the fine ether was soon gradually changed in its hue from the dim obscurity that reigned over the face of nature, and to a gradual and progressive enlightenment of the whole scene; for some time there was scarce a shadow, gloom pervaded the scenery, and indistinctness; but as the east became gradually lit

up, every object in nature—in the order of its size and position—became gradually developed to the sight.

It was curious to observe how a world grew out of the chaotic scene that lay around; tree after tree became visible, and mass after mass began to become apparent; a brighter glow could each moment be observed, and shadows on the earth became also more and more defined; hill and dale, and even the bold forms of the distant mountains appeared, and the huge forms threw a long shadow upon the sweet vallies beneath.

These vallies and the lower portion of Spain are well wooded, and among the many beautiful productions may be reckoned no less than eight different kinds of oak; among which is to be noticed the cork oak, the beautiful foliage of which and the other species form one of the greatest charms to Spanish scenery. The dark patches of pine near the mountain's brow stand suddenly out in full relief against the light that shines behind them.

Thus the early morn is breaking upon the slumbering inhabitants of this beautiful land; the first golden streak that glances from the east is like a molten beam of fire, and the heavens become tinged with its beauty, and a sunny glow spreads itself over the face of nature, giving all things a brighter colouring, and rendering them more distinct to the eye.

The golden and almost fiery streak that first stood on the horizon has given way to the brighter and more powerful light of the whole luminary. Nature is indeed indebted to the sun for its beauties, as well as for the many benefits that vegetation confers upon man. The aged trees now cast long shadows, and the yet deep but beautiful, shaded vallies are like dark spots that require a nearer approach to enable the observer to penetrate their deep shades.

The sun's high course in the heavens is the signal for thousands of warblers to strain their throats in the praise of the might, majesty, and beneficence of the Creator for such boons as we see on all sides.

The many beautiful and bounding creatures that may now be seen seeking their food forms an addition of no ordinary character to the scene; fawns, deer, and the whole tribe may be observed quietly feeding by the banks of some gently flowing river, while the wolf may be seen occasionally stealing like a thief in the morning's light to his craggy lair, from which the monster will not issue till darkness again envelopes the earth.

Such was the morning when the cavalcade of Don Jose emerged from the thick foliage of the forest into a cleared space, which revealed the palace of Aranjues, the favourite resort of the Queen of Spain, since she had become disgusted with the profligacy of the court, and wearied of the cruel and neglectful conduct of her husband.

Don Jose appeared to have the very highest opinion of Lazarillo, that is to say, the sort of high opinion which just suited him, for he considered the boy felt so bound to him, that he was thoroughly to be relied on for evil purposes as well as for good ; accordingly, now that he had arrived at the palace, he turned to the page, and said,—

"Come closer, boy. Are you aware that this is the abode of the Queen of Spain ?"

"I have so heard, sir."

"'Tis well. You see yon garden which surrounds the palace on three sides. Thither I am going to wait for the queen, who is accustomed at early dawn like this to walk there. Your duty will be to hover near at hand, and give me timely notice of any intrusion on my privacy."

"It shall be done, sir."

"Be watchful and vigilant, Lazarillo, and you will not go without your reward."

Don Jose then made greater speed up the entrance of the palace, and being known, of course, to the attendants, he was at once received with all the courtesy which an individual of his rank and power, whatever may be his merits, always is made welcome to at the hands of menials, who measure all men by what they are, and not by what they ought to be.

The major-domo of the queen's household met him in the hall, and in answer to the question if the queen was yet stirring, he replied,—

"Signior, such a morning as this will not pass without her majesty taking her accustomed early walk in the garden—I expect her each minute now. Shall I have the honour to announce your excellency?"

"No, no, I will walk in the garden, and so wait her majesty's coming."

The major-domo bowed low, and Don Jose, after an expressive glance at Lazarillo, to put him in mind of what he had to do, passed completely through the lower rooms of the palace, and emerged into the garden, followed closely by his page, who was beginning to fear that he would not be permitted to search for Don Cæsar, whom he was becoming now so painfully anxious to see. Even this feeling, strong as it was, however, could not prevent the page from being enchanted with the beauty of the garden.

Long and shady walks were frequent, and even necessary in such a climate as that of Spain; but that was not all, for there were many that were ornamented with the beautiful and gorgeous flowers that come to perfection under such a sun.

The long walks diverged from one point, and were evenly and geometrically laid out, with shorter paths branching from them. The point at which the walks met, was ornamented by a beautifully constructed fountain, whose ever-falling waters threw a cooling and grateful influence around, while the senses were soothed by the gentle murmuring sound.

Scarce anything is so grateful to the senses as this, and especially so where sights and odours are pleasing. The beautiful flowers were spread out in beds, or arranged in groups, or by the side of some lone spot, rendered fragrant by their presence.

Like a place destined for the abode of the happy, it was a scene of never fading beauties and delight—serene and calm, a spot where no intrusion is ever experienced—a spot, indeed, where existence might glide by, and finally, like the setting sun, sink in splendour as the darkness of night envelopes the world.

Life would here be a dream of bliss, and death would leaving the world in darkness, while the spirit fled in light.

Not a few of the long walks were provided with seats and bowers, in spots which were the most favourable for views and prospects, for there were others in these extensive grounds, while there were many that were secluded and shaded by copses of trees, evidently intended for use during the hours of noon, when the sun is at its meridian.

All, in fact, that could assist to make that spot a second Eden, was there congregated, and dull and spiritless would have been the mind that failed to appreciate such a scene of unrivalled beauty, where art made no war with nature, but only assisted to place her in her most exquisitely beautiful attitudes.

When they were fairly in the garden, Don Jose again spoke to his page, saying,—

"Now, boy, you will conceal yourself at the back of one of these arbours, in such a position that you will be able to have a clear view of this gate through which we have just passed, as well as of another, you may from here see the gilt railings of, just by yon citron tree."

"I see the gate, sir."

"Good. Now find out some spot which commands a view of both, and at the same time affords opportunity for concealment. I will be in the immediate vicinity, and should you see any one enter the garden, it shall be your duty to give me immediate notice, for I do not choose to be remarked or overheard by any of the queen's attendants."

The page bowed, and as Don Jose seemed impatient, he hastened to find for himself a place in the garden which possessed the requisites as to situation Jose had pointed out. This was not a matter of much difficulty, and the small agile frame of Lazarillo was soon effectually concealed among a mass of vegetation, near to one of the delicious arbours with which the garden abounded, while he had a tolerably clear view of the two entrances.

Scarcely had he accomplished this, than he saw coming from the palace, by the same way that he and Don Jose had approached, several persons. The first was the major domo who had received Don Jose so civilly, and he opened the gate and stood by it in a respectful attitude, while a lady, plainly attired, and with a pale, beautiful face, that rivetted the attention of the page, passed through it.

Then the major domo said something, which no doubt was an intimation of the presence of Don Jose in the garden, for he indicated with his hand in that direction as he spoke. Upon this, the queen, for it was she, turned to the attendants who were about to follow her, and seemed to dismiss them, for they returned to the palace, and she entered the garden alone.

Don Jose waited until she had got so far among the trees that she was not in the immediate sight of any one from the palace, and then, emerging from one of the arbours, he knelt on one knee, with the greatest appearance of deference and respect. Lazarillo was sharp of hearing, and by changing his position a little, he managed to gather distinctly the greater part of the conversation that ensued between the innocent and accomplished queen and the wily courtier, whose brain was so full of the most unholy projects and plans, in the execution of which he cared not what misery he inflicted, or who suffered death, danger, or disgrace.

"Rise, sir," said the queen ; "we would willingly dispense with such homage as this."

"Madam," replied Don Jose, as he rose, "I hope I

shall ever know my duty to my queen. I have dared to intrude thus early on your majesty, to explain how much I tried to obey your wishes in one particular, and how sadly I have failed."

"Failed, sir!"

"Yes. Your majesty was desirous that mercy should be shown to Don Cæsar de Bazan."

The queen clasped her hands, as she exclaimed,—

"You cannot come to tell me that so poor a boon to the Queen of Spain, as the life of one condemned to die, has been refused?"

"With grief, your majesty, I have."

"Can this be possible? But, Don Jose, you promised my officer such a length of respite as should enable me to plead with the king for that mercy which should be the brightest attribute of his kingly state. Have you deceived me?"

"Alas, madam, you will not censure me when you hear all. Heaven is my witness how I have striven to do your majesty good service in this matter."

"An awful abjuration, Don Jose."

"But excusable, your Majesty, because it is so very sincere. I shall be able briefly to state how your majesty's wishes have been contemned and set at nought."

"Go on, sir; go on."

"Knowing your majesty's most gracious pleasure, I, as minister of the Crown, ventured, on my own responsibility, to have the execution of Don Cæsar de Bazan put off for a week, pending which period I hoped that the anger of the king would lessen, and he might be induced to listen to the voice of pity."

"It was put off?"

"I ordered it, your majesty; and after that, your majesty will recollect, I was favoured with a ring, which was my authority for acting in your majesty's name in this business: knowing, however, too well, how extremely jealous his gracious majesty is of interferences with what he considers his own prerogatives, I knew that no time should be lost in getting his sanction to save Don Cæsar. Alas! alas!"

"Go on, sir. Waste not your time in idle regrets; tell me what happened, plainly and distinctly. Do not keep me in suspense, while you adorn your narrative with flowers and rhetoric."

These words were uttered in a tone of irony, which gave Don Jose some uneasiness, inasmuch as it induced in him a belief that the queen was not quite so simple as he imagined her, but really had serious suspicions of his good faith. He, however, continued, in much the same manner,—

"Feeling that no time was to be lost, I seized the first, as I thought, favourable opportunity to address my royal master on the subject, when, to my surprise and consternation, he burst into an ungovernable fit of rage—accused me of being a traitor to him and his interests—spoke more words of disrespect towards your majesty than I dare permit to pass my lips, and, on the moment, heated with passion and excitement, he ordered the execution of Don Cæsar."

"His execution?"

"I threw myself at the king's feet——"

"His execution?"

"But he would not retract. He spurned me from him, and poor Don Cæsar—the noble—the chivalrous—the kind-hearted—the old friend of my boyish days, was murdered! I can call it by no other name, your majesty."

"Murdered?"

"Forgive these tears, and this exhibition of emotion before your majesty, but the fate of this brave nobleman moves me much."

"Gracious God! Oh! Philip—Philip, how art thou changed."

The queen gave signs of much emotion, and it was some moments before she again spoke. Then she said,—

"If, Don Jose, you have acted as you say in this matter, I thank you."

"If, your majesty! Gracious saints! Can your majesty doubt my faith and willingness, to die to serve you?"

"I want no such proof of faith and loyalty. Farewell, sir; farewell. You have given me too much cause for sadness to allow me longer to enjoy the beauty of this fair morning. I will now at once make a communication to the king, which, I hope, will suffice to let him see we never can again be happy together. I wish to leave Spain at once."

"Leave Spain? Oh, your majesty, recall those words, and, ere you leave this paradise—made so more by your presence than its own beauties,—listen, while I unfold to you the dreadful reason why the king would listen to no appeals for mercy towards Don Cæsar de Bazan."

"The reason, Jose? What reason can there be but the wild caprice of a bad heart?"

"Ah, your majesty, there is another reason."

"Let me hear it, with a hope that it may yet be some palliation of the dreadful act of that man's death."

"Would it were; oh, would it were; but, I regret to say, that far otherwise is the circumstance which, quite by accident, I ascertained was the cause of the exceeding rancour of the king against Don Cæsar de Bazan."

"Go on; go on."

The queen turned aside, as if half afraid to hear Don Jose's statement, and yet, unwilling to close her ears wholly against it; while he proceeded, in a whining, hypocritical tone, to add,—

"Don Cæsar de Bazan had recently married a young and beautiful maiden;—need I say more than that the beauty of the Countess de Bazan has proved fatal to her husband?"

The queen cast a look of agony at Don Jose, and then, with a slow step, she moved towards the house.

"Stay, madam," he cried, as he followed her. "Yet a moment stay, and hear me swear, that with a full appreciation of your wrongs, I, from this moment, devote myself to your service—become your champion. To-morrow let us meet again."

"No, sir," cried the queen, "never again; even this meeting should never have taken place. Within an hour, one of my suite shall proceed to the king, and demand for me an interview, where I will, myself, to his face, proclaim what you have told me."

"Madam——"

"Aye, sir, such shall be my course of action—I will put it to his kingly word, before Heaven, to tell me if your tale be true. If he deny it, I shall demand —"

"What, madam—what?"

The queen turned upon him with a look, that even he, with all his effrontery, shrunk before; and then, in a low, but firm and distinct voice, she added,—

"Your head!"

Before, then, he could recover himself sufficiently to make any reply, she was gone. Don Jose crossed his arms upon his breast, and stood for about a minute in deep thought.

"A failure," he muttered; "a dead failure—she will demand my head, will she? Humph—Philip might be in a good humour, and grant the little indulgence; but I must be beforehand with her gracious majesty, who, by all the saints, I never imagined had half so much courage—nor perhaps has she after all. But if I loved her before this, now I adore her—she has spoken of my head—well, let that be the stake, I will lose it, or gain the beautiful, haughty, scornful queen."

He then looked towards the arbour where the page was concealed, and in a loud voice he called,—

"Lazarillo! Lazarillo!"

"Here, sir," said the boy, coming towards him.

"You overheard my conversation just now?"

"I did."

"Humph—I like your answer. Now, mark me, boy, you are vacillating between life and death—life with many charms, or a sudden painful death. Keep my counsel, and you have all to hope; betray it, and were you in the centre of the earth hidden, I would find a means to drag you out, and crush you. You understand me?"

"Perfectly."

"To horse, then, to horse. We must have a gallop for Madrid. To horse, boy, to horse—follow me."

Don Jose strode through the lower floor of the palace, followed by Lazarillo. As the boy, however, was about to close the door of one of the apartments behind him, he felt a hand upon the lock on the other side, and in a moment the queen appeared before him. She laid her hand upon him, as in agitated accents she said,—

"Boy, I saw you in the garden. You heard my discourse with Don Jose?"

"I did, your majesty."

"You are young, and should be innocent. As you have faith and hope in Heaven, answer me, truly, according to your knowledge, were his words true?"

"False, madam, as his own heart."

"Lazarillo," cried Jose.

"Go, go," said the queen; "we shall meet again."

The boy kissed her hand, and then hastened after his master, who had mounted. Lazarillo sprang upon the horse on which he had ridden from Madrid, and in an instant, at a smart trot, which was very soon changed to a gallop, the minister and the small suite he had with him were making towards Madrid.

The conversation he had heard between the queen and Don Jose, had fully opened the page's eyes, as to the real character of his new master, if he had had any doubts on that subject before; and during the ride to Madrid, he resolved to remain no longer in his service than should be sufficient to render some of his plots abortive, and do what good was possible for Don Cæsar, for whom he entertained so strong an affection.

He began now to understand several matters connected with the intended execution of Don Cæsar, of which he had before been in strange and perplexing doubts; and it was a subject of great delight to him, that he had had such an opportunity of unmasking the hypocrisy of Jose to the queen, although, upon reflection, he felt conscious he had been a little too hasty, because he could not know for certain but that the king was quite open to the charge of seeking Don Cæsar's life for the disgraceful motive which Jose had imputed him; but upon the whole he was glad he had said what he had to the queen; as to his own knowledge, there was quite enough falsehood in Don Jose's statement to warrant a strong presumption that it was altogether a tissue of misrepresentation.

Jose, during his ride to Madrid, fully made up his mind what he meant to do; and what conclusion he came to we shall shortly see. In the first place he went direct to the king, who had not yet risen; but who, upon the request of Jose, saw him in his chamber.

"I have been to Aranjues, your majesty," said Jose. "The queen sent to me, to know if I thought your majesty would consent to her absence from Spain, which she seems most anxious to take place."

"Absence from Spain!"

"Aye, your majesty; she will send you a messenger with some such request, and, if I mistake not, at an early hour to-day. That messenger will be one of her suite, and, I would stake my head, it will be one to whom, quite by accident, as I was taking a near cut thorough the garden of the palace at Aranjues, I saw her majesty, with more tenderness than perhaps discretion, give a ring."

The king sprang from his bed, as if electrified, and with a gesture of fury, he cried,—

"What mean you, Jose? Speak—say all you think, or know, or by all the saints in Heaven, I'll kill you. Do—do—you suspect my queen? I—I am calm—speak to me—tell me all. Death and fury! I am wonderfully calm."

CHAPTER XXI.

THE ASSASSINS.—A DREADFUL DEED.—DON JOSE'S PROGRESS.—THE RECEPTION OF DON ROTONDO.

As the king spoke these words, he commenced hurrying on his apparel, and his eyes gleamed with passion, like two fiery meteors, and he trembled so excessively, he could scarcely dress himself, and was compelled to accept the assistance of Jose, who added,—

"I have told your majesty all I have to tell. The fact is, that the queen did give a ring to one of her suite—who it was, by name, I cannot tell you; but it was given with a look of love, as if she would have said,—'Let me escape from Spain, where you will be out of danger, and I will be yours and yours only.'"

"Fiends!"

"Yes, your majesty; but, still—after all, your majesty, there is no proof of aught wrong."

"I will kill her."

"Nay, your majesty must think better of such a deed. Already your majesty is in receipt of a remonstrance from his holiness, the pope, on account of your neglect of your wife."

"True, true."

"And any harshness of yours now, without ample proof, would bring down the excommunication of the church upon you, and, perchance, dismember your kingdom."

"But, am I, a king, to suffer this indignity, unrevenged—am I, Philip of Spain, to be thus tampered with? No, by Heavens! I will—I must have vengeance!"

"Which your majesty can have. Leave your queen to her own thoughts at Aranjues; as for this messenger of hers, when he shall come, let him find how dangerous it is to tamper with royalty. Take his life if he have the ring, for by that test we shall know he is the right person."

"Of course he shall die."

"I will find one who—in the outer chamber, or say upon the staircase of the royal closet, whither he can be invited to come—will be his executioner. What says your majesty; have I your licence for the act?"

"Most certainly, slay him; d——n! slay him; our queen shall henceforward be watched. Quit Spain she shall not, for now I do much suspect her motive; I will think over this affair, and yet devise more revenge. Am I, a king—an absolute monarch—not one of those puppets of royalty, who affect to rule by the voices of the people, to endure such great indignity? No; by Heaven she shall know what it is to insult majesty. I must have revenge of her, as well as upon the audacious wretch who has dared to lift his ambitious eyes so high."

"Might I implore your majesty to be content with punishing the audacious man, who, no doubt, will soon be here, on the message I have mentioned to you?"

"You plead for her?"

"Most humbly."

"She was never a friend of yours, Don Jose; the last time she mentioned you it was not in flattering terms."

Jose's face was flushed for a moment, and then it became paler than before, as he said,—

"Your majesty, I will not allow myself to feel more hurt than will warrant me, in grieving that the Queen of Spain should do me such injustice. It would be, perchance, too bold of me, to ask what her majesty was gracious enough to say of me?"

"Not at all," said the king, who, like most passionate men, when he was angry, was angry with all the world, and glad to make everybody uncomfortable. "Not at all; she said you were a crawling hypocrite."

Jose bit his nether lip, until it was completely divested of all colour, and then he replied,—

"I do most sincerely hope, that some day I shall stand better with her gracious majesty, than at present."

"You have great patience, Jose, or great tact," said the king.

"A little of both; and most heartily at your majesty's service."

"'Tis well; you need not heed what the queen says or thinks of you: a jealous woman always decries her husband's friends, for she thinks, or affects to think, them all necessarily her enemies."

"Most true, your majesty; I may understand, then, that I have your royal leave, and full licence, to act in the affair which I have been so bold as to mention, in a manner which shall place all chance of a stain on your majesty's honour out of the question."

"Kill him!" said the king, with bitterness. "Kill him! The very suspicion shall be death."

Jose rose, and bowed himself from the room.

The change in his demeanour, when he left the presence of the king, was always most remarkable. He did not seem the same man, and there was no degree of submissiveness or humility exacted of him, by Philip, that he did not transcend to his inferiors, whom he considered every one, but the actual monarch, and him he despised, and, as we have seen, made an unconscious agent in the advancement of his own base and most dishonourable intrigues.

That the queen would adhere to the resolution she had expressed, and send a messenger to the king, praying for leave to go from Spain, and, possibly, by letter, too, upbraiding him for his infidelities, he had no doubt; for well he knew she was not one who shrunk from anything which she considered just and honourable.

That the messenger, if he ever reached the king, would do him, Don Jose, some mischief, he thought probable, because, should it be proved that the queen was aware of the dark intrigue that was in progress with the Countess de Bazan, Philip might well say to him, Don Jose,—"From whom could she have obtained such information, but from you, or some one whom you tell of my most private affairs?"

Under these circumstances, then, Jose was resolved that the queen's messenger never should reach the king; but solely on account of his having the misfortune to be her messenger, he should perish beneath the daggers of assassins. Too, often, already, had Don Jose made assassination one of the means which helped him to power, and he had no difficulty whatever in forming ready tools to carry out any murderous project which his brain suggested. In less than half an hour after his interview with the king, during which he had contrived to inflame that monarch's mind so much against his queen, Don Jose had two assassins placed on a narrow, dark staircase, which led to the chamber of the king, where he was accustomed to give audience to persons of note, and messengers on very urgent business, with whom a personal interview might be important.

This department was called the royal closet, and when Don Jose had made all his arrangements, he stepped into the ante-chamber, and sought the lord who was in waiting, and whose duty it was to take charge of any messages for the king, and to ascertain who were to be admitted to audience, and who refused. Of course Don Jose's instructions were presumed to come direct from the monarch, and implicitly obeyed accordingly.

"His majesty," said Jose to this personage, "expects a messenger from the queen; when he shall come, you will please to let my page know, who will have instructions where to take him."

Don Jose had sent for Lazarillo, who was present when this order was given, and indicated by Don Jose.

The officer promised obedience; and then Jose whispered to the boy,—

"You will take charge of the messenger, when he shall come from the queen, and crossing the courtyard with him, you will tell him that the king will see him in his royal closet. The low arched door, with the gilded panelling, conducts to that apartment; it shall be open, and you will leave him to ascend alone, saying, that above he will find some one to usher him into the presence of the king."

"It shall be done," said Lazarillo.

"Mark me; you had better not ascend the staircase."

The page bowed, and Don Jose, quite satisfied that he had arranged everything very comfortably indeed, went home to his own breakfast, which he had as yet been by far too busy to waste a thought upon.

He was quite right, as regarded the queen's intentions to send one of her suite with letters to the king, and, naturally enough, she selected the one she most esteemed, and considered the most trustworthy, to perform the dangerous, and, indeed, what may be called the fatal errand. She lost no time in despatching this messenger, for Spain had become hateful to her, and she had no difficulty in giving credence to what Don Jose had told her regarding Don Cæsar and the reasons why so much rigour had been shown to him, because, although a more wicked and detestable act than any that had preceded it, she judged, from what she knew already of the king's conduct, that such things might be done.

She wrote a feeling and a proud letter, in which she demanded that she should be freed from the shackles of an alliance which, since it had become distasteful to him, had become a pain and a reproach to her—she offered to forego anything for the repose and peace of mind she should enjoy, could she feel that she was no longer his wife—she begged him to act with candour, to assist her in procuring a dispensation from the pope to annul the marriage, which now, instead of an honour, was a stain and a public reproach. Together, with all this, she charged her messenger to explain fully to the king, that she knew of the intrigue with the Countess de Bazan—that she had her information on that from a good authority; and if the king should ask what was that authority, she charged her messenger to use no disguise, but to explain at once that it was from his confidential minister, and friend, Don Jose, she had obtained the news that had induced her to think her wrongs had reached a climax, which required imperatively some strong step to rectify.

All this, of course, would have been highly prejudicial to Don Jose. He might have succeeded in stultifying the judgment of the king sufficiently to enable him to get over the consequences of such a communication; but then, again, he might not, and he was, as we see, not disposed to take the chance of such an affair. His shortest way of getting out of the difficulty was by the assassin's dagger, and then he knew he should be able tolerably well to dictate every word of the message which should be sent back by the king to his much-wronged and insulted consort.

The messenger dead, he knew then that he could do as he pleased; and, by placing the act on the king's shoulders, when next he saw the queen, he should be able to increase the breach between them, by filling her with horror at the deed, while she would shrink from placing any one else in similar fatal circumstances.

Really, Don Jose de Santarem was a skilful politician, and quite a great man in his way!

*   *   *   *   *

Jose had not been gone from the palace above a quarter of an hour when a horseman arrived, the state of whose steed and apparel showed that he had ridden hard. He flung himself from his horse, entered the great hall where he announced that he was a messenger from Aranjues, with a letter to the king from the queen.

The officer of the guard on duty would have taken the letter from him, and let him depart with an assurance that it would be delivered; but the queen had given him private instructions that he was to wait, for in the letter was a request that the king would see and converse with her messenger, who was a nobleman of her household, and who would inform him more than she chose to disclose herself by writing of her reasons for urging so instant and immediate a separation.

Under these circumstances, he was conducted to the person to whom Don Jose had already given his instructions, and he, turning to Lazarillo, said immediately,—

"This must be the expected messenger from her majesty, whom the king desires to see in the royal closet, and whom you are to conduct."

"Doubtless," said Lazarillo; and, addressing the queen's messenger courteously, he requested him to follow, and he would lead him to an audience of the king.

Little did poor Lazarillo suspect that he was leading that ill-fated messenger to a terrible death, or no consideration on earth would have hindered him from warning him of the treachery that was intended him. He was as yet not sufficiently acquainted with Don Jose's mode of doing business to draw any such deduction from the present arrangements; and, not dreaming of the horrible deed that was about to be consummated, he handed the fated man towards the gilded door which had been mentioned to him by Don Jose.

"Did I not see you at Aranjues?" said the messenger.

"You did, signior; I have been but a few hours from there."

"You are in the service of Don Jose, then?"

"I am."

"Truly, then, I wish you a better master."

"Thank you," said Lazarillo, by an impulse he could not resist, although he felt, at the moment, that it was imprudent thus to acquiesce in a condemnation of Don Jose to a stranger, whose good faith he had no means of testing.

They had now arrived at the gilded door, and Lazarillo said,—

"This door, I am told, leads to a staircase which will conduct you to the royal closet, and you will find some one in waiting who will introduce you. Why do you pause, signior?"

"I was only looking up to the sky," said the messenger. "It never seemed to me so beautiful."

"Indeed?"

"No; it either has some new charm to me, or I never fancied it half so lovely; strange thoughts sometimes come over us! You will think it very odd now; but, just at this moment, there has come to my recollection a thousand reminiscences of childhood—of friends long since passed away."

"It's odder still," said Lazarillo, "that you should speak to me of such matters. We are strangers."

"We are, and yet I feel impelled to say some kind words to you, boy. I was born in Andalusia. How vividly does my old ancestral home rise up before my eyes! My mother, too—my father—sisters! How strange that all these thronging fancies should so suddenly possess me. Through this door, you say? Thank you; I am in a strange mood of mind. Farewell, young sir—God bless you! Am I mad, or going mad?"

He pushed open the door, and passed through.

"A curious fellow," said Lazarillo; "and now, as Don Jose did not say he wanted me immediately, I wonder if, by any possibility, I could get a conveyance to Aranjues, so as to look for Don Cæsar? I could go and be back again, perchance, before I was missed. I will to the streets; and, if any mules be going in that direction, I will bargain for leave to accompany them."

So saying, the page dashed from the court-yard, and left the palace, where so foul a deed of blood was about to be committed, and the horrors connected with which, he, by his sudden absence, happily escaped.

The messenger ascended the staircase, till he came to the first landing, where, seeing no one, he stamped with his foot, to give notice of his presence. Still all was quiet, and he had no resource but to descend again, or to advance unaided and unheralded. He decided upon the latter course, and reached the landing of another flight. There a door stopped his further progress; indeed, there were three doors on that landing, one on each side of him, and one immediately in advance, which really led to a small chamber, immediately communicating with what was called the royal closet.

The other two doors, although of full size, and richly ornamented, only conducted to cupboards, in which there was not much more space than would accommodate one more each. They were occupied on this occasion.

The messenger hesitated a moment, and then he placed his hand on the lock of the door immediately before him. That was the signal for action; the assassins emerged from their places of concealment. One stride brought them up to their victim, who, hearing a noise, turned his head, and saw his danger, and fully understood it in a moment.

There was no time for action, and scarcely enough for one cry of alarm, when two poniards sunk up to their hilts in his back, and were as rapidly withdrawn again.

He threw up his arms, and, with a shrieking voice, cried,—"Oh, God!" Then he turned backwards upon his heels, and fell headlong down the steep staircase bathed in blood.

The first landing did not stop him, and he still fell, till he reached the door at the bottom of the staircase, which, not being fastened, was flung open by the blow which the murdered body gave it, and the corpse, presenting a dreadful spectacle, rolled into the courtyard. There was then a convulsive movement of all the limbs; the hands opened and shut with frightful vehemence; a gurgling sound issued from the throat, and the dying man, in his mortal agony, bent himself back till nothing but his head and his heels touched the marble flags, with which the court-yard was paved. Then a gush of blood poured from his mouth; he breathed along with it his last sigh, and the body fell straight and dead upon the ensanguined stones.

*   *   *   *   *

The assassins, when they had withdrawn their poniards from the back of their victim, stood upon the defensive, like men who knew their business, for past experience had told them what desperate struggles a dying man will sometimes make ; but such did not occur in the present instance, and, when they saw him fall backwards in the manner we have described, they knew that all was safe, and their job was over.

Coolly wiping their poniards in the lappels of their coats, they gazed after the body, as it bounded from stair to stair.

"He'll stop at the landing," said one.

"Will he though?" cried the other. "There he goes. Now, by all the saints, he'll be in the court-yard in a moment."

"Stop him, then. Our perquisites may fall into other hands. We must have the rifling of all we kill."

"Aye, to be sure. D—n him, there he goes !"

The two bravos, when they saw the body knock open the door, and roll into the court-yard, hastily descended ; and, having assured themselves there was no one there, they stepped out, and, taking hold of the now dead man by his heels, they dragged him inside the doorway, and one held him along the stairs, while the other, with practised dexterity, robbed the corpse of every article of value it had about it.

"Not much," he growled ; "not much, but I suppose about what might be fairly expected."

"Is there any letter ?" asked the other. "Don Jose bade us be careful to search for one, and let him have it."

"Here is one."

"To whom addressed ?"

"To the king."

"Then, that what's wanted, Nicole, you may depend. There's a reason for all things, and this fellow might have lived over to-day but for that letter."

"So I suppose."

"What a lot of blood there is in him."

"Ah, you may say that; but come on now to Don Jose. He will be impatient ; and, recollect, we have only as yet received half of our reward."

"Ay, true ; come on, come on."

The assassins were provided with a written pass by Jose, so that they had no difficulty in passing the palace guard, and in a few moments they were hurrying through the streets towards the splendid mansion of the minister.

Such visitors were well enough known at Don Jose's to be always announced, and they had not been five minutes in his house before he was with them.

"Well," he exclaimed, "have you done it ?"

"We have, signior. When did we ever undertake a little delicate commission, such as this, and not do it ?"

"'Tis well. Was there any disturbance ?"

"None."

"And the body ?"

"Is on the staircase."

"Good. Let it be found there by the palace guards, and let them make as much of the affair as they like. Now give me the letter of which he was the bearer."

"Here, signior."

"Now, Nicole," cried the other ruffian, "where's your manners, you beast—eh ? Why don't you wipe the fellow's blood off the letter before you hand it to a gentleman ?"

"Wipe it yourself ?"

"There, there, that's the way."

"Really, gentleman," said Don Jose, "you are too particular. There's your money, and permit me the honour of bidding you a very good morning."

He made a courtly bow, and the assassins returned it as well as they could, and then left, declaring to each other as they went, that, after all, say what people would, Don Jose was quite a gentleman.

"And," said one, "he knows how to behave to brave men."

"And men of honour."

"Ah, he does; let's go and drink."

"A good resolve ; we will get drunk, comrade, now till all the money is gone ; that's the rule, I believe."

"It is, and a good one, too ; come on. Hurrah ! Don Jose is a gentleman; there's no mistaking him. He knows how to behave to old Castillians like us. Ah ! we are distinguished characters, comrade, and no man knows that better than Don Jose de Santarem."

When the minister was alone, the ghost of a smile crossed his features, and he said,——

"Those are remarkably useful fellows. They only require a little management, and when, in spite of that, they get troublesome, I can always manage to place them in the hands of the hangman. That's a comfort."

He then, without the least hesitation, opened the letter the queen had addressed to the king, the purport of which we have sufficiently explained to the reader to render a transcript of it unnecessary in this place.

"As I anticipated," remarked Jose. "Her messenger had full instructions to explain everything, and I might have been placed in an extremely awkward position. An answer shall be sent to this before mid-day, which I think will stop any communications from her majesty for some time to come."

"The Marquis de Rotondo," announced a servant.

Don Jose knit his brow for a moment, and then he said,——

"Admit him."

"My noble patron," cried the marquis, "excuse the great liberty I take in calling, but since you and his majesty did me the extreme honour of announcing an intended visit to-day, I have made such preparations as I hope and trust will astonish you quite. I—— I have a full private band—I have dancing—I —— "

"Marquis," said Don Jose, "will you excuse me ?"

"Oh, certainly."

Don Jose took his plumed hat, and left the room.

The Marquis de Rotondo waited four hours ; but Don Jose came not back, and then he summoned an attendant, to whom he said,——

"Is your master coming ?"

"I don't know, signior."

"Has he gone out ?"

"He has, signior."

"God bless me ! How strange ; but it must have been absence of mind to forget me. Well, bless my heart—how odd—but not at all disrespectful. Oh, dear no. It is quite an anecdote of absence of mind in a great—I may say an illustrious, person; and I wanted to speak to him about the appointment of head keeper to the puppy dogs — and — and — oh, dear me, what a thing ambition is !—now, there is one situation which, if I could but procure, would crown my happiness. Ah, ah !—oh, dear ! If I could but be green stick in waiting on the royal guinea pigs,— but I must not grasp at too much ! No, no ! I will keep my ambition down — down for the present— but time may do wonders, and make me yet, before I die, a green stick."

CHAPTER XXII.

THE MEETING OF THE PAGE AND DON CÆSAR IN THE STREETS. — THE FETE AT THE MARQUIS'S, AND MARITANA'S INTERVIEW WITH THE KING.

ALTHOUGH Don Cæsar might manage to pay his debts by acting upon the superstitious fears of his creditors, he was not in so good a position for replenishing his finances, and he found the morning growing on apace, without having any vivid idea of where to procure a breakfast, although his sensations of wanting one increased each moment.

Don Cæsar's sensations and reflections kept pace with each other, and he could be said to be exceedingly unanimous. Thought and feeling were one within him, though it was by no means the better, since each grew momentarily more disagreeable and sharp.

To be in the streets of Madrid at an early hour, without either home or place where he could call for a breakfast—call, he might, it was true—there was no hindrance to such an amusement; but then it would have been productive of nothing that was beneficial. Much noise and hoarseness would have been the only results of such an action, and Don Cæsar did not attempt it.

The morning was yet early, and the sun scarcely risen to the neighbouring hill tops; but there was a beautifully serene atmosphere, without a cloud to be seen, or cast a reflection on the earth, or to absorb a single ray of his light.

The night clouds had long since cleared off, and nothing but the clear morning air was now between heaven and earth—bracing and beautiful in the extreme. This was the pleasantest part of the day, and in which you could move about without being suffocated by the great heat.

This was scarce any consolation to Don Cæsar; for he could scarce feel much pleasure in anything that was likely to increase those sensations of hunger; he now felt, on the contrary, he would have been much inclined to have worshipped any divinity, if she came to him in the shape of a substantial breakfast.

Morning was growing on, and yet Don Cæsar saw no appearance of breakfast; he could not but think it was very unlucky, and scarce knew what to do, or how to get through the day.

Upon that point he had sundry suspicions that he would have to dine in the same economical manner he had breakfasted, and tea likewise, if there were no better luck in store for the unfortunate Don.

People now began to move about, and the *bourgeoise* began to clear out their shops and houses, and set them out, in order that they might present the most attractive appearance to the eyes of the passengers.

Don Cæsar looked around, first on one side and then on the other; but there was no difference—all were equally unlikely to procure the necessary meal.

"I would scarce mind," soliloquised Don Cæsar, "quarrelling with some one; anything to get up any kind of stimulus, rather than the stomach stimulus; it is so very imperative."

He now drew towards the house of a respectable-looking tradesman, whose wife was busily engaged in gossiping with another of the same class. Don Cæsar went towards them, and heard the following conversation.

"Ah!" exclaimed the first speaker, with a deep sigh; "my husband is so terribly jealous."

"What! Gil Mino?"

"Yes."

"Well, well, I should never have thought that of Gil Mino."

"Nor I, before I married him."

"Then why don't you cure him of it? I am sure I would not quietly sit down with any man who was to be jealous of me; I'd let him know who he was jealous of. I would lead him such a dog's life. Jealous, indeed! Oh! oh! oh!—he! he! he! Well, I am sure ——"

"Why, how can I help it? He storms, and raves if I say anything to him, that it is quite fearful to look at him!"

"I'd look at him! I'd give him good cause to be jealous of me, I would."

"Would you, now?"

"Yes, I would."

"But how?"

"Ah! I know."

"But I don't."

"There's the difference, you see, between us; I am a woman of spirit, and all my acquaintance and friends know that I don't care a rush what my husband says, and so, if he ever attempts to frown, or say anything to me unseen or unheard by those who are about, I immediately expose him."

"Yes; but what can I do?"

"Invite somebody that he don't know, and who isn't afraid to talk to him if he grows angry about it."

"Indeed! What would be the use of that?" replied the first; "he would be sure to scold directly the visitor had gone, and I should be no better off than before."

"Yes, you would."

"I don't see how."

"By threatening, every time he attempted to scold, to invite the same visitor again, and expose him to him."

"Ah, that's a capital plan. I wonder I never thought of that before; but then I had no such visitor as could talk to my husband; he's not afraid of anybody."

"Ah, but you should have somebody who is above him in rank—a fine, dashing cavalier! with a long rapier."

"Oh, la!"

"Ah, that's the way to do it. You don't mean that you don't know any such?"

"Yes, I do."

"Then I pity you very much, and really think you must remain a meek, snubbed, and dutiful wife. But I must now go in, for breakfast time is coming round very fast, and I must see to that, as well for my own sake as my husband's, who really is very furious when anything happens to disappoint him of his meals, and I don't think anybody would do any good with him if he were at all hungry, or the matter in dispute was respecting anything to eat and drink."

Thus she turned suddenly from her companion, who remained standing by the side of her own door, unable to determine what she should do, and being unable to do anything, because she had not the necessary means, and therefore she sighed again, saying to herself,—

"Ah, I wish some kind fairy would have compassion on me, and teach my husband a lesson, and then I could do as other people do, and not be taken to task for it."

"The fairies have heard your wish," said Don Cæsar, "and have deputed me to aid you in your undertaking."

As Don Cæsar said this, he advanced towards the spot where the bourgeoise was standing, and saluted her most gracefully, at the same time advanced his sword.

The woman gave a sudden start, and uttered a half kind of exclamation.

"Be not alarmed, my dear madam; the matter is easily done, and no harm can result from it."

"But," said the woman. "how can it be done? I can't understand ——"

"Certainly not; for I have not told you how you are to act."

"Who—I?"

"Yes, you. All you have to do is to invite me to breakfast with you, and say nothing at all about it to your husband; and if he speaks to you, say that I am there to answer for myself."

"But—but ——"

"You may depend upon my discretion. He shall not blame you for what you have done; and if at any future time he should attempt to ill-use you, you can always threaten him with a renewal of my visit."

"Oh, la!"

"Yes; it is astonishing that husbands should be so cruel to their wives. If you were my wife, Lord help me, how I should doat upon your sparkling eyes and cherry lips. Ha! ha! ha! by Jove! I'd sing all day, and dance all night; but no, that wouldn't do, and you'd get tired of it, and, now I think of it, so should I."

"Have you a wife, sir?" said the dame, making a curtsey.

"Who—I? Eh?"

"Yes, you."

"Yes—no; that is—I believe so. You see, she's an imaginary creature, and will be mine when I get her. Yes, that's it."

"Ah! I am afraid you are a sad man," sighed the good woman.

"Not at all—never merrier;—I am so near you and—and breakfast," said Don Cæsar, internally.

"Doubtless you belong to the court?"

"Court! Oh, yes; look at my sword—I am a gentleman, you may depend. You were cut out by nature to be a lady."

"Oh, dear!"

"Yes, you were. Not that I say so, because anybody would say the same who had once seen you and the court."

"Well, I have often wished I could have seen the queen and the courtiers; it must have been a charming sight."

"It is, I assure you; and, one day or other, you'll come to the court, to a certainty."

"Shall I?"

"You will. But come, you had better see me seated at the table before your husband enters, as a great deal depends upon that."

Indeed, there was much to depend upon it, as Don Cæsar knew, for upon that depended his breakfast.

"Come this way, then," said the female; "he is not yet down, and will be so surprised to see you, I am quite sure."

"So am I," replied Don Cæsar, "and that's the greatness of the joke; 'twill make him the more cautious how he acts for the future, for he may otherwise meet with more of your acquaintance whom he does not know of; and, indeed, he'll think you have many more, and so behave properly, lest you should call upon any of them when he is away."

"So he will. I never should have thought of such a thing, if you hadn't said so. Dear me, what men you courtiers are, to be sure."

"Indeed, we are fire-eaters."

"Fire-eaters!"

"Not literally speaking, only figuratively."

"What's the difference?" said the good dame, thoughtfully, not being able to comprehend the difference.

"You have been to a theatre, have you not?" said Don Cæsar.

"Yes, sure I have; that is, before I was married, for my husband never takes me there now—he's too jealous to do that."

"That must be amended."

"It ought, sir."

"Well, you have been to a theatre, and seen the actors drink out of goblets?"

"Yes."

"Well, they don't do so; it is merely figuratively drinking, and not reality."

"Indeed! and do you mean to say that the ladies and gentlemen, dressed so fine, really do not eat and drink when they sit down to their feasts?"

"No more than they really cut one another's throats; it is all pretence."

"Oh, what a shocking world this is; to think that people pay their money, and after all be deceived!"

"To think that people didn't cut their throats when they were paid for doing so! Well, I must say than it is a disappointment; but there is one thing in favour of their not doing so, and that is, you see, they would get speedily used up, and then there would be an end of the supply."

"But, what shall I do? I declare there's only one great chair, and my husband ——"

"Will scold you if you give it me."

"Well, I declare! you know what one is going to say," said the dame, amazed.

"Yes, I know it. Give it me—it is no use in adopting half measures, because they have to be repeated; and when you have an unpleasant duty to perform, it should be well done, so that there is no need of doing it again."

"True—that is very true, because we should then doubt its efficacy."

"Exactly. We'll commence breakfast before he is down, and by that means begin the attack by confounding and confusing him."

The good dame herself was confused and confounded, besides somewhat nervous, and very much delighted with her new visitor, who talked and rattled on without giving her time for reflection, or he feared he might be compelled to breakfast in the metaphorical style, and not at all in the real and actual way in which mortals usually perform their game of meals.

The breakfast was soon ready, and they both sat down, Don Cæsar laying particular stress upon the injunction that she was to say yes to everything he asserted, and to back him in all he said, and, by that means, the husband could say nothing; whereas, if she failed, he would say much more.

"I wonder," thought Don Cæsar to himself, "if I shall be fortunate enough to succeed in performing the service the good dame wants; however, I shall not fail to talk the husband down; if not, I'll treat him to a bit of the ghostly."

Steps were heard upon the stairs, and the dame exclaimed,—

"There is my husband!"

"Never mind," said Don Cæsar, throwing himself back in the chair, and sipping some chocolate very leisurely.

The door opened, and in stalked the husband, whose brows knitted when he perceived his wife had began her breakfast; but he had advanced close to his own large easy chair without perceiving Don Cæsar, and turning to him, he started, and looked in intense astonishment.

Don Cæsar returned his gaze with much steadiness, and there was an appearance of hardihood and strength about the don, that perfectly staggered the petrified husband, who could neither speak, nor move from the spot he stood on.

"W—what d—d—d—do you want here?" at length he stammered out.

"Breakfast," was Don Cæsar's reply.

"Who told you to take it at my table?"

"Your wife."

The bourgeois gave a start as if a cannon had exploded close to his ear, and, turning to her, he said, in a tremulous tone,—

"I—is this true?"

"Yes," replied his wife, but without looking up, for she felt somewhat dubious of the step she had taken.

"Sit down, man," exclaimed Don Cæsar; "you cannot take your breakfast in that posture; let me advise you to sit down, and take your breakfast while it is hot. Your wife and I have seen each other before this moment; have we not?"

"Yes," replied the good dame.

The man did sit down, but why he could scarce tell, he was so bewildered, for he had hitherto been so despotic, that he could scarce believe his own senses

that his wife had dared to invite any one to his table without even first consulting him, and that individual a stranger, and a man.

Don Cæsar motioned the wife to place before him his breakfast, and employed himself with some viands he found to his taste, but which, he having an extraordinary appetite, disappeared with remarkable celerity.

The husband ate what was before him, and looked alternately at Don Cæsar and his wife, and then at the sword he carried, and remained silent, unable to form any precise notion of what he had better say or do, or whether he hadn't better do and say nothing.

This last was likely to be the case, but that Don Cæsar, having concluded a hearty meal, felt little inclined to prolong his stay at so silent a table, so he rose and said,—

"I shall now bid you and your amiable lady a good morning, and trust that you will not be in any way displeased with her."

"Displeased! Pray who may you be? I shall insist upon knowing that," cried the husband, starting up as though a spell had been broken, and he was suddenly released.

"Do not insist too much, my good friend; my name you may hear, and would scarce like to hear, if I were to name it."

"You are some vile impostor!"

"No; I am Don Cæsar de Bazan!"

"Who?" screamed the tradesman.

"Don Cæsar de Bazan! Are you deaf? I have done you great honour in breakfasting with you; be more civil for the future to your amiable wife, or I'll visit you again."

"He is dead! He was executed!"

"If he were, I am his spirit."

"Impostor!"

"No, no; I am Don Cæsar de Bazan."

As Don Cæsar said this, he rose to quit the room, when who should be entering the apartment but his own diminutive tailor.

The man of measures, who had heard of his execution, and regretted it because he lost his debtor, stared at first, and then gave a deep groan, saying,—

"The spirit of Don Cæsar de Bazan!" He sunk down, and Don Cæsar, looking mysteriously at his host, nodded to him, and then stepping into the street, he soon quitted the neighbourhood.

If Don Cæsar was a wonder in the streets, so was Lazarillo, for he no sooner got free from his imperious master, than he sought some conveyance that would carry him to the forest of Aranjues, to there seek for Don Cæsar; as it was, he was spared the journey, for they met within a short time after the above occurrence.

CHAPTER XXIII.

THE UNEXPECTED APPEARANCE OF DON CÆSAR.— THE MINISTER'S FRIGHT.—THE QUARREL AND ITS CONSEQUENCES.

WHILE the Marquis de Rotondo was waiting for Don Jose, the latter had gone to the former's house to see Maritana, which he preferred doing while the troublesome marquis was from home.

To avoid the trouble and *eclat* of his carriage, and the necessary attendants, and besides drawing upon himself more observation than he at all times chose, as well as perhaps the novelty and change of the thing, Don Jose determined to walk, and walk he did.

He congratulated himself also upon the happy manner in which he had brought so much about already, and that more was certain to follow it. He had, however, certain misgivings relative to the probable amount of trouble he should have to overcome the scruples of Maritana.

This was somewhat unexpected, and yet a great man like Don Jose could not see anything like a determination not to yield to the king—his talents at intrigue and success assured him she was to be overcome.

But then how would the king like these delays? Charles was, he knew, fickle, and was likely to change, and should he do so, then some other of his plans might be deranged.

"How lucky it was I was able to make that matter of Don Cæsar right. Say of myself what I may, I deserve, at least, credit for being unexampled and unrivalled in intrigue: the stroke of policy connected with Don Cæsar will of itself prove that, I imagine."

Thus he talked and reasoned, until he reached the marquis's house, which he entered without hesitation or ceremony.

In the meantime, Maritana herself was much bewildered by her station in society, and her peculiar seclusion, which she could not make out or the motive for it.

True, it was said the queen said she must be content, and she was so; but she could not, nevertheless, forbear putting some few questions to herself, which she was unable to answer satisfactorily, but they haunted her mind.

True it was, also, that she had nothing to complain of as regarded the treatment she experienced from the Marquis de Rotondo and the marchioness, who acted towards her with great civility, and although they admitted that she was their niece, yet they would afford her no explanation of the circumstances connected with her birth whatever.

Then, they lodged her in one of the best rooms in the house—handsome and lofty, with every luxury that could drown the senses in beauty and splendour.

The window stood open, and a portion of the fine gardens belonging to the marquis could be seen from it; beautiful groups of rare plants and marble statues were to be seen here and there, forming different scenes of great beauty and diversity.

Fountains played, and birds sang with the most enchanting melody; all was there that could make earth a heaven.

Maritana looked upon these things, and was not insensible to their beauties—she was not insensible to the change around her; wealth and luxury had their charms for her. Yes, she thought of all, and saw all, but there was yet something else she desired to see beside all the pomp and magnificence that surrounded her.

The gaily and beautifully furnished saloons—which were not the only objects that her mind dwelt upon—she could see and admire; but they did not satisfy in lieu of other, and, to her, far dearer and more worthy objects than were those she gazed upon, and so much admired.

While these thoughts were passing through her mind, Don Jose was announced. The very name had become hateful to her, and yet she dared not refuse to see him, for to whom else could she look for a hope of extrication from the world of anxieties that pressed upon her mind? To whom else could she propose the questions which she felt she had a right to ask of him?

She directed that he should be admitted, and then, in the brief interval that elapsed before his coming, she strove to arrange with what distinctness she could the questions to which she was resolved, if possible, to obtain categorical answers.

Jose made no doubt of a reception from Maritana, although he had ample tact sufficient to feel that he had become hateful to her, and that she heard with ears of suspicion every word that came from his lips. But what mattered that to him? What cared he for the breaking heart of the poor Maritana, provided he succeeded? and success seemed within his grasp in achieving those results upon which he had, like some desperate gamester, staked his all.

And yet Don Jose was more than a desperate gamester, for he was not satisfied to go on winning. As the prime favourite of the king, because he was the minister to his pleasures, he had opportunity of accumulating wealth beyond his most enthusiastic expectations. As the minister, too, who was presumed to direct the affairs of state, he had necessarily great power—greater power than the throne itself—at least, greater opportunities presented themselves for its exercise, and power has no charms if unused. It became a mere abstraction, like the miser's gold, at once a possession and not a possession—a paradoxical good, which may for a time amuse the imagination, but wants at last the semblance of reality.

Therefore, we say, had Don Jose more power than the King of Spain, because he came daily, hourly into contact with those upon whom he could use it. He had abundant wealth, and yet was he far from being satisfied.

It may appear strange in our views of the duties and responsibilities of a minister of state, that a man like Don Jose was able to combine such a public situation with the mass of private business which seemed to occupy the whole of his attention; but the reader must bear in mind that Spain, at the period of our narrative, was neither liberal nor revolutionary; a long series of despotic monarchs had reigned tolerably peaceably, dictating the affairs of state themselves, or, if that was too great a labour, allowing some bold, bad man, like Don Jose, to assume the reins of government, or some enlightened statesman, like the celebrated Cardinal Anderoni Vieschi, who, some years afterwards, did so much for Spain, and raised it higher in the scale of nations than it had been for two hundred years previously.

Moreover, in governments of such a character, there are no politics properly so called. There is none of that perpetual squabbling for place and power, which, after all, perhaps, forms one of the greatest safeguards of constitutions, upon the principle that the quarrels of rogues are generally advantageous to the honest. To one man alone, in such a pure despotism as Spain presented, was ceded power. He had but to say, "do this," and it was done. He had but to keep the nobility around him in tolerable unanimity of spirit, and all was right. The people had nothing to do with the system, except to pay for it, and that was done, where such an amount of popular ignorance prevailed, as if it were one of the consequences of existence, and as little to be resisted as the changes of the seasons, or any bodily infirmities.

To govern, therefore, under such circumstances was a task which might be very easily discharged with a moderate share of comprehension. It was only in the foreign policy of Spain that tact and mind were required, and such were shown; but then the foreign policy of Spain was managed almost solely by the church, among the members of which were men of profound ability and acquirements. The king was a puppet; the nobility insolent, wealthy, and overbearing to all but the monarch; the people ignorant and superstitious. Truly, Don Jose was not much vexed with affairs of state, and might well combine in his own person the jackall to the king's pleasure and the minister of state.

But still, as we have remarked, he was not satisfied. His was one of those minds which never cry enough. There were no limits to the height of Don Jose's aspirations, and, consequently, like some miscalculating gambler, who imprudently always plays double or quits, he was sure to lose sooner or later.

He never would be content to stand upon the firm basis of a certain amount of power which he had obtained, but he would always place himself upon the slippery edge of some new acquisition which he longed for, and a fall from which must have hurled him to destruction.

He was clever, but he had the one great fault of clever men, and that was, in fancying that everything was to be done by finesse. He had scarcely yet, with all his talent, got far enough to feel that simplicity was a far more powerful weapon than deceit. In some cases he did certainly see his way by the light of such a philosophy; but not in all. He was a plotter and a schemer, and when he presented false motives of action to people around him, even if he succeeded in making them believe them true, he could not tell that they would be fully understood, or that, because they would have acted upon his politic and logical brain, they would produce a similar effect upon others.

He had but one rational excuse for the present ambitious course he was pursuing, and that consisted in fact, that as he had mainly contributed to the breach between the king and the queen, a reconciliation between them would induce certain explanations that might terminate in his disgrace. When he found himself, as he sometimes did, questioning his own discretion, he consoled himself with that argument, and it was by no means a bad one.

But we have been led into this digression unwittingly in our anxiety to place such a character as Don Jose's fairly before our readers—a character too common in all grades of life, and one which affords not only a curious and amusing, but an instructive study.

There are none of our *dramatis personæ* who require the dilating upon that Don Jose demands. The king was but a sensualist, and a man of weak mind and strong passions—a man who might be swayed for good or for evil, according to those among whom he might be placed; but who, perhaps, with the common perversity of human nature, was more easily led to the latter than he would have been to the former.

The queen was one of those gentle, quiet spirits which endure much, until fairly aroused to action, and then they display an energy of character, that no one previously gave them credit for possessing. She was, at this period of our tale, nearly on the verge of such an exhibition.

Maritana our readers can easily judge of. Enthusiastic, generous, ambitious, but not ambitious enough to draw a sense of right and wrong in its pursuit, panting for all those luxuries and delights which make the charm of youth, and possessing, as the stamina of her character, a native integrity of soul which never could be shaken.

Lazarillo, the page, was open and candid as the day. Such a mind and intellect as promised great things, if properly directed. Full of feeling, no bad sign in early life, and bold as any human being could be.

And what shall we say—now that we have been led to take this view of the actors in a drama—what shall we say of Don Cæsar, the wise, foolish, discreet, reckless, brave, noble, careless Don Cæsar? He who never thought harm to any one, and yet did harm to many. Alas, he had one great enemy, who was always leading him astray, and that was, himself.

* * * * *

To resume. Maritana kept her eyes fixed on the door of the apartment with an expression of great anxiety, and when it was flung open by an attendant, and Don Jose de Santerem announced, her colour went and came with rapid transitions.

Jose's countenance was calm and unruffled. No one, to look upon it, would guess the world of passions which lay hidden beneath that staid, steady expression of cool indifference. There was a studied grace in his bow, and an affectation of courtly urbanity in his tone, as he said,—

"May I presume to hope that the fair Countess de Bazan is in the enjoyment of that health which all her friends wish her?"

"Don Jose," said Maritana, "you do not come here to compliment me, nor do I wish for any lessons in courtly insincerity."

"Insincerity, countess—whoever heard of insincerity at a court, and at the court of Madrid, too, of all places? Oh, countess, you must have had some evil adviser since I last had the pleasure of seeing you."

The air of bantering with which these words were spoken, could not be misunderstood even by one as unused to such a mode of discourse as Maritana, and she replied, while a slightly heightened colour betrayed that she was not insensible to a sensation of offended dignity,

"Don Jose, if your errand here is really to convince me that you can be insolent under the guise of compliment, you may spare yourself the pains, for I can well believe so much of you already."

"Nay, now ——"

"Peace, sir, peace. I have questions to ask, which should receive most explicit answers, if they do not."

"I am, as you know, the slave of your wishes, lady. Ask what questions you please. Depend upon receiving such answers as shall be congenial to the natural candour of my disposition. Alas, how much I have suffered from a too nice sense of honour, and a too scrupulous adherence to the truth, which, really, now that I am seeing more of the world, I almost begin to think ought not to be spoken at all times."

Maritana made a gesture of impatience, and a slight pout of the lower lip showed how much she despised such hypocritical language as Don Jose was now addressing to her.

"Answer me, sir," she said, "what I shall demand of you. I want no discourse on morality from you. Who did I wed in that large place, which seemed half chapel, half prison."

"Don Cæsar de Bazan, Count of Orfilla, chevalier of the most noble order of ——"

"Enough, enough. I want no herald's list of my—my husband's titles and honours."

Maritana's voice trembled, as she pronounced the word husband, for she felt how proud a title that was, when she could use it as regarded him who had all her heart, and who had raised her from her lowly state to the high rank she then enjoyed.

"As you please," said Jose, carelessly. "However impolite it may be to interrupt me, you see I am not at all put out of my way."

"You sought the interruption, sir. You say you had the queen's commands to see me united to him whom my heart had long since acknowledged as its master."

"I had; and a ring she gave me, which was to be my authority so to act, I have still in my possession."

"'Tis well. Then what man was that who was introduced to me, when I expected him whom I loved, and whom I have sworn to honour!"

"Maritana, Maritana—I beg your pardon, countess I should have said—you are, by asking that question, directly opposing our gracious queen's wishes, and placing yourself in such direct opposition to her plans, that you risk their entire defeat."

"Plans, Don Jose?"

"Yes, plans. You know that the king and queen are not on the best of terms."

" I have heard so much."

" Well, then, as this marriage has been a pet affair of the queen's, it will require some tact to get the king to approve of it. Moreover, Don Cæsar was, and is, in great disgrace with the king, and it is her majesty's wish that a reconciliation should be effected, which should come along with the knowledge of Don Cæsar's marriage to you. You understand."

" But this strange man ?"

" Ah, he was a part of the queen's plan."

" All this mystery ?"

" Parts of the queen's plans."

" The singular mode of my marriage ?"

" All the same."

" The absence of my husband ?"

" Those things are all arranged by the queen. They are all parts of her plan."

" Then what am I to do ?"

" Wait."

" Until when ?"

" Until the queen has matured her schemes, Maritana. Let me ask you if I have not performed all that I promised to you, even to the very letter."

" You have, and yet I am wretched."

" And this is gratitude," said Don Jose, elevating his eyebrows. " Well, well, if I really did not look for a reward in another and a better world, I should feel myself very much hurt indeed. Are you not surrounded by luxuries ? Have you not numerous attendants at command ? Are you not a countess—the *protege* of the queen ?"

" I am—but yet ——"

" Oh, you are unreasonable."

" Tell me, Don Jose, is this affected relationship between me and this Marquis and Marchioness de Rotondo true or false ?"

" Hush ! hush ! What an uncourtly mode of expression. Between you and I, I rather think that it's only ——"

" What—what ?"

" A part of the queen's plans. Hush ! hush ! Not a word about it. Seem to believe it."

" Don Jose, you will drive me mad !"

" Pooh—pooh ! Maritana. Look forward to a pleasant release from all these little embarrassments. The day of eclarcissement will come soon ; far sooner, perchance, than you expect. What should you say, now, if actually to-night you were to see your husband— your real husband ? What if I could persuade the queen to allow Don Cæsar to kneel at your feet—to utter to you words of love ?"

" He does—he does love me ?"

" To adoration."

" He speaks of me—of me, Maritana ?"

" Continually, with rapture. What if I should so manage that you should have an interview with him this very evening ; would you then accuse me of falsehood and dissimulation ?"

" No, Jose, no—oh, no ! Let me but look in his face—let me but see his smile—let me but hear him say the words, ' Maritana, my wife,' and I shall be happy."

Tears gushed to her eyes, and she turned aside to hide the gush of emotion from Don Jose, who, with a great flourish of a richly embroidered and scented handkerchief, said,—

" I am much affected ; but it shall be done. Countess, you shall be gratified ; I give you my word."

" You—you will keep it ?"

" Keep it ! Do you doubt my honour ?"

" I never shall, if you keep this promise. Oh, Heaven be thanked, he is not dead."

" Dead ! Who told you he was dead !"

" I overheard the Marquis de Rotondo intimate so much ; but, when I questioned him, he declared I was wrong, for he had never mentioned the name of Don Cæsar, although his protestations made me suspect he had."

" Countess, your penetration, since your brief residence here, has surely been sufficient to let you know that the Marquis de Rotondo fills one other office besides those of stick in waiting and comptroller of the royal pugs."

" What situation ?"

" That of court fool, for which he is eminently designed by nature. Think of nothing that he says, for he knows nothing. Do not allow any silly nonsense of his to trouble you."

" But you cannot be surprised that such a statement gave me the most acute uneasiness."

" Why, truly, not ; but after all, countess, if you should even hear from any one else that Don Cæsar was dead, you must not be at all surprised ; for are you not aware that he slew an officer of the royal guard, during the carnival ?"

" And was saved, as you told me, at the intercession of the queen."

" Good ; and yet should you hear even a circumstantial account of his death—should you be told how and where it happened ——"

" I should die."

" No ; that would be foolish. What you ought to do instantly—on the moment ——"

" What—oh, what ?"

" Is to think it is part of the queen's plan."

" The queen's plan is very complicated."

" Now that is an ungrateful speech, Maritana, after all she has done for you. I cannot give you credit for that speech. It is one unworthy of you."

" And yet the plans of the queen are complicated. I feel most thankful to her—most grateful. It is impossible for any human being to feel stronger emotions of gratitude towards another, than I feel towards the Queen of Spain ; but still I say, I do dread the result of these complicated plans."

" That arises, lovely countess, from your ignorance of the usages of the court. Everything there is complicated ; but be assured that nothing can shake your dignity, or make you other than the Countess de Bazan you have become. Listen to no one but myself. Rely on nothing but what comes from my lips ; for I and the queen alone know the real state of affairs, and we make no confidants. Whatever any one else may say, can be nothing but vague surmise, and, as such, unworthy of your consideration. To attend to any one but me, will only give you endless mortification for literally nothing."

" I am necessarily so circumstanced," said Maritana, sadly, " that I can seek information from no one else."

" 'Tis better that it should be so ; and now listen to what I shall propose to you, as the means by which I can keep the implied promise I have made you, to introduce you to your husband this evening."

Maritana did listen, for that was a theme which touched her heart nearly, and Don Jose continued,—

" To-night there will be here a fete. It is got up by the Marquis de Rotondo, to honour some guests he expects. You will make your appearance, and, doubtless, be the admired of all eyes. In the midst, however, of all the brilliancy and beauty of the scene— for it will be both brilliant and beautiful—give orders to have your carriage announced. I will accompany you in it to the palace."

" The palace ?"

" Yes, Maritana, to the palace, where the king gives an entertainment likewise. There you shall find Don Cæsar in disguise."

" And I shall see him ?"

" You shall. It will be my care to bring you together ; be discreet, and say nothing of this to any one."

"I will be dumb as the grave. But you will keep your word, Don Jose; for this is not the first time my ears have been deluded by the words of hope, which have failed in fruition."

"You may trust me; and, as I am a living man, I swear to you, Maritana, you shall this night see your husband, Don Cæsar de Bazan!"

"I will be guided by you. At what hour shall I order my carriage?"

"At ten."

"It shall be done."

"Then, lovely countess, allow me to take my leave, wishing you all the joy you so much deserve, and convinced that I shall at length have justice done me in your heart. Ah! would that I were the happy, happy man, who is so ardently expected by such beauty! Would that instead of the simple, poor Don Jose, I were Don Cæsar de Bazan."

Maritana shuddered as she thought that the exchange would be to her anything but agreeable.

"Your varied charms," continued Jose, "must perforce assail every heart. Oh! if I could but hope that you would give me but one smile for the pains I have taken in perfecting your happiness, I should then ——"

Maritana walked from the room without deigning a reply to this speech, so that Don Jose was left to finish it as he thought proper, which he did by adding,—

"I would then jilt your royal lover, and endeavour to make you my own until I was tired of you. But no matter—I fly at far higher game! The queen! the queen for me!"

He strode down to the hall of the marquis's mansion, and was about to step into his carriage, when a messenger, in the livery of his own household, respectfully addressed him, saying, in as humble a tone as he would have used to a monarch,—

"The king desires your attendance."

"I am going. What else?"

"The man is taken who sent you a letter warning you of a plan against your life."

"To the torture with him!"

"But he says he wishes freely to tell all he knows, and ——"

"To the torture with him! Let him tell what he pleases first, and then to the torture with him, in case he knows more, which he will not tell."

The messenger retired, and Don Jose, ordering his coachman to drive to the palace, threw himself back in his carriage, very well satisfied with the result of his interview with Maritana, whose scruples he had succeeded in lulling for a time, if not entirely quieting; and that evening he fully intended should bring affairs to a crisis, and open her eyes to the cruel deception which had been practised upon her.

Meanwhile she, little suspecting what an evening of terror that was really to be, waited with the greatest impatience for sunset, when the entertainment would commence at the marquis's, and she might expect the arrival of Don Jose.

CHAPTER XXIV.

THE PAGE AND DON CÆSAR.—THEIR INTERESTING CONFERENCE.—LAZARILLO'S OLD MASTER.

DESPITE his strong opinion of the impolicy of Don Cæsar being in the streets of Madrid, there was no one in the whole world whom Lazarillo could be more delighted to see; and for some time he almost forgot the dangerous and precarious situation of his friend in the joy of meeting him and seeing that he was in health, and wore his old smile, which, though it had such recklessness in it, still possessed a magic that no one could withstand. It is strange, but no less strange than true, that there are characters which we love more for their faults than we can many others for their virtues;

but the reason of that must be found, not in any anomalous state of human nature, but in the fact that your very virtuous people are commonly very disagreeable, and disdain to make goodness and temperance and discretion pleasant.

There are haply exceptions, but, as a general rule, such is the case; and hence was Miss Edgeworth prompted to say that those who made the truth disagreeable committed high treason against virtue—a saying admirable alike for its philosophy as for the loftiness of its diction, and adding much to our admiration and appreciation of our authoress, from whose pen have flowed an immense number of practical truths in the most graceful of forms.

There was to the page's mind something so romantic, so noble, so chivalrous, about Don Cæsar, that he thought no human being could be like him—he was the *beau ideal* of all that his young imagination had pictured of a gentleman and a friend. His carriage—his reckless gaiety—his commanding handsome person—the wild generosity of his nature—all had charms for Lazarillo; and he carried his devotion to Don Cæsar almost to the length of adoration.

Cæsar smiled as he saw the half alarmed yet delighted expression of the page's face, when they had walked together some distance after this chance meeting in the streets; and, with a view of calming his fears, he said,—

"My boy, you fancy that I am in great danger, I dare say; but you must correct that notion; I am a ghost only, and as such not liable to human accidents. The air of Aranjues did not agree with me, so I felt myself compelled to come back to dear delightful Madrid, notwithstanding it is the place of resort of most of my creditors. No one will interfere with me, you may depend; I have a number of reasons for feeling tolerably well convinced of my own personal safety."

"Have you really, Don Cæsar?" said the page. "Thank Heaven! I am so delighted to meet you! Ah, who would have thought that we two should be walking now in the streets of Madrid after the terrible danger you were in! and how much you have done for me, dear Cæsar! How can I ever leave you! How grateful I feel towards you! How I love you!"

"Done for you, my boy? I have not had it in my power to do much for you. It is I who am your debtor for my very life. I have here the twelve bullets you gave me which you took from the arquebuses of the guard, and I shall keep them, Lazarillo, as a memorial of your devotion to me. Here I have them all snug in my pocket, when but for you they would have been disagreeably distributed about me."

"But, Cæsar, you must hide yourself somewhere—you must find some place of concealment—for, suppose some enemy were to see you and denounce you? I might not be again able to save you, even if I would give my life to do so—and Heaven knows I would most readily."

"I have thought over my position, Lazarillo, and I think it is a safer one than it at first sight appears. Those who were entrusted with my execution have failed in carrying out their orders, and therefore will not feel inclined to bring disgrace on their heads by making a stir about it. If I let them alone, you may depend they may leave me alone. All Madrid knows of my execution—none of my escape—so that convinces me that the authorities at the prison, if they suspect the real truth, have prudently said nothing about it, but let the affair blow over."

"Heaven send it may be so!"

"It is so, I feel convinced; and, now, how do you get on with Jose?"

"He is a villain, Cæsar—a most abandoned villain! I have heard much of him since I have been in his service—short as that time has been—and I feel convinced that he is engaged in a mass of intrigues, which your death was necessary to the completion of. He fancies you dead, of course—he congratulates himself upon that event; but what are his real objects in all that he is about, I am certainly at a loss to fathom. He has been seeking to inflame the jealousy of the queen by wishing her to believe that the king is enamoured of your countess."

" My countess? oh, by the bye, of course I have a countess. I am a married man. Really I sometimes forget it entirely—there is a Countess de Bazan."

" There is indeed!"

" Well, it's rather an odd question for a married man to ask; but can you give me the least idea of who my wife is, Lazarillo ?"

" No—no."

" You have not seen her ?"

" I have not, Cæsar, since you yourself saw her in the prison, and then, as you know, she was so closely veiled, it was impossible to discover a single feature."

" True, true, but I was in hopes you might have acquired by now some little information upon that subject."

" I have none further than what I have told you, namely, that Don Jose did mention to the queen that there was a Countess de Bazan of whom his majesty was much enamoured, and that such constituted the reason why you were condemned to death so suddenly; of course, he meant her to believe that he was innocent of any participation in so vile a scheme; but I found an opportunity of letting the queen know how false was such an inference, for if any such intrigue is on foot, it is, I am convinced, wholly and solely the work of Don Jose, and no one else."

" You are right, Lazarillo," said Cæsar, " you are right. Jose is a villain, and the day may come soon, when I shall tell him as much to his face. This intrigue, which you overheard him mention to the queen, may or may not be a reality, for so sinuous and intricate are Jose's actions, that one may well doubt that which he asserts. There is, however, some mystery in the whole transaction, which it is just as well I am alive to fathom. I have given my name to a woman, and if my imagination does not deceive me, to a young and fair one, and it shall be my care to see that she does not dishonour it. My appearance may be unexpected, undesired; but I will not rest till I have found out this Countess de Bazan. Have you any notion, Lazarillo, of where she is ?"

" None whatever. That she was taken away from the prison in Don Jose's carriage after your supposed execution, I do know, but she is not to my knowledge in his house."

" And you have no clue as to who she is ?"

" None—none; I dare not ask questions of any one, and even if I were to do so, and run the risk of it coming to Don Jose's knowledge, I much doubt if I could get any information, for I believe he treats me more confidentially than he does any one else, and what I do not know, it is not likely any other member of his household is acquainted with."

" True, true ; you are quite right, Lazarillo, quite right ; I must trust to accident to make me acquainted with these matters, which, at present, bear so very mysterious an aspect. Chance may befriend me, and yet I may be able to confound the machinations of Don Jose."

" I would not remain in the service of such a man an hour," added Lazarillo, " but I have a hope that by so doing, I may be able to acquire for you some information. Who knows but she whom you have wedded may be wealthy and noble, and as anxious to see you as you can be to see her. She may be kept from you by Don Jose, who, no doubt, has some intrigue on hand, in the conducting of which to a suc-

cessful termination, he fancies he has made you a tool."

" Such may be the case, boy ; but I confess I view this matter of my marriage now much more seriously than I did at the time it was contracted."

" Do you so ?"

" Yes. Then I fancied myself on the verge of the grave, and it mattered little to me then what became of the name of Bazan—I am the last of my race. The Bazans were born under some vagrant planet, for all have been wild, reckless, and improvident. Some have died in the ranks of the army, some in foreign services, some in duels; for somehow our swords always hung very loosely in their scabbards, and were drawn upon small provocations, so that what with one mode of exit and another, the Bazans, with the exception of myself, have all taken leave of the stage of life. This fact pressed itself upon me, when Don Jose made the offer to protect you, and give me the death of a soldier in preference to that of a common malefactor, if I would bestow my name upon a woman. There was nothing to give but the name, and I gave it freely ; but now that I have retained life, honour forbids that I should be careless of the reputation of my house, which, in honour, is spotless still, whatever may have been the amount of the indiscretions of some of its individual members. For these reasons, then, I will search out her who goes by my name, and I will force her to renounce it if she be unworthy, or protect her in its assumption, if, as my heart would fain believe, I find her a victim of Don Jose instead of herself an intriguante."

" Let me implore you to do nothing rash," said Lazarillo; " for my sake, be cautious."

" I will, boy; you shall not be jeopardised by me."

" Nay, you misunderstand me; I spoke not with any view to my own safety, but yours. It is because you are dear to me that I implore you to be careful in what you undertake, and not needlessly to expose yourself to danger. If there be anything to require personal risk, rather let me do it, Don Cæsar, than place yourself in peril."

" Generous boy," said Cæsar, with a tone of feeling that contrasted strangely with his usual careless manner, " if ever my star be again in the ascendant, you shall have cause to rejoice in making such a brotherly friendship with Don Cæsar de Bazan. But who is that coming towards you ?"

The page looked in the direction Cæsar pointed, and beheld his old master the armourer approaching.

" Stand aside, Don Cæsar," cried the boy ; " he may know you, and he is a man of implacable resentments."

Cæsar smiled as he half hid himself in a doorway, while Lazarillo's old master, the armourer, quickly advanced, and so anxious was he to reach the boy that he never glanced at his companion.

" Rascal !" he cried, " you young villain ! where have you been all these days—where have you been masquerading ? Come to your work, you young villain—to your work !"

" Why, who are you, old maniac ?" said Lazarillo, assuming in a moment all the bold pertness of manner which characterised him when we first introduced him to the reader.

" Why, you rascal, do you pretend not to know me ?"

" Let me have a good look at you. Tell me who you are."

" Why, the armourer, to be sure, who has charge of the arquebuses of the guard."

" Very good. When I want anything done in that way, I'll patronise you."

" Now, you young villain, if you don't come back immediately to your work, I'll—I'll knock you down.

I'll have you taken up, you rascal, I will. Come home this moment."

"Hush, old man. Is it possible you take me for Lazarillo, your late apprentice?"

"Late apprentice! Confound your consummate impudence. Late, indeed! You are my apprentice still, and I will soon let you know as much if there be law in Madrid. I do not leave you now I have found you, and, remember, you have not another Don Cæsar to bring his neck to a halter on your account."

"True. Don Cæsar is dead."

"I know it—I know it; and serve him right, too, for interfering in other people's affairs."

"But, is it possible you were not aware that your apprentice was so full of grief at the death of his friend Don Cæsar, that he drowned himself?"

"Drowned himself, you villain! Why, you are he. I know you well enough, despite the masquerading, comical dress you have on."

"Old man—old man, you are deceived. Touch me not, or you will rue the consequences. I am your apprentice's ghost."

"Ghost!"

"Yes, ghost. Don Cæsar's ghost walks about with me in the streets of Madrid. We can make ourselves visible or invisible when we please."

"Now, was there ever such impertinence. I ——"

"Do you doubt it?" said Don Cæsar, suddenly stepping up to the side of the page. "Do you doubt it, old man? You know me?"

The old armourer, who had no doubt in the world of Don Cæsar's death, for he had received from some of the guard, who were in the habit of coming to his shop, a circumstantial account of his last moments, and how he had fallen with a dozen bullets in his body, was so panic-stricken at the sudden appearance of the man, who, in his mind, was, as the song says, " very bad, indeed," that he no longer doubted the ghostly pretensions of Lazarillo, but dropping on his knees, he began bellowing for mercy, in a voice that would soon have collected a crowd, had not Lazarillo put a stop to it in his own way, by saying,—

"Now you know us, old man. I told you we should disappear when we pleased. You see us one moment, and the next you don't."

The old armourer wore a very high, steeple-crowned hat, and as Lazarillo spoke these words, he, with one blow on the top of it, sent it down completely over its owner's face, who was in immediate darkness.

"Come on," cried the page; and he and Cæsar walked rapidly away, leaving the armourer lying on his back, roaring for help to all the saints in the calendar, and kicking and plunging like a galvanised frog.

It was not then his fault if the whole of Madrid was not soon made aware of the fact that two ghosts were perambulating the city, for he told the horrible tale to every one he met, and with so many additions, too, that no one could hedge in a doubt as to the supernatural character of the meeting.

"It seems, Lazarillo," said Don Cæsar, " that the news of my execution has spread rapidly enough. I have met with no one yet who is not aware of it."

"The guard have gossiped of it," remarked the page; " and it is better it should be so, for it gives you liberty of action which you would not otherwise have, and will save you from interruption."

"Certainly. I will keep up my ghostly character, Lazarillo; and, in the meantime, do you get for me what information you can concerning my countess."

"I will. Where shall we meet again?"

"In the church of San Lorenzo. There are long, dark aisles there where we can confer at leisure. I will be there twice in each day—once immediately after morning mass, and again, one hour before sunset. If you can come to me, do; and if I do not see you, I

shall suppose you occupied with Don Jose, and not blame you for lack of punctuality."

" 'Tis a good arrangement," said Lazarillo. " I dare say I shall be able to meet you."

"What the deuce are you doing with your hand in my pocket, boy?"

"Oh, nothing—nothing. I—I hav'n't got any more."

"More what?"

Don Cæsar felt in his pocket, and found that the page had slipped in several pieces of money. He shook his head as he added,—

"Lazarillo, I know you would be pained if I were not to accept this money from you; and Heaven knows, I have too few friends to inflict any uneasiness on the best, the firmest, and the most esteemed of them all."

"Do you speak this of me?" said the boy, as the tears started to his eyes. "I am but a poor page at best, and you are a Spanish grandee."

Don Cæsar warmly grasped his hand as he replied,—

"The Spanish grandee need not be such a brute as to be dead to every sensation of gratitude. You are my friend, Lazarillo, if you will own the title. I shall never find a better. Farewell, and remember our appointment."

The page could not speak, but he wrung the hand which was placed in his. He tried to say, " God bless you, dear Cæsar," but the words died away in an indistinct murmur, and Don Cæsar, with one of his old smiles, cried,—

"Adieu—adieu, till we meet again. May you live a thousand years, my Lazarillo."

The boy stood rooted to the spot, looking after him till he was out of sight. Then he turned his steps slowly towards the splendid mansion of Don Jose, much pleased at his meeting with Don Cæsar, and determined to stir heart and soul in his affairs, let the risks or consequences be what they might.

"I will discover for him," he thought, " who this Countess de Bazan really is, if it be possible; and, perhaps, by diligence and perseverance, I may find out what Don Jose is aiming at by all his plots and plans. I will closely watch him, and it will go hard with me but I find him out. Knowing that I overheard his conversation with the queen, perhaps he will not be so particular in keeping other matters from me. I wonder what success her Majesty's messenger had with the king. It seems to me that Jose will find it very difficult to meet that messenger, and exculpate himself. Perhaps I shall hear how he has done so. What a surprise it will be to him some day to find that Don Cæsar lives."

Don Jose was not at his own house when Lazarillo reached it, and so, according to general orders he had received, always to keep as near to his master as possible, in case of any confidential messenger being required, the page hastened to the palace, whither, he thought it more than probable, Don Jose had gone.

The minister was not there, for, in point of fact, he had not concluded the interview with Maritana, which we have recorded in the preceding chapter; so Lazarillo having the *entree* to the hall and vestibule, mingled with the court pages and resolved to wait for his master.

There was a youngster, about his own age, lazily lounging upon a couch, and picking his teeth, who said to Lazarillo,

"Have you heard the news?"

"What news?"

"Oh, nothing particular; only a man has been poniarded in the small court-yard."

"What! here!—in the precincts of the palace?"

"Yes, and the king has sent for Don Jose. He

seems ferocious about it, and his eyes blazed like two coals as he looked at the body from a window."

"Indeed."

"Yes. We hav'n't had an assassination here for some time. It has disturbed the monotony of to-day. Oh, by the bye, you belong to his excellency the minister, don't you?"

"Yes."

"Is he liberal?"

"Yes, yes; but who is the man who has been murdered?"

"They say he belongs to the queen's suite."

"Do you know him?"

"I do not, by name, though I have often seen him about the court."

Lazarillo's heart beat audibly, and a thrilling sensa-tion of horror ran through his veins. Then he again said,—

"And has no effort been made to take the assassin?"

"What would be the use?"

"How! what do you mean?"

"Why, most likely, he has already taken refuge in the sanctuary of the cathedral."

"Ah, that sanctuary!"

"But, between ourselves," said the page, in a whis-per, "there may be, perhaps, a more powerful reason why he is not taken."

"Indeed!"

"Ay; somebody in power may know more of it than they care to confess."

Lazarillo now passed out of the hall, and made his way, with sad misgivings, to the court-yard, where

he had so recently parted with the queen's messenger. The body lay where it had fallen—a cloak was thrown over it, which had sunk down to the still proportions, and made the spectacle one of more terror to the imagination, if possible, than would have been the uncovered witness of the frightful tragedy that had been enacted.

The boy trembled, and well he might, before he could gain courage to lift a corner of the cloak and look upon the face of the dead man; and yet he felt impelled, by a strong feeling of curiosity, to know if it was the queen's messenger, and if Don Jose had really taken so desperate a means of preventing the letter and explanations with which he was charged from coming to the ears of the king. A sickening sensation came over him, and he turned a death-like paleness as he stooped to lift the portion of the cloak that covered the face. His hand shook, and for a moment every object swam around him. Then he raised it—one glance was sufficient—with a shudder he dropped the ensanguined covering and staggered from the spot, whispering to himself in horrified and startled accents,

"It is he!—it is he!—it is he!"

Then Lazarillo had to lean against a column for some moments before he could recover the shock that dreadful spectacle had given him sufficiently before he could proceed to the hall again. He drew a long breath as he said—

"The villain Jose! The murderer! This is his work, and, oh! God forgive me, I was the unconscious agent who conducted that murdered man to so horri-ble a death. I must leave this service, or it will kill me. Justice cries aloud against this monster, Don Jose, and if I remain longer in his service it shall now be as well to take measures to punish him for his crimes, as for the sake of my dear friend Cæsar. Oh, who could suppose that he and Jose belonged to the same species—alike, but, oh! how different. The one a man, the other a fiend in human shape."

As Lazarillo reached the palace front again, Don Jose's carriage dashed up, and the minister alighted with as serene a countenance as if that day had not added the guilt of another murder to his soul.

He saw Lazarillo, and, as he passed him, he said—

"Wait here within call—I may want you."

The boy could not speak to him, but turned aside with a shudder, which Jose took no notice of, but, with a courtly smile, passed through the troops of lacqueys who received him, and gave his name to the major domo, who loudly echoed it up the grand staircase until it reached the king, who was waiting with the most frightful nervous impatience for the arrival of his villanous minister.

CHAPTER XXV.

THE RING.—THE KING'S RAGE.—PREPARATIONS FOR THE FETE.

WELL did Jose know with what extreme impatience he was looked for by the king, whose ears he had so abused with false insinuations against the queen, and whose mind he had so effectually succeeded in warping from what was right and honourable, to the perpetration of acts at which humanity might well blush, and which are ten times more monstrous when achieved by those who know they are not amenable to human laws for their villanous actions.

It required no courage—no fearlessness of consequences, on the part of Philip of Spain to connive at a cold-blooded murder; and now he was waiting with the greatest impatience—for what? To know if the deed were, even in his opinion, justifiable by the circumstances, *after* it had been committed.

The moment Jose showed himself in the room, where the monarch had endured some hours of tantalising suspense, he sprang to his feet, and, almost verifying the description of the lad, who had described his eyes as blazing like coals of fire, he, in a voice hoarse and grating from passion, cried,—

"Now, Jose, now! The ring!—have you the ring? Resolve me that doubt at once. The messenger is dead. Had he about him the queen's ring?"

"He had a ring, your majesty."

"Quick, quick! Let me see. Tamper not a moment with our impatience, or, by heaven, Don Jose, your head. Oh!—this—this is—the—ring. It was found ——"

"Suspended by the ribbon your majesty now sees about it."

"Yes, yes."

"Around his neck."

"His—his neck?"

"Reposing on his heart. It remains for your majesty to identify it if you can."

"I—I gave it her myself."

Don Jose clasped his hands and cast his eyes upwards, with a groan, as if he would have said, "What dreadful wickedness there is in world, if we innocent, pure-minded people, did but know it."

The king, perhaps, had had some hopes that Don Jose's story would turn out to be imperfect; but this evidence of the ring was too conclusive—well he knew the glittering bauble. In better, happier days, he had himself presented the jewel to the queen, and now, to see it again, invested with such damning suspicions, was gall and wormwood to his heart. He seemed absolutely staggered by the completeness of the evidence against his queen, and for some moments was silent, like a man who has received some unexpected blow of fate, which is too great for expression in any words.

Don Jose was not deceived by this terrible calmness. He could well in his mind predict the storm it was the precursor of, and when the king did recover himself, it was to burst into such a perfect fury of rage, that even Jose turned pale, and felt a momentary alarm at the tremendous manifestation of the passion he had raised.

Jealousy in its most aggravated aspect showed itself on the king's face. His eyes seemed starting from their sockets, and every muscle of his countenance was convulsed. He dashed the ring on to the floor, and stamped wildly upon it, till the room shook again, and the wondering attendants, who heard the uproar, turned pale, and asked each other what was going on.

"Would it were her heart," he cried. "Would it were her heart that I was thus crushing beneath my heel. Curses on her; curses, the bitterest that hate can forge!"

Alas! Philip saw the mote in his queen's eye; but how entirely he overlooked the beam in his own.

"My liege," said Jose, "I pray you moderate this transport of passion. Remember who you are."

"Moderate—moderate. Speak of moderation to a hurricane I know I am a king—a dishonoured king!"

"Nay, sire."

"Peace, I say. I will have her heart's blood."

"Not without more proof than such a solitary circumstance as this can afford."

"Proof, proof! what more is needed?"

"I admit, your majesty, that there are grave grounds for suspicion; but, with humble deference to your majesty, permit me to suggest that it is possible the queen may be innocent, and yet this man have become possessed of her ring."

It was no part of Don Jose's policy to bring affairs to a decided crisis between the king and the queen. All he wished was thoroughly to exasperate both parties, so that the breach between them should be so wide that anything in the shape of a reconciliation should be utterly out of the question. Now, therefore, he wished to allay the storm he had raised, and only leave as its result the stinging effects of strong suspicion—a suspicion which would effectually prevent Philip from paying any attention to his queen, or lending an ear to any just remonstrance or true statement that might reach his ears from her, even despite all that he, Jose, could do to the contrary.

He felt that he might not always succeed in intercepting any communication that should come from Aranjues to Madrid; and, therefore, his policy was beforehand to damnify either letter or message that the unhappy and much maligned queen might find a means of sending to her husband.

"This is strange conduct, Jose," cried Phillip. "You furnish me with proof of my dishonour, and then you set yourself up as the apologist of my queen."

"Not as her apologist, your majesty; but pardon me if I suggest that in an affair in which the honour of a king is at stake, suspicion is not enough warrant for action against a queen."

"What—what mean you?"

"I would say this ring affair is amply sufficient to induce you to look with suspicion upon any communication that may reach you from the queen."

"Communication!—think you we would stoop so low as to receive any communication from her?"

This was just what Jose wanted, and he added,—

"As your majesty pleases; and, moreover, I think that special care should be taken that the queen does not leave Spain secretly, and her actions ought now to be thoroughly watched."

"They shall—they shall."

"I could easily find trusty persons to hover round Aranjues,—aye, even to make members of her very household; and, in addition to that, if your majesty grants me your permission to make visits myself occasionally, I think I may pick up enough to give you the peace of mind which would result from the dispersion of your most justly awakened suspicions, or, by confirming them in their worst form, enable your majesty to act as becomes a king, whose honour has been attacked in its most tender point."

" My judgment tells me your advice is good," said the king ; " and yet 'tis hard to follow it."

" Your majesty, I am sure, would regret any hastier or more violent proceedings."

" Perhaps I should. The church, too, would be upon me instantly, and to silence the thundering anathemas of Rome I would need some strong, unimpeachable case against the queen, who seems so great a great favourite there."

" That is a just and wise remark, your majesty. Have but a little patience, and all will be clear, one way or the other, to an absolute certainty."

" Well—well, I will have patience, although my blood rebels against it. Oh! for revenge—ample revenge! I shall know no peace of mind now, sleeping or waking, until I have avenged my honour as becomes a king."

" Your majesty must endeavour to solace yourself for these sad disagreeables by the sweeter society of one who, I am sure, will become very dear to you."

" Ah! you mean Maritana?"

" The Countess de Bazan, niece of the Marquis de Rotondo, who is your majesty's very humble servant."

" Talking of that lovely girl, Jose, I should not be at all surprised were our queen to use that as some extenuation of her own conduct."

" Oh, scarcely possible ; the cases are so very different."

" Certainly ; I am a king, and, of course—of course ——"

" Must have royal pleasures."

" Just so. It would be hard, indeed, if a monarch could not amuse his leisure without his queen taking advantage of the little affair."

" Very hard—very hard, your majesty ; and yet, from what your majesty knows of your queen, were she to get any notice of this little affair of the Countess de Bazan, no doubt she would think herself extremely ill used."

" She would ; but I have always found, Jose, that women were the most unreasonable of God's creatures."

" Your majesty could not have made a juster remark, and, for the present, to have a consideration of this affair with your queen, and to talk of more agreeable matters, permit me to say that, if to-night, which may be easily done, a little fete be got up here, I will manage to bring the countess to some private room, where your majesty can have an interview with her free from the chances of interruption."

" Shall I not go to the marquis's, then ?"

" I should advise not ; but, if your majesty will wait here, I will engage that soon after ten o'clock the lovely Countess de Bazan shall be here."

" She will come ?"

" Oh, willingly."

" Then I may well for a time forget my faithless queen, whose head shall ultimately pay the penalty of her rashness, when so much beauty awaits me. Make what preparations you please, Jose ; I give you power to act. Throw open, if you will, the grand reception-rooms, and this night, let me hope, will make me happy in the love of Maritana. How does she take her new state, Jose ?"

" Like one born to it, and bred from infancy in royal saloons."

" 'Tis well; the strongest passion ever I conceived for woman that girl awakened in my breast. She shall, she must be mine, Jose, and, the greater the difficulty, the greater the conquest."

The king, as he finished these words, inclined his head slightly, and left the room by another door than that at which Don Jose had entered. When he was fairly gone, a demoniac smile crossed the minister's countenance, and he picked up the queen's ring from the floor.

" 'Tis not much injured," he muttered, " and may be useful yet. Truly, this little diamond, with its small circlet of gold, has caused its share of mischief, —truly there was a royal exhibition of passion, and how wonderfully it calmed down. Yes ; Maritana shall to- night know her real situation, so far, at all events, as regards Don Cæsar. Then, if she will not yield, the last resource must be a declaration on the part of her royal lover, of who he is, and surely the brilliancy of such an intrigue will smother the scruples of the street dancer. But, at all events, let what may occur as regards Maritana and the king, I have poisoned his mind against the queen most effectually, and can now turn all my attention to her. She is something less or more than woman, if I cannot goad her to a retaliation against her husband."

Don Jose, then, with the same pleasant-looking smile that had shone upon his face as he entered the palace, left it ; and, stepping into his carriage, ordered that he should be driven home, where he intended to dine, and then dress for the fete at the poor duped Marquis de Rotondo's, who was busy making active preparation for the reception of his rascally patron, who had got so the upper hand of his weak intellect, that he dared not call his soul his own, if Don Jose had chosen to assert the contrary.

Most anxiously did the poor neglected queen of Philip of Spain wait the return of the trustworthy messenger she had despatched to the palace with her letter, and such full instructions to enable him to answer any questions which the king might think proper to put to him.

Hour after hour passed beyond all reasonable calculation of the time it should have taken him to go and return, even allowing for a considerable delay at the palace, and still he came not. The anxiety of the queen rose to a great height, and she could no longer conceal from the ladies of her suite, or the immediate personal attendants who had followed her to the secluded residence she occupied, that some important and alarming matter pressed upon her mind.

More than once she thought she would send another messenger in search of the first one, and then she would chide herself for her own impatience, and make up her mind to let another hour elapse ere she would allow her imagination to picture any of the crosses or accidents that might have happened to him whom she had taken into her confidence.

The queen, to her credit be it spoken, never for a moment suspected the fidelity of her messenger. Many persons, in her situation of painful suspense, would have fancied that they had been in some way betrayed—perhaps to Don Jose, against whose interests the letter was sure to act ; but she had no suspicions, and her anxiety was painfully depicted upon her countenance.

The reader will not have failed to remark that the anger of the king was so strongly excited by the whole affair, and that he had become so perfectly furious at the sight of the ring, which he so well knew belonged to the queen, that he had quite forgotten even to ask Don Jose if the murdered messenger from Aranjues had been the bearer of any letter ; so that— not that he would have scrupled at any untruth on the occasion—Jose was spared the trouble of raising one to suit the question.

Little, then, did the queen suspect that at the very time, and long before, she was vexing herself at the unaccountable delay in receiving an answer to her letter, that it was quietly reposing in the drawer of a cabinet at Don Jose's house, from whence it was not again likely it would ever emerge to the light of day, unless it might be wanted as an assistance in some forgery of Jose's, for he made no sort of difficulty in setting people by the ears by forging notes, one from the other, where he had facilities of imitating the hand-writing with fidelity.

But at length the shades of evening fell upon Aranjues, and the queen absolutely despaired of the return of her messenger that day, and yet her imagination could supply no plausible conjecture to account for his absence.

The real truth never for one moment crossed her imagination ; that so atrocious a deed as the murder of one simply charged with a mission from her to her husband, whatever cause of disagreement they two might have, should take place within the very pre-cincts of the palace, was too monstrous a notion ever to enter, of its own accord, into her thoughts.

It was some hours now after sunset that she rose from prayer, and intimated to her attendants her de-termination to go to Madrid herself.

They knew far better than she the implacable nature of the king, and the horrible character of Don Jose. Her aged major domo threw herself at her feet, crying,

"Let me implore your majesty to put off this reso-lution until the morning—then you will be able to reason upon it with a calmer judgment. After all, some trivial accident may have delayed the messenger, which, when explained, will only excite wonder that it was not before thought of. Do not, I pray you, for our sakes as well as your own, do not go to Madrid merely on the suspicion that some wrong has been done to him whom you have honoured with your con-fidence."

Her other attendants joined in the same prayer, and the queen's was not a spirit to resist the entreaties of those whom she knew loved her, and were willing to do her any and every service in their power.

Tears gushed to her eyes as she looked upon the commiserating faces around her, and she said,—

"You shall not implore me to aught reasonable in vain ; I will wait till to-morrow."

"Heaven guard your majesty !"

"I know," she added, "there is no one here who would not advise me to the best of their ability, and I know, too, that the oppressed heart does not always dictate the wisest course of action to its owner ; I will wait till the morrow, and Heaven, in its mercy, then send me happier tidings."

"Amen, your majesty ; all may yet be well."

"I would fain leave Spain ; I have no wish longer to force my presence on one who once loved me, but who now, alas! loves me no more. If my husband can find more satisfaction in the life that he is leading than in my affection, I am willing to go. Heaven grant that he may give me leave !"

The major domo having got this promise from the queen, as soon as, without any show of hurry, he could leave her presence, did so, and, hurrying to the lower part of the lodge, he sought out a youth named Fer-dinand, who was his grandson, and, taking him by the arm, led him into a private apartment, and, having closed the door, he said to him, in a serious tone,—

"Ferdinand, my boy, you, in common with all of us, love the queen, and would do anything for her."

"Anything in the world, bless her !" said the lad, fervently.

"Well, well, you know she this day early sent a messenger to the court, with a private letter to the king, as well as verbal instructions of the most secret and delicate nature ?"

"I know a messenger started, grandfather, and he said he was for Madrid ; but I know no more."

"Well, well, I now tell you. He has not returned, and the queen much fears that some evil has befallen him, in consequence of the machinations of her enemies. She talks of proceeding herself to Madrid, in the morning, to learn his fate, and such a step would sure to be construed to her prejudice, and,

perhaps, make her position much worse than it is at present."

"Yes—yes."

"Well, then, what I want you to do, my good boy, is, between this time and to-morrow's dawn, to ride to Madrid, and ascertain what has become of the queen's messenger, and get back again."

"I'll do it, grandfather, never fear."

"But be careful, Ferdinand. Put thyself in no more danger, boy, than shall be absolutely necessary to serve your queen. If in that cause there should be some risk, meet it fairly, and bravely, and becomingly ; only do not, by any rashness of youth, make danger where none else would be."

"I will be discreet."

"Do so, and Heaven protect you. Remember, you have to go to the palace, and ascertain if the mes-senger from the queen arrived, and if so, when he left."

"I am off."

The lad was soon mounted on a small, fleet horse, to which his light weight was nothing ; and walking the animal quietly, until he got some distance from the palace of Aranjues, so that the sound of its feet should not reach the ears of the queen, he then put it to its speed, crying as he did so,—

"For Madrid—for Madrid ! Hurrah ! what a glorious ride !"

The old major domo having thus adopted the only course which seemed likely to have the effect of pre-venting the queen's journey to Madrid, which he found would be to her prejudice, and which the reader knows would have been frightfully so under the circum-stances of the king's awakened jealousy, retired to re-pose, and, before another hour had elapsed, the calm-ness of sleep reigned in Aranjues on all eyes, except the queen's, and she wept bitterly the whole of that night, as busy fancy conjured up a thousand distressing images of the past, and anticipations of coming woe in the future. She thought of how happy she had once been, and, as is always the case in present misery, she thought of the contented past, where reigned the calmness of peace—a very heaven of delight.

"Alas—alas!" she cried ; "our pains and miseries in this world are all positive and actual ; our pleasures but negative, consisting of the absence of anguish only. Joy has no existence. Would that I were dead !"

*　　　*　　　*　　　*

The faint dawn of morning broke upon the tops of the tall trees, and upon the roof of the summer palace of Aranjues, and still the queen had not slept. She rose, and with now a fixed determination to proceed to Madrid, she commenced, without awakening any of her tiring women, to dress herself for the journey. She had nearly completed her arrangements, and was about to order a horse, and command that two of her household only should accompany her, when the sound of horses' feet coming towards the palace, at a hard gallop, fell upon the ears.

"He comes—he comes !" she cried, and a gush of tears started from her eyes, as she sunk upon her knees and offered up a brief prayer and thanksgiving to heaven.

Nearer and nearer came the horseman, until she heard him dash into the court-yard. Then, with a terrible and heart-breaking anxiety, she waited for some one to come to her. Some seconds elapsed, which to her seemed hours, and no one came. She hastily walked into the adjoining apartment, and rang for an attendant.

The old major-domo himself answered the sum-mons, and at the same moment several of the ladies of her little court came by another door into the apart-ment.

"Speak—speak!" cried the queen. "Tell me what news? Some one came from Madrid."

The old man knelt before the queen, and in saddened tones, he said,—

"Yes, your majesty, it was my grandson, Ferdinand, whom I sent for news, to spare your majesty your journey of this morning. He has returned."

"And what of my confidential messenger?"

"He has been murdered."

The queen clasped her hands, uttered a deep sigh, and fell back insensible into the arms of her attendants.

CHAPTER XXVI.

THE FETE AT THE MARQUIS'S.—THE MYSTIFICATION OF ROTONDO.—THE MARCHIONESS'S CHARMS.

THE labour of the Marquis de Rotondo in superintending the getting up the fete was great and most important. The good marquis was here, and there, and everywhere, and grave consultations were held between the marquis and his major domo; and when all was arranged according to his wish, the marquis walked up and down the principal apartment where the guests were to assemble, reviewing all the arrangements, and making such trifling alterations as to him appeared to be requisite.

In truth, the appearance of this magnificent apartment would have done credit to a much more able and cultivated mind than that which could be ascribed to the marquis, who was a creature of fashion, of imitation, and could scarce be a frequenter of gay scenes, and a court, without being somewhat imbued with the same taste, and a desire to imitate the gorgeous scenes that he so frequently witnessed. Besides that, the necessary appliances were always at hand, in the shape of servants and means.

The room was a long one, splendidly appointed, both as regarded the decorations and the furniture. The most elegant and costly designs were visible on the walls, and the gilding that relieved them threw an air of lightness and elegance over the whole, that gave a charm to everything, and struck a stranger with a sense of the magnificence and grandeur of the place, as well as the wealth of the owner.

There were large glasses hung up at either side and end of the saloon, so that the visitors were reflected on either side or end as they passed along, and this gave an idea to those who entered the place that it was of much larger dimensions than it really was; though it was, as we have said, a lofty and spacious saloon, capable of holding a vast number of visitors.

These glasses had the effect also of multiplying the lights and ornaments, and confusing the minds of such as were not used to such a display, so that they could neither tell nor imagine either limit in space or number.

The carpets were most costly, and felt like velvet under the feet. The hangings were gorgeous; the sides were lined with tables, on which were spread costly *bijouterie* and many little elegancies far too numerous and minute to describe.

But one thing must not be forgotten; the splendid and beautiful tinted flowers that ornamented certain portions of the apartment.

Such was the apartment which the Marquis of Rotondo walked through with his hands behind his back, and his red face with his white moustache, and first turned one way and then another, so that he could occasionally view his own person.

"Yes," he said to himself, "I think everything is now arranged. I think Don Jose, my dear friend Don Jose, will approve of what is done; and his most gracious majesty cannot but be gratified at what has been done for his special entertainment."

The Marquis of Rotondo walked backwards and forwards, and felt quite gratified with the result of his own doings.

The Marchioness de Rotondo now entered the saloon, and came sailing along in all the dignity of conscious beauty, rank, and — what is ungallant to say — years; besides, this was so disguised by art, that we are hardly justified in alluding to so unpleasant a theme.

"My dearest marchioness," said the marquis, going to meet her with a juvenile and anxious air, "my dear marchioness, I declare you are daily more charming and more beautiful; indeed, you are, a-hem—yes."

"Oh, marquis," replied she, with a modest side-long glance at the happy husband, "do you think so?"

"Think so, my charmer,—think so? I believe so. Don't I believe so—don't I know it? Oh, marchioness, you hardly know the exquisite nature of your charms."

"Ah, you flatterer," replied the full-blown marchioness, playfully handling her fan.

"I flatter!" cried the marquis, with a start; "dearest, loveliest of your sex, believe me, I am as sincere and as devoted an admirer as when I first knew you."

"Dear, dear," exclaimed the marchioness, with another playful flutter of the fan.

"You are as beautiful as you were. Ah, let me see—thirty years ago. Time does not touch you, dearest."

"But he will."

"Oh, no, no; those charms of yours are exempt from the touch of time. Envious age has no power over you. You are, as I always recollect you, lovely, charming, and youthful."

"Oh, but you are partial, marquis. Your love makes you think so. Now, do you really think I am beautiful?"

"Do I not? Does not every one think so? You are the object of every one's admiration, the theme of every one's praise. Are you not? Why, even Don Jose says so."

"Oh, Don Jose is a very nice man."

"Oh," said the marquis, with a grave shake of the head; "Don Jose is my very good friend, and a man of singular discernment."

"Oh, he is very intimate with the king, is he not? and a very gallant gentleman."

"He is; and, as I said, a discerning man, and one fully capable of appreciating merit, my dear marchioness, and by his aid I expect to be made a stick in waiting. Indeed, I am but waiting the proper moment in which I shall become a stick. What honour!"

"What honour!" ejaculated the marchioness, lifting her hands, and playing with her fan, at the same time she continued to throw killing glances at the marquis, who was as delighted as if it had been a courtship.

They now quitted the saloon, but presently the marquis returned, and shortly after was followed by Don Jose, who walked up to him, saying,—

"Marquis, excuse me, but what a charming creature that marchioness of yours is. I never saw her like."

"Didn't you, now?"

"No, I assure you she is really enchanting. She is, really—quite—a-hem. You perfectly understand me, marquis."

"Oh, perfectly—perfectly. Well, I do think myself she has not altered in the least since I first knew her."

"If she has, it must be for the better. Do you know, marquis, I think you must have some secret means of perpetuating beauty, and rendering it immortal."

"No, no; I assure you it is simple nature; there is no art, Don Jose."

"Then nature has done more for the marchioness than she has done for any one else; you ought to prize her."

"So I do—so I do! I adore her—I love her—nay, Don Jose, I worship her!"

"She is worthy of it."

"She is—she is—I feel she is! Do you think his majesty will be pleased with this sort of thing—eh, Don Jose?"

"Yes, doubtless he will."

"When will he come here?"

"You will not know."

"Not know?"

"No."

"Why?"

"Because his majesty will be pleased to come disguised."

"Aye, but I haven't seen him among any of the numerous guests that throng these halls, Don Jose?"

"But I tell you, marquis, he will come disguised, and therefore designs not to be known; and if you should know him, let me whisper a little advice in your ear."

"Eh—what?" inquired the marquis.

"Don't know him."

"Don't know him!" repeated the marquis; "eh? what!—ah!—hum!"

And the marquis walked about, apparently under the impression that he was compelled to see the drift, but yet was perfectly innocent of understanding anything at all.

"Marquis," said Don Jose, somewhat amused by the marquis's grotesque efforts to appear cunning, but not wishing to show too much contempt, he continued, "you are a discerning man, like myself—you know a little of the world, its ways and manners."

"Yes, yes," said the marquis; "as you are pleased to say, Don Jose—why I do see a few things, and I dare say I may yet———"

"Exactly. Now, if the king comes here in a disguise, he don't want to be recognised—you can see that?"

"Yes, I can."

"Then, if you were to recognise him, you must not attempt to know him."

"Not know his most gracious majesty?" inquired the marquis, much bewildered.

"No; he would scarce thank you for seeing through his disguise."

"Oh, indeed!"

"He will, however, be so well disguised that there will be but little chance of your knowing him."

"Indeed; but I don't see any one mysterious; I don't see him; when will he be here?"

"I don't know—at least, I must not say; 'tis a great secret, you see."

"Oh, yes—I see."

"The best way for you to act," said Don Jose, "will be to believe everybody is his majesty in disguise."

"Oh, yes, I see; but then, if I know they are not his majesty?"

"Why, then, let that make no difference to you, but continue to follow my directions; and should you chance to see his majesty, take no particular notice, because he will not be pleased if you do."

"Very well, Don Jose; you understand his most gracious majesty's wishes, and therefore I will follow your advice."

"Do so, and you will find what it is to contribute a little to the royal pleasure."

"Exactly; oh, yes; I shall be a stick doubtless before long."

"You may depend upon that."

Don Jose now quitted the apartment, and a number of the guests came forward and passed through the saloons; wines and the most delicious fruits were spread about; the rooms were splendidly lit up, and music rendered the whole scene like one of enchantment.

There were none who could refrain from praising the marquis's taste—his wines—and, above all, his marchioness; indeed, to praise the latter was to gain a welcome to the house and all it contained.

Many, indeed, were the congratulations that were made to the marquis and marchioness, who received them without the least suspicion as to their genuineness, and felt happy in the deceit that was universally practised among their visitors towards them.

More than once was the marquis congratulated upon the youth and beauty of the marchioness, of which he was exceedingly proud.

Now loud bursts of music came upon the ears of the guests, and the stately dance became the amusement of the grandees by whom the marquis's fete was attended; for, notwithstanding his extreme folly and dotage, the marquis's balls and fetes were well attended by the grandees, on account of the marquis's rank and riches, for he was descended from one of the oldest houses in Spain.

Hence he was received well go where he would; and his known rank and riches were enough to ensure his saloons being filled with the highest and gayest of the Spanish noblesse.

The dancing was of a stately character, and the many dancers lent a gaiety and animation to the scene, which it would have wanted notwithstanding the beauty of the festal halls.

The splendid and gay dresses of the Spanish nobles and that of their dames, indeed, rendered it a scene worthy of being recorded. Many of these were soldiers by birth and rank, and their costumes were also extremely handsome, so that, taken altogether, few more novel, pleasing, and gorgeous scenes of splendour could, perhaps, be met with out of Spain.

The sounds of music filled the air. No part of that princely mansion was there to which they did not penetrate. The very menials appeared to take pleasure in the scene before them, and their features betrayed satisfaction.

The visitors roamed about and enjoyed the good things collected together especially for them on this occasion; but yet there was one who wandered through this festive scene with anything but a festive spirit.

This was no other than Maritana, who, however well she was treated by the Marquis de Rotondo and his marchioness, yet she was not satisfied. She wandered from room to room, and beheld the many happy faces whom she saw all around her, and she sighed in her own loneliness, when she behold many of the stately dames threading the dance, or walking through the lofty halls; for each had a protector—some one upon whom they could call in the hour of need for succour and support; but for herself she saw none such; she was alone, and he to whom she had been so mysteriously united was not by her side, to render either that love or homage a beautiful woman looks for at such a moment. Her marriage appeared like a widowhood. She sighed for the appearance of him who was to put an end to her uncertainty and her sorrows, for sorrowful enough she felt since her singular marriage, despite the gay scenes around her, and the promises of her self-styled relations the Marquis de Rotondo and his marchioness, as well as those of Don Jose, whom she was impatient to see.

The Marquis de Rotondo walked from room to room, filled with the notion that he would be profoundly polite to every person; for he was not to know which was which, or who was who.

He had been completely mystified by Don Jose, who

had informed him that the king would not be known when he came, and that he would be so disguised that even he, the Marquis de Rotondo, who knew the royal person so well, would be unable to recognise it

This had given the marquis some trouble, for he did not think it barely possible that a king, however wrapped up, could, by any transmogrification become merely an ordinary person to look at.

Much puzzled and perplexed, he approached Maritana, who was looking at some dames who were engaged in the amusement she herself would have felt happy to join; but she was too melancholy and too sad of heart.

"Ah!" exclaimed the marquis as he approached her, rubbing his hands; " do you not enjoy the fete, Maritana?—is not the saloon a beautiful and handsomely fitted up one?"

"Yes," replied Maritana, "it is all that could be desired; but there are other things required to make the heart glad besides music and dancing."

"Yes, yes," said the marquis, " to be sure—that is very right; but have we not all here—all that pleases the sense or mind?   We have choice and rare wines, the pleasantest and most costly viands and confections —indeed everything that is to be had in Spain?"

"You have—you have," replied Maritana; " and yet these things are not those that I allude to."

"Then what can you see wanting?" said the marquis, looking round.

"Nothing that appertains to your entertainment, marquis. 'Tis all beautiful, grand, and magnificent."

"Ah! I thought I had been successful in bringing together all that was necessary to ensure a splendid fete, such as would gratify even a monarch."

"No doubt, when a monarch had nothing else to desire."

"Eh?"

"I mean, however, that there is so much to be revealed respecting myself."

"Oh, yes—ah—indeed," said the marquis, looking a variety of ways, and endeavouring to hit upon some plan of escaping from being questioned on a matter he was profoundly ignorant of.

"Have you seen Don Jose?"

"Oh, yes; he was here some time back, and will be here presently, if he is not here now," said the marquis.

"Had he any one with him?"

"Not then."

"Cannot you tell me anything respecting my relationship to you?"

"I—really—I—but Don Jose can."

"Ah, I see, Don Jose is the answer to every question I ask. He is the depository of all that is mysterious."

"Truly Don Jose is like to be so, from his position of king's minister, and his constant attendance upon his most gracious majesty."

"And the queen."

"Oh, ay, surely he is. Don Jose is in a great many places and posts, and that reminds me he has many posts to dispose of."

"Has he a great many things to dispose of to his friends?" inquired Maritana.

"Oh, yes; there is no knowing what he can or cannot do."

Maritana paused a moment, and the marquis affected to see some one whom he must attend, and at once quitted the apartment, leaving Maritana to herself and her reflections.

She gazed upon the splendid apartments, and upon the happy, or apparently happy, throng who passed through the festive halls. She thought that with wealth and splendour surrounding them on all sides they at least must be happy; while, though she was in the midst of it, she felt herself an alien to it all. She had not the feeling, the knowledge that she was entitled to wealth, rank, and splendour, that she saw blazing around her on every side. She possessed not the knowledge that usually produces that feeling of confidence and independence that so much conduces to all the amenities of high life, even in Spain.

She had not long remained in this dream-like reverie, when Don Jose entered the apartment, and paused to contemplate the beautiful girl who had been thus far the victim of a variety of circumstances that might or might not conduce to splendid misery or misfortune, but which results depended only upon the firmness of character unusual on such occasions.

Don Jose himself was in no hurry to proceed to break in upon the privacy of Maritana; on the contrary, he patiently awaited until she should turn round and see him.

This was not long first; for Maritana moved from the spot, and was about to quit the apartment, when Don Jose said,—

"Maritana."

"Ah!" she exclaimed, turning round short.

"I beg pardon—I should have said the Countess de Bazan."

"Don Jose," returned Maritana.

"Yes, I have come to see you, Maritana."

"To keep the promise you made me?"

"Not this instant."

"Why?"

"Because the moment is not come."

"At what hour?"

"At ten o'clock," replied Don Jose; "and you see it has not yet arrived at that figure on the clock of the marquis."

"It has not," said Maritana. "Another weary half hour to wait."

"A weary half hour, countess? Why? Can time be weary when there is so much beauty, both to catch the eye, the ear, and entrance the senses? Can you be weary in such a place?"

"When the heart is sad, the senses are but little influenced by all these things, Don Jose; sadness is an antidote to it all."

"Indeed! and why then sad, countess? There is enough to make the heart glad."

"There may be; but you know I am yet unacquainted with many things, and I am anxiously awaiting to see the marquis, whom you have promised I shall see."

"My carriage will be here presently, and then you shall see him as I promised."

"I am impatient to behold him; but are you sure, Don Jose, there will be no more unpleasant mistakes?"

"None; all will be revealed to you."

The hour of ten chimed, in a silvery tone, from the clock, and Maritana started at the sound, and, when the last stroke ceased to reverberate, she said.—

"'Tis the hour, Don Jose."

"It is."

"I will immediately attire myself to attend upon you."

"Do so, countess, and I shall await your return to this room."

Maritana quitted the apartment, leaving Don Jose alone, well pleased with the progress affairs had made.

"Well, well," he said, "considering the tools I have to work with, I may congratulate myself upon the modicum of success that has hitherto attended them; but, most of all, I am quite satisfied that the greatest impediment to my success is removed, for Don Cæsar is dead. Yes; that was a great and successful stroke of policy—many a minister would have fallen; but, then, I have no scruples, and Don Cæsar, thank the fates, is dead."

CHAPTER XXVII.

THE HASTY JOURNEY OF THE QUEEN TOWARDS
MADRID.—THE RETURN TO ARANJUES ON MEETING
DON JOSE'S MESSENGER.

THE queen was more than an hour in recovering
from her swoon after hearing of the death of her messenger, and then she did so with a painful struggle;
it seemed to her attendants as though to return to life
and consciousness was to her no welcome or happy
circumstance, and she shut her eyes for some moments,
as if to collect her scattered senses, and assure herself
that all she had heard was not a hideous dream,
caused by some unforseen freak of the imagination.

Her attendants surrounded her, and scarcely a dry
eye had one of them—her grief appeared to affect
them all; and, animated by one kind wish, they
exerted themselves until returning animation assured
them that their labours were not unavailing.

"She lives—she lives!" exclaimed the Lady Inez.
"God be thanked—our dear queen yet lives to bless
us!"

"Amen!" said the ladies, with one accord.

"Do you think her majesty is in any danger?" inquired Lady Inez of the medical men who was called
in on the spur of the moment.

"No," he replied; "but much depends upon circumstances. What might cause a fever and severe
illness in one person, would probably pass off harmless
in another. We cannot usually tell for a short period
after recovery."

"Heaven grant that she may be spared that infliction. Alas! she suffers enough in mind already, and
that would, indeed, be a sad conclusion to misfortune."

"Time will show," said the physician; "but I do
not apprehend very severe results. See! she is recovering from her swoon. I will now leave her in
your hands, and, should my services be required, you
will send for me. I shall not quit the palace."

The physician now quitted the apartment, and the
queen again opened her eyes, and slowly looked
around her.

The ladies spoke not; they remained perfectly quiet
until the queen should speak, lest they should be premature. It was thus they afforded the Queen of Spain
an opportunity to recall all the preceding events to
her mind.

At length she said,—

"Inez."

"Yes, your majesty," said the lady.

"Is it real? Is all we have heard a dream—a
mockery? It cannot be real."

"I would I could say yes, your majesty; but, alas!
I cannot. The news your majesty has heard I cannot
falsify. They are, alas! too true; much too true."

"Then we will proceed at once to Madrid."

"Madrid!"

"Yes, Madrid, Inez. We will go instantly."

"Impossible, your majesty—impossible. Let me
beg, entreat of your majesty ——"

"Nay, Inez, nothing is impossible, that nature is
not violated by its execution."

"Your majesty's health ought to make it impossible, then," replied Inez.

"No, no; health and everything ought to give
place to the urgent necessity that induces me to do
this. I must go, Inez. I will go—it is imperative."

"Heaven forbid that we should do aught to thwart
your majesty's will. We would die to serve you."

"I know it, good Inez. I feel you speak the truth.
I cannot doubt you."

"Your majesty does us no more than justice; but
on our knees let us implore your majesty not to go to
Madrid."

"I must see the king."

"If you will risk your own health, which is so dear
to us all, let us implore you not to attempt to see his
majesty under the influence of such passions as he
must now be animated by."

"Yes, yes, I will see him. I will boldly accuse
him. I will learn whether all that I have endured,
all I have heard, and all that has been done, be not a
dream; and if I find, as I believe, that Charles has
become the slave to his own base passions, and in
the hands of—God forgive me if I err in judgment—
a base, truculent minister, who would pander to the
vices of royalty to maintain an undue ascendancy,
then I will demand a divorce, and obtain the aid of
my own family to get the marriage annulled."

"My gracious lady," said the weeping Inez, "believe me, we share your grief; but think, oh! think
again, before you adopt any such terrible resolution.
You know not what may be the result of any hasty
step."

"It is no hasty step, Inez," replied the queen. "Go
and give orders that we will at once proceed to Madrid;
tell them that everything must be in readiness for our
departure in less than an hour."

"Will your majesty take your physician's advice;
he is in the palace?"

"No, no, it is now no time to accede to such request. We feel ourselves equal to the task, and did
we not it should be done. Go, Inez, go."

The weeping lady quitted the apartment not the
less sorrowful for what was passed than she was for
what would probably ensue.

There was, however, no help; and seeing the queen
was resolved, she thought the best she could do would
be to offer no opposition to her orders, as by that means
some little fatigue would be saved, and tranquillity be
gained for the unhappy queen, who certainly was much
in need of it.

The queen retired to her boudoir, and immediately
began to attire herself for the journey; and since her
swoon, she breathed not a sigh nor shed a tear, but
made what preparations she deemed necessary to meet
the king.

The palace of Aranjues was quickly a scene of bustle
and confusion—men were running about at all quarters,
and in less than the appointed time everything was in
readiness for her instant departure for Madrid.

Great as had been the hurry and confusion, none of
it was observable. Everything had been arranged as
it was ordered, and every attendant was at his post—
so much can the merest wishes of royalty perform;
and in this instance, if ever there was a labour of love
performed by servants for even a royal mistress, it did
in this instance fully bear out such a name.

"The train is ready for your majesty," said the Lady
Inez. "I have seen it, and believe there is everything
that is necessary present."

"We thank you, Inez; you are ever ready to obey
our slightest wishes."

"It is my duty, my gracious queen, and glad am I
to do all that can in any way please your majesty—
though I would rather have done anything else than
order what it has been your majesty's desire I should.
Something tells me that his majesty will be more angry
than ever."

"Under such circumstances, Inez, it becomes imperative upon us to act with decision and dignity. The
dreadful fate of my unfortunate messenger makes me
tremble while I think of it. I cannot—will not believe that Charles could devise such a thing of himself,
and probably our presence may be the means of detecting the source whence this crime emanates, and then it
will be some good gained, if it be but as a warning
against future evil, or justice may be done upon those
who executed this wicked act."

"Wicked it is indeed; but does your majesty not

think that you are going to the fountain-head of danger, whence all the troubles spring, and where even your majesty may run great personal risk."

"Surely not, Inez; the king would never employ the assassin's knife against the life of his queen—he could not do that!"

"No, no, your majesty; but those who have done this—who have instigated his majesty to consent to this deed, if he have done so, may perchance for their own safety attempt more, and even raise their hands against your royal person. Crime does not stop short

in its career because it encounters the good and virtuous."

"There is much truth in what you have said, and yet I will go. I understand the nature of the danger I shall have to encounter, but do not think it at all imminent. The only danger I run will be the king's anger, but under such circumstances this must be braved."

The Lady Inez said no more; she could not move the queen: she had urged every consideration she could think of, and had been unsuccessful, and would

say no more, but set about attiring herself to attend the queen. She with a deep sigh quitted the boudoir, and proceeded to her own apartment.

In a few minutes more the whole party were ready. The queen, followed by her own attendants, instantly quitted the palace, and entered the royal carriage, which was standing in the palace court-yard. There were a number of armed attendants, who either mounted the carriage or rode horses by the royal carriage, as well as some outriders, who were likewise armed, according to custom, but without the knowledge or wish of the queen, who however was too much absorbed in thought to take any notice of what had been done by them.

She entered the carriage, and then the palace gates opened, and the whole cortege moved out of the court-yard into the forest of Aranjues.

The queen leaned back in her carriage, and appeared to be absorbed in reflection, and saw not—looked

not—at the many beauties the forest presented at each turn of the road; she was by far too painfully occupied by her own reflections to see or value aught around her; and her attendants, seeing the state she was in, forbore to break in upon her reverie, however painful it might be. There are times when the silence of sorrow and grief is sacred, and such were the thoughts of the queen's attendants, and this prevented them from attempting to break the silence that reigned during this part of the journey.

They had not yet quitted the forest of Aranjues, when they saw at a distance a horseman at full gallop towards them. This caused some degree of speculation among the attendants of the queen, and they endeavoured to ascertain by his dress and appearance whence he came.

This they could not do at first, because of the great distance, but that was diminished each instant by the speed of both the messenger and the cavalcade. Perceiving he was bound to the palace, by his route, the Lady Inez at length broke silence by saying,—

"There is a messenger coming towards us, your majesty; he may come from Madrid."

The queen looked towards the quarter indicated, and saw the approaching messenger, who, recognising the royal cavalcade, called out to them to halt, as he had a message to the queen. He then rode up to the carriage in which the queen sat.

The messenger made a profound reverence to the queen, and awaited her pleasure with a packet in his hand ready to deliver it.

"Whence come you?" inquired the queen.

"From Madrid, most gracious lady," replied the messenger, with a profound reverence.

"What have you there?"

"A letter from Don Jose to your majesty," replied the man.

"Take it, Inez," said the queen; "we will see what this crafty man has to say. It may be of importance to know what even such a man as he says."

The Lady Inez took the letter, and handed it to the queen, who opened it, and read the letter Don Jose had written to her to induce her to remain at Aranjues.

He merely informed her that the king was dreadfully enraged at something or other, and that, for her own safety, she had better remain at Aranjues, and not to think of coming to Madrid.

"What has happened, most gracious lady?" exclaimed the Lady Inez, who had watched the various expressions of her countenance. "Pardon me for thus boldly questioning you, but my devotion to your majesty will I hope be my excuse."

"Read that, Inez. What can be that arch-traitor's reason for thus attempting to persuade me to return to Aranjues, or at least to remain there?"

Inez took the letter, read it attentively, and became much alarmed at its contents. She feared she knew not what might be the result, but she felt that there must be some vile plot afloat to injure the good queen.

"You are terrified, Inez," said her majesty. "Shall I not go and confront this villain, and unmask him to Philip, and thus confound all his vile plots, by what he appears to dread more than all else—my presence in the capital."

"Indeed, gracious lady," replied Inez, "I think you had better even follow the directions of that letter, specious as it is."

"What! take the advice of my enemy, Inez—of a man who—God forgive me if I wrong him!—would stop at no piece of iniquity? Surely it would be to further his plans, and perhaps our own destruction."

"That can never be, gracious lady; but you know not how the king's mind may be possessed against you by this artful and wicked minister, and your majesty may only irritate the king by your presence when he might possibly desire you should be at Aranjues."

"Indeed, let us join the Lady Inez, your majesty, in imploring you to return to the palace. Your majesty may incur the anger of his majesty, who may be led away and deceived by this Don Jose; and Heaven knows what may be the result, should your majesty fall into any of the wicked snares laid to injure you!"

"How can I be injured, save by the loss of his majesty's affection?"

"But what may be lost only in a degree, may be lost entirely. Misunderstanding may be increased, and colour may be given to any vile calumny, by doing so. Let us entreat your majesty to defer your visit a few days, at least."

The queen considered a few moments, as she thought over the different arguments that had been urged to induce her to delay her departure from the palace of Aranjues.

Turning to the messenger, she said,—

"Tell me truly, as far as you know, how is the king and Don Jose engaged?"

"He was at the palace, I believe, your majesty, when I left Madrid."

"Were there any fetes?"

"I believe there was one or two in contemplation," replied the messenger.

The queen remained silent for a few minutes, as if she were thinking deeply upon the events that had passed; but was scarce able to decide on what course of conduct to pursue; each way she turned appeared to be objectionable, from some one cause or other, and at length she sighed deeply, and said,—

"I know not what to do; this is a crisis I had not anticipated. To stay here would be acknowledging myself deserving of the unworthy treatment I have received; and to go on might be to hasten on a matter that Heaven knows I had rather there never had been cause for!"

"Do, dear lady, return to Aranjues; the king will become convinced of your innocence, beauty, and resignation. It is not in the nature of things that such qualities should go without their due reward—it must come in time."

"Ah, well!" sighed the queen, "that time may be on my death-bed, Inez; but I will delay my departure an hour or two—perhaps altogether. Inform the people that we will return to Aranjues," added the queen.

"Have you any commands for my master, Don Jose, your gracious majesty?" demanded the messenger, who had been a spectator and hearer of all that had passed.

"I have none," replied the queen.

"God bless and save your majesty!" replied the messenger, as he quitted the side of the carriage.

The queen graciously returned his salutation, and he immediately returned to Madrid.

It was with a heavy heart the queen returned to the palace of Aranjues. She was much troubled in her mind, and felt more than she was even willing her attendants should see.

She was, however, so well beloved by them, that her misfortunes were theirs also, and her grief was shared by them, and they equally felt the sad and deserted condition of so good and beautiful a woman as the queen.

Silence was scarcely broken, and but little conversation was carried on. Her majesty leaned back in her carriage, apparently absorbed; and a tear was observed to fall from her cheek.

At last the palace-gates were opened, and admitted them once more into the court-yard of Aranjues. The queen looked up at this splendid building, and a thought crossed her mind that how bitter did all the grandeur around her assort with the feelings that now possessed her heart.

Pomp and grandeur of themselves cannot give happiness—neither can the possession of the most exalted virtues ensure happiness. They render their possessor more worthy. Happiness on earth depends upon a combination of circumstances often wholly beyond our control; and if ever that was the case, it certainly was that of the unfortunate and beautiful queen of Philip of Spain.

CHAPTER XXVIII.

THE JOURNEY TO MADRID.—THE INTERVIEW BETWEEN THE QUEEN AND THE BISHOP OF TOLEDO. —ANGRY ALTERCATION WITH PHILIP.

THE queen at once proceeded to her apartment, and when she arrived there, she was about to throw herself upon a couch, when her attention was attracted by a crucifix that stood at one end of the apartment, near a large window.

The blind had been disturbed, and the sun's rays penetrated unimpeded through the beautifully stained glass window, and fell in a strange flooding light upon the cross. The light came from behind, and the form of the cross was bold and prominent; the colours of the light, diversified by the stained glass, gave it altogether a strange and singular appearance, such as the queen had never before seen. It was, indeed, most striking.

For a moment she paused to look upon the strange scene, and then she felt the natural impulse of a pure and faithful heart, in a season of affliction, to seek for aid and consolation in prayer.

Obeying this natural and beautiful impulse, she threw herself before the emblem of Christian faith, and there offered up supplications to the Throne of Grace for aid to enable her to bear with the afflictions with which she had been visited, and to be spared their continuance. She prayed that the heart of her husband Philip might not be estranged from her, but that truth and virtue might prevail.

The sun changed its course, and its rays were more oblique, and now shone directly on the features of the Saviour, and he appeared to look down upon her with an indefinable expression.

She gazed wistfully at the image, and then exclaimed, in a voice of confidence,—

"Yes—yes—it is—it must be so! I will accept the omen. I will look to none for protection and assistance, save in God alone. He rules the hearts of his creatures and of kings; in Him will I trust, and into the arms of His servants will I throw myself for protection.

"The church will grant me aid, and exert its influence to obtain the justice I shall demand. I wish not to impose myself upon Philip; it would be unworthy of me, and I would sacrifice my love, rather than it should be the means of binding him to an object he must, I fear, loath and detest, else he would never act in the manner he has done.

"I will to Madrid this very day. I will no longer remain here to abet his wickedness; for quiet and tame acquiescence is certainly abetting him in a line of conduct alike injurious and dishonourable to himself and to me."

A feeling of relief stole over her mind, and she felt her grief sit lighter than before, and a holy confidence took the place of grief and sadness, and she was now enabled to look forward to the putting into execution a plan she had formed in her own mind.

Before, she was at a loss what to do. Overloaded with affliction, she knew not to which side she could turn for aid and consolation. Now she was more tranquil under the same load of grief, for she believed she saw the means of exchanging her present unhappy condition to one in which, at least, she could not be supposed covertly to permit the conduct of the king to pass unnoticed.

When her attendants rejoined her, they were amazed to see the change in her demeanour, quiet resignation having taken the place of great and active grief; calmness had succeeded the outbreak, but they knew not the change that had been effected, nor by what means.

"I hope your majesty is recovered from your great grief this morning," exclaimed the Lady Inez. "We feared some terrible catastrophe."

"Thank you, good Inez, I am better. Not that I think less of my griefs—not that I think that I have less cause to grieve; but I have a stronger and more powerful consolation, and have more hope than I had then."

"Ah, your majesty cannot conceive what happiness I feel, while I hear you talk thus."

"Yes, there is a change."

"I am so happy you have given up the idea of going to Madrid, your majesty. I argued the worst of consequences from it."

"And I the reverse."

"Indeed, your majesty!"

"Yes, I think that the greatest good is likely to result from it, and have determined to go in a few hours' time."

"But has your gracious majesty considered the anger of the king?"

"I will brave that."

"God grant you a gracious reception, and make it instrumental to your happiness."

"He will, Inez. I have had a sign."

"A sign—oh, what?"

"Nothing but what is simple; but it has made me decide upon this course, and has given me great confidence in myself and the justice of my cause. I am no criminal seeking for mercy."

"No, no, your majesty, we are all aware of that; but there may be powerful reasons for abstaining from visiting Madrid."

"And yet, I have made up my mind to go. I have yet more powerful ones to urge me on, and my duty leads me to do so."

"I trust in Heaven, gracious lady, and your right," said the Lady Inez, with a sigh.

"Ah, there we agree, Inez. It is to Heaven and its servants that I trust."

"How, your majesty?"

"I shall seek the active aid of the church. The clergy will not refuse to lend their influence and succour to one situated as I am."

"No, no, surely not; but will not that measure widen the breach between yourself and his majesty? The clergy are a powerful body."

"And when that power is exerted in the cause of truth and injured innocence, it is a blessing to a nation."

"It is; and I trust your majesty will find its power sufficient to throw its shield around you, and protect you from all harm."

"Amen! Inez."

"Your majesty will not be persuaded to remain at Aranjues, then?"

"No, Inez."

"How will your majesty proceed? Go to Madrid, or to the palaces of the clergy?"

"I shall proceed to Madrid, and then ascertain who are in the city that are likely to aid me, and then either send or go to them, as may appear most convenient."

"Had I thought your majesty would have done this, I would not have entreated your majesty to return to Aranjues; but I feared you might have had an abrupt interview with the king, who would perhaps, have believed that you were unwilling to obey him, and Heaven knows what the plotting of your enemies may have induced him to believe."

"I will know all, Inez. I will know what they mean, and what they have said or done that can have any connection with my name. To let this go any further, without an attempt to stop calumnies and injustice, would be to cause more."

"Oh, your majesty ——"

"And more than all, I do not seek any reconciliation that may be distasteful to the king. If my presence be a clog to his happiness, let me be separated from him, nay, divorced. Our connection is now unequal, while he has neither love nor regard for me. I will quit Spain."

"Heaven forbid your majesty should be reduced to

that extremity ; but if your majesty will go to Madrid, when will you have the carriages ready ?"

" As soon as the sun begins to decline, so that we may reach Madrid in time to see those whom I purpose seeing."

The Lady Inez quitted the apartment of the royal lady, and proceeded to give the necessary orders for the journey.

The queen, besides her intention of throwing herself for protection on the clergy, thought that her presence would probably disconcert Don Jose and some of his schemes, for his messenger had returned, fully possessed with the idea that the intended journey had been effectually put off, and her presence in Madrid was now not likely to prevent any plot of his from being carried on.

This, too, was a motive to persevere in her original intention of visiting Madrid. Since she had a settled plan to pursue, the queen had not exhibited that grief she before indulged in. Other motives now actuated her conduct, while other feelings filled her bosom. It could not be expected that injustice and neglect should fail to sow the seeds of anger, and a wish to enforce justice, or escape from the humiliating position which she at that moment maintained, despite her efforts to avoid it.

The day wore on, and high noon was passed ; the sun's rays were fast losing their greatest power ; they became more angular, and the forest trees of Aranjues threw lengthened shadows across the paths, and afforded an opportunity for those who chose to stroll about thus early to walk beneath their shades.

It was at this moment that the royal grooms were busily employed in getting in readiness those things entrusted to their care, and an hour later the scene was much enlivened by the harnessing of the animals, and soon after the travelling equipage was waiting for the queen.

The Lady Inez thought she would have persuaded the queen to remain ; yet seeing, by her royal mistress's tone and manner, that she had determined upon one line of conduct, she did all she could to further those plans and ends she believed her royal mistress desired to succeed in, and the best way she could do that, she believed, was by implicitly obeying her, and seeing her orders were promptly executed.

There was, however, little need of her superintending care ; the virtuous queen was too well beloved by all not to make it a point of honour among her domestics to see who should best obey her wishes.

" My gracious lady," said Inez, entering the apartment, " all is ready for the journey, just as you desired it should be."

" I have ever found so much readiness and willingness among my people to obey me," replied the queen, " that if it were only from that motive alone, I shall shed many a tear when I leave Spain. I shall always think of them."

" Heaven send that your majesty may not be compelled to have recourse to so extreme a measure. It may happen that the powerful prelates that are in this country may render this quite unnecessary. They have the power, and I do not think they lack the will."

" We shall see," replied the queen ; " unfortunately, of late, the king has paid but little attention to the councils of these wise prelates ; but come, we will at once enter the carriage."

The queen, followed by the Lady Inez and her attendants, quitted the palace, and in a few minutes more the gates of Aranjues closed after the royal cortege, which wound its way through the forest, presenting a beautiful and picturesque scene.

The desire the queen had of reaching Madrid at an early hour in the evening was communicated to the

drivers, and they proceeded at a rapid rate towards Madrid.

It was at the busiest hour in the evening that they entered that city.

The first place the queen determined to go to was the residence of the Bishop of Toledo, the only prelate whom she knew to be in town. To his mansion, therefore, she at once desired to be driven, and finding, upon inquiry, that the bishop was within, she desired to be shewn to his apartment.

The prelate at first was not aware of the quality of his visitor, until he saw her, and then, with a profound bow, he said,—

" Welcome, most gracious lady, to my humble abode. Such an honour I had not thought in store for me."

" Alas, my lord," replied the queen, " I come to throw myself upon the power of the church, and the generosity of its servants."

" Whatever your majesty can desire of them that is theirs to give, to none would it be more readily parted with than to the good and beautiful Queen of Spain."

" Alas, my lord, I want only what they are best qualified to give."

" Then your majesty may command us," replied the bishop.

" I want counsel and assistance," replied the queen, " and the power of the church to aid me in obtaining justice."

" You shall have both, gracious lady," replied the bishop, " as far as the unworthy servants of the church have it in their power to aid you in your desires."

" I expected no less at your hands, and I have not been deceived."

" Inform me, gracious lady, what may be the nature of your wishes ?"

" You must all be well aware that my husband, his majesty, takes but little pleasure in the company of his consort."

" With sorrow, I must confess, we know it too well," replied the bishop.

" I have every reason to believe that he is much aided by his minister, Don Jose—Heaven pardon me, if I wrong him—in seeking other pleasures than his honour and my happiness will permit him to indulge in."

" Don Jose is powerful, and has the king's confidence, but he holds it in consequence of his pliancy in matters not to be lightly mentioned."

" I believed as much. I have been sorely aggrieved by him. His majesty has neglected me, and treated me in a manner highly reprehensible, and seeks the company of others to the exclusion of myself from that place in his affections and position near him which I am entitled to."

" True, most true."

" My honour and happiness are alike injured—ruined by this line of conduct."

" I deeply regret it."

" If I am an object of dislike and disgust to the king, I do not seek to compel him to a forced appearance of regard, that must be as painful to him as it would be to me."

" Certainly—certainly."

" Then my object would be, of course, to free both the king and myself from an union that is no longer agreeable to him, and painful to me from that cause, and the dishonour it brings upon me."

" A divorce, then, is what your majesty aims at ?" said the bishop.

" It is," said the queen ; " and, considering all things, the only course that is left open for me that I can pursue without the charge of selfishness being urged against me by the king."

"There are none who could charge you with such a feeling."

"I do not know that; but such is my object, and to obtain which, I count upon the power and goodness of the church."

"Your majesty may be sure of our aid; but you would then cease to be Queen of Spain," replied the bishop.

"I know that; and I should seek an asylum somewhere out of Spain."

The bishop was thoughtful for a few seconds, and then he said,—

"It will be a matter of much difficulty, I see; but we will do what can be done; but, before we take any step in this matter, there must be some meeting among ourselves to deliberate upon the nature of our proceedings, and what support we may receive from Rome."

"And, in the meantime, what course would you advise me to pursue?"

"You had better see the king, or, at all events, go to the palace, assume your place, or, if he object, to beg him to allow you, thus affording you an opportunity of alleging that you have been refused to be allowed to take your proper place; besides, an interview between yourself and the king may tend either to remove the cause of complaint, or of giving you a greater right to pursue the line of conduct you have resolved to pursue. There is a cardinal here to whom I will relate all that has happened; and, with his powerful co-operation, I doubt not but some good may be done."

Much more good and sound advice did the bishop give the queen, and by the time she arose to quit his mansion, she felt much more re-assured, and then at once resolved to proceed to the palace.

When she arrived there she was astonished at finding everything as though a splendid fête was about to be given.

She entered the apartments that were usually occupied by herself and suite when she was in Madrid. It would appear that no news of this unwelcome and unexpected return to Madrid of her majesty had been named to Philip, whose head was occupied with other thoughts, and he was not aware of her presence until he accidentally met her in a saloon.

"Ah, madam!" he exclaimed, "what brings you to Madrid, when you were supposed to be at the palace in Aranjues?"

"I have come to Madrid on purpose to obtain some explanation."

"Explanation, madam! this is unbearable! cannot I transact the affairs of the state, but you must demand an explanation?"

"I sent a messenger to you."

"I cannot attend to you."

"But he was murdered."

"Well."

"God of Heaven! and can you sanction such deeds? and has the majesty of Spain sunk so low that it must employ the dagger of the assassin to execute its missions?"

"How dare you, madam, speak thus? This is insolence, and must be repressed. You must back to your residence at Aranjues."

"Nothing now remains for me but to seek some asylum out of Spain, where I can spend my days free from dishonour."

"Free from dishonour! Oh, yes, madam; doubtless you would be freer out of Spain than you are in it; but I know all, madam."

"This is scandalous and unjust. I will throw myself into the hands of the church; dishonour and neglect cannot always be borne with honour. I cannot sanction all that has or may happen by the aid of cringing sycophants and unscrupulous counsellors. I cannot submit to such injustice. I do not desire you should be forced to endure my presence; divorced from you, I may know peace of mind, if not happiness."

"Ah, madam, it is true; however, if you do not return to Aranjues, I will. The same roof does not cover our heads at the same time."

"But Don Jose ——"

"I'll hear nothing. Either you go or I; do cease, therefore, to trouble me."

As the king spoke, he abruptly quitted the apartment, leaving the queen bewildered by what had taken place, and unable to decide on the spur of the moment what she should do under the circumstances.

CHAPTER XXIX.

CÆSAR'S SUDDEN APPEARANCE.—JOSE'S CONFUSION AND CLEVER ARTIFICE.—THE BRIDE OF THE PRISON.

ALONE as was our friend Don Cæsar in the streets of Madrid, and not choosing, for various reasons, among which the most prominent was a dread of getting his young friend Lazarillo into trouble, to make himself known to any of his old associates, it is not at all to be wondered at that he sought amusement whenever anything of a bustling character seemed to be going on.

By the liberality of the page he was released from the immediate pressing necessity of taxing his wits to procure the various meals of the day, which, at stated hours, his stomach told him were so very desirable; so that, really, the Don was thrown completely into a state of mental vacuity, unless something should occur of a character to save him from ennui.

To be sure he had ample materials for thinking in a careful consideration of the circumstances which surrounded him, but his was one of those happy dispositions which do not brood over distressful images, and which, with a truly pleasant facility, succeed in casting off, with amazing rapidity, all gloomy meditations.

"I can do nothing just now," he thought, "without running a great risk of compromising my friend Lazarillo; and as I would rather have those twelve soldiers of the guard pointing again their arquebuses at me than such a thing should happen, why, I suppose I must even content myself as I am."

Few of those who had been accustomed to see him in the faded finery which he had cast off in prison never to resume, would have recognised him now in the modest, plain suit for which he had exchanged the rich costume which Don Jose had placed at his disposal. Moreover, he enveloped all the lower part of his form in the ample folds of his cloak, and as he slouched his hat down far over his ample brow, there was very little chance of recognition, unless he should choose to give any one so fair a chance of knowing him as he had done his old friend the tailor, or his equally old friend the wine-merchant.

From street to street he paced, absorbed in serious reflections as to what a very different appearance the city now wore that the carnival was over, to what it did when the wild revelry of that period of licensed enjoyment was at its height. Occasionally he rested himself in some of the public gardens, and the thought had just occurred to him where he should take up his lodgings for the night, which was rapidly approaching, when he heard proceeding from a superb mansion, in the immediate neighbourhood of where he happened to be, such sounds of mirth, jollity, and gaiety, that, by an irresistible impulse, he immediately made his way towards it, and at a glance recognised the mansion as that of the Marquis de Rotondo, of whom, during his, Don Cæsar's, court career of extravagance, he had so often made a butt against which to hurl the shafts of his wit.

"Fools have fortune," said Cæsar, as he paused opposite the brilliantly-illuminated mansion; "now, the owner of yon house has scarcely brains enough to enable him to go through the ordinary duties of society, and yet here he is surrounded by all the most lavish gifts of fortune, living in the midst of all that can delight the senses, or improve the imagination ; paying for a thousand luxuries which he wants the capacity to enjoy, and fancying himself a great man because his mansion swarms with court gallants, who come to taste his exquisite wines, and listen to the music which he can pay for ; while they survey their unsightly persons in the mirrors that adorn his state apartments and reception saloons.

Through the jalousies of the windows Don Cæsar could see the gay faces of the guests, as they flitted to and fro. He could hear laughter mingling with the soft strains of melody which came from unseen musicians ; and, with a feeling of interest which he could not resist, nor did he attempt to do so, for amusement was what he sought, he stood under the portico of an opposite house, and pleased himself by listening to the music which the marquis had provided for the enjoyment of his guests.

Oh! could the crafty, politic, far-seeing Don Jose have imagined but for one moment that the man upon whose death he had so frequently felicitated himself was so near at hand that some couple of dozen steps would have brought them face to face, how sudden an alteration such a piece of intelligence would have made in his plans, and how urgently he would have continued to chance the order of events for that night, upon which he had expended so much ingenuity, and which, in their involuted course of action, partook so strongly of his artful, designing disposition.

How little he imagined with what ease he could have at once performed his promises to Maritana, to the spirit of them as well as to the letter ; but so it is with such exquisite plotters and schemers as Jose. They build an admirable superstructure of designs upon what they think a foundation, which is unstable, and so they find themselves, and all their airy castles, wrecked in an instant by some untoward event, which has transcended all human calculation.

It was nine o'clock, and the music went merrily on, and still Don Cæsar kept his post beneath the portico, watching the flitting faces which passed and repassed the windows, and drinking in, with the soul of an enthusiastic admirer, the strains of melody which poured forth into the night air, subdued sometimes to a more exquisite softness than the notes could possibly present to the ears of the guests themselves, who were nearer than our friend to the source of the melody.

Sad thoughts began to creep over Cæsar ; thoughts of what he then was, contrasted with what he might have been. He thought of the ancient glory and renown of the Bazans ; that renown which had won for them the undying fame in the history of their nation, and which even then descended to him, and visited him with privileges and immunities which many of the wealthiest nobles of the court sighed for in vain.

He thought of the time when he was the centre of some such a gorgeous throng as that which crowded the saloons of the half idiotic Marquis de Rotondo—when music, at his bidding, had filled the air with a heaven of sweet sounds—when rich wines had flowed for him—when courtly compliments had met his ears—when beauty had smiled upon him, and the soft, silvery accents of affection had reached his heart.

" What am I now ?" he said, half aloud ; " what am I now ? What was I once, and what might not I have been with the commonest prudence ? Nay, it scarcely required even prudence ; but I was mad and reckless, and this is my reward—a penniless wanderer in the streets of that city which once rang with themes of my wealth and magnificence—a proscribed man, with

a price upon my head if it were but known that I lived. My only security consists in the belief that I am in my grave. Oh, Cæsar, Cæsar, what follies have you not been guilty of! When all the wild extravagancies of youth are reckoned up, what a fearful catalogue of follies against you would they make ! Indeed, the shorter plan would be to reckon up the few acts of madness which I have not done, and then at once state that I pleaded guilty to all the rest."

This was a very salutary state of mind for Don Cæsar to be in ; but, unfortunately, like most repentances, only came when the means of folly no longer existed, and consequently was just a little too late to be of any practical benefit.

The time crept on, and still he stayed gazing at the Marquis de Rotondo's house, the doors of which were wide open, as was the custom, and the hall filled by lacqueys, in rich liveries, who announced the guests, as one by one they came or took their departure from the gay scene.

He heard many a name that was familiar to his ears, and by about half past nine the street became tolerably well filled with carriages drawn by mules, the servants attending which kept up a chatter of conversation, and were, for the most part, attired in liveries of a necessarily expensive description.

Don Cæsar now was thinking of going, for the music had ceased, and he had just drawn his cloak closely around him, when he heard a neighbouring church clock sound the hour of ten ; and, before the sounds had well died away upon the night air, he was startled as if a cannon-shot had fallen at his feet, for a servant of the Marquis de Rotondo's came to the door of the mansion, and, in stentorian accents, said,—

" The Countess de Bazan's carriage !"

" The what !" thought Don Cæsar ; " oh, it was some mistake. The Countess de Bazan ?—and yet, why should it not be so ? She will rank with the highest of the court with my name ; and, no doubt, she is a guest here. By Heaven! what a chance is this. I have not waited here for nothing ; I may have, after all, a chance of getting a sight of my wife."

In an instant he dashed among the throng of carriages, and reached the door of the mansion just as a splendid vehicle drew up to it. One glance sufficed to show Don Cæsar his own arms richly emblazoned on the panels. He could now no longer fancy that his ears had deceived him, and he at once entered the house ; and, amid the confusion in the hall, was unnoticed, and, without question or hindrance from any one, he ascended the grand staircase with a tumult of feelings at his heart that deprived him for the moment of all power of reflecting upon the probable or possible consequences of what he was doing.

*   *   *   *   *

Don Jose stood looking at himself in a mirror, with such a nice, placid comfortable sort of smile upon his face, that it was a thousand pities to disturb it. He was waiting for Maritana, who had gone, pursuant to arrangement, to prepare herself for her appearance at the palace. All had gone on beautifully smooth, just as he, Jose, wished it. Nothing was amiss—he was succeeding nicely in all his schemes. That evening he would be able to keep faith with the king in placing in his power the beautiful Maritana, who had been so basely betrayed. That night he would tell her he had kept his word with her by introducing her to her husband. Truly he had managed it well—admirably ; and what a great comfort, too, it was, that Don Cæsar was dead. Ah ! that was a matter for deep congratulation, for had he been, by any weakness, permitted to live, what mischief, thought Don Jose, he might have made with all my plans.

Then Don Jose smiled again, and looked at himself more complacently than before, as he muttered,—

" Maritana may yield to the king, fancying him her husband, whom she has sworn to love ; but she won't like him, for Philip, to tell the honest truth, is desperately ugly, while I—a-hem! I flatter myself I owe some of my promotion at court, and many of my successes, to a personal appearance, which no one can find any particular fault with."

Alas! that great men should have such moments of vanity ; but so it is ; Don Jose felt so comfortable, and happy, and contented, as he stood opposite the magnificent mirror, that he began to think himself quite a minion of fortune, and one of the handsomest men, if not actually the handsomest, man in the world. He gave his mustachios a killing curl, and adjusted the large collar which he wore, as he added,—

" Maritana will become mine, of course. She will, on account of her marriage, think it virtuous to love the king, supposing him to be Don Cæsar, and she will find it pleasant to love me, because I am Don Jose. There's nothing like getting the better of people by arraying their virtues and their religion against them. Now, there's Maritana, she will consider herself bound to acknowledge the king as her husband, because, forsooth, she has mumbled some words at the altar. Ah! I have, thank my stars, no such scruples or prejudices to overcome."

The glass into which Don Jose was looking formed the door of the room, which was a large and handsome one, opening into another immediately communicating with the great staircase by a corridor. Just as the smile upon his face had almost deepened to a laugh,—just as he was at the very height of his self-felicitation, and plunged in as profound an admiration of himself as any reasonable man could wish to be, he saw, by the aid of the glass, the door opened, and Don Cæsar de Bazan walk deliberately into the room.

Don Jose was not the sort of man to be a believer in apparitions ; he was well schooled against sudden shocks and surprises, and very much prided himself upon the manner in which he could subdue all awkward signs of emotion ; but here was a circumstance that no human philosophy could combat against. A dead man—one whom he knew to have been executed—one whose death he had managed himself to almost see accomplished, open a door, and walk as deliberately into a room as if nothing at all was the matter.

Every muscle of Don Jose's body became perfectly rigid. The blood seemed to settle round his heart, and then to become as cold as ice ; his very breathing was suspended, and then he stood like a statue, glaring at the mirror in such an agony of soul and body, that his own face became absolutely frightful to look upon in its convulsed agony of terrified expression.

That it was a being of another world all his fears at once told him, and when he saw Cæsar advancing towards him, he thought, or rather he felt, an absolute conviction that his last hour was come.

It was not until Don Cæsar was so near to him that he could have touched him, that terror broke the spell which had rooted Jose to the spot, and then, with an absolute shriek of horror, he turned round and cried,—

" Keep off—keep off—spirit of the dead ! There is extinction in your touch. I know it. Mercy—mercy! Have some pity on me."

He sank on to the floor in an attitude of supplication, while his face, being destitute of every particle of colour, looked like that of some disinterred corpse.

Don Cæsar folded his arms, and looked sternly at him, as he said, in accents very different from those he usually used,—

" Don Jose, where is my wife ?"

" Your—your wife ?"

" Yes ; where is my wife ?"

" Don Cæsar. You look like Don Cæsar."

" No cavilling, Jose ; where is my wife ?"

A faint suspicion ; and, oh ! what a relief it was, began to come over Jose that, after all, the being before him might be flesh and blood, and, rising slowly to his feet, he said,—

" Just tell me, for Heaven's sake, are you an inhabitant of this world, or some pretended spirit, which has assumed the likeness of him whom I believed dead ?"

" I am a living, breathing man, like yourself, Jose. I am Don Cæsar de Bazan. You know me. I much suspect that my death would be more satisfactory to you by far than my living ; but as that is a question which personally concerns me materially, I prefer the latter, however inconvenient it may be to you ; and since I am, by your assistance and contrivance, a married man, permit me to inquire where is my wife ?"

" Then you are no ghost," said Jose, with a long drawn breath, as he wiped the perspiration from his face, which had been induced by the dreadful state of fever to which he had been so suddenly reduced.

" Certainly not."

" But how could you escape the fire of the guard? I heard the report of the arquebuses ?"

" I bear a charmed life. I caught all the bullets, and here they are. Would you like to count them? There are twelve, I assure you."

" There is some damnable jugglery in this," cried Jose, as he knit his brows, and stamped with rage.

" You are right," said Cæsar. " There is too much jugglery by half, and it all lies at your door. I have come for a few explanations, Don Jose, and I will have them ; but, first and foremost, be so good as to introduce me to the Countess de Bazan."

" Your escape, Don Cæsar, from execution," said Jose, after a pause, " is to me inexplicable ; but permit me to offer to you my congratulations."

" Judas!" said Cæsar, " you will not succeed in again betraying me under the guise of friendship. Jose, I heard you ; my death—after I had answered your purpose, by bestowing my name upon some one—was necessary to you. I live, and therefore you are bitterly disappointed. Whatever intrigues hung upon that circumstance you must now give up, for I have no intention of dying to oblige you."

" My dear Cæsar, you ——"

" Psha! this is folly. I have come to ask you for my wife."

" But she is not here."

" Indeed ! Then, who is using the Countess de Bazan's carriage, with my arms emblazoned on its panels ? It waits below—if not for its fair owner, who else ? Don Jose, you look confused—the conscious lie shows itself on your face."

" You are not a good judge of expression, Don Cæsar," said Jose. " I was only surprised that you should have taken up the notion that your wife was fair !"

" Fair ! I cannot be mistaken—" she is beautiful !"

" Indeed !"

" You know she is, Jose. I touched her hand—it was soft and gentle as a babe's ; I heard her sigh—such a sigh never came from other than a young and tender heart ; her figure, manner, but most of all that hand, which was not concealed from me, convinces me she is beautiful. She is my wife—my countess ; she holds now the honour of my ancient name in her keeping. Don Jose, I will see her, and she shall know that her husband lives, perhaps, to confound her as well as you."

Don Cæsar spoke these words with an energy which convinced Jose that a remarkable change had taken place in the character of the once careless, rattling, heedless spendthrift ; and he bit his lips with intense vexation, as he fancied himself nearly at his wit's end to know what to do.

"I thought he said you were a great enemy to matrimony?"

"I was, but I *am* married, and therefore I *will* protect my honour. If I had been in my grave, what would it have mattered to me? I am the last of my race, and, had that same woman bore my name for a few years longer, it could not then have hurt any one; but now I live, the affair becomes of vital importance. Once more, Don Jose, I demand at your hands my wife."

Jose was thinking what on earth he should do to get rid of the man temporally, whom he was congratulating himself he had got rid of altogether; and not many minutes was it before a daring scheme suggested itself to his crafty and politic brain, which was no sooner conceived than he at once proceeded to put it in action.

Putting on a serious face, he said,—

"Don Cæsar, you think harshly of me without cause, and you accuse me of making a victim of you to my schemes. You may not believe it, but the fact is, I did all I could to save your life; but the king was resolved, and had I persevered further, I should only have ensured my own disgrace without benefitting you in the least."

"We will drop that portion of the subject," said Cæsar.

"Well, well. To come, then, at once to your wife; I assure you I meant well by you, and now that you are alive, I think it is my duty to consult your wishes."

"Now you talk reasonably," said Cæsar.

"But, permit me to observe," added Jose, "that, if you do not find her so beautiful as your imagination points out to you now, it is your own fault, for the interview is of your own seeking."

"She is lovely!" exclaimed Cæsar. "My heart tells me she is all that love could wish. Once more, Don Jose, I demand to see her."

"She is here."

"You admit so much? Then no power on earth shall keep her from me!"

"Do not trouble yourself, Cæsar; I have neither plots or plans contingent upon separating you from your wife. If you will see her, you shall; but, once again remember, the interview is of your own seeking."

"It is; I give you all that. Produce her, Jose; let my eyes feast upon her charms, and I shall be happy!"

"Very good; but before you do so, let me make you one offer. You know that you stand in danger of your life; how you have escaped the death the king condemned you to, it matters not—the condemnation still hangs over you—and if I chose to give an alarm, you would be at once seized, and consigned again to prison."

Don Jose, even while he spoke, could not entirely conceal his deep vexation at the thought that it was really not in his power to execute this threat, in consequence of his having actually sent to the prison Cæsar's pardon a few hours after his execution, in order that the fact might come to the queen's knowledge that he had done so, coupled with the insinuation that it was the king's fault that it was too late.

"I know all that," said Cæsar, impatiently, as he slightly touched the hilt of his sword.

"But," added Jose, "I will not betray you; on the contrary, I will provide you at once with the means of quitting Madrid; I will place in your hands a thousand crowns, if you will give me your word of honour as a gentleman to go at once."

"Not for a million."

"As you please. Wait here a moment, and I will bring you your wife."

"Jose," said Don Cæsar, "if you play me false, beware! I wear a sword, and know how to use it."

Jose raised his hand in refutation of any idea of treachery, and then left the room. Scarcely had he been gone a moment, when the Marquis de Rotondo, at a half gallop, came in, crying,—

"My lord! my lord! the guests wonder what has become of your lordship, and I have been hunting everywhere for you, and so has my wife, the beautiful and universally admired——Oh! I beg your pardon, sir—I thought Don Jose was here. Lord bless me! I can't call to mind who you are, but it seems to me as if I had seen your face somewhere."

"No doubt," said Cæsar, "I often go there."

"Eh? oh! Pray, sir, I suppose my beautiful and universally admired wife invited you? Pray, sir, who are you?"

Cæsar walked to and fro, betraying considerable agitation of spirits; and then, suddenly turning to the marquis, he said,—

"Is the Countess de Bazan here?"

"Ye—yes—no—that is, I don't know. God bless me! Don Jose never told me what to say if such a question was asked me. What an odd manner this fellow has!"

"What do you mean by no and yes, idiot?"

"Idiot! Well, that's civil in one's own house! Are you aware, sir, that I am a green-stick? Idiot, indeed! I am quite sure my wife, whose beauty is so universally admired, has too exquisite a taste to invite any such bear as this to the house."

"Psha! confound you and your wife too."

"Now if this was not a big fellow, I'd let him see what a Rotondo could do; but, after all, he may be a coward. I'll—I'll try—I'll certainly try."

Don Cæsar was still pacing to and fro, and the marquis went after him till he turned, when they were face to face.

"Sir—oh—oh—sir, you have spoken a disrespectful word of my wife, who has been the pride and admiration of the court for more than five-and-forty years, and, sir—oh—sir ——"

"Well, sir?"

"I—I despise the—the nothing—nothing. Bless me, he ain't a coward after all—he'd run me through in a moment; I can see that with half an eye; and then what would become of my lovely wife, and who could be got to fill my court offices as I fill them? Nobody—nobody. Down, down, rebellious heart, and keep me from fighting. I will sacrifice my own feelings of courage to—to expediency—yes, expediency. Sir, I have the honour of going away."

"Go to the devil."

"How very abrupt—and in my own house, too. Oh, if it were anywhere else I should boil over, and have some terrible revenge; but as it is, I will do nothing—nothing at all, however dreadfully aggravating it is."

The marquis was upon the point of leaving the room, when he started back upon encountering Don Jose, who was with great ceremony conducting in the Marchioness de Rotondo, veiled so closely that scarcely any one but her husband could by any possibility have known her.

The presence of Don Jose, however, was a check upon any expression of his sudden surprise, and the cold look with which the minister regarded him, made him recoil back a step or two, and the words " my wife," died away upon his lips before he could give utterance to them.

Don Cæsar, the moment he saw the veiled figure brought in by Don Jose, had no occasion of doubt but that in her he beheld his beautiful incognito, his bride of the prison, to whom, although he had never seen her face, he had become, from the very romantic cir-

cumstances connected with their marriage, passionately attached. A sensation of joy came over him, which affected him so much that he trembled and was scarcely able to speak or move, but stood with his hands clasped, and in an attitude expressive of his admiration and hopeful feelings.

"My wife—my bride!" he said, "my own beautiful bride!"

"Damn it!" cried the marquis, "what do you mean? Your wife, do you say?"

"Yes, yes, my own—my beautiful! Let me lean on you a moment, my friend. You are a stranger to these extacies I dare say, and I never experienced them before."

"Lean on yourself, and be d—d to you," returned the indignant marquis.

"Marquis," said Don Jose, "do I really hear such language from you? I am shocked!"

"But——"

"Peace—peace! do you allow no one to have any feeling but yourself? I am indeed both astonished and afflicted at your strange behaviour."

"Oh, look at her!" exclaimed Cæsar; "there is a magic in her movements—she is my own, my bride, whom I never thought to have seen again; when I went to my death I dared not think of her, lest my courage should vanish, and I should, in my despair at the loss of such a treasure, meet my doom in a manner unworthy of a Bazan."

"He's mad!" cried the marquis; "they are all mad, or else I'm mad. I don't know if I am on my head or my heels—indeed I don't know which is my head and which is my heels; perhaps I ain't myself at all, but some one else—what will become of me? I don't know if I am anybody or nobody, or behind, before, or nothing to anything."

"Don Cæsar de Bazan," commenced Jose.

"Good gracious, ain't he dead?" screamed the marquis.

"Receive your bride!"

The marquis sunk on a chair, and Don Cæsar, with a rapid step, advancing to the veiled marchioness, exclaimed, while his eyes sparkled with rapture,—

"This is indeed a moment of pleasure—one which I have dreamt of, and pleased my fancy with the fond hope of one day bringing about, if courage or perseverance could do so much; my wife—my treasure—my beautiful—my countess—chosen of my heart——the devil!"

He had removed the veil, and beheld the venerable countenance of the Marchioness de Rotondo, on whose cheeks artificial white and red lay in sufficient abundance to warrant the notion that it was put on with a trowel and taken off with a pickaxe. A simper sat upon that mouth which was only prevented from shutting by two dragon's teeth. She would have cast a loving glance at Don Cæsar, but an unhappy squint made the tender language of the eyes look as if it was addressed to the chandelier, instead of to him, against whose heart the artillery of so many charms was directed.

"Behold your bride!" said Jose; "she whose unknown charms have been your thoughts by day, your dreams by night—your prison bride, the beautiful incognito, the ——"

"Devil!" added Don Cæsar, as he staggered nearly into the lap of the bewildered marquis.

"Are you he," said the marchioness, "whose

tender sighs have so long haunted my repose—are you ——"

"No, madam; I—I am not—it's some dreadful mistake—I don't feel very well, but yet I am sufficiently master of myself to know that some terrible mistake has arisen. Madam, I do not on any account insist upon your keeping your veil removed; the very air might injure those charms. Heaven defend me, marquis, ain't she a fright?"

"A fright!"

"Yes, a perfect basilisk, a sort of gorgon's head. Fancy any one being condemned to live with such a monument of ugliness—oh, gracious!"

"If you don't like her yourself," screamed the marquis, "don't try to make other people uncomfortable. Damn it, I—I'm mad, stark staring mad!"

"No wonder, if you have got such a wife as I have. Here's a dream of romance blown to the winds! My dear marquis, be so good as to allow me a chair; I feel rather faint, upon my honour. Jose, I forgive you—my eyes are opened now. What a mouth—what tusks! Now, marquis, tell me candidly, did you ever see such a damnably ugly woman in the whole course of your life?"

The poor marquis danced again in the agony of his soul, while Don Jose mightily enjoyed the scene; and the marchioness, who was too far off to hear any of the dialogue between Cæsar and her husband, endeavoured, with an amiable simper, still to attract the attention of the former, who Don Jose had told her was really desperately in love with her, although he was a little mad, and she was not at all to be surprised at anything he should say or do as a consequence of his malady.

He had, likewise, to provide against interruption, sent a servant to desire Maritana not to quit the house for ten minutes, by the end of which time he expected to have fully got rid of Don Cæsar, who had so unexpectedly and so inopportunely turned up, as if to thwart his plans, at a moment when he was congratulating himself upon having brought them so near a triumphant conclusion. But, then, as physicians tell us, a robust state of health is the most dangerous condition we can be in, so is it with human projects; they are never in so ticklish a state as when they appear to be nearly crowned with the most complete success.

CHAPTER XXX.

THE BARGAIN BETWEEN JOSE AND DON CÆSAR.—THE INTERRUPTION AND THE FIGHT.

JOSE now stepped up to Cæsar, and laying his hand upon his arm, he said,—

"You have sought this interview, Cæsar. I do not now attempt to keep from you the information that it was love for you which prompted this lady, at such an extremity of your fortunes, to wish, at least, for a memorial of you continually, by bearing your name. Look at her. Do you not see affection beaming from her eyes?"

Don Cæsar actually groaned, as he replied,—

"My fortunes were never in this extremity before. Jose, just be so good as to give that alarm you talked of a short time ago. I consent to have my sentence carried out. Better be shot than persecuted by such a fright. Marquis, there's a look. Just fancy yourself, now, tied to that woman for life."

"As a gentleman and a man of honour," added Jose, "you cannot now retract. I told her how ardent you were in pursuit of her, and it was only by that argument I induced her to see you. The news that you lived had a startling effect upon her; but when I told her you loved her—that you had named her your prison bride, your beautiful incognita, she replied to me, in heart-stirring accents, ' Don Jose, I will see him. I am, as you know, rich; but he shall have with me all the gifts of fortune, and in his arms I ——' "

"That'll do," said Cæsar, as he gave his countenance a twist, expressive of great agony. "Do be so good as to call the guard."

"No, no. Go and speak to your wife."

"My wife! Gracious Providence, my wife!"

"She is a very good woman."

"By Heavens! she had need to be. A person who is neither useful nor ornamental had better be out of the world altogether."

With tardy footsteps Don Cæsar approached the marchioness, but he took care to pause before he got within arm's length; "For who knows," thought he, "but, in the ardour of her affection, she might embrace me," and then, in perturbed accents, he addressed her,—

"Madam, the—the—noble—I may say, the exquisite condescension you have shown in consenting to this meeting, never will be forgotten. It has given me a shock, madam, which is quite enough to put me in a cold perspiration—no, I mean, which must awaken the liveliest terrors—I mean, sensations of profound fright—a—a—gratitude. Your exquisite beauty, madam, I will not mention, lest you should think me a flatterer, which is a character I despise—a-hem!"

"Oh, sir!"

"I am dreadfully poor."

"And I rich."

"I am over head and ears in debt."

"I can pay them."

"I'm going to be hung, or shot, or something of the sort, I assure you, madam, as Don Jose can inform you. In fact, at this present moment, I have no pretensions to be alive. I ought to be dead. I am dead in law, and if you will therefore be pleased to consider me so in fact ——"

"Oh, no, I cannot—I will not," said the marchioness; who, considering the very brief instructions she had received from Don Jose, played her part well. "Oh, no! I will shield you from all harm. I will pay your debts, and petition the king for mercy."

"Don't, madam, don't. I am a dead man—I am indeed; and, besides, can I—ought I—will I—dare I take advantage of such noble generosity? No—no. Perish into all sorts of fragments the thought. Madam, if you had been less generous than you are, I might have stuck to you like a leech. Madam, I might have tormented you! but now I scorn to do so. I will not be outdone in generosity, and, I assure you, rather than allow you to make such sacrifices for me, I will go to the very devil. Farewell, madam, farewell! My heart is full; I cannot say any more. I only hope that what I have said is explicit. Jose, why the deuce don't you call the guard? Did you, in all your life, ever see such an extraordinary-looking woman?"

"She is certainly neither young nor beautiful, but her virtue is great."

"Oh, don't let me interfere with it. I am unworthy of her quite. If I can't escape in any other way, just be so good as to have me executed as soon as convenient, will you? You don't look well, marquis."

"Well? How the deuce should I look well? Why, that lady, sir, whose charms you don't seem to appreciate, is no other than ——"

"Peace, marquis," said Jose; "you don't know what you are talking about. That is the Countess de Bazan."

The marquis lay down on a couch, and placed the pillow over his face.

At a signal from Jose, the marchioness appeared to be quite overcome by her feelings, and left the room, after giving utterance to what she thought a sigh, but which, to Don Cæsar's ears, was more like a howl of defiance.

"I regret, Don Cæsar," said Jose, "that you don't seem pleased with your wife."

"Thank you. I am extremely obliged for your commiseration."

"Do you now feel disposed to accept a pension of a thousand crowns per annum, and quit Madrid, renouncing all claim upon your countess?"

"What?"

"A thousand crowns."

"Why, you don't mean to tell me that I am to get a thousand crowns for giving up that horror? You are jesting, Jose."

"Indeed I am not; and if you will sign a paper to the effect that you give up all claims upon your wife, and that you will leave Madrid within four hours, never to return to it, you shall receive a pension of one thousand crowns per annum."

"My dear Jose, you electrify me! Sign a paper—I will sign a hundred papers if you please. A thousand crowns to give up my wife! Hurrah! Why, I would have gone to execution willingly to get rid of her. I'll sign. You are, after all, Jose, infernal hypocrite as you are, my best friend; for if you have made me marry the Gorgon who was just now here, you point out a mode of release."

"Hush! this affair must be between ourselves. I must get rid of the Marquis de Rotondo. Marquis—marquis!"

"Yes, I'm here. Who's who now? Am I somebody, or nobody, or somebody else?"

"Allow me the honour of opening the door for you, marquis."

Jose opened the door of the apartment, and made a very low bow. The poor marquis had no resource but to go away, in obedience to this mute command of the man who held his very soul in bondage; and with a feeling of such absolute bewilderment, that he nearly fell down stairs, he left Jose and Don Cæsar alone in the room where so strange a scene had been enacted.

"Here are writing materials," said Jose, assuming an air of as much indifference as he could, and yet being scarcely able to conceal the exultation he felt at the manner in which he was succeeding in deceiving Don Cæsar. "Will you at once, under your own hand, ratify the bargain you have just concluded?"

"Will I? Of course I will, my dear fellow. The least delay is an age of agony. Dictate the conditions, and if I never wrote anything legibly in my life before, you may depend I shall this most interesting document."

Cæsar sat down as he spoke to a table, upon which were writing materials, and seizing a pen, he waited for Don Jose to commence the dictation of the document which was to release him from, decidedly to his mind, the most terrible and awful embarrassment he had ever encountered.

Jose stood a few paces behind him, so as to conceal the exultant expression of his countenance, and thus commenced the dictation of the paper:—

"I Don Cæsar de Bazan, Count of Orfilla and Chevalier of the Order of our Lady of Loretto, &c.—"

"Yes, yes—go on."

"Do hereby, on the word of a nobleman——"

"On the word of—a—noble—man. Go on."

"Renounce utterly and entirely all right—all title——"

"All right—all—title."

"To my countess, to whom I was privately married in the chapel of the prison of La Guardina——"

"Capital! Go on. We cannot be too precise in a description of her. Shall I put in that she squints, and paints, and——"

"No, no; by no means."

"Very good."

"I renounce all the legal rights of a husband——"

"Yes, don't I."

"I renounce all claim whatever upon her, or control over her actions——"

"Certainly. Let her do just whatever she pleases."

"And I solemnly pledge myself never to come knowingly near her, or to molest her, or to write to her, or seek her society, on any pretence whatever——"

"What an useless paragraph; but here goes. I have written it. Is there anything else?"

"And to leave Madrid within four hours on condition of receiving an annuity of one thousand crowns, to be paid by Don Jose de Santerem."

"By—Don—Jose—de—Santerem. Is that all?"

"It is. Now sign the paper."

"Ha, ha! Upon my word this is a nice morning's work, Jose. Ha, ha, ha! how desperately ugly she is. You can have her yourself, Jose; she would suit you, for you are not the handsomest man in the world, you know. Ha, ha, ha! The idea—my countess!—my beautiful incognito—ha, ha, ha!"

"Sign the paper."

"I will in a minute; but I can't help laughing, to think of my fancying she was a beauty. I—I—ha, ha, ha, ha, ha! I have certainly dreamt of an angel and thought it was my wife. Now, candidly, Jose, did you ever see such a fright?—ha, ha, ha!"

"The paper—the paper!"

"Don't be impatient. She tried to look loving, too, upon my soul she did. One eye seemed directed to the ceiling, and the other into yon adjoining apartment. It was too rich, ha, ha, ha! I shall kill myself with laughing!"

"But the paper! Sign the paper, Cæsar."

"Yes, of course. There's time enough, I say. The marquis seemed hurt because I didn't admire her. Oh, gracious! Is she any relation of his?"

"No, no—none whatever; but conclude this business first, and then laugh as much as you like. I will laugh with you then if such be your humour."

"Will you? I never saw you laugh in my life. Here goes—'Cæsar de Bazan.' There's a large dashing signature. Stop a bit, let me underline that part where I promise not to come near my lovely countess. That part I wish particularly to look emphatic, as if it were no joke. I don't intend it for one; and now, I suppose, I may laugh."

Don Jose stepped forward to take the paper, upon which Cæsar's hand still rested, when, from the adjoining apartment, which was used as a thoroughfare to the grand staircase, and of which a view could be obtained from where Cæsar was sitting, there came the sound of footsteps, and a page, in the gorgeous livery of the Marquis de Rotondo, said aloud, according to the custom of the age—

"Way for the Countess de Bazan!"

In another moment Maritana, attired in a splendid costume, and preceded by several lacqueys, crossed the inner room before the astonished eyes of Don Cæsar, who, at the sound of the name of the Countess de Bazan, had sprung to his feet and regarded the fair apparition that met his gaze with an intensity of astonishment that, for an instant, deprived him of all power of action.

It was but for a moment though that Don Cæsar's surprise stood in the way of his energy: unhappily that moment had been sufficient to carry Maritana from his sight. Resuming all his energy and all his courage he tore the paper which he had just written and signed into many pieces, as he exclaimed—

"A juggle after all!—a trick, Don Jose—a trick! By heaven I ought to have known you better. She is the living reality of my dreams of beauty!—she is my beautiful countess. A trick! a trick!—but thank God failed in the moment of its fancied triumph."

"Hold," said Jose, who was, for the moment, goaded to desperation at the failure of his plan—"hold, you pass not from here a living man."

"Ha!" cried Cæsar, "has it come to this? Welcome, Jose—my sword rests not in its scabbard."

"Guard! guard!—help! help!" cried Jose, as the swords rung together, and the next moment his weapon was wrested from his grasp, and he was at the mercy of his foe, who, had he been a more vindictive opponent, might at once have rid the world of Don Jose and all his plots and artful machinations. Intent, however, only on following the beautiful being whom he had heard addressed so very opportunely as his countess, Cæsar contented himself with dashing aside his disarmed antagonist with a vehemence that flung him to the further end of the apartment, and then he disappeared down the grand staircase with a rapidity that set all pursuit at defiance.

The beautiful Maritana, little suspecting how near she had been to him who held her heart in such secret bondage, had heard angry words, and the clash of swords, and such sounds had added wings to the speed with which she had descended the great staircase. She gained the carriage in an incredibly short space of time, and it was not until she was seated in it, that she remembered she had to wait for Don Jose, who was to accompany her.

By the time Cæsar reached the hall, the numerous throng of lacqueys that were in it had taken the alarm, for Jose's cries had reached their ears, and some half-dozen of them, with more zeal than discretion, threw themselves before Cæsar, and received as their reward, some very uncomfortable lunges from his rapier. Still the delay was something, and it enabled Don Jose to descend the staircase, rush past his late opponent, and gain the carriage where Maritana was sitting, in great alarm.

"To the palace," he said to the lacquey, who opened the door of the vehicle for him. "To the palace—quick, quick."

He flung himself into the vehicle, and the coachman, who well knew his master's humour, lashed the mules who drew it into a gallop, so that just as Cæsar dashed into the street, sword in hand, despite all opposition, the carriage on which was emblazoned his own arms, and which really contained her whom he had a right to call his own, rolled off at a speed which made pursuit madness.

Don Cæsar, however, was in no mood for calculation, and he rushed after the vehicle at headlong speed, until he fairly lost sight of it round several turnings, and was compelled to stop from sheer exhaustion.

"A pretty night's business this," he said, as he dashed his sword into its scabbard. "The villain Jose—but yet I will foil him. All I have now most particularly to guard against, is assassination, for if report does not belie him strangely, he is a man who never scruples to adopt means of getting rid of an enemy. Eugh! how warm a fight and a race, coming one upon the other quickly, make a man. By the mass, I should not wonder if I have hurt some of those scoundrels who stood in my way in the marquis's hall."

He took off his plumed cap to allow the cool night air to play upon his brow. The night was getting very dark and cloudy, and there he was, with a world of fresh information concerning his own affairs, and yet in as great perplexity as ever, to know how to apply it, so as to meet his views. One thing, however, he had achieved, which was a set off against many other evils, and that was, that he had satisfied himself that she who bore his name, was indeed all that his fancy could have loved to picture her.

The glow of pleasure that pervaded his heart, as he thought of the beauty of the face that had beamed upon him for a moment, did not last long, for soon it was alloyed by a still more fanciful feeling.

"She is beautiful," he thought, "but what motive can she have had in becoming my countess but a few moments before my death, which must have been known to her? How fares my honour in the keeping of such an one? It seems to me by the transient glance I had of her, that I had seen her face before. It comes across me like the dim shadow of a dream. When, or under what circumstances I have seen her, I am baffled to think; but no matter, no matter, circumstances have much altered. I have now a pursuit in life, a great object to urge me on. My wife is young and beautiful, she is mixed up with the intrigues of the villain Jose. Of that there can be no manner of doubt, and she uses the name of Bazan, perchance to enhance the value of her services, or her charms. By Heaven, I will not endure so much indignity. I must have been a madman, so easily as I did to lend myself to the infamous views of such a man as Jose, against whom I should with great earnestness have warned any one else, and yet to whose machinations I have so heedlessly lent myself."

Don Cæsar replaced his hat, and in a melancholy mood strolled towards the Prado.

"I am married," he muttered, "and she who has courted my name, shall find that it is a dangerous as well as a high sounding and honourable possession. She shall find that in adopting the title of Countess de Bazan, she has accepted a trust which she must render an account of, or rue the consequences. Now, if I could but meet my young friend, Lazarillo, to let him know what has taken place this evening, I should esteem it a lucky stroke of fortune, for I much fear his interests will be compromised, by my being found alive, instead of dead."

The prado was nearly deserted, so that Don Cæsar, as he paced to and fro, with unequal strides, which denoted the disturbed state of his mind, was not likely to be interrupted in his uncomfortable reflections.

At length, after much more consideration than he usually gave to any subject, he suddenly said,—

"I will to Don Jose's house, and endeavour to see Lazarillo. He may be there, and by going boldly, I may succeed in getting an interview with him, and putting him upon his guard, in case Jose should question him concerning his knowledge of my being in existence."

Acting upon this resolution, he made the best of his way to the minister's magnificent mansion, and considering how little likelihood there was of any of the household, with the exception of Lazarillo, knowing him, he boldly entered the hall, and demanded to see the young page.

It so happened that Lazarillo had not followed the minister to the Marquis de Rotondo's, but he had been commanded to be in waiting before eleven o'clock, at the palace, in case he was wanted on any confidential matter. Had Don Cæsar been five minutes later in making up his mind to call at Don Jose's, Lazarillo would have been gone; and, indeed, as it was, the boy had reached the hall previous to leaving, and when he heard his name pronounced in the well-known accents of Don Cæsar, he was exchanging a word with another of the pages of the minister.

It seemed to Lazarillo such a height of indiscretion for Don Cæsar to come there, that he almost dropped down with fright, when he heard him speak. Rushing towards him, and taking him by the arm to lead him away, he said,—

"I am here, I am here. Good God, Cæsar, how could you think of placing yourself in this danger?"

"To avert a greater," said Cæsar. "Can you come out?"

"Yes, yes; I am going to the palace."

"Is your rascal of a master at home?"

"No."

"Has any carriage come here with my arms emblazoned on its panels?"

"No—no—why do you ask?"

"For good and substantial reasons, my friend Lazarillo. I knew your master was not one of the most virtuous men alive, but from a little conversation we have had to-night, I find him the most thundering rogue I have ever heard of."

Lazarillo made a dead stand, and looked at Don Cæsar with an expression as if he thought he must have gone mad—decidedly mad.

"What's the matter?" said Cæsar.

"The matter—the matter!"

"Yes."

"Why—why you talked of a conversation with Jose! Does he know you are alive?"

"He does, but he don't seem at all pleased with the news."

"Gracious Heaven! what has happened?"

"Why, Don Jose and I had some conversation, which ended in a fight."

"You have killed him?"

"I might have done so, but really I was in too great a hurry to kill anybody. Listen, Lazarillo, and I will detail to you the events of this evening, which have been of a tolerably romantic character, and which, if they lead not to something yet more fortuitous, will very much surprise me."

Don Cæsar then related circumstantially to the wondering page all that had occurred at the Marquis de Rotondo's, concluding by saying,—

"I felt how very important it was that you should be made acquainted with all this, Lazarillo, because no doubt Jose will speak to you upon the subject, and glad am I that I have had this opportunity of doing so."

"And I too, Cæsar," said the page. "I should not have known what to say had he commenced questioning me. There is much in your narrative to surprise me."

"There is, indeed. But you cannot conceive how ugly the pretended Countess de Bazan was."

"That must have been the Marchioness de Rotondo whom Don Jose had persuaded to act the part."

"You don't say so?" said Cæsar. "By the gods, then, that accounts for the horror of the poor old marquis, when I made some remarks to him about his own wife. Oh, what a night of cross purposes this has been!"

"It has, indeed, Cæsar."

"But if this mock Countess de Bazan was ugly, how resplendently beautiful was the real one. Oh, Lazarillo, she was indeed lovely. Come, boy, help me to a guess of who she is."

"That I cannot."

"You cannot! Search your memory for some court beauty with a form of heavenly grace, the face of Hebe."

"I don't know one."

"But she must be somebody, Lazarillo."

"Very likely. But although the pages here have told me there was a Countess de Bazan residing at the Marquis de Rotondo's, I have had no opportunity of seeing her, and I nor they cannot hazard a guess of who she is—or rather who she was."

"I will find her were Jose to hide her from me in the centre of the earth. I will now make it the one sole object and aim of my existence to obtain an interview with her who was so anxious to obtain my name, and force from her an account of how she has used it."

"Oh, be careful, Cæsar—Don Cæsar, beware of Jose. He stops not at even assassination."

"Oh, I guessed as much."

"For my sake, Cæsar, do nothing rash. Leave the matter with me for a day or two, and trust me I shall get you some news of who the lady is."

"I will not be rash, Lazarillo, you may depend I will not be rash. I am not the man I was. Many circumstances have combined to make me think more deeply, and not the least is my affection for you, my boy, for I owe you much love as well as my life."

"Then for my sake, Cæsar, you will keep out of Don Jose's way."

"I will, unless, as it happened to-night, some very strange circumstances throw me again into collision with him,—trust me, I will be very careful, and do you endeavour, all you can, to learn for me some particulars of this lovely woman, who lords it so well as the Countess de Bazan. By Heaven, I love her, Lazarillo, but she must be pure as unsullied snow, or even her wondrous beauty shall not save her from the just contempt of my injured honour."

"I am even now," said Lazarillo, "going to the palace, in obedience to Don Jose's commands."

"The palace? There, then, he has taken my wife."

"Indeed!"

"Yes. The mules—confound the brutes—who drew the carriage, galloped off at so furious a rate, that to attempt to follow them would have been madness, and yet I did so, but of course they soon distanced me. The palace, no doubt, was their destination."

"Doubtless, and there, then, I may chance to hear something of this Countess de Bazan."

"You are sure to do so."

"Depend upon me. But let me implore you, Cæsar, to keep away; you may be my destruction as well as your own by any precipitate act. You will give Jose a certain triumph over you if you are not discreet. Remember that the sentence still hangs over you—remember that Jose has the daggers of assassins at command. Let me implore you not to come near the palace to-night."

"I yield, Lazarillo. For your sake I will not."

"I am satisfied. Let it be for my sake, if you will. To-morrow morning I will meet you in the Church of the Veronica, and then, no doubt, I shall have news for you."

"Be it so. Good night now, and Heaven protect and speed you."

"God bless you, Cæsar; when once I have discovered all I can for you, I will leave the service of this rascal, Jose, for rather would I beg my bread from door to door in Madrid, or live upon nuts and wild figs in the forests of Andalusia, than I would feast upon countless delicacies at the cost of a man whom I cannot but hate and despise."

"Fortune," said Cæsar, "may yet smile upon me, Lazarillo, and if she does, she shall spare you a sunny glance, or she may give me her frowns. You are to me as a brother, Lazarillo, and what may be mine shall be as much yours. Adieu till to-morrow. Be scrutinizing, but run into no danger for my sake. Adieu—adieu!"

CHAPTER XXXI.

THE DESERTED PALACE.—THE CONSPIRATORS.—THE TRAITOR'S DEATH.

IN one part of Madrid there existed, and probably does exist even to this day, a large and deserted palace, or mansion, that had been thus uninhabited for many years, indeed, the oldest inhabitant knew not the time when it had been occupied. The family to whom it formerly belonged were supposed to be extinct, and hence it was that there was no one who attempted to appropriate it to his own use, save the bat or vermin, that roamed about free and undisturbed.

It was a large and gloomy-looking place, and had for ages resisted the efforts of time to destroy its strong built walls. The doors too were heavy and strong, and hence it was that the idle beggars of Madrid had not disturbed the colony of rats that took up their residence there.

It was built of stone, and the doors were formed of oak, studded with large iron bolt heads, that gave it the appearance of a prison, or fortress, rather than anything else. The windows looked like black plates of iron, and long had they been since the accumulated dirt had been disturbed by the hand of man. It was altogether a spot of most hideous and disagreeable appearance—from which the timid and superstitious would shrink, and cause unpleasant thoughts to arise.

It had, moreover, the reputation of being the abode of evil spirits, for on more than one occasion had a strange unearthly figure been seen in its vicinity, and one or two even went the length of asserting that they had seen such figure enter through the great door, and disappear. If this be true, it must have been a spirit, since nothing but the most subtle essence could have gone through an oaken door of many inches in thickness, and not leave a vestige of a sign behind.

These things procured for the deserted palace the favour of being let alone, and even its very neighbourhood became almost deserted, and after a certain hour at night few cared to go near it.

The interior of the palace was strikingly grand; there was not much ornament about, but its features arose from the great simplicity and size of the different apartments, and this added very much to its gloominess.

The dust laid thick upon the floors, and the room gave no echo to the foot as it passed over the boards; the stone passage even sounded not to the iron heel of the cavalier.

It might, indeed, be called the palace of silence and gloom—a palace in which a hermit might dwell, condemned to thoughts of death and perpetual repentance.

Beneath the large apartments on the ground floor, were a large range of rooms and cellars, the extent of which were unknown and unguessed at, many of them difficult of approach, some almost impassable, because not known, and nearly undiscoverable.

There, was, however, one large room that had several entrances, with large and strong doors; it was of great extent, and would have held several hundred people, as well as giving room for entertainment. It was supported by two rows of strong stone pillars, of eight each, and besides these, the walls were of great thickness, and were fully capable of bearing the weight of the superstructure.

But stranger than all this, is the scene that now is open to us. This large subterranean hall is filled with human beings; torches glare from one end of the hall to the other, and a deep, but strong red glare, fell upon their sable dresses and fierce countenances.

The torches had been placed in a convenience attached for that purpose to the pillars—so that no less than sixteen torches threw their united glare upon the fierce countenances of the men who stood in the centre of the hall, each with his sword drawn, ready to strike down intruder or traitor that should venture there.

A better representation, or idea of Pandemonium, and a council of evil spirits, could not possibly be conceived, than the scene which we have endeavoured to picture to the reader.

The conspirators, for such they were, stood face to face on either side of a rude table, at which sat one who, from the peculiarity of his dress, was no less than a cardinal, and several ecclesiastics, who wore the dress that indicated they belonged to the celebrated order of Jesuits.

The rest were men of note, though their dresses were plain, and each wore a cloak that drooped from his shoulders. Their large hats and drooping feathers gave them a singular appearance; indeed a stranger or more fearful assembly can scarce be imagined in the wildest dreams.

The cardinal arose, and, glancing down from one side to the other of the conspirators, he said in a grave voice—

" We are all here ?"

" Yes—yes—the whole."

The cardinal then took a written list of names, and called them over, each one answering to his name, until he finished.

" There have been no defections," he said, satisfactorily. " All have been true. The oath—my brethren —the oath."

The oath was then responded to ; it was a deep and fearful ceremony ; and the oath by which they bound themselves not to make known the fearful league they had entered into to any human being, father, mother, wife, or child—not to give notice or warning to any one whatever by any word, sign, or token—but that they would, themselves, not only keep these things secret, but would charge themselves with the execution of anybody who had, in any manner, broken the oath by which they were bound, in the slightest degree—their swords should pierce his breast, whatever might be his kindred to themselves, even to the nearest.

While this solemn vow was being uttered, each man held his drawn sword in his hand, as if ready to strike that instant, if it were necessary. After this ceremony was performed, the Cardinal di Vinci said, addressing them,—

" You have all met, according to the promise mutually made at our last meeting. It was then agreed to adjourn, for the purpose of obtaining the co-operation of some powerful ally, whose active aid might come to us, should not remonstrance and argument induce our king to grant our urgent prayer for justice."

" We did—we did!" echoed the conspirators.

" And have we not just cause for this ?" inquired one of the nobles stepping forward. " I, Don Guzman de Segovia, declare, that there is no chance of obtaining from Philip of Spain, governed as he is by a vile, truculent, pandering minister, as Don Jose is, those rights and privileges, and that justice we are entitled ; we have been grievously wronged, brethren."

" We have—we have."

" Has not the sanctity of our homes been defiled— our wives and daughters debauched ?"

" Yes—yes."

" Have we not been imposed upon, injured, our rights trampled upon ?"

" Yes—yes."

" Then we have had good cause for seeking justice in the only way it can be obtained ; we must take it, since it be not given."

" We must—we must."

" Then, again, have not unjust fines and imprisonments been levied and imposed," said another conspirator, " and our kindred are endangered as well as ourselves, if we reproach this Don Jose ?"

" True—true."

" It is time, then, for men, for Spaniards, to be up and doing—'tis time that he, whom we love and honour as our king, should be made sensible of the great danger, both to himself and state, by the permission and impunity with which these things are daily done, through his connivance, or at least under the auspices of his minister, Don Jose."

"True—true."

Another conspirator now stepped forward, and spoke in a clear distinct tone—

"And besides all these things that you have alleged, and each of which is a sufficient justification of our present position, there are others, and not least of which are the numerous and even daily assassinations that take place in all quarters."

"It is so—it is so," echoed the conspirators.

"These cannot always be accidental and unprovoked murders, merely caused by the desire of plunder in the outcast."

"No—no."

"If it had been, how comes it that those who thus fall are always some one who was opposed to Don Jose—some one who is obnoxious to him, or who can be no longer of use to him. For a man who knows his secret cannot be safe; he knows not the moment when Jose will deem it necessary to have the unfortunate being's life."

"Too true," they murmured.

"I have lost a brother—he, too, opposed both king and Don Jose; he was disposed of, as no doubt they considered that they would do better to rid themselves of an adversary."

"This is also too true."

"Again—no quarter of the town is safe, from the most frequented places in the public squares to the outskirts of the town, and in the most wretched and retired quarters of this great city. How does it always happen, I say, that none of Don Jose's friends ever fall?"

"That hand that can direct the dagger always discriminates between friend and foe."

"That is the secret; then down with Don Jose, say I,—down with the base and truculent minister who only lives that other men may die; whose only capacity is that of being able to cater for the pleasures of the king, and cares not how the country benefits by the counsel of the wise, nor how ill it prospers under such abominable practices."

"Bravo—bravo!" shouted many of the conspirators, and many of the others cried,—

"Down with Don Jose!"

"Besides all these, my brethren," said the Bishop of Toledo, "there is another, which, though you may not injure directly, yet which you cannot see exist without shame to yourselves, and injury to your future welfare? What has not the church suffered?—her ministers treated with indignity—their counsel and warnings neglected, and their rights invaded. What can we do but seek to restore those things which have existed and flourished together for ages, but which are now thrown away as useless. I tell you, brethren, that secular power is nought of itself, and must bring with it the seeds of destruction.

"Do we not see an instance of this in the state of affairs at this present moment? It is our duty to enforce such an alteration as shall render all the affairs of state flourishing. Heaven sanctions the means to such an end, and we must have the aid of Heaven, or we are nothing—our purposes are vain and fruitless, and the church is one of the oldest and most hallowed institutions the land possesses. These things must be amended, and the nobility, in unison with the holy church, will be the means of effecting this happy change."

"'Tis agreed," said several voices.

"Then," continued the cardinal, "there remain but the means to be considered."

"And they," continued the Bishop of Toledo, "are to be found. But there is one more topic I wish to advert to, and that is the scandalous private life our king lives; the cruel and unjust treatment that the beautiful and virtuous queen receives is unworthy a gentleman and a christian monarch."

"Shame! shame!" echoed through the vaulted room, and the fierce visages glowed in the red glare of the torches, giving a ferocious appearance to the whole assembly.

"This unfortunate and virtuous lady is as beautiful and pure of heart as she is gentle and good. She throws herself into the arms of the church, to whose influence and advice she bows. A restitution of her rights is sought; but that will be no impediment to us, since it will be for the church to advise a divorce or an accommodation short of that. You see, it will add strength to our cause, and is one of those incidents that spring up to aid a good cause by an accession of strength."

"This is a point," said the cardinal, "that may be made much of; yet it must be treated delicately, and, act which way it will, good will result to us as well as to the queen."

"But," said one of the conspirators, "she must not be permitted to know our secret; that would be to court destruction."

"Ay, ay," said several voices.

"Exactly," returned the cardinal; "the queen would deem it her duty to inform the king. No, no; this cannot be contemplated for one moment, it merely forms another item in our catalogue *raisonnée* of grievances, which are enough to cause some states to levy war against their lawful sovereign."

"It is—it is."

"We are Spaniards, noble men, not the toy of a monarch, nor the tools of a vicious minister," said another of the conspirators. "Our faith and station demand reparation, and such we will have if we wring it by force from Philip."

"We will—we will!"

"But," added another conspirator, "we must be united—we must be strong from unity, and also from numbers; having engaged in such a cause as this, it would not be well to precipitate it, and hazard defeat for want of maturity."

"No—no!"

"If we were to do this, to what deaths should we not subject ourselves. The king might pardon us, as he did Don Cæsar, when it was too late. Alas! poor Cæsar, he had many faults, many extravagancies; but he had also great virtues, brethren—many great virtues."

"He had—he had!"

"Again, we must not succeed short of a complete and full success, for if Don Jose lives as minister, and he once becomes acquainted with our persons, he would not hesitate to rid himself of powerful enemies, and, more, successful enemies. What would be our fate?"

"The assassin's knife!"

"Truly it would. We should dare not walk in Madrid after dark; we should scarce be safe in our own mansions, and surrounded by our own servants and friends. Even our very chambers would be but a lurking place to conceal some assassin who was waiting his opportunity to rid Don Jose of an opponent."

"That is but too true a picture of the present," added another of these mysterious individuals. "I have heard that it was but yesterday that a man was poinarded in the very palace itself, and his body lay in the court-yard, and excited no surprise."

"Horrible—most horrible!"

"And, more, report speaks that such things are not looked upon as rarities, which says but little for the morals of a court, when it can look upon assassination with indifference."

" We must not tempt the assassin's knife; there is no courage in that."

" None—none, my friend; but how, then, are we to proceed? We must do something. Our meetings must not end in empty vapourings."

" No," replied the cardinal; " but we must proceed cautiously, because the first step must be followed by others, and, unless we are prepared for what must follow, we shall probably be defeated. If one proposition fails, let us have another to succeed it of greater efficacy. Should persuasion fail, let us have recourse to argument, then demand; and, finally, should all fail, the sword must do its office, and right us."

There was a momentary pause among the conspirators, who looked in each others' faces, and then, sternly grasping their drawn swords, exclaimed in one voice,—

" Then our swords must right us, and may God aid our arms."

Silence being again restored, the cardinal looked at several papers that he had with him, saying, as he took one in his hand,—

" This letter assures me of the support of the holy see. His holiness, the pope, blesses and consecrates our meetings, they being for the restoration of the rights and influence of the church, and of those nobles who have been grossly neglected, and whose houses have been outraged by the wild conduct of the king, aided and abetted by the minister."

" The removal and disgrace of this minister must be one of the objects for which we are thus met in solemn council."

" It is—it is," responded the remainder of the conspirators, with a readiness and fervour that plainly showed what kind of estimation Don Jose was held in amongst them.

" Then," continued the cardinal, " we have a powerful ally in the person of the French monarch, who views with disgust the conduct of Philip towards his nobles, men who are second to none in rank and birth. The peers of France are not thus to be treated, and they yearn towards their brethren of Spain."

This appeared to produce considerable excitement, and an appearance of joy.

" With such a powerful ally as this we shall soon be able to speak boldly to Philip, and compel his attention; and if he will not accede to our demands, and mark us out as objects of his aversion, the revenge of his minister, then, indeed, a body of French troops, under the command of an able general, will be ready at our call to march to our support, and with such as the laity in the country can raise, will form a force which it will be in vain that Philip may try to meet in the field."

" It will—it will."

" So far our views are aided by France. The French ambassador at court here is our friend; he will exert his whole influence with his own court to further our just desires."

" And what may be the price of the interference of France in our affairs?" inquired one of the conspirators.

" She merely requires that she shall be indemnified for her expenses, and that some articles that will be proposed by way of treaty, shall be advocated by you. France is our near neighbour, and a barrier between Spain, and all the world beside."

" The mountains defend our frontiers," remarked one of the conspirators.

" And while Spaniards are Spaniards, they need no one to keep an enemy out at that quarter; the passes may easily be defended," said another.

" It may be so," replied the cardinal; " but when there are dissentions, when shall we be safe? We must either give up our hopes, and those objects for which we meet, and have sworn to pursue until they are attained; if we refuse aid, we destroy ourselves, and lose all hope of effecting the good we desire."

" Besides," added another, " we are not bound to allow Frenchmen more than we deem just."

" Certainly not."

" If France aid us, should we be compelled to have recourse to the last argument, we should, doubtless, owe her a debt of gratitude which we could not hesitate to pay; but this can never extend so far as to interfere with our rights as a nation, nor our honour."

" Most certainly not," said the cardinal.

" Then what have we else to fear?"

" France may require more of us in return than we grant to any other nation."

" And if France do for us more than any other nation, why should we not do, in like manner, more for her? that is, allow her some honourable privilege, or admit some of her produce at a less duty than others; or, perhaps, enter into a treaty offensive and defensive—there can be nothing in all this that can be at all inimical to us."

" No, no."

" I do not like French intrigue," replied the former speaker; " but, nevertheless, since the general feeling is in favour of the addition of strength, I will not object to it. I yield my private opinion to the majority; though, I must confess, nothing but deceit and vanity ever was seen in a Frenchman."

" This being agreed to," continued the Cardinal de Vinci, " I have drawn up a proposition for the signature of the French ambassador."

" That signature will never be obtained."

" Indeed! Why?"

" Because it would, if it fell into the wrong hands, cause a war, or a serious rupture between the two courts, and involve the ambassador, who would, on that ground, refuse it."

" That point I have thought of before," replied De Vinci; " and if he object to sign it, which, as you say, I believe he will, we cannot, in justice to him, urge him to do so; since, to involve the two nations in difficulties, would only be to injure ourselves; at the same time, it would not aid our cause."

" On the contrary, it would attract attention, and we should be left in the shade. Popular opinion would be drawn to the side of the king, who will then be too strong for us to coerce. Don Jose will still continue minister, and we shall continue to be oppressed as heretofore."

" That cannot be borne," exclaimed the conspirators; " we are here met for a specific purpose, and we will carry it out, despite all that can be urged against it."

" And sooner than I would submit to Don Jose, I would throw myself into France, and submit even to a foreign yoke, which must be governed by equity and mildness, or it could not exist, than calmly stand by and see daily injustice, and daily assassinations take place. It is really too horrible to stand still and even think of it."

" And I," said Don Gusman, " am ashamed of the manner in which the affairs of state are carried on; neither honour nor justice is cared for; appearances are not even of any consequence; and, when that is the case, a state is fallen low indeed. We are the contempt and pity of foreigners. As a nation, we have not the influence of a nation beyond our own frontiers. We can be insulted with impunity, and if we are not invaded by the army of a foreigner, 'tis not so much owing to our own power, as to the jealousy which the possession of our fair fields would create in the minds of contemporary nations, and the eagle would be obliged to lose her prey in defending it."

"It is a most true statement of our degraded condition," replied another of the conspirators. "We cannot hesitate. France, with all her notions of glory and aggrandisement, will be the most fitting ally for us under our circumstances, because she can always resist her, should there be any necessity; and, besides, the jealousy of her neighbours would be a sufficient security for our integrity as a nation. We can fear nothing from her, while we may hope everything ——"

"Hush!" exclaimed the cardinal, in a listening attitude. "What sounds are those?"

A breathless silence ensued, each one listening to catch the slightest sound while he held his breath. They grasped their swords as men who have determined to die at bay, rather than submit to the tender mercies of an enemy whom they hate and detest, and whose faith they cannot trust.

"It is my secretary," replied Don Gusman.

"I have strange suspicions of thy secretary, Don Gusman," replied the Bishop of Toledo; "there is something in his appearance that strangely compels me to believe that he is, or would be a traitor, upon the opportunities that has been afforded, or will be. I fear him."

"If I thought him capable of what you insinuate, my lord bishop, my own hand should be the first to strike the blow to rid us of a suspicious man—one wanting opportunity to become a traitor."

"Money to such a man would be a great temptation," said another of the conspirators.

"I believed I saw him near Don Jose's but the early part of the forenoon."

"Indeed!"

"Yes; and, moreover, by inquiries I have made I learn that he has recently conveyed away treasure from your palace. It may be his own; but then it looks as if he were preparing to guard against some event that he calculated would render your palace unfit as a place of security; and I have an anonymous warning in which I am told that he has copies of certain letters to which my name is attached."

"There are none that can in any way commit you," replied Don Gusman; "they only relate to preliminary matters, and can by no means criminate any one."

"I am aware of that; but an insignificant link can connect a long chain."

"Then he shall die!"

"It were better that he should die, than the good cause fail and those assembled perish. I absolve all who may take part in the deed," said the cardinal. "It is a deed of necessity, and one of punishment."

"Strike when he enters!" said Don Gusman.

"Hush!—hush!"

A tall, lean man, with a shifting eye, who looked cautiously around without seeming to do so, now entered, with some papers in his hands. He advanced towards Don Gusman, who, when he came near enough to plunge his sword in his heart, said,—

"Die, traitor!"

The blow of Don Guzman was not a single one, for at least a dozen swords were at the same moment plunged into the unfortunate man. His eye glazed in a moment; he uttered no cry—but he stood, or was held up by the swords of the conspirators; and when they withdrew them, the body fell with a heavy sound on the cold pavement.

"Thus die all traitors!"

"Amen!" added the Bishop of Toledo.

The cardinal then pronounced a prayer, and said, in a low tone,—

"Let the body be buried in some of the vaults, and we will pronounce a burial service over it; an honour he would not have received under other circumstances—he died because it was necessary to our safety."

The conspirators wrapped the body up in a cloak, and, lifting it between them, they carried it to a vault, in the floor of which was a trap-door: this was opened; and, as the body was held over the aperture, the burial service was hastily pronounced by the cardinal, and the body lowered; then, at a given signal, they let go—the body fell; they listened for a moment; and, as it fell, the sound returned was as though it had fallen into water.

The aperture closed, and the conspirators returned to the stone hall where they had first met.

They then agreed to accept the assistance of the French, and settled some minor points among themselves. Their prospects were discussed; but all appeared to condemn the king for his culpable neglect of their interests and the nation's; and at the same time they devoted Don Jose to destruction—this man they hated.

At the termination of the meeting a long prayer was uttered by the cardinal, which was responded to by the Bishop of Toledo.

Suddenly the lights were extinguished, and the whole party were enveloped in the most complete darkness; but their silence was as complete. They quitted the stone hall; and, with noiseless steps, they sought their homes through the streets of Madrid—unseen and unknown. None could tell how they got in or out of the deserted palace.

CHAPTER XXXII.

MORNING IN MADRID.—THE CONFESSIONAL.—THE INQUISITORS.

THE morning broke upon Madrid in all its beauty and freshness. The cool air and gentle wind produced an effect scarce understood in a more temperate climate. Here the great heat caused by the almost vertical rays of the sun at mid-day is intense; and scarce any animal or human being moves about, save under the direst necessity.

Grateful, therefore, is the morning breeze to the Spaniard; 'tis at this hour he hurries to enjoy the delicious coolness that pervades the air, and oft at this hour seeks the confessional, and purges his soul of the yesterday's sin.

The first gray tinge of light is speedily followed by the whole of the sun's beams, for he quickly rises, and throws over mountain and plain a sea of sunlight, that gives life and animation to countless multitudes of beings who live and breathe in its beams.

Not a cloud dimmed the atmosphere, nor cast a momentary shadow upon the scene below; all was beautiful as spring; but it gradually warmed, as at each moment the sun was gradually rising higher and higher.

The long shadow of the steeple of the great church gradually shortened, and the fine building became illuminated, and every architectural ornament became visible and distinct, forming a picture too vivid and beautiful to be easily forgotten.

People were now abroad, moving about as though the mid-day of a more northern climate had come—but no, the Spanish day is only morning and night; mid-day and midnight are alike devoted to repose.

The church was a beautiful and handsome building, and the interior was well worthy the exterior. There was no lack of beauty and ornament, which was unsparingly, but tastefully, laid on; but what is an excess of ornament in a small building, in the large and lofty one before us was by no means more than what good taste would sanction.

The tall marble columns, the beautifully decorated tombs and devices of various kinds, formed a scene one might well dwell upon and admire; then the large windows, which were most beautiful from the devices that were done with stained glass, and when the sun shone in the morning through the eastern window, the marble pavement was a sea of the most beautiful colours, and appeared like enchantment.

To stand and gaze upon such a picture would carry the fancy to realms of thought, making the gazer forgetful of the world to which he belonged.

In one corner of the church was placed the confessional—some boxes, where the penitents entered and confessed to the priest; neither party was visible to the other, there being a partition; through a small aperture the penitent made his confession, and through which the confessor gave the remission that was sought.

The priests usually attended; sometimes some other ecclesiastic, and even a cardinal; but that was rare, and an occurrence scarce ever dreamed of.

This morning, the penitents had nearly all been, and quitted the confessionals. There yet, however, remained one box, at which sat a priest, waiting to see if any chance penitent might come.

A man entered the church with a somewhat unsteady step; he was enveloped in a dark cloak, and his hat was slouched down over his face, so as to render recognition difficult, if not impossible.

He paused and looked round, to ascertain if any one was watching for him. He gave an uneasy glance, but, seeing no one, he walked straight to the confessional, which he entered, and carefully closed it after him.

He fell upon his knees and removed his hat, which he flung down, and appeared excited and much alarmed from some cause.

"Well, my son," said the confessor, "hast thou come in the sincerity of thy heart to confess?"

"Yes, holy father, I have, and to pray to the servants of the holy church to be merciful to me, for my sins are heavy."

"Speak out thine errors, my son; say that the leprosy of thy soul be not past cure. Speak out, and repent."

"I do repent."

"Go on."

"Resolve me, father, a question that will either save me from committing sin, or cause me to make atonement for the past."

"Speak on."

"Is it good to keep a solemn oath?"

"Yes, my son—proceed."

"But I may not proceed if that be so; for I have done that which I fear to think of, and my oath binds me to secrecy."

"Ah!"

"It is so, holy father."

"But the church has power to bind and to loose; therefore, proceed. Absolution shall be granted thee if there be need of it; but no oath can bind thee to secrecy at the confessional—'tis altogether wrong."

"But life may depend upon my secrecy, holy father; I tremble lest I should do more mischief one way than another."

"The secrets of the confessional are never revealed, and, therefore, thou canst not fear anything from speaking out upon what thou dost know; it may be you will do wrong to keep such a secret. An unlawful oath is not binding, and no oath is binding that causes thee to withhold aught from thy confessor; for if thou dost, who shall make peace between thee and thy God! My son, my son, why hesitate! I fear for your salvation—I fear for your faith!"

"Oh, no—no, holy father; I am convinced—I am

convinced! I never doubted the efficacy or power of the holy church."

"Proceed, my son, proceed!"

"Last night, holy father, there was a dark and secret meeting held."

"Ah!" exclaimed the confessor.

"Yes, holy father. The object of this meeting was to concoct measures by which the king would be compelled to do justice to certain of the grandees of Spain."

"Go on—go on, my son," said the priest, in a sudden and energetic tone.

"It was supposed that he has been led by his minister, Don Jose, to commit these acts, and that to ensure the fall of that minister would be to ensure the success of the scheme."

"Ah!"

"We met in the deserted mansion, long since without an owner; there we met in numbers."

"Were there any of the church there?"

"Yes, holy father, there were several. The Bishop of Toledo and the Cardinal de Vinci."

"Ah!—proceed."

"Then it was proposed to call in the aid of the French, in case we were not strong enough to force Philip ourselves. That I objected to, but I was borne down by many voices. French intrigue had made its way even to the very council of the secret brothers, and influenced the majority."

"What happened then?"

"There was much discussion, and the grievances of which we most complained were enumerated, and of these, the secret assassinations were attributed to Don Jose."

"Go on."

"Then it was said that the secretary of Don Gusman was a traitor."

"A traitor?"

"Yes; they said he looked like a traitor, and was condemned to be murdered in cold blood."

"And was he murdered?"

"He was. The unfortunate man entered the place where we were, and when he came into the midst of us, a dozen swords pierced his body, and it was some minutes ere they withdrew, and the body stood up erect, as though it had become rigid, until the swords were withdrawn, and then it fell. After that, it was carried in a cloak to a vault, into which it was thrown, the burial service being said by the cardinal."

"Proceed."

"The cardinal absolved us from the deed, and soon after that the meeting dispersed."

"And you ——"

"Returned to my own home; but the scene made so strong an impression upon my mind, together with the fear of the interference of the French, that I regret I ever joined the secret association, and bitterly repent it."

"My son, your case requires a short consideration. Wait here a few moments, and I will return to you anon."

"I will wait, holy father; but pray have a merciful consideration. I will make amends for the evil I have done. I will propitiate the church, by giving to the value of ——"

"Stay, my son," said the priest. "I must away; but do thou remain here until I return."

"Yes, holy father."

The priest rose, and quitted the confessional, but, when he emerged from it, it was easy to perceive his brow was flushed and troubled, but that subsided almost immediately, and a contracted brow and compressed lip were all the signs that remained of any mental disturbance.

He was by his habit a cardinal. He was the Cardinal di Vinci, the president of the very secret conclave that the unfortunate conspirator now denounced.

He immediately quitted the church, and whither he went could not be seen, but he was soon out of sight of the church.

Little suspected the unfortunate penitent who was in the confessional—of the mistake he had made. Little did he think the confession he had just made was uttered to the man of all others from whom he would most willingly have kept it secret.

Little did he dream of what awaited him; little did he think of the tremendous power that would ere long be brought to bear upon him. He remained in the confessional, not dreaming of the evil that awaited his leaving it.

He thought of the sin he had committed in joining a set of men who were so ready to shed blood with so little provocation, and who were willing to sell their country's liberty to unscrupulous and vainglorious Frenchmen.

His thoughts occupied him for some time, but he at length began to think the return of the priest was delayed for a long time, and to suspect that the holy father had forgotten him.

He, however, awaited his return patiently; he could not quit the confessional then, as he had not received absolution. Indeed, he would subject himself to much inconvenience, if he did so, and perhaps draw upon himself a severe penance for so doing.

It was certain, however, that a great length of time had passed since the priest had quitted the confessional, and something must have happened of which he knew nothing, nor could he know.

Somewhat uneasy, he determined to quit the box, and walk about the church, until the confessor should return to him.

He stepped outside the confessional, and then a sight presented itself, that sent the blood from his lips to his heart. It was two of the officers of the Holy Inquisition, who immediately seized him, one on either side.

If the advance of civilization in Spain has done nothing else of a congratulatory nature, it has at least sufficed, if not entirely to extinguish, to give a great blow to the awful power which, for ages, was exercised by the priesthood, under the name of the most Holy Inquisition for the discovery and the suppression of heresy.

It was some minutes ere the unfortunate man who had been seized by the officers of the Holy Inquisition could recover from the shock into which he had been thrown by this sudden and unexpected occurrence, an event of such a fearful and dreadful nature, that it was enough to cause a weak man to fall insensible, and would blanch the cheek of the most courageous.

"This is some m—m—mistake," he stammered out, as he instinctively drew back.

"We cannot make a mistake—the officers of the Holy Inquisition know their duty too well to mistake their prisoner."

"I meant not to dispute it; but I was at confession; and knew you also the fact, that I was in the execution of the appointed ordinances of the holy church?"

"You will have justice done you; we are not your judges."

The prisoner trembled, but he still walked onwards with an officer on either side of him to prevent an escape.

The Inquisition was a most fearful institution, and when once the ponderous doors of its prison were closed behind a prisoner, he seemed to have lost all hope, his spirits sunk within him, and nothing but the most terrible pictures of cruelty and torture unheard of filled his mind.

The unfortunate conspirator could not account for this, to him, most unexpected occurrence; he ran over in his mind such of his acts and sayings that he thought at all likely to have caused the accusation of heresy, as he not for a moment doubted that he was seized for such a crime.

They arrived at the prison of the Inquisition, a black and fearful looking prison, which was never passed by any one without a shudder of horror at the recollection of the atrocities that were committed there; and it was not without a visible shudder that the prisoner stepped over the door-stone.

The few passengers who had noticed them, hurried from them as though they carried about some contagious disease; indeed, so great was the terror that the Holy Inquisition inspired, that none would have offered him even a glass of water had he been dying for it.

The doors closed, and the prisoner was hurried through a court-yard; entering some dismal passages he was carried to a distant part of the building, and thrust into a dismal cell, into which came just sufficient light to enable the wretched prisoner to see its extent.

It was small, damp, and strong; there was a stone pillar, to which was screwed a heavy chain by an immense staple.

This was a sight that made the unhappy man shrink with horror; however, he was not thus secured, but it made him feel nevertheless the utter hopelessness of his case.

In an agony of despair he threw himself upon the cold stones and shed tears. He was a man who could and who had faced death and danger in battle from open foes; but no courage could fight against the horrors and tortures of the Inquisition—it appalled the strongest and firmest, for there was no mercy, and no hope—to be accused was to be condemned, and condemned was to suffer only such tortures as man, not God, could invent.

"What can I have done—what can I have said that should thus condemn me to these walls, from which none ever escape save through the gates of death? My confessions have been regular, my faith sincere—what could I have done, or even thought?"

The poor man beat his breast in his despair, but he could find no consolation, and no clue to the cause of his incarceration; how long he might remain there without even knowing the cause of his imprisonment, or of what he was accused, he could not tell.

In the extremity of his grief he became insensible; he had swooned.

How long he remained in this state he could not tell, but when he awoke the sun's rays were evidently sinking, and it was verging towards eventide.

Oh! how the unhappy prisoner longed to be on the Prado,—to enjoy the evening walk, the hour of coolness and enjoyment. He feared to hope that he might once again partake in the pleasure of such a scene; for the walls of the Inquisition were too thick and too strong to admit of an escape, and the hearts that kept the keys were steeled against all human emotions—fear, love, and mercy found no place in their bosoms; while hatred, cold-hearted cruelty, and revenge, alone were there, and these were called into being by envy, ambition, and avarice.

It was some minutes after he had opened his eyes, ere the unfortunate prisoner could recollect where he was. By degrees he, at length, remembered how he came there.

He lay there recollecting and recalling to his mind the events of the day; he recollected the mysterious disappearance of his confessor; then the two men who took him into custody, and his being brought hither, but why he could not possibly imagine. As soon, however, as he became conscious of where he was, he started to his feet, with a cry of anguish and despair.

"Great God!" he exclaimed, "can you thus doom your creatures to destruction, as though it were but sport!"

He would have said more; but the sound of approaching footsteps stopped him. He listened attentively, and could distinctly hear the approach of more than one person. The steps were heavy and measured. Oh! how his heart ached, he knew not why, at the sound of those footsteps! How his attention was inexplicably rivetted to them! he could neither think nor hear of anything else; he had no mind for aught else. Those mysterious steps! and yet, why should they be mysterious? He knew not—he could not guess; he breathed short, looked with a longing look at the departing sunlight.

The persons approached the cell-door; they stopped, and the pulsation of the prisoner's heart stopped also, and he staggered a pace or two; but the current of his blood became restored, the door opened, and the two men entered the cell of the unhappy man.

For some moments no word was spoken by either the prisoner or the two men, who stood near the door regarding the prisoner with cold, but bloodthirsty eyes; they were stout, resolute men, of middle age; their heads were covered with black caps, which did not hide the coarse, curly, raven hair beneath, though this was now tinged with grey, presenting a colour well suited to their dispositions and calling.

They were dressed in black garments, and bore something in the shape of a pall; it was coarse, and like sackcloth, but it was black.

Thus they stood, regarding each other for some moments, until one of the men, looking at the sun's rays, said,—

"Prisoner, prepare for death!"

"For death!" said the unfortunate man, in a solemn voice; "and wherefore?"

"We are not your judges, or accusers; but——"

"But what?"

"Your executioners."

"When must I die?"

"When the last beam of sunlight shall quit the wall yonder." And he pointed to the spot where there yet lingered some rays.

"Mercy—mercy!"

The men shook their heads.

"The time is so short; I cannot—cannot prepare to die in so short a time. Think how dreadful it would be to be hurried out of life to eternity with all my sins rank upon my soul. Oh! surely the church will grant me time."

Again the men shook their heads, and looked at the sunbeams.

"Oh! a confessor—let me have a confessor; that, at least, will be allowed."

"No; it will be useless."

"Oh, no, no; besides, I have some important state secrets to divulge. I must have a confessor; you will be rewarded for this act of leniency."

"No, no; you confessed this morning."

"I did—I did; but, oh! to whom was it? Since that confession, I have been brought here. To whom did I confess?"

"To the Cardinal di Vinci."

These words were no sooner uttered than the prisoner sprang to his feet with a cry of anguish. The men looked for the sunbeams; they were gone; and, before he could utter another word, they had buried their long poniards in his bosom, and he fell dead.

CHAPTER XXXIII.

INTERVIEW BETWEEN DON JOSE AND THE MARQUIS.
—THE LETTER.—THE CONSOLATION OF A GREEN STICK.

THERE was some stir in the streets of Madrid as a body of the guards were marched through the streets; not that this was very unusual, but it did not happen to be the relief hour, and the route they took was an unusual one—it led them to the city prison, where Don Cæsar de Bazan was supposed to be shot.

They stopped there, and summoned the gaoler of the prison, who was much amazed to see such a body of men, and he began immediately to look among them for the prisoner or prisoners that they had brought with them; but they were not to be seen.

"You are numerous to-night, gentlemen. Pray, have you any special company? Confound my cough. Eugh! eugh!"

"Where's the governor?" said the captain of the guard, in reply.

"Ah! the governor. Eugh! eugh! Well—eugh! I suppose there's something particular afloat. Any state prisoner—or—or—eugh! eugh!"

"The governor!" repeated the captain of the guard, impatiently; "I wish to see the governor. Soldiers, take position by the gate."

This order was immediately obeyed, and the old gaoler opened his eyes in astonishment, and stopped short in the middle of his cough, and made an effort to speak, but could not.

"Tell the governor I have a communication to make to him, and must see him immediately; and, if you are not more handy in your office, I must order a halberdier to assist you in your errand, by the application of the smallest portion of the end of his bayonet."

This had the desired effect, for the old gaoler found the use of his legs and speech, and said, as he hobbled out,—

"I'm going, good captain—I am gone."

This was the fact, for at that moment he disappeared, but in a short time after the governor appeared, following the gaoler. He appeared very much astonished, and said,—

"I am informed that you desire to see me?"

"I do, sir. I am commissioned by Don Jose to take possession of the prison, and place certain of the authorities under arrest."

"Am I to consider myself so placed?" inquired the governor.

"I have no instructions to that effect, though as your people will be replaced by these men, your authority will at least for a time be abrogated."

"Exactly," replied the governor; "there is one more question I would inquire."

"And what is that?"

"Why," replied the governor, "I should be glad to have some explanation as to the motives for this alteration; for, being so suddenly done, it is scarcely honourable for me."

"I am embarrassed at the question, for I have no other answer that I know of, but that it is according to Don Jose's orders."

"But there is little etiquette in Don Jose's mode of transacting business with those who are inferior to him in station."

The officer shrugged his shoulders as though he thought so too, but declined saying so in words, and then he said,—

"I have got further orders."

"What may they be?"

"To place under arrest the gaolers."

"Indeed! that is somewhat unusual."

"It is my orders."

"I will send them all hither to you; but you had better station men in their places, else they will not know where the keys belong."

"That may be as well."

The officer sent a small party with the governor to take possession of the wards, and when he returned, he had in custody the twelve arquebusiers who had done duty at the execution of Don Cæsar.

"What is all this about? what am I accused?" exclaimed the old gaoler; "eugh! eugh! there's been no escape, and nobody executed by mistake. Eugh! what have I done?"

"Don Jose orders it."

"What have we done? the royal guard were never thus used before. 'Tis an indignity never offered to us before."

"Don Jose orders it."

"But why?"

"I don't know, but I have orders to do it; and he who has the shrewdest guess, may communicate with Don Jose."

"Well," exclaimed the gaoler who had been so terrified at Don Cæsar's supposed ghost, "I can't think what it can be about. True, I have seen Don Cæsar's ghost, and perhaps it's because the prison walls won't hold ghosts, that we are thus treated, or some such likely cause. Was there ever the like known before?"

The officer made no reply, but carried out his instructions according to what were Don Jose's wishes, and a complete exchange was made in the prison.

The guard were very indignant, and complained loudly of their treatment, which they declared could never be sanctioned by the king.

* * * * *

Don Jose in the meanwhile sat in his own mansion, much vexed and annoyed at what had happened. The sudden appearance of Don Cæsar had been a great blow to his felicitations, and one so entirely unexpected, that it could scarce be provided against.

He had been foiled in his attempt to put Don Cæsar off,—the trick of presenting himself with the Marchioness de Rotondo had failed just at the moment of success.

In the first moments of his anger, he had dispatched a company of troops of the line to take the city prison under their keeping, and to place the whole of the functionaries in that place under arrest, believing that there must have been some collusion, direct or indirect, to favour the escape of Don Cæsar.

He could not account for his escape under any other supposition. The guard must have been privy to it, and fired over his head, and the gaolers must have aided his escape afterwards.

Acting upon this belief, the soldiers were sent, and we have seen how they carried their instructions out to the letter.

The unfortunate Marquis de Rotondo, who had been in a state of mental botheration ever since he had heard Don Jose call his beautiful marchioness the Countess of Bazan, and driven frantic by the remarks of Don Cæsar, who had not been particularly complimentary, determined to visit Don Jose, and obtain some explanation of what had occurred.

With this view he proceeded to the minister's house, scarcely knowing, as he said, whether he was in Madrid, or out of it, or whether he should find Don Jose's house where it formerly stood; indeed, he was rather disappointed to see that it still stood where he had usually found it, and it had not been removed to some other spot, and another building substituted in its place.

The marquis rubbed his eye, however, before he felt quite assured that he was not mistaken, and that his vision did not deceive him.

Having satisfied himself that Don Jose was there, the marquis desired to be announced to him, which was done by one of the pages, and the marquis followed on the page's heels.

Now Don Jose was in no humour to see and be bored by the marquis, who, notwithstanding his immense subserviency and extreme pliancy, and the intense admiration and respect he had for Don Jose, yet he could not at all times be plagued by him—he wanted time and patience for the amusement.

Don Jose slightly bowed to the marquis as he entered, which the latter returned with much formality, at the same time saying,—

" Good morning, Don Jose—that is, if this be the morning ; for it may be midnight, for all I can affirm to the contrary."

" Well ?"

" It may be so, Don Jose ; but I can't tell if I be a Rotondo, or a Jose, or a—a—the devil himself knows what."

" What do you desire, marquis ?"

" Why, I believe, I want some explanation—some a—a—that is—I scarcely know anything—but am I myself, or somebody else besides myself? I don't know."

" It may be the latter ; but, as far as I know, you are what the page announced you to be—the Marquis de Rotondo."

" I'm glad of it—very glad of it."

" Of what ?"

" That they know me, for I couldn't recollect myself—at least, I should have been fearful of trying to do so. But some disagreeable discovery was to take place, and I was to find myself a dead man, which is next to a dead man finding himself alive."

Don Jose bit his lip with impatience, and said,—

" Well—well. Go on."

" Ah ! there comes the difficulty. Do I recollect the occurrence of last night ? Didn't something extraordinary take place ?"

" Yes—yes."

" I am right—I am right ! Well, how dreadful ! Is my marchioness my marchioness, or is she somebody else—or who is she or is she not ? And are we anybody, nobody, or something of all three ? I can't tell whether I am upside down, anyhow, nohow, or nothing. Where am I, or ain't I ?"

" Your questions are so singular, and require so much wisdom to understand them, that it will take time to answer them."

" Ay, truly ; but most of all am I disturbed respecting my beautiful and charming marchioness. She, the light of Madrid, the star of the court, the—the loadstar of my existence. I am concerned about her. What's to be done, Don Jose? how am I to act ? I can't make it out. Pray explain to me the meaning of what occurred last night. I can't understand it. Is the marchioness my wife, or does any one else claim her ? and then, who is she ?"

The marquis had worked himself into a frenzy of feeling, and walked about swinging his arms, quite unable to repress the feelings of despair which possessed him, when the idea of finding the beautiful marchioness, whom he so much adored and admired, might not be his own, but some one's else.

During one of these raving fits, he turned round to speak to Don Jose, but the room was empty, save that he himself was there. For some moments the bewildered marquis began to think himself bewitched, and began to endeavour to recollect if there had been anybody there when he came in, and that he had not been either talking to himself or to a shadow.

He was, however, soon convinced of the fact, and attributed the sudden disappearance of Don Jose to a fit of absence of mind, to which the great are often subject.

Don Jose, in the meantime, being tired of the conversation of the marquis, as he required more knowledge than he (Don Jose) chose to impart, silently quitted the room, and strode through the hall, where his lacqueys were waiting his orders.

Don Jose's carriage was at the door, in readiness to convey him whither he chose. He stopped a moment to give some orders, and then descended the steps to the carriage.

There was no one about at the moment, save a man dressed in a sombre-coloured cloak, the ample folds of which completely enveloped his person and concealed it, while the large slouched hat was pulled down so low, that it entirely concealed his features.

Just before Don Jose reached the carriage, this person stepped forward and stood between him and the carriage, at the same time holding in his hand a letter, which he extended to Don Jose, as if he desired that he would take it of him.

The action of the stranger alarmed Don Jose, who stepped back a step or two and placed his hand upon his sword, as if he expected an attempt at assassination.

He perceived the fear that actuated the minister, threw the letter down at his feet, and quickly passed on and was lost to sight.

" Take up the letter," said Don Jose, to a page who stood by.

The page did as he was desired, and held it towards Don Jose, who did not yet think it prudent to touch the epistle, lest it might contain any concealed means of destruction, for the minister was somewhat apprehensive of assassination, and was well aware that there were few who loved him, and all those who pretended implicit submission to his wishes did so because they knew that he had much to give, and had it in his power to avenge any slight in no light manner.

" Open the letter," said Jose, after a moment's thought, and the page did so accordingly, and when Don Jose saw that it contained nothing mischievous, he took it, and entered the carriage, saying, " To the palace."

Don Jose read the letter and re-read it several times, and appeared to be deeply concerned at its contents. It was as follows :—

" If Don Jose will give the sum of five hundred crowns, he can give him information of one of the most desperate plots that ever existed, and which affects the position of the king and his own life."

The letter then stated the means by which he was to signify his assent to the proposition which had been made.

" I have had some inkling of this before, but I know nothing of the particulars—but this may be of use as a clue to the mystery. I will use it."

The carriage now stopped at the palace, and when Don Jose alighted, he called to him one of his pages and gave him some whispered instructions, and then he entered the palace, while the page took his departure to some other part of the city.

After the departure of Don Jose the Marquis de Rotondo waited with some impatience for the return of the great man, whose absence he so much deplored at that moment.

" He will be back soon, and then I can satisfy myself—he will not be long—as soon as he recollects he has left me here he will return and apologise; how unpleasant it must be to him to be thus forgetful of his visitors ; it must cause him many unpleasant reflections, for it is not every one who knows as well as I do that it arises from absence of mind, and not any desire to affront."

Consoling himself with these thoughts he waited a little more than two hours, and finding that the minister did not return, he was compelled to quit the house, believing that the minister's absence of mind might continue all day, and he would then, perhaps, be forgotten altogether.

"However, I'll not mention it, lest he should feel hurt at his own forgetfulness."

The marquis now hastened back to his own abode in a great fume, and hardly indulging in a hope that his residence might remain on the same spot where it stood, previous to his going to Don Jose.

He determined to question his marchioness as to what was the matter, and when he reached the saloon where he had been so bewildered the night before, he met her there.

"My dear, charming, marchioness, you who have been the idol of my soul, the charm of my eyes, and the hope of my days, are you really the same, or am I anybody else, and who are we?"

The marchioness became somewhat alarmed lest the marquis was losing his senses.

"What is it you say?" she inquired. "I really do not recollect having ever heard you speak in this way before."

"I never recollect anything of the like nature happening before."

"What has happened?"

"Why, how was it that Don Jose called you the Countess de Bazan? Have I any ears, or haven't I ——?"

"I can't tell, my dear, how he did it, nor why he did it; but I suppose he must have had some motive."

"Some motive—some motive! Yes; but what I can't understand is, why my marchioness is to be called somebody else's countess, that's what I don't understand."

"You must remember that Don Jose is our patron, and that you are a green stick, and that ought to be some consolation."

"Yes, I am; I know I am a green stick, and that I have been ambitious, and have succeeded; certainly there is some balm in that. Well—well, I suppose Don Jose knows best, and I shall know more in time."

CHAPTER XXXIV.

THE PALACE. — THE KING'S IMPATIENCE. — THE DREADFUL INTERVIEW.—MARITANA'S DESPAIR.

KINGS, although not the most punctual people in the world in their own movements, seem to consider they have a prescriptive right to be dreadfully angry with any one else who may err in that way.

Certainly one of the cardinal virtues is punctuality; with it the affairs of life, if they do not glide smoothly on, at all events glide much smoother than they would without, and if it has not the positive chance of bringing with it success in all instances, it, at least, has the positive tendency to turn defeat into something much less annoying than it otherwise would be.

Moreover, there can be neither comfort nor prosperity of any long continuance without it, as those persons have woefully found who have disregarded it.

If ever any one was in a mood to descant upon its virtues on the evening, the proceedings of which we have to some extent recorded, that person, if we may be permitted to speak of him so irreverently, was Philip the king of Spain.

Don Jose was to have brought the beautiful Maritana to the palace by a particular hour; that particular hour came, and no Don Jose—no Maritana.

The king paced to and fro in a small apartment, where he awaited the minister in quite as great a rage as any of the humblest of his subjects could have been in. The "divinity that doth hedge a king," somehow does not exercise much effect upon royal tempers, and Philip was very like some fretful man, and no king at all.

Alas! the spread of literature and the arts is sadly at variance with this same "divinity" of kings. People have begun not only to suspect and assert that crowned heads, after all, are just like any other heads; but that, in some instances, they are below the average excellence of common heads—what a sad thing for kingcraft! We may expect that the day may come when human nature will contrive to do almost without kings and queens altogether, and when that shall arrive another glorious light will not be long in bursting upon the human mind, and that will be the notion that priests can be done very well without, and that no man requires a go-between to place himself officiously between him and his Creator.

But we are a long way off such a consummation, and one circumstance has recently gone far to prove that we are. That circumstance consists in the fact, that a newspaper, which occupies its columns every day in a stupid bigoted controversy as to whether a person should preach in a black frock or a white one, is not shelved by general consent as a thing at variance with the intelligence of the age. While the *Times* newspaper exists, it is a living proof that there is a large class of bigots and noodles in the world, and the manner in which that journal panders to the bigotry and brutal ignorance of its readers, shows amply that its proprietor calculates upon the existence of a large class possessing those feelings and habits.

But to resume. We have said that Philip of Spain was very impatient that Jose did not, according to arrangements, make his appearance by about ten o'clock; but when a quarter past ten came, and no arrival, the royal temper became thoroughly waxed.

Then half-past ten was the time, and Philip became furious. What added, too, as much as possible, to his bad state of nerves was, that there came upon his ears continually all the merry sounds of enjoyment from the saloons of his own palace, for many guests had been invited, with the hope that Maritana would be dazzled by the brilliancy of the throng among which she would suddenly find herself, and her judgment and feelings would be carried away in the vortex of pleasure.

This was all very well if it had been comfortably carried out as intended, and at the time intended; but the non-arrival of Jose made every sound from the state rooms indicative of mirth and enjoyment gall and wormwood to the most gracious king.

Perhaps there is nothing so jarring to the feelings, when they are put much out of sorts, as to hear others enjoying the easy hours as they swiftly fly, and, by their tones and manner, betraying how easy and comfortable they are.

Some poet says, "When I am happy I'd have all things happy, that all around should be a breathing gladness;" and we much suspect that the gentleman who penned such a sentence might, perhaps, with far more truth, and more in accordance with the principles and feelings of human nature, have said,—

"When I am uncomfortable, I should like everybody else to be so, too, and nothing is so annoying as the contrary."

At all events his majesty, Philip of Spain, had a strong feeling that way tending, and when he heard the musicians of his own private band playing a lively air, it would have given him infinite satisfaction to have crammed their instruments down their throats, till the royal temper had recovered from its present state.

"Curses on that scoundrel, Jose," he muttered. "How dare he thus tamper with me? When he comes he will have some well arranged, excellently united excuse; but I will not mince it, and he shall find, however I may choose to honour him in familiar moments with my conversation, that I am still a king."

Fuming and fretting thus, he waited another quarter of an hour, and then, with stealthy steps, and a tone of such reverential respect, that any one would have supposed him addressing a divinity, a page appeared and announced the arrival of Don Jose.

Of course, Philip could not have the least idea of the extraordinary circumstances which had occurred at the Marquis de Rotondo's to delay Jose. They were circumstances which, probably, not another man in Spain would have been able to struggle through half so successfully as he had done; and the wonder was that he ever that night got to the palace at all with the Countess de Bazan, considering how very inopportunely, 'for his plans and projects, Don Cæsar had not only turned out to be alive instead of dead, but had actually made his appearance at the very time and place of all others which were most inconvenient.

Had not Maritana passed, as she did, towards the grand staircase, and, for an instant, in all her wondrous beauty, beamed upon the ravished eyes of Don Cæsar, there can be no doubt but Jose would have been successful in inducing the former to leave Madrid, under the influence of bitter disappointment, at finding his supposed countess so very different a person from what he had pictured her to his warm, fervid imagination.

But it is such little circumstances that disturb the finest woven and the most elaborate plots. As one word of truth has often power over heaps of falsehood, so one trifling event, which has not at all been pre-arranged, will derange the most artfully constructed scheme that the politic brains of man could conceive.

The immediate danger, however, from Don Cæsar was past, for Jose knew well that all pursuit of the carriage, even if the Don should get free from the lacqueys in the hall, would be fruitless, and he knew, likewise, if he even got Maritana under the palace roof, that she was beyond the power of Cæsar.

When the mules, therefore, dashed off from the door of the Marquis de Rotondo's house at the speed we have recorded, Jose threw himself back in the carriage and drew a long breath of relief; and he felt he had reason to thank his stars on several grounds, not the least of which was, that on the impulse of a moment, which, in his cooler judgment, he could but bitterly condemn, he had had the temerity to cross swords with Don Cæsar, and escaped the consequences in the shape of a foot of cold steel through his body.

The perspiration stood upon Don Jose's brow as he thought of this, and he could not help saying to himself—

"What an escape! Don Cæsar is one of the best swordsmen in Madrid, and I am quite certain if he had not been in such a tremendous hurry he would have run me through at once. I must take care not to give away such another chance."

Maritana was trembling with alarm at the riot she had heard going on in the marquis's hall. How little she suspected its cause, or that it arose from the efforts to reach her of him whom alone she would have gladly welcomed to her heart.

"You tremble," said Jose. "I suppose you heard the clash of swords, and, woman like, are alarmed."

"I may well be," she replied. "What was the cause of the tumult?"

"A cavalier who had taken too much wine had forced himself into the house."

"Indeed."

"Yes. Nothing further. These little affairs frequently happen; but, countess, leave your thoughts to other matters. This night I will keep to you my promise, and you shall be introduced to your husband."

"To Don Cæsar?"

"Assuredly. Are you not the Countess de Bazan? You are now proceeding to the palace, so that you cannot doubt how much the queen has interested herself in your welfare, or she would not invite you there."

"Shall I see the good queen?"

"Well, I cannot say exactly, but it is very probable. You will, however, be introduced to the nobles, and fully recognised to-night as one of the brightest stars of the Spanish court."

"I wish for no admiration but from him to whom I have already given all my heart."

"But your beauty will command admiration, and even Don Cæsar will feel a pride in seeing the looks of approval and surprise that will be cast upon his beautiful countess."

"To please him I would be ambitious of applause."

"You will please him. Oh! countess, what a brilliant career you have before you, dating from this night. Your fortune is certainly now in your own hands. You can make or mar your own destiny, countess."

"If you are acting fairly by me, Jose, it cannot be marred."

"And that I am so, you will soon admit. I have no motive to deceive you. I am the agent of the queen in the whole of this business, and am merely carrying out her majesty's most gracious commands."

By this time, for the distance was not great, the carriage had reached the palace gates, and as Maritana knew well that there could now be no deception as to the place to which she was brought, she began to give more ready belief than she had hitherto done to Don Jose's promises and protestations of good faith.

He saw the change in her countenance from doubt and hesitation to more assured feelings, and he said,—

"You see, Maritana, I am keeping my word. Here is the palace. Can you have any doubts remaining?"

"Scarcely," she replied. "Time, Jose, will show if I have done you an injustice."

"You will find you have, except when you have relied upon my honour."

"You know I have had cause to doubt it."

"Not really, though apparently."

He assisted her to alight, and the royal pages in waiting announced, from one to the other, the name of the Countess de Bazan, as she accompanied Don Jose towards the principal saloon of the palace, which was one blaze of lights, and thronged with the most brilliant company.

Jose was right in supposing that such a scene would have a powerful effect upon an imagination like Maritana's. He watched her countenance, and he saw it glow with animation and pleasure as the rich strains of music broke upon her ears, and she saw the gorgeous assembly into which she was about being introduced. How far such a feeling was likely to confuse her judgment, or influence her feelings, when she should find the heartless trick that was about to be played upon her, will soon be seen.

The announcement of the Countess de Bazan attracted general attention among the king's guests, for although it was familiar enough to the ears of all, it had not been heard within those walls for many a day.

But if curiosity was excited in the first instance by the mere announcement of a name, how quickly was it changed to feelings of admiration when Maritana, in all her radiant and exquisite beauty, burst upon the enraptured sight of the throngs assembled in these gorgeous apartments.

Every one was anxious for an introduction to the lovely creature who leant upon the arm of Don Jose, but he took no notice of the appealing looks that were directed towards him, but walking up to an aged nobleman whom he was intimate with, he said in a low voice,—

"I have, Don Carlotti, to pay my immediate respects to the king; may I trespass upon your goodness so far as to leave the Countess de Bazan in your charge; and let me remark to you, that she does not like any questions or remarks concerning her husband, Don Cæsar, as he is in some difficulties at present on various accounts."

"But there was a report of his death," said the nobleman.

"That was premature," replied Don Jose, with a slight cough, and then he was about leaving, but Maritana laid her hand upon his arm, saying,—

"Your promise, Don Jose, your promise."

"Shall be performed," he replied. "I go now but to make the necessary arrangements."

Maritana released him, and he left the hall, getting himself, as we have already stated, announced to the

king, of whose impatience Don Jose could make a very fair calculation before he saw him.

Maritana attracted all eyes. Established court beauties were neglected by previously attentive courtiers, who wished to pay their devotions to the new star of beauty that had so suddenly appeared in the court galaxy.

Eager questions of "Who was she? Where did she come from? What are her connexions? How long has she been Countess de Bazan?" passed from lip to lip, and not a little wonder was excited and duly expressed that so much beauty could have, up to that hour, existed unknown.

And yet many of those present had seen the dancing girl in the streets of Madrid with scarcely a passing glance; but then, to be sure, Maritana was wonderfully altered—she was gorgeously apparelled—she was a countess, and the events of the last few days of her existence had imparted an entirely new expression to her features.

No wonder none recognised in her the street musician. In the first place, she had, as we say, much altered; and, in the second, the idea of this being one and the same person was too absurd to be entertained for a moment, even if any fancied resemblance had suggested itself.

We have seen that even Don Cæsar, familiar as he had been with the face of the beautiful Maritana, knew her not as the Countess de Bazan, although, as he remarked to the page, there was a something about her face, transient as the glance had been that he caught of it, which haunted him like the dim remembrance of a dream.

Don Carlotti performed the office which had been set him, and quietly repressed any attempt to question Maritana of Don Cæsar, while she cast her eyes with intense interest from one to another of the glittering forms which flitted before her eyes, with the hope of detecting, beneath some guise, him whose image was treasured up in her heart, and whom she loved with a devotion now, that, perhaps, owed part of its intensity to the romantic circumstances under which she had been married to him, and the great difficulties which appeared to be in the way of their meeting.

With a saddened aspect, she ceased her scrutiny of the guests, for she knew he was not there, and she suffered Don Carlotti to conduct her to a seat, where she was out of the immediate throng, and yet could obtain a good view of all that was passing, as well as hearing the sweet strains of exquisite music that floated through the saloons.

Jose made up his mind to be amused at what he knew would be his reception from the king, and when he heard that monarch, in a voice which was quite sufficiently indicative of the rage he had worked himself up into, desire the page to admit him, he gave a half smile, as he muttered,—

"I will astonish him by the news I bring; but first, I will amuse myself with his anger."

Philip of Spain was very far from being the most captivating man in the world. When he was angry, his countenance always assumed a dark shade instead of a flushed one, as is commonly the case, or a pale one, as is sometimes met with. Now, in the light he stood, as Don Jose, with a low bow, entered the room, his face looked almost black, he had worked himself up to such an amount of bad temper at the three quarters of an hour's disappointment he had experienced from Don Jose's delay.

For a moment he did not speak, and Don Jose made another bow lower than the first. Then, in a hoarse, husky voice, the king said, slightly stamping with his foot as he spoke, and bending on his minister a most diabolical look—

"So, sir, you have come at last?"

"At last, your majesty."

"My majesty would bestow upon you but your deserts by demanding an apology from you that would leave you a head shorter. Do you hear, Jose?"

"I do, your majesty. But by such a process your majesty would lose your most faithful servant."

The king pointed to a time-piece, and Don Jose made a parade of going up to it to see the time. At that moment it struck eleven, in soft, silvery notes.

"Eleven o'clock," he remarked.

"Well, sir?"

"I said eleven, your majesty."

"And you were to have been here at ten."

"I was; but a little circumstance prevented me, which, in all the chapter of accidents, was least likely to occur."

"Your were always good at excuses, Jose."

"I hope my humble merits have gone further than that in your majesty's service."

"I don't know that. Am I to suffer so much indignity as to be kept an hour in suspense?"

"Sire, hear me. I assure your majesty that the cause of the delay is not to be attributed to your devoted servant. An occurrence took place ——"

"Pshaw! Have you brought Maritana to the palace?"

"She is below."

"Ah!"

"But first permit me to put your majesty in possession of a piece of news, which will create in your mind profound astonishment, as well as account for the delay of which your majesty so justly complains, and for which I should feel myself so very culpable without the excuse I shall have the honour to submit to you."

"Say on. What was it?"

"I repaired to the Marquis de Rotondo's, and every-

thing was proceeding well and smoothly, according to arrangement. Some short time before ten, I desired the Countess de Bazan to prepare herself to accompany me to the palace."

"Well—well."

"I am as brief as possible, your majesty. I waited her coming in a room where there was no one but myself—a room removed from the public saloons of the house. A few moments only had elapsed, when a man made his appearance."

"What man?"

"Don Cæsar de Bazan."

The king started back a few steps as he said, slowly,—

"Don—Cæsar—de Bazan?"

"The same. He whom your gracious majesty and I have more than once congratulated ourselves was dead."

"But—but he must be dead."

"He ought to be dead."

The king sank into a chair, and fixed his eyes upon Don Jose with a look of mingled terror and amazement.

"I knew," added the minister, "that your majesty would be almost too surprised to credit what I report to you, but such is the fact. The Don Cæsar de Bazan who was condemned by your majesty to death, and who we had the strongest possible reasons to suppose was duly executed."

The king drew a long breath as he remarked,—

"This is indeed an extraordinary circumstance. There is some treachery here, Jose; look to it, and see that a proper meed of punishment falls on the heads of the guilty. By the mass, are our judgments to be set at nought in this way? Are we a king?"

"It is almost, your majesty, beyond my comprehension to imagine how he escaped."

"By the connivance of the gaolers, of course."

"But I all but saw him executed."

"Indeed!"

"Yes; I heard the arquebuses which were to herald him to death; and from a passing glance I had of the court-yard when the execution, as I believed, took place, I saw his dead body lying."

"You do indeed surprise me. Are you quite satisfied of the identity of him you saw to-night?"

"Quite; I know Cæsar well. He would have followed the carriage, containing the Countess de Bazan, hither, had I not fought with him, and at my sword's point succeeded, not without trouble, in keeping him off."

"Why did you not kill him?"

"Don Cæsar is an adroit fencer. I was more anxious to get here with the lovely Maritana than to take Don Cæsar's life. I knew your majesty would justly be impatient."

The king rose and traversed the room, biting his lips, and then he turned abruptly to Jose, saying,—

"Jose, see to this. Don Cæsar must be taken and again executed."

"But your majesty forgets the pardon."

"Ah, true. The guard, Jose, that fired at him, must have been leagued with him in this business. They must, each man of them, have purposely missed him."

"No doubt."

"They shall meet with adequate punishment; and as for this Don Cæsar, who is so much in the way, why—why—Jose ——"

"He must be put out of the way, your majesty."

CHAPTER XXXV.
THE REPROACHES OF MARITANA. — INSENSIBILITY. —THE VILLA IN THE SUBURBS OF MADRID.

THE king was silent for some few moments after this notable speech of Don Jose, and then, waving his hand, he said in a low voice, as if he would rather hear no more on that head,—

"I will leave that to you, Jose."

"Your majesty, I presume, bestows upon me full powers of action?"

"Certainly, certainly."

"Then I may venture to say such is my zeal in your majesty's service, that Don Cæsar de Bazan will not trouble the world long with his very untoward presence."

"Enough, enough."

Jose bowed.

"Now about Maritana. Is she prepared to meet me?"

"She is prepared to meet Don Cæsar de Bazan. There may be a little difficulty when she finds that the Don Cæsar she is introduced to is not the one she expected; but I do not anticipate that she will be very cruel. The gaiety and glitter of the court may greatly influence her, and if soberer feelings should prevent such matters from bewildering her judgment, she must, believing herself to be your wife, resign herself to her condition, and that she will perhaps think it is as well to do with a good grace as a bad one."

"You think, then, I shall be successful?"

"Unquestionably."

"I am all impatience to behold her."

"I will bring her to this apartment. Your majesty is aware of the device by which I mean to induce her to look upon you as her husband, and feel it her duty to do so?"

"You told me, Jose, you will assure her I am the real Don Cæsar de Bazan."

"I will; and should your majesty experience any very cold reception from her, I will be near at hand, and, if necessary, corroborate the story you can yourself tell her."

"Do so. Now, Jose, bring her hither."

"If your majesty will step into the adjoining apartment, I will bring her to this, and then, informing you she is here, you can go to her."

"Agreed," said the king; and he repaired to the next chamber, while Don Jose again sought the brilliant saloons on the ground floor of the palace to bring poor, devoted Maritana to her fate.

She was waiting for him in a state of anxiety that painfully showed itself upon her countenance, and when he approached and whispered in her ear, "Now, Maritana," she said,—

"The queen is not here, Jose. I should have felt more confidence had the queen been here."

"Her majesty is certainly not here," said Jose: "but she will come at a later hour of the evening. If you like to wait till then before I introduce you to your husband you can, and I will tell him as much."

"No, no. He is here, then?"

"He is in the palace."

"But not here?"

"Not in these rooms. The queen has not yet quite succeeded in making her peace with the king, and, therefore, she advises that he should not show himself in the saloons."

"It is for his safety's sake, then?"

"Most certainly. Don Carlotti, I return you a thousand thanks for your care of the Countess de Bazan."

The old nobleman bowed, and Don Jose walked with Maritana through the rich apartments, and conducted her towards the more private rooms of the palace.

She trembled excessively, and a vague feeling of some coming evil came over her mind. More than once she looked in the countenance of Don Jose, and she thought she never saw " villain" so strongly marked upon it in her life before.

He appeared, by some sort of intuition, to be aware of what was passing in her mind, and as they went, he strove to dispel, as much as possible, the fears and suspicions that were crowding round her heart.

"Countess," he said, "what a happy and brilliant destiny is yours. Does not your heart rejoice that your destiny has developed itself in such glowing colours?"

"I scarcely know," she replied. "This is not a moment in which I can analyze my feelings, Don Jose."

"But you should be happy."

"God grant I may! I have been happy as a poor wanderer in the streets of Madrid, and, as you say, I should be happy now, surely."

She glanced at her once splendid attire, and, despite her reason, a sigh came from her heart.

"Humph," thought Jose, "the royal lover will meet with more trouble in his suit than he calculates upon. However, he cannot blame me; I can bring the beautiful Maritana here, but I cannot make her love him, or induce her even to assume the feeling. He must take his chance like other wooers, but, for my own part, I have great doubts indeed of his success."

A few minutes sufficed to reach the room in the one adjoining to which the king was waiting, and there Don Jose said to his lovely companion—

"If you will wait here, you will, in a few brief moments, be in a situation to acknowledge that I have kept my word with you, Maritana."

"Is he near?"

"He is. You will soon behold him."

"Don Cæsar."

"Of course, Don Cæsar."

"Then there is no mistake, no juggle? God forgive you, Don Jose, if you have played me false."

"Now this is too bad," said Jose, shaking his head with the air of injured innocence. "This is really too bad, after all the pains I have taken in your service, Maritana. But no matter—no matter—the day will come when you will do more justice to my motives than you do now."

"If I have done you an injustice, Don Jose, I shall not shrink from saying so much."

"Then I shall have the honour of hearing such sentiments flow from those lovely lips."

Don Jose made a low bow, and then entered the next room, where the king was again getting his impatience up to the boiling point.

"Have you brought her, Jose?" he inquired.

"I have."

"She is ——"

"In the next room."

The king at once walked to the door, and, in an instant, was in the presence of Maritana, who, hearing footsteps, had half risen from her chair, and was bending forward with eager anxiety to catch the first glimpse of him whom she hoped to see.

A half shriek of alarm came from her lips when she saw the king, and her terror was much increased by his advancing towards her with a warmth of manner, and exclaiming—

"Maritana, my wife—my countess—my love!"

"No, no," she cried, "no—not you—not you."

"Not I!"

"No, you are not he. There is some deception; I have never seen you before—I loathe you. You are not Don Cæsar de Bazan. Oh, God, I am deceived again!"

"Deceived! Not by Don Jose! Gracious Heavens! what is the meaning of these transports? Is this the way, Maritana, you show your gratitude to him who has made you a countess."

"You are not that man."

"What! doubt my own identity to my face?"

"You know you are not Don Cæsar de Bazan. He is noble, generous, handsome ——"

" And I."

She shuddered, and turned aside her face in too expressive a manner to be mistaken.

The king's countenance assumed its dark shade, as, in a voice struggling with passion, he said—

" Oh! Maritana, this is, indeed, a poor reward for me, after, at the request of the queen, I have stooped from my high estate to ally myself to you. How can you treat me thus? I love you, Maritana."

" Oh, horror!"

" I love you."

" Oh, that you hated me!"

" Hate such beauty—such perfection—impossible! Are you not my countess—my wife?"

" No—no—no."

" This perverseness is beyond all calculation. I wedded you in the prison. The vows I then made I will now fulfil—you are my bride."

" Now, God of heaven protect me," cried Maritana. " You know you are not Don Cæsar de Bazan. He is my husband. You are an impostor, sir."

" An impostor?"

" Yes. How dare you name yourself Don Cæsar de Bazan. You know you are not he."

" This is strange language, madam."

" It is true. There is some dreadful imposition attempted. You are not my husband, and the villain Jose, as I half suspected, has played me false."

" He has played me false, madam, for, by his account, you were most desirous of being introduced to see your husband."

" To my husband, but not to you."

" I am he."

" It is false—false as your own and Don Jose's hearts. You are not Don Cæsar de Bazan."

The king's anger was roused, and he grasped the wrist of Maritana with painful tightness, as he said—

" I understand all this well. Some low passion has found a home in your heart, and you would repudiate your marriage in order to be left to the indulgence of it. Too well I understand this affected anger at my claims."

" If so," said Maritana, " why came I hither full of hope? But you know the falsehood of your own words. You are not Don Cæsar de Bazan—show me likewise that you are not a ruffian, by removing this grasp from my wrist."

The king let her hand drop, as he said between his set teeth—

" You do not escape us—I mean me—thus. Do not suppose it—I have made you my wife. What ho! Don Jose, your evidence is wanted. Don Jose, I say, come hither and speak to this stubborn girl."

Jose advanced boldly from the inner room.

" Who am I?" said the king.

" Don Cæsar de Bazan," replied Jose.

" And this lady?"

" Your countess."

" 'Tis false," cried Maritana. " Jose, well you know the falsehood your tongue utters."

" Nay, madam," said Jose, " you are labouring under a most grievous error, but still one which you will rejoice to rectify, I have no doubt. You contracted a marriage in one of the public prisons of Madrid."

" I did, but not to him."

" There you are in error; you did not see your bridegroom. You were content to wed, so that it raised you to a height you had often looked up to with the dazzled eyes of mad ambition. Is not that true?"

" It is. I have lived to see my error. Oh, God! that I should have been so blinded to the joys of the state of freedom and happiness I was in as to grasp at what should ever have been beyond my reach, and

fancy happiness was to be found in those gaudy trappings, and an empty sound."

" You should have thought of that before, Maritana," said Don Jose; " no one could be more eager than you were to embrace the opportunity presented to you of becoming what you now are."

Maritana covered her face with her hands, and wept bitterly, while Jose exchanged a significant look with the king, and then, after a slight pause, resumed—

" He whom you married while your face was covered by an impenetrable veil, now stands before you."

" But the name?" cried Maritana. " I know Don Cæsar de Bazan well."

" Listen, and you will speedily understand the mistake you have made. The Don Cæsar de Bazan whom you knew in the streets of Madrid, I assure you, was an impostor. He is dead."

" Dead?"

" Yes; immediately after your marriage with this gentleman, who is the real Don Cæsar, the impostor was shot in the court-yard of the prison."

" Shot—shot?"

" Yes, by a party of carbineers of the guard."

" Great God, I heard the sound!"

" Can you doubt now, Maritana, or shall I bring you a hundred witnesses from the halls below to tell you this is Don Cæsar de Bazan."

" Oh! kill me rather."

" No," said the king; " live for me and joy."

Maritana shrunk from him.

" I am rich," he resumed, " beyond your most sanguine expectations. You shall not have a wish ungratified; I have power and wealth that shall anticipate your every caprice. Smile upon me, my beautiful countess, and give the greatest possible effect to the kindness of the queen by loving the husband she has provided for you."

" Ay," said Jose, " how happy you must now feel, Maritana. What a glow of satisfaction must irradiate your heart!"

" You do well to mock me," she said; " I deserve it; but hear me now solemnly swear ——"

" Nay, Maritana," cried the king, " take no rash oaths. Be mine, and as happy as love can make you."

" Let me leave this place; restore to me the poor apparel, and the guitar, which I once despised; let me once again, as the street dancer, know what it is to lie down at night without a pang."

" Impossible."

" Take back these gauds. Oh, how I hate them now!"

She flung from her the magnificent bracelets she had worn; and then, overcome by excess of feeling, she sunk upon a chair, and seemed on the point of lapsing into insensibility.

Perhaps it was only the hateful touch of the king' as he laid his hand upon her shoulder, that recovered her; she shrunk back, as if an adder had stung her, exclaiming,—

" Touch me not, sir; I never can be yours."

Rage flashed in the eyes of the king, as he replied—

" You shall; you are mine, and nothing shall keep me from you. You are my wife, and, willing or unwilling, I will exact from you all the obedience due to a husband. Beware how you provoke me; you have no resource."

" I have one; you are wrong!" she cried, with sudden energy. " I have a resource.'

" Indeed!"

" Yes; in death."

" I am not afraid of your availing yourself of it."

" You know me not. Rather would I die a thousand deaths, than live with a consciousness that such as you had power over me."

"To your chamber!" cried the king, stamping with rage. "To your chamber, minion."

"Nay," she said, rising, "I will throw myself on the queen's protection. If she will declare to me that you are my husband, I will tell her how hateful such an union is to me, and beg her to get for me the protection of the church."

"The church! Think you the church would aid you?" said Jose. "Indeed, lovely countess——"

"Who bade you interfere?" cried the king, furiously. "Begone, sir; but be in waiting."

Jose bowed, and made his exit as quickly as possible, for he saw that his royal master was in no mood for anything in the shape of argument.

Then, turning to Maritana, the king added,—

"You are mine, and nothing can take you from my arms. I have toiled to make you mine, and I will reap the reward of my labours. You are my wife."

"Welcome death rather."

"Pshaw! a woman's threat."

"You will find it no idle one. Approach nearer to me, and perchance you may be in some danger."

"Now, by Heaven, I like you all the better for this Amazonian spirit—my fancy is palled with yielding dames. You add a zest to your beauty by the difficulties you throw in the way of its possession. On my soul, I love you."

"Hold!" cried Maritana, as a thought suddenly struck her; "hold! you say you are my husband?"

"I do, and, in saying so, say truly."

"You married me in the prison?"

"I did."

"I did not see my husband; my eyes were hindered from performing their office, but my ears were not; he who wedded me spoke to me. I made him no answer; but the words he uttered sunk deep into my heart. I never can forget them."

"No one wishes you."

"What were they, then, sir?"

"What were they?"

"Ay, what were those words? If you are the man I wedded, you surely know what you said to me at the moment of our nuptials? Speak, sir; what were those words addressed to me at such a moment by my husband?"

The king looked confused for a few moments, and knew not what answer to make to such an appeal. If Jose had been present he could have got out of the difficulty, he thought, for probably he had, while in the prison, heard the words alluded to, but to send for him to answer a question of so home a nature, was out of the question.

"You cannot answer me," added Maritana. "Your looks proclaim the fraud you would perpetrate, if your silence did not. Well you know you are not my husband; neither are you Don Cæsar de Bazan, who has my heart."

"And so you would decide against my claim, because, upon the question of a moment, I cannot recollect a few frivolous words which I have uttered?"

"You never uttered them. Stand aside, sir, and let me pass. In your countenance you show yourself the conceited villain that you are."

"Villain, madam!"

"Yes, sir, villain. I believe that I am under the same roof which shelters the king. Would that my voice could reach him, to proclaim to him how innocence was assaulted even in his royal palace, and what a villain Don Jose, his minister, is, as well as what unprincipled associates he has."

"The king would favour my suit."

"The King of Spain favour one like thee!"

"Ay. They say his majesty is himself fond of beauty, and surely he would not throw an obstacle in the way of my possession of it."

"Let the king be what he may, he dare not be the dishonourable wretch you would paint him. He must be a gentleman. He cannot forget that he is a king. He would—he shall protect me."

Stung by a variety of conflicting feelings, and not less by a bitter consciousness of the infamous manner in which he was behaving, than by any other mental sensations, Philip took refuge in a rage from his compunctions, and, advancing towards Maritana, said aloud,—

"I will put an end to so profitless a discussion. Since fair words, justice, and persuasion, will not make you mine, force shall. You may shriek, but no one here dare hear your cries. Maritana, you must and shall be mine."

"Never!" she cried, and, as the king laid his hand upon her arm, she drew a small poniard from her breast, and very nearly succeeded, by one well-directed thrust, which he escaped only by a hair's-breadth, in ending the profligate reign of the evil-passioned Philip of Spain.

"Ah!" he exclaimed; does the bee carry a sting?"

In an instant he wrestled with her for the dagger, and her strength was not sufficient to enable her to resist him. Wresting it from her hand, and casting it to the farther end of the chamber, he exclaimed, in a brutal voice,—

"Now, scornful beauty, I have deprived you of the power to do more mischief, you had better, with a good grace, yield."

"My lord—my lord!" cried Jose, rushing into the room, and laying his hand upon the king's arm; "the Pope's nuncio."

"D——n the Pope's nuncio!"

"But—but ——"

Philip tore his sword from its scabbard with frightful vehemence, as he shouted,—

"Die, caitiff! How dare any one ——"

But Don Jose disappeared like a shot, and Maritana, rushing into the adjoining apartment, flung open the window, and cried aloud, in a voice that made itself heard above the music and the hum of conversation in the saloons,—

"Help—help! Courtiers, help—help! oh, help!"

Quite overcome, then, by the effort, and the agitating interview she had gone through, she dropped in a swoon upon the floor, while the king stood with his sword drawn, nearly foaming with rage, and yet irresolute what to do.

Gladly would he have sacrificed some one to his vengeance; and feeling sure that Maritana could not escape from the adjoining room, he turned the key in the lock, and then dashed out into the corridor, with a view of finding Don Jose, and making him suffer for his temerity in interrupting him. As he reached the corridor he heard the music suddenly cease, and a rapt silence pervaded the palace. He no longer doubted that the Pope's nuncio had indeed arrived, to launch at his head some thundering denunciation of the church.

CHAPTER XXXVI.

THE POLITICAL SPY.—THE CONFERENCE.—THE FEARFUL INTERRUPTION.

DON JOSE'S messenger sought an obscure part of the town, which he threaded as though he had been used to do so, either from long habit or from former knowledge. He entered a long street; it was narrow, but the houses were of such a class that they might or might not contain respectable inhabitants; that is, they might be people who were pretty well off in the world, or they might be adventurers, worth nothing; and many were men who pursued callings of various kinds, from the profession of physic and law to the poor author, who urged his already overwrought brains to satisfy his own wants and the unfathomable gulf of a printing-office.

The house that the page stopped at was one of a peculiar appearance, when once observed with care, though to the casual observer there was nothing by which it might be distinguished from those abutting on either side of it.

It was tall and dingy like the rest, and the lower windows were secured by iron staples, while the door was, like its fellows, dirty, and by no means of any pretensions; it bore a look of remarkable strength that was not seen in others; but it was only seen upon a close inspection, and a skilful person in these matters could easily perceive that there was an air of quietness and repose affected, and that the inhabitant was one who, however mysterious he might be, had the good things of the world about him.

The page rang a small bell, which was not heard, but the door was speedily opened by a stout porter; the door swung noiselessly upon its well-oiled hinges.

"Is Signor Monserino within?" inquired the page of the porter.

A signal was the only answer, and the page stepped in, the door closed, and the porter, followed by the page, entered the passage, and passing through a door into an apartment, in which were several seats, but ill lighted, he said,—

"Wait here a moment, and I will announce you to my master; you are from Don Jose, as I percieve by your livery."

"I am—you have seen me before."

"Yes," replied the porter, and opening a green door softly, he was beyond hearing; in a few minutes he returned saying,—

"Follow me."

The page arose, and passing through the same door and a second, entered a room in which a man sat with his back to the door.

"A messenger from Don Jose," said the porter, who then withdrew.

The room was a small one, filled with a variety of matters, and well furnished; there was a good carpet, so that the tread of the foot was not heard there were boxes with papers and books. The page remained a moment silent, and then Signor Monserino turned and faced the page.

He was a tall, dark man, with deep-set eyes, and sallow complexion; his raven hair hung matted upon his shoulders, and altogether he was a most uninviting person, and yet this man could be quite the reverse when it suited his pleasure or his business to be so.

"Do you come from Don Jose," he inquired, in a strange, harsh voice.

"Yes."

"And he wants me?"

"He does."

"Where is he at this moment?"

"At the palace."

"Does he want me there?"

"I don't know; his instructions were to say you were to be with him as soon as possible.

"Very well, I will be so."

The page quitted the room, and was soon joined by the porter, who afterwards closed the door after him.

*   *   *   *   *

Some few hours after this, Don Jose and Signor Monserino were seated together in a small apartment; there was a pause of a few moments, which was broken by Don Jose saying,—

"I have sent for you, Monserino, to entrust an affair to your management, and one, too, that will require great care and caution. Can you be successful in such a case?"

"I must first be acquainted with the case itself; but

you know my way of doing business, Don Jose. I never yet failed through want of care and caution."

"No; you never did, I admit; but this is a serious case, because I have no clue."

"Indeed! and yet you have information?"

"I have."

"From whom?"

"I know not, and in that consists the chief difficulty," replied Jose, thoughtfully.

"Are you sure the information is correct," inquired the spy.

"I have no other surety of it than its probability, and my own belief that it is so."

"What is it?"

"A plot that has been concocted by I can't tell who, and held in Madrid."

"Indeed! Then what is the aim or object of it? You are acquainted with that."

"I am informed that the position of the king and my life is threatened."

There was a pause of many minutes, during which both Don Jose and Signor Monserino appeared to be buried in deep thought, and after some time the latter broke it by saying,—

"This matter affects you as well as the king."

"Of course it does."

"Then it cannot be that you have to fear this only from your own enemies or those of the king, but from those principally who hate you and your policy, and the king in conjunction—they are political enemies."

"Yes; that is true enough."

"Then whom do you consider as the most rancorous personal and political opponent you have."

"I'faith," replied Don Jose, "I can hardly tell, there are many of them; 'tis the fate of successful men to make enemies."

"You must recollect those whom you think as being most likely to be engaged in some such desperate undertaking."

"Why, it is needless, I tell you, there are so many of them," replied Don Jose.

"It is needful," replied Monserino. "It is needful to the discovery, for I can see, without some such aid, I shall not be very likely to succeed in my undertaking of discovering the plot."

"Well, then, I know none so hearty in their hatred, or so unprincipled in their conduct, at the same time more hypocritical, than the Cardinal di Vinci," said Don Jose.

"Leave a churchman alone for that," replied the spy; "it is his peculiar privilege; he can cultivate those feelings in secret, and exhibit them under the cloak of religious sanctity."

"Besides him, there is Don Gusman; he is a bold, violent man; he, too, is a steady and strenuous opponent of mine, who would glory in my downfall, as much as he would reap."

"I know them both well," replied Monserino, and will proceed to place them under surveillance immediately."

"And how do you expect to learn anything of the plot?" inquired Jose.

"If these men are engaged in it," replied Monserino, "I shall discover as much, because I will watch them, go where they will, and then, if they go to any place where meetings are held, I must learn it by the members engaged, and then, it will be hard but I obtain more information; it is scarcely possible I should lose a clue once given, but, you see, if I have not correct information given, that is, if these men have nothing to do with it, all subsequent exertions are useless; there is nothing so essential as a good beginning."

"I see, I see; well, well, your plan is a good one, but you have all the information I can give you; you must therefore, if they don't do, have a few more names of my acquaintances, and try again."

"And now, Don Jose, about the pay?"

"It shall be most liberal."

"I may depend?"

"You may; you are too useful a man to be neglected, therefore do not let money matters be any impediment."

"Exactly; but will you advance a little, by way of putting me in funds, as I must use the gold as I go on."

"Very well—take this purse, and it is a heavy one, and begin your task."

Monserino took the bag of gold proffered to him, and finding it weighty, deposited it carefully in his own pocket.

Monserino quitted the presence of Don Jose, with assurances that he would put his plan in force immediately, and begin the surveillance at once upon either of the individuals who had been named to him.

The spy put another of his own choosing upon one of them, while himself watched the other during the day.

Monserino placed a watch upon the actions of the Cardinal di Vinci, as the churchman, he was sure, required less trouble to watch than a layman, and he himself watched Don Gusman.

The day passed with but little alteration, but towards evening there came several persons, who called at Don Gusman's, men who were opposed to the supremacy of Don Jose. Among them were several whom he recognised, and this induced Monserino to think he was in the right.

The hours passed away. Not for one moment did the spy let his eyes repose on any other object, lest he should miss something of the greatest importance; his greedy eyes devoured each trivial circumstance, and he noted the names of all he knew by sight.

This done, he prepared to make a night at the same watch. Soon after that, he perceived the Cardinal di Vinci at a short distance, coming towards the mansion of Don Gusman. He immediately concealed himself, and then saw the cardinal enter the abode of Don Gusman, and he was followed by his own man.

It was now getting late, and Monserino muttered to himself,—

"The plot thickens. Something must be got from this," and he approached his own man, who had not perceived him.

"What has happened?" he said to him in an under tone, when no one was nigh.

"The cardinal has been busy to-day."

"Aye, has he so? Well, relate to me all you know as quickly as you can."

"Then it was this:—the cardinal has been to several people to-day, and there appears to be something on foot; he has had two messengers from the Holy Inquisition, and has appeared very uneasy; he has, I said, been to several people, and there have been several people to him; and, moreover, there appeared to be something that made them all cautious and suspicious. I had the greatest difficulty in keeping near, without being seen or suspected."

"You may now return and watch the cardinal's abode, and see who comes there, and where they may go to."

The man gave a sign, and passed away like a shadow.

Monserino himself placed his hands upon the arms he always wore, and drawing his cloak around him, he awaited with impatience the result of this meeting, for such to his mind it evidently was.

It was some hours ere there was any appearance of a break up among the party at Don Gusman's, and had the risk not been so great, he would have endea-

voured to have procured information of what was going on, by attempting to get into the house under some pretext or other, if he could not get in by stealth.

Monserino was a man of great daring and courage, full of expedients and excuses; and, moreover, he was cat-like in his movements, endowed with great foresight and cunning, joined to great perseverance and patience; he had by these means overcome obstacles that had been sufficient to deter and discourage all others, and had often baffled them.

It was near midnight when some of the guests at Don Gusman's quitted his abode, and appeared to disperse themselves through the streets of Madrid.

Monserino, however, did not stir from his post, but remained there until he saw the two principals. Don Gusman and the Cardinal di Vinci came out, though both were disguised to escape observation; but the spy was too well acquainted with their persons to mistake them, and they passed close by him without their perceiving him, and he heard the Cardinal de Vinci say, as they passed,—

"He is dead. We have nothing to fear, however. I have taken the precaution of having the meeting held in another apartment further to the rear of the premises."

"That is well," replied Don Gusman.

No more was heard; and when the two had proceeded to some distance, Monserino stepped from his hiding-place, and followed the conspirators.

This was a matter of no easy performance, and they were cautious in the extreme; sometimes retraversing the street they had before gone down, and more than once Monserino had to shelter himself beneath some broken pillar or doorway, or in any place that served to screen him for the moment from his observers.

After all this circuitous travelling, they came near to the old mansion before spoken of, and the conspirators then slunk into their house of meeting, with as little noise as possible, and as quickly as they could.

By the time they had got in, Monserino had arrived at the door, and could distinctly hear the last man's tread along the hollow passage. As the sounds died away, he produced a skeleton key, and opened the door.

This was an anxious moment to Monserino, who listened for some minutes with the deepest attention to every sound that might be heard, for he well knew that, if caught, his life was forfeited, and yet he persevered.

All was silent, and he crept silently towards the stair-head, and there he again paused, but he was nearly surprised; for another conspirator came in after him, and he had but time to slink into an empty room, when the stranger passed him.

With a cat-like step, he followed him, until he saw him go up a staircase, where he followed him, and then he entered a room, the door of which closed immediately after him.

Monserino paused some moments, and heard the conspirators were engaged in conversation with each other.

He then searched along the walls until he came to a door, where he paused, and finding the door open, he gently pushed it, and entered the apartment, and found, to his great satisfaction, that he could distinguish all that passed.

The cardinal had been engaged in reading the names over, and all answered but one, and that was the unfortunate man who had been poniarded in the cell of the Inquisition.

"Friends," said the cardinal, "the last name will not be answered; he has ceased to exist; he is no more.

"There was proof given to me that he was a traitor—he had even confessed the existence of the conspiracy, and we were nearly betrayed; but I took measures in accordance with my oath, which binds me to you, and you to me. I am the judge who condemned him, and ordered his execution. Have I done right?"

There was a momentary pause, and then the conspirators replied, as with one voice,—

"Yes—yes! he deserved death!"

"Then proceed we to business."

"But why have we met in this room instead of the hall below?"

"Because we might be watched; because, as there had been a traitor—though I am in my own mind convinced that there are none aware of our objects besides ourselves—I thought that it would, nevertheless, be better to meet in another part of the premises."

"That I think equally prudent with making the traitor pay the penalty of his treason on the spot."

"True—true!"

"And now, friends," said the cardinal, "I have not yet had an interview with the French ambassador, and, therefore, have not his ultimatum. I do not yet know to what extent we may be relied upon for our purpose."

"When may this be learned?"

"In the course of to-morrow," replied the cardinal, "I expect to see him."

"Is there any certainty of that?"

"Yes; but why ask the question?—have you any doubts respecting it?"

"None. I inquired, because, if there were any doubt, it would be better not to meet again until the night following the day on which you are sure you will ascertain all that we desire to know."

"That will be to-morrow night; for to-morrow morning I shall see his excellency."

"Then to-morrow night will be a meeting for further deliberation."

"Yes, we shall meet not to deliberate upon the necessity of action, but upon the means and the nature of our first step."

"Good—good."

"Such I believe to be our wishes."

"It is—it is."

"Yes," added Don Gusman, "most truly, cardinal, have you said it is our intention, nay, our wish and hope. Inaction does not become Spaniards, when their rights and privileges are trampled on, the clergy ill-treated, and the nobles put aside; this cannot be allowed to exist, nor shall it, while there is one amongst us who boasts the proud title of Spaniard."

"Bravo—good!"

There was a general exclamation of approbation at these expressions of sentiment, that so well accorded with their own feelings.

"Well, then," said Di Vinci, "we will adjourn until to-morrow at midnight, and then we shall have time to form some definite plan of operations, because we shall know exactly what we have to depend upon."

"Yes, we can all turn the matter over in our minds, and each by doing so much will aid the general plan, as being better prepared to discuss whatever may be proposed."

"Exactly," replied the cardinal; "I and Don Gusman will have by that time some plan which will be submitted to your approval."

This being all agreed, they gave each other the mutual assurances that they would be true and faithful, and harbour no treason one towards another, but would league, weal or woe, for life and death.

This done, they all left the apartment, and proceeded cautiously down the same way they had entered the deserted building.

Monserino paused, and scarce drew his breath, until the last sound ceased to reverberate through the stone passages, and then he crept to the door of the next apartment, and listened with breathless attention; but no sound met his ear, and then he crept towards the stairs, which he descended.

Once did Monserino start; he ran against an old door, which immediately fell upon him. In the fright of the moment, he believed himself seized, and drew his long, keen poniard; but a moment's reflection taught him the nature of the impediment, and he replaced it, though he was much shaken by the suddenness of the shock; but he shook it off, and in a few moments more he stood in the street.

After a cautious survey to ascertain if he had been watched, he at that hour of the morning proceeded at once to the mansion of Don Jose.

Servants were always awake there, and such men as Monserino could always gain admission to the minister at what hour soever it might be, and when he entered the yet lighted hall, he soon aroused some of the sleepy serving men, and desired some of them instantly to awaken Don Jose and inform him that he desired to speak to him upon business of importance.

This was done; and one of them returned, saying to Monserino,—

"My master will receive you, signor; walk this way."

Monserino was shown into a splendidly furnished bed-room. On a couch of the most costly fittings and furniture lay the minister, anxiously looking for the entrance of Monserino.

When the door was closed, Jose called out to him, saying,—

"What news Monserino, eh?"

"The best."

"Indeed! have you discovered them?"

"I have."

"Then that rascally cardinal was one of them, I'll be sworn."

"You are correct, Don Jose; he and Don Gusman are the leading members of one of the most dangerous conspiracies I ever heard of."

"Indeed! then that accounts for the courtesy with which he treats me. Ah! ah! ah! shallow-pated fools, to think that Don Jose is so easily blinded by outward demeanour!"

"Their meetings have been held at midnight in the old deserted mansion or palace, that has stood so many years without an owner."

"Indeed!"

"Yes, and they expect the aid of the French ambassador to assist them."

"Ah!"

"Yes; the Cardinal di Vinci is to see him to-day and arrange plans definitively, and they went in a body to plan and discuss the nature of the first step they intend taking."

Don Jose paused for some minutes, and appeared buried in reflection, and then he said to Monserino,—

"Tell me exactly the kind of place they meet in, and where you were?"

"I should say it was a large room, and an empty one, by the sound of voices; and the room I was in, from what I could guess by the uncertain light that I had, was a smaller one—as suppose one very long and lofty room, divided unequally by a thin partition, through which you could hear every word that was uttered by any one in each room."

"Then the partition is very thin between the two rooms."

"It is."

"Would a musket-ball go through it, and take effect at the other end of the apartment?"

"Most certainly."

"Then give me writing materials."

Don Jose then wrote a short note and delivered it to Monserino, saying,—

"This note will authorise you to obtain the aid of thirty of the guard, and to take them at once to the house and secret them in the same room in which you were, examine the other, and I will be with you before the hour of meeting; the guard must be there before daybreak, else some accidental wanderer may betray us."

At the head of thirty resolute men, commanded by a captain, Monserino entered the desolated mansion; carefully did he watch and efface any footmark, and when the whole party entered the apartment, they piled their arms, and waited in silence for the events of the night.

Daylight came, and Monserino examined the room in which the conspirators met; it was such as he had guessed, and the room in which he had stationed himself looked out into a garden now rank with weeds.

Long before the hour appointed, Don Jose was present with the party stationed, and made careful examination into the nature of the place, and with devilish glee he ordered the soldiers to face the partition, ten kneeling, and the next ten stooping, so that the three tens could fire at one instant, when he gave the word.

The sounds of footsteps approached, and there was scarcely a breath drawn—not a hand or musket moved. It was near ten minutes or a quarter of an hour before every one of the conspirators were supposed to be present.

Then Don Jose distinctly heard the voice of D. Vinci calling over the muster-roll, and then the solemn oath was repeated, the congratulations of the conspirators, and the adherence of the French ambassador, who would aid them with influence, money, and men

How Don Jose laughed in his heart at the confidence of these men—how he gloated over the stunning effect of the surprise he was going to bring down upon them.

He had taken the precaution to have the window of the room, in which he and the party were stationed, opened, to get rid of as much as possible the effects of the concussion.

He stood ready to give the word, with his hands raised to his ears, ready to stop them, but yet listening.

"Down with tyranny—down with Don Jose!" exclaimed the conspirators, in answer to some remarks of Don Gusman. This was the signal of their fate, for Don Jose waited but for some such thing as this.

"Fire!" shouted Jose, in a stentorian voice, which sounded yet louder in the momentary stillness that reigned.

The signal had been waited for with some impatience by the guard, who were tired of their posture, and they fired as if by one intent.

It is impossible to describe the effect it had—it was deafening—the crashing of the fragile materials of the wainscotting, the dense smoke by which the place was filled, the recovery and re-loading of arms by the guard, all formed a picture easier to be imagined than described.

CHAPTER XXXVII.

TERROR OF THE CONSPIRATORS. — THE SCENE OF DESTRUCTION.—THE DISPOSAL OF THE PRISONERS.

It would be difficult to describe the scene of confusion, consternation, and dire dismay that took place among the conspirators. It was perfectly indescribable.

The sound of Jose's voice, when he gave the word to fire, was distinctly audible to them, and it sounded like a voice from above, and produced an effect perfectly electrifying; and then, before thought came to their aid, or even instinct caused them to shrink from the concealed enemy, came the iron shower, crashing and tearing through the flimsy partition that separated them from their enemy, and striking them to the earth dead, dying, and wounded.

The very house re-echoed, nay, shook to its very foundation; the doors rattled, and the windows became shattered, and fell out. Don Jose and his party could not for many minutes recover from the effect the shock had upon their hearing.

They could not even hear the groans that were uttered by the expiring and the maimed for some seconds.

The conspirators, when they saw their numbers decreased by about one half, and that that half were wounded, dead, and dying, saw that they had been betrayed. For a moment they staggered beneath the shock, and the few who were not thoroughly bereft of their faculties for the time, made frantic efforts to escape, and some of them succeeded; for, as we have said, Don Jose and his party were stunned with their own work for some moments.

They, however, soon recovered, and rushed from their place of concealment, and endeavoured to enter the next apartment, which they found however had been secured.

A delay of some minutes now ensued, and the guard then beat the door in with the buts of their carbines. They entered the room, and were immediately met with a discharge of small arms, such as pistols, and a desperate attempt was made by some who remained to cut their way through the guard.

But this was the last attempt of men who sought but an instant death; for, though several of the guard were killed, yet they received the conspirators upon the point of their bayonets, and many were killed.

All was enveloped in darkness. The concussion had extinguished the lights; the rooms were filled with smoke, and the smell of gunpowder was very strong.

The groans of the wounded were sufficient to inform Don Jose of the success of his scheme, and how that minister's heart glowed like a fiend at this sign of the effect his plans had secured.

"Lights!" cried Jose, "lights! Let me see who are the friends of the king and the state."

The torches were soon lighted, and then a scene presented itself to their view. The room had been built for a saloon, and was ornamented with various devices on the walls and ceilings.

There, in the middle of the room, and at the further end, lay the dead bodies of the unfortunate conspirators; others were dying, and many were wounded, and some stood with their drawn swords, endeavouring to effect their escape from the window, which was at a great height from the ground.

The floor was literally drenched in blood, which ran in streams from one side of the room to another.

There was a pause of several moments' continuance, during which Don Jose examined carefully the features of those who lay helpless on the floor, and then said to the guard,—

"Secure your prisoners!"

This was not done without a slight struggle; so hopeless did it appear to them to surrender, they expected no mercy.

The officer, seeing there would be some more blood spilt, cried out to his men to keep together and reload, and then advance upon the recusants, whom he then called on to surrender.

This had the desired effect, and they at once surrendered themselves to their fate.

"Where is the Cardinal di Vinci?" inquired Jose, in a disappointed tone.

"He is not here," replied the officer, looking over the dead and prisoners.

"And Don Guzman?"

"He is also not here."

"Some have escaped," said Don Jose. "How could that have happened?"

"That may have happened immediately after the men fired, by some means unknown to us at present."

"We shall have them, and the punishment their deeds deserve with ——"

"Who talks of punishment?" exclaimed a dying man, as he raised himself upon his elbow, while the blood flowed fast from his wound. "Is it you, Don Jose?"

Don Jose nodded.

"You who have brought many brave men to this, and ——"

"I! You came here for traitorous purposes, and you have now been punished, and you, of course, blame any one but yourselves, as though the slain robber should complain of the fate he provoked."

"False-hearted liar!" vehemently replied the dying man; "you first drive men to band together for their own safety, and then you reproach us with having done what you have compelled."

"I compel! I am but the minister of another's will," replied Don Jose; "but of what use is it to talk thus to a prisoner?"

"You are a sycophant—a mere pander! one who, to prosecute his own ambitious end, will descend to any meanness—to any act, however unmanly and derogatory!"

"Cease to speak—your last moments are at hand. Seek the aid of a confessor."

"I need none."

"Your passage will be shorter; but perhaps your friend the cardinal has secured you a safe conveyance."

"Impious man! do you not know that he who dies in a righteous cause, merits eternal felicity," replied the dying man.

Don Jose shrugged his shoulders, and said to him in reply,—

"Well, well, I would not undertake the voyage upon such a hope, and under such assurance. It would be doubtful."

"I have faith."

"You require it at this moment."

"Yes," replied the conspirator, "I do, and have it; and hence I die without sorrow or regret for the course I have taken."

"You die then without repenting of the mischief you have caused; but regret that you have not been able to cause more evil than this."

"The evil is of your own committing, and not ours."

"Ah! ah! ah! But come, soldiers, do your duty; bind the prisoners, and march them to the prison to await examination."

"Before that is done, I would speak to you. I have but a few moments more to live."

"Say on."

"I wish to speak to you unheard by others—it concerns you to know."

"I am willing to be in ignorance of it. Therefore speak out or not at all."

"Well, then, take this, with the curse of a dying Spaniard, and a grandee of Spain."

So saying, the conspirator drew forth a small pistol, and levelling it at Don Jose, fired, but without effect; the ball, it is true, grazed his cheek, but scarcely touched the skin.

This was enough to cause Don Jose to start, and become exceedingly pale. He was much enraged, and would have inflicted death upon the unfortunate conspirator, but the moment he perceived that he had failed in his object, he fell back and expired.

The conspirators were all bound, and such as were capable of walking, were hurried off to the prison, while a guard of about ten men were left in care of the wounded, with the promise of sending them speedy relief.

On looking out of the window, at the end of the room, it was evident that several had attempted to escape that way, and several lay in the court-yard beneath, unable to rise, having been disabled by the fall; while it was quite possible that some few, by great good fortune, might possibly have been able to escape that way.

Then cautioning the guard against a surprise, Don Jose and the prisoners quitted the deserted mansion, and he proceeded himself towards his own abode.

The consternation of the immediate neighbourhood of the spot where all this had taken place was very great. The people were mostly in bed, and they were awakened by the heavy discharge of musketry; they were unable at first to tell what was the cause of the alarm.

Some supposed that an earthquake had been felt, while others imagined that some explosion had taken place, while others, nearer to the spot, imagined some awful occurrence had taken place—perhaps the old building itself had fallen to the earth with such a terrific crash.

They immediately proceeded to their windows, but, at first, this gave them no satisfaction; for they could see nothing, save that the old building really stood where it did.

Soon after, however, about twenty of the royal guard were seen to come out of the house with a number of prisoners. They were certainly prisoners, because they were bound to each other, and marched in the centre of the guards.

This was food for speculation to those who saw this occurrence; but their view was but momentary; the party passed onwards, and was lost in the darkness of night.

Don Jose saw the prisoners enter the city prison, and reminded the captain of the guard of the necessity of reinforcing the troops at various points, as well as relieving those in the place they had but just left.

CHAPTER XXXVIII.

THE EMISSARY FROM ROME.—PHILIP'S RAGE.—THE BREAK UP OF THE FETE.—THE SECRET INSTRUCTIONS TO JOSE.

WE left Philip of Spain in the spacious corridor which was at the head of the grand-staircase of his palace, listening for a moment to the music which resounded from his regal halls, and then, from its sudden cessation, becoming at once convinced that the news brought to him by Don Jose, of the sudden and most unwelcome, as well as unexpected, arrival of a messenger from the Pope, was indeed too true.

Philip was a superstitious man, if not a religious, but that answers the purpose of churchmen and priests just as well, and, perhaps, a little better. He stood for some seconds, revolving in his mind what he should do in such an extremity. At one moment his temper got the better, and rage, at the interference of the head of the church with his private affairs, governed him wholly; then, again, before he could take two steps towards the staircase, a creeping fear came over him that some dire disasters would surely fall to his share if he should be indiscreet enough to anger the church.

Thus he stood irresolute for some five or ten minutes, during which a stillness, as of the grave, pervaded the palace, and he began to tremble at being alone.

The courage of the king was not of an enduring nature. It rather consisted in ferocity when thoroughly roused, but it was not of that order which springs from reflection, and now a sensation of absolute cowardice came over him, because he was alone and there was no one to provoke him.

His hand trembled so much that he could scarcely manage to get the point of his sword into the scabbard when he tried to sheath it, ere he should, as he had now made up his mind it was necessary for him to do, descend to the grand saloon and there receive the messenger of the Pope, who, at that time of day, when superstition held mens' minds in worse bondage even than it does at present, was privileged to come when he pleased and thunder the denunciations of the representative of St. Peter at the head of any monarch who in any way offended the majesty of the Papal dominion.

It must not be supposed that Philip's immorality had provoked the censure of the most holy Catholic Church. Oh, no! monarchs might be as immoral as they liked, always provided they, to an extent which satisfied the Church of Rome, succumbed to its influence; but Philip had not done so. He had, on more than one occasion, shown a strong disposition to be too independent, and, in one or two cases, he had not listened to the suggestions of the body of cardinals with respect to the use of certain large properties, which virtually lay in the gift of the crown, but which, for many years, had been allowed to be at the disposal of the Court of Rome for ecclesiastical purposes.

Philip's extravagancies had made him lay hands upon all such waifs and strays, and, therefore, a grave discussion had ensued in the apostolic chamber with regard to him, and it was agreed that he was not quite the thing.

It was easy, after the determination had been come to that the church was to wage war against a king, to find some other excuse than that one in the conduct of the monarch, and, accordingly, Philip's conduct to his wife, and the intrigues he carried on, contrary to his vows to her, was the thing pitched upon to attack him with.

That the messenger from Rome should pitch upon the precise hour he did to disturb Philip's felicity by a visit, was a little bit of private professional malice of the Jesuit who came in that capacity, and well he knew that his employers would back him out in any aggravations he could add to the papal bull of which he was the bearer, and which was thrown out merely as a feeler to see what sort of humour his most Christian Majesty, Philip of Spain, was in.

The king would now gladly have seen Jose to ask him some particulars before he himself descended to the hall, but he had, by his sudden violence, sufficiently frightened that admirable minister to insure his not disturbing the royal cogitations for some time.

Send for him Philip would not, so he had no other resource but unaided to walk into the hall, like any one else, to ask the intruder what it was he wanted.

This was rather an undignified situation to be placed in for a king, but there was no resource, and accordingly Philip slowly descended the staircase.

His approach was seen, of course, by some of the royal attendants before he reached the entrance, so that he had not the mortification of opening the door for himself. There was a general rush to do him honour. The doors were flung wide, and a gentleman of the household disturbed the stillness that now reigned in the grand saloon, by announcing, in a loud voice, to the assembled company,—

"The king—the king!"

All eyes were turned to the door, and in another moment Philip walked in with that strange, black look upon his face which always came over it when he was much distracted by anger, fear, or any other strong and violent passion.

The courtiers shrank back, for they anticipated a very disagreeable scene indeed, and the only person who looked insolently at his ease was the Pope's messenger, whose dark and sombre attire contrasted oddly enough with the splendid and glittering jewel-bespangled costumes of the wealthy nobles of old Spain by whom he was surrounded, and who looked in some cases the dissatisfaction they felt at the interruption which had been given to the brilliant entertainment they had just begun to get into the spirit of.

A magnificent chair was brought for the king, upon which he sat himself down without saying a word, and then pulling his plumed hat still further down upon his brows, as if he would have said,—

"It is my prerogative to be covered, and I wish all to take notice of it," he fixed his eyes upon the messenger, who himself probably began to think there would be something in the shape of a disturbance, and, perhaps, such a defiance of his authority on the part of the king as was unknown in the archives of Europe.

"Philip of Spain," he said, "I appear before you as a humble messenger from the great head of the most holy Catholic Church."

Then he paused awhile, as if he would have said,—

"I must know what humour you are in before I proceed."

After this pause had lasted an unreasonable time, Philip said, in a strange, sharp, cracked voice,—

"We are here."

"His holiness," added the messenger, "sends greeting, with all loving-kindness, but much regrets that the fallibility of human nature as exhibited in your majesty, forces upon his holiness to transmit to you a decree more in the shape of an admonition than as a punishment, although the punishment is grievous."

"We are of opinion," said Philip, "that this had better been matter for our private ear."

"No," said the messenger; "such were not my instructions, and I am but a humble instrument."

"You look—very—humble," said the king, with a tone of sarcasm, which could not be mistaken.

The messenger bowed, as if in acknowledgment of a compliment, and said, meekly,—

"His holiness will much rejoice when it is reported to him in what a gentle and Christian spirit your majesty has received his most holy message and humble messenger."

"Go on," said the king.

"I had instructions, if your majesty objected to receive me publicly, to post the Pope's message on your palace doors, and who would have dared to take it down?"

The king half rose from his seat, but he sat down again instantly, as if discretion had come to his aid, and merely waving his hand, he said, with a sickly smile,—

"Go on—go on."

"His holiness prohibits your majesty from confessing or receiving absolution from any member of the church, until you shall have communicated with him and explained certain matters which it is no part of my instructions to enter into."

"This is excommunication then," said the king.

"Not properly so called," replied the messenger. "I have performed my mission, king of Spain, and now take my leave with the same humility with which I have approached you."

The amount of this humility seemed to consist in turning his back coolly upon the king, and striding out of the room with all the ease and nonchalance in the world.

"Sir messenger," cried Philip, in a loud voice, "take back, as my answer, ——"

"Aye—what?" cried the messenger, turning hastily

"Your majesty—my liege—oh, sire, be careful!" cried several of the courtiers, as they flung themselves at the feet of the king, for much they feared the dreadful consequences of a decided rupture with the court of Rome, which, although powerless in itself, yet had power to stir up all the nations of Europe against any obnoxious sovereign, and so fight out its battles with other people's means.

"Speak," added the messenger. "Philip of Spain, what is your answer which you commenced so loudly?"

"Submission!" cried the king's confessor, stepping forward, while the members of the court closed around the king, and earnestly besought him to be calm. "Submission!"

"Is that the king's answer or yours?" said the messenger.

"The king's," said a dozen voices, and the throng of courtiers opened, and Philip, without rising, slightly inclined his head.

The Pope's messenger strode from the hall, and, before another minute had elapsed, the palace was free from that most unwelcome of all guests that had set foot in it for some time.

Fear and consternation sat on every countenance. The fete was now virtually at an end, and curiosity alone detained many in the saloon, who would else have hastened to quit it, for, with the superstition of the age, they now considered the palace as unholy, and almost a damned place.

It seems strange to us, now that the yoke of superstition is shaken off by so many minds, that the church should ever have acquired so tremendous an influence as it had in the days of Philip the Second of Spain.

Such, however, was the fact. Kings were made and unmade by the court at the Vatican with the greatest ease, and the whole of Europe may be said to have been virtually under the dominion of the bold, daring, insolent, rascally churchmen who formed the conclave at Rome, and in the hands of whom the pope himself was a mere puppet, kept for show, as the head of a system, like our own gracious Queen Victoria and all her babbies, by the Grace of God, &c., &c.

Alas! times were indeed changed for popes, when Napoleon made the representative of St. Peter, sorely against his inclination, come to the Tuileries.

Even in our own day, we find that if there is any one class of men more insolent, overbearing, and intolerant than any other, it is the class of churchmen and their supporters; and many a smirking fashionable clergyman of the present day would be, if he could, the denouncing priest of three hundred years ago; but, thank God, we have changed all that, and as we find that, by the progress of improvement, every man can be his own anything, almost, we do not see why any man should not, at all events, be his own parson, and so get rid of the whole tribe of black drones wholly.

*   *   *   *

The moment the Pope's messenger was fairly gone, that gratifying fact was communicated to Philip, who thereupon drew a long breath, and said,—

"Where is Jose?"

"Here, my gracious liege," said Don Jose, emerging from behind the royal chair.

"Follow me."

The king rose and strode towards the door. When he reached it, the thought seemed to cross him for the moment, that he was treating his guests rather scurvily, and turning, he lightly raised his hat from his head, by way of being amazingly civil. Then he left the saloon, and immediately upon his footsteps followed Jose, with such a solid, vacant-looking countenance, that no one, to look at him, could have possibly devised what was going on in that prolific brain of his.

When the king had thus abruptly left the hall, the nobles knew, by his touching his hat, that he meant good night, and, consequently, they suspected that the sooner they left the better.

From mouth to mouth ran the opinion that it was better at once to break up the fete, and no one dissenting, no more dances took place, and the guests began rapidly to leave the palace, where, had all things gone smoothly, they would have kept up the festivities for at least several hours longer.

There was the dashing about of carriages, the rearing of insubordinate mules, and the usual amount of bustle which accompanies the departure of a number of persons in equipages. All this lasted nearly an hour, and by then the last guest had gone, and the royal mansion presented its usual interior aspect of subdued quiet and gorgeous repose.

The king, meanwhile, had led the way to his private cabinet, and, flinging himself into a seat, he said,—

" So, Jose—so we are at length bearded in our own palace. This is an evening's work I little looked for."

" Nor I, your majesty."

" How should you—how should you? How, indeed, could any one? This quarrel, Jose, with the court of Rome will not be easily arranged. It is too public, and well you know as well as I, that where the holy conclave at the Vatican wishes its denunciations public, as this has been made, it is with a view of enforcing some public submission on the part of the person against whom it is acting, which will be more degrading in its exactions than I shall, probably, be at all likely to accede to. That is the policy I know that is invariably pursued. You, Jose, as well as I, must know that."

" It is so, indeed, your majesty. But I am not without hopes, in this instance, that matters may be more satisfactorily accommodated than your majesty supposes."

" No, Jose, they will not. It is part of the artful policy of Rome—a policy I have always set my face against—to degrade now and then a king, as an example, forsooth, to other monarchs."

" Upon some of the petty monarchs of Europe that scheme has been tried and succeeded," said Jose; " but it will hardly be adventured, upon slight grounds, with so powerful a monarch as the King of Spain."

" But if the pontiff be obstinate, Jose, what can I do? You know, as well as I, how much I, in my own heart, despise all these priestly machinations, but you likewise know that, king as I am, I am but one man against many."

" Your majesty shows yourself to be a profound philosopher as well as a king. I should humbly suggest, that a letter be sent, in your majesty's own handwriting, to the Pope, explaining matters."

" Explaining matters! How the devil can I explain matters, Jose? There is nothing to explain. I suppose it's that Cardinal de Vinci's doings, because he has ferreted out some of the disagreements between us and our queen, as if that was any affair of his. How can I explain?"

" I should send a large sum of money."

" Money! I have no money."

" But your majesty, like all other gracious kings, can tax the people to the tune of enough to pay off the conclave of St. Peter's, for I have not a doubt but your majesty's application of some revenue which holy mother church thinks she has a right to, is at the bottom of all this bitterness shown to your majesty."

" You think so?"

" On my soul, I do!"

" Then you have, I am sure, special reasons for so doing. You must think of a tax, Don Jose, that the people will grumble the least at, you know, for already there is much dissatisfaction."

" There is; but I think I can so manage, by adding to some taxes and taking from others, and lying with regard to them all, as to mystify the people, and make them believe that something is being done to relieve them of a burden, when, in reality, a new one, and that of no inconsiderable amount, is imposed. You understand me, your Majesty?"

" Not quite; but that is of no consequence. Get the money, and get it quickly, by fair means or by foul. Of course, we know the people must pay, however the question may be mystified, and they may be deceived."

" Exactly, your majesty. What's the use of ' a people,' but to huzza when the monarch graciously appears, and pay cheerfully for his state, and equipage, and general expenses?"

" Certainly—certainly. I believe, Jose, that is the properly recognised view which monarchs and ministers have, from time immemorial, taken of a population."

" And will continue to be the view taken," added Jose, " while the world stands, your majesty."

" No doubt—no doubt. But now of this girl—this Countess de Bazan, around whom more difficulties seem to be thrown than ever I could have imagined possible. You heard the alarm she made?"

" I did, your majesty, and it was heard likewise by many of your court. I saw significant glances interchanged. Nothing in my hearing was said; but yet there can be no doubt but the outcry she made will be subject-matter of much remark among the courtiers. By Heaven! she made herself well heard throughout the palace, and no one could miss knowing that something unusual was going on."

" Confound her virtue," said the king. Is it assumed or real, think you, Jose?"

" Real; and that makes the conquest, no doubt, worth so much more in your majesty's eyes."

" Of course it does. But we must not create scandal in the palace on any consideration, Jose. I think it a bad plan to have brought her here at all."

" Her obstinate resistance has made her residence here a trouble."

" True; she must be removed, Jose, to that place which, although ostensibly yours, is really mine— that place devoted to intrigue, where all are secure and discreet."

" Your majesty alludes to the villa a league from Madrid, en route to Aranjues?"

" I do. Be it your care, Jose, to have this beautiful but mad-brained girl removed thither. The opposition she has made to me has but maddened my desire. She shall be mine."

" Your majesty has but to will it. I marvel she is so silent in her chamber."

" I locked the door, Jose, and, no doubt, finding escape impracticable, she has resigned herself to patience."

" Probably. Have I your majesty's permission to seek her?"

" You have. I shall myself seek no other interview with her here, for now that the curiosity of the court is once awakened, I cannot say, even in my own palace, I shall be free from spies and listeners."

" Most true. And now your majesty will permit me to say, that I cannot help thinking some studied complaints of your queen have drawn down upon you the visitation of to-night. I would recommend, before the letter be written to the pontiff, that you see the queen."

" I see the queen, Jose ! I'd as soon see the devil himself."

" May I, then, with the leave of your majesty, make a seeming passing call at Aranjues, and try if I can, without direct questioning, discover if such is the case ?"

" As you please—as you please ; but the queen, you know, has such a bad opinion of you, that I do not think you will succeed."

" With your majesty's gracious permission, I will attempt even what would seem to be impossibilities."

" Go, then, when it suits you ; but first see to the proper bestowal of the Countess de Bazan at the villa."

" It shall be done."

The king nodded, as a signal for Jose to leave him, and the minister bowed himself out, and at once betook himself to the apartment in which Philip had taken the precaution to lock Maritana previous to his interview with the pope's messenger.

" 'Tis, after all," muttered Jose to himself, " perhaps better as it is. If Maritana be now removed at once to this most inaccessible retreat, I can easily find means to convince the queen of what she yet, I am sure, doubts, that the king keeps a mistress to supply her place. I will either hurry the queen into some act of violence, which shall be her destruction, or she shall yield to me. Humph ! she said that she thought I was playing a bold game, and she named the stake if she won—my head—well, well, be it so. My head or hers. If she will not be mine, I will so contrive that she shall seem sufficiently guilty for Philip to feel himself justified in putting her to death. Already are his suspicions that way awakened, although this affair of the ring has really made less impression on him than I thought it would. Either his mind has become, by his own irregularities, indifferent to the supposed guilt of his queen, or he is satisfied with the death of the poor devil who was supposed to have been honoured by such a gift from her majesty.

" I daresay, now, that was really a very inoffensive kind of man in his way; but he, unfortunately for him, stood in my way, so, like all things and people, who happen to be in the way of the great designs of Providence, he got crushed. I do but copy the wisdom of Heaven, for that is precisely the way in which it conducts the world's affairs ; namely, relentlessly to sacrifice individuals to arrangements.

" A stone falls from a high building by a principle and an arrangement of nature, and were the best and wisest man beneath, it would not swerve a hair's breadth from its even course to spare him from having his brains dashed out. That is being systematic, and so am I. Surely it must be sublime to imitate the glorious mode of proceeding adopted by Providence, so I shall continue to do so, and having made arrangements, woe be to those whom chance or evil fortune may make stand in my way."

Thus reasoning, this bold and daring sceptic, with a mocking smile upon his countenance, passed on towards the chamber of the beautiful and persecuted Countess de Bazan.

He turned the key into the lock, and, at the first glance into the apartment, he thought she was gone ; but a second assured him she was there, and lying upon the floor insensible, or nearly so.

He raised her up in his arms, and the movement recovered her.

" Maritana," he said ; " countess. Lovely and incomparable being, look up. All love you, and, therefore, can you wonder that I, too—Humph! she is awakening from her swoon ; I must be cautious yet. Maritana—Maritana—Maritana."

" Where am I ? Oh, Heaven, where am I ?" she said, faintly.

" In perfect safety."

She opened her eyes, and gazed on the countenance of Don Jose. Then disengaging herself with loathing repugnance from his arms, she cried,—

" No, no ; not with that face near me. You are my evil destiny ; away—away ! I loathe you, while I tremble to behold you. You are a fiend—an awful fiend. You are not human."

CHAPTER XXXIX.

MARITANA'S ILLNESS. — THE PHYSICIAN.—THE ASSASSINS.—LAZARILLO'S ENDEAVOURS TO SEE THE COUNTESS DE BAZAN.

MARITANA felt too weak almost to stand, and she gladly availed herself of a chair to sink into, at the further end of the apartment. Then tears came to her relief, and as they flowed freely from her eyes, she did not, despite even the presence of Don Jose—and it is always mortifying to show emotion before those we hate—attempt to stem them, for she felt much relief by them, and that she was now more capable of taking her own part, and resisting the dreadful tyranny of the profligate minister.

When, then, her emotion had subsided, she turned her eyes upon him with flashing indignation, and, in a voice of reproach, beneath which even he recoiled for a moment, she cried,—

" Villain—deceiver—double villain ! Now, indeed, I know you, and can well believe all that I have ever heard of villany and fiend-like malice coupled with your name. You have now thrown off the mask, and never again can you attempt to deceive me by your false promises. Don Cæsar is my husband, and if he be dead, I will remember that I am his countess, and have his honour, the honour of his name in my keeping. If he be alive ; and, oh, grant Heaven that he may be so, he will yet exact from you, Jose, a fearful retribution."

" Indeed, lovely one," said Jose, " you are much mistaken."

" I have been, but am not now."

" The Don Cæsar whom you know is dead. Your husband is the veritable man, and the honourable gentleman you have this night, in defiance of your vows, treated so badly."

" 'Tis false—false !"

" Nay, I should not wonder if he were actually to hate you."

" Oh, that he would. Oh, that he would."

" What a strange prayer for a wife. But I happen to know he loves you with that sort of passion which gathers strength from opposition. You cannot escape him, lovely countess : and although you affect not to be obliged to me for the favour I have done you in promoting your interests so much, you will, I feel assured, be of a very different opinion."

" You talk in vain, Jose. I have now no hesitation in my mind concerning your character. Never again, for one moment, can you delude me into a belief that you are my friend."

" Well, then, Countess de Bazan, since you reject the fair course which is open to you. Since you will have me as an enemy, instead of a friend, know that, despite all you can do, and all you can say, I will place you in the arms of your husband. I have sworn it, and you know, or you ought to know, that I am by far too religious to break my oath."

" Religion and you are as the poles, asunder."

" That's your opinion."

" I know it, villain ! You but profane the sacred word by uttering it with those blaspheming lips. But your conquest over me may yet not be so easy as you imagine. I know I am in the palace of the king, and even yet I may find some gallant heart which will aid me, some strong arm to rescue me. Tremble, Don

Jose, for you may have cause more to dread me than I you."

" I never trembled."

" There will come a day when you will learn to do so."

" Indeed! Let it come. I am one who fears nothing, because he believes nothing. I have but one great point of faith at present, and that is in thy beauty."

The door at this moment was dashed open, and the king stood on the threshold.

" No more of this," he said, in a subdued voice. " No more of this."

Jose started as if a thunderbolt had fallen at his feet, and, despite his assertion that he never trembled, he did so now most strongly and perceptibly.

" I—I," he stammered. " I only ——"

" Peace! Enough," said the king. " Countess, it is very far from my wish or desire to make you unhappy. Very far, indeed; but you cannot be ignorant that you are beautiful."

" Should I be, therefore, persecuted?"

" And being beautiful," added the king, without noticing her interruption, " I cannot choose but love you."

Here he paused, as if expecting an answer; but Maritana now, after one shuddering glance, turned her eyes from him.

" You do not now love me; but you will learn to do so," he added. " Lovely creature, opposition but increases my love. This persevering rejection of the suit I plead but increases my wish to call you mine. The church has united us. Then I knew but little of you. It was—was ——"

" In obedience to the commands of the Queen," said Jose.

" Yes, yes. Although I had seen you, and adored you, but not to the extent I do now."

" You had better leave her," whispered Jose, to the king. " She is in a very dangerous mood."

" Pho, pho!"

" But your—a-hem! I mean my worthy friend, Don Cæsar de Bazan; perhaps to-morrow your lovely and accomplished countess will be better prepared to smile upon your affection."

" Never!" cried Maritana; " never!"

Even as she spoke, and before the words had well left her lips, she made a sudden rush, and passing the king, who had left the door slightly open, before he was aware, she dashed into the outer apartment, and without an instant's pause, she then gained the corridor, and the head of the grand staircase, before either Jose or the king could sufficiently recover from their first intense surprise to stop her.

Jose and the king then at one and the same moment appeared to become aware of the urgent necessity there was for pursuing the flying girl, and they both made a rush together to the chamber door with such unthinking violence, that they ran against each other, and both fell sprawling on the polished floor in the outer room.

" D——n!" cried the king.

" Curse you!" shouted Jose.

" Take that," said Philip, and drawing the short dagger he always wore, he made a tremendous stab at Jose's head with it, but the weapon only passed through his hair, slightly grazed his ear, and then sunk deep in the flooring.

Jose was infuriated, and grasped the king by the throat, and shook the Lord's anointed with a vehemence that threatened scarcely to leave a breath in his body.

All this was the work of a very few brief moments, during which neither party had had time to reflect; but soon reason came to the aid of both, and instantly releasing each other, they rose, and looked bewildered in the direction Maritana had so suddenly taken.

" My liege," cried Jose, dropping on his knees, " pardon me for allowing my temper for one moment to get the better of my humble duty to your majesty."

Philip glanced at the dagger, which was quivering in the boards, and said,—

" You had very nearly, Jose, been past asking for pardon; but let this be forgotten. Go after that girl—secure her. I must not be seen, or some officious fool will tell her who I am. Go, Jose. Quick, quick."

Don Jose was off in a moment, and the king sat down on a sofa, to recover some of his lost breath.

" Was ever an intrigue," he muttered, " so troublesome to a king? In this affair there seems to be nothing but pain, and mortification, and endless disappointments. I have received more insults, more personal indignity in the prosecution of this one amour, than I could sum up in my whole reign beside; and what progress have I made—literally none. She seems to have a hatred to me, which transcends all belief. Well, she shall be mine, nevertheless. I will not be foiled. No; by force she shall be mine, if no other method shall present itself."

With this worthy and pious resolution, Philip waited with what patience he could command for the re-appearance of Don Jose, who, he knew, could have no great difficulty in capturing the lovely fugitive, because her leaving the palace was a matter of impossibility, closely guarded at every outlet as it was.

In the meantime, Maritana, after a moment's pause, had made a rush down the grand staircase, and gained the saloon, where, had the numerous guests with which it had been so lately filled still have been there, she would have produced, no doubt, a very extraordinary sensation.

As it was, all she met was a terrified page, who, when he saw her coming towards him, made his escape as quickly as he could, because she looked like one bereft of her senses.

Maritana pursued him, for as he was the first person she had seen, she did not exactly wish to lose sight of him; and when he found such was the case, his flight became a perfect race, and he stopped not till he gained the grand vestibule, when he rushed in among the guard there stationed, crying with all his might,—

" Murder! help, help! here's a mad woman in the palace. Help, help! murder!"

" 'Tis I who should cry for help," said Maritana; " oh, if you have the hearts of men, aid me. Where is the king? Let me throw myself at his feet, and claim protection. Help me. The king—where is the king?"

The guard and the pages who thronged the hall looked amazed and terrified, for so sudden an apparition as that of a beautiful female in so much apparent disorder, was to them a most mysterious circumstance.

" She's mad," cried the page, " she's mad;" and the proposition being the only one offered, met with general approval, and one and all shouted,—

" A mad woman! a mad woman!"

" Secure her instantly," cried Jose, at that moment making his appearance on the staircase.

" Not yet," cried Maritana, and she caught up from among a pile of them one of the arquebuses of the guard, and presented it at Don Jose.

The action was so sudden, that had Jose not had the presence of mind to throw himself back on the staircase, there might have been an end of his career, for scarcely had he done so, when Maritana discharged the musket, and made the palace echo again with the report.

Then dashing the unloaded piece on to the stone flooring of the hall, she made a rush through a half open door she saw, with the hope that it might lead to freedom; but on the other side were five stone steps, down which she fell, and striking her forehead as she did so, she for a second time that night lapsed into a state of insensibility.

"D——n!" said Jose, as he scrambled to his feet. "Twice to-night have I had narrow escapes from death. I shall dread the third time."

All that had occurred in the vestibule had occupied a space of much shorter amount of time than it has taken us to record it, and when Jose called aloud, as he now did to the guard,—

"Secure her! she is unarmed!" they were much surprised to find him alive, for the general opinion was, that the shot had taken effect, he had fallen so exactly almost at the moment of the discharge of the arquebus.

Alas! poor Maritana, she was now an easy conquest, and at Don Jose's command was carried back again, and placed on a couch in the chamber from whence she had recently fled with so much precipitation.

Those who bore her thither, and knew as well they did that those were the private apartments of the king, had their own thoughts on the matter, but a palace is not exactly the place in which to utter one's own thoughts, be they of what complexion they may, so everybody kept a remarkably prudent silence, and Don Jose told them it was a prudent silence, and that it would be prudent exceedingly not to break it on any account.

The king, when informed of the accident that had befallen the Countess de Bazan, at first threw increased blame on Don Jose, as well as on everybody else; and when Jose, during a pause in the monarch's invectives, said,—

"Your majesty will surely admit that I ran into quite enough danger to secure her, for she fired an arquebus belonging to one of the palace guard full in my face, the king replied,—

"And I suppose your head was so hard, Jose, that it resisted the bullets successfully. Between you and I, I do believe that this young girl will be the death of you."

Jose turned a little pale, for the prediction to him was a disagreeable one, inasmuch as it chimed in too well with his own uncomfortable surmises. He, however, changed the subject, by saying,—

"Does not your majesty think that a physician had better be sent for?"

"Truly, yes, if she be badly hurt."

"May I send?"

"Take care that you get a discreet one, who will not babble about having been in the palace."

"Trust me, sire, for that. There is a clever little leech resides not far from here, who I will get."

"Do so, then, for this long insensibility of the lovely countess gives me some alarm."

Don Jose left the room, and while the king, who by this time had got a little nervous, sat watching Maritana, he proceeded to the hall, where of the first attendant he met, he said,—

"Have I been inquired for by any one?"

"Yes, my lord," was the answer. "Two persons, who showed a written pass from you, are in waiting, but they desired that you should not be disturbed unless you asked for them."

"Good. Where are they?"

"This way, my lord, if you please. This way."

The attendant led Don Jose to a small room, where were seated none other than the very two assassins who had performed so horrible a deed upon the unfortunate queen's messenger, whose only crime was, that he was selected for his trustworthiness by his royal mistress, to be the bearer of her letter to the king, which the reader is aware was intercepted by such diabolical means by the infamous Don Jose.

At Don Jose's appearance, these two gentlemen rose and greeted him with that mock respect, but really insolent familiarity, with which such characters feel that they may greet their employer who have brought themselves down to their level by the common principle of criminality.

"We have been here some time, noble sir," said one, "for we received your message; but—but—ho—ho—but ——"

"But what?"

"We have a grievous complaint to make."

"Of what nature? I am in no mood for frivolity, so say what you have to say at once."

"Why, we would scorn a frivolous complaint, we would. It's beneath us. The real fact is, most noble sir, that we have been here now some hours, and have had nothing to drink."

"Pshaw! This is not my house."

"We know that, sir—we know that."

"We wishes as it was," said the other.

"You are very kind; but you see, as it is not, I cannot make you so welcome to its cellar as otherwise I might. There is gold for you. You can serve yourselves well at the next wine shop, no doubt."

"Spoke like a oracle," said one of the fellows, as he placed in his pouch the gold coin which Jose threw to him.

"Now you may suppose," said Jose, "that I should not have sent for you for nothing."

"Certainly not, noble sir."

"I want you to do a little job for me with your stilettoes. There is one Don Cæsar—a bold, daring fellow, and one who can use his weapon well."

"Ha! ha! signor—we don't care about that. We are above fencing completely."

"I believe you are. But do you know the man of whom I speak?"

"Used he," said one, "to wear a long rapier, which would stick through a hole in his threadbare cloak?"

"The same," said Jose. "You know him, I see. He must die."

"He shall."

"And that quickly, too. Half as much again as the usual price will be paid if he be disposed of before four-and-twenty hours have elapsed."

"We will find him."

The ruffians made towards the door, but Don Jose stopped them, saying,—

"Hold! Before you go on that errand, I have another of minor importance, but still one which must be done first. In the neighbourhood there resides a surgeon, named Pepito."

"We know him."

"Good. He must be brought here as soon as possible; but he must not know where he is conducted. When you get him here, you will let me know by sending me a messenger from the vestibule."

"We will manage it."

"But you must be careful to do him no injury, for he is wanted here in the exercise of his art."

"Very good, noble signor—very good."

"The details I shall leave to your own experience and judgment in such cases."

So saying, Don Jose walked from the room without any further ceremony, and his two friends, after consulting together for a few moments, left the palace.

Their first step was to proceed to a shop in the vicinity, kept by a man who dealt in charcoal; and while one of them held him in conversation concerning the present market prices of his commodity, the other stole one of the large sacks in which he was accustomed to pack it. A whisper informed the one who was talking of the success of the experiment, and then declining any purchase just then, he left likewise,

and, in a few moments, they stood at the door of little Signor Pepito, the learned leech.

The little doctor, in answer to the tremendous hammering they kept up at his door, popped his head out at an upper window, and demanded,—

"Who is there?"

"Oh, Master Pepito," cried one, "do you know Geroni, the charcoal-dealer, good sir?"

"Yes, yes."

"Well, sir, he was standing by his own door, and then you see, sir, down he fell, and they say it's all about what they call a vessel."

"A blood-vessel," cried the other. "He's bursted one, sir."

"Indeed!"

"Yes, sir. He always keeps open so late, you know, sir. It's past midnight now, and no doubt as that's the cause of it."

"Well, well, I will come to him directly."

"A thousand thanks. May all the saints protect you for a humane man as ever was."

"Now, Matteo, just hold open the sack," said the other. "Close to the door, if you please, and we'll manage this matter as pleasantly as any little affair of the kind could be managed."

The sack was held open, and in the course of about five minutes Doctor Pepito opened his door, and skipped out right into the arms of one of the scoundrels, who, seizing him in a very scientific manner round the waist, tipped him up before he was aware of

it, or could utter an exclamation, head foremost into the sack, the mouth of which they closed in an instant.

"Now, take your end, and I'll take mine," said Matteo; and this being done instanter, the two fellows walked off with the little doctor at a good round pace.

When he had recovered a little from the first shock of his surprise, he cried,—

"Murder! murder!"

This produced a good shake, and an admonition to hold his tongue.

"Murder—murder! watch!" he cried again; and this time he got a hearty kick, so he began to think it would be prudent to be still, and, with a groan, he gave himself up to his fate.

These assassins had a pass from Don Jose, so they made their way into the same waiting room in which he had held his brief interview with them, and where he joined them now again in a few moments.

"You have him?" he said.

"We have him here."

"An admirable contrivance. Follow me."

Don Jose himself let the little doctor out of the bag in the chamber where Maritana was lying; but, in the interim, she had come to her senses, and after being urged to look at her head, which she had struck in her fall, the doctor declared that no mischief was done, although, if she had not rest, mischief might ensue, and thereby he saved Maritana that night a journey to the villa in the outskirts of Madrid which had been spoken of by the king.

"Now, sir," said the doctor to Jose, "whoever you are, let me beg of you to let me walk back, instead of being carried in a sack."

"Oh, certainly," said Jose; "step this way, sir."

The little doctor followed him outside the door, where the two assassins were waiting, and before he could utter a word of dissent, he was again in the sack, and being carried down stairs as comfortably as possible, with the exception that they were not particular, and held his head downwards, instead of his feet.

He was taken to his own door, and there laid down and left to chance, for his captors returned again to the palace, to get some money in advance of Don Jose, on account of the projected assassination of our friend, Don Cæsar.

*   *   *   *   *

But what has become of Lazarillo all this time?

Upon leaving Cæsar, he had made his way direct to the palace; but Don Jose, since he had become aware of the fact of Don Cæsar's existence, had become suspicious of Lazarillo, and he left a message in the grand vestibule, that when a page in his livery should come, word was to be immediately brought to him of the fact.

Accordingly he was so informed, and then he wrote upon a slip of paper the words:—

"Lazarillo, go at once, without a moment's delay, to Aranjues, and there wait my coming.

"JOSE."

In the paper he folded a couple of gold pieces, to enable the boy to pay any necessary expense *en route*, and thus was the page compelled to leave a scene of action which, within the last few hours, had become trebly interesting to him.

He went at once to Jose's stables, and selecting a fleet, small horse, of the beautiful Andalusian breed, he, with a heavy heart, set out for the queen's palace at Aranjeus, little suspecting he was sent there merely to get him temporarily out of the way; for at that moment Don Jose did not contemplate a journey thither, although that he did so afterwards, we know, from what passed between him and the king.

CHAPTER XL.

THE RETREAT —THE OMEN OF THE WHITE HORSE.
—DON JOSE'S MESSENGER.

ONE league from Madrid was a kind of mansion, or retired residence, ostensibly belonging to Don Jose, but, in fact, it was the property of the king, for whose convenience it had been occupied.

A high wall surrounded the whole extent of the house and gardens, which were large, and this wall was lined with a thick row of tall trees, whose branches were so long and so thick that they interlaced each other.

It stood on an eminence—the highest ground in the neighbourhood, and could be seen from many places; but the windows were all inwards, and none in the outward walls of the house, so that, view it from what quarter you would, there could not be any of them seen.

The house itself was so built within its own grounds, that even those within could scarce obtain a view of the scenery by which it was encompassed.

The rooms were splendidly furnished; every luxury and convenience that wealth and rank could procure were here to be found.

The gardens were laid out with care and taste; there were many shady walks, and there appeared to be a predominance of umbrageous vegetation, where those who desired it might walk without being exposed to observation.

Indeed, from the manner in which the house was built, something in the shape of two-thirds of a circle, the whole of the windows being on the inside, they concentrated the view to one spot, and just at the opening of the circle rose a magnificent conservatory, and the small space between this and the mansion was laid out in tasteful walks, along which were cultivated the most beautiful flowers, whose blossoms made the place look a second Eden.

This delightful spot was consecrated to the intrigues of the king, and here more than one tragic occurrence, so common in those days, had taken place. Here lived, or, rather, lounged and idled, a set of servants picked out by Don Jose, and whom he knew to be confidential men, and who accepted of their service upon the understanding that they were to take no notice of anything that might happen within the mansion.

Indeed, they knew that discretion and silence were necessary; for, though they were well paid, and had little to do, yet they had a master who would neither scruple, nor find it difficult, to get rid of an indiscreet servant. Therefore, under such circumstances, they could be implicitly trusted, and more than one event of a serious character had been transacted.

The apartments assigned to them for their use were much superior to those usually made use of for a similar purpose in Spain, and there were more than enough of them to do three times the labour that devolved upon them.

They lounged upon benches, and smoked between meals, and passed their time in conversation which often turned upon matters that had occurred within the walls of that singular dwelling.

"Ah, Pedro," said one of these menials, "we shall have something to do soon; I am sure we shall be disturbed."

"And how know you that, Martinez?" inquired Pedro, languidly.

"The old sign."

"What old sign? I know of none save extra wages." said Pedro.

"I dreamed."

"Of what?"

"Of the white horse, to be sure. When there's anything to be done, I always dream of the white horse."

"You were troubled with the night-mare," suggested another.

"No, no."

"But it is very likely; I don't know anything else that would happen after the supper you ate last night."

"Pho—pho!"

"But, come, tell us all about it, for I like to hear about the marvellous."

"Well, you know, I dreamed of the white horse, and then, as a matter of course, we shall have somebody here a visitor."

"And why?"

"Because I have ——"

"Oh, that's enough; you have said that before, and we know it, but we have no proof of the truth or justice of your signs of the times. It never happened so before, that ever I heard of."

"But it has."

"Relate it, then."

"Well, then, there was the case of the foreign lady who came here, and was kept here some months, and then taken to France."

"Well?"

"She was here some time, and before she came I dreamed of the white horse, and before she went I did the same, and she had not been gone many hours before Lequard Isabella came.

"Now," said Pedro, winking at his companion, "I think it is not easy to say whether the white horse indicates a departure as well as an arrival."

"Well?"

"In that case, if anybody was to go out, you would claim to have your prediction considered as fulfilled."

"Ah, but there's nobody to go out."

"Oh, yes; if I went out that would be enough for an omen-monger."

"No, no."

"But I dare say it will be all the fulfilment you will have."

"It will not."

"At all events, it is a doubtful case—it is equal chances, I think."

"And so think I."

"But there was the case of Donna Camilla; before

she came I had the same dream, and she didn't go away at all."

"How so?"

"Oh! don't you know about that?"

"No."

"Well, we never speak of things out of school, but we are all right here."

"Right enough."

"Then you must know that one night I had a dream of the white horse, and I was laughed at for my pains; however, I knew that when I had that dream something was sure to happen immediately afterwards, and so I said. Well, all that day passed and nobody came—we hadn't heard anything of Don Jose or the other—you know who I mean?"

"Aye, aye."

"Well, when we were all locked fast asleep, we were awakened by a thundering knocking at the outer gates; well, we had scarce time to dress, before they were almost broken in, indeed they would have been entirely so, had they not been of great strength. They were no sooner opened than a courier rode in.

"'Lights—lights,' he called out, 'prepare the state apartments instantly.'

"'What's the matter?'

"'I don't know,' exclaimed the courier, 'where's Paulo?'

"'Here am I,' exclaimed the steward.

"'Then here's a despatch—make haste and read it. I have ridden hard, and have scarce left the carriage an hour, and the delay in opening the gates has given them almost time enough to overtake me.'

"Then Paulo began to shout and call, and give directions, till he was almost frantic; nobody knew what they were doing, or why—when, suddenly, Paulo was at his wit's ends, by hearing another thundering application for admittance.

"This time the gate was opened at once, and a carriage with four mules, covered with foam and reeking hot, entered the court-yard.

"'There now,' said I to Paulo, 'who's right now?'

"'What about?' said he.

"'The white horse.'

"'Curse the white horse,' said he, in a rage, 'you had better not bespeak such trouble again, it's all through you.'

"'I said no more—but in another moment Don Jose stepped out of the carriage, and led a lady forward, and they entered the reception room.

"Of all the beautiful women, she was the most beautiful I ever saw. She looked very hard at us, and I thought she appeared to have some suspicion that all was not right; but a look from Don Jose, of course, cleared the room of servants, and they both remained together for some time, and then she was left to herself.

"'Paulo,' said Don Jose.

"'Yes, signor.'

"'Attend to me. You must be watchful and respectful to the lady, and when she is visited you will attend to nothing she says, as she will be in good hands.'

"Of course we understood very well what was meant, and acted accordingly.

"The next day the king came."

"Hush—no names."

"We are alone, and nobody's present but knows well enough whom we mean; well, he came, and it appears they were not good friends, for the gallant is not the most favoured by nature, a little of the grim about him, and the lady did not like him, and he was repelled.

"A day or two more passed, and then he came down again, but this time it appeared as though he was determined not to be foiled, but he would succeed by some means or other.

"A great deal of squalling ensued; screams were heard all over the place, and, after a time, she escaped, and ran all over the house; the king's face appeared to be scratched, and he was dreadfully chafed, and called upon us to catch her.

"Well, well, we tried hard, and came to a room where she had taken refuge, and had secured the door on the other side—we were at a loss what to do.

"'Break it open, and force her away,' said the king, in a furious tone.

"We did this, and in another minute we were all in the room.

"Donna Camilla, however, had gained the balcony, and when she saw us advance, she jumped down into the garden.

"The height was great, and we hesitated to follow that way.

"'You will not be outdone by a woman—a mere girl? Twenty doubloons to he who secures her first!'

"Over the balcony went six or seven of us, and a desperate race commenced. We had gained upon her, when, seeing she could not escape, she looked up to Heaven, saying,—

"'May God forgive my sins! but death before dishonour.'

"Then, with a sudden motion, she darted past us, and plunged head first into the well, an old, monkish place, built many ages back.

"This was an unexpected occurrence, and we all stood aghast—nobody moved or spoke—and the king walked up to the edge of the well and looked in, and then coolly walked away, and ordered the carriage, and left the place, without anything more saving throwing a heavy purse for our trouble, and we were, of course, silent on that and every other occurrence that happened here."

"Of course."

There was a sudden summons at the gate, and an instant commotion ensued among the men, and a courier entered, delivering to Paulo a despatch.

"The white horse," muttered Martinez, loud enough to be heard by Paulo, "is a sure prediction after all is said and done."

"We must break up," said Paulo; "visitors will be here to-night; we must prepare. This is from Don Jose, and he expects everything to be in readiness. Did I not tell you, friends and comrades, that something would happen? Trust me another time, and you will do well."

"But, then," said one, who was rather sceptical—and what a sad thing it is, that, in all well-grounded faiths, there will be always found some one who will be sceptical, and want more substantial reasons for anything than will satisfy everybody else,—"but, then, you go on prophesying all the year round, and so you are sure to be right some time or another, and what makes the singularity of the thing is, that we never hear of your failures."

"Indeed, indeed. If we were all bound to furnish you with comprehension, as well as with facts to exercise it upon, you might, by general competition, be a very clever fellow; but, as it is, you are no better than a fool."

"Disputing, as usual," said the courier, as he dismounted from his horse. "Here you are, all of you, a set of well-paid, well-fed, idle vagabonds, with really nothing to do, and the consequence is, you do nothing but quarrel."

"Nay, now," said one, "I am the most peaceable-disposed man in the world: but if folks will quarrel with one, what is one to do?"

"Psha! No more of this. I came from our master, Don Jose, and he commands that everything should be got in readiness for a visitor."

"Did he say distinguished visitor, good master courier, can you tell us?"

"On my faith, I think he did."

"A—a—hem!"

"What do you say a—a—hem for?"

"Hush! We happen to know who the distinguished visitor is. Come and take a cup of wine with us, and we will tell you. We are not all of us wanted to light up the saloon surely. Come this way, good sir courier."

"Ah, my friends," said the courier, as he surrendered his horse to one of the attendants, "I have a shrewd suspicion myself on that head."

"Have you?"

"Yes. Don't give the animal any oats. Let him cool first, and,—do you hear?—rub down his coat with a handful of hay. He is quiet as a lamb; but I have ridden him rather hard; for Don Jose, even if he is in no particular hurry himself, likes everything done quickly that is done for him, as if his life and everybody else's depended upon it."

"Ah, that's his character; but, however, he is a good master to us, and so we have no reason to find fault with him on any account. Now, who do you suppose, master courier, the illustrious personage is, eh?"

The courier looked amazingly knowing, and winked several times; after which, he said,—

"Why, I don't know that it's prudent to say what we think always; but we may say what we don't think, I believe,—eh, my friends?"

"Ah, to be sure."

"Well, then,—on my faith, this is as pleasant a cup of wine as ever I tasted,—well, then, I don't think, mind you—I don't think on any account—for to think such a thing would be quite absurd—I don't think that the illustrious personage, for whom this villa is prepared and so well guarded, under the orders of Don Jose, is the King of Spain."

"Oh, dear no," said everybody, "oh, no, nor we—nor we! How could we think so for a moment?"

And then they all laughed uproariously, as if they were the cleverest fellows in existence, and they looked at each other and nodded, as much as to say,—

"This courier is no fool, not he."

They did not, however, neglect to get as rapidly as possible into a state of readiness to receive Don Jose; for, although they were informed by the courier that he had showed no appearance of an immediate haste when he left, yet well they knew the strange rapidity of his movements, and that, in order to deceive people as to his intentions, he would be one moment lying on a sofa, as if he was not about to move for hours, and the next in the saddle.

The fact was, that Jose had sent this courier to the suburban villa before Doctor Pepito had given his verdict against the removal of Maritana that night; so that the domestics were left in a state of painful and wondering suspense till the next morning; for, as to sending any one to say he was not coming, that was a piece of politeness he never for one moment dreamt of.

CHAPTER XLI.

THE ADVENTURES OF A NIGHT IN MADRID.—DON CÆSAR IN THE PALACE VAULTS.—THE DISCOVERY.

DON CÆSAR, when he quitted the page, walked about the streets of Madrid in deep thoughtfulness; the past came before his mind like a dream, and such a one that, for the first time, he deemed it worthy of grave consideration and thought.

He walked about the streets for some time, quite heedless of where he was going; indeed, he knew not that he was going at all, and certainly he had no place to go to.

It would have been luck if he had, and he would have deemed himself a fortunate man indeed to have had some place where he could have sought a few hours repose and rest.

It was past midnight, he knew not how much, as he neared the church of San Nicholas, and there, beneath the deep shadow of the structure, he paused.

"Where on earth shall I go to?" was Don Cæsar's mental inquiry, as he suddenly awoke from his reverie, and looked about him; "where shall I go? A walk in Madrid by moonlight is all very well when there is an object in it, and an end to it. True it is I have both; the one is to pass the time away between this and morning, and the other is that it will terminate when the hour of meeting Lazarillo at San Veronica shall arrive."

Cæsar looked first one way, and then the other; but saw no object that would at all decide him in his choice of road—all appeared alike—one was not before the other—one was as long and wearisome as the other, and they would all lead him to a chain of different streets.

While thus considering within himself, Don Cæsar suddenly became aware that there were some persons at no great distance from him who were engaged in serenading a house; there were two, one was engaged with a guitar, and the other was standing by.

"Well," thought Don Cæsar, "this is an adventure. Who can they be serenading at this hour? Surely they are true lovers, and worth more than a passing glance."

With this curiosity Don Cæsar crept closer to the party, and, having nothing better to do, he listened to the music.

"For," thought he, "it will pass the time away 'twixt this and morning."

Don Cæsar leaned against the projecting part of the next house, and then he calmly awaited the termination of the serenade.

The sound of the voice and guitar ceased, and the gallant looked up with a disappointed air at the balcony—no one appeared to thank the giver of the serenade for the pleasure afforded by his entertainment.

"I think that my fair friend heeds but little my passion."

"Little, indeed; and, were I in your place, I would either give up the chase, or hunt out the rival that supplants me."

"But I don't know who he is."

"Exactly; if you did, you would not have to find him out."

"But it is impossible."

"Nothing is impossible to a sincere lover. I would hunt the place, and put a spy on her actions, I would."

"But would it be honourable?"

"Surely it would, since all stratagems are alike honourable in love and war; and, when there was no other course left me, I should certainly have recourse to them."

"Well, well, I know not what to do, but will consider what can be done more at leisure; if I thought that I could, by setting a watch upon the house, discover the cause of her coldness and indifference, I would do it."

"It will so, depend upon it; she would never be indifferent without a cause."

"Ah! it must be so."

"And, if that course do not do, a perseverance and determination on your part to prosecute your suit, and you are sure to be rewarded for your pains."

"I would I could think so, and yet hope does whisper some consolation to me."

"To be sure it ought; and yet, were it my own case, I should act differently."

"How?"

"I would give up the chase as one that was like to be too long and wearisome, and without a sufficient reward when the object was gained. Wives are not scarce."

At this moment they both turned from the house, the lover thinking it useless to remain there any longer, when they came upon Don Cæsar, whom they saw not till they came close to him.

The lover's mind was instantly fired at the thought that he had at length found out the rival of his affections, and the favoured of his mistress. The thought was madness.

"Oh, detested rival!" he exclaimed; "fortune has at length delivered you into my hands, to chastise your insolence and presumption."

"As to fortune," replied Don Cæsar, "she has played me some tricks, and she must still be jade if she has delivered me over to you; indeed, it would be singular if she interfered in the quarrels of Spanish gentlemen, and yet I know not wherefore we should quarrel, fair sir."

"Would you shrink from defending your love with the sword?"

"Certainly not. I wear a sword and can use it, at least, so I have heard."

"'Tis well. But there is one chance for you—give up for ever the beauteous Isabella, and declare, upon your honour as a gentleman, that you will never see her again."

"Faith, I cannot do that, since I never saw the lady you have spoken of."

"'Tis false! You speak thus to escape the alternative I propose. Coward! dare you neither acknowledge the fact nor draw to defend yourself?"

"I have denied all knowledge."

"You have, to save your own base self from chastisement. Be it so; but it shall not avail you. Draw and defend yourself, if you dare."

"Well," exclaimed Don Cæsar, "I used not to require a second invitation to such an encounter; but I admit of late I have grown careful, having promised to do so; but, since there cannot be any help, my good sword must play its part, and I will do so likewise."

"You have the honour of encountering," said the stranger, with some pomp, "one of the best swordsmen in Madrid, and a member of one of its most noble families."

"Two great honours at once," remarked Don Cæsar; "and I could make the same reply to you, changing, however, the name of Madrid into the more extensive meaning one of Spain."

"This is boasting," cried the other. "Come on; such as this must be punished."

"It will be dangerous to attempt so much. Am I to encounter one or two?"

"One. What do you take me for?"

"It matters not. You have settled the preliminaries; we may as well begin, since you are so bent upon it, and not waste our precious breath in magnifying the occasion."

The stranger cast loose his cloak, and, drawing his rapier, advanced in an attitude, and Cæsar did the same. After a few passes, that assured him he had no novice to deal with, the stranger became cautious in his movements, and Cæsar said, as he for a moment drew back,—

"Are you satisfied?"

"You must give up the lady."

"I know her not," replied Cæsar.

"It is mere subterfuge," replied the stranger. "Did I not find you near the house?"

"You might."

"I did. Were you not waiting till I should go away, that you might receive those marks of affection that are mine?"

"Hardly. Had it been so, I should have come and disturbed you at once, and it would have gone hard but you had taken to your heels."

"Enough—insult to injury—enough!" and the stranger rushed upon Cæsar with fury, and for some moments with address. It was not a very difficult matter for one accustomed to his weapon as Cæsar was, to choose his opportunity and disarm his adversary, who fell with a groan to the earth.

Don Cæsar paused a moment. His first emotion was to fly, in case he should by any accident be detained if the guard came up, and he knew that he had more than ordinary reasons for retaining the liberty he possessed. The fallen man, however, exclaimed,—

"Fly! I am not hurt seriously. Fly, else you may be taken by the guard."

"Are you hurt?" inquired Cæsar.

"Not seriously, and shall be able to reach home by the aid of my friend."

"Well," said Cæsar, "it is over now, and I regret it; but I had no choice, yet I can assure you I never saw the lady about whom we have quarrelled."

"On your honour?"

"On my word of honour, as a Spanish gentleman, a word I never yet profaned."

"I believe you, sir. There is something in your voice and manner that assures me you are sincere. I I would I had not been so hasty. I beg your pardon."

"Name it not; I will assist you if you need more aid."

"No—no; seek your own safety."

"Farewell, then," said Don Cæsar, after having assisted to bind the wound, and place him on his feet again.

Don Cæsar walked quickly away from the spot where the encounter had taken place, towards the palace.

"If fortune does not find me in house and fare, she, nevertheless, provides me in adventures. I would indeed she would change the character of them, and place me in ease and plenty, for I have had the reverse for some time. Somehow or other, fortune is said to be fickle; but, in good truth, I never found her so. She has constantly stuck by me through misfortune, and never yet wavered by veering towards good. Some of these days she will, perhaps, leave me, and I may be happy and prosperous.

"Yes, happy and prosperous! Those are strange words for Don Cæsar to utter; yet I am now a married man, and that is sufficient to account for many strange things. I have new thoughts, indeed a new life before me, if I can but seize upon the beginning. It is like the first step one has to take upon a ladder; but at this moment I cannot find the first step, and so am unable to climb it."

Thus conversing with himself, Don Cæsar continued to walk onwards without any definite object, somewhat wearied, and devoutly wishing for daybreak; but that was yet distant, and he had some hours yet.

"How to employ my time I know not," thought Cæsar; "that is beyond my art; but, I suppose, it will pass along, however heavily that may be."

He thought he heard at that moment a cry for help. It was at some distance, and he could scarce distinguish what it was; but yet he thought it was such a cry, and Don Cæsar's ears were ever open to such a cry as that, and he hastened a little onwards, in hopes to catch the sound again, and thus direct him to the spot whence it came; for, at that moment, he could not tell whence it came, or even in what direction it lay.

"Surely it was a cry," muttered Don Cæsar, as he listened attentively.

There was the same cry again, but it was much closer at hand.

"Oh, there it is again!" he exclaimed, hastening forward. "I thought I could not be mistaken in the sound. Some rogues, I suppose, who are setting upon some of the guests returning from the fete, probably, of the Marquis de Rotondo, or from the palace. Ah, well! and yet they may be able to inform me of something I most desire to know."

The thought no sooner entered his mind, than he disengaged his sword-arm from his cloak, and drawing it tight round his body with his left, he hastened to the scene of the disturbance.

He was but a few minutes ere he reached the spot. There was one man leaning his back against the wall, and defending himself against the combined attack of several ruffians, whose object was to rob him of the costly jewels he wore.

The stranger had evidently been a guest at some entertainment, and was returning homeward, and had, no doubt, drunk more wine than usual; but he defended himself with great resolution.

"Stand off, you ruffians," he exclaimed, "and I'll pay some of you. Here, guard, guard, help! The rogues are ever away when most needed, and a man may be robbed without their hearing his cries."

Don Cæsar saw how matters were, and drawing his sword, he rushed in among them, crying out at the same time,—

"Rescue! the guard are at hand."

The effect was magical; the ruffians no sooner felt the sword of Don Cæsar among them than they fled, after receiving one or two wounds.

"Thanks, stranger, thanks; you deserve my utmost thanks, and I shall be happy to put them into any tangible shape that you may be pleased to point out."

"I am a Spanish gentleman, and, therefore, what you have said is enough; besides, the trifling service I have performed is amply repaid by the knowledge that it has not been entirely thrown away."

"It has not," replied the stranger; "they would have robbed me but for your timely arrival, the dogs. A gentleman cannot traverse the streets of Madrid now of a night, but he is to be subjected to these risks; or, rather, a certainty of being robbed."

"Most true," replied Cæsar; "especially, loaded as you are with jewels; 'tis a great temptation to such men as these."

"That is very right; but I have just quitted the mansion of the Marquis de Rotondo's, who has given a fete to the nobility."

"The Marquis de Rotondo's!"

"Yes; and, as it was well attended, I could not go dressed like a hermit."

"Certainly not."

"Then these rogues set on me as I was returning home, having come hither on foot; but I did not certainly think of being robbed."

"You have lost nothing?"

"No; thanks to your timely aid, I have not; else I might have lost all, life included, the rogues."

"You have come from the Marquis de Rotondo's, you say?" said Don Cæsar.

"I have."

"Did you see a Countess de Bazan at the fete?" he inquired, with a little consideration.

"Yes, I did."

"Is she there now?"

"No, she has left."

"Can you inform me where she went to?" said Don Cæsar, eagerly.

"To the palace," replied the stranger.

"To the palace! are you sure that she went to the palace? With whom?"

"Don Jose."

"Indeed!"

"Yes, I heard Don Jose give the order himself to the pages."

"I thank you, sir—I am obliged to you," replied Don Cæsar.

"You seem interested," remarked the stranger, in some surprise.

"I am so. Farewell."

"Farewell."

Don Cæsar had quitted the spot but a step or two, when he turned and said,—

"Pardon me; but can you inform me who this Countess de Bazan is?"

"I really do not know more than this,—she is said to be the niece of the Marquis de Rotondo, and is very beautiful."

"A niece of Rotondo's."

"Yes."

"And gone to the palace with Don Jose," said Cæsar, musingly; "to the palace?"

"Just so."

"Thank you, sir. I bid you good night," said Don Cæsar, as he turned away.

"Good night," replied the stranger. "Good night, and thank you."

Cæsar, however, heard him not—he was too deeply immersed in his own thoughts; but, at the same time, the stranger looked after him, muttering,—

"Well, he is a strange fellow, after all; who can he be? There is something noble in him, notwithstanding he is not dressed in first style. What can he want with the guests at Rotondo's, I wonder? Some of Don Jose's spies; but, no, he is too frank and brave to be a spy. Well, well, I can't make it out."

So saying, the stranger sheathed his sword, and resumed his way homeward.

As for Don Cæsar, he was proceeding towards the palace, without thought of where he was going to.

"To the palace," he muttered; "to the palace, and in the company of Don Jose. What infernal machination is now going on? As certain as there is a Heaven above, they shall answer with their lives for all that may be done in which my name and honour may be compromised."

Don Cæsar now approached a low wall that runs round the back part of the palace, and its sides.

A sudden thought struck him, that if he could enter the palace unperceived, he should, perhaps, be able to render some service to the beautiful being who bore his name.

After a little thought he returned to make the venture, and, with a sudden bound, Don Cæsar had caught at the top of the wall, and threw himself up to the top. He listened, and heard no one; he looked attentively about, but saw no one.

"The coast is clear," thought Cæsar; "I will get down here."

Suiting the action to the word, he jumped down, and found the court-yard was not so far down as the foundation on the other side.

The place he had got into was desolate, and no one was to be seen or heard. Don Cæsar hunted about for some time, endeavouring to find some entrance into the palace, without success. At length he came to a small door, an old Moorish structure, apparently studded with nails, and looking very formidable.

"This may do," he muttered to himself, "if one can but get it open; though how that is to be done has to be found out."

He tried to pull it open, and many other modes, but none would answer, and at length he drew back in despair, when the thought occurred to him that it might open inwards, or, at all events, it would not resist his weight, if thrown forcibly against it.

He instantly rushed against it with much force—

the door gave way, and Don Cæsar was precipitated down some deep steps, and felt himself at length upon some flagged flooring.

Don Cæsar looked about him, or, rather, he endeavoured to do so, for he was enveloped in the most pitchy darkness; he could see nothing, and, in his attempts to penetrate this place, the glare of his own eyeballs was the only thing he was conscious of.

After a few minutes, his eyes became habituated to the darkness, and he even thought that from one particular spot he could perceive a single beam of light.

Curious to ascertain if this were not merely a freak of fancy, he arose carefully, and, with much caution, went towards it; at first he was disappointed at finding it was only a projecting point of a passage or something; but when he came to examine the other side of it, his joy was great, when he perceived a lamp standing evidently but recently trimmed.

"This will serve me as well as another," said Cæsar, and he took it from its place. "These passages, or vaults, ought to lead upward somewhere or other; it is usual to do so; but time and patience will enable me to overcome much, and now that I am a married man, I may be supposed to have a good store of that commodity."

Cæsar now entered a long narrow passage of peculiar structure; it was damp and unwholesome.

"This was formerly the vaults and dungeons," thought Cæsar,—"here, many an unfortunate man lingered out a wretched existence, which was perhaps terminated only by the knife of the assassin."

He still pursued his way, but saw nothing that would lead him upwards, and, at length, he emerged from beneath an archway into a broad space.

Here he stood for the space of a moment or two with his drawn sword, holding the lamp above his head, endeavouring to pierce the gloom by which he was surrounded.

There appeared to be several passages, branching away, or it might be an immense dungeon, in which many prisoners were confined at one time.

This latter conjecture appeared to be the true one; for the pillars had, each of them, one or more rings, with massive chains to them, ready to secure the body of any unfortunate being who had the misfortune to displease the powers that be.

"Men who were brought here," said Don Cæsar, "were those that they dare not bring to trial, because there was no offence with which they could be charged; but they had done or said something that caused them to be considered dangerous in the eyes of the ruling powers."

On looking around more carefully he perceived the body, or, rather, the skeleton, of some unfortunate being who had died there. The chain still lay beside it—clasping, even in death, the fleshless waist of the sad remains.

Cæsar was much shocked at such a spectacle; there lay the skeleton at full length, the flesh entirely gone, through decay and vermin, though some of the garments yet remained beside it—a sad memorial.

"Poor unfortunate man!" muttered Cæsar, "your end was an unhappy one."

He turned from the sight with a feeling of disgust and melancholy, when another sight as bad as the former met his eyes.

This was the body of a knight, who lay in complete panoply of war, as though he had been suddenly seized and hurried to this dismal place of death.

There he lay extended on his back, with his vizor open, which displayed the ghastliness of death, his hands clasped above him; the iron chain encircled his waist and his feet, but his hands were left free.

Beneath his head lay his sword, at least, the handle and a part of the blade, which had no doubt been broken in the contest, in which he had been worsted, and made prisoner.

Near him lay his shield, against the very pillow from which was suspended the chain by which he was confined. Altogether, a more melancholy spectacle Don Cæsar had not seen; but, sighing, said,—

"Poor knight—perhaps, after fighting bravely for thy country's sake, thou hast come to such an untimely end, and that, too, by the villanies of such men as Don Jose, for such men have lived in all ages, and the true and valiant have often been compelled to succumb to such tricksters."

Don Cæsar now turned from the scene, and endeavoured to explore his way about from passage to vault, and from vault to passage, until, fearing he should be unable to retrace his footsteps in time, he made the best of his way back.

This was not effected without some trouble and a few mistakes.

"Once more I breathe the fresh air of Heaven," muttered Don Jose, as he neared the entrance of the vault. "This I think is the niche from which I took the lamp; 'tis nearly out."

And so saying, Don Cæsar replaced the lamp, and made his way to the mouth of the vault where he had entered.

When he came here, he saw that it had been some time daylight—he sprang up the steps, and was in the court-yard in another moment, almost blinded by light, exclaiming, at the same time,—

"By heavens, I shall be too late for my meeting with Lazarillo."

He immediately made for the wall; no one was nigh—and the height not being so great upon this side as on the other, he was soon on the top of the wall, and in another minute he was in the street; then hurrying onwards, he soon disappeared, going towards the quarter in which the church of San Veronica was situated.

CHAPTER XLII.

ARANJUES.—JOSE QUESTIONS LAZARILLO.—THE SPY. —CÆSAR'S IMPATIENCE.—SUNSET.—THE WATCH UPON THE PALACE.

DON CÆSAR waited at the church of San Veronica until his patience was exhausted, for Lazarillo came not, and had he known how impossible it was for him, Lazarillo, to have been there, he would long since have quitted the spot; but Don Cæsar did not know this, and hence it was that he waited at the church for some hours, fully persuaded that some unforeseen event had happened to detain Lazarillo, and at the same time he was equally well satisfied that as soon as he was at liberty he would hasten to him.

This hope appeared so reasonable, that he indulged in it till near mid-day, when he could not but believe some accident had occurred to the boy; or that, perhaps, Don Jose had suspected that there was a correspondence between them, and that that had brought the youth into trouble.

It is astonishing how a person, situated as Cæsar was, without the power of ascertaining the cause of Lazarillo's inability to keep his appointment, will conjure up causes, one after the other, until they can no longer bear with their own excuses, and Don Cæsar determined that, if Lazarillo did not shortly come, he would go and satisfy himself of the nature of the cause of his absence.

"Confound it, what hours have I spent wandering about Madrid, and here have I been since morning, and I am burning with impatience and anxiety to learn who and what this countess of mine is; but, stay, I ought not to be hasty, he may be, at this moment, seeking to ascertain what I most desire to know, and yet this is dull work here; I had better go to Jose and make the inquiries that will at once satisfy me, and set my doubts at rest."

Thus muttering to himself, he quitted the church, and walked towards the residence of Don Jose, choosing the shady side of the way, for the sun was high, and the heat of the day was great.

He was not long in reaching the mansion of Don Jose. Cæsar paused, and passed the open door before he entered; he could not, however, see aught of Lazarillo, and he entered. At first he was unnoticed, the servants being idle, and, for the most part, asleep, until he bestowed a hearty kick upon one, who immediately rose up, with an angry expostulation on his lips; but, on looking in Cæsar's face, he saw something there that told him he had not such a one to deal with who would tamely submit to any impertinence, and he wisely held his tongue, and waited until Cæsar spoke.

"Is Lazarillo, Don Jose's page, within?" at length inquired Cæsar.

"No," replied the man.

"Where is he gone, then?"

"To the palace."

"To the palace?"

"Yes."

"Is Don Jose there?"

"I believe so."

Don Cæsar, after a moment's thought, quitted the house, and determined to proceed at once to the palace, and inquire whether the page had been there, or was there then.

"If Don Jose is there, my countess is there also; no doubt that something or other will turn up to give me the information I so much desire."

Don Cæsar, therefore, traversed the distance between Jose's mansion and the palace with somewhat hasty strides.

*   *   *   *   *

In consequence of what had occurred, Don Jose determined to visit Aranjues—everything was in a state of abeyance for a short time—he had settled the affair relative to the conspirators—Maritana was not fit for removal, and the page, Lazarillo, was safe at a distance from Madrid.

In pursuance of his determination, Don Jose sought his own mansion, and ordered a small retinue of servants to attend him on his progress thither.

Full of thoughts of the most diabolical tendency, he, Jose, rode at the head of his suite, without exchanging a word with any of them until he came within sight of the tall trees of Aranjues.

"Ah!" he muttered, "she must and shall be mine; she knows not the extent of my power, and if we must try our strength, it will go hard but that I prove the stronger.

"And as for Lazarillo, now I am about to see him again, I will make some inquiries of him. He may be ignorant that Cæsar lives; but if he knew it, I doubt not but that he would abandon me, and become attached to Cæsar, if, indeed, he would not become a cunning spy upon my actions, and a serious hindrance to my intentions."

When Jose arrived at Aranjues he sent for Lazarillo, who was all anxiety and impatience to get back to Madrid, as he feared the worst from Cæsar's impatience, who, he believed, would go about the city inquiring after him, and running into all sorts of dangers in his endeavours to find him out, which it was very unlikely he would do.

As soon as he received Don Jose's summons, Lazarillo entered the presence of his master, who cast on him a keen and scrutinizing glance.

"Lazarillo," said he, "has anything of importance occurred since you arrived here?"

"No, signor; nothing that I have either heard or seen."

"What have you been about?"

"Executing your orders, signor."

"Indeed! what were they?" said Jose, not noticing at the moment what he alluded to.

"That I should wait here till you came, which I have done."

Don Jose gave a dry cough at this answer, and then paused.

"You recollect Don Cæsar, Lazarillo, do you not?" inquired Jose, after a moment's thought. "Yes, you must do that."

"Yes, signor; I could not forget him. Oh, no; it would be to act ungratefully."

"It would so, then. But it is said that he was shot."

"Yes, poor Don Cæsar, such was his fate; many a worse man lived when he died."

"Truly, a-hem! that is according to taste; do you recollect anything of his death?"

"No; for I could not look upon that cruel ——" Lazarillo stopped.

"Nay, speak on; it is of no consequence; the king is not here to hear you."

"Well, signor, I could not look upon the execution of such a brave and gallant gentleman, and one who had done so much for me; and, indeed, it was through me that he met such a fate."

"Well, well, it is reported that he lives; do you know aught about it?"

"I would that he was alive, signor."

"You would quit my service?" said Don Jose, suddenly.

"Signor, there can be nothing of the kind happen; for a dead man cannot well come to life again, I should think."

"One would think not, indeed. You have heard nothing of the report?"

"Nothing at all, signor; besides, I could not believe a man, with half-a-pound of lead in his head, administered in the shape of bullets by the royal guard, could at all recover the shock produced."

"Nor I, boy; but listen to me; have you seen aught that could cause this rumour? have you seen this Don Cæsar?"

"Who, I?"

"Yes, you."

"No; surely, signor, you don't think me superstitious, or frightened at a shadow?"

"No—no, that will do; you may leave me, and send up Pedro."

"Yes, signor," said Lazarillo, glad to escape from this conversation, which was, to say the least of it, very alarming to him; for he knew Jose too well to believe that he would hesitate but little, either in putting himself or Cæsar out of the way by means of assassination.

He quitted the room, and seeking the domestic named by Don Jose, he said,—

"Pedro."

"Well," remarked Pedro, "what do you want now?"

"Don Jose wants you."

"Does he?" said Pedro; "he is always wanting some one or other."

"You had better be quick; or, at least, tell him I informed you of it immediately, because he is in no humour to be trifled with."

Up went Pedro, and had no sooner entered the apartment in which Don Jose was, than the latter said,—

"When next I send for you come at once, and don't stand to think about it."

"Yes, signor," stammered Pedro.

It has often been said, that none but the brave deserve the fair, and that a faint heart never won a fair lady, and we may add, that none but the adventurous deserve, or, indeed, ever enjoy the bursts of rapture that thrill the traveller's bosom; no, that is his due, and his alone.

The moon's beams threw dark and broad shadows across the streets, and in some that were narrow the whole street was thrown into one deep shade.

Now, at places, might be seen some suspicious-looking man wrapped in his cloak and broad hat, stealing along with a stealthy step, and anon he would vanish under some archway, when he heard the footstep of another. But even at the hour of midnight these places in Madrid are not destitute of busy beings, as in all large capitals there are those who love the night better than the day, probably because their deeds are better shrouded by midnight's sombre mantle than they would be while the sun yet lingered above the horizon. With such, however, at present, we have nothing to do. Let us turn our attention now to the interior of the palace, in a small apartment of which sat Jose and the king, looking like the guilty men they were, diabolically plotting against such innocence, and truth, and virtue, as were represented to human eyes in the actions of poor Maritana, who, by this, felt, indeed, how preferable would have been her lowly estate, which she had spurned, to the terrors and anxieties she had since suffered.

The light which was in that small room was a dim one, and they conversed in low tones, as if they feared the very walls would hear and relate again their guilty machinations.

"You say she sleeps, Jose?" remarked the king.

"She was sleeping, sire."

"'Tis well."

"I believe exhausted nature has sunk into repose. She has made such efforts to escape, and so loudly protested against being kept a prisoner here, that she must by this time be tired out completely."

"I wish, Jose, she would remain in sleep till we get her to the villa."

"That is not very likely, your majesty."

"No; but yet it would be very desirable, indeed, Jose. What is the time now?"

"It wants but a few minutes to midnight."

"Then we must be stirring. How have you arranged?"

"A carriage with one postillion, and his livery concealed by a large cloak, will, exactly at twelve, drive up to the side entrance of the palace. Into that carriage I will have the countess immediately placed. On her head shall be placed a cap and plume, and around her shall be wrapped a cloak, so that her sex will be disguised, even should any one notice the proceeding."

"Good—good."

"Then your majesty and I can go with her, and an hour places us in absolute security from anything like interruption."

"It could not be better arranged. About it at once, Jose—about it at once, and all will be well. By Heaven! we have much trouble in this matter, but that will but enhance the value of success and victory."

"As your majesty remarks," said Jose, "the affair has been a most singularly troublesome one, and full of cross accidents. I have myself, during its progress, chanced my life more than once."

"Go, go. Hark! The midnight hour is pealing from the church towers. Go, Jose; I shall not now be satisfied, or at ease, until we are far from Madrid. By-the-bye, have you put that Cæsar out of the way of doing mischief?"

"I hope, and, indeed, have every reason to believe,

from the nature of the means I have used, that he is no longer in a condition to be troublesome. I ——"

"Well, well, I want no particulars—no particulars, Jose. It is enough to know that he will not be in my way. Quite enough. Now for the lovely countess."

Jose left the king, and when he closed the door behind him, he muttered,—

"Philip, I think, grows scrupulous occasionally. He forbade me giving to Maritana a sleeping draught; but I have done so, nevertheless, or I believe she would have continued as active in her opposition to everything now as at first. She will, however, not recover until we reach the house, where, when she does recover, she may cry for assistance in as loud a voice as she likes, without a remote chance of getting any."

＊   ＊   ＊   ＊   ＊

Don Cæsar was still waiting anxiously. He had made up his mind to remain till midnight; but when he heard that hour given forth in solemn sounds by the different clocks of the city, he still felt loth to move, and in a few moments he congratulated himself that he had not done so, for he saw a carriage, drawn but by one pair of mules, drive up to the private entrance of the palace.

The postillion was enveloped in a large cloak, and now he dismounted from the mule, and muttered some execrations expressive of his dislike to do duty at such an hour.

Scarcely had he been at his post a moment, when Don Jose made his appearance. Cæsar knew him in an instant; indeed, the moonbeams fell full upon his face. He merely glanced at the carriage and the man, as if his object was to see that all was ready, and then, without saying a word, he retired again.

"Now," thought Cæsar, "am I convinced some villany is in the wind. How to discover and thwart it is the question."

After a few moments' consideration he determined upon a vigorous and bold manœuvre, which few men but himself would ever have thought of, or risked the execution, for it was one likely to involve him in much danger and trouble; but Don Cæsar was not the sort of person to be deterred from any adventure from consideration as to how he was to get out of it again. That he left to chance and his own inspiration, aided by his courage and indomitable perseverance at the moment; so he no sooner conceived a scheme of action than he at once made up his mind to its execution.

"If done at all, it must be done at once," he said, and, even as he spoke, he crossed over the way to the postillion, who stood nearly in the shadow of the portico of the palace.

"Friend," said Cæsar, "you have a night job, and you don't half like it, I can easily perceive."

"Dear me," said the postillion, in a jeering tone, "you must be some great conjuror."

"Perhaps I am; shall I relieve you of your work to-night?"

"No; but if you like, I'll give you some to do."

"Of what nature?"

"By cracking your troublesome, inquisitive pate, when you can find occupation in applying vinegar to it."

"You are a funny fellow."

"I wish I could return the compliment, for you are only a fool."

"Well, now, this is pleasant," said Cæsar; "I was afraid I should have to knock you down without any provocation at all."

"Were you, indeed. Take that, then, for a commencement."

The postillion struck at Don Cæsar; but the latter parried the blow, and returned it with such good intent, right in the middle of the postillion's face, that he fell backwards, and hit his head so hard a knock against the base of one of the stone columns, that there he lay as still as a mouse.

Cæsar dragged him completely into the shadow of the building, and laid him as neatly along the wall as he could. Then he took the cloak from him, and likewise his cap. The latter he placed on his own head, and, wrapping himself up in the cloak, he assumed the whip of the man he had vanquished, and waited anxiously the result of his adventures, which had begun so oddly.

Scarcely had he completed these arrangements, when the small private door again opened, and Jose looked out.

"All right, friend?" he said.

"All right," said Cæsar, in an assumed voice.

"Good," said Jose. "Mount your mule—mount your mule at once."

Cæsar had no resource but to comply; but he still kept an eye on the small door, from whence now issued Don Jose and another person who was with him, supporting a third, who seemed quite unable to walk. This third party was wrapped in a large handsome cloak, and had on a cap with some magnificent feathers in it, and looped with diamonds.

"Who can that be?" thought Cæsar.

Alas! how little he suspected it was her whom he had already obtained so transient a glance of, and who now filled his whole thoughts, and was the key-stone to all his actions—the beautiful being who went by his name, and had been before his ravished eyes at the Marquis de Rotondo's for a moment as his countess—his bride of the prison, whom he now loved with all the fervour of the most romantic attachment.

Yet such it was, and Maritana, supported on one side by the king, and on the other by Don Jose, was, thus disguised, literally lifted into the vehicle to which her husband, Don Cæsar de Bazan, was about to act as postillion.

"Where Jose is," thought Cæsar, "I shall most likely get news of my countess, so I will continue this character I have assumed until some better chance presents itself."

Of course Jose, with his habitual caution, had told the supposed postillion to mount his mule first, in order that he might not be in a good situation to recognise the king, and now Jose himself leant out, and succeeded in closing the door.

"Postillion!" he cried.

"Ay, my lord," said Cæsar, still in the assumed voice, which was as different as possible to his own.

"You will drive fast."

"That's all very well," thought Cæsar; "but where to, is the question. Never mind, he will stop me if I go wrong."

With this Cæsar laid the whip on the mules, and off they set at a great rate. They had not proceeded far, however, before he heard a volley of oaths from Jose, and, upon drawing up, the minister, in a voice of passion, exclaimed,—

"Villain! Are you drunk? Is this the Aranjues road, rascal? You were told which road to take, you scoundrel, by me this morning."

"Was I," thought Cæsar. "That's a mistake; but no matter, I know now which road to take." Then he said aloud,—

"Pardon, signior, I had forgotten."

"Confusion seize you!" muttered Jose. "This is ever the way, sire; we are always getting troubled by subordinates."

"Caution, Jose, caution," said the king; "do not call me by any name but Don Cæsar de Bazan."

"She sleeps soundly."

"Which convinces me you have given her the opiate."

"Will your majesty forgive me? Zeal for your majesty's service, I own, has induced me to act as I have done; and I think, if your majesty will please to reflect, you will still think it is for the best I have acted."

"Say no more—say no more," cried the king; "I am sufficiently satisfied on that head."

Don Cæsar knew the road to Aranjues well enough, although he had never achieved that journey in any capacity assimilating with his present one, into which his inherent love of adventure had perhaps as much forced him as his deep anxiety to trace Don Jose wherever he should go, with the hope of, by such means, obtaining some satisfactory account of his own countess, whom he had, upon so very slight an acquaintance, contracted so enduring and powerful an affection for.

"What a devil this postillion is for driving," said the king.

"He does go at a tremendous pace," said Jose. "I should not wonder, by his furious speed now, and his mistaking the road before, to find him in a state of intoxication when we arrive."

"Which we shall quickly enough do now," added the king, "if we have not our necks broken by the way."

"True, true—shall I stop him?"

"No, no. The fellow don't seem a bad driver, although so very fast a one. I was more fearful at first of him than I am now."

So Don Cæsar was allowed to proceed, and, to tell the truth, he did dash on at a pace which was quite sufficient to warrant any one not over timid in having reasonable fears; and had it not been that he, Cæsar, hoped to make some discovery of interest to himself, by taking Jose and his companions safely wherever they might wish to go, the probability that nothing would have amused him more than upsetting the carriage at once, and giving that worthy minister, as well as every one in his company, a good chance of a broken neck, for that his countess, she who had for a moment blazed upon him in all her beauty, was one of the party, could not for an instant cross his imagination; so on he drove safely enough, though recklessly, and perhaps a little savagely.

Madrid was soon left some distance behind, and the direct high road to Aranjues, which is one of the best and most frequented out of the city, was gained, along which the mules dashed without interruption, for it was not an hour when any travellers were likely to be on the road.

The city of Madrid is not so encumbered with extensive suburbs, stretching far and wide into the open country, as London. The dense mass of houses were passed, and the sweet open country burst upon the sight, without any of those disagreeable adjuncts in the shape of half finished building operations, which have so many years past now made what would otherwise be pleasant suburban districts about London, so very full of discomfort.

Cæsar spared neither whip nor spur, and when any rut occurred in the road, the occupants of the carriage got a jolting, which knocked them together, whether they would or no. More than once Jose's and the king's head came in contact, as if they were both bent upon discovering which was the hardest.

The king swore, and Jose apologised, while Maritana, under the powerful influence of the narcotic which had been administered to her, slept soundly on, knowing nothing, and undisturbed by all the joltings of the vehicle in which she was conveyed.

"You have given her, Jose, a powerful dose," said the king; "she has all the semblance of death upon her."

"She breathes."

"True, she does; but I would rather this measure

had been avoided, even while I confess how safe a one it is."

"It is a very safe one, your majesty. It is one by which you may silence all scruples on the part of this young maiden. Your majesty, I presume, quite understands me?"

"I do, Jose, but reject the suggestion. I cannot stoop to so much baseness as that."

"Your majesty is surely needlessly particular," said Jose, with a scarcely suppressed sneer.

"Have a care, sir," said the king, in a voice which the minister knew well foreboded mischief, and he immediately said,—

"God forbid I should suggest anything that your majesty disapproves. I am your majesty's most humble servant ever."

"Enough, enough," said the king. "Name the subject no more, Jose. Where are we now?"

"At the rate we have been travelling, I should say we must be near our destination."

Jose looked from the carriage window as he spoke, and then he said to the king,—

"A very few minutes will now conduct us to the gates of the chateau, where your majesty, thanks to Providence, has passed some very happy hours."

"Jose," said the king, who appeared to be needlessly at such a time raking up all the smouldering remains of his virtues, "Jose, I do not approve of so ribald a mode of talking."

"Ribald, your majesty? I thought I had reached that amount of virtue which becomes piety."

"Peace, peace. Does your postillion, think you, now know where he is to stop?"

"I doubt if the knave does, since he went so hugely astray at his first starting; but I will speak to him."

Jose again put his head out at the carriage window, and called to Don Cæsar, who therefore drew up the mules.

"Do you know where you are going to, sirrah?"

"No," said Cæsar, in the assumed tone of voice he had first put on, and which had so effectually deceived Jose.

"Fool," muttered Jose; "drive on till you come to a light wall on your right hand; half way or thereabouts down it you will see a low gate. Draw up there."

Don Cæsar made no reply, for he wished to say as little as possible, but again applying both whip and spur to the mules, away dashed the carriage again at a more furious pace than ever.

"Confound that rascal," muttered Jose.

"He deserves death," said the king.

"And perhaps may have it," added Jose. "When a man like that gets out of temper with his employers, I think he is always better out of the world."

"Certainly," said the king, who now appeared all of a sudden to have forgotten how scrupulously virtuous he was getting a short time since.

"I dare not trust myself to speak much to Jose," thought Don Cæsar, "or I shall lose temper, and let him know, perhaps, who I am, with a vengeance. The infernal scoundrel! I will not lose sight of him, let him go where he will."

In the dim light now which was beginning to show itself across the early morning sky, Don Cæsar saw at some distance in advance, what appeared to be a thick wood, and then came in sight below the tops of the trees, which in reality belonged to the thick plantation that was around the little chateau, he saw the commencement of the stone wall which had been mentioned by Jose.

He now slackened the speed of the mules, and Jose remarked,—

"I am glad the fellow has grace enough to stop at all; I feared we should have had some trouble with him, but now he seems to know the place."

"Hush! be careful—she moves."

Heavily, as if disturbed by some dream, Maritana tossed her arms to and fro, and moaned.

"She dreams," said Jose; "it is the nature of narcotics when their influence is subsiding to produce restlessness."

"There—we are just in time."

"I presume so, although I thought her sleep would have lasted much longer than this."

"She is still again."

"And may so continue for hours."

Don Cæsar strained his sense of hearing to catch, if he could possibly, the muttered words he heard spoken in the carriage; but he could not make out one word distinctly, and after a few moments, he gave up the attempt in despair.

"What will happen next?" he thought. "Here we are at the low gate mentioned, and where on earth it leads to, I am at a loss completely to conjecture."

He now drew up the carriage quite close to the gate, and was in the act of alighting from the mule on which he had ridden, when it was opened, and a flash of light came from within, although he could see no one whatever.

"Remain where you are, postillion," cried Jose.

"Indeed!" said Cæsar.

"Ah! dare you reply to me?"

"No, signor."

"I will remain where I am for a moment or two," thought Cæsar, "but no longer."

He loosened his sword in its sheath, for he thought a fight now one of the most probable things in the world, and as that was an affair to which he had not, nor ever had, the slightest possible objection, he waited, with more composure probably than he would, without such a hope, have exhibited, the termination of the adventure — an adventure which none but himself would have ventured, under any such circumstances, with such great odds against him, to undertake at all, but which positively suited his chivalric nature.

CHAPTER XLIV.

THE DISCOVERY AND THE FIGHT.—CÆSAR'S ESCAPE.
— MARITANA'S RECOVERY FROM HER SWOON. —
CÆSAR'S ESCAPE FROM THE GUARD.

THERE was now light enough to distinguish surrounding objects, and Cæsar, having drawn up, was considering what would be the best course to pursue, determined to keep to the saddle, until compelled to dismount by circumstances.

Don Jose, on the other hand, attempted to open the door of the carriage, but could not; from some reason or other the door was fast, and so hard had it stuck, that all Don Jose's efforts were insufficient to open it.

Finding this to be the case, Don Jose began to call for the postillion to open the door; but he heard him not, or paid no attention to their cries, in which he was joined by the king; and then Jose commenced kicking and hammering, to attract the driver's attention.

"Open the door, postillion—you knave, do you hear me? Open the door."

"They are making noise enough," thought Don Cæsar, "and I suppose a scene must take place, and a discovery as well, and yet they may pass me without knowing who I am, or even seeing me."

"Open the door, you infernal knave!" shouted Jose, kicking and hammering, "open the door—do you hear?"

"Yes, yes, I hear," thought Cæsar, "and you'll not be pleased when you know I do; but as I have undertaken the performance of the character, so I must go through with it."

Don Cæsar accordingly dismounted the horse he rode, and approached the door of the carriage, which he opened, and Don Jose immediately stepped out, saying,—

"What means this delay when I called to you to o—— Damnation!"

The cause of Jose's sudden break in the midst of his displeasure, and the utterance of the exclamation that followed, was his casting his eyes upon Don Cæsar, whom he instantly recognised, and believing himself to be in immediate danger of assassination from Cæsar, whom he could not but regard as his enemy,

He was perfectly paralysed, and tumbled back in an undignified manner into the carriage, without any regard to etiquette, pale and trembling.

The king was much amazed at what occurred, and scarce understanding it, but believing there was some kind of opposition, disturbance, or assassination, attempted by the postillion, he drew his sword, and, without any thought as to consequences, made a lunge at Don Cæsar, who, seeing his danger, stepped on one side, and avoided the thrust.

The king's thrust not taking effect, he overbalanced himself by the force of the attempt, and tumbled headlong out of the carriage, and lay sprawling upon the ground.

Don Jose saw the accident, and believing there was great danger, immediately called for aid by shouting,—

"Guard—guard! help—help! here are assassins! help—guard!"

In another moment, the guards, that is, the armed servants, hearing the noise, rushed out with what weapons they could seize, swords and arquebuses, and a general *melee* ensued with Cæsar, who was, by the activity of his movements, here, there, and everywhere; and they believed they were contending with half a dozen persons, and more than once exchanged blows with each other; but after a short period the clatter ceased, and the enemy became invisible—he had escaped.

"What is all this about, Don Jose?" inquired the king.

Don Jose shrugged his shoulders, and looking around him, said,—

"In faith, your majesty, I cannot well tell; but I saw a demonstration of hostility on the part of the postillion."

"Do you know who he is?"

"I only know that he is a postillion, and nothing more."

"It is very strange. What could be the cause of such a sudden and inexplicable attempt?"

"That I cannot tell, save that he must be seized with a sudden fit of madness. I expected instant assassination, and was not in a condition to defend myself, and checking myself so suddenly, I fell back into the carriage."

"And I out of it," muttered the king between his teeth, angrily.

Don Jose pretended not to hear this—he could not say anything but what would tend to anger the king; he, therefore, shifted the subject, saying,—

"He is now gone, your majesty, and I hope the interruption will not be repeated, and we may proceed."

"It is very strange," again muttered the king; "have these knaves got him? he could not surely escape them."

"Have you taken that fellow prisoner, you knaves?" said Don Jose.

"No, signor," replied the steward; "in the con-fusion he has got off, some how or other—I cannot tell."

"Confusion, indeed! what could you be at to let one man escape you?"

"One man! I thought there had been several," replied the steward.

"Then you ought to have had one at least, if you had been men."

"Had we better not carry her out, your majesty, for the opiate will soon cease to have any effect?"

"Yes—yes," replied the king; "let it be done at once."

Two of the attendants were called by Don Jose, who were ordered to carry Maritana, wrapped up as she was with the cloak, into a certain apartment, where she would be left by herself till she became conscious.

Don Jose was very much chagrined at what had occurred; he was more, for he was terrified, for he knew not by what inexplicable means the postillion had become metamorphosed into Don Cæsar.

How could Don Cæsar have come there, was a question that he could not answer; and another was, Did he know that Maritana was there also? and if he did, what was likely to be the result of such knowledge, he knew not, and trembled to think; he, however, must be got rid of by some means or other—if he were shot or stabbed, so much the better; then he, Don Jose, would be relieved of a disagreeable and fearful enemy.

When the king first inquired who it was, Don Jose gasped out he did not know, for he would not have informed his majesty that Don Cæsar was living for a trifle—it would have thrown suspicion on himself, and he feared to do it.

Don Cæsar's singular escape from the prison, and the fate to which he was condemned, was to him inexplicable, save on the supposition that there had been collusion between the prisoner, his gaoler, and the guard. This he could scarcely credit, and yet it was the only probable supposition.

Had he admitted the existence of Cæsar to the king, it might have caused some embarrassment, and he would have believed that he, Jose, had been guilty of deceiving him, which would very likely produce a rebellion in the king's mind, and go far towards his downfall.

While Maritana was left to herself, the king and Don Jose entered an apartment prepared for their reception, the latter being very ill at ease, and could reply to the questions put to him with an ill grace, for the suddenness of the whole affair, and the surprise of seeing Don Cæsar, was so great, that he had scarce recovered himself from it.

However, he did recover from it, and conversed with the king, and shook off from his mind any second thought about the affair. Indeed, the king was scarcely the man to remember anything but an indignity, and caring but little what might happen, he gave himself up to the joys of anticipation, and questioned Jose about Maritana's state of mind regarding himself.

That wily favourite enlarged upon this subject, and Maritana's beauty, and kept the king in a pleasant humour. * * * *

Maritana, when she was carried into the room prepared for her reception, was laid upon a couch in a reclining posture, and a female soon after entered the room, who was to await upon her.

This was the duenna to whose charge Maritana was given—a big, coarse woman, past the magic period of "fair, fat, and forty"—the first quality had become wanting, and the fair dame became sun-burnt and coarse; the second she was to perfection, and blousy; forty she had seen some six or eight years.

This woman entered the room with the air of a person of consequence who filled a highly responsible, confidential, and respectable situation in the house. She walked along like a mountain of flesh, tenderly nurtured. She gazed upon Maritana a minute or two, and then said, in an affected voice,—

"Dear me, what girls these men are fond of; for my part, I can't see what they can see in such little things to take their fancy—not I. Well—well, taste is everything, and must be complied with. She must surely soon awake—ah! she moves."

Maritana did open her eyes for a moment, but she felt sick and giddy, and could not bear to look about her; she considered for a few moments, and endeavoured to recollect the past, but her brain was in such a whirl that she could scarce recollect anything.

She again opened her eyes, and with more success, but she could not recognise where she was; the room was strange—it was quite different to any she had seen before, and the furniture also was entirely different from what she had before seen.

"God of Heaven!" she exclaimed—"what is the matter—where am I?"

As she spoke, she lifted herself upon her elbow, and began to look round the room, and her eyes encountered the woman of whom we have spoken, who said,—

"There is nothing the matter, my little dear; do not flurry yourself, and be sure that you are quite safe."

"Quite safe—quite safe!" muttered Maritana, pressing her hands against her head, as if endeavouring to repress its throbbing, and trying to recollect what had passed. "Where am I—tell me, where am I?"

"In Don Jose's mansion. He! he! you know Don Jose, I'll be warranted."

"Don Jose, yes; but this is not his house; I was never here before."

"But Don Jose has more than one house, my dear," said the woman.

"Oh, merciful Heaven! what will become of me—where am I?"

She sat up on the sofa, and gazed wildly around her.

"Come, come," said the big woman, "do not be cast down. It is all for the best, and you'll be rich and beloved. Take my advice. I know what things are; for believe me, I have seen a little. Be complaisant, and you will be sure to make your fortune."

"Ah! do you talk thus to me?"

"And why not, pretty one? Am I not doing you a benefit by reconciling you to your fate? Am I not acting friendly—am I not giving you counsel that I know to be good?"

"And who are you?" inquired Maritana, with some energy, and so suddenly, that the fat dame gave a start, and pressing her hand against her heart, replied in a languishing tone,—

"Dear me, dear me—how you alarmed me. I am very nervous and delicate. Why, you see, I am sent here to do you any good office that I can."

"I need none. I would be alone," replied Maritana, who felt a great disgust at the woman's appearance.

"Well, I am sure; but I am not so sure that I may do so; however, I will go into the other room; you'll be solitary here, and glad of my company. Ah, I'm going."

Maritana motioned her away, and the woman then quitted the apartment in no very good humour.

Maritana moved not from the couch. The little exertion she had made to speak to this woman caused her brain to become confused, and the whole place appeared to be in motion. This was the effect of the opiate, which had not entirely quitted her.

Her thoughts, too, were confused; she could not trace the events that had preceded her appearance in that place. She could recollect the fearful scenes she had gone through, and the palace—yes, she could recollect the palace.

Yes, she must have been drugged and brought there insensible. At the thought of this, she started to her feet, exclaiming,—

"Holy Virgin, save me! What can these men mean? What is all this mystery about? Why am I subject to all this treatment? Should dishonour be their motives, I would sooner perish than submit. I mistrust that man Jose. He is a sycophantic, mendacious man. This could never have happened but for him.

"Ha! what is that? God of Heaven, there is more firing! Oh, it reminds me of the dreadful prison scene—the scene of slaughter to one I don't know but who was most near and dear to me. My God! forgive me; my brain whirls round, I know not what I say."

The firing continued, and was mingled with shouts and execrations.

"What can this mean?" she ejaculated. "More firing; some juggling of Don Jose's. Another execution, perhaps. I will see what it means, if possible."

There was a window in the room, which she opened into the balcony, and into which Maritana immediately stepped.

The court-yard and garden was a scene of uproar and confusion, and the flash of fire-arms, succeeded by the reports echoed through the place.

Presently a man, pursued by others, jumped to the top of the wall, waved his sword, and jumped down on the other side; just at the moment several guns were fired at him, but missed him.

"Gracious me!" exclaimed the fat woman, re-entering the room, "what can be the matter? I could faint, and would do so, too, but the sound of fire-arms makes me so nervous; and then I'm responsible, too, and might be kicked out by Jose, who doesn't stand about trifles."

She then went to the window, where she saw Maritana, and fearing she was going to escape, she laid hold of her, and dragged her into the room, saying, as she shut and fasten the window,—

"What, can't you keep out of harm's way? When bullets are flying about, it is very dangerous, and death to stop 'em."

The noise that had been created was occasioned by the discovery of a stranger on the premises, and that stranger was no other than Don Cæsar.

It would seem that Don Cæsar, when he made his escape, did it effectually, because he rushed in at the open gates, while those round the carriage only looked for him on the outside.

Here he for a time concealed himself, and would, no doubt, have been unmolested; but he unfortunately stumbled over one of the armed servants, who, knowing him to be an intruder, attempted to seize him. This, of course, Cæsar would not permit, and a fight was the consequence; and, finding himself no match for his antagonist, the fellow called out lustily for help, which came, but not before he had been wounded.

Immediately there was a furious onset made upon Cæsar, who, for a moment, sustained the shock; and, skilfully availing himself of their impetuosity, he eluded them, and broke away, and made the best of his way towards a low wall. He was hotly pursued, being repeatedly fired at; but the men, being so close, scarcely waited to take aim; but his good fortune did not desert him in this extremity; he gained the wall, sprang up, and in another moment was safe on the other side.

CHAPTER XLV.

DON JOSE'S INTERVIEW WITH THE QUEEN. — HIS
COUNSE.—LLAZARILLO'S INTERVIEW WITH THE
QUEEN, AND HIS RETURN TO MADRID.

WE will now relate to our readers the particulars of
the interview that Don Jose had with the unfortunate
queen after he had questioned Lazarillo respecting
his knowledge of the existence of Don Cæsar.

The queen was reluctant to grant the interview he
sought; indeed, she would not have consented to it,
but she was anxious to know something more respecting the fate of her messenger, and, if it were possible, to ascertain how it was he had been assassinated,
and by whose orders.

She had a strange misgiving; she believed that Don
Jose was at the bottom of it; she could not disguise
from herself the fear she entertained, that the king
himself had given his consent to it, else how could it
happen that it had caused little or no sensation in
Madrid. It was, therefore, with a heavy heart she
consented to the presence of Don Jose, who bowed low
when he entered the royal boudoir.

The queen, for some moments, scarcely deigned to
notice the man she so much feared, and hated for his
many crimes, his baseness, and want of those qualities
which she herself possessed so eminently.

"What," she said, after a while, "what is it that
brings Don Jose again into our presence after we had
so recently dismissed him?"

"The exigencies of the times, gracious lady, must
be my excuse, and a desire for your welfare, also,
animates me."

"Indeed, Don Jose, methinks you have a singular
way of manifesting your desire to do good; for, as yet,
much mischief has been the result of your interference
in these affairs."

"Madam, I may be unfortunate enough to lose
your majesty's good opinion; but fortune never yet
sat constantly on any one's shoulder, and my advice,
if followed, may not be productive of the result
desired."

"But the advice itself has been more than suspicious, and the attempts to do our pleasure have been
more than questionable."

"I am not all-powerful, gracious lady; and when
what is desired runs counter to the pleasure of a king,
it does not come within the category of possibility to a
subject."

"Very well reasoned; but how was it our unof-
fending messenger was assassinated within the precincts of the royal palace?"

"Alas! madam, I would rather have but little to
say upon that unfortunate affair."

"And why, Don Jose? Are your hands too deeply
stained with blood, that they shame your conscience,
and you revolt at the bare contemplation of that in
our presence which finds such ready participators out
of it?"

"Then, madam," said Jose, with offended feelings
of innocence, "I must admit I knew that the unhappy
man was murdered."

"Cold-blooded wretch!"

"I am not, at least, deserving of such an opinion
as that which you have been pleased to express concerning me, and I must say that which I would otherwise have said nothing about. I am not the cause of
the death of your gracious majesty's messenger."

"Who was, Don Jose?"

"The king, your majesty," said Don Jose, watching
the effect this announcement would have upon the
queen.

For a moment she appeared struck with a thunderbolt, and hid her face between her hands; but she
suddenly recovered herself, saying,—

"No, no, you tell me an impossibility; the majesty
of Spain could never stain his hands with blood in
such an atrocious manner."

"You say right, gracious lady. The majesty of
Spain was not soiled by any contact with the blood of
your messenger. Oh, no; there were plenty who
would offer their daggers and to step in between the
king and such a deed. His majesty certainly did not
do the deed."

"What would you insinuate, then?" hastily exclaimed the queen.

"That though his gracious majesty did not strike
the blow, yet he was pleased to order it to be done."

"And you were the willing minister of such an
order?"

"Far from it, your majesty. I did all that I could,
all that I dared to do, and ran some personal danger
in attempting to avert the fate that was in waiting for
the unhappy man."

"And he suffered assassination, then, within the
palace?" exclaimed the queen, much affected at the
recital.

"Yes, most gracious lady. The deed was done on
the private staircase, close to his majesty's private
closet."

"Oh, Heaven; what a horrible crime! Surely
there cannot be so much wickedness in the world?
And my letter—what became of that?" said the
queen, quickly.

"I do not know. I dare say the king had it. Indeed, I have reason to think he had, because he spoke
in great anger respecting you afterwards."

"Indeed, by taking the life of my messenger. He,
at least, was innocent of any cause of offence."

"His majesty will not hold any direct communication with you. He is more than ever enraged against
you. He would not hold any kind of intercourse, and
even forbids your appearance at court. His anger is
extreme."

"And wherefore should he do all this? In what
have I deserved it? I am not conscious of having
done aught to anger him, and certainly I am innocent
of having done anything for which I might be deserving of censure."

"That may be, your majesty; but it is not always
the innocent and pure that escape misfortune and
suspicion."

"Misfortune I may not escape; but, surely, suspicion I might."

"Your majesty will pardon me ——"

"How, sir! dare you to our face express a doubt?
Do you judge others by your own insincerity of
purpose?"

"You have so long tamely submitted to the king's
unkindness, that even his majesty may think that fear,
or some other motive may be the cause of your silence.
Those who know your majesty will know to what
source to attribute this—to patience and sweetness
of disposition; but there are those who don't so well
appreciate your majesty's character as I do."

The queen looked at Don Jose with emotions of
scorn and contempt, and did not deign to reply to
him for some moments. At length she said,—

"It is strange that evil men should ride triumphant
through the world, their evil deeds bringing them fortunes and impunity, while all that is noble and
virtuous should be the victim of treachery and
deceit."

"Your majesty must be guided by yourself in what
course you would pursue under such circumstances;
but as your majesty will not probably deem any advice
that savours of worldly wisdom, or coming from me,
as worthy your attention, I need scarce offer it."

"I fear your sincerity, Don Jose," replied her
majesty.

"I have fallen, unhappily, under your majesty's displeasure," replied Don Jose, "and hence it is I appear culpable."

"Look at and remember your deeds."

"I am not the prime mover of all that happens in the state," said Don Jose; "and because my position brings me almost in contact with what your majesty most abhors, yet I am by no means chargeable with, or responsible for it, since my earnest endeavours are not sufficient to check it in a slight degree."

The queen sighed, and said,—

"What can be the reason that the king treats me with such cruelty? I am persuaded that you, Don Jose, are well acquainted with that secret, if I could depend upon your answer."

"Alas! madam, you have before guessed too surely the reason. The king's time is occupied in gallantry; but yet I think that your majesty must be misrepresented to him by some one who has his ear."

"What can I do?"

"I would advise you to proceed to Madrid, gracious lady."

"Indeed! Why, that is the reverse of what you advised before."

"Your majesty would not venture upon sending again, I presume?"

"No," replied the queen, with a shudder, "I would not, indeed."

"Were your majesty to do so, your messenger would, I fear, meet with equally as sad an end as the first."

"Another should not tempt the same fate for me," she replied.

"Then your majesty must go yourself, or remain and be acquiescent of all that is done, and suffer neglect."

"But you advised me not to do so before; now you wish me to see the king. How do you reconcile these things?"

"Because the case, I believe, is much worse now than before. His majesty is completely set against you, and will attend to nothing that you say; indeed, his dislike to you amounts to a rage and perfect madness."

"Then my best place is evidently to remain here till an opportunity occurs."

"Your majesty knows how far what I have said is the truth, by what has already passed, and how far he is disposed to attend to you."

The queen could not but acknowledge that his consort was extremely violent, and would not hear what she had to say, and she was ordered back to Aranjues with no courtesy or kindness.

"The king ordered me to remain here, and I do not see that I am justified in disobeying him."

"Then your majesty needs no advice how to act; but your majesty, of course, will be aware that his majesty will have no check upon his actions at Madrid."

"Alas! what check am I? But if I were to go to Madrid, it would be entirely useless, for he would not see me."

"That may be, and it is, I know, the fact. To go to his majesty would be the last of my thoughts, and I should certainly not advise you to do so, since you would be unable to obtain a hearing."

"Of what use would such conduct be? You speak in riddles."

"Not if your majesty will hear all."

"Proceed, then."

"With your gracious permission, I will. Your majesty will require the mediation of some powerful person, who has the right of audience, and the will to exert it."

"Ah,—I see; you would make yourself the mediator. I see—I see—the cloven foot then appeared, despite your disguises."

"Pardon me, your majesty. I do not propose myself as the mediator; had I the interest and the power, I would have done it unasked; but I have not."

"What do you mean?"

"That your majesty should go to Madrid, and throw yourself on the protection of the church, and obtain among them the aid, advocacy, and protection of that powerful body."

"There is certainly something reasonable enough in all this," replied the queen, musingly; "and yet I distrust the advice, because of the giver. You do not do it without motive."

"I can have no bad one, your majesty, since you place yourself and your affairs entirely beyond my reach."

The queen paused; she could see nothing in this that would at all be improper; nay, she had already done so, but nothing had come of it; she had heard nothing more.

"I have done what you advised," replied the queen, "ere this."

"Indeed, your majesty; pray, what may be the success of the plan?"

"I have heard nothing at all about it, and I presume it has failed."

"May I inquire, most gracious lady, the name of the churchman to whom you entrusted your cause?— for then, perhaps, I may be able to inform you of the probable cause of its failure, or non performance, whichever may be the case."

"It was the Cardinal di Vinci."

"Ah, he is in no favour; he is, indeed, looked upon as one who is plotting against the state, and, indeed, he is known to lean to the French interest, and I am not at all surprised that you have heard nothing about it."

"Why?"

"I doubt whether it has ever reached the king's ears, and if it has, it would be quite useless."

"To whom could I apply under such a state of things?"

"I should say to none better than the Abbe Perigord. He has influence with the king, because he has great influence with the clergy, and is held in high estimation by the court of Rome."

"Indeed."

"Yes; and, besides which, he is known as a man of letters, and such a one that even his majesty will not slight."

"I scarce know what course to pursue," exclaimed the unhappy queen, much afflicted at the position in which she found herself placed. "I may be running from one danger to another, like a mariner in an unknown region, surrounded by sunken rocks."

"Your majesty cannot go wrong, and I say this the more willingly, since the execution does not rest upon myself; but that is the course I should advise you to adopt, and may your majesty be successful in the issue."

"The Abbe Perigord," said the queen, musingly, "I have heard, is often at court."

"Not often, gracious lady, only when the king has leisure to receive him and others; not that the abbe would absent himself; it would be remarked. He is too much feared and respected not to receive the praise of all who come in constant contact with him."

"I fear he could do little towards softening the king's heart towards me."

"He could not compel justice," replied Don Jose. "It is beyond the power of man to control the passions of another, and this is especially true in the case of his majesty."

"I would not have the king forced to live with me, for forced affection I could not endure. No; I would seek another asylum, where I could repose in peace and serenity, and look upon the past as a dream."

"The abbe would aid you in whatever was your wish, and whatever appeared just, as your majesty's wishes certainly are though it is to be hoped that that extremity will not be forced on; but all things may be in time accommodated, and resume their wonted course; he would use his influence, which, as I have said, is very great, both with his holiness and his majesty."

The queen shook her head, and appeared doubtful and uneasy.

"Should your majesty go to him—as, if you come to Madrid at all, your only course would be to go to his palace, and there remain; for, if you attempt to see the king, he will be more than ever enraged against you, since he will believe you wish to intrude upon his privacy, and he will immediately quit the palace, and the breach will be rendered more desperate."

"I know not what to do," said the queen, thoughtfully; "I have already attempted to put this advice in practice, but it failed."

"Your majesty applied to one who has been discovered to belong to traitors, who would have deluged Madrid in blood."

"Aye."

"Yes, your majesty, and therefore 'tis unlikely that you would ever succeed, or that even your complaints would ever reach the ear of his majesty, much less could you benefit by them."

"But that I doubt the adviser, I shall almost be inclined to follow the advice."

"Let the merit of the advice and your majesty's own wishes be your guide; I have now done all that I can, and will, with your majesty's permission, withdraw, having given your majesty such counsel as it was my duty to give."

"I am not sure that I shall adopt this advice, Don Jose; but, should I do so, I will write and inform you of my determination, so that you may inform the Abbe Perigord of that step I shall have taken before I can reach his abode."

"Certainly, your majesty; I shall be happy to obey your orders, and shall remain at Madrid until I have the honour of receiving your majesty's wishes."

With a profound bow Don Jose retired from the royal boudoir.

He had scarcely quitted the royal apartment, when Jose resumed his wonted step, and he strode through the apartments elated, and filled with pride. A sinister smile crossed his dark features.

"She will wait, will she? Was ever man more fortunate? The very thing I most desired, but should not have dared to ask it. Well, my head or hers is the stake, and I think I have the odds in the wager. But now to Madrid, there to wait for this promised epistle."

He immediately quitted the palace, and, mounting his mule, he, with the few attendants that were with him, quitted the precincts of Aranjues.   *   *

Lazarillo had seen Jose depart; but he had not been invited to attend him, and he knew not what course to pursue.

"Doubtless," thought the page to himself, "he has been here to hatch up some devilish scheme for mischief; I would I could baffle him, and render his visit nugatory."

The page walked up and down the long alley in the garden, in anxious meditation, willing to do something, but unwilling to obtrude himself upon the queen, or how to begin an interview with her, if he saw her, he knew not.

At length, however, he made up his mind to risk all, and throw himself upon the queen's indulgence, and request an interview with her. This was readily granted, and Lazarillo soon found himself in the presence of the queen, whom he had before seen.

"You seek to speak with us, good youth," said the queen, kindly.

"Yes, gracious madam. Am I right in saying that my master, Don Jose, has been here?"

"You are, and may you speedily find a better master."

"Amen," said Lazarillo, fervently.

"You, too, doubt his honesty, my good youth, and you should know him."

"I do."

"And what does your knowledge teach?" inquired the queen.

"That he is capable of the most cold-blooded treachery that man can be guilty of, and a man with every vice, and no one good quality to give a single light to so dark a character."

"Upon my word," said the queen, "your picture is most unpromising. What can you allege as a motive for your opinion?"

"Facts, gracious lady."

"Relate them."

"First, then, with regard to the unfortunate Don Cæsar. He promised to exert his influence to save him."

"He promised me that."

"And, had he done so, he would have succeeded; but he had a motive for acting otherwise."

"Ha! had he so?"

"Yes, gracious lady, When Don Cæsar lay in prison, Don Jose came to Don Cæsar, and offered to procure him the death he preferred—he was doomed to be hanged—if he would marry and give his name to to a lady, who was to be veiled, and who was not to speak during the ceremony."

"Indeed! and was it done?"

"It was, and your majesty's name was very frequently made use of by Don Jose to further his object."

"Good Heaven! and dare he ——"

"He dare do anything, your majesty, that would favour his own views. After the marriage, the unfortunate Cæsar was led out to execution, and within a few moments after he had pronounced the solemn vows of marriage."

"How dreadful!" exclaimed the queen, shuddering at the recital.

"I had been the unhappy cause of Don Cæsar's death, and my terrors were great as I remained by and saw all this. Gratitude would have willingly made me take his place, if that had been possible."

"Poor boy!"

"While Don Cæsar and the guard were drinking to the health of the Countess de Bazan, I drew all the bullets of their arquebuses."

"Indeed!"

"Yes, and Don Cæsar fell from the anticipated shock, and was left for dead. That night he and I escaped from the prison."

"Then he lives?"

"He does."

"Heaven be thanked so foul a murder has not been committed on so brave and generous a gentleman!"

"Indeed, your majesty, he does indeed bear the character you have given him."

"But Don Jose—is he aware of the existence of Don Cæsar?"

"He was not for some time; but he has seen him once, and appears to dread him, and I fear, that if taken, the original sentence may be put in force against him; and I wish him to be concealed, or at least out of the way of Jose's people, for I am sure he would have him assassinated to get rid of him quietly."

"What a terrible bad man this minister is!" exclaimed the queen.

"Yes, gracious lady, he is, indeed, a bad man. I could not have believed any man could have been so bad, till I knew him."

"Then what became of the lady who was married to Don Cæsar?"

"That I can hardly say; but Don Jose has been often to the Marquis de Rotondo's, as well as at the palace, and his majesty has been much with them."

"Heavens! what can be the meaning of all this? It is very mysterious."

"Yes, gracious lady, and your name is very freely used, to sanction anything that may be said or proposed by Don Jose to this lady."

"And can he have such audacity as to use my name to sanction his villanous schemes?"

"Oh, yes, Don Jose dare do anything that is vile and unworthy, and especially when he has once poisoned the king's ear."

"Ah, it must be so! All my miseries have been of his inflicting, and perhaps the very advice he offers to me he offers because he thinks that from so polluted a source I should never take advice, but act directly contrary, and thus gain credit and his object. Who is the lady thus misused?"

"I do not know, neither does Don Cæsar even know; but he is most anxious to ascertain, for he knows not for what dishonourable purpose his name may be used."

"This is, indeed, a terrible state of things that you have related to me, Lazarillo, and yet I am so poor, so powerless, that it is not in my power to aid him, or prevent any wickedness from being perpetrated. Even my messenger was assassinated. Can you tell me anything relating to that sad and terrible affair?"

"Alas, madam! I fear I was the innocent cause of his death."

"How! You?"

"You shall hear, your majesty. When Don Jose came from the king's private closet, he said to me, ' Lazarillo, I expect a messenger from the queen; you will see him, and take him to the door that leads to the private staircase of the king, as he will receive him in private; and when you have done that, you may come to my house. Do not go up yourself, but leave him to go by himself, or you may expose yourself to danger.'

"I did as I was desired, and little did I think I was sending the poor fellow to his death. Alas, but I was not aware of the extent of Don Jose's wickedness; the next I saw of him, was his lifeless body in the courtyard, with two ghastly dagger wounds."

"My God—my God!" exclaimed the queen, as she fell into a seat, and swooned.

Lazarillo was distracted—he knew not what to do, but immediately ran and called for assistance, and when he saw the queen in the hands of her attendants, he withdrew from the apartment.

What course to pursue he scarce knew, but he wished to be at Madrid. Jose had sent him there to remain till he came. Don Jose had not, at that moment, contemplated a visit, and as he, Lazarillo, had general orders to follow Don Jose about, he determined to follow him to Madrid.

His period of absence from Madrid had been ended by Don Jose's arrival, who had, in the exultation of the moment, forgotten to give him any fresh orders.

The moment he thought of this, he obtained a mule and set off from Aranjuez to Madrid, with all the haste he could make.

CHAPTER XLVI.

LAZARILLO'S ADVENTURE UPON THE ROAD TO, AND ARRIVAL AT, MADRID.—HIS JOURNEY TO THE RETREAT.—THE VERY CLEVER SERVANT.

IT was late in the day when Lazarillo quitted Aranjuez, and he hastened onwards with all possible haste for Madrid, which he wished to reach in good time.

He spurred his mule onward, and proceeded at a good round pace, and passed on the road the retreat or villa of Don Jose, and this brought him within a league of Madrid, and this distance was decreased to one half, when he slackened his pace a little to allow himself to reflect upon what he was about.

"There can be no doubt but that Don Jose must be aware of the existence of Don Cæsar: that is certain; and his object would be to get him put out of the way, and assassination is the readiest way of doing that; indeed, if there were any other, Don Jose is not the man to adopt it. Use is nature with him, and he is so used to that, that he would use no other.

"Well, where is Don Cæsar? I trust he is safe from the daggers of Don Jose's minions. One consolation is, that if he have half a chance they will pay dearly for an encounter with him; but it is taking him unaware that I fear; the best man may be slain by a child under such circumstances, or he may be overpowered by numbers."

Just as he had muttered these words to himself, three men darted out from beneath the shade of some tall trees and seized his mule, and desired him to stop.

"Hilloa!" cried Lazarillo; "what is all this about? I do not carry a treasure that you pounce upon me as though I were a regiment of horse concentrated into one."

"Come—come," replied one of the ruffians, "let us have as little of your impertinence, or we may throw you into the brook, my gay youth."

"La! it appears to me that there are three of you to do it, now; if there had been but one, for instance, like yourself, why, it would have been questionable whether you wouldn't have felt my riding-rod across your face."

"Ha! ha! ha!" laughed one of the other ruffians, who appeared to enjoy the laugh at his fellow-assassin; but turning to Lazarillo, he said, in a threatening tone,—

"Come, enough of this; have we not seen you in company with Don Cæsar?"

Lazarillo instantly became alarmed, and hesitated before he answered; this being seen by the men, one of them said, in a severe tone,—

"No prevarication, as you hope for your life; tell us truly—have we not seen you recently in the company of Don Cæsar?"

"I am sure I cannot tell what you have seen, but I have been in his company."

"And you know him?"

"Do you think I can always choose my company?" inquired the page.

"And why not?"

"Because if I could, I would take an opportunity of doing so now."

"Where is Don Cæsar?"

"That I cannot possibly tell."

"Where do you come from?"

"From Aranjuez."

"Where are you going to?"

"To Madrid."

"What for?"

"I don't know. I am following my master, Don Jose, and, therefore, know nothing unless he tells me, which is not likely."

"I believe you," replied the man. "Well—well, you are alone, and may, therefore, continue your journey. There is no reason to do anything with him, I think," he added aside to one of his companions.

"Oh, no; never give ourselves more trouble than necessary," replied the other.

"There, go on, and be discreet."

The page needed but once inviting to do that, and soon put his mule into a smart gallop, and was shortly out of sight.

"Well," thought Lazarillo, "no harm has happened, and much good may, because it will enable me to inform Don Cæsar that he is looked after, and that Don Jose has appointed attendants to wait upon him, who will save him the trouble of existing for the future.

"But where to find Cæsar I do not know; that is the question; he has not fallen, else he would not be looked after by those people, and as to going to the church of San Veronica to-night, I might as well go to the Holy Sepulchre.

"Where shall I go now,—to Jose's? no; I will at once go to the palace. Cæsar is more likely to be about there than anywhere else, and I shall there learn more than by going direct to Don Jose."

With this determination he immediately turned his mule's head towards the palace, where he arrived. It was late, and there were but few persons about.

Don Jose's livery, however, procured him unmolested admission to the interior, where he met with an old servant, who wandered about the establishment as a sort of inspector, who, when anything happened out of the ordinary way, he was called upon to give directions as to what was to be done; to him Lazarillo now spoke, for he had, on one or two occasions, spoken to him, and the old man became very communicative to him.

"Have you seen Don Jose?" inquired Lazarillo of the old domestic.

"Yes, sir page, I have."

"Is he here?"

"No, he is not, indeed. By the way, that Don Jose, your master, is a strange man. There are strange doings of late."

"Are there?"

"Yes, sir page, between you and I, and I know it will go no further."

"Oh, certainly not," replied Lazarillo; "we know the deeds of the great are only spoken of under the rose."

"Certainly."

"And are never known, except among those who are in the midst of the scene of action, as you and I are."

"Yes—yes, that is certain; you are, I see, a discreet courtier."

"One must necessarily be so to have anything to do with such people as we serve."

"Ah! you may say that," said the old man, with a

shrug of the shoulders; "I have seen some things that would astonish strangers to court life in Spain."

"But what has happened lately," inquired Lazarillo, "that you speak so mysteriously?—where is my master?"

"Ah, my young friend, there is more there than meets the eye."

"I dare say; but that is so common a case, that I am not at all surprised at it; indeed, after what I have seen these few days past, I shall never be surprised at anything, however singular and strange."

"You are right to say so; I learned that many years ago."

"But of Don Jose!" exclaimed the page, somewhat impatiently; "I am in search of him. I may be blamed for my delay."

"Oh, you'll not be wanted to-night, at all events," said the old man."

"How is that?"

"Why, Don Jose is with the king," he replied, significantly.

"And the king?"

"Is with Don Jose," answered the old man, smiling at his own pleasantry.

"And where are they both?"

"Together."

Lazarillo was angry, and could have cursed the old man for a fool, for he had no humour for jokes and other things; but he checked himself, and said,—

"Ah, you have seen much in your time—there's no contending against you."

"No—no," sighed the old man, shaking his head, and smiling complacently; "I have not been here a matter of five-and-forty years for nothing, you may depend."

"I can believe you," replied the page; "but, touching the whereabouts of Don Jose; you can, if you will, let me into the secret, I know."

"They are at a certain house within a league of Madrid."

"Ah!"

"Yes—you know where."

"Scarcely; for you have not yet told me," said the page.

"Well, then, you know the Retreat—a quiet little nook, about a league from this city. This is, of course, confidential."

"Strictly."

"Well, then, it is a villa of Don Jose's, with servants all in his livery; indeed, the place is believed to be Don Jose's."

"I know the place."

"Well, that's where they are."

"The king and Don Jose?"

"Yes, and somebody else."

"And somebody else," repeated the page, in astonishment. "Some mischief is afloat," he added, musingly.

"That may be a very likely story. I cannot pretend to understand the matter at all. I cannot make it out, anyhow."

"You can't, eh?"

"No. The Retreat I know, from what has been whispered among a few such as ourselves, ostensibly belongs to Jose."

"Exactly."

"But, then, my gracious master goes there sometimes, and plays up the devil's pranks; because, you see, my master is complaisant, and doesn't much care what the world says of him."

"I know that full well."

"Exactly; but, then, you see, having no character to lose, he has none to keep, and, of course, he doesn't care what's done at a place supposed to be his."

"Well."

"Now, his majesty must be somewhat careful; because, you see, he is the king, and it might be of some consequence—and there has been a rumpus between him and the pope—and he has gone there; and, from precedents, I should have said he went there to carry on an intrigue that was like to cause him some trouble, because he never goes there when he finds the ladies kind at home."

"Then you mean, if a lady won't fall in love with his majesty, and he takes a temporary liking to her, he has her taken there because she cannot escape him?"

"Exactly; high walls, master page, and servants with no ears—what can be better planned, or where can anything be done more securely, I should like to know?"

This was another scheme of villany exposed to Lazarillo, and he, too, had just passed the very spot.

"Who was the third person that went?"

"Can't tell; there was much mystery about it He, or she—the former, I believe—was hurried out between them in a large cloak, and cocked hat, and they drove off like fury."

"I will go after them."

"Surely not."

"Yes, I have general orders to follow Don Jose everywhere."

"You'll get into disgrace."

"I have thought of it deeply, and I think I ought to go. Good night."

"Good night, if you will go, and may you meet with no accident."

Lazarillo mounted his jaded mule, and set forward on his journey, much doubting the propriety of the step and the issue; but he was soon recalled from his fears and doubts by his mule stopping at the gate. He rang, and was admitted, being in Don Jose's livery, without question, by those whose office it was to attend to the gate.

This facility of entrance was an agreeable surprise to Lazarillo; for although he had made up his mind to endeavour to effect a passage into the chateau, by representing himself as specially attached personally to Don Jose, he did not think the claim would be quite so readily acknowledged as it was.

The place, of course, to him was quite new, and yet he thought it better not to show any feeling of surprise at anything he saw, so he strolled with as easy an air as he could assume into a large hall, which he saw was occupied by some servants, who stared at him when he came with looks of great surprise.

"Why, where do you come from, youngster?" cried one.

"Madrid," said Lazarillo, as he carelessly threw himself into a seat. "Where do you come from?"

"From Madrid! You look as if you had come from your mother's apron string."

"And you," said Lazarillo, "from robbing your master's wine-flagon, if one may judge from the ruby beacon you carry before you by way of a nose."

"Death and fury!"

"Oh, put yourself into as great a passion as you like. For my part, I consider it too fatiguing."

"Now, by the mass ——"

"Leave the lad alone, Lopez," said another. "You began it with him, and you know well, or you ought to know, that a Madrid page is equal in sauciness to the very devil."

"Nay, my friend," said Lazarillo, with a smile, "you spoil your advocacy by damaging your client. I think myself civil spoken."

"And so you are, I dare say. You belong to Don Jose?"

"I do; my coat shows you as much. I am his confidential page, and go with him everywhere."

"So I should have said, for you are the first one of all his household he ever brought with him here."

"Indeed."

"Yes; and so you are highly favoured. You know place, no doubt, and its useful purposes?"

"Oh, yes—yes."

"He'll tell us," whispered one, "who the lady is who was brought hither to-night disguised *en cavalier*."

"Aye, boy, do you know the name of the favourite?"

"I do not," said Lazarillo. "She is here, of course?"

"Oh, of course."

"From whence there is no escape?"

"None—none."

"And yet," added Lazarillo, "do you know, my friends, I cannot help really pitying her."

A roar of laughter was the reply to this, and Lazarillo felt convinced that nothing was to be gained by working upon the sympathies of the domestics, who were too much inured now to such adventures to think anything of them in a moral point of view. He felt himself, therefore, to be perfectly unaided, and that if he were to do anything for the Countess de Bazan, it must be alone, if indeed, his information should turn out to be correct, and it should really be the wife of his dear friend, Don Cæsar, who was in such dishonourable hands.

He was invited by the domestics to partake of some refreshments, of which, to tell the truth, he was greatly in want, for such had been the rapidity of his movements lately, as well as his great anxieties, that he had not thought of supplying his ordinary wants.

He was sparing of the rich wine which was freely offered him, and, perhaps, all the more freely, because his entertainers hoped to get from him all the tittle-tattle and correct news of the court. But Lazarillo soon became too much immersed in his own thoughts to be in a talkative humour at all, so that his audience were disappointed, and soon, by degrees, they left him to himself completely, which was just what he wanted, for then, without exciting more than a mere passing remark, he came and left the hall.

The romantic idea had taken possession of him that during the night he might possibly succeed in rescuing the Countess de Bazan, and he felt that the first step towards even such an attempt must be to see her, and induce her to have sufficient confidence in him to allow him to make the effort.

How to reach her he had not the least idea, or in what part of the house she was, so that it behoved him to be especially careful in his walk through the chateau, which was so zealously guarded from intrusion from without.

If, instead of discovering the countess, he should chance to light on Don Jose or the king, he felt certain that he should be ordered to leave the place, even if no worse suspicions were entertained respecting his motives for coming there than that he was an intruder from ignorance; so he wished, before such a meeting should take place, to secure an interview with the Countess de Bazan.

"I will explain to her," he thought, "should I be fortunate enough to find a means of speaking to her, all that Don Cæsar has done for me, and then I will ask her how I could be such a monster of ingratitude as not to devote my whole life to his service. Surely she will then trust me."

Suddenly then Lazarillo paused; for, with an acuteness scarcely to be at all expected from a lad of his age, a new thought struck him, and it was a painful one.

"What," he said, "if, after all, she is unworthy of him. I know not who and what she is. If she is unworthy, alas! poor Cæsar! you will, indeed, wish then that you had fallen under the arquebuses of the palace guard."

Painful as this thought was, still it was but a supposition, and the page would not give so much weight to it as to induce him to abandon his enterprise.

"No," he said, "no. I will seek her, and endeavour to judge for myself. If she be as good and virtuous as report speaks her to be beautiful, I will risk my life to rescue her. If I find her otherwise, and indifferent about Don Cæsar, I will at once leave this place, seek him out, and we will together bid Spain adieu for ever. It will no longer be a home or a country for him, and then it will have no charms whatever for me."

Thus reasoning and determining, Lazarillo commenced his search through the chateau, of all the localities of which he was quite ignorant, for the Countess de Bazan.

He ascended the first flight of stairs he saw, for he thought it much more probable she should occupy some chamber above those on the ground floor. All was perfectly still, and, although he now walked slowly and cautiously from room to room, yet he saw no one, heard no one, nor could he observe any indications whatever of the chateau being inhabited by any persons besides the servants he had seen below.

"And yet," he thought, "they admitted that Jose was here. I will persevere yet awhile."

Before he entered any more, he placed his ear close to the panelling to listen if any one was within, but as he invariably, throughout some eight or ten rooms, found that no one was in any of them, he, without a thought, grew a little more bold, and opened several more, after a very slight investigation.

Now he came to the end of one suite of apartments altogether, and he found that to reach another, which ran at right angles to the former, he had to cross a wide landing, from whence descended another flight of stairs to the lower part of the house.

He hesitated but a moment, and then crossed the landing, and opened the door of a room beyond.

The instant he did so the sound of voices struck upon his ears, and he at once shrank back, as he heard Don Jose exclaim in a tone of anger.

"Who's there—who dares disturb my privacy? Who's there, I say? By heavens, I'll know! Speak, knave, and say your errand."

CHAPTER XLVII.

MARITANA IN HER NEW PRISON.—HER TERRIBLE STATE OF FEELING.—JOSE'S MOCK CONGRATULATIONS.—THE PAGE, AND JOSE'S SURPRISE AND ANGER.—THE ARQUEBUS AND THE ORDER.

It will thus be seen that by a singular combination of events the whole of our characters have chanced to assemble at that suburban villa which had been the scene of so many atrocities.

Here we have Philip of Spain, the licentious, crafty monarch, who cared for no rights, divine or human, so that he accomplished his own fell purposes.

We have Don Jose, a man of ability with the morality of a fiend—a man so utterly destitute of all sensations of goodness, that when we meet such a character, and contrast it with its opposite, we wonder that the same class of beings can exhibit such remarkably different varieties.

We have, too, at this suburban chateau, the page—and the Countess de Bazan, who has suffered so much to be great; and last, although far from least, we have Don Cæsar, who, after all that had occurred, was not at all likely to leave that neighbourhood to which his suspicions were now so strongly excited.

*   *   *   *   *   *

The moment the words of Don Jose, from the room

which he had so incautiously opened, reached the ears of Lazarillo, he dashed across the landing-place, and was ensconced behind a column and effectually concealed.

In another instant Don Jose came out with a light in his hand, and stood in an irresolute attitude on the landing.

"Who's there?" he cried,—"who's there?"

All was still, and now the king came to the door of the room, and, in a low and agitated voice, said—

"What was it, Jose?"

"I know not, sire, unless the door was not securely fastened, and a sudden gust of wind opened it."

"The morning breeze is blowing."

"It is. I hear it among the trees, which makes me think such a solution of the alarm probable."

"Who would have ventured, Jose, to interfere with us here?"

"None. None."

"Then it must be as you say."

"I think it must. I am sure I may depend upon all here now, your majesty. I think it must have been the wind, which comes, I find by the light, with a strong current up this staircase even now."

"And yet, Jose, how strange an affair that was of the postillion."

"It was, sire."

"There must have been some treachery."

"No, sire, I think not. Upon consideration, I am only inclined to think the man was mad drunk."

"I wish we were sure, Jose."

"I think we may be, your majesty."

"Well, then, come in. The countess is, I am sure, upon the point of recovering from her swoon."

"It would be well to call the woman whom your majesty has sent away."

"Aye—true. The first sight of you or I might produce a dangerous relapse. Come in, Jose—come in."

Don Jose, with a troubled countenance, left the landing-place, which was, in consequence of the rapid approach of daylight, now nearly as light without the candle he had carried as it had been with its assistance.

Lazarillo, however, was in no hurry to emerge from his hiding-place, for well he knew the crafty disposition of Don Jose. He was amply rewarded for his discretion, for in about ten minutes the door was opened so suddenly that it seemed as if done by magic, and Don Jose made a thrust with his sword outside, which, if Lazarillo or any one else had been there, would have speedily rid them of all earthly troubles and concerns whatever.

"Ah!" he said, as he did so, and he looked around him disappointed to observe no one.

The king stood close behind him with a lamp in his hands, held up as high as he could.

"There is no one," said Jose. "It must, of course, have been a false alarm. I have no longer any doubts whatever."

"Nor I. Come in."

They both retired, and closed the door.

"That was clever enough, Master Jose," said the page to himself, "and very like you, indeed; but now I believe the danger to be passed."

It seemed to Lazarillo that by a bold experiment he might at once put an end to all suspicion, and with a tact that did him infinite credit, he thus achieved his object.

There was a very brisk breeze blowing, and Lazarillo waited until there came a gust of unusual strength, which could not but reach the ears of both Jose and the king, and then he rapidly walked towards the door, unlatched it, and in an instant retreated again to the place of concealment he had chosen for himself behind the column.

Jose and the king were outside in another moment, and after a slight pause the former said—

"There, I said it was the wind."

"You were quite right, Jose," observed the king. "There can be no manner of doubt upon the subject now whatever."

"Certainly not. I have often known a sudden gust, such as came just now, to open doors."

"And I—and I."

They both retired into the room again, and now the page had no hesitation whatever in stationing himself exactly outside, to listen to what they should say to each other.

So completely were all the suspicions of Jose and the king now removed, that they conversed even in a higher tone than before, so that Lazarillo had no difficulty whatever in hearing them, and he did accordingly hear the following colloquy, which, to him, was deeply as well as very painfully interesting.

"If she still continue obstinate," said the king, "and we find that neither entreaties nor menaces will move her, what is to be done?"

"Your majesty loves her?"

"To distraction."

"Then you must call her yours. This chateau has already had its share of such celebrity."

"It has Jose. But somehow I do not feel so firm in my resolves as concerns this girl. I do not mind confessing to you, that her high-souled virtue does alarm me, if not awe me."

"Awe your majesty?"

"Yes, Jose. For the first time in my life I have felt such a feeling, although a king."

"In—deed!"

"It is a melancholy truth Jose,—a very melancholy truth, because, when we come to consider that kings are—are, in a manner of speaking—you know, Jose—"

"Precisely, your majesty."

"Exactly."

"I am of the same opinion."

"I thought you would be, because it is a rational view to take of the matter—a very rational view, I may say. But about this girl, Jose. If persuasion of any kind will avail, I should be far better pleased than if any other measures were to be adopted. I love her, and the more violently, because I have never yet met with so much opposition to my wishes."

"Exactly, your majesty."

"You pair of rascals!" thought Lazarillo.

"Then, you know," added the king, "I am quite tormented at present about the queen and this affair between me and the church of Rome. By heavens, Jose, it would seem as if I were condemned to be crossed at every turn by everybody in everything."

"A few seeming crosses," remarked Jose, "at the outset of an adventure, ought not to deter your majesty from the consummation that is just within your grasp. You would not fly from victory, because it is not quite, but only nearly gained."

"But the consequences, Jose,—the consequences. Victory is one thing, but if we are to be beaten for it afterwards, it is another."

"Very true, your majesty; but that is not what your majesty need apprehend from the court of Rome."

"But the minds of men are so bowed down by that enormous power which is wielded by the Vatican, that makes it irresistible."

"No such thing," replied Jose; "if your majesty will recollect that in all the contests which the court of Rome has had with European princes, it has not universally met with success."

"Granted; but what then?"

"Why, in proportion as they have been boldly faced by their adversaries, they have invariably drawn back, and become more humble; for your majesty may take it for granted that the court of Rome would sooner itself submit than lose the submission of a prince, even though the submission was merely nominal."

" But this nuncio makes very high demands, and there is so much publicity, that they could not well draw back without a contest, and for a successful one the minds of men are not yet prepared."

" That cannot be of a certainty predicated until tried; but I would meet the court of Rome in any-thing but the spirit of concession—nay, I would treat them with a haughty indifference becoming a king, who governs despotically, as your majesty does, and as one possessed of the supreme power of a great na-tion. Do this, and the court of Rome will be alarmed, and their conduct, now so bold, will become changed to civility, and your majesty's pleasure will be con-sulted, and then, by a trifling concession, you may gain whatever point you desire; they will be glad to secure your submission, if it be given ever so much like an act of favour to them."

" Well, well," replied the king, "let that pass; I am not well pleased with these functionaries at the best."

" Truly they would pretend to judge of the wants and pleasures of men who live in the world, and of which they are perfectly incapable of appreciating, from their very position, with regard to it."

" Certainly."

" Your majesty will bring this matter to a con-clusion while you may, and thus prevent all future opposition to your wishes."

The king shrugged his shoulders, and said, as he walked across the room,—

" No, no, Jose, that will not do; I never did yet, and I never will."

" I am amazed," said Jose.

" Indeed, I see no cause for it," replied the king; " she is insensible and inanimate; in that state I leave her till consciousness returns. I could not think her a human being, while lying there in that state."

Don Jose, in his own heart, could not help cursing what he called the silly qualms of the king, and thought that every delay would cause him more danger, for he was perfectly aware of the vicinity of Don Cæsar; but he could not gain an entrance there, and therefore there could be no danger; but yet the vicinity to such a man as Cæsar, to whom his villanies must be known, produced an uncomfortable feeling in his breast.

" Your majesty, no doubt," said Jose, suddenly recollecting himself, " will be glad to quit this room, since it is so close to Maritana—indeed, you will re-quire some refreshments."

" I am fatigued," replied the king, " and think I could take some wine. Is there anything to be had in this place ?"

" I have cared for all that, your majesty. In the room below is a cold collation, and some excellent wines."

" Lead the way, Jose," said the king,

Lazarillo had scarce time to withdraw from the door, and secrete himself in his hiding-place, when Don Jose, followed by the king, entered the passage.

Nothing was spoken by either as they passed down the passage, and Lazarillo listened to their retreating footsteps with anxiety.

" Now," he thought, " I shall have an opportunity of discovering who the Countess de Bazan is, and whether she be worthy the name she bears. But I must be cautious."

Lazarillo waited some time, but could hear no sounds; but even then he crept softly from his hiding-place, and after listening to the sounds of the king's and Don Jose's voices in the room below, he went back, and peeped into the room they had just left.

All was silent and quiet, and Lazarillo quickly and lightly stepped in, and approached the door leading into the room in which Maritana was lying.

He listened at the door; a low murmur met his ear, and a sob. He did not hesitate any longer, but opened the door and gently entered the room.

There was Maritana, seated, in a kind of half stupor, on a couch, with her head lying on her arm, almost insensible.

Lazarillo paused. He knew instantly who the Countess de Bazan was. He paused again with as-tonishment, and gazed at her.

" Maritana—Maritana!" he exclaimed, in the ex-tremity of his surprise.

Maritana slowly lifted her head, and looked towards the page with an effort, as if she could not overcome her inclination to sleep, and said,—

" Who calls me by that name? Have mercy, Hea-ven, and protect me!"

" Who has brought you here? But I need not ask you," he added, suddenly checking himself. " It could be no other than Jose."

" Ah! you have pronounced the name of one who is bringing and has brought on me a dreadful calamity."

" Say what has happened? What would you have?" inquired Lazarillo.

" Protect me from Don Jose; save me from his evil machinations. Surely the queen never wished me to suffer thus. Oh, no, no! She is too good, too kind, too noble. What—what am I saying? My head wanders, my heart beats. Oh, am I delivered into the hands of such men? Aid me! Save me—save me! or I shall die—ay, die mad!"

She gazed about her so frantically while she spoke, that Lazarillo felt the utmost pity and commiseration for her, and was about to whisper some comfort to her, and to assure her that she had friends, who would work their utmost in her behalf, as well as that Don Cæsar, her husband, yet lived. But he had no time to utter a syllable, for he heard the handle of the door turn, and caused him to think of his own safety, which he knew was compromised.

This, unfortunately, happened to be the only mode of egress from Maritana's room, and what to do he scarce knew.

Now the cause of this disturbance was, that Don Jose having quitted the king for a few moments, for some purpose or other, the king took it into his wise head that he would for once steal a march upon Don Jose.

He therefore left the room below and stole up stairs, and it was he who disturbed Lazarillo; and just as the door opened, and the royal head was popped in, it met with a salute, rude and daring, that caused the door to fly open, the candle the king carried to go out, and the royal person to fall flat on the floor.

Lazarillo, driven to an extremity, and finding no means of escape, did the only thing that under such an emergency presented itself to his mind, and that was, to seize the couch pillow and fling it at the king the moment he appeared with the light in his hand, and before he could see who was in the room.

This was so well timed, that it had the desired effect, and the result is as we have stated, the prostration of the royal person.

The instant Lazarillo saw the effect produced, he rushed to the door, and as there was no help for it, he scrambled over the king, who lay in the way, endea-vouring to rise, and was soon out of the room.

" Murder! guards! help—help!" shouted the king, scrambling and sprawling about, and either through fear or amazement, was unable to rise, be-

cause his efforts to do so were so ill-directed for that purpose.

"Guards, guards! murder! help, Jose, help!" shouted the king, more alarmed than ever at his own inability to rise.

In another moment Jose, who had heard the shouts of the king, but was rather puzzled to say where they came from, made his way through the room below, to the room above, where he found his majesty in the undignified posture described.

Having assisted the king to arise, he inquired if his majesty had been hurt.

"No, no, I believe not," replied the king; "but I can hardly tell what has happened."

"You were in the room below, your majesty, a few moments ago."

"Yes, I was," replied the king, looking round, "and I came up here with a light, intending to see how matters stood, and whether Maritana had recovered or no."

"Yes, your majesty," said Jose, who stood listening anxiously to what the king said.

"Well, I hardly hardly know what followed, but I opened the door. and thought I saw somebody there, when suddenly something happened, I don't know what, that threw me down, and extinguished the light."

"Indeed, your majesty, I cannot understand it at all; there could be no one there; but we had better question Maritana."

"Be it so," replied the king; "I could not be thrown down by nothing—something must have struck me, though I cannot tell what it was."

"A blow—there would have been marks left if there had been one."

"It was with something soft," replied the king; "something quite soft."

"A soft blow, your majesty?"

"Yes, but hard enough to knock me down, man," said the king, testily.

They now entered the room in which Maritana sat trembling, for they had taken the precaution of shutting the door, and speaking in a low tone together.

"What is the meaning of this, Maritana?" inquired Don Jose. "Is it thus you greet your lord?"

Maritana spoke not, but her breast heaved and fell so, that shewed the terror she was under, and she averted her eyes from the king, as though she feared to look at him.

"There was some one else in the room," exclaimed the king; "who was it that used me so rudely, when I attempted to enter the chamber?"

"Is it not my chamber?" gasped out Maritana, but in a low, subdued tone.

"Your chamber?"

"Yes, surely. I am not denied the poor right of privacy. I cannot maintain it against two such as you, though I have endeavoured to do so against one."

"You did it?" exclaimed the king, in astonishment, and Don Jose elevated his eyebrows. "You struck me down?"

" I know not what I did," replied Maritana ; " but I must suffer outrage when intruded upon by two."

It is impossible to describe the unpleasant astonishment of Philip, or the strange sensations and thoughts that came crowding to the brain of Don Jose.

" Holy Virgin!" exclaimed Maritana, " protect and pity me."

" Come, Jose," exclaimed the king, " we will leave her awhile; and you, madam, prepare yourself to receive your lord in a more befitting way than in that you have just received him."

Without waiting to hear any reply, Don Jose and the king quitted the apartment, leaving Maritana once more to her reflections.

" Do you think, Jose," said the king, " that there was no one in the room besides Maritana when I entered it ?"

" I think not, your majesty ; there is no other entrance."

" But could they not have escaped while I was on the ground ?"

" No, your majesty, I must have met them coming up-stairs ; besides, there is no one who would dare act thus—there is no motive, and that is a strong proof that she speaks the truth."

" And yet I thought I saw some one."

" Your majesty must be deceived," replied Don Jose, confidently, " though, I must say, I did not expect that Maritana would have used such means as that."

" Nor I ; it seems to me that there are more than usual unpleasant circumstances attending this affair."

When Lazarillo had got clear of the king, he heard Don Jose moving about below ; and, fearing he should meet him, he betook himself to his old hiding-place, and there remained until they were fairly engaged in conversation ; and then, again quitting it, he sought the servant's-hall.

Here he mixed with the servants, and talked with them for a short time ; and then, knowing that Don Jose must soon become aware of his presence, he determined that he should know it from himself in preference to its reaching him from any other person ; accordingly, he wrote on a slip of paper to Don Jose, stating that he had arrived, and awaited his orders, and sent it to him by one of the domestics.

CHAPTER XLVIII.

CÆSAR'S NIGHT'S LODGING.—LAZARILLO'S DESPAIR
OF FINDING HIM.—HIS LETTER TO THE QUEEN,
AND JOURNEY TO ARANJUES.—THE RECEPTION.—
MORNING AT THE VILLA.—THE KING'S RAGE
AND IMPATIENCE.—EXPLANATIONS.

IT may be well imagined that Lazarillo waited with no small degree of anxiety the answer of Don Jose to his message, and when a servant came to say that he, Lazarillo, was to follow him, he did so with some serious misgivings as to whether Jose, in his unscrupulous mode of treating all who, by any combination of circumstances, might be in his way, might not think proper even to take his life.

" I will defend myself," thought he, as he loosened in its sheath the short dagger he wore, which was, most probably, far more ornamental than useful. " Even he shall not find me a passive victim. This, however, is a risk I am compelled to run, for the news of my being here from any other lips than my own would have instantly been an assurance of my doom."

Jose was seated in an apartment just at the top of the great staircase, and, when Lazarillo was introduced, he motioned to the attendant to withdraw, and said nothing until the door was closed upon them. Then, in a voice of assumed cheerfulness and confidence, he said,—

" Well, Lazarillo, what brings you here ?"

" A fleet horse, and your lordship's commands," said the boy, with an unabashed air.

" My commands ?"

" Yes, sir. You ordered me always to follow you, if I had no positive commands to the contrary, and here I am."

" But how did you know where I was ?"

" I considered it to be my duty to find out."

" Indeed ! Do you know, Lazarillo, that this place is dangerous to the health of any one who comes to it unbidden ?"

" I scorn danger in the performance of my duty."

" Where is Don Cæsar ?"

This question was put so abruptly, that any one but so acute a person as our young friend would have been taken by surprise. Not so he. His reply was instantaneous.

" I don't know."

" You don't know ! I would I knew, for, upon a review of all the circumstances connected with him, I think he might now fairly claim to place himself in a position of high honour and large emolument about the court. Ah, Lazarillo ! I cannot forget that Cæsar and I were old college friends. My heart yearns towards him."

" Does it indeed, sir ?"

" It does—it does."

" I sincerely hope you may find him. Can I be of any immediate service to your lordship ?"

Jose felt that he was foiled, and a rapid argument flitted through his mind, to the effect of,—" Shall I kill this lad, or attempt so fairly to attach him to me, that his great abilities—for they are great—may be all used in my service solely ?"

He could not completely make up his mind, so he resolved to give the subject more mature consideration. He had not the shadow of a thought but that the page had only just arrived when he had sent up news of his presence, and that circumstance tended greatly to his preservation.

" You can remain here," Jose said, after rather a long pause. " You can remain in this house until you receive further orders from me. But mark me, Lazarillo, if you but, in the most distant manner, give a hint to any one of aught you see or hear, while within these walls, you may depend that your death is certain. Even I cannot save you were I to wish to do so. The king, Lazarillo, would most assuredly have your life. You understand me ?"

" I do, my lord. Your words are plain."

" Let them sink deep into your heart. On the other hand, boy, I don't mind saying to you, that, situated as I am, a quick-mettled lad like yourself might be of infinite service to me. Attach yourself to me, Lazarillo, wholly, and you may depend that upon each proof I have that you really work for me, and me alone, faithfully, I will shower such golden favours upon you, that you shall bless the day your happy destiny gave you the favourite minister of Philip of Spain for a master."

" My lord, you shall not find me backward in my duty."

" Enough ; now go and wait for my further orders. You had perhaps better take some repose while you can."

" Then I shall not probably be wanted for your lordship's service yet awhile ?"

" Probably not till morning."

Don Jose waved his hand, and Lazarillo immediately left the room, and proceeded to the lower part of the chateau.

It was nearly morning then, for the sun was rapidly rising, and in a short time its full blaze of power would be above the horizon ; but yet the hour was an early one, and the page sat himself down in the deep recess of a window, to think upon what course he could pursue that would be the most likely to be favourable to the rescue of Maritana, whom he now felt was too much surrounded by the power of Jose to be taken from the chateau by his individual means.

"It must be," thought he, "some bold, sudden, and desperate scheme that shall snatch her from the power of the king and Jose. I am in no condition to do so. Thank Heaven, too, that Cæsar is not here; for well I know that, casting aside all thought of personal danger, some desperate project would come into his brain, in the attempted execution of which he would be murdered. Yes, I thank Heaven that he is not here. But, what can be done?"

He remained for some moments still in thought, and, then, rising, he said, in a low tone,—

"I shall not be wanted till morning—that means till the ordinary hour of stirring; for it is morning now. I shall not be missed if not asked for. What is to hinder me from riding to Aranjues? I am already some distance on the road, and the morning air is cool and favourable to speed; my horse is rested. The queen, and the queen only, can now save this much persecuted Countess de Bazan. Could I see her, and explain to her the position of affairs in this chateau, she would make an effort to rescue the countess from her dreadful situation. Dare I? Of course I dare; what is there within the compass of my means I would not dare for the happiness of Don Cæsar.

"He loves his countess, and well he may, for she is loveliness itself. That she is an unwilling inmate of this place, I have seen enough to know full well that point is clear and satisfactory. For Aranjues, then— to Aranjues! I will risk all, dare all, in this one expedient to save the countess from Jose and the king."

Upon a little further consideration, Lazarillo thought that as time would be urgent with him, and that he should arrive at Aranjues at an hour when, probably, the queen would not be stirring, he had better commit to paper a very brief outline of what he had to say. At all events, such a course might assist him, and it could not possibly impede him.

Accordingly, he procured writing materials, and, in the course of ten minutes, he produced a note, addressed to the queen, wherein he stated the situation of the chateau, hinted at the purposes for which it was used, and stated that both the king and Jose were there, having succeeded in carrying off the young, innocent, and beautiful Countess de Bazan, who, from so cowardly a step having been taken as regarded her, might look forward to the most dastardly and dishonourable usage.

He, likewise, in the most solemn terms, insisted upon the unimpeachable virtue and innocence of Maritana, and, upon that ground, he urged the queen to hasten to the rescue of one of her own sex from dishonour, even although the villain who would accomplish her destruction was the king himself.

Lazarillo's heart and soul were in the composition of this brief note, and it was written with extraordinary facility and energy.

When he had finished it, he at once proceeded to the stables, and saddled his own horse, without attempting to make any concealment that he was going to ride from the chateau. Had he betrayed any desire to do so, doubtless, Don Jose would, by some officious person, have been at once informed, and his suspicions, of course, awakened.

As it was, however, Lazarillo owed all his safety to the openness of his actions, by which he induced a belief among the domestics of the chateau that there was no concealment, and, consequently, none of them had anything to tell.

Within less than half an hour from the moment he left the presence of Don Jose, he was mounted, and passing out at the garden gate of the chateau. He walked his horse for some distance, so that the sound of his feet should not reach the ears of Jose, as well as to prevent the domestics of the chateau from thinking that he was bound on some hurried expedition, which might have created in their minds speculation and consequent conversation.

Then, when he was so far from the chateau that all apprehension on these points was at an end, he urged his steed to a gallop, and his light weight being no impediment whatever to the progress of the animal, he went at a tremendous pace on the road towards Aranjues.

*   *   *   *   *   *   *

It was well that he just left as he did; for, had he been another five minutes, he would have been seen to leave the place by both Jose and the king.

That danger occurred thus: when he had, as he thought, quite fixed Lazarillo by the brilliant promises he had made him in his service, he sought the king, who had resolved upon trying once more the effect of a personal interview with Maritana before he had recourse to violent measures. The fact was, that Philip was as arrant a coward as ever stepped, and the unexpected opposition he had met with from Maritana frightened him. In all his previous intrigues, he had never encountered one who, with so much stubbornness of virtue, defied him, and hence the singular vacillation of his conduct; consenting to adopt all the rascally suggestions of Jose at one moment, and then, the next, from some pretext or another, delaying their execution.

When Jose now sought his presence, he found him in an extremely nervous state, and it was easy to be seen that fears and superstitions of all kinds were at work upon him.

"Oh, you are come, Jose," he said. "What is the hour?"

"It is early morning, your majesty."

"Well, Jose, I am told that the countess still remains in a state hovering between insensibility and despair. I will see her some hours hence, when she may be more composed."

"As your majesty pleases."

"This is the last time, Jose, I will ever set foot within this place. After this affair, you may break up this establishment as soon as you please. It is hateful to me. I am convinced, Jose, that things not human are about it. I have heard strange noises—seen forms that have, I think, no mortal existence—because it is contrary to all belief that there should be any one here not in the express service of yourself, and I will confess that, from the moment I set foot within this place, a feeling of dread crept over me, which I have tried in vain to combat with."

"Indeed."

"It is too true, Jose."

"Oh, let me pray your majesty to shake off these idle fears."

"You call them idle, because you do not feel them. I wonder if really the sentence pronounced against my receiving any communion with the church has produced this effect."

"I should think not," said Jose, drily, "but faith goes a long way."

"Jose, Jose, I have ever remarked that you sneer at things which all other men think holy."

"Not so, your majesty. I have the highest opinion of religion, and no one can be more convinced of its necessity than myself for the common people."

"And why for them only?"

"Because they require some wholesome restraints, and superstition is the best I know of."

"Wherefore?"

"Because it is indefinite."

"Well, then, Jose, this is a subject upon which you and I have talked before, and we will not now renew it. You say it is only morning."

"Your majesty will find that such is the case if you will permit me to extinguish the lights, and draw these massive curtains, which so effectually exclude the light of day."

"We will leave this room, Jose," said the king, rising. "A turn in the garden will, perhaps, dispel the gloomy feelings that now haunt me."

"No doubt—no doubt."

Jose and the king passed out of the apartment, and, crossing the corridor, they descended to the staircase which led to the lower part of the building, which was but of one story in height.

Half way down the staircase was a wide landing, and a large, ancient window, filled with magnificent stained glass. The window was covered with a thick blind; but Don Jose paused at it, and, as he withdrew the blind from before, he said,—

"From here your majesty will see that the sun is rapidly rising, and the life and gaiety of daylight is coming."

"I see," said the king. "Thank you, Jose, I am much better now. How different one feels by daylight than by night, when the soul grows gloomy along with the gloom of nature. By Heavens, I am not the same creature I was but an hour since."

Philip of Spain was not the only man to whom the shades of night brought sad and distressful thoughts. To how many is the sun's decline a fearful sight? Men of crime answer, and in your answer be truthful to say what damning tortures you endure during the long hours of night, when the imagination holds her empire in the brain, and then rise up, in all the fearful distinctness of reality, the shadows of evil deeds, which, in the broad light of day, have no existence.

*   *   *   *   *   *

But what has become of our friend Don Cæsar, who went through so much danger to get to the chateau of Don Jose, and then went through so much more to get from it again?

Our readers will remember that he miraculously escaped death from the arquebuses of the guard. He seemed to have a charmed life. Perhaps Heaven really does interpose to save those who have yet not quite achieved all the purposes of their being, and so he was saved from what might have been inevitably death to any one else. Certain it is, he leaped from the wall of the chateau unhurt.

The height was rather considerable, and, for a moment, he felt a little stunned by the leap; but he quickly recovered, and plunged into the neighbouring forest of tall trees, which adjoined to one part of the garden of that sequestered and little known building.

Then he paused, and made a sort of personal examination of himself to ascertain that he was unhurt.

"All's right," he cried. "Thank you, friends, for nothing. You certainly rewarded me by a shower of leaden bouquets, and I only wonder that none of them reached me. I suppose it was not to be. My hour has not yet come; but what now to do next, I must confess, puzzles me considerably. Humph! I have not taken much by this adventure. Don Jose is a rascal; but that I knew before. It's a decidedly awkward case. Here I am alone, a league from Madrid, with no means of reaching it but those with which nature has gifted me, namely, my legs."

Cæsar sat down on the gnarled roots of an aged tree while he spoke, and a sensation of great fatigue came over him.

"I could walk to Madrid," he said; "of course I could, tired as I am, but when I got there, it would be yet very early morning, and I should feel the necessity, as I have been a night adventurer lately, of seeking some repose. Now I do not see why I should not seek it here, and yet be in the city time enough to take my chance of meeting my young friend at the church of San Veronica, whither, I dare say, he will repair every morning, till he does meet with me."

Don Cæsar's sleepiness grew upon him each moment, and he spoke slower, and with less distinctness.

"I have had enough fighting for to-night, and I should not be at all surprised if I have hurt somebody. Indeed, I am rather inclined to think I have, but if the subordinates of great scoundrels will put themselves in the way of getting six or eight inches of a rapier in their stomachs, why, how the deuce can I help it? Ah, ah!"

Here he gave a very terrific yawn.

"Of course I can't help it, and it is no sort of business of mine to seek to help it; so that's all settled. All's right—what a thundering rogue that Don Jose is, when one comes to think of him. I shall never be quite satisfied till I have given him his deserts."

He now lay down under the old tree.

"And as for my beautiful and most incomparable countess, who ought, bless her heart, to be here, lying down comfortably in this bed,—no, it ain't a bed—well, well, no matter. I will seek her still; she is my wife, and I will have her, though ten thousand Don Joses stood in my way, and tried to say me nay. Ah! how sleepy I am. Good night. Eh? Did anybody speak? very good—who said you did? Good night—I feel tolerably comfortable. Kind insects of all sorts and descriptions, be so good as to keep out of my ears and mouth while I sleep, if you please. Good night to you all. Good night—good ——"

Don Cæsar fell fast asleep—sleeping far more happily beneath the boughs of that aged tree, more calmly and serenely than many a monarch beneath his canopy of state.

Oh, what wealth would many, who have made the discovery that wealth is not necessarily happiness, give, to have had the capacity to sleep so calmly, so soundly, and with such a dreamless happy slumber as Don Cæsar de Bazan—poor, persecuted, and nearly friendless.

Hour after hour slipped by, and there he lay in such a deep, deathlike sleep, that unless some extraneous cause awoke him, he was not at all likely to get to Madrid by the time he had anticipated, and fully intended, before he gave way to the enticing influence of repose, which had come over him so stealthily, and yet so strongly.

Not even the sound of the horses' feet which Lazarillo bestrode, awoke him, and yet the page passed close to where he lay, little dreaming that he was so near to the person whom he held in such dear esteem, and for whom he had adventured so much, and would adventure so much more, if it were required of him, even to the utmost danger of his life.

But, perhaps, it was better as it was. Had they met, perhaps Lazarillo would not have proceeded in the decidedly good course he was taking, and by the advice and guidance of the rather headstrong and heedless Cæsar, he might have run into great danger. On he galloped, until the towers of Aranjues suddenly burst upon his sight.

As Lazarillo urged his tired steed towards the grand entrance of Aranjues, he observed that it was open, and that a crowd of lacqueys and attendants were about it. From these indications, he had no doubt that the queen was going forth. He hastened forward his horse, and rushed into the court-yard, amidst the attendants, who were hurrying to and fro.

"Where is the queen?" demanded Lazarillo, of one of them, and he had to wait for his answer.

"She isn't here," replied the man.

"I see that," replied Lazarillo; "my eyes tell me as much as you can. I want to know where she is, and not where she is not?"

"May be," replied the man, "but I can't tell you any more than I know."

Lazarillo inquired first of one and then of the other, but could obtain very little satisfaction from any; the fact was, Don Jose's livery was not to their taste—they hated the man, and, from principle, disliked his attendants.

"I must see the queen immediately," said Lazarillo. "I have important business to speak to her about."

"You have, have you?" replied the man, curiously. "Well, then, will you take a word of advice, eh?"

"It must depend upon its nature," replied Lazarillo.

"Then have patience, for it strikes me your business must put up with delay."

"That we shall see," replied Lazarillo; "but I expect I shall not have to wait, for yonder I see the queen coming."

This was the fact. Her majesty was coming along the stone corridor that led to the hall, from which descended a few stone steps, to the spot where the carriage was waiting.

Here it was that Lazarillo was waiting her appearance among the lacqueys and attendants, and when she descended these steps, he kneeled on one knee, and presented the letter in that posture to the queen, who immediately recognised Lazarillo.

"Gracious lady," exclaimed Lazarillo, "will you deign to read this letter?"

"From Don Jose?" exclaimed the queen, looking at the letter with distrust.

"No, gracious lady; I have written it, in case I could not see you."

"Remain here while we read the letter," said the queen, who took it, and retired to one of the apartments in the palace.

"The delay you promised me," said Lazarillo, to the man who had spoken to him first, "is likely to be yours, for you will have to wait for your ride."

"Do not crow before you are out of the wood, young gentleman."

The queen, in the meanwhile, having read the epistle written by Lazarillo, nearly fainted when she came to read the letter through.

When her attendants had somewhat recovered her, she sent for Lazarillo, and said to him, in a faint voice,—

"You wrote this letter; and, therefore, can tell me, of your own knowledge, if this be truth. Speak boldly."

"It is the simple unexaggerated truth, gracious lady," replied Lazarillo.

"This chateau is a league this side of Madrid, and is ——"

"Ostensibly Don Jose's."

"Exactly. Do you know it, any of you?" she inquired, turning to the servants, who were gathered around her.

"Yes, your majesty, we know well enough that Don Jose has such a place; but it is very private, and no one can get into it, and there are some strange tales whispered about it."

"Then I will go, Lazarillo."

"Heaven speed your majesty, it will be a work of mercy and true benevolence to save one from such a fate."

The queen was visibly affected, and her attendants, one and all, besought her not to quit the palace for such a place.

"The servants," said one, "are usually armed, and I think your majesty will run great risk in going there."

"It must be done," replied the queen. "Nothing else will have the effect of saving this unfortunate lady from the dreadful fate that awaits her, and she has been dragged into this lamentable state by the use of my name, too. It really is dreadful."

"Yes, your gracious majesty," replied Lazarillo to the inquiring glance of the queen.

"Do not go, your majesty. We implore you not to go. Order us to go anywhere; to do anything, and we will cheerfully do so, though it be to do death."

"I thank you," replied the queen, "for this; but what danger there may be I must meet myself, Lazarillo."

"Yes, gracious lady," replied the page, stepping forward as the queen beckoned him.

"You had better return, and, most probably, before you have returned there long, I shall be there also."

"Thanks, gracious lady. You are ever ready to peril all in the cause of truth and honour, and may your majesty's endeavours be effectual, and conduce to your own happiness."

The queen was violently agitated by the contents of Lazarillo's letter, and appeared almost undecided when he left her.

Leaving the presence of the queen, he at once entered the court-yard, and, remounting his horse, quitted Aranjues, making the best of his way towards Madrid to the chateau, where he had left Don Jose and the king together.

The morning had now broken some time, and by the time he reached the villa it was broad day, and had been so for some time. He rode into the court-yard and dismounted.

"Where, young gentleman, where have you been to?" inquired one of the lacqueys. "Why, you ride about for your own pleasure, sure."

"It matters little for that, when I go, and when I come back, since you don't have to wait for your breakfast till you see me again, eh?"

"Why, as for the matter of that," replied the other, "it may be so as regards myself; but there are others who may make your laced jacket fit too close to your shoulders for your comfort."

"It will be a sight when its done. Who has been troubling themselves about me?"

"Oh, nobody of consequence after yourself, only I thought Don Jose might have had the will, as I know he has the power, of giving saucy pages proper chastisement."

"Has he inquired for me?"

"Yes, repeatedly," replied the fellow, "and now I'll leave you to digest the meal that is in store for you."

"Stay a moment; you need scarce be in a hurry; having said so much, you may say a little more. Where is Don Jose?"

"Somewhere up stairs, I believe; but I cannot tell you well where."

"And he is very much chafed about it, is he?" continued Lazarillo.

"Yes; he has inquired after you several times—at least six or eight."

"He wants me very badly, and I must see him immediately."

"You had better, for he left orders with us to the effect that the moment you returned, you were to go to him."

Lazarillo said no more, but giving his horse to one of the grooms to look to it carefully, as it had suffered much from fatigue and exertion, he entered the villa, and proceeded in search of Don Jose, whom he found alone.

"Lazarillo," said Jose, when he saw him.

"Signor," said Lazarillo. "I am here."

"Pray tell me how you have been employing your time since I saw you last?"

"In riding, signor," replied Lazarillo, with much *sang froid*.

"In riding!" repeated Don Jose; "and wherefore in riding? I took you as a personal attendant upon myself, and did not contemplate that you would act thus whenever an opportunity occurred. What induced you to act thus?"

"You did not require my attendance, signor, and I was tired ——"

"How did you know but I might have wanted you at any time—as, indeed, I have wanted you?"

"But, signor, you told me that you should not require me yet awhile, and I had no other orders at all."

"Then because you have no immediate orders, you deem it necessary to be running all over the country?"

"No, signor, not so; but having nothing else to do, I took a little exercise. I couldn't sleep, and yet was drowsy, and the fresh air recovered me."

"Humph!" said Jose, scarcely understanding this. "Pray where have you been?"

"In the forest, signor."

"Riding about alone in the forest at this time in the morning, Lazarillo? Did you not meet with any one in your rounds?" inquired Jose.

"No one, signor, that I cared for."

"But it was imprudent, if not dangerous, to go out thus."

"Indeed, signor, I had no fear; and had I met with any one, your livery would have protected me from all harm."

"I am not sure of that, boy; for when men hide and skulk about they care not to whom a coat belongs; if they want it they will take it; and let me tell you, Lazarillo, you have escaped some danger."

"I was not conscious of it, signor; but, at all events, I am safe back again, and have received no hurt."

"You may thank fortune; but be more careful for the future; and, do you hear, mind me, and do not for the future quit any place where I send you on such frivolous pretences."

"I attended to your orders, signor."

"Continue to do so, Lazarillo, and attend to me. I have waited some time to speak to you, as I wish you to perform a piece of duty."

"Yes, signor," replied Lazarillo, curious to learn what was the nature of the duty required of him, and also breathless with anxiety, lest it were of a nature to precipitate the events he most wished to protract.

"It is to place you sentinel at a particular window. You can perform the duty well enough, I believe?"

"Yes, signor."

"Then follow me, and I will show you your post."

Lazarillo, following Don Jose, quitted the room in which they had been speaking, and going up the private staircase, came to a corridor.

It was the same that opened into the room in which the king and Don Jose had held their conference, and through which room Lazarillo had entered the apartment where Maritana had been left.

The corridor ran to a stair-head—the principal one, and a large round, or bow window, with a balcony on the outside. Here Don Jose stopped, and turning to Lazarillo, he pointed to the window, saying,—

"See you that window, Lazarillo, which commands a view of the country round for many miles?"

"Yes, signor," replied Lazarillo.

"You know the use of an arquebus?" inquired Don Jose.

"Yes, signor. I have not cleaned the arquebuses of the royal guard so often but that I know how to use them."

"Exactly; so I thought," replied Don Jose; and going to a closet, he pulled out one, which he handed to Lazarillo, saying,—

"Take that, and examine if it be loaded properly."

Lazarillo did as he was directed, and sounding with the ramrod, soon ascertained that it was loaded, and on opening the pan, saw also that it was duly primed.

"It is quite right," he said, when he had finished his examination.

"Then you will stand here—this is your post; and if any one attempt to enter the house, you will fire upon them."

"Yes, signor," replied Lazarillo.

"Be vigilant and faithful," replied Don Jose, as he quitted the spot.

Lazarillo looked after Jose, and when he had gone, he opened the window and gazed out upon the scene that presented itself to him. The morning was fresh and balmy, while the fresh gale came laden with the perfumes of the blooming flowers that grew around in the gardens beneath.

CHAPTER XLIX.

MARITANA'S MORNING THOUGHTS.—THE ATTEMPT ON THE FIDELITY OF THE ATTENDANT.—JOSE'S APPEARANCE.—THE VIOLENT INTERVIEW.

Now that the excitement and intense anxiety which Lazarillo had been subjected to had so far subsided that he felt he could do no more than he had done to serve the cause of his dear friend, Don Cæsar, the page began to feel the effects of the fatigue he had undergone.

While there was still something for him to do—while he saw, or fancied he saw, that by any exertion of his he could benefit Cæsar, or at all advance his cause, he had stood up nobly against every feeling of lassitude which might be fairly expected to come over him; but now all that was past. He had done all he could; he had deprived himself of rest, of food, and he had suffered along with those severe privations, to one so young, much mental anxiety. He had warned the queen—he had spoken to Maritana, although so ineffectually, and now he felt that he could do no more.

He leant against the embrasure of the window, with the arquebus which Jose had given him hanging listlessly on his arm, and a strong desire to sleep began to creep over him.

In vain he battled with this wish for repose—in vain he shook himself—in vain he exclaimed,—"I must not, I will not sleep." Nature was too potent for him, and would assert her sovereign sway.

The trees grew to his eyes indistinct, and he no longer heard the sweet carol of the forest birds. Once or twice the arquebus nearly slid from his relaxing grasp, and then still saying,—"No, no—I must not sleep," he placed it in a corner by the window, and crossing his arms upon his breast, he sat down upon the old-fashioned seat which was there.

"I can rest," he murmured, "without surely going to sleep, although my eyes are so heavy, and somehow I can hardly open them. How strange it is, but my eyelids seem pressed down by heavy weights. Yet—I—I will not go to sleep, for I am on guard, and—and who knows—ah, who knows ——"

Lazarillo's head drooped forward on to his chest, and in another minute he was in a deep, dreamless sleep. For all he knew, the chateau might have been attacked and carried by storm, and anybody might have made an assault upon it, for the slumber that had come over him was one of those which result from sheer fatigue, and which are so very difficult to shake off, until the bodily powers have become invigorated by a long continuance of it.

The morning advanced. The bright sun rose above the houses—above the trees—above the dim mountain tops, which were perceivable in the far-off horizon, and Lazarillo slept soundly and happily.

There was one, however, in that haunt of vice whose repose was neither sound nor dreamless—whose forced sleep was haunted by all kinds of fearful images, and who awakened on that lovely morning, which, under happier auspices, would have inspired joy and delight, but to feel all the horrors of captivity, and the terrors of expected violence.

That one was Maritana, Countess de Bazan, whom nothing had preserved, probably, from the most ruffianly treatment, but the awakened superstition of the king, which led him to shrink from attacking the virtue he had taken such pains to betray.

Yes, she as yet owed her preservation not to any latent feeling of honour or nobility of soul in Philip of Spain—not to any relenting of his wicked purpose, but to the real fact that several circumstances had occurred to awaken his fears of the supernatural—fears which, during the career of the monarch who occupies so prominent a place in our pages, made themselves conspicuously manifest.

When, however, the daylight fairly came, these phantoms of the imagination always dispersed, and the king reverted back to all his dark and evil thoughts and suggestions once more.

When Maritana awoke she was dazzled by a stray sunbeam which had found its way through a crevice of the massive curtains that had been drawn across the window of the apartment in which she was, and placing her hand over her eyes, to shut out the painfully bright effulgence, she exclaimed,—

" Is it a dream—is it a dream ?"

" What dream ?" said a woman, who had been appointed to watch her, stepping up to the couch on which she lay. " What have you been dreaming about, madam ?"

Maritana shuddered, as in a low tone she added,—

" It is real—it is real. Oh, Heaven, look down upon me and protect me ! Save me—save me ! I am punished surely enough for my mad, wild, unreflective ambition. Save me from the hands of the monsters in human form who have brought me here !"

" Well, I'm sure, madam," said the woman ; " you pay a very bad compliment indeed to a gentleman who is so much enamoured of you that he has taken no end of trouble to bring you here to this place, which is quite a palace in miniature, and which possesses all the charms and luxuries in the world."

" Peace—peace," said Maritana, " if you be human."

" Human, indeed ? I should think I am human. Well, I am sure ; some people get into habits of making a desperate fuss about nothing at all. Really, now, I wonder how many beauties would be glad of one-half the opportunities you enjoy."

" This style of conversation is insulting," said Maritana. " From one of my own sex I ought, at least, to be free from language which a wife should never hear."

" A wife ?"

" Yes. I am the Countess de Bazan. If you are a menial, know then the gulf which separates us."

" Bless me ! here's airs—well, I never. You may be half a dozen countesses, for all I care, although I believe you are really about as much a countess as I am. I know your situation without you telling me, I'll be bound. You had better be civil, I should say, for you can do yourself no good by insolence."

Maritana was silent for some moments, for she disdained to answer that woman's words ; but then a thought struck her that, after all, hardened as the female was who was thus placed in attendance upon her, she, Maritana, might be able to secure her services in escaping from the house to which she had been so cruelly carried.

" This woman," she thought, " can have but one motive in becoming what she is, and that must be an interested one. If I can convince her that she will gain more by befriending me than betraying me, she may do me good services."

Impressed with this idea, Maritana at once attempted to put it into execution, and addressing the woman as calmly as she could, she said—

" Attend to me. Of course you are paid for keeping a watch over me ? I cannot believe but what your present situation in life must be a repugnant one, for you cannot be destitute of all feeling, however you may feel the necessity of assuming a callousness of demeanour which is suitable to what you have to do. If I make it worth your while to act for me, instead of those who now employ you, will you feel inclined to do so ?"

" You cannot," said the woman.

" Indeed I can. I have some reason to believe that the Queen of Spain would be a friend."

" The queen ?"

" Yes. If so, you would be certain of a good reward, besides immunity for the past, by protecting me. More than that, too, I am owned as a near relative by the Marquis de Rotondo, and although he is a man not much gifted with intelligence, still he could not but be grateful in some substantial form to you, if it were proved you had saved me from this place."

The woman had been tutored by Don Jose what to say, in case Maritana should ask her any questions, and now she said,—

" This house belongs to your husband. I really cannot understand what you have to complain of."

" There is some cruel trickery practised against me," added Maritana. " I am the Countess de Bazan ; but he who owns this house, and calls himself by that title, I am convinced is not my husband, but some impostor who would personate him. Heaven only knows if he, to whom I was really married, be alive or dead. My fears frequently assure me that he must have fallen a victim to his enemies, and then, even in the moment when such despairing thoughts take possession of me, something seems to whisper, ' Come, courage—courage, Maritana ; Don Cæsar lives, and you will be happy yet.' "

" And you would tempt me to assist you ?"

" I would—I would."

" Without, I dare say, a coin of any description to place in my hands. Do you take me for a fool ? No, no. You have made a mistaken calculation. You are here in your husband's house, and I am quite sure he has some very good reasons for his conduct towards you. I suspect there has been some affair of gallantry connected with you, and that your husband is naturally angry."

" That tone and manner does not deceive me," said Maritana. " You are now acting a part—you are merely repeating a lesson which has been taught to you."

" You can think as you please, madam, but all your promises cannot move me to be unfaithful to those who have placed me here. You don't know your extreme good fortune."

" You will not aid me ?"

" Certainly not."

" Then upon Heaven and myself must I rely. Now I make a determination that I will brave death rather than be made the slave of him who has usurped the title of my husband. I am driven desperate, and let them beware who have made me so. Can I have some refreshment ?"

These last words were spoken in so altered a tone that the woman was rather amazed, but she replied,—

" Oh, certainly ; I have orders to supply you with whatever you wish."

" Then let me have food."

" I thought she'd come round," muttered the woman, as she stepped into the next apartment, where were some cold viands and wine which were purposely placed there. "All her pretended grief is non-sense. They all come round very comfortably after a little while. I've heard that hunger will tame a lion, and I don't see, if that's the case, why it should fail in taming a girl who has nothing in the world to recommend her but a baby face, which it is a wonder to me how any man can be such a fool as to admire."

When the woman had left the room, Maritana, for a moment, covered her face with her hands, and uttered a deep sob. Then, as if ashamed of such a display of weakness, she looked up more courageously, saying, in a low, sweet tone,—

"Yes, I will eat, that I may have strength to defend myself. I can die, and I will die; for what is death compared to dishonour? I am faint now from want of food; I will eat so that I may the better be able to defend myself against a villain; and there may be another chance, as a consequence of my demanding food—she comes—she comes! Let me school my features to apparent serenity. Will she bring me a knife?—will she bring me a knife?"

The woman now made her appearance with a tray, on which were eatables and drinkables. Maritana eagerly scanned the contents, and much pleased was she to observe a long, sharp-looking knife, which the woman had brought without the least suspicion of its being put to any other than its legitimate use.

"Here is breakfast," she said, as she placed the tray before Maritana, who made no reply, but in pursuance of the resolution she had come to, commenced eating, in order to recruit her strength. At the same time, she kept an eye on the knife, which she resolved, if she could get possession of, should serve her as a defence against any and every one; for she made up her mind she would not part with it but with her life: she was indeed desperate. Her aversion to the king, who represented himself as Don Cæsar de Bazan, and whose real rank she little suspected, was to the full as strong a passion as she bore for him whom she believed to be her husband in reality; and, with a romantic, chivalrous feeling, she now made up her mind to die rather than disgrace the name she gloried in possessing.

The timid, shrinking spirit which had once been a characteristic of Maritana, had now, to all appearance, entirely deserted her, and she became devoted as a heroine, who was resolved to conquer the adverse circumstances in which she was placed, or perish in the attempt.

The woman who attended upon her had not the least idea or suspicion that Maritana had any other motive in asking for food than merely to get rid of the feeling of hunger, and, consequently, she had brought her the knife quite unsuspiciously. Indeed, the woman began, when she saw Maritana taking the food, to have a very great contempt for her, and to think that her speeches concerning the oppression of the circumstances in which she was placed were all so much moonshine, and much she congratulated herself upon the fact that she had not listened, with any show of acceptance, to the offers which had been made to her by Maritana.

"She is like all the rest," muttered the woman, "who have ever set foot within this house. At first, all fire and indignation; and then adapting themselves to the circumstances in which they are placed, as if it had been all arranged in their own minds beforehand."

The attendant, however, was doomed to be very soon undeceived in her calculations, for now Maritana had taken as much of the food as she thought necessary, and she turned to the woman, saying,—

"With one exception, you can take these things away."

"One exception! what do you mean?"

"I mean to retain the knife."

"The knife!"

"Yes. For my own protection I shall retain it. I am in a desperate situation. I have no hope of succour but from my own resolution, and that is now indomitable. No one shall disarm me of this weapon in safety. Attempt it at your peril."

"Are you mad?"

"Not so; although I have suffered enough to drive me mad. Beware, I say. Approach me not, as you value your own safety. If you are so devoted to your infamous employers that you will risk your life in their service, come on. The mischief and the misery be all upon your own head."

As Maritana spoke, she placed a chair between her and the woman, so that if the latter had attempted to disarm her of the weapon, she must, always provided Maritana retained her resolution, have run the most imminent hazard of having it plunged into her breast.

This was a contingency which, however great might be the woman's devotion to the interests of Don Jose, she evidently had no sort of inclination to place herself in the way of encountering, and accordingly she commenced reasoning with Maritana, instead of contending personally with her, for she naturally enough expected great blame from Don Jose, for being so confiding as to place so awkward a weapon within the grasp of one situated as Maritana was.

"This is great folly," she said; "you will bring harm upon yourself by such a proceeding as this. For Heaven's sake lay down the knife. Give it to me, I implore you."

These words, if anything was wanting to do so, fully convinced Maritana of the power she possessed, by having armed herself with such a weapon, and she replied,—

"No, I do not part with this knife until death forces my hand to relax its hold."

"But I will befriend you."

"I will not trust you."

"I swear I will befriend you. Surrender the knife, and I will do all I can to rescue you from your present painful position, for now I am convinced, which I was not before, that you are perfectly serious in your wish to escape from this house."

"Once again, I will not trust you," said Maritana. "You are now too late to make such an offer. I am armed, and I will not surrender the weapon which may rescue me from dishonour, even though it be at the expense of my very existence."

"I am stronger than you are," said the woman; "I command you to lay down the knife, or it will be my duty to use force."

"Attempt it," said Maritana.

A thought seemed to have struck the woman, that after all, if it came to the moment of action, so young, and apparently delicate and gentle a girl, would not have nerve enough to use the weapon she had possessed herself of. It was a last resource, and no sooner was it conceived, than it was attempted to be carried into effect.

"I must and will take that knife from you," she cried, and she made an affected rush forward to do so, in which she just went a little too far, and before she could retreat, she got rather an ugly cut across the arm, which immediately bled profusely.

The sight of her own blood alarmed the woman beyond measure, and she fairly believed now that she should be murdered if she made not an immediate escape. With a cry of pain she fled towards the door, while Maritana said, calmly,—

"I warned you."

Before then the terrified and bleeding attendant could open the door, some one else did so from the other side, and in her eagerness to escape, she rushed precipitately into the arms of Don Jose, who by command of the king was coming to see if Maritana was awake, and what frame of mind she was in.

An oath burst from the minister's lips, and he involuntarily laid his hand on his sword.

"Murder! help!" cried the woman.

"Peace!" shouted Jose, as he dragged her into the room again, and closed the door. "What is the meaning of these frantic cries?"

"I am killed."

"Killed? by whom? you are bleeding."

"There—there is the murderess. Go not near her, she is armed—she has gone mad."

"Ha!" cried Jose, as he placed himself immediately behind a table, and looked at Maritana in speechless wonder, while she stood with the knife uplifted, prepared for action.

"I am not mad," she said; "I am not mad, but I am armed, and I will defend myself."

never will be his. You may kill me, but I never will consent to be his, Don Jose. Villain! betrayer of innocence! cowardly assailant of a woman, I defy you!"

Don Jose bit his lip, as he strove to assume a careless air, and after a brief pause, he said,—

"Indeed, Maritana. You defy me. Is this your gratitude for all I have done for you? What a dreadful account I shall have to give to our good and gracious queen of your conduct. My mind bleeds for you, really. Be better advised, Maritana. Abandon this vein. You never looked so little like yourself. What has beauty and intelligence like you to do with knives? Oh, it is horrible. See how this poor woman bleeds. You have surely much injured her. Lay down the knife—lay down the knife, Maritana, and remember who you are."

"I do remember who I am," she said; "and with that remembrance I likewise do not forget who you are. You are a villain, of such a black and monstrous dye, that the hand which slays you will have rid the world of one who is to it a disgrace."

"You are mad."

"You are in danger, Jose."

"Eh? danger?"

Don Jose made a movement towards the door, for he fancied it just possible that Maritana might make some sudden spring upon him, and do him some serious personal injury, before he could take any means of warding it off. Coward as he was under all circumstances, and only nerved into some show of courage when passion sometimes for a moment would overcome the dictates of prudence, which was, in his estimation, by far the better part of valour, he had no fancy for falling a sacrifice to the just indignation of Maritana.

"You are afraid," she said, "and well you may be. A guilty breast trembles even at a woman's arm."

"Now, how foolish you are," he said. "You know well you will be disarmed. You cannot hope for any other result."

"D——n!' said Jose. "How came she by that knife?"

"It matters little, Don Jose," added Maritana, "how I became possessed of this weapon. Suffice it to say, that with it I will defend myself, and I dare you, or any one whose intention I have reason to suspect, to approach me. Grant me a free passage from this house, and I will injure no one. Refuse it to me, and there must be bloodshed. I care not if I myself perish. I shall have preserved the name of Bazan in honour, and shall have died as becomes me."

Don Jose seemed paralysed for a few moments by Maritana's words and attitude. Then he said,—

"Good God, countess, whence has arisen this sudden accession of fury? do you know where you are?"

"Yes, too well. I am in the house of some villain, whither I have been betrayed by you. I now more clearly understand my position. I have been the victim of some diabolical plot. The man whom you have introduced here as my husband, I utterly repudiate. He is not Don Cæsar de Bazan—he cannot be—I

" Who will disarm me ?"

" Not I—I have no fancy for becoming the victim of a woman's fury, but there are those whose duty it will be to run the risk. By this outrageous conduct you do not in the least better your condition. This is your husband's house. You are in his power, and he will not resign you."

" The grave shall part us !"

" Nonsense—nonsense !"

Don Jose turned and left the room, closely followed by the woman, who, although she had succeeded in stanching the blood that flowed from her wound, had no disposition to stay and run the chance of another stab with the formidable knife which Maritana had shown she could use so effectually.

Jose made the best of his way to the king, to whom he related the new posture of affairs, and the very embarrassing position in which Maritana had been able to place them all.

" But," said Philip, angrily, " do you mean to tell me, you could not disarm a girl of a knife?"

" Your majesty ought to know," said Jose, " that when a woman is thoroughly furious, she is more than a match for a man. I do not believe that she could be easily disarmed. I am, indeed, quite sure she would do some one, if not herself, were she driven to desperation, a serious injury. There is but one chance of overcoming her, and taking from her the means of mischief. Close behind where she is standing on the defensive, is a concealed door behind the arras. If your majesty could, while I hold her in conversation, creep quietly through that door, and seize her arm, we might succeed in taking the knife from her hands."

" Agreed," said Philip, " I will do it. Come on, Jose—come on. We cannot allow her to remain in such a state of mind. Come on ; I know the passage that leads to the small door in the arras. When you see me upon it, do you make a feigned attack upon her, and then I will clasp her from behind, and you can easily wrest the knife from her."

Jose followed the king from the room ; but he made a determination in his own mind that he would be most especially careful of his own safety, in the feigned attack he was to make upon Maritana.

" It's all well enough for Philip," he thought, " but I do not see any particular reason why I should run into danger on his account, nor, indeed, will I ; so if there be any knife business, let him himself take the consequences of his own amours. I have higher objects of ambition, than to sacrifice myself to the rage of a woman armed with a carving knife. Let Philip reap, along with the pleasure, all the danger of his intrigues."

CHAPTER L.

DON CÆSAR ON HIS FOREST COUCH.—HIS DIFFI-
CULTY IN PROCURING A BREAKFAST. — NEWS
FROM THE CHATEAU.

CERTAINLY the king's project was the only feasible one for overcoming the resistance of Maritana, and preventing her doing some serious mischief to some one, or to herself.

Much as society at large, and those in whose fortunes we are particularly interested, would have gained by the death of Don Jose, yet we own we should have been unwilling for that death to have ensued from the hands of the beautiful and gifted Maritana. Not that any set of circumstances could well be conceived which would more amply justify her in such an act than those in which she had been placed by the cruel and dastardly artifices of that man ; but well we know that when calm reason and reflection should again have resumed their sway in her mind, that it would have been a source of shuddering horror to her, and of a whole life's

regret, to think that with her own hand she had taken the life of any human being, however despicable a specimen of humanity the individual might be who had become the object of her vengeance. Therefore, although we cannot but feel acutely for poor Maritana, we are glad that Don Jose had not the courage to place himself in the way of the keen edge of the avenging steel she had in her hand, for if he had done so she would, without doubt, in the present excited state of her feelings, have made an attempt to bury it in his heart.

To tell the truth, too, the king's courage evaporated just a little, as he made his way towards the small door in the arras which Don Jose had mentioned to him. Guilt can never be truly brave, although it may possess a brute ferocity which sometimes makes it scorn danger, and Philip of Spain was no exception to the principle that

" Conscience doth make cowards of us all."
Before he got half way to the place mentioned, he turned to Don Jose, and said, doubtingly,—

" Is she very ferocious ?"

" She is, sire, most ferocious. Had she not been so, I should hardly have troubled your majesty."

" Then she may be insane."

" Possibly, your majesty ; but certain it is that she is most desperate, and I do now begin to despair, always provided that your majesty does not get rid of some of the scruples which your majesty suggested last night, if Maritana, with all her charms, will ever be yours."

" Curses on her obstinacy."

" Amen."

" Who would have thought it, Jose, that a girl could make so determined a resistance, and even show that she preferred death to the pleasure of such an intrigue as I could offer her. Do you think a declaration of who I really am would dazzle her ?"

" I do not."

" Indeed! Is she so much of a philosopher that she can resist a king ?"

" I would not advise your majesty to make the experiment, because I am quite convinced it would end in nothing but the most absolute humiliation. You have no chance of success by any appeals to her."

" Then what chance have I ?"

" Force or insensibility."

The king was silent for a moment, and then he said,—

" I will yet have another interview with her, and endeavour to convince her how very irreligious it is for her to behave in the manner she does towards her husband, whom she has sworn to love."

" But she now denies that fact, and declares in the strongest terms her absolute conviction that your majesty as an impostor."

" Ah Jose, your looks are enough, as I have frequently found, to create suspicions in any quarter. You have a disingenuous face, Jose ; there is abundance of cunning in it, but no honesty."

" And yet," said Jose, with a sneer in his tone that gave full point to his words, " and yet I have had your majesty's countenance in this affair from the first to the last."

" Enough," said the king, " enough, Jose. You forget who you are, and who I am."

Jose made a low bow, and put on a look of the most profound concern, for he was certain that he had given the king a Rowland for his Oliver, which he never failed to do when Philip had the indiscretion to make any remarks of a derogatory nature to his minister, who thought himself extremely ill-treated to be called a rascal by the very man in whose service he had committed so many dishonourable actions.

They had now reached the head of the staircase, and Jose, for the first time, saw how sound asleep Lazarillo was.

"By the bye, what boy is that?" said the king.

"A page of mine, sire."

"Can you rely on his fidelity?"

"I think I can; at all events he is not scheming any harm now, for I never saw any one sleep so soundly."

"Do not awaken him."

"As your majesty pleases."

Jose stepped back, for he had advanced to give Lazarillo a good shake by the arm, and then the two passed on again till they reached the point where they must separate, each to take the road which they had mutually agreed upon.

Jose proceeded to the chamber of Maritana, while the king walked down a narrow passage, which led to the door in the arras, of which mention has been made. When Don Jose had left Maritana he had not omitted to take the precaution of locking the door immediately behind him, so that, although she was alone, she had no chance of escape except by means of the window, and to have made an escape that way, would have been certainly to have got rid of all her cares at once, for the height was so considerable, that nothing could have saved her from absolute destruction.

When alone Maritana soon discovered all this, and as she would, by casting herself from a window, commit suicide, she resolved to await the course of events, and to defend herself with the knife, according to her fixed mental resolution.

The moment the door of the room was opened, and Don Jose again made his appearance, she rushed to her former place of refuge, beneath the massive chair which had before saved her from surprise by the sudden attack of the woman she had wounded. Of course now this was the very place to which Don Jose wished to induce her to go, for immediately behind it was the small door in the arras, at which he each moment expected the king to make his appearance.

"Maritana," he said, "really now consider how foolish is your present conduct."

"Keep off, sir, as you value your life," was her firm reply.

He saw the arras move gently, and he gathered more courage.

"He who loves you, Maritana, is rich and generous. He is your husband. He has made you his countess. He adores you. Why, therefore, oh, why will you continue to treat him with so much disdain?"

"Don Jose, you are again in danger," said Maritana.

The secret door was slowly opened, and the king appeared.

"Reflect a moment, lovely Maritana," added Jose, as he advanced a step towards her. "I really, in common duty to my dear friend, the real Don Cæsar de Bazan, must deprive you of the knife which you have so very imprudently, to give it no harsher term, possessed yourself of."

"Don Jose," said Maritana, "you think I am not serious. Be warned. Come but within my reach, and I will find a sheath for this knife in the worst heart that ever beat in human bosom."

"Are you resolved, fair one?"

"I am. So help me, Heaven."

"Amen, my beautiful amazon," said the king, and in a moment he had snatched the knife from the hands of Maritana, who, with a cry of dismay, rushed forward, to the great terror of Jose, who at the moment was not quite sure if she was disarmed or not. Leaving the king to take his chance, the chivalrous minister fled from the room, nor stopped until he was the whole length of the corridor from any danger, after which, finding that he was not pursued, he paused to take breath and inquire of himself what was to be done next.

A little ashamed, then, of his pusillanimity, he slowly walked back; but he paused at the door to listen to what was going on inside, and scarcely had he done so, than it violently opened, and the king ran against him, exclaiming, loudly,—

"Hold, hold; repent of your rashness, girl. You are surely mad. D—n, Jose, why do you get in my way? She threatens to throw herself from the window if I don't leave her at once."

"But the knife?"

"I have cast the knife through the casement."

"Then she is unarmed?"

"Yes; but the window—the window. She declares she will cast herself from the window, and if she does she will be dashed to pieces upon the marble flags of the court-yard, even if she escapes death from the projections of the architecture. What on earth can I do, Jose?"

"Come away, at present, your majesty. Come away. While she is in this mood nothing can be done at all. She must become in time exhausted. So much violence will wear itself out shortly, and we must watch an opportunity to remove her into some other apartment, where she cannot put such frantic threats into execution."

"But this is monstrous, Jose. Here have I been in this dull wretched chateau, Heaven knows how many weary hours, exposed to all kinds of disagreeables, and not a whit nearer my original object than when first I came."

"The opposition is most unexpected," said Jose; "but your majesty will have all the greater honour from victory."

"I don't know that, Jose. I begin to suspect I shall find it difficult to retreat with a good grace from an affair, the difficulties connected with which increase each hour."

"Let me entreat your majesty to be patient. I will yet devise some scheme which, while it shall respect all your majesty's scruples, shall yet be successful in bending this stubborn beauty to your purpose. She must—she shall be yours. I swear it."

"Yes; but ——"

"Nay, your majesty has known me manage far more troublesome intrigues than this."

"Yes, but ——"

"Oh, trust to me, your long-tried faithful Jose. He who is so very fertile of expedients, that if one fails, then shall arise, phœnix-like, from its very ashes, a host of others. Be assured, sir, that half an hour's consultation will enable us to mature some plan which shall at once put an end to this most annoying state of suspense under which it is, indeed, most shameful that majesty, an anointed king of one of the greatest nations of Europe, should for a moment suffer. Be calm, —I pray you to be calm."

The king suffered himself to be overcome by Don Jose's persuasions, and walked with him to a room on the ground floor of the chateau, where they held a long consultation, and while that is proceeding, we cannot do better than turn our attention to our friend, Don Cæsar, whom we left in so profound and so pleasant a sleep, beneath the shadow of a cork-tree in the wilderness which was immediately adjoining the chateau from which he had been compelled to make so precipitate a retreat.

The sleep of Cæsar was sound and prolonged. Hour after hour flitted by, and there he lay, dead to the world, and to himself, and to all the cares and anxieties which had beset his waking thoughts. The night had passed away. The first faint light of the dawn had fallen upon him. The birds had sung their salutation to the morn, and had hopped about and above him with curious eyes. Myriads of insects had buzzed like notes in the sunbeams above his head. The sun had climbed high in the heavens, and the business of this working world had all began, ere Don Cæsar de Bazan gave the least sign of awakening from the prolonged and deep refreshing sleep which had visited his senses.

Then, suddenly, as a bright sunbeam found its way among the leaves of the old gigantic tree beneath which he slept, and fell full upon his eyes, he opened them, and looked upwards at the green canopy of vegetation with a look of amazement.

It takes some seconds for the most active intellect to recover from such a state of somnolency as that which had for now so many hours steeped the senses of Don Cæsar de Bazan in oblivion. His question, therefore, to vacancy of " Where am I ?" was not much to be wondered at, the more especially as it was almost immediately succeeded by the words,—

" Oh, I recollect perfectly; I laid down for a nap beneath this tree. Bless me, how stiff I am in all my joints ; I wonder, now, if it is to-day or to-morrow."

With some difficulty (for, somehow or other, sleeping in the open air, although all sorts of animals do so with such perfect impunity, has not so good an effect upon the human subject) he commenced looking about him.

" It's morning," he said, " as it should be when a fellow gets up ; but I am afraid I have overslept myself. The sun is high in the heavens ; let me consider, when did I go to sleep ? Oh, I recollect now perfectly. Last night, or, rather, early this morning ; so, unless I have slept for a whole day and a night besides, I have not been altogether such a sluggard, and, now that I am getting the use of my limbs again, I do feel wonderfully refreshed, at the same time, that I am wonderfully hungry."

Don Cæsar looked up and down, and all round ; but nothing in the slightest degree suggestive of a breakfast being at all comeatable, he added,—

" I have serious thoughts that I shall be starved. No supper last night—that I recollect perfectly ; no breakfast this morning—that is a present, and a shockingly disagreeable fact. Humph ! that sort of thing won't do ; I feel as if I could devour an elephant, with the exception of his tusks. Really, I never felt so desperately hungry in all my life ; what's to be done ? that's the question, and, like that question usually, it is so much easier asked than it is answered."

Don Cæsar took another serious thought of his position, and then he said, suddenly,—

" There's no help for it ; I must walk to Madrid, and take my chance on the road of getting something to eat. That's the only chance I have, and I'm afraid it's a poor one—a very poor one ; but here goes. By staying here I only increase the extremely famishing state of my interior. I shall have a meal presently in my inside ; it's a very hard case ; there's a little streamlet I see winding its way among yon trees. I wonder, now, what's the amount of actual nourishment in a quart of spring water ?"

Don Cæsar approached the little brook, [which he found to be wider, and a much more considerable stream than he had thought it. Just as he had stooped, and made a cup with the hollow of his hand, to get some up, he heard a voice say,—

" I can lend you a tankard, sir."

" Hilloa !" he exclaimed, rising to his feet, " who's that—eh ?"

Turning, then, in the direction of the sound, he saw a well-dressed, neat-looking young peasant girl, who had a basket on her arm, and a pitcher in her hand.

" My dear," said Don Cæsar, " what sylvan goddess are you ?"

" Lor, sir !"

" You are a divinity, and I am at your service, and as hungry as any man can very well wish to be. Do

you think you would excuse me, in your great kindness of heart, if I were to eat you up ?"

" Not me, signior ?"

" Yes : I could eat a dragon."

" Saints preserve us, signior ! Have mercy upon a poor girl, who is going to her brother, Juan, with his breakfast. Oh, sir, spare me !"

" What was that you said about breakfast ? Pray, my dear, be as explicit as you possibly can upon that head, and I shall owe you my very best thanks. I owe everybody something ; but I never had so fair a creditor before."

" You ain't mad, signior ?"

" Mad ? Oh, no, my princess—my rural divinity. But, about this breakfast you mentioned ?"

" Why, sir, my brother is a cork-cutter."

" A corn-cutter. Well, well."

" No, signior, a cork-cutter, here in the forest, and he has a great appetite, you must know, so I have to bring him what he calls his breakfast, at this time of the day ; for, by the mass, what he takes the first thing in the morning he calls only a whet, and a snack, and all that kind of thing, signior ; so, in this basket, I have ——"

" Good God ! what ?"

" A fowl—a Bologna sausage—a ——"

" That'll do. Don't stand upon ceremony, my dear, you see before you a man with ten appetites rolled into one. There's something about the air of this place that must be highly favourable to digestion, for I am quite convinced that, unless I speedily give my stomach something to digest, it will begin to digest itself, and, when it has got through that, it will commence upon the rest of my inside, and who knows then what might be the consequences ? Oh, you angel ! what eyes ! what a chin ! what a brow ! what lips ! oh !"

" Well ; but, signior, you wouldn't kiss them ?"

" I could eat them."

" Lor ! bless me. Take Juan's breakfast rather."

" I intend, rather ! Oh, cold fowl, bless you ! Oh, Bologna sausage, I shall pay my respects to you, and thou, wheaten bread ! My dear girl, fill the tankard at the stream, and we will eat and talk, and wash all down with that pure element which I so much admire, when I can't possibly get anything else."

The bewildered girl allowed Cæsar to take her basket from her arm, and commence devouring the contents in such an uncommon style that the fowl was a skeleton, the bread had disappeared, and the Bologna sausage was reduced to very small dimensions, before she had time to think of the consequences as regarded the voracious young cork cutter, her brother Juan.

" I feel decidedly better now," said Don Cæsar, as he made a minute examination of the basket, and convinced himself there was nothing but straw in it. " I am quite, in a manner of speaking, a new man."

" Well, sir, I'm glad you are better," said the girl, with a dubious expression of countenance, as she looked at the basket. " You hadn't a bad appetite as a part of your illness."

" By no means, my dear. Now, what recompense can I make you for placing me under so serious an obligation ? Will another kiss be considered at all satisfactory ?"

" Well, I'm sure, signior, it's like your impudence ; I think the best thing I can do is to hasten home and get Juan some more breakfast, or else he'll be leaving his work and coming in like a roaring lion."

" Will he, indeed ? Well—well, farewell, nymph of the cold fowl and Bologna sausage ; when I forget thee, may I want a breakfast worse than I did a short time ago."

The girl tripped away, and Don Cæsar, now that he was so much better able to do so, began more seriously to reflect upon those matters which the imperative calls of hunger had for a time banished from his reflections if not from his memory.

"I am now ready," he soliloquized, "for any adventure. I am in receipt of a breakfast, and I do not find that my sword has suffered from its night's bivouac. What shall I do? What is the next step I can pursue in the now great object of my existence—the discovery of my countess?"

Don Cæsar now began to regret extremely that he had been so eager to quit Madrid, for, by so doing, he found he had deprived himself of all means of communication with Lazarillo, who certainly was, if any one was, in a good position to get for him information regarding not only the movements of Don Jose, but who and what his wife was, and what connections she had about the court.

"Well," he said, "I am not very far from the city, and now that I am much refreshed, and as I have certainly taken nothing by my motion of coming here, I think I cannot do better than make the best of my way at once back again."

As far as regarded following Don Jose, he could not now, of course, be aware of whether Jose had not proceeded to Madrid again. Indeed he considered it highly probable that he had done so, for well he knew that the minister was so much immersed in the factitious politics of the period, as well as in a hundred private intrigues of his own, for place, power, and influence, that it was not likely he could be long spared from the principle scene of his labours.

"He must certainly have gone to Madrid," said Cæsar, as all these various causes and considerations forced themselves upon his mind. "I can have no rational doubt of it, and, therefore, there go I at once, in the hope that Lazarillo may still haunt the church of San Veronica in search of me."

Scarcely had Don Cæsar made this determination, and taken a preliminary glance round him, to see in what direction he should go to get by the nearest route into the high road, than he heard some one advancing towards where he was at a brisk pace, and he stepped behind the tree, beneath whose friendly shelter he had left in order to reconnoitre the stranger.

The man, for it was a man who approached, was a stout fellow, and one whom many persons would have feared to encounter single handed. He carried in one hand a large leathern bottle, which it would appear as if he was going to fill at the stream which was so close by, and from which Don Cæsar himself had so lately quenched his thirst.

By his side hung a short stick, which looked capable of doing much execution in the hands of a strong and resolute man, and his whole appearance denoted that he possessed the former quality, whatever may have been his pretensions with regard to the latter.

Whether he was a peasant residing in the neighbourhood, or some one sent from the chateau, there was nothing whatever in his dress to determine, and as that was a point which Don Cæsar wanted very particularly to know, he made up his mind that, by fair means or by foul, he would know it.

As Cæsar surmised, this man made his way towards the brook, and with much grumbling and growling to himself, in so low a tone as to be quite unintelligible, he proceeded to fill his leather bottle.

Don Cæsar then stepped from behind the tree, and stood calmly waiting till the man had done his task, and turned round to go from where he came, when they met face to face.

"Who the devil are you?" said the fellow, who was so amazed that the sudden and unexpected appearance of Cæsar had made him give a great jump.

"My friend," replied Cæsar, "who I am is of very little consequence to you, but as to who you are, may be of very great consequence to me; allow me to ask you, then, in your own elegant phraseology, 'Who the devil are you?'"

"Find out," said the fellow.

"That's just what I mean to do. Who are you?"

"You are an impudent fellow enough," said the man, as he threw down the leather bottle of water. "What suppose now I tell you that I'll see you damned first before I let you know?"

"Why," said Cæsar, "the consequence of that will be, that I shall be under the necessity of compelling you."

"You compel me?"

"Precisely. I want to know if you come from yonder chateau or not, and what is more, I will know."

"You will know?"

"I will."

"Do you see I wear a sword?"

"I do, and hope you know how to use it. I shall be able to compel you to answer the questions I have to ask of you in a much more gentlemanly and quiet way than as if I was compelled to adopt some harsh means of proceeding,—at a word now, if you don't answer me all questions I choose to ask you, I shall give you most likely a cracked crown and a ducking in the brook besides."

CHAPTER LI.

THE RUFFIAN DEFEATED.—AMPLE INTELLIGENCE.—A BOND OF SECRESY.—DON CÆSAR'S DETERMINATION TO ENTER THE CHAMBER.

IF surprise before characterised the expression of the man's countenance, as far as that expanse was capable of showing any expression at all, intense astonishment now succeeded, for the fellow was a bully of the first class, and never before had met any one who questioned his strength and prowess.

For some moments there was a pause by mutual consent, and the fellow eyed Cæsar, as if he were doubtful of his own capabilities to contend with him for a moment or two. But he saw nothing in Cæsar that made it a very dangerous contest. Cæsar was not so big, so heavy, or so tall as himself, and he therefore considered him in the light of an easy antagonist. True, he saw that Cæsar was cool and undaunted, and, moreover, there was something in the expression of his eye, that told him he was resolute and courageous.

To men of this class, this was reckoned but little, for they ever look upon bulk as the only criterion of strength and courage, and he replied to Cæsar's last words, after he had finished his survey, by saying,—

"Yes, I do know how to use it, and I reckon you will find that out before long."

"It may be possible that your reckoning may be false, my good friend; you may reckon without your host, and find your mistake out only when it is too late."

"Ha, ha, ha! upon my soul, one would think that you were old enough to know better. I like to meet with such a man as you, because it gives one an opportunity of teaching a lesson."

"Or rather of learning one," replied Cæsar; "fellows like you must be taught humility. Your insolence is unbearable, and must be better fed than taught, but you must be compelled to know your station, since you forget it."

"I forget it. I should like to see what you would now do? By St. Jago, I never heard a man talk so before. I have whipped better and sturdier fellows than you, and I suspect you will follow the yelping dogs I have kicked with my toe."

"Now, it strikes me," said Cæsar, "that you will

not leave this place until you have been well chastised for your insolence, for a more arrant knave and fool I never met."

"Knave and fool! whom do you call by such names? I'll have you know, Signior Puppy, that I will open a vein for you, let out a little of your warm blood, and cool your courage and arrogance."

"Draw, then, if you dare, and attempt it," said Cæsar, coolly; "you are a mean, cowardly bully, and as such I will treat you; and, moreover, you shall not stir until you have satisfied me respecting all that I may think proper to require of you."

"You will, will you?" said the fellow now through rage; "we shall see, we shall see; but to begin with, take this as an earnest of what is to follow."

So saying, the burly ruffian drew his short, two-edged sword, and rushing at Cæsar, suddenly made a desperate cut at him.

Cæsar saw his object, and stepping on one side so as to avoid it, he instantly drew his own rapier, and stood upon the defensive.

It was not without a curse that the fellow recovered himself, and irritated by the failure of his cowardly attempt to catch Cæsar unprepared, as well as feeling assured in his own mind of an easy victory, that he rushed on Cæsar with the view of at once bearing him to the earth by his superior weight and strength.

In this, however, he was foiled; and do what he would, he found that his antagonist, whom he had so much despised, resolutely kept his ground, and the point of his rapier always at his breast, so that he could not rush in upon him without first spitting himself upon Cæsar's sword—a thing he had the least possible stomach for.

Cæsar, in his own mind, was more desirous of disarming his adversary, so as to place him at his mercy, and thus enable him to get the information he desired; for if he killed him, he would be of no further use to him.

The man was dangerous to encounter, because Cæsar did not fight with the same spirit of extermination. The bully, however, began to grow angry; he had never before met with so much skill and coolness, and never before had been so much opposed and baffled, and redoubled his efforts upon Cæsar, thinking he must gain ground from fatigue with fighting with one who was so much heavier.

The forest rang with the clashing of the swords, and no one was near to see the fight. However, irritated almost to madness, the ruffian showered his blows and thrusts, which Cæsar skilfully avoided; and at length his antagonist, making a blow at him with all his strength, somewhat overreached himself, and before he could recover himself Cæsar had seized his sword hand by the wrist, and there held him, with his sword at the fellow's throat.

"No, no, I will not sully the bright blade of my Toledo with such blood as stagnates in thy veins," said Cæsar; "another punishment awaits thee."

As he uttered these words to the amazed and terrified ruffian, he suddenly reversed the sword, and struck the fellow with the bright steel hilt such a tremendous blow on the head, that he instantly fell extended at full length upon the green sward, and insensible.

Cæsar paused a moment and wiped his brow, and gazed upon the now inanimate ruffian who lay at his feet.

"In truth," he said, "he is a big and burly ruffian; and, with teaching and a little sense, he might be made something of; but, as he would say, there's no converting an old pair of hose into a silken doublet; he is what he is, and won't be anything else for love or money, and that is the whole truth.

"He is not dead," he continued, as he gazed upon him, "though the crack I gave him has gone far to-wards fracturing his skull. However, he's no use so; I want him to speak, if for anything."

So saying, Don Cæsar went to the leathern bottle which stood by untouched, and emptied the contents upon the head of the prostrate man, who lay without motion, and when the last drop had escaped from it, he began to breathe and snort; and then Cæsar, to aid and quicken the revivication of the lump of humanity, bestowed a few such hearty and well-directed kicks, that he soon began to cry aloud for mercy.

"Get up, then," said Cæsar, "and not lie there idle and helpless; you are big enough, and, one would think, able to get up."

"Oh, signior," said the man, "I am done—I am done for. Oh, my head."

"Curse your head; get up and answer my questions, otherwise I may bestow a little more chastisement upon you."

Thus admonished, the fellow endeavoured to get up, but only succeeded in crawling to a tree, and propping himself up in a sitting posture, he glanced around him, completely frightened and subdued.

"You are quite aware now that you are at my mercy," said Cæsar, standing before him with his sword in his hand.

"Yes. Mercy, signior—I crave your pardon; but I didn't know ——"

"You didn't know that I could successfully combat with you, you rascal; but you see I have, and now there you lay at my mercy; and if I spare your life, I expect that you will earn my forbearance by answering my questions—honestly, if such a thing be possible."

"I will, signior; I will do anything you desire of me," replied the fellow, who was now as humble as he had before been insolent and overbearing.

"And answer them truly, too, for if I find you tell me one falsehood, that moment shall be your last. Mind, I know how to keep my promise as well as I know how to make it. Do you hear, sirrah?"

"Yes, signior, I hear, and will do what you desire without any reservation."

"Good. Now tell me whence do you come?" said Cæsar.

"I come from the chateau yonder among the trees; you can just see it from yonder hillock," said the man.

"I know the place which you mean," said Don Cæsar. "Pray tell me to whom does that chateau belong, and wherefore do you come here?"

"I belong to Don Jose, and I come here every morning to get water to take back to the chateau," he replied.

"Indeed! well, then, tell me who is there Who was it that came down there last night?"

"Don Jose," replied the man.

"Aye, but who else?"

"Two other persons."

"Take care, sir knave; answer me truly, and no evasions, or my sword will find its way through your doublet. Tell me who it was that came with Don Jose?"

"I don't know who they are," replied the man; "I have seen one before, but I don't know him."

"And the other?"

"Is a woman," said the man—"a lady, that they brought with them."

"That is an abominable lie," exclaimed Don Cæsar. "I followed them all the way, but saw there were three men there, and no female at all—one of them was insensible, and that is all."

"Ah, signior," replied the man, "what I have told you is the truth—the female was disguised."

"Disguised! say you?"

"Yes, signior; she was wrapped up in a large cloak with a hat over her head, and insensible when they carried her in."

"Do you know the Countess de Bazan, fellow?" said Cæsar, after a pause of some moments.

"No, signior, I never heard of her."

"Do you know who this lady is," he inquired, "that Don Jose brought?"

"No, I do not, signior, I never saw her before; indeed I only saw enough of her to know that it was a female, and that she was also insensible."

"Well, well," replied Cæsar, "but who was the other man who came with Don Jose? you have seen him before, you say, and must surely know him."

"I do not, signior; were you to kill me I could not tell you anything more relative to him."

Don Cæsar considered within himself if there were any further information that he could extract that would be of any service to him, but could think of none. Lazarillo he knew did not come down, and yet he might have come at another or subsequent period; he determined to inquire, and said,—

"Do you know if Don Jose has a page of the name of Lazarillo?"

"Yes, signior, he has."

"Is he at the chateau?"

"He is, signior; I left him there when I came out to fetch the water. He came after Don Jose came some hours."

This was important information, and Don Cæsar pondered as to what he could best do; whether he would send a message to Lazarillo, or take his chance of meeting him—then, what should he do with this fellow?"

"Can I trust you to go back to the chateau?" inquired Cæsar.

"Oh, yes, signior, you may—you may watch me, and I will go straight back."

"I dare say you will—I can very readily believe that; but you are not gone yet. Can you go, and, at the same time, keep your peace as to what has happened, eh?"

"Yes, signior, you may depend upon it I would not even name it to a confessor. I mean to be silent, indeed, signior; I would cut out my tongue sooner than say a word about it."

"Oh, I dare say so, you promise so willingly and so much; besides, you have such a hang-dog countenance, that at once belies all you say. I can't believe you."

"Oh, never mind my face, signior; I swear to be true. My face will be better when I am better, signior."

"And that will be many a long day first, I'll be sworn. No—no; you'll remain as you are till you are hanged, and then you will be better, much better; and, moreover, you may be indiscreet, so I have come to the determination of leaving you here."

"Yes, signor, I will stop here. I cannot, indeed, get away; I am powerless."

"Oh, I shall leave you so. Your own sword-belt and the straps of the leather bottle will help me to ensure your safety, for some time at least."

So saying, Cæsar knelt down, and, having sheathed his sword, he took the fellow's belt off, and by passing it beneath his arms, secured him to the tree, so that he could not move or escape without aid.

"Now," said Cæsar, when he had done, "if you attempt to escape, or call, I shall return, and your life will be forfeited."

"Indeed, signior, I will not say a word—not a sound shall escape my lips."

"It is well. I shall be within hearing for some time, and should I have occasion to come back, you will also have occasion to remember it, if you live afterwards."

"I am quite quiet, and will remain so," said the fellow, who was thoroughly subdued and terrified.

"It will be well for you. You know what it is to contend with me, and, before any chance passenger could help you, you would be a dead man."

"I understand, signior. You shall find that I will be true to my word, and you may reckon upon me; for it is not my interest alone that causes me to be true, but, as you say, my safety depends upon it also."

"It does."

"Then I should be a fool indeed to endanger it, signior, helpless as I am, and I feel no inclination to encounter more than one danger a day. I have had enough, and must be content."

"If you retain that frame of mind," said Cæsar, "you may reckon upon my forbearance, and your own safety."

Don Cæsar now turned from the spot, and walked slowly away. He thought within himself that the aspect of affairs had suddenly changed, and he should give up his intended journey to Madrid. It was evident to him that the parties were near him, and therefore there was every probability of something taking place that would materially alter his views.

He was anxious, too, now that he had begun this adventure, to go through with it, as Don Jose would, if possible, he had no doubt, remove the scene of action without the sphere of his observation, by starting to some new quarter, whither he would not have an opportunity of following them. This consideration induced him to desire to see Lazarillo, though how to do so he had no idea.

The day was somewhat advanced, as he judged, from appearances, for he had no means of ascertaining with accuracy. However, as he walked through the forest, the sun's rays came downwards through the intricacies above, which told him it must be somewhere near noon. The tall trees shaded him from the heat of the day, but Cæsar thought but little of it; he was desirous only of getting into the chateau, but how, was another matter. He, however, wandered on through the groves of trees towards the quarter in which it was situated.

CHAPTER LII.

THE DIFFICULTIES IN THE WAY OF ADMISSION TO THE CHATEAU.—THE KEY BELONGING TO THE BULLY.—THE GARDEN.—THE ENCOUNTER.

THE information which Don Cæsar now possessed of access at once altered all his views as regarded returning to Madrid. The facts, which had been disclosed to him by the man with the leathern bottle were detailed under a feeling of so much evident fear, that he did not for a moment doubt their accuracy. Indeed, there could be no special motive on the part of that man to deceive him, although there were some powerful ones to induce him to be both truthful and explicit.

"The fellow's story is correct enough," thought Cæsar, as he paced to and fro on the sweet green sward, which grew so delicately pale beneath the overhanging branches of the old forest trees. "It tallies with what I actually know, and, therefore, I cannot doubt it. Oh, Heaven! could I but have surmised for one moment that the half-insensible form which, from the cloak in which it was enveloped, and the hat and plume it wore, I imagined, of course, to be a man, was a female, how different a course of conduct would I have pursued, and how difficult would the scoundrel Jose and his rascally associate, be he whom he may, have found it to arrive at his journey's end. My heart, too, tells, as a confirmatory testimony, along with all other circumstances, that it was she whom I love. My countess—she whom I have made a vow to search for unceasingly, whom I drove hither, and allowed calmly enough to be taken into that abominable house by Jose. The very thought is madness."

Don Cæsar paced up and down, stamping and

fuming at such a rate, that the terrified man, whom he had fastened to the tree, expected nothing less than that his death would succeed such a working up of the passionate feelings of his conqueror.

"Oh, signior," he said, in a whining tone, which was so very different to the bullying, insolent one, which he commonly assumed, that his most intimate friends could not have imagined him by it,—oh, signior, pray have mercy upon a poor fellow. I have told you all I know. I swear by every saint in the calendar ——"

"Peace, fool!" said Don Cæsar, "I am not thinking of you."

"I am very glad to hear it, signior, and I was only afraid."

"Peace—peace!"

The man thought it prudent to hold his tongue, and he did so accordingly, much wondering in his own mind what could have put his vanquisher in such a fume.

"My countess," said Cæsar; "my beautiful bride,—you whom I saw but for so brief a moment,—my own dearest,—that I should have acted as postillion to the carriage which actually conveyed you to I know not what danger—that I should have been sufficiently near to you to have snatched you from the arms of your oppressors, and not have done it. Oh, such thoughts are madness—positive madness. I must now do something desperate, as well as efficacious, to release my tortured mind from them."

He drew his sword, and, turning to the man, he said,—

"What is the force at the chateau?"

"The force, signior? Oh, there are half-a-dozen men, besides Don Jose and his friend, whom I don't know, and the page, whom they call Lazarillo, and two women."

"Humph!" said Cæsar. "Then I shall have on my side myself, the page, and the two women, I suppose."

"Signior?"

"Well, what?"

"Did you say the two women?"

"I did. I always have the women to side with me."

"Oh! but signior, you don't know what sort of women those are; now, I happen to know too well what one of them is, for she happens to be my wife, you see, and of all the devils that ever stepped, or spoke, or breathed, hang me if she is not the very worst."

"Indeed! Well, well, if I cannot count upon the assistance of the women, I must frighten them into being passive. I will storm that chateau, or my name is not Don Cæsar de Bazan."

"What, signior, are you Don Cæsar de Bazan?"

"I am."

"I have heard talk of you, then. I heard Don Jose mention your name."

"Indeed!"

"Yes, signior, I did. He said you were a bane to his very existence, and when such a man as Don Jose takes up that opinion, I think that usually they don't long remain in this world to trouble him."

"I owe you some thanks for your caution," said Cæsar; "but I am as well aware of the rascality of that man as any one can possibly be. I know him to be unscrupulous as to what means he employs to accomplish his ends. He is a villain, every inch of him."

"He is, indeed, signior; and if you let me go back to the chateau, I will do all I can to assist you; and, perhaps, be able to render you very material service, indeed."

"Say you so?"

"I do, signior. I do think Don Jose a great villain—a very great villain; and surely it would be quite an act of virtue to assist in circumventing his vile plots and plans."

"So it would. You are, however, in his employment, and must have known how bad a master you had before now."

"I did, signior, partially; but I never saw the matter in so clear a light before. If you will let me go, signior, I pledge myself to act for you to the very best of my ability."

"My friend," said Don Cæsar, with a very provoking look, "your conversion does you much credit; but the fact is, it is a great deal too sudden to be relied upon—I do not. Heaven forbid that I should doubt its sincerity for a moment, and if no evil consequences could result, practically, from trusting you, you should be completely and unhesitatingly trusted; but, as it is, I decline doing so at present. You see, my friend, how dreadfully suspicious the contamination of this wicked world makes us. It's quite melancholy to think of."

The man bit his lips and muttered a curse, which Don Cæsar took no notice of; but, being quite sure that he could not escape from the hands in which he had secured him, he walked off in the direction of the chateau.

How to procure admission to the house where he entertained no sort of doubt that his countess was imprisoned, Cæsar had no definite idea; but he made up his mind to reconnoitre the garrison, with the hope of somewhere finding a practicable mode of entrance. As to encountering the force which would be displayed against him when he should succeed, if he were to be so fortunate in getting into the chateau, he was resolved to face it; and, relying upon that indomitable courage, which is as armour of proof to its possessor, and his admirable and unequalled skill in the use of his sword, he considered himself as a good match, even for half a dozen men who merely fought because they had the wages of a bad master, and whose heart could not be in the conflict.

"Besides," thought Cæsar, "I may not encounter them all at once; if I could get at them, now, a couple at a time, I should be able to manage them nicely; but, as regards that, I must just take my chance. I will not, while I have life left, desert you, my countess, and I have now but one prayer to Heaven, which is, that I may find you, when we do meet, as worthy in mind, and in virtue, as you are beautiful."

With these thoughts in his mind, Don Cæsar reached the chateau, when it suddenly struck him that, possibly, from his friend, who was tied to the tree, he might get some available information as to the best mode of effecting an entrance to the house.

"Perhaps I can make that rascal, who thinks himself so very cunning," said Cæsar, as he retraced his steps, "tell me of a means of obtaining admission to the chateau, without risk or labour; I will ask him—it is, at all events, worth a trial."

The man, when he saw Don Cæsar returning, and no very violent demonstration of hostility upon his countenance, began to hope that he had reconsidered his proposal, and meant to trust him, which gave him much satisfaction, as, in such an event, he firmly meant to betray him, and procure, for so doing, a handsome gratuity from Don Jose, who, to tell the truth, never scrupled to pay underlings well, which, however, may be accounted for by the fact that it is very easy and comfortable to be generous with other people's money.

"I suppose," said Cæsar, "you have every facility for getting back to the chateau easily, my friend?"

"Oh, of course, signior, I am very much trusted; indeed, I assure you, I can go in and out at my pleasure."

"But how? Now, if I were to trust you, how

could you get back to the chateau, and let me in without letting the household know that you were introducing a stranger?"

"I will tell you, signior; I have a key."

"Oh, you have a key?"

"I have, signior; it lets me in by a little door in the garden-wall, so, you see, if you will unbind me, and allow me to go, I will see that the coast is all clear, and then come back again, and let you in. And sweetly I will let you in," thought the fellow to himself.

"That's kind of you," said Cæsar; "but, my friend, don't it strike you that if I have the key you mention, I could let myself in?"

"Eh, signior?"

"Be so good as to give me that key. Quick, fellow, I am in no mood for delays—quick, I say!"

Don Cæsar drew his sword about an inch from the scabbard, which so alarmed the man that he at once produced the key from his pocket, and from that moment gave up all hopes of of mollifying Don Cæsar, and procuring his liberty.

Don Cæsar took the key; and, giving a comic sort of nod to the fellow, as much as to say, "You are outwitted, and you know it," he strode off to the chateau again, determined to walk round the walls until he found the small door of which the man had spoken.

"Here is one of my difficulties overcome," said Cæsar; "and, perhaps, after all, the most difficult of them. Once let me obtain an entrance to this place, and surely then I shall be able to accomplish something towards the liberation of my countess."

All was silent around the chateau, and nothing could be seen but the castellated top of the building, and the high wall, which shut out from observation any other part, and which, as he surveyed, Don Cæsar could not help thinking would even have defied his powers to scale. Perhaps, however, if he had not had the key which was to procure his admission, he would not so readily have given way to such an opinion, but have buoyed himself up with hopes of accomplishing the feat, had it even been ten times more difficult than it really was.

Such minds as his never allow themselves to make much of difficulties and dangers, but always underrate them when they consider that they have to be overcome. When they are so overcome, frequently a revulsion of feeling will take place, and all the dangers will be fully admitted which before were scorned.

So overgrown was the wall in every place with huge creeping weeds, the growth of many years, that Cæsar was particularly careful in his scrutiny, in order that he might not miss the little door which had been mentioned to him. After he had traversed about half-way round the wall, he, to his joy, observed a little door hidden among the ivy so much, that it was by mere chance he happened to espy it.

In another moment he applied the key to the lock, which it operated upon easily, and Don Cæsar, with a throb of hope at his heart which he cared not to repress, and the name of his countess (the beautiful incognita) upon his lips, once again stepped into the magnificent garden which surrounded the chateau, and which the infamous Don Jose had placed at the disposal of his majesty of Spain for the very worst of purposes.

"Here at last," he said,—"here at last!" And as he spoke he loosened his sword in its scabbard, for he knew not how soon he might require its use. "I am here at last, with more information to guide me, and more certainty in my actions than I have yet had, during the progress of the pursuit for her who bears my name. Let those beware who now cross me in that one great object of my existence."

There was no one within sight, and the same rapt silence reigned within the garden of the chateau as had characterised the exterior of it. The fact was that Jose and the king were at that moment in deep consultation; Maritana was weeping, and Lazarillo was sleeping; while the domestics were assembled together in one apartment, conversing in whispers, for when their imperious master, Don Jose, was present in the house, they knew that they dared not disturb him by the least appearance of noise or rioting.

Cæsar, however, did not like the air of profound repose which reigned over the place. He would have been glad to have seen some indications of life and energy, and such a rapt silence brought a disagreeable impression to his mind that all was not well with her whom he was willing to encounter so much danger to see.

Advancing from the immediate neighbourhood of the door, he made his way down a narrow walk, bordered on each side by tall thick orange plants, and listened attentively almost at every footstep he made for some sound indicative of life in the chateau.

He had closed the garden gate after him, and he had taken the precaution to secure the key, as well as to ascertain that it fitted tolerably well on the inside, because he knew not what might occur to make a sudden retreat highly politic and desirable.

Suddenly now he paused, for he thought he heard some one approaching. He listened attentively, but the sound had ceased; then again, just as he was on the point of proceeding, they were renewed, and he became convinced that footsteps were approaching the path in which he was, and from the sound he thought that more than one person would soon be in sight. Of this he was further assured, by hearing voices as if in cautious conversation, and he had just time to conceal himself among the orange trees, when two persons came in sight of where he was.

One of these persons Don Cæsar at a glance recognised to be Don Jose—the other he did not know.

They were conversing in a low tone, but, as Jose's evil destiny would have it, something possessed him to stop exactly opposite to the part of the garden where Cæsar was concealed, and then and there to carry on some portion of his conversation with his companion, who was one of the servants of the chateau, but the one in whom Don Jose placed confidence and trust, and in command over all the others during his absence from home.

"Now, Martinzi," said Jose,—for such was the name of the man,—"you will be specially careful in attending to my instructions."

"I will, my lord," was the reply.

"At dark to-night I must have a horse ready caparisoned for me, you understand, and waiting at some private entrance of this place."

"It shall be as your lordship desires."

"It must be a fleet steed, for I have got to go to Aranjues, and possibly back here again, without being missed, good Martinzi; so you will understand that during my absence you will keep up the delusion that I am still on these premises."

"I understand your lordship—it shall be done."

"That is right, good Martinzi. I know of no man who can lie with so good a face as yourself."

"Oh, your lordship is too good; I am but a humble imitator of those who have a far higher genius for such matters than I can ever aspire to."

Martinzi bowed as he spoke, so that Don Jose could not avoid feeling that the very equivocal compliment was meant for himself. But he was not exactly the sort of man to be disconcerted at such a trifle, not he —on the contrary, he was rather amused than otherwise, for it put him forcibly in mind of how he treated the king, and he said,—

"You are quite right, Martinzi. Continue, I pray you, to hold good models in your eyes, and you may in time become quite a great man. And now listen to me most particularly."

"I do, my lord."

"I have reason to suppose that there is one about this neighbourhood still, who has been, who is, and who I fear will be, the greatest pest I ever in my life encountered."

"Indeed, my lord!"

"Ay, Martinzi, you may well be astonished; but there is one who seems to bear a charmed life on purpose to vex and annoy me. It is too bad, but such is the case."

"May I presume to ask the name of the atrocious individual?"

"Oh, yes; his name is Don Cæsar de Bazan."

"And this lady, now in the house ——"

"Ask no further questions, Martinzi, lest you get too wise, and die of that disease. You understand me?"

"I do, my lord, understand that it is dangerous for any one about the court of Spain to know too much; but let me assure your lordship that if I seem at all inquisitive, it does not arise from a feeling of curiosity, but a wish to know so much as to enable me to serve your lordship thoroughly."

"I am willing to believe so, Martinzi. And now, as regards this man—this Don Cæsar de Bazan. He is bold, daring, strong, brave, and the best swordsman in Spain."

"High qualities, my lord."

"Very disagreeable ones, indeed—very disagreeable ones, you should say, my good fellow. He will, if the humour takes him (and it may), make an attempt to get into this house; nothing will deter him, if he does think of doing so, and therefore I warn you to be most particularly on your guard against him."

"I will, my lord. But such an attempt must end in his destruction. Who could scale the wall?"

"I have faith in the wall. But he would think nothing of ringing at the postern, and then pushing and fighting his way in, despite all the opposition you could bring against him. Therefore, when any demand is made for admission here, be sure you take a good look at the person before you open the gate a single inch."

"I will, my lord."

"That would not have been a bad plan," thought Cæsar to himself. "I give the rascal credit now for that scheme; and, if I had not already made good an entrance here, I should certainly have adopted it. It is a capital plan to get into a place. Ring at the door, and then knock down whoever may come to open it; it saves a world of trouble. Truly, the simplest means of accomplishing objects are ever the best."

"I shall attend to your lordship's instructions most particularly, your lordship may depend upon it, as I always do."

"Good! then I have no more to say to you at present, further than that I shall not forget you in the shape of a handsome gratuity when all this present little intrigue is over."

"I humbly thank your lordship."

They both then walked towards the house again, leaving Don Cæsar certainly with some extra information as regarded the movements of Don Jose, but with nothing new upon the subject so near and dear to his heart.

"Confound him!" said Cæsar; "while he was being so very confidential, if he had said something about my wife, now, it would have been just as well, and might have assisted me a little in that which I have to do. However, I must be guided by circumstances. Oh! that my young friend, Lazarillo, would take it into his head to come strolling this way now."

Of this there was no chance or likelihood, and Don Cæsar was about to proceed again down the path towards the house, when he heard a loud voice say, from the immediate neighbourhood of where he was,—

"Who's there?"

Cæsar looked about him, but he could see no one,

and then the inquiry was repeated, and he began to think that some path must run parallel with that in which he was, but that he could not see it in consequence of the thickness of the hedges that there abounded.

When this idea occurred to him, he said,—

"It is I—it is I!"

"Who the deuce are you?" was the next question.

"Come and see!" said Cæsar.

"That will I," said the voice. "I think I know your voice: you are that drunken varlet, Lopez, and I have no doubt you have been at the wine flagon as usual; but, now that Don Jose is here, an example shall be made of you, you may depend upon it. Just wait where you are till I can come to you."

"I will," said Cæsar. "Come along."

"Now, hang your impertinence!" cried the voice. And Cæsar heard footsteps, at first as if in rapid retreat, and then in advance, which he accounted for by the winding nature of the pathway which would conduct the man towards him.

Cæsar drew his sword, for he knew not what sort of an antagonist the man might be, or how sudden an attack he might make upon him, and scarcely had he done so when he was confronted by one of the servants of the chateau, all of whom seemed to have been picked out on account of their personal strength.

An exclamation of surprise came from the man's lips when he saw Cæsar, who said,—

"Now, friend, you see I am not Lopez. What have you to say to me?"

"A stranger?"

"Yes, a stranger! Do you question my right here? If you do, you have a sword, and why not use it?"

"Perhaps you have wandered in here, signior, without knowing the nature of the trespass you were committing. If so, I will shew you the way out, and say nothing about it, for if you are discovered here by any one less scrupulous than myself about shedding blood, your life would assuredly be taken."

Cæsar was puzzled now what to do, but he would not condescend to act the hypocrite, and he replied,—

"My purpose here is hostile, I will not deny it, and I regret to meet with any generosity from you."

As he spoke he allowed the point of his sword to drop, and stood completely off his guard, for the words of the man had inspired him with a confidence in the absence of danger. At this moment, however, the fellow, who had buried his hand in his breast, where he had a dagger concealed, suddenly made a treacherous spring upon Cæsar, as he exclaimed,—

"Fool! I will teach you to intrude here when you are not wanted. Take that."

Had not Cæsar providentially at the instant stepped aside, the poniard would have been buried in his heart. As it was, the assassin missed his aim, cunning as he thought himself, and his arm went completely over Cæsar shoulder, while the sharp edge of the dagger ripped up a portion of his clothing, and at the same time slightly grazed his shoulder.

CHAPTER LIII.

THE FATE OF THE ASSASSIN.—DON CÆSAR'S PROGRESS IN THE GROUNDS OF THE CHATEAU.

IF anything whatever could rouse the anger of such a man as Don Cæsar to a height nearly above all control, it certainly was such an act as that which had been attempted to be perpetrated.

He could forgive any man for active opposition. He could forgive any one for doing his best, even in a bad cause, after he had once embraced it; but the base, cowardly act of attempted assassination he could not look over, and it at once, in his opinion, placed the man who strove to perpetrate it far without the pale of all consideration.

It was indeed little sort of a miracle that Cæsar did not thus fall most mysteriously by the dagger of that scoundrel in the grounds of Don Jose's chateau. Had he been a little less active, a little less self-composed or observant, the poniard must have found its way to his heart, and ended a life which was of such important consequence to the happiness of others.

Such a life, too, as Don Cæsar's, is, we conceive, of importance to society; for where so much generosity, so much honour, and so much chivalrous bearing are united in one individual, it seems as if nature had made him as a pattern piece of work,

"To give the world assurance of a man,"

and as such he becomes valuable to the community in which he lives, and moves, and has his being.

Such was Don Cæsar. And even for his very failings we would fain claim some kindly considerations. They were but spots in the sun—flaws in the diamond, which proclaim it real. He had failings, but they were generous ones. He was rash—a heritage of generous minds; he was headstrong in running into danger; but although no one could defend the prudence of the means he adopted, even in carrying out an undertaking, no one could by any possibility dispute the purity of his motives, or the exalted nature of the object he strove to attain, perchance so rashly.

Of all men living, then, he should not perish by assassination; and glad are we to be enabled to record this his escape from the greatest danger which had ever assailed him, and the signal and complete discomfiture of the ruffian who had aimed at his life by such desperate and unworthy means.

It had something strange in it how any one man could so far commit himself to so bad an action in the service of another, the more especially as such partilar service could not be contemplated beforehand as at all likely to become necessary, and, therefore, could have formed no part of the bargain between Don Jose and this one of his many infamous and unscrupulous dependants.

But there are men so inherently bad and cruel, that they commit such actions as these quite con amore. There are men who prefer an assassination to a fair contest, even if victory were certain to be with them, because their minds are warped and crooked, and their ways partake of a similar deviation.

Of such materials was the scoundrel composed who had made so atrocious and so utterly undefensible an attack upon the life of Don Cæsar.

But if it be a principle of some minds to exult in such modes of action, there is another feeling which invariably accompanies cruelty and deceit—namely, cowardice. The man who has the mind adapted to use the knife of the assassin is always a paltroon and a cur of the very first water. There may exist all the disposition and savage ferocity to do mischief and to exult in bloodshed, with the physical courage to perpetrate one of the deeds the vitiated mind pictures to itself as pleasant to see.

Perhaps the most abject object in human nature is a foiled assassin—one who has attempted a despicable crime, but who has been arrested at the very moment when, with fiend-like exultation, he had made in his own mind sure of his victim.

What a sudden revulsion of feeling takes place in such characters. At once they sink from the tiger to the jackall. At once abject fear takes possession of them, and their cringing meanness is only to be equalled by their former wickedness.

When this fellow, then, found that his dagger had missed its aim—when he found that he was in the grasp of the man against whose life he had made so dastardly an attempt, and that that man, too, was calm and cool, and held him with a grip like a vice, he began to humble, for he thought his last hour was come indeed.

All nerve deserted him. He shook like an aspen-leaf. The dagger which he would willingly have sheathed in the heart of Don Cæsar dropped from his relaxed grasp, and a pallid hue came across his face as he strove, by looks of the most abject humility, to beseech the mercy of the man to whom he would have shown none, and who was so nearly falling a victim to his rascality.

"Mercy, mercy, signior!—oh, mercy!" he gasped, as he strove, but in vain, to slide from the powerful grasp that held him.

"You monstrous villain!" said Cæsar.

"Mercy, mercy!"

"Despicable in your actions—despicable still more, if that be possible, in your cowardly appeal against their consequences. How dare such as you ask or expect mercy from me? Villain! a thousand deaths were too poor a punishment for such base treachery. Were you mad, that you have thus thrown away your life?"

"My life—my life!" gasped the writhing wretch. "Oh, grant me my life, and I will be your slave."

"My slave!"

"Yes—oh, yes; I will be your abject slave for ever. Why not? I have always been some one's slave, and no one ever spared my life before, because — because ——"

"Because," said Cæsar, "perhaps you succeeded in plunging your poniard into their hearts, as you would have done into mine. Villain! Think you I could demean myself by taking service of such as you are? No, I must rid the world of you."

"Oh, have mercy upon me, signior! Have some mercy upon me! Spare my life."

"I must think of some means of preventing such a wretch from any longer encumbering the earth with his presence."

"No, no," howled the cowardly ruffian, as he wept abundantly. "Oh, no. You are too brave and generous to kill me. You will spare me, I know."

"You have deprived yourself, by your own act, of all right to draw upon anybody's generosity."

"But, but consider, great signior. You see I do not call for help from the chateau, as I might. I have no wish, you perceive, to get you into trouble. None whatever, you understand, noble signior, or I should call for aid."

"Which would be your last cry in this world," said Cæsar. "Call for it as soon as you will."

"Mercy! You choke me, signior."

"I don't intend to choke you. That's too easy a death for an assassin, and I cannot pollute my sword with your blood. Let me consider. Humph! I must certainly find some mode of disposing of such a scoundrel."

"I have a wife, signior. For her sake spare me."

"Spare your lies, villain, and leave me time for reflection. You a wife, indeed; what woman would take to her arms such a wretch as you are?"

"I have indeed, signior. And I have children."

"Children?"

"Yes, signior."

"An assassin children? Now, this is monstrous. How dare you have children? What right has such a man as you with any household ties? Are you sure you have children?"

"Oh, quite, signior."

"Well, I will take your word for it. I had a notion of letting you go before, as being unworthy of my vengeance; but now, for the sake of your children, in order that their father's pernicious example may be removed from their eyes, I feel myself, however un-

willingly, bound to become your executioner; so die you must, and shall."

"Oh, good signior, forgive me; I have no children."

"Why, how now," cried Cæsar, as he gave the fellow a kick across the shins that made him dance again. "Is this the way you traffic with your very existence by lying to my very face?"

"Mercy, mercy."

"Have you a wife?"

"No, no; oh, dear, no."

"I'm glad of that, for the honour of womankind," said Cæsar; "I thought you could not possibly have a wife, you scoundrel. How dared you malign the sex!"

"No, signior, I didn't mean to malign anybody. All I want is my precious life, signior."

"And so you go floundering about among a collection of lies, experimenting to discover which is the most likely to effect your purpose."

"My life—my life!"

"Let me consider, you infernal rascal. Let me consider how I shall dispose of you. Is that a well yonder?"

"Oh, signior, it is a well; but—but ——"

"You would rather let well alone, I suppose."

The fellow made an ugly attempt to laugh, because he thought it might please his captor for him to do so; but Don Cæsar looked as stern as possible, and said, in a cold tone,—

"What are you laughing at?"

"You—you made a joke, signior. You made a joke."

"No such thing; but, however, you will have some leisure to laugh when you are down the well, where I mean to put you."

"D—d—down the well?"

"Yes."

"It's—it's got some water at the bottom of it, signior. I shall be drowned. Oh, only think what a dreadful death."

"Do you think it worse than having some eight or nine inches of cold steal plunged into one's heart?—because, if you do, you may choose that instead, and the instrument by which it shall be inflicted can be your own poniard. Choose now."

"No, no; God help me, no!"

"The well ——"

"Mercy, mercy, signior!"

"Or the dagger?"

The fellow glanced wildly around him. There was no help near. Had he raised his voice he certainly would have been heard in the chateau; but then Don Cæsar's hand was upon his throat, and that he felt was a hand that could collapse upon his windpipe rather closely, so that should he attempt to call out, the first cry would in all human probability be the last, and his ghost, if he had one, would only have the melancholy satisfaction, if ghosts have satisfaction, of seeing how embarrassed his conqueror might be.

Taking, then, this view of the subject, it was not politic to call out for any assistance; and, besides, as regards the well, the fellow happened to know that there was not a great quantity of water at the bottom of it, so that he might have a chance of escape from it by some means, even if his conqueror should, upon which he had he had some doubts, actually insist upon his descending into it.

"Noble signior," he said, "I hope you will have mercy; but if you will do the one or the other, I—I—think I will be drowned in the well."

"Very good."

Cæsar dragged him towards the well's brink, and making the rope into a noose at one end, he slipped it over the fellow's neck, who directly took the idea that he was about to be hung, and such terror seized possession of his soul at the moment that he nearly fainted away.

"You may have it round your neck if you like," said Cæsar; "but it's all a matter of taste."

Half dead with fear as he was, he took the hint, and slipped the cord below his arms, and breathed a little freer than before.

"You are a stupid as well as a malignant hound," remarked Cæsar. "I have more compassion on you than you have on yourself. You would have been hung, as you really richly deserved, for your abominable treachery, but for me."

"But, signior, you do not mean to make me descend the well."

"I have no time for argument. Please to go."

Another kick sent the alarmed ruffian over the well's brink, and Cæsar just held the rope sufficiently to prevent his being actually dashed to pieces as he reached the bottom, by concussions against the sides.

When he found, then, by the slackened appearance of the rope, that the fellow must have got down as far as he could go, he drew his sword and severed it, saying,—

"Now, my friend, I think you will have time to ruminate upon the hazardous consequences of attempting assassination."

The man made no sound, and Don Cæsar walked from the spot, certainly free, but with no very distinct idea of what he could do next towards the rescue of his countess, should it really be her who was in the chateau.

He began now sensibly to feel the increasing heat of the day, and as he walked up a cool, shaded avenue, the delightful fragrance of many flowers came upon his senses. The hum of insect life, too, met his ear, and, as now and then a soft gentle wind swept across the orange and lime trees, it carried with it a delicious refreshing fragance, which at any other time would have attracted the attention and admiration of Don Cæsar, but which now passed him by unheeded, as his mind was intent upon matters of an all engrossing nature.

"Shall I at once," he said, "make a bold dash into the house, and cut down every one who attempts to oppose my progress in search of the darling treasure of my heart, or shall I reflect, for her sake, upon some means less hazardous to my own life, of rescuing her?"

This was a prudent way of putting the questions, which was quite a novelty to such a man as Don Cæsar, and it was no imputation on his courage that he did so. Far from it. It was one of the natural results of affection towards another in such a mind as his.

While he stood alone in the wide world, the last of his name and race, and when he had nothing to care for, and knew of no one who would mourn his death, he allowed the natural bravery of his disposition to run riot unchecked by the least impulse of reason. He cared not to give himself the trouble to think if this or that impulsive undertaking was dangerous or not. What was it to him? He had nothing to lose but his life, and that, for all he knew and believed, there was no one to regret.

Acting on this feeling, the wild recklessness which had characterised him when first we, with the reader, made his acquaintance at the carnival time in the streets of Madrid, was at its height, and he was as willing to fight one man as twenty, and as willing to do either as to eat, or drink, or make merry, or join in the dance or the frolic of the moment.

But now he thought that some one loved him. The delicious and novel feeling had come over him that now there would be tears shed for him—that he was of importance to some one. That the happiness of a fair and beautiful being, perchance gifted with all the nobility of virtue, was in his keeping, and, consequently, whenever he had time to think he became more reflective and careful.

"She, perhaps, loves me," he said. "She is, perhaps, helpless, and surrounded by enemies. She, perhaps, thinks of me as the only person who can rescue her, or who will feel sufficiently impressed with a desire to do so. I may be her only hope—there might come upon her heart utter despair if I were dead—who knows what moral influence upon such a cowardly scoundrel as Don Jose the mere knowledge of my existence may have. I will be careful, wonderfully careful. I, who was never very careful before, will now become very much so, indeed."

By the time Don Cæsar had arrived at this abstract conclusion with regard to the advantages of discretion, he had likewise reached the corner of a raised terrace, which was in the garden of the chateau, and which was to be gained only by a flight of steps.

Anticipating a good view of the house from this terrace, and, possibly, hoping that it might conduct him quietly into some of the lower rooms of the place, he at once ascended.

As he had supposed, he now got a very good view of the chateau, because he was lifted above the mass of vegetation which adorned the garden.

He stood surveying the house for some time, and letting his eyes rove from window to window, in the hope of seeing some indications of the presence of her who engaged so much of his thoughts and best feelings. In this expectation, however, if it amounted to such, he was mistaken, for he saw no one whatever, although at one of the windows something that looked like a human head, fixed his regard for some moments.

The extreme stillness of the object, however, made him think he was mistaken, and now he walked forward on the terrace, and saw that it had another rise, which was likewise to be reached by some half dozen steps, and he perceived that when on that additional height, he should be on a level with a long range of narrow windows, through one of which he thought surely there would be no very great difficulty in getting.

Had Don Cæsar forgotten the admirable lesson of caution he had been giving to himself? Surely he had, or in such a dangerous locality as he was now in, he would not have omitted to look behind him, and around the garden occasionally, to see if he were an object of observation to any one.

More particularly was such caution necessary, since he had ascended the steps of the terrace, for now there were no trees and shrubs to screen him from the sight of any of the creatures of Don Jose, who might be prowling about the chateau.

Alas, he did not look behind him—he cast no observant eye into the garden. If he had, he would have seen, indeed, that danger was thickening around him, and that a busy preparation was making to put an end to all further trouble on his account, in this world, at least.

The fact was, that he had not been on the terrace many moments, when he was seen by a servant of the chateau, who was so much bewildered by the cool manner in which he appeared to be walking there, that at first he was inclined to say nothing of it, conceiving that he must be there with the cognizance of Don Jose.

Still the man did not know him, and as he had heard of the alarm that some one was endeavouring to enter the premises, he thought it just worth while to get the opinion of a fellow-servant upon the matter, and accordingly he hurried into the hall of the chateau, and brought out one, to whom he said, as he pointed at Don Cæsar,—

"There, what do you think of that?"

"Think of that?"

"Yes. Don't you see that tall fellow walking on the terrace, and looking so inquisitively at the house?"

"By the mass, I do."

"Then who is he?"

"Why, how should I know who he is? If you know, I suppose that enough, stupid?"

"But I don't know."

"You don't?"

"No; and if you don't know him, he's an interloper here, and Don Jose will be the death of us all, for keeping, as he will say, such a poor watch in the chateau, as to allow a stranger to enter its grounds. Good God, some one must have left the garden door open. What shall we do, comrade?"

"What shall we do? Why, fetch Don Jose at once, and if he don't know the signior, he will very soon tell us what to do."

Don Jose was fetched, and the stranger pointed out to him. An oath came from his lips, which made the men jump again, and in an instant Jose darted into the chateau, followed by them in amazement and terror.

"An arquebus, an arquebus," he said; "quick—give me an arquebus."

Half a dozen were immediately produced.

"Loaded?" said Jose.

"All, all, noble signior—all."

Jose seized one, and was about to rush into the garden, and try his hand at a long shot at Don Cæsar, when his usual caution and cowardice overcame his suddenly formed resolution, and he paused.

"No," he muttered; "it can be done safer, much safer. Take each of you an arquebus—rank yourselves up at the foot of the terrace, and when I give the word, fire at him. Such a volley will surely kill him, unless he have a charmed life, which, by Heaven, I have sometimes been inclined to believe."

The servants did as they were ordered, and by the time Don Cæsar reached the second flight of steps which led up to the higher part of the terrace, all was ready to fire a volley at him, and every arquebus seemed pointed fairly at him, so that his death now appeared to be quite certain.

As for Don Jose himself, although, surely his amount of danger was amazingly small, he took good care not to come out of the chateau again while the proceedings were pending; but kept himself snugly just within the doorway from which the servants issued.

"Hark ye!" he said, in a low tone; "you will take the word to fire from me, but mind that you take a good aim at him, and every one of you shall receive a dozen crowns."

Liberal Don Jose! Again, with other people's money, were you earning golden opinions.

"Are you all ready?" he said.

"We are, my lord," was the muttered response—"we are."

Some of the men did not half like the job, and the arquebuses shook in their hands. Now there ensued a deathlike stillness, and Don Jose, who considered that even if his victim were to look round, still his death would be certain, said, in a sepulchral voice, which was not entirely free from agitation,—

"Once!"

The stillness that ensued seemed more than natural, and he hastened to say, in a quiet tone,—

"Twice!"

Then intense anxiety and curiosity to see Cæsar fall, impelled him to step about one pace from the shelter of the chateau, and he shaded with his hand the sun from his eyes, as he saw Cæsar steadily ascending the second steps of the terrace.

"A fairer mark could not be had," he muttered. "Don Cæsar de Bazan, your hour has come. Nothing now but some miracle can save you, and the age of miracles is past, as I have ample reason for believing."

He still kept his eyes fixed on Cæsar, and then he said,—

"Fire!"

The discharge of the arquebuses instantly followed, and when the smoke cleared away, Don Cæsar was gone.

CHAPTER LIV.

THE PROGRESS OF THE QUEEN.—THE ROBBERS OF THE WOOD OF MEUOJOREER.

THE queen, after the departure of Lazarillo, was quite undecided what course to pursue. She had almost determined in her own mind that she would accede to the request of the page, and proceed at once to the chateau where Don Jose and the king were at that moment.

Again she would argue, that to appear in such a place, and among such men, would scarcely be seeming on her part. How could she account for her knowledge? She hesitated, and was troubled to think of the result either way.

What if she should be refused admittance? This she thought highly probable. In that case, she would even precipitate matters, and render the situation of Maratina even worse than before, by any unavailing attempt at assistance, as both suspicion and opposition would be awakened.

Distressed in her own mind, and greatly disturbed, the queen had almost forgotten her own causes of unhappiness in her sympathy for that of the unfortunate Countess de Bazan, and for Don Cæsar also; and seeing the little good she could do was more than likely to be counterbalanced by the great evil she was sure of causing, she came to the conclusion that she would defer going.

However, upon second thoughts, she reversed this determination, because she believed it was her duty to attempt something, and, if she failed, the failure ought not to be attributed to the fact merely of her attempt to do good, but to something precedent to that attempt; to no new passion, but to the existence of the old one.

Thus, if she went, and a great disturbance was to arise, and Maritana suffer, and she herself be baffled, it must be attributed to the existence of the king's and the minister's bad passions, designs, and pre-determined intentions, with regard to Maritana; and not that their purposes were merely the result of her interference—on the contrary, they would surely pursue their intentions in spite of all she could do to prevent them, and her intention could cause no new misery, though they failed in averting the old one; and, moreover, who could tell that it might not have the desired effect, until the event was discovered? No one could; therefore she was determined not to throw a chance away, but go.

"Inez," said the queen, who had been seated in a thoughtful mood for some time, while these considerations were passing through her mind, "Inez, I will go."

"Go! gracious lady—say, rather, that you will not go. Your presence would, in such a case, and at such a place, bring fresh insult and even danger to your majesty."

"Indeed, Inez."

"Yes, my lady;—think well over it: have you not been driven away from Madrid—and have you not, in a manner, been confined to Aranjues?"

"Confined to Aranjues, Inez! what do you mean? I heard nothing of that."

"Did you not, gracious lady, know that the tone and manner in which the king ordered you to return hither, was equivalent to telling you to consider the precincts of this place your future residence, and the boundary of your majesty's liberty?"

"No, Inez, no—I did not understand it in that light."

"Such I think it was meant, and, therefore, I think it unadvisable for you to take this journey."

"But, under such circumstances, I feel I am right in going."

"Scarcely, your majesty."

"The journey is one of mercy—intended to save a young and beautiful woman from destruction—from dishonour. Can I, a queen, hesitate to do such a deed? Surely I cannot—I cannot."

"Let me implore your majesty not; recollect that there is not the remotest chance of your ever being able to do the least service. Success might, indeed, compensate your majesty, but you will run needless danger without hope, and the certainty of stirring up the king's hatred and anger in a yet stronger degree than ever."

"All this might have its weight, Inez, against a less important reason to urge me on than the one I have."

"Might I hear it, your majesty?"

"You may. It is duty—my duty as a queen—urges me on. There is a beautiful and suffering creature on the point of being cruelly dishonoured, and it seems to me that both duty and humanity point out to me the course I ought to pursue. My interference must be productive of some good; they will, indeed, perhaps refuse any request I may make, but they cannot commit so odious a crime while I am present, and should I obtain a sight of her, I can, at least, take her under my protection."

"But such a thing, your majesty, would not be permitted."

"Not permitted?"

"No; your majesty could not obtain admittance; and then, once in, they would take very good care that your majesty went to no part of the place save where they chose, and then you could be of no service—the danger you run would never be compensated."

"Yes; my own conscience would compensate me. I had done all that I could; and, however I might lament the failure, yet I should feel it less to recollect that I had not been wanting upon the occasion."

"Alas! alas! gracious lady, your own generosity and goodness of heart will cause you more misery and more unhappiness. I hope it may cause you no danger; but I dread and anticipate the worst."

"Say no more, Inez; but tell my people to get ready."

"Your majesty will go?"

"Yes."

"May I not implore ——"

"Nay, Inez, go and tell them to have all in readiness."

"I obey your majesty."

"Do so; I shall be ready very speedily for the journey."

"Since your majesty will go, no time or pains shall be spared."

"I would have it so."

Inez quitted the apartment, and proceeded to give the necessary orders for going to the chateau of Don Jose.

The queen was seated in her boudoir, when an old grey-headed man, her steward, who held a confidential situation in the household, and who was much respected for his fidelity, and the general tenor of his life and conduct entered, and said,

"I pray your majesty to forgive the intrusion of an old servant, whose very life he would gladly sacrifice rather than your majesty should be injured."

"What do you want, Pedro? You are an old and valued servant, and I would hear anything you have to say for that reason alone; but you must be brief, for I am about to quit Aranjues for a short time."

"It is about this very journey," replied the old man, "that I would speak to your majesty."

"Say on, then," replied the queen; "you, too, are not infected with idle fears?"

"Idle fears they are not, your majesty," said the steward, shaking his head, gravely; "I know Don Jose, and the chateau your majesty intends to visit."

"You do?"

"Yes, your majesty."

"What of it?"

"It is a dangerous and a dreadful place, your majesty. It is peopled by Don Jose, who has hired the servants for two qualities, that your majesty would scarcely dream of," said the old man.

"Indeed?"

"It is true, your majesty; strength and perfect unscrupulousness."

"Horrible!" said the queen; "but why two such dangerous qualities?"

"That they may the better answer his purpose, they are well paid, and, at his word, will commit any enormity; and this they well understand before."

"It is very dreadful to say this, Pedro; do you really believe all this?"

"Oh, yes, your majesty; I know it well, too well to have any doubt of it. These men had their situations either to commit any robbery that may be required of them, or to take no notice of any that may be done by others."

"Indeed!"

"They are ruffians of the worst class, your majesty, and will not hesitate to commit any deed."

"But what have I to fear from such men?" inquired the queen.

"Everything, your majesty—everything. They would not hesitate to commit any enormity even against your majesty."

"You must be in error."

"Forgive me, your majesty; but I am an old man, and have been too long in your majesty's service to tell an untruth. They both would do it, and dare do it. If Don Jose should have the mind to seize your majesty here, I believe it could be done."

"You tell me more than I would have deemed possible."

"But not more than what is true."

"Do you know if any one else goes there besides Jose?"

"I—oh! your majesty ——"

The old man was about to speak, but suddenly checked himself as though he had, upon second thoughts, better not say what he first intended.

"Speak out," said the queen, "and tell me truly what you know concerning the place and its inmates."

"They do say, your majesty," replied the steward, "that the king himself goes there in private, but it would be worth a man's life to say so."

"Indeed!"

"Yes, your majesty; and to follow his majesty there and find him, at a time above all others when he least desires it, would render him exceedingly angry, and more lives than one would be sacrificed on the occasion. I hope your majesty will forgive me, but your majesty is so beloved by us all, that we would all sacrifice our lives for you, if we could aid or defend you; but then your majesty must be sacrificed."

"I will think of this," said the queen.

"Heaven send your majesty may be saved from this journey. I am sure it will turn out to your disadvantage."

"I will not go. There, peace. Now leave the room, unless you have any favour to ask for yourself."

"Nothing—nothing, your majesty. We want for nothing here, while your majesty remains here to reign over us. God bless your majesty."

As the old man rose up, she could perceive tears trickle down his cheek, as he turned to quit the apartment.

The queen was sensibly touched by this piece of feeling on the part of the old man, and was for some time buried in deep thought, and informed Inez she would not go, and she might countermand the orders she had given for the journey.

This was gladly done by her attendants, who rejoiced at the thought that their royal mistress would not quit Aranjues.

"Your majesty cannot tell how thankful we all feel for this kindness. We were all certain of some dreadful accident or other, if your majesty had seen the king, or trusted yourself there."

The queen made no reply, but remained for a long while buried in reflection; for while they would not attempt to disturb her, it was an escape, they thought, from her present misery, and they all remained at a distance.

It was nearly an hour ere the queen spoke to any one, and then she called Inez to her, saying,—

"I have taken a new resolution respecting this affair of the Countess Bazan."

"Indeed, your majesty."

"Yes; honour, duty, and justice impel me, and I will proceed to this much-dreaded chateau."

"Your majesty——"

"Nay, seek not to deter me."

"We would not for our own sakes, but for your majesty's."

"I will go, Inez. I will brave it out. I will endeavour to succour her, be the consequences what they may."

"Your majesty will do as you please, and your majesty has our prayers for your safety. But, gracious lady, do consider the consequences to yourself."

"I have considered all things, and, in spite of all, have I come to the conclusion that I must go. Therefore, Inez, see that we are not delayed."

"It shall be as your majesty wishes. Allow me, gracious lady, to order the escort to be a full one."

"We do not need that; there should not be any appearance of force; but we shall require sufficient to protect us on the road, and no more."

The Lady Inez then proceeded to the proper officers of the household, and gave the queen's orders, and they were soon in the way of being fulfilled.

There was an immediate stir in the palace of Aranjues, and all immediately knew that the queen had altered her intention, and would shortly depart for Don Jose's chateau, when they expected there would be a scene of some kind or other.

It was not long before the queen was ready, and, accompanied by Inez, and two more female attendants, entered the royal carriage, and then the gates of Aranjues were once again thrown open, and they issued forth under the care of a small escort.

It was a beautiful sight, and few would have thought that the queen, who could command such luxuries, was, perhaps, one of the most unhappy beings in her own dominions, and that there were many whose lightness of heart and peace of mind she envied, if she could be said to envy any one.

But such is the case. We may have many things, and yet the heart yearns for what we have not, and few, seeing the gay equipage, would have thought it contained one of the most unhappy, at the same time the most amiable of ladies in the whole Spanish dominions.

They wound their way through the forest of Aranjues, and finally quitted it by the road that led to the wood of Menajoues, through which they must pass before they could arrive at the chateau where they were bound to.

This wood they traversed, and then they entered the wood of Menojoreer. The scenery was wild and enchanting, the road irregular, and there was altogether less art and arrangement here than in the forest of Aranjues; this, for a time, excited the attention of the queen, who expatiated on the various beauties that presented themselves to her, and in some measure dispelled the gloom that appeared to be overspreading herself and her attendants.

"Why are the escort riding around the carriage, and sending some of their number to scour through the grounds on either side of us?"

"Because this is a place well known for the number of its robbers, and the bands are both numerous and strong."

"I have heard something of this," said the queen; "but they will not attempt to touch us; our escort will prevent that."

"Yes, your majesty, it will, I hope; and yet they have dared do many things; but they, perhaps, will not be on the watch."

This, however, was soon settled; for as the queen was watching the motions of one of the privates, who was scouring round a certain part of the road, a white wreath of smoke came curling up, a flash, as of fire, and a stinging report came across at the same time; the man fell from his horse.

"Good Heavens!" exclaimed the Lady Inez; "your majesty, we are attacked by the robbers. Heaven preserve your majesty!"

"It will not desert us in our need, I am sure," replied the queen.

An order was given by the officer commanding to drive on with the utmost speed, and a portion of the escort was ordered to ride with the carriage, while the others were ordered to make an attack upon the road in front where the fire had come from. This soon brought on a conflict, for the robbers were there posted, but being strongly secured by their position among the trees and brushwood, the queen's party were much amazed, and lost several men before they could come at them hand to hand. By this time the royal carriage arrived, and men were seen on each side of them; several shots were fired, and blows were exchanged, when a stentorian voice shouted out,—

"Hold, and surrender, while your lives are spared!"

The queen's escort yet resisted, and much blood was shed by them in their unavailing efforts to protect her, until, at length, they were either slain or taken prisoners.

There was a cessation of firing, and a parley appeared to be carried on among the robbers. At length, some came to the carriage, and said,—

"Now, ladies, we shall request you to alight."

"What do you want with us?" inquired the queen.

"What would you have?"

"Whatever we can get," was the surly reply of one of the men.

"Is it our lives or our money?"

"Your lives are worth but little to us; but if we could get anything for them we should take them."

"You want our money, then?"

"And your persons, ladies; so have the goodness to come down, or we must enter and carry you out in our arms, and that would be an easy task."

The queen, followed by the ladies, was then conducted among the trees, to a place that had the appearance of a wild and tangled thicket; but they found a hut-like built place, made of wicker-work, somewhat of the coarsest, and overrun by weeds and climbing plants, so that nothing but the closest scrutiny on all sides would enable any one to detect it.

There were some rude seats and chairs, and utensils of the rudest character that could be imagined. In going to the place, the queen saw several of her escort lying dead and bleeding on the earth.

"What do you desire of us?" inquired the queen. "You surely will not kill those who are now at your mercy?"

"Oh, no," replied the man, "we only kill those who resist."

"But have they no right to resist?"

"Yes; but, as in any other case, we are the strongest, and forest law is our law; we never yield where we can conquer. Sit down, and ask no more questions at present."

It will be remembered by the reader, that for many years the state of Spain was such that all the nobility, and even royalty itself had been often engaged in affairs of attack and defence with the robbers that infested the roads and forests of Spain—indeed, none dare travel without an armed escort.

What made these bands of marauders more desperate and dangerous was, the fact that the frequent political convulsions, which take place there, and bloodshed being nothing strange, the peasantry are inured to scenes, and once drawn from their legitimate way of life, they have a disrelish for industry ever after, and become one of the roving bands of "Free Companions," as they styled themselves; many of whom did not confine themselves merely to robbery, but detained their captives in prison until they could obtain ransom.

It is not many years since, in our own country, one of the royal family, a princess, was stopped and robbed on Hounslow Heath.

It is therefore scarce a matter of surprise that the Queen of Spain should be so detained by a lawless band of men, there being many such at that time nay, at this day, in Spain.

The queen saw no end to her danger, and that of her attendants, and she was much grieved at the bloodshed she had been the cause of, but she knew not what to do, or what to say.

The robbers were mostly engaged in securing the escort, and plundering the carriages and the bodies as well.

They now returned to the shelter, and having piled up what they obtained, the head of the gang turned to the queen, and said,—

"Will you give me your jewels and trinkets, or shall I take them?"

"I will give them to you, and that freely, if you will shed no more blood."

"Why, what can that be to you,—you are not hurt?"

"I am more hurt to see my people thus around me dying and wounded, than if I had myself been hurt."

"There are few who think as you do," replied the robber; "but that's not our business. What ransom can you procure?"

"Ransom!"

"Ay; money for letting you go. You will then re-gain your liberty."

"And my people, too?"

"Ay, if you will ransom them, they may go, too."

"If you knew how poor I am, though in the midst of riches, you would scarce require so much. You cannot either be aware of the jewels you have there."

"I see; but they are too large to be of any good."

"Indeed."

"Yes, they had need be a queen's to be genuine," said the robber.

"They are a queen's."

"Ah!—what?"

"They are a queen's."

"Are you a queen?"

"I am the Queen of Spain."

"You the Queen of Spain?"

"Yes; I come from Aranjues. Inquire of my people and they will tell you the same. I am incapable of a falsehood."

"If you are the Queen of Spain," said the robber, "you shall quit these woods free, and I will aid you to do so."

"Then you will do me an acceptable piece of service."

The robber immediately summoned together his band, and the prisoners were unbound, and the carriages turned towards Aranjues, whither she immediately proceeded.

It was impossible for her to go on to the chateau; some of her own people were dead, and some were wounded; others were much terrified at meeting with such a numerous and desperate body of men, who were capable of sustaining a regular engagement.

For their sake, as well as her own, the queen was glad to get back to the palace, where they could obtain every assistance which they so much needed.

The queen sighed bitterly as the party wound their way through the forest roads, to think that she had failed in her intentions, and from such a cause—the most lamentable of any.

Again the towers of Aranjues appeared in view, and when the gates opened to receive them, they breathed and believed themselves safe again; while their appearance excited the utmost consternation among those whom they had left behind them.

The gates were closed, and the queen alighted from the carriage, and once more sought the privacy of her own apartment, there to offer up a prayer for her own safety, and for the welfare of those who had unfortunately been sacrificed.

CHAPTER LV.

DON JOSE'S SPY.—THE DEATH.—THE PROCEEDINGS OF THE CONSPIRATORS IN MADRID.—THE IN-QUISITION.

LET not the reader imagine that so wily a man as Don Jose was without any knowledge of the state of affairs at Aranjues; on the contrary, he was tolerably well informed, for he had taken the precaution to leave behind him one on whom he could rely, because it was his interest to be faithful, and with whom he had left strict injunctions to inform him of any attempt the queen might make to quit the palace of Aranjues, or to hold any correspondence with any one in Madrid. Indeed, a man like Don Jose was not likely to be without those instruments of power so noxious to mankind in general, but so common to great men, namely, spies. No person in whom he ever took interest, from whatever cause it might spring, was he ignorant of his movements, and everything connected with him that was supposed to be secret was known to Don Jose.

The spy system was carried on very extensively by Don Jose. He, indeed, would have been sacrificed long ere this, and it was by these means he had successfully combated his enemies, and discovered more than one plot against the life of the king, and by this means he was frequently enabled to injure an opponent who was too powerful to combat fairly. These things had given him much of the ascendancy he now possessed, and helped him to keep the elevated position he had attained.

The worthy left by Don Jose in the palace of Aranjues was much puzzled at the queen's conduct. He could not tell whether she would go or not, and when the old steward came among the attendants in the hall, they all asked him what was the determination of the queen.

"She will not go," replied the old man. "Heaven be praised, she will not go; I have persuaded her off that."

"You are certain, then, she will not go?" inquired the spy.

"I am."

"Thank Heaven! It is a desperate place to go to, and among such men."

It was with grief and surprise that the old man heard that the queen had altered her mind, and had determined upon going to the chateau of Don Jose; and the spy would instantly have set out on his journey to Don Jose, but that he feared that the queen might again change her mind, and then he would carry false intelligence, and he was pretty sure that the reward in such a case was likely to be anything but pleasant.

"Has the queen gone?" he inquired of the old man.

"Yes, the gates are now closing upon her," he replied, shaking his head.

The worthy instantly proceeded to the stables and obtained a horse, and mounting it, set out for the chateau. To do this he had to overtake the queen's party, and get there before she could. He rode hard, and taking a circuitous route, he arrived at the chateau before, as he believed, the queen could. In this conjecture he was quite right, but he knew not the accident that had been the cause of her detention.

"Now," thought the worthy, "how am I to get in? They don't know me here, and I have the queen's livery on; that will be quite enough to prevent my seeing Jose, or perhaps from being admitted."

He stood a moment in doubt how to act, whether to summons the people to the entrance, or to effect an entrance himself.

"I know how, and will get in. Once in, they will not oppose my seeing Jose; besides, the gardens are open to the house, and he will see me."

With this determination he was moved to seek for a proper spot where he could effect his purpose, and having found it, he mounted on the wall that surrounded the dwelling by means of climbing the tall chesnut trees that surrounded the walls, and having got up one of these, he gently glided on the top of the wall.

Here he stopped, considering where he should effect his descent, and he perceived at some distance from the spot he stood on, a small building that would assist him in his descent, and towards it he cautiously crept on the wall.

Don Jose had given strict orders to shoot anybody that attempted to enter the chateau by any illegitimate means. Knowing, too, that there had been an attempt, the men considered that there was something serious in the order, and were, consequently, on the alert.

It so happened, that the unfortunate spy had chosen the only dangerous way to get in, in his anxiety to be clever, and, while creeping upon the wall, he was espied by one of the servants.

The news was immediately spread among one or two, and several guns were coolly levelled at him, and fired.

A shriek and a bound in the air was all that was heard save the heavy dull sound of the body, as it fell to the earth among the leaves on the other side of the wall.

*   *   *   *   *

In no part of Europe, Italy scarce excepted, were the terrors of the Inquisition more dreaded than in Spain. The natural cruelty and blood-thirstiness of the Spaniards, as well as their proneness to superstition, was well typified by this institution, and in none were more horrors and injustice committed and perpetrated.

The Inquisition was an immense pile of irregular buildings; in one part were cells, and in another, places fitted up for the reception of the officials, and another for the performance of the necessary proceedings connected with the institution.

The room in which the Grand Inquisition sat was a large room, exceedingly gloomy, well hung with black, and these long black curtains divided the room into several compartments. One end of the room was fitted up with a high chair, with lower seats on either side, and a low table, with seats arranged before it, and round the sides.

The high chair was occupied by the grand inquisitor, in his long black robes, and his square-topped hat. The lower seats near his own were occupied by other inquisitors less in rank than himself, and the table by familiars, who acted as scribes and clerks to the inquisitor, and his companions in office.

On either side of the inquisitor were two large wax candles, and several others at the table where the scribes were seated. Beyond this was a large space hung around with black cloth, giving it a terrific and fearful appearance, sufficient to strike terror to the stoutest heart.

They were evidently awaiting the coming of some more who were to be tried, and who were placed in peril.

"These men," whispered one of the inquisitors to the chief, "have already suffered much I believe?"

"They have."

"When will their sufferings terminate?"

"In a day or two."

"One way or the other."

"Yes."

"Will they be permitted to go at liberty again?" inquired the same individual.

"No."

"I think it wise."

"It is. They are no longer useful, and therefore noxious. They may fall into the hands of enemies to the cause, and be terrified into disclosures inimical to us and our hopes."

"Have you any idea of the cause of the interruption you experienced?"

"Don Jose."

"Are you sure?"

"Yes."

There was a pause of a few moments' duration, when the chief inquisitor said,—

"You see, brother, the secrets of the confessional aid us in supporting the good cause, and, but for that, destruction would often be our fate. It is through that we hold men in such subjection, and can rise upon the wrecks of the baser kind, who want the sense and courage to act for themselves. Bah! they don't deserve pity."

"True, and but for the terrors of the holy Inquisition men would scarce be under any control."

"Exactly. To control the mass of mankind you must resort to the strong arm: reason is not intended for them, only for the few, and they are very few who have a tolerable share of it."

"It is true; it is too precious a gift to be thrown away."

While this conversation was going on the sounds of some one approaching put a stop to it, and then four men entered the room, having with them two wretched looking, emaciated beings.

They were placed on a kind of rude litter, and then the two men to each stood further back than when they first deposited their burthens.

There was a long pause, as though the inquisitors were desirous that the wretched men before them should recover the use of their faculties before they asked them any questions.

The chief inquisitor was so shrouded by the drapery and his dress, that he could not be seen sufficiently plain to be recognised again. This individual was no other than the Cardinal de Vinci, the chief conspirator, who had been missed in the late attack upon them; neither the bullets of the guards nor their bayonets were doomed to be his destruction.

Knowing the intricacies of the old palace so well, he had made use of the knowledge he possessed to elude the pursuit, and, as the conspiracy was evidently blown, there was but one other that he cared about saving.

These two quitted the place together, leaving the remainder to make the best of the affair they could; sink or swim—escape, or fall into the hands of the enemy. In himself, he well knew his ecclesiastical character and rank would protect him from all the assaults of justice.

It was some of his late associates that he was now about to try, and condemn to a cruel death. Do what they might, they could not escape the cruel policy pursued by the cardinal and his party, causing them to be perfectly indifferent to the sufferings they caused.

The pause now ended, and the cardinal, the chief inquisitor, turned to one of the prisoners, saying,—

"What is your name?"

"Martinez del Roto."

"What rank?"

"Grandee Count of Roto."

"And your's?" turning to the other prisoner.

"Velasco Volez."

"What rank?"

"Count of St. Domaieto."

"You are accused of being engaged in a conspiracy against the king."

No answer.

"Are you guilty?"

Still no answer.

"If you don't answer the interrogations that we put to you, measures will be adopted that you can scarce conceive, and under which you will sink."

"To what end do we answer such questions as those you ask us?"

"To the end that you speak the truth, and conceal nothing from the holy Inquisition."

"Nothing is concealed."

"Were you not leagued with many more individuals against the state?"

"I was."

"Where are they?"

"Many of them are dead. Of the others, I know nothing. Some escaped, some were killed, and some taken prisoners. I was one of the latter."

"Do you repent?"

"Could I suffer all I have suffered, and not repent?"

"It is for the wicked to suffer; but who were your companions?"

The respondent remained silent, and the question was repeated, and still receiving no answer, the same question was put to the other, who said,—

"I have no wish to live, and yet I do not wish to die with a broken vow upon my conscience."

"You are to hold more sacred some such as the church recognizes."

"And yet ——"

"Peace! hear what I say. You are compelled by the church to confess all to your spiritual teachers. Reservations are not allowed in any case."

"But an oath ——"

"Cannot be held against the church, which has the power to bind and to loose. The church dissolves such bonds."

"Can the church ——"

"Hold! how can such impious thoughts cross your mind at such a moment as this, when you know not but that you are to appear shortly before your Maker."

"Holy father, I have no doubt about the power of the church; but my oath was so terrible, that I ——"

"Feared to divulge it?"

"Yes."

"Then I dissolve such bonds of secrecy as being contrary to the holy church, and the tenets of the Christian religion."

"Indeed."

"Aye, and had you so died, you would have been an outcast in the world to come."

"And yet I fear. To divulge is so treacherous and so bad."

"Then prepare to endure torments that you have no conception of. Your contumacy shall be punished."

Then, turning to the other prisoner, he said,—

"Are you prepared to endure the torments about to be inflicted upon your companion; the rack has no tender mercies; but every limb will be dislocated, and your sinews strained till they crack and swell, till you have not strength to sue for mercy, or shriek for water."

The unfortunate man was visibly affected, and shook in every limb, and could not answer for terror.

"If they refuse they will be executed, and die a painful death."

The other inquisitor nodded.

"And then, if they confess, they are disposed of as enemies to the holy Inquisition."

"I see there is only a choice of deaths, without the knowledge beforehand of which they can choose."

"Precisely."

"Now, prisoners," exclaimed the inquisitor, "have you made up your minds as to what you will endure?"

There was no answer.

A sign now from the chief inquisitor caused one of the familiars to ring a small bell, and immediately one of the large black curtains was thrown on one side, and two men were seen standing beside a small moveable furnace, and there were several fearful looking instruments beside them.

They stood motionless, their arms bared to the shoulder, while their grim and ferocious countenances bespoke almost a pleasure in the occupation they were employed in.

Another motion brought them forward, and at a word the red-hot pincers were taken from the fire, and seizing the wrist of each of the prisoners, they stood as though they expected the signal from the grand inquisitor.

"Prisoners, once more the question will be put to you. Do you still continue in your contumacy? Will you, or will you not, give up the names of your companions in the conspiracy?"

"Is there no medium course that can be adopted?"

"None."

"Cannot we write the names down upon paper?"

"You can."

"Then I will do so."

"And I."

"Give them both writing materials," said the inquisitor.

These were at once placed in their hands, and that being done, the inquisitor turned to the two familiars, saying,—

"You may retire for the present."

The unfortunate men looked at these fellows as they carried their fearful apparatus away, and shuddered to think of the cruelty that they had so narrowly escaped, and happy that for a time such agonies were not in store for them.

The lists took some time to write, and during this the inquisitors commenced a conversation among themselves.

"What do you think," inquired one, "will be the end of this affair?"

"The death of these men," said De Vinci.

"I mean of the attempt to turn the king from his course, and ministers."

"This will end in the destruction of those who attempted it; while, at the same time, something more will rise from its ashes."

"And crush Don Jose."

"Aye, his time is not yet come, but come it must. Never did minister in Spain hold his way against the church successfully to the last."

"Nor serve such a master as Philip, year after year, with the same success that he has done; but the largest rivers have the greatest number of windings, but it does not prevent their waters being discharged into the ocean."

"And into the ocean shall Jose be plunged at last—I am sure of it, or there is no faith in Madrid."

"The king, too, will grow tired of the life of pleasure, or rather debauchery, he leads, and then he would naturally throw Jose off."

"Exactly. And there is a new change like to take place. His holiness the pope has sent a remonstrance to the king, and though he would like to treat it with contempt, and pay no attention to it, yet, thanks to the influence of the church and the people, he will not be able to struggle successfully against the clergy."

"It never has been successfully accomplished in a Catholic country—the clergy must be triumphant."

The lists were now done, and the chief inquisitor said—

"Are these lists quite complete?"

"They are."

"Are no names omitted."

"None that we believe."

"You must be certain—the church cannot be temporised with in this matter."

"On our faith, as members of the church, the lists are correct—as correct as our memories will enable us to make them."

Di Vinci took the lists, and carefully perused them, and he knew they were correct. His own name was amongst them; he smiled, for well he knew that he could not suffer, and the document would be suppressed. In fact, the whole of the inquisitorial body were at the bottom of the conspiracy, but, of course, the lay criminals only were the sufferers, it would be against the common order of things for a cardinal to suffer—in Spain, too, of all countries.

"You may now retire," said De Vinci to the unfortunate criminals.

"May we hope for mercy?"

"You may."

"May we expect ——"

"Yes, whatever you please," said the cardinal, with a motion of the hand. "The Holy Inquisition cannot commit injustice."

"Heaven be thanked," said one of them, "and bless you for this mercy."

"Holy father, your goodness is such that it emboldens me to ask when we may once more see our families?"

"It cannot be immediately. We will consider of it."

With this evasive answer to the two unfortunate men, who were already in great danger of dissolution by the course of nature, he hurried off. They yet clung to life, and would have, perhaps, been restored to health had they then been delivered to their friends; but De Vinci had other intentions.

"You will, doubtless, not allow these men to escape."

"No, no; it would not be prudent, for two reasons."

"Name them."

"The first is, that the punishment would not be deemed sufficient by the authorities, and then a civil process would be gone through."

"But they could not do that after being discharged by the ecclesiastical authorities."

"They could not, but they would no doubt attempt it, and that would cause a strife upon a point we wish to avoid at this moment."

"Exactly."

"And then it would involve a more important matter; by letting them go, we may be starting up and preserving testimony against ourselves, either to be used at the present moment or at a future opportunity."

"I see."

"Therefore it is better these men should die, and trouble us no more."

"That is true."

"Our policy is this, and it is a good and correct one—that whoever is not for us is against us."

"Excellent."

"And again, one that has been useful in important and secret matters, will, in time, make use of his knowledge either against us, and become a dangerous enemy, or he may become too importunate a servant, and therefore he is to be got rid of, and rendered harmless on the first opportunity."

"Exactly. You speak of laymen?"

"I do; all ecclesiastics are under the dominion of the church, and are servants of the church, and would be punished to the last extremity, were they disobedient or refractory; but there is no fear of that."

The mustering then broke up, and the chief inquisitor gave some whispered instructions to the officials, and then disappeared.

The two unfortunate prisoners who had been induced, in the hope of mercy, and to escape the horrid cruelties that were about to be practised upon them, to make a confession of the name of their accomplices, were hurried back to their prison.

Before, however, they were taken to their cells, they were taken to a long room that had several windows in it, and some strange looking apparatus.

Here they were deposited for a time, while their conductors were busy in arranging some machinery in proper order.

To their horror they found that it was an execution apparatus; for strange as it may appear, they were ordered out to instant death. There was no use in remonstrating, or begging for mercy—all their prayers and entreaties were alike disregarded by these stern men, who did not even reply to them, but placed them in the chair, and life was soon extinct; for the method of strangulation they adopt is always certain and instantaneous in its effect.

Their bodies were thrown on one side till a convenient opportunity occurred to bury them, and then the transaction was forgotten, as if it was of no moment, or had never happened.

CHAPTER LVI.

THE RETURN TO ARANJUES. — THE OUTLAW'S MISFORTUNES.—THE PROMISED PARDON.

DURING their progress through the wood of Menajorees, there was a general and perfect silence reigned throughout the queen's retinue, or such of them as remained. They were yet in the domains of the robbers, and were still in their power, though they were promised safe conduct by them, and even one of the number rode with them, followed by others at a little distance, to protect them, and ensure them from further violence.

The queen leaned back in her carriage, and appeared lost in thought. She was very pale, and occasionally a slight shudder ran through her frame, and sadness sat upon her soul, for several of her people lay weltering in their blood.

The good queen could not avoid deploring the terrible results of evil passions, and the violence to which men would hurry when they had any object to pursue or obtain. To despoil herself and those about her, these men had been guilty of murder, nay, of treason, and lifting their hands against their sovereign—wickedness appeared to be a part of human nature almost inseparable.

The results of her attempt to reach the chateau alone were sufficient to pain her; she grieved for the loss of several faithful servants—they had ever shown the most marked willingness to die for her, but that made her grieve the more; she had not too many friends, that she could afford to lose them thus, and it cast a deep gloom over her countenance.

Moreover, she had not to mourn the disaster alone, that was not enough of itself; but there was the probable results of her inability to reach the chateau to be considered. The consequences she had striven to avert, which she had encountered and risked so much danger to prevent, would now be consummated.

These considerations caused her much uneasiness, and a deep sigh now and then arose, plainly telling her attendants the nature of her reflections. To see their good and amiable queen melancholy and tristful, was cause sufficient to make them alike melancholy; if she suffered, they suffered too, for their sympathy was deep and sincere, without ostentation.

The scenery around them was of the same grand and wild character they had so much admired while journeying through it previous to their present disaster; but with what different feelings did they contemplate it.

The inartificial and tangled thickets gave it a look of terror, while the gigantic trees towering above the rest, looking almost sublime, added a deeper gloom to the scene, and caused the gazer to have greater fears of personal safety, and wish himself well out of the place, and in the well-cultivated parts and the plain open road again.

Disturbances such as they had met with greatly disturb the imagination, and what the mind was willing to admire as the most beautiful and sublime thing in creation before, has a very different appearance, and produces very different emotions on the mind, after such an occurrence. Sublimity becomes fearful, and the beautiful becomes suspicious and gloomy, and it loses all those many little adventitious aids it received from the peculiar state of the mind, when it first becomes acquainted with things in which it is disposed to regard them satisfactorily.

The retinue by no means gloried in the wild appearance of the place; they looked, and looked again, but hey were not satisfied—for they anticipated a new gang of freebooters to spring up from behind every thicket, and make a new attack upon them.

"Inez," said the queen, breaking out of her fit of silence,—"Inez."

"Yes, my gracious lady; what would you desire of me—what can I do to render this terrible scene less dreadful to your majesty?"

"Nothing, Inez, nothing. I regret what has happened, because it has caused so much misery and desolation."

"Who would regret sufferings and death for your majesty's sake?"

"I know the devotion of those few by whom I am surrounded, but it is that that makes me the more grieved for the dreadful scene we have gone through."

"It was a dreadful scene, your majesty," replied Inez, "and the more so, from the extreme danger your majesty ran on the occasion."

"My danger was not greater than that of others; and, perhaps, had a stray bullet pierced my heart, my troubles had been over, and the dangers that I have so repeatedly caused others would be at an end."

"Do not talk thus, I implore your majesty," said Inez. "No more has been done or suffered than duty dictates; and though it was sad and dreadful in its results, who could have anticipated such a dreadful encounter?—not your majesty, I am sure."

"Indeed I did not."

At this moment they were interrupted by an altercation between some of the escort and the robbers

"You shall come no nearer," exclaimed one of the men.

"Do not disturb yourself, my good fellow," said the robber; "I merely wish to ride up to the carriage."

"But you must not."

"If I chose to say I would, you could not hinder me."

"We will see that."

"Do not tempt your fate. But for the lady's sake, you should be a dead man before you could have time to beg for mercy, I promise you."

"What is the matter?" inquired the queen of one of her attendants, who was riding by the carriage.

"That fellow wants to ride alongside the carriage."

"Let him do so."

"Yes, your majesty," said the man, much astonished; and then, turning back again, he said, respectfully,—

"Will your majesty trust him?"

"Yes, we must."

"We will all die around your majesty before he should do it."

"No, no; I command you to allow him to come here. I will have no more contention with these people at all—it can answer no purpose whatever. Go and tell him to come hither."

With this positive order the man instantly rode up to the robber, saying,—

"You are to come to her majesty, and see that you conduct yourself something decently; for, though you may be the strongest, yet it will not save your life, if you are any way uncivil."

"My good fellow, do not work yourself into a fury, or I shall be obliged to hang you to yonder tree, as an example. I have done so before now, and I am persuaded that you cannot do better than be civil to your superiors."

The man made no reply, for he knew it would be useless to remonstrate; and, besides that, there was something of superiority in the manner and words of the robber that betrayed him into involuntary respect, and he made way for him.

Riding up to the carriage window, he bowed civilly, and then said,—

"My journey will soon terminate, your majesty, and I am desirous to hear if you have any wish to express that we can execute for you."

"I fear that my wishes or prayers would have very little effect."

"I must first know, please your majesty, and then I can tell you truly whether they be such that they can be performed."

"I would that yonder misguided men would turn from their dreadful course of life, and pursue some honest livelihood."

"Ah! your majesty," said the robber, "yonder men have sinned too deeply against the law ever to hope for such a consummation; indeed, many of them would not do so, being disbanded soldiers—men who have never been used to a regular course of life—and some who have suffered unmerited misfortunes, and great injustice; and, disgusted with society, they have chosen the only means of existence consonant with their tastes and wishes."

The queen remained thoughtful for a few moments, and then said,—

"I can make much allowance for such men; but you are aware that such a course is not justifiable, either before Heaven or earth. You have no right to inflict evil upon others, because you have been badly treated by some one else."

"The logic of what your majesty says I am ready to admit; but when feeling and necessity are often so strong and significant, logic has but a poor chance; on the contrary, men's passions are easily enlisted, and they soon learn to make reprisals, and enjoy the fruit of their revenge upon mankind generally."

"You ought to know the fallacy of such arguments; you have held a better position in society than that in which you now appear."

The robber was silent, but bowed.

"Tell me," continued the queen, "have you not held a different rank?"

"I have, your majesty."

"And may I not hope to do one good act, by recalling you from the state I see you in, and so unfitted for your ——"

"Your majesty is right; I once held a rank that was somewhat different to that I now appear in; but unmerited misfortune has been the cause of imbruing my hands in blood."

"I am sorry to hear you say so," replied the queen; "but there is hope yet; I would do all I could to aid you in so laudable a design as a return to society."

"I fear that cannot be done; I was once a captain of cavalry, and did some service in the war that was then raging; and, when the peace came about, I became acquainted with a beautiful and accomplished lady, the daughter of my superior officer. We loved, and, after some opposition to our marriage, we were united. I was then happy, and wished for a change in life; but a change came, and one I could not have anticipated."

Here the robber appeared deeply affected, and paused for a moment or two; but then he resumed,—

"My wife was false; she had been basely seduced by one of the most powerful noblemen in the kingdom of Spain. I discovered all, and instantly challenged my enemy; but he feared to fight me, and exerted his power to get me thrown into prison, upon a charge of treason.

"I was innocent, and contrived to escape, after I had been there some months. I swore I would be revenged, and I took the first opportunity of putting my vows in force.

"I met him, and he endeavoured to avoid me; but I would not let him. He attempted to call for aid, but I swore I would kill him if he did. He might fight and slay me, but he should fight, and if not, I would kill him outright. He trembled, the coward, and did endeavour to fight, but his coward heart caused him to become paralysed, and he fell.

"Of course, I was hunted from place to place, and called a murderer. A price was put on my head, my prospects and character ruined, and a criminal. What was I to do, but seek the woods again? There were some bands of desperate adventurers who did not scruple to seize upon other people's to supply their own wants. I joined them, and was gladly received; for my military knowledge was looked upon by them as the rarest qualification I could possess, and thus I have been since."

"Will you not give up this kind of life, and endeavour to become again what you once were?" inquired the queen.

"I would gladly; but society has lost all charms for me, my happiness is wrecked, and I have no hope —no wish."

"You should have my best wishes—I would endeavour to protect you, obtain your pardon, and restore you to society."

"Gracious lady, I know not how to thank you; but I could scarce accept it. It would but drive me back again, as it would be so well known."

"It would not. No soul need know it, save the king; and you should either be in some employment near my person, or have a commission in some of the regiments on foreign service or stations."

"That, indeed, would be a thing I could accept. Your majesty has offered more kindly to me than ever I believed human being capable of doing."

"Will you accept my offer," inquired the queen, "and give me your word that you will for ever abandon the life you now lead with these men?"

"I solemnly pledge myself to do so. Your majesty shall never have cause to say you regretted the act of kindness and benevolence you have done."

"You will then dismiss these men, and ride with my attendants?"

"I cannot do that, your majesty."

"Why not?"

"Because I should be pursued by them, and most probably fall a prey to them, as well as those with your majesty. The best way will be this,—I will return with them, and take the first opportunity of escaping from them; and, with your majesty's permission, I will seek safety in the palace of Aranjues."

"Do so, and, depend upon it, you shall find it to your advantage."

"Will your majesty pardon me the crime I have been guilty of in taking part with these men against your suite?"

"You have it."

"Farewell, gracious lady, and be assured I cannot forget your kindness, or be ungrateful."

The queen bowed to the robber, who reined in his steed, and allowed the whole party to go by, and then lowly returned towards his companions.

The queen was visibly affected by the tale of the outlaw, and that, with her terror and anxiety, occasioned by the recent events, she appeared to be very ill, and when she arrived at Aranjues she was scarce able to rise, and required aid to descend from the carriage, and ascend the steps, and reach her chamber, which she had scarce done when, unable to hold out any longer, she fainted away in the arms of her attendants.

CHAPTER LVII.

CÆSAR'S MIRACULOUS ESCAPE.—THE LEAP AND ITS RESULTS.—DON JOSE'S FEELINGS OF SATISFACTION, AND ORDERS TO HIS DEPENDANTS.

OF course, we much regretted that the imperious nature of all the various incidents we are compelled to get together during the progress of our narrative, compelled us to leave our friend Don Cæsar in so very critical a situation.

We are now, however, enabled to resume a consideration of his peculiar position, and to relate what occurred immediately upon the clearing away of the smoke arising from the discharge of the half-dozen arquebuses.

When the smoke did clear away, and that was quickly, for there was a light puffing wind setting in in the direction from where the servants of Don Jose stood, towards where Cæsar was standing, he had entirely disappeared.

In consequence of the wind being in the direction it was, the eyes of those who fired the arquebuses, as well as of Don Jose, were completely shrouded by the dense column of blue vapour, which receded from them, until it got clear of the terrace, over the parapet of which it scattered itself, and then, but not till then, was Jose enabled to say, as he drew a long breath of exquisite relief,—

"He is gone!"

Those who had fired the arquebuses lowered their weapons, and gazed inquiringly at the spot which but a moment before had been traversed by Don Cæsar, and then they looked at each other, as if they would have said,

"What, on earth, has become of him?"

"Oh, we have blown him over the parapet," said one.

"Of course," added another, and that became the generally received opinion on the subject.

As for Don Jose, he was inclined to think with them that Cæsar had certainly gone over the parapet; but as to being blown over, that was quite another thing. His own impression was, that Don Cæsar, with the suddenness of the surprise, must have jumped over, and fallen dead, of course, below.

How near Jose was to the truth in all but the most essential particular, we shall presently see.

The servants who had thus executed the orders of their imperious master, now looked to him for further instructions how to act; and he, recovering from the first rush of feelings that came over him of a congratulatory nature, of having got rid of Don Cæsar at last, after he had been so very troublesome to him for so long, said aloud,—

"You have done well. He must be dead; I will go and see."

He marched a pace or two towards the spot were it might be supposed the dead body of Don Cæsar was lying. A fiendish satisfaction sat upon his countenance, and he was exulting in the prospect of looking on the remains of his enemy, when a servant emerged from the house, and, addressing Jose, said, hurriedly,—

"May it please your excellency, your excellency's friend is impatient to see you, and know the cause of the firing."

Jose paused. He well knew that the report of the arquebuses must have reached the ears of Philip, and no doubt filled him with the liveliest alarm. He dared not dispute the mandate; so, although it was with reluctance he gave up the idea of visiting the dead body of Don Cæsar, he turned towards the servant, and said,—

"Say I shall be with my friend directly."

This delusion of not pronouncing the king's name in the chateau deceived no one, but Don Jose kept it up notwithstanding, so that Philip, who was known very well, was called the "friend" instead of the king, when spoken of to Jose.

Although now a more urgent duty called him away, and he could not go himself to gloat over the cold-blooded murder he believed he had committed, he felt the full necessity of taking some steps immediately to dispose of the remains of Don Cæsar, and with that intent, turning to his followers, he said, in a lower voice,—

"Find out where he lies, and, if it be a very quiet spot, let him still lie in it, and tell me of it; if he be at all in the way, drag him among the underwood and there leave him, until I shall decide upon what shall be done with him."

The servants received these orders respectfully, and, as Don Jose turned into the chateau to seek the king, they, with not the most willing steps in the world, marched in the direction of the spot immediately underneath the parapet of the terrace, where they made up their mind (and that was why they trembled) that a sanguinary sight would present itself to their gaze.

"Do you like this job?" said one to his next comrade, in a whisper.

"I neither like nor dislike it," was the reply.

"Well, I don't like it at all."

"Oh, you are too tender-hearted, you are, ever to get on."

"There you are wrong. It isn't from tender-heartedness that I don't like it, I can tell you."

"Why then?"

"Because it's a decided extra, and we ought to be better paid for such things, we ought."

"Well, there is something in that."

"Hark!" said another, suddenly. "Hark, comrades, did ye not hear a groan? Mind ye, I don't mind firing an arquebus at a fellow, but it does make me uncomfortable to hear him groaning about it afterwards. That's the way I view it."

"You are a coward."

"Am I—am I? Don Jose would hardly have had me here, if he did not know that I was bravery itself. By-the-by, now, I tell you what strikes me most amazingly forcibly."

"What, what?"

"Why, that we ought not all of us to have left the chateau, for fear Don Jose should want anything, for you know that there is no one there to attend to him but that stupid Sebastian."

"Come, come. You are afraid to face the body. Say so, and you shall go, but if you will not own that truth, you shall come along with us. Will you, or will you not?"

"I afraid—I afraid to face a dead body! Come now, that's too bad—a vast deal too bad."

"You won't confess it?"

"Oh, if you wish it—if it will give you any satisfaction to hear me confess it, I don't mind doing so, you may depend. I am too good-tempered by a vast deal, that's the fact, and just to please you all, I will confess it, and we will imagine I have said I don't like to face a dead body, gentlemen and old Spaniards, if you please."

So saying, the coward, who thought nothing of firing a loaded arquebus at an innocent man—one whom he had no quarrel with, and who, for all he knew, might be really the least deserving of such a fate of any human being, walked hastily off in the direction of the chateau, leaving his comrades to look for the dead body, and to make what they could of the dreadful spectacle when they should come to it.

The distance was not great, although from the disposition of the paths, and the jutting out of a large corner of the terrace, it was much greater than as if they could have proceeded in a direct line towards it. However, they reached it or fancied they had reached it in a very few moments, and paused at which they could have sworn was the identical spot upon what the murdered man must indubitably have fallen.

A feeling then of intense surprise crept over them, not unmingled with some superstitious fears; for, not only was there no dead body there at all, but there was not the least appearance or trace of any one ever having been there. No blood—no impression among the plants, as of a heavy substance; no disorder—no appearance whatever of any kind or shape of any such catastrophe having occurred, as that which they were each individually prepared, if it were necessary, to make oath that they were the authors of.

There was a deathlike stillness among them for some moments, and then one, in bold accents, at all events, even if they were assumed, said,—

"Oh, we cannot have got to the place yet."

"Or we have passed it," said another.

A third shook his head very gravely, as he said,—

"Look up, and you will see the corner of the terrace, which we know is close by the stairs."

All looked up, but still, familiar as the place was to them, some were still sceptical, and would rather believe that they had mistaken the shape, position, and general bearing of the terrace, than that anything so much more extraordinary as the disappearance of a dead man, almost before their very eyes, should happen, for that transcended all belief.

"Convince yourselves," said he who had been so positive regarding the precise locality; "convince yourselves, if you have any doubts, by one of you going at once to the very spot where we saw the man. Who will go, and settle the question by holding his hand above the parapet?"

No one seemed exactly to relish the undertaking—perhaps from a dread of quitting the main body—so he who had made the suggestion had no resource but to abandon it or go himself; and, as every one has an attachment to his own suggestion, he chose the latter alternative, and at once started off, saying,—

"I'll go—I'll go. Keep a sharp look out, comrades, and you will see my hand held up at the very spot where he stood when Don Jose gave the word to fire, and we pulled the triggers of the arquebuses."

All eyes were turned upwards in the direction where the expected hand was to be, and as the man ran fast, they felt certain he would not be very long in getting round.

"There he is," cried one. "There—there."

And there he was, sure enough, just above them, holding up his hand; but, not content with that, he, to the wonder and surprise of his friends below, suddenly shot over, head foremost, and fell in the midst of them, with such a hard, sudden, and sickening dab, that it was quite clear that he would never again be among the living.

He fell exactly on his head, and although the ground was not hard enough to fracture his skull, yet it sufficed amazingly well to break his neck, which was accomplished, and after one convulsive movement of the arms, he was a corpse.

Terrified and paralyzed by the unexpected event, the men stood like statues for the space of about half a minute, and then, as if suddenly acted upon by some mental machinery which affected all alike, they turned round, and made off in the direction of the chateau, leaving their dead comrade behind them, and resolved to endanger themselves no longer by looking after the dead body they had gone to seek, since they had in so abrupt and startling a manner been introduced to one they did not at all expect to see.

The door from which they had issued, when ordered on the murderous errand with the arquebuses by Don Jose, was that for which they now strove, and consequently there was an opportunity of taking a glance towards the terrace again from that same point of view.

Had not the last man among them been so impressed with the danger of occupying that position as to be continually looking behind him, they would probably not have had a further trial of the nerves which awaited them, and their terror would have been confined to its first effect; but, as it was, he made a discovery which not only paralysed himself with abject terror, but enabled him to add wings to the flight of his comrades.

Standing on the upper flight of steps leading to the higher portion of the terrace—in precisely the same spot, in precisely the same attitude as when they had fired half-a-dozen arquebuses at him, and looking as

unconcerned as anybody possibly could,—was Don Cæsar de Bazan.

"Look! look! Oh, look!" cried the man. "There he is! A ghost! a ghost!"

"Where? where?"

"There—on the terrace! There he is—the ghost!"

"A ghost!" was now the universal shout, and tumbling over each other in the wildest state of confusion, the whole party made their way into the cha-

teau, lost to all sense of caution, and shouting as they went,—

"A ghost! a ghost! The ghost of the dead man on the terrace! Murder! murder! A ghost! a ghost!"

The reader may well imagine with what an air Don Jose sprang from his seat, when such a tumult of sounds met his ears, as he was explaining to the king how he had so snugly disposed of Don Cæsar in the chateau, and how utterly impossible it now was for him ever again to trouble with his evil presence the ruffled majesty of Spain.

There was quite a look of pleasure upon Jose's countenance as he announced so agreeable a fact to Philip, who was in such a state of nervousness from the shock he got at the sudden discharge of the arquebuses, that he trembled in every limb, and glared at Don Jose with a wild sort of bewildered look, as if he scarcely understood the words he uttered.

"Never more, your majesty—never more," he said, "will this turbulent Don Cæsar be the least trouble to you. He is gone, and with him a terrible load of

anxiety off my mind. I do believe he was one who would not have scrupled to lift his hand even against the majesty of Spain itself."

"Think you so, Jose? Would he have dared to interfere personally with us, think you?'"

"I have no doubt he would—I have no manner of doubt upon the subject; therefore, that he is disposed of, is to myself, as it would be to every faithful servant of your majesty, a matter of great satisfaction."

"Satisfaction indeed! Well, it may be. Then the noise which—which certainly a little surprised us, was occasioned by the discharge of firearms?"

"It was, your majesty. Don Cæsar had actually the dreadful and unprecedented audacity to come here. But now his lifeless body lies in the garden."

"Have it removed—have it removed, Jose. I like not such sights. Have it removed, I say, Jose. Deaths may be highly necessary and politic, but still we should endeavour, as shortly afterwards as possible, to get rid of the effects and appearances. So, Jose, lest the corpse should come in my way, you will see that it be carefully removed, as well as all traces of its repugnant presence."

"Your majesty's orders shall always be attended to. I have already given directions that the dead body should not be allowed to meet the sight of any but those who necessarily were engaged in the execution."

"'Tis well—'tis well. The countess is now, then, fairly mine, without hindrance from any one. I do not, by the remarks I make, impute any blame to you, Jose; for I believe you have striven hard, and done your best; but, really, so troublesome an intrigue as this I never entered into or heard of. It is perfectly fearful, and could I have anticipated one half the danger, trouble, and inconvenience which has arisen through it, I should have hesitated to engage in it, notwithstanding all the beauty of the Countess de Bazan."

"Be of better cheer, sire. Cæsar is no more, and

the greatest trouble of all is, consequently, past and over."

" I will think so now, Jose. I am quite willing to think so now, but my nerves are terribly shaken by what has occurred, and I feel but the shadow of myself."

" A cup of generous wine will restore you, sire."

" No—no. No wine. Have you heard any news from Aranjues lately, Jose?"

" None, my liege."

" The quiet and silence of my queen is ominous. Much I fear me that she is making insidious efforts to involve me still further with the church."

" Timely concessions will, from a powerful monarch, at any period conciliate the pontiff."

" Ay, but the sort of concessions demanded by the court of Rome are always of a fearfully expensive character. There is great talk made about religious penances and humiliations, and then tacked in, as if it were of no moment, is some subsidy of large amount, or the condition of ceding some province or rich principality. By Heavens, Jose, the church is of a grasping nature!"

" All churches ever have been, your majesty, and it is not a very hazardous prophecy to say that they ever will be."

" True—true—most true. Not a doubt of it. There is no such thriving trade in the whole world as superstition. Send some one to Aranjues, Jose, on whom you can rely, to ascertain among our queen's household the state of affairs there."

" It shall be done, your majesty."

" Let it be done quickly, too, Jose. I am anxious on the subject, and before another hour has elapsed, I think I will pay another visit to my fair prisoner here, who may, perhaps, be wearied of treating me with so much disdain. Should she, however, persevere beyond all reason in rejecting my suit, I will adopt your advice, Jose, and the same stupefying drug which brought her here quietly, shall overcome her senses."

" 'Tis a good plan, your majesty."

" And yet one to which, as you know, I am much averse. Do you think a declaration of who I really am would move her and dazzle her judgment?"

" I do not, my liege."

" Well, well. There might be danger in that. Let it be—let it be. Were she to know that it was the King of Spain who knelt to her as a suitor, and then by some means to effect her escape from here, there might be much scandal and many disagreeable consequences."

" Most assuredly, your majesty—most assuredly; and though the escape of any one from here is a matter of almost physical impossibility, yet it is well to guard against everything. I will now despatch some one at once to Aranjues."

" Do so—do so, and then come back to me."

Jose left the room, and, after a moment's thought, he said,—

" I may as well send the page, Lazarillo. He is of no service here, and may be an hindrance. Besides, he has no connexions there of any kind. Yes, he will do well enough. I will get rid of him, and by the time he comes back, I may, perhaps, not be here at all. Moreover, if he suspects or ascertains what has happened to Don Cæsar, he will endeavour to thwart me and my plans in some way. He will be well out of the house; but if I see about him the least symptom of disaffection, I will put it out of his power, very quickly, to be a trouble or a hindrance to anybody. I will take his life; but not yet—not yet. I may, perchance, attach him wholly to my interests, and, should I do so, such a lad might do me much good service."

Lazarillo was still posted at the corridor, where

Jose had placed him with his arquebus. The sudden discharge of musketry had startled him, as well as every one within the chateau, and although he was far, very far indeed, from guessing at whom the arquebuses had been fired, yet he felt very anxious to know.

He had, too, his own private reasons for feeling considerable anxiety upon the subject, and, when Don Jose came in sight of him, he was leaning over the corridor wall, endeavouring to catch some sounds which might give him information upon the matter.

He heard the tramp of feet, and the general noisy symptoms of a good deal of commotion in the chateau, and had not Jose suddenly touched him on the arm, probably he would have risked his displeasure by descending to see what really had happened below in the garden.

It was provoking that the window at which Lazarillo had been stationed did not command a view of that part of the garden where the scene, of which we have already given a description, occurred, so that he just had a knowledge that something was going on, without being in the least able to make out what it was.

He started when Don Jose touched his shoulder, and immediately placed himself in an attitude of defence.

" Humph! You should not allow disturbances below to attract your attention at all. I want you to go to Aranjues."

" To Aranjues, sir?"

" Yes. Why do you echo my words?"

Now, it was the very last thing the page wanted to do, to leave the chateau at such a juncture of affairs, and to be sent so unexpectedly and suddenly away, was provoking in the extreme. In a moment he made up his mind that he would not go if he could possibly help it, but how to avoid it was the trouble and the mystery. However, Lazarillo had an active imagination, and was seldom much behindhand in expedients. He made a bold effort to remain.

" My lord," he said, " I pray you, then, before I go, to place some one in whom you can repose implicit confidence at this window."

" Why so?"

" Because an attempt has been made to get into the chateau through it, within the last hour."

" Indeed! You did not tell me?"

" I feared to leave my post to tell you, and now I tell you as soon as I can utter the words."

" What style of person? By heavens, why did you not use your arquebus?"

" The attack was sudden, and I was drowsy, but I did use my arquebus."

" Aye?"

" Yes, my lord. I could not discharge it, but with the heavy but-end of the weapon I warned the intruder off. He fell somewhere ——"

" On to the terrace, which winds round here?"

" Probably, my lord. He had a shaven crown, and said something about the Pope, and the curses of the church, but that was nothing to me."

Jose strode to and fro, muttering to himself,—

" These confounded priests. They are making an attempt on the chateau. They must guess that the king is here. There is not one of the household who would resist them but this boy. Superstition has a strong hold on all but on him. So he struck one of the shaven crowned rascals down, did he? Ha, ha, ha! 'Twas well done. Very well done, Lazarillo. Ha, ha! You struck him down?"

" I did, sir."

" And you felt no compunction?"

" None in the least."

" Not one for his priestly appearance?"

" Oh, no."

"I am afraid, Lazarillo, that you are not very religious?"

Don Jose said this with a smile, which implied that he thought it a very good thing indeed.

"I am not very," said Lazarillo. "I lay claim, my lord, to a little conscience, which I think goes farther than a great quantity of religion."

"Very true. Lazarillo, I have altered my mind. You shall still continue to keep watch at this window, and some one else shall go to Aranjues; and mind me, boy, if any priest should make his appearance here, or any one in an ecclesiastical habit, be sure you fire your arquebus in his face."

"I will."

"It is for the good of the church I speak. There are many young priests who can get nothing to do, so I want to make a few vacancies among those who enjoy, and have enjoyed too long, the good things of this life."

Lazarillo signified his acquiescence, and scarcely able to conceal his joy at being permitted to remain at the chateau, he resumed his watch in the recess of the window.

Jose walked away, muttering to himself, as he went,—

"And, besides, if there should be a great disturbance about the resistance made by this boy to the agents of the church, I can throw it all on to his shoulders, and if needs be, sacrifice him completely to the resentment of the priesthood. By heavens, it is something, now-a-days, overridden as we are by these bloated ecclesiastics, to find anybody who will knock one of them on the head. I had not an idea that Lazarillo was half so valuable."

It was indeed something, at that time of day, to find some one who would, as Don Jose energetically remarked, knock a priest on the head, for superstition was the prevailing characteristic of the whole nation, as it always is of some barbarous nations, under which category Spain might very fairly then be classed.

Even assassins—men who for a few silver rials would take the life of any one, had, forsooth, their religion, and were ever ready, while their hands were reeking with the blood of some victim, to pay homage to some of the rudely sculptured images of the Virgin, which occupied niches in every public situation.

Religion then, like religion now, was supposed not to teach men to be virtuous, but to cover a multitude of sins, only then it was coarser in its mode of action, and there were not so many fine gradations of superstition as there are now.

Of course such a man as Don Jose found his interests decidedly opposed to those of the church, and he had made the court of Philip of Spain almost too hot to hold the confessors, who, of right, claimed a place there. Hence had arisen the ticklish aspect of the king's affairs, as regarded the clergy; and had Jose been a high-minded man, and capable of taking comprehensive national views, instead of lending all his energies to the accomplishment of his own petty and private ends, he might, with the talent he undoubtedly possessed, have struck a heavy blow to priestly supremacy in Spain.

But such was not his great object. As he went on in his career of private aggrandisement and ambition, he had no objection to give as many side blows to those who opposed him as he possibly could, but he was no patriot; and if the clergy had gone with him and held him up for a model of a minister, and winked at his vices, he would have been just as willing to bespatter them with praise as he was now to have them knocked on the head with the brass-bound but-end of Lazarillo's arquebus.

How far he pursued a fearfully mistaken policy in fighting against a system he could not conquer, we shall quickly see.

CHAPTER LVIII.

INSURRECTIONARY MOVEMENT IN MADRID.—CONFLICT BETWEEN THE POPULACE AND THE GUARD.—THE BURNING OF DON JOSE'S MANSION.

DURING the progress of these events, that were likely to have a most inimical effect upon the happiness of individuals, others were occurring upon a more extended scale, and involving the safety of a much greater number of persons.

There was a large body of the inhabitants of Spain who were highly dissatisfied with the state of the government, which they termed tyrannical and unjust; and what rendered it yet more oppressive was, that the system pursued was variable, so that no man could safely say he knew the extent to which he was amenable to the laws, either criminal or fiscal. This was a great evil, and when we come to consider that the administrators of the law were, for the most part, people who took their tone, and followed the example of their superiors, and were generally influenced by bribes and presents, we shall feel no surprise that such dissatisfaction should exist.

There was another cause for dissatisfaction, and that was, the lax tone of manners and morals that ran through the Spanish court, and which, of course, influenced all who had any pretension to breeding or fashion, and the consequence was, there was many a family whose happiness was disturbed and for ever destroyed by the propensities thus engendered by the court in the youth of the principal families in Madrid especially, and as the provinces are usually not behind the provinces in these matters, the evil spread far and wide.

Thus was caused a great and general feeling of dissatisfaction, which was fostered by the turbulent among the nobles, and, more especially, among the clergy.

These latter had used every art to urge the people to create some disturbance, and proceed to force and open hostilities, for, as it will be remembered, the secret conspiracy, which embraced so many individuals of the first consequence in Spain, was discovered, and the far greater portion of them were either killed or taken prisoners.

This was a great blow to the party, for it discouraged them from meeting, especially as they could not discover the means by which Don Jose had become possessed of their secret. They, however, determined to push the populace on to commit acts of hostility by sowing the seeds of sedition among them to effect that purpose.

It was no difficult task to do this, especially where there were so many real grievances to complain of. Daily were fresh matters of complaint growing up between the two classes, and the breach was daily becoming wider and more perceptible.

Strange it was that none of the countries saw, or would demonstrate if they saw, the rupture that would soon take place. The commonalty were treated as though they were born to put up with the wrongs inflicted upon them by the rich.

There was in Spain, indeed in Madrid, a demagogue, by name Petro Caracas; he was the very man of all others to lead the mob of Madrid; he was their darling orator, the man they deemed most fitting on earth to govern Spaniards, and the one of all others to be most trusted by the people.

This man had been a soldier; had seen service, and had been promised promotion, with both honour and profit.

His ambition and self-love had been injured, as well as being unjustly treated. There could be no objection to granting him a rank or a pension, because he had come of good family, and even decently educated; but he was what is termed a troublesome fellow, and, moreover, was no favourite of any one. Hence it was he was shelved.

This was an offence against himself he never forgave; and, moreover, in his attempts to obtain justice he met with many personal insults, which he could not return or resent; all this he treasured up, determined to be revenged, if he could not be righted.

This man was very popular among the mob of Madrid, and he took care to take a leading part with them, and carefully seized every opportunity of increasing his own powers, and damaging his enemies, by declaiming against them as a body, and pointing out the injustice and indignity with which they were treated by their superiors.

The absence of the king greatly tended to increase that dissatisfaction—not that he was beloved, but it was something they could seize upon to quarrel about —for nobody could tell where he was gone to, and that was something mysterious.

During the king's absence the nobility, unrestrained, led the same dissolute life, of which the king himself set the example; but they were unrestrained by his presence, and the consequence was a scene of riot and confusion occurred nightly in the city of Madrid, in which the inhabitants were often sufferers. Their wives and daughters were often insulted with impunity, and when the common people rose *en masse* to repel anything of the kind, the guard was called out, and some of the ringleaders of the rioters, as they were termed, were taken and punished for the disturbance that was created.

This exasperated the mob to fury, and Petro Caracas lost not the opportunity to inveigh against the aristocracy and the rulers of the nation, whom he characterised as an idle, dissolute mob, fit for the commission of crimes against the social laws, and unfit to govern them, or to make and to administer good laws, for they were the first to break through them.

The mob testified their approbation by loud shouts and angry menaces; and many a deep oath was taken that the next time they were molested they would take a severe and exemplary vengeance upon those who should venture to act towards them as the noblesse had hitherto done.

Petro Caracas was well beloved by the populace, and was thought the best leader they could have, because he was by birth and education superior to the common herd; and he had been a soldier, and therefore a man of action, and the best calculated for such an office. Moreover, he had been ill-used; in addition to which, he possessed a rough kind of eloquence just suited to the tastes of his hearers, which he managed with some skill, and had a happy knack of keeping his hearers always in good humour with himself, and securing their attention.

A night or two after this, an occurrence took place that brought on a popular tumult of no ordinary nature.

A young gentleman of good family and connections, accompanied by two or three persons of distinction, made an attempt to enter an artificer's dwelling, with the intention of carrying on an illicit and disgraceful intercourse with his daughter, who had received the gallant before, not knowing who he was.

The father met the stranger, and then ordered him out; he resisted, and was put out by force. Being heated with wine, he and his friends determined to force the house and enter, despite the owner's consent.

He, however, met them, and resisted; and before aid came, he was killed by one of the party, and it was believed by the aggressor himself.

There was immediately an *emeute*: people were running from all quarters, and a desperate struggle took place between them who arrived first to revenge the death of the murdered man upon his murderer;

but he was defended by his friends with their drawn swords, and as they retreated, followed by the infuriated populace, they called for the guard.

The guard came, and endeavoured to rescue them from the populace, but unsuccessfully, and two of them were slain. A stronger detachment of the guard were sent for, and all the available force of the capital was ordered under arms.

In the meantime, the inhabitants were not idle; the priests, and some of the nobility who were in league with them, immediately aided in the tumult, which they endeavoured to give a political tone.

Petro Caracas was immediately sought, and arms were suddenly distributed by some unknown individuals among the people, and they were thus impelled suddenly to oppose those stoutly whom they had before feared so much.

There were leaders who sprang up amongst them, men whom they knew nothing of before, who urged them on in martial and stirring words, and placed them in order, instructed them, and pointed out the means of offence and defence.

Cries were heard in all quarters; the populace were called to arms, and "Long live the constitution!" "Down with the king!" "Down with Jose!" "Down with the spies and assassins!" "Liberty for ever!" "The people for ever!" were shouted everywhere.

These cries, and many others, were uttered and shouted, as the guard came down in increased numbers, and immediately charged upon the people, expecting they would give way as usual to the weight of men, and the terror of the sword.

In this, however, they were mistaken, for they were received in a manner they had no recollection of before. The streets were torn up, and the road rendered uneven, and barricades erected; this, in some measure, gave it the effect it was desired to have, to break the line of the troops, to render their charge less effectual, less simultaneous; and to give time to those opposing them to assail them in this state.

The guard was everywhere received with shouts of defiance and derision, and a sharp fire of small arms.

This was altogether unexpected; the guard wavered, and at the same instant it was attacked in front by the populace defending the streets, and its rear was endangered by those that followed them; added to which, small bodies collected in the streets, and made desperate sallies on their flanks.

Thus endangered on all sides, the guard gave way and fled, leaving one half their number dead in the streets. Still it was looked upon as a mere riot; the people were highly incensed, but an increase of men would soon bring them to their senses, and a little hanging or strangling would atone for all things.

With this view the guard were called out almost to a man, and also a small body of troops of the line were ordered out, headed and officered. But the people, elated with their success, were now ungovernable; and being armed in a manner without precedent, felt themselves stronger and more daring than any mob in Madrid within the memory of man.

It would no longer appear to be a mere riot; people talked of a constitution, of equal rights, and the destruction of the monarchy; of displacing one king and replacing him with another, with more limited power, and, above all, the total destruction of Jose.

This man was most cordially hated, and, indeed, the king appeared to be but little more respected—if he were it was not on account of his personal qualities, but rather from the habitual deference it is usual to show to the title.

However, there was but little time to spare, and none for thought. The guard and troops came on in a gallant and soldier-like manner, and some cavalry belonging to the household troops came down at a canter, but could not act with effect, on account of the nature of the ground, which had been broken up and barricadoed in every available spot. The infantry, however, acted better, and drew up quickly to the charge, and were received by the people with a galling but irregular discharge of small arms, and afterwards a desperate conflict ensued.

The people gave way, but disputed the ground at every inch ; but it is questionable if they would have stood their ground, had it not been for the throng behind them. They could not recede, there were such dense masses of human beings coming up to their aid. They did, however, give way slowly, and for some distance, but this was the cause of their victory.

When they had given way some few dozen yards, there was a street that ran across, and this was also barricadoed and filled with armed men, who, no sooner did the troops appear, than, discharging their arquebuses at them, they gave a loud shout, and an instant and simultaneous rush took place, and they were charged on both flanks ; and at that moment a fresh impetus was given to those in front, and they charged afresh upon their assailants.

The struggle was terrific, but it did not last long. The troops were broken, and they fled on all sides ; they were pursued, and more were killed in the pursuit than in the fight, yet a full third of the number were left dead on the field.

The discomfited troops fled towards their barracks, and there endeavoured to fortify themselves against the multitude by placing a piece of cannon on the walls, and manning every available spot for defence—even the wounded were compelled to do duty at some posts. But this was of no avail, the whole of the populace of Madrid were now in arms, the greater part of whom were reeking with blood ; and they were not easily pacified—success intoxicating them ; and the more ignorant and brutal the subject, the sooner does it take effect.

"To the barracks! to the barracks! men of Madrid!" cried Caracas. "Once obtain possession of that, with the surrender of the troops, and all is your own."

The first discharge of the piece of ordnance that had been placed on the walls greatly abated their ardour, but Caracas was not intimidated by this, and again urged them on, heading them himself, and then shooting down a man who was about to fire it again, the mob soon carried the walls by assault, for they completely surrounded them. The guard fought desperately, and having secured itself in a strong position, asked for terms. Quarter was offered them, if they laid down their arms ; but they desired to walk out with their arms. As the populace required arms, they refused, and the carnage was about to recommence, when they surrendered. They were allowed to depart, but the officers were detained prisoners.

There was a tremendous stir in the city of Madrid. No one could tell what was happening, what had, or what would happen ; no one could understand what was the meaning of all this, but they believed there was a change going on, and this they all deemed advisable.

The authorities were completely at fault, and dared not stir out for fear of being recognised by the mob, and ill-treated—perhaps killed.

The rioters, in the meantime, called a council of war in the barracks, to deliberate upon the next steps to be taken, for there were many of them who were alarmed at their own success ; but they were, however, urged on by many of their number, and their leaders spoke out boldly, and even priests were not wanting in exhortations to induce them to persevere in the course they had begun ; at the same time, renounc-

ing the cause of the state, which they declared was so bad that it had brought down the wrath of Heaven.

In the barracks they met, and held a kind of council of war. Petro Caracas was there, and he was chosen by acclamation as their general, and in him was vested a kind of arbitrary authority, for which he was responsible to no one.

He then addressed the multitude in his usual style, and described the injuries and indignities they had received from the court ; their lives and properties were not safe, and their wives and daughters, instead of being a blessing to them, too often proved a curse, for it brought down the licentious nobility upon them, and they were seduced, in many instances, from their duty ; and, if not, force was not unfrequently resorted to to effect what fraud could not, and hence it was a poor man's dwelling was not safe.

If they resisted, and punished their aggressor, they were cruelly treated, and heavily fined and imprisoned ; and what for ? Because they had only defended the sanctity of their own homes, and the integrity of their families.

Now they had suddenly succeeded in punishing their aggressors, and it behoved them to take such steps, now they had the power, to secure themselves against evil treatment ; for, so sure as they were contented with the punishment of those who had angered them, so sure were they to feel the effects of the revengeful spirit of the nobles.

"They would," he declared, "seek those out who had borne arms, and taken part in this just rising, and beheading and strangling would be the order of the day, without mercy, and the mines would be peopled by the inhabitants of Madrid.

His advice was, therefore, to aim at a higher object —a free constitution—in which their lives and properties would be better taken care of and respected.

To seize, therefore, the points of defence (for, if they should fail in their grand object, yet a lesser one would be gained—that of making terms for themselves) was his urgent advice, and that, too, without loss of time.

These were pointed out, and the houses and buildings that abutted on the entrances into Madrid were to be taken possession of, for the purpose of defending the city from any attack of the troops coming from the provinces.

Bodies of men were at once despatched to these several points ; and, as many of them were in the hands of the troops and authorities, they were not relinquished without bloodshed, many of the defenders, however, escaping into the country, and spreading an alarm wherever they went, or wherever they sought refuge.

Madrid was a scene of the most terrible confusion : everything was suspended ; the civil authorities durst not act ; they were overpowered and overawed ; they remained within their own houses, where they were not fortunate enough to escape to the provinces.

The news spread like wildfire through the city among the nobility, and these proud and haughty men were fain to take what precautions they could against being singled out by the vengeance of the mob, and sacrificed to the resentment of men whom they had treated as dogs.

The servants, too—a race always at variance with the people, and who ever seized an opportunity to exert their native insolence, the offspring of ignorance and fancied superiority—these men often committed acts of petty tyranny, and pushed them back with rudeness and violence whenever they had the power or excuse to do so—now trembled with abject fear as they heard the wild hurras of the mob, and the roll of musquetry.

Thus passed a long and dreadful night ; every one

predicted a revolution was at hand, and there were but few who could by any means tell the cause of the first outbreak

The darkness and mystery that enveloped the whole affair was so great, that it increased the terror of those likely to become objects of popular discontent greatly. These people ran hither and thither, endeavouring to escape, and yet they feared to do so, fancying they were observed and watched on all sides by the populace.

The attacks were carried on against several of the different places that were in the hands of the government, and even several of the forts were seized and garrisoned by the people.

The prisons were all broken open, and the prisoners let out, as a matter of course, and many profited by the occurrence to regain their liberty, which they could not have done for some years.

The monks, and the agents of the superior clergy, were at work. The Cardinal de Vinci was among the foremost, and it was the presence and advice of such men as these, who possessed, or were supposed to possess, great influence with Heaven, that gave the rioters greater courage and spirit than they would otherwise have had, and caused them to persevere in the line of conduct, that had began by accident, but was seized by these artful Propaganda, and turned to their own purposes with a readiness and forethought, that proves, beyond doubt, that such things had been foreseen and anticipated.

The houses of their oppressors were attacked by the people, and the astonished domestics were terrified almost to death when they perceived there was no escape.

Everything was done that could be done to propitiate the multitude; but this was of no use; they were dragged out, and were left, half dead, from violence and fear, while the mob roamed through the splendid apartments and saloons, so gorgeously decorated, and destroyed the furniture, paintings, and ornaments of every description.

Morever, many of the people did not scruple to appropriate several of the articles that were of a portable and costly nature, while all the rest were collected in a heap, in the lower part of the house, and then piled up with many combustible matters, and then they were fired.

It was with a shout of joy the populace welcomed the appearance of the flames, as they rose gradually, each moment, however, gaining more force, and rushing up with greater rapidity and drowning sound. The flames now sought the house, and the whole building was soon enveloped in the destructive element that had been called in to aid them in their projects of revenge.

Thus far they stopped to witness the success of their movement, and when fully assured it would be completed, they moved on to the execution of their original intentions.

The news of the firing of Jose's mansion soon spread throughout Madrid, and, ere morning dawned, there were several more mansions blazing in Madrid, and the nobility obnoxious to the people were in the utmost alarm for their own safety, as well as that of their property.

Indeed, the populace were now in possession of two-thirds of Madrid, and bad men seized a magazine, and were rapidly distributing arms and ammunition among themselves, fortifying every available point with such means as they possessed.

Among one large body of men that had been despatched to secure some place, was observed a man in the garb of an ecclesiastic, who urged the people on to deeds of violence; and, by his side, were several men, who, though disguised, it could easily be seen they were of the better class. Their jewelled swords told a tale they would have concealed; but they concealed their features, and prevented identity—all they cared about. There could be but little doubt but this was the Cardinal de Vinci, and such of the conspirators as are yet alive and at liberty.

Suddenly this cry was heard from this band of traitors,—

"To Jose's!—down with Don Jose! Burn—burn him down! Fire his house!—search him out!"

As everybody hated Jose cordially, there was an excellent opportunity to pay off old scores, and exhibit the love they bore this public man, whose virtues were certainly equal to their love.

The cry was instantly caught up, and echoed from mouth to mouth, and a tremendous huzza was shouted from the throats of the many-headed, who now swept onward with a whirlwind-like force to the street in which Jose's house stood.

Another shout rent the air, when they arrived there.

CHAPTER LIX.

THE CHASE THROUGH MADRID.—THE MARQUIS DE ROTONDO'S DANGER, AND FORTUNATE ESCAPE.

THE morning now broke upon Madrid, and the sun looked down upon the burning of many of the best houses in Madrid; for, as is usual, in these cases, the ire of the multitude once raised, and having found vent in one particular direction, it continued to pour out to the utter destruction of everything that opposed it.

Thus it was. The people, in addition to securing such places of strength as were available for their own purposes, yet they omitted not the exertion of that power of vengeance they now possessed, and which they might soon be deprived of.

It would appear that they thought it wise to exact all the power they possessed, and punish at once those who had been so long obnoxious to them, and who would surely take vengeance upon them, should they ever get the mastery.

It was this reason, therefore, that induced them to act thus, to strike, if possible, terror into them, and prevent, on a future occasion, a similar tyrannical exercise of power and wealth, by the recollection of former terrors, which might be renewed, should they be driven again to extremities, and compelled to rise.

Thus passed many hours, and many serious occurrences took place in the streets, and those who heretofore would have had the rabble driven before them, were now compelled to put up with a reversal of the case, and were glad to fly before them, and were happy to do so.

Among those who were thus placed was the Marquis del Minho, who had made himself particularly obnoxious to the people, both on account of the connections he had with those who so often with impunity insulted the commonalty, as on his own account, since he had often been brought into collision with the people, from which the latter, as was usual, came off second-best.

Besides that, he was well known at court, and leagued with their enemies, the king and Don Jose, and one of those who appeared to take pleasure in loading them with imposts and restrictions.

This man's house was surrounded and attacked—his people were ordered to come out and save their lives by an immediate abandonment of the mansion and all it contained to pillage.

The marquis had taken refuge in his house, believing himself safe, and had armed his servants and prepared to make a vigorous resistance; but when he saw the number of his enemies and their arms, he at once found that there was no hope; moreover, he as well as his people were now but too well aware that the mob had, after a deadly conflict, defeated all the military authorities in the city at that moment, and to desist would be but certain destruction.

Neither would his people resist—they loved life better than their master, and were not prepared to undergo certain death for no earthly purpose.

"You had better all go out in a body, as they require," he said. "There is no hope of maintaining the place against them; if there had been, by Heaven I would give these knaves some work."

Upon this the doors were thrown open, and the men and women quitted the mansion and were permitted to depart, and amongst them was the marquis himself, who passed out in the midst of them, and had nearly got off, when his cloak betrayed him to the people.

"There is the marquis!" shouted Caracas, at the head of the mob.

"Down with the Marquis del Minho!" shouted the mob.

"Stop him—seize him! Hang him up to his own windows!"

"Strip and whip him through the streets of Madrid!" shouted Caracas.

The marquis no sooner heard these shouts than he felt assured that they would put their threats into execution the moment he was caught.

He therefore waited no longer, but, getting his cloak about him, set off at a speed that astonished the mob, who, however, started off in pursuit of him. The chase was a long one, and the marquis was ahead, yet the pursuers were stout, and would not give up the chase, but kept him in sight and hunted him half through Madrid.

More than once he was nigh being taken by the mob, in consequence of passengers attempting to seize him as he rushed onwards; these he either eluded or cut down with his sword, for he believed it to be a chase of which life was to be the prize.

At length he suddenly turned a corner, darted across the street, and then disappeared, where, no one could tell.

The fact was, he had reached the Marquis de Rotondo's mansion, which had been carefully secured, and just at that moment one of the servants had opene' the doors to see if anything was going on.

Quick as lightning, the marquis, who just saw it, dashed in, knocking the terrified porter clean down by the force of his entrance.

"Murder—fire!" shouted the man.

"Hold your tongue, you knave!" exclaimed the marquis, who had fastened the door with the speed of thought.

"Mercy!"

"Hold your noise, or I'll run you through! Do you not recollect me?"

The man got up, and, looking the marquis in the face, pronounced his name, and then the marquis, motioning him to be silent, listened for the mob.

They came in numbers—hallooing, shouting, and cursing; at the same time they paused and looked about.

"If they inquire for me, say I'm not here," said the marquis, dropping some gold pieces into the porter's hand.

"Yes, my lord," said the man, respectfully bowing, "you may depend upon me."

"Is the Marquis de Rotondo within?" inquired the Marquis del Minho.

"Yes, my lord, he is."

"Then announce to him my name."

The porter immediately called a page, and desired him to announce the Marquis del Minho to his master.

The page soon returned, desiring the marquis to enter, for Rotondo knew the marquis was a great man,

and one who had some considerable influence at court, and as a matter of course he was an individual of consequence, and to be well received.

The marquis met him on his entrance with a low bow, saying,—

"My dear marquis, I am happy to see you—how I have longed to see you—it is an age since I have seen you. What happy circumstance is it that has produced me so much pleasure?"

"Why, as to the happiness—hem—my dear Marquis de Rotondo, we may as well say nothing about, save indeed, the happiness of your seeing me, and my seeing you. You see that, marquis?"

"Undoubtedly. I must be blind not to see anything so perceptible. It is a happy and felicitous way of rendering it obvious—a happy cause."

"Happy cause?"

"Yes; that is—didn't you say so, my dear marquis?"

"No, no, there was no happiness in the cause at all."

"Eh—what—I thought," stammered the marquis, much puzzled.

"You see there is much happiness in the fact, but little in cause."

"Ah, ah! I see—exactly," replied the Marquis de Rotondo, not understanding at all what was said or meant.

"The fact is, marquis, I have been hunted," said the Marquis del Minho.

"Hunted?"

"Yes, veritably and truly hunted."

"God bless me, I never heard of such a thing. Hunt a marquis! Impossible!"

"It is nevertheless true. You are aware that all Madrid is in an uproar, and all the people are killing and slaying, robbing and pillaging, right and left."

"Yes, yes, I have heard of that, and that they have not even spared Don Jose's mansion—it is burned down."

"Is it? Well, then, he and I am equally obliged to the mob."

"You?"

"Yes; only he has the advantage of me; he is not in Madrid. I didn't expect they would spare him, nor myself either—we have too much power and influence at court to be their favourites. The hounds—I would I had cannon to sweep them away by the thousand."

"Ah, it would be a good clearance of the villains, I must say; but, dear me, what audacity, what presumption, to attack the wealthy and powerful."

"Yes, yes; but what will not these people do, when hallooed on by their demagogues and leaders, when indeed they have been successful in their first resistance to the properly constituted authorities. 'Tis like the course of a river that has been dammed up, and at length its waters find some little flaw, and then succeed in making a breach, which, unchecked at first, is the cause of the whole stream following, and carrying death and devastation till it has subsided."

"Ah, that's very true; but there's no getting out of Madrid."

"I shall endeavour to do so, and see if I cannot alarm the king, and bring the troops quartered in the provinces down upon them. Something must be done."

"Yes, you are right, something must be done, and by whom should it be done, save by the nobility? These misguided people must be brought to a sense of their inferiority, and punished."

"Ay, and most richly shall they reap the reward of what they have done, and a pretty harvest will they reap."

"By-the-bye, it was fortunate that my house was at hand for you."

"Yes it was; and it was fortunate, also, your man was passing out at the moment, or I should have been caught before I had got in."

The marquis had thrown his hat and cloak upon the seat where the Marquis of Rotondo's was laying there before.

"I think, Rotondo, these people will be soon gone."

"Exactly, they are going away by degrees. They don't know you are here."

"No, no ; if they did they would fire the place, and set their hell-hounds upon us in a very little while."

"Indeed!" exclaimed the Marquis de Rotondo. "A-hem! When do you think of going to the king, eh?"

"As soon as I can quit Madrid, but not an hour before ; but, then, I am not sure when that can be, because, if I were seen going through the streets I might, as, indeed, I should certainly, have them after me, and I should be again placed in great and imminent peril."

"Exactly, so you would."

"There is one way, I think I could contrive to get away without suspicion."

"Name it, my dear marquis, name it. I shall be delighted to hear it. I will do anything that may be required of me to produce so desirable an end, for Madrid will be a heap of ashes before many days are over."

"You are perfectly right, it will ; but will you walk with me through the streets, as I think thus I may escape detection ? You are generally known and respected, else you would not have escaped, and I shall not be noticed."

"Indeed! I see what you would have," replied the Marquis de Rotondo. "What would have become of you if you had fallen into the hands of these people ?"

"I should be dead long ere this. Their morbid thirst for blood would have induced them to take my life. When will you go, marquis ?"

"I will go with you when you please," replied Rotondo, not ill pleased to hear that the marquis was about to quit his house, for, while he was there, he endangered its safety ; and, moreover, he was a man to be obliged, and hence he did not care if he did escape, as either way he would be benefited by the occurrence.

Once in the country, he thought he would then soon be released from fear by the speedy approach of the royal troops, which would, of course, soon march to their succour in the capital, and he would be the sooner relieved from the serious fears he began to entertain for his own safety, and that of his beautifully adorned mansion.

"The coast is clear, marquis, is it not ?"

"Oh, yes, not a soul to be seen anywhere ; they are all busy elsewhere."

"The rogues. But make sure of it ; send out, and then let us go, if the report be favourable to the undertaking."

The marquis did as he was requested, and sent a trusty servant out for intelligence, with which he soon returned, saying there was no one in the neighbourhood, and the people were all engaged in some other part of the city.

"Then now is the propitious moment," exclaimed the Marquis del Minho ; "allow me to take your arm, Rotondo, and all may yet be well."

"With pleasure ; yes, certainly. Marquis, you do me a very great honour."

So saying, the Marquis del Minho, took his friend's cloak, and he, on the other hand, was adjusting his on his own shoulders, which done, they proceeded into the streets of Madrid.

Now it so happened that the Marquis del Minho's cloak, which graced the shoulders of De Rotondo, was of a peculiar and singular shade, and one that was well known to the populace, on account of the expensive and curiously wrought trimmings about it; and he was anxious not to be seen in it, as it no doubt would lead to his immediate detection.

They had passed through several streets, and they were beginning to congratulate themselves upon the good fortune that befriended them, when a man who was crossing the road made a dart at Rotondo's hat.

The marquis stepped on one side, perfectly aghast at this want of respect and ceremony, and Del Minho instantly struck him down, saying,—

"That is the quickest way to get rid of him. Come, we must now exert our speed ; you go one way, Rotondo, and I will take another ; we may thus divide them and escape."

"Yes, certainly."

"But we must run."

"I fear I can't run ; never did such a thing in my life ; don't think it possible ; so undignified."

"Well, well, I must, so farewell ; they may not hurt you, but I know they would me ; but I would advise you not to trust them ; they have no notion of your dignity."

So saying, the Marquis del Minho set off, leaving the Marquis de Rotondo to do the same if he chose : but he was not long in making up his mind about it, for, seeing a mob approaching, attracted by the cries of the man who had been knocked down, he gathered up the cloak around him, and stepped out at a good round pace.

"Down with Del Minho! chase him! hunt him! see, there's his cloak! that's him! shoot him, shoot him!" shouted the mob, and these terrific shouts reached the ears of the unfortunate marquis, who now fully believed they had made a mistake, and took him for the marquis, his friend, and that he should be a sufferer by that mistake; that he, a green stick, would be beaten by sticks of all colours, and perhaps meet with an ignominious death. He groaned in his heart, became red in the face, puffed and blowed, and ran like a greyhound, for fear "pricked him on."

Notwithstanding fear urged the marquis on, yet his short stature and bulky protuberant portion of his person in front, was ill calculated to support a lengthened hunt. His heart beat quick—his lungs found scarce room to play in. The marquis had lived so well that he could scarce find room in his person for more fat than it already contained, and which he knew now to be considerably more than was useful in such gymnastic exercise as he then, perforce, was indulging in.

The mob gained upon him despite all his exertions, and he was near going into fits at the idea of a green stick being handled by anything less than royalty.

"Huzza!" shouted the mob ; "down with the Marquis del Minho; that's him—see his cloak—that's his cloak, and he's in it too—huzza!"

These were dreadful sounds to him ; though he heard these words, yet the thought that he was bearing the cause of the mistake on his own shoulders, and had he been perfectly sensible of it, it would yet have been questionable whether he would have been collected enough to cast the obnoxious garment from him ; however, as it was, he retained it the tighter.

Almost fainting with exertion, and panting dreadfully, he arrived at a shop—it was a tailor's shop, and in he rushed, clean over the counter, upsetting divers articles which stood in his way ; even the tailor himself was upset in his impetuosity, and he only stopped when he found himself in a back room, in the midst of the tailor's family, consisting of his wife and daughter, a pretty and good-natured girl of more than the ordinary share of understanding, as well as beauty.

"My good people," exclaimed the marquis, "save me. I am a green stick."

"A what?" exclaimed the tailor, seeming in great wrath.

"A green stick, my good man."

"Don't good man me; do you think I am to have my house invaded by such unruly ruffians? You shall taste the sweets of a seasoned stick."

"Now—my—why, my good fellow, don't you understand? why ——"

"Pshaw—I'll not stand it."

"Yes—but ——"

"Out with you."

"But the mob."

"I don't care for the mob; they'll hang you, not me; the mob pay people, you don't."

"Save me, my good, dear young ladies," exclaimed the marquis, quite terrified, and he let the cloak and hat fall to the ground as he spoke.

Whether it was the effect of the rich dress the marquis wore, his sword and jewels, or whether the tailor's wife was softened by being termed, by implication, a young lady, is not certain, but this much is certain, she turned to her angry husband and said to him,

"You ought to be ashamed of yourself to treat a gentleman and a nobleman in this manner, instead of which, you ought to be grateful he has so much honoured you."

"So much honoured me, indeed. Yes, I was honoured by Don Cæsar de Bazan, and I can show his honour on my books."

"And he will pay you, father; he will, I am sure," exclaimed his daughter, earnestly; and turning to the marquis, she added, "you must not think my father unwilling to serve you, sir, if he can; but your haste has disturbed him."

"Yes—yes, I was rather hasty, I admit; but I hope the fact of having a few hundred men who were ready to kill me at my heels, will excuse me for that."

"Certainly," said the tailor's wife; "shut the door, my dear; don't you hear the people at a distance? if they come in they will make free with your goods without ceremony."

The tailor was subdued, and sneaked off to shut the door, and save his shop from intrusion; he had not done so too soon, for the mob rushed by in great numbers, hallooing and shouting, as though the object of their pursuit was still in advance of them.

"There," said the marquis, "they would not show me any mercy if they were to catch me; they would not wait for any explanation, I am sure; if explanation were required, it would be only when too late. What a state of things!"

"Why do they seek you?"

"Because they mistook me for the Marquis del Minho," replied De Rotondo.

"And who are you?" inquired the tailor, who had now returned to the room.

"I am a green stick. I am the Marquis de Rotondo," he added, with a dignified bow.

The little tailor was horror-struck at the indignity he had offered the marquis, for he well knew his great wealth and magnificence.

"I am very sorry I didn't know it before," he stammered out, "or I wouldn't have asked any questions."

"Don't name it," said the marquis, blandly, waving his hand, and recovering his breath a little.

"Will you sit down?" said the wife, offering a chair.

"Thank you," said the marquis. "I never ran before in my life, and you can't think what an extraordinary effect it has had upon me. I never was so hot before, and what a horrible sensation of choking it has upon me, too."

The wife made no remark, but going to the cupboard, produced a bottle of wine, which she set before the marquis, with a glass in a homely fashion.

"Thank you," said the marquis, pouring out a glass and swallowing it, which he repeated three times, while the tailor rubbed his hands, and looked on, not knowing what to do, what to say, or what to think of what he saw.

"Very good, and most welcome," said the marquis; "never wanted anything so bad in my life before; and at the same time, never relished anything so much. Oh! these are terrible times."

"Is there not a Countess de Bazan residing at your mansion?" inquired the daughter, after some thought, and with an effort.

"Yes—yes, there was."

"Who was she?"

"I really—eh—oh—I don't know."

"You have heard of Don Cæsar de Bazan?" she inquired.

"Yes; he was a graceless dog; spent all his money, and in debt."

"Yes," said the tailor; "so he is in mine, and will never be out."

"I am sure he will."

"I am sure he won't," replied the tailor, snappishly. "I wish I might be mistaken."

"But," inquired his daughter, with much interest, "is the lady who bears that name his wife, or any other member of the same family?"

"I really don't know. Don Jose never told me. I never heard."

"Do you know who the countess is, and to whom she is related?"

"She is related to me, I believe."

"Believe!"

"She was lost, then found and recovered, and was related to me; how, why, or when, I don't know; but Don Jose does, I suppose. I don't know why she was lost, or why she was found; all I know is, there was such a person in my house; but she left with Don Jose; he gave me no explanation, but he took her to some of her husband's friends, I suppose; and that's all I know about it. Dear me, what an escape I have had."

CHAPTER LX.

THE SERENADE AND ITS MISTAKEN OBJECT.—CROSS PURPOSES AND THE DENOUEMENT.

THE mob who had so ruthlessly pursued the Marquis de Rotondo, and caused that great man to take refuge in the house of the tailor, pursued its way, fully believing that he was ahead of them, and this induced them to increase their speed in the pursuit lest they should not catch him. He was, therefore, comparatively safe for some time, at least; perhaps, more so than he would be even in his own house; for who would think of finding a marquis in a tailor's shop? no one. It was not the soil in which such things were found; so the occurrence was but an accidental one.

The marquis drank some of the wine set before him; he had suffered much from the terrible fright, and the exertion he had been forced into for the sake of self-preservation. It took him longer than he anticipated to recover himself; for now all the distressing symptoms he had before endured, without feeling them, were at an end, and he was sorely puzzled as to how he should go home.

"Well, my good people," said the marquis, "you shall be rewarded for your hospitality. You shall learn what it is to oblige a marquis—a green stick; and I don't know but something more by this time, for we of the old nobility do not know to what exalted station we may suddenly be called upon to fill."

"Oh, honoured sir—my lord," stammered the little tailor, "make my house your own. I wish all the nobility and grave ones had been like you."

Here the tailor's daughter gave a shrewd shrug of her shoulders, as much as to say, that she thought some of them might be none the more pleasing for such a change in their persons.

"We can't all hold the highest offices," said the marquis; "only the great and the wealthy do that; and it is those only who have rank, station, capacity, and abilities that can hold them; indeed, if there were more places than applicants their state would be ruined; and hence it is, some are born for great offices, and they get them; how could they, indeed, do otherwise?"

"Exactly, worthy and great sir," said the tailor, cringing into a half standing and half sitting posture; "but now I wish they were all honourable like yourself. You see we should not suffer by them in that case."

"Suffer!"

"Yes."

"How do you mean?"

"By their getting in debt."

"Debt—debt! what's that?"

"Why, having things of a poor man, and then never after paying him for them, as I have known some do."

"I never did so; oh, no. I pay everybody. I don't owe anything. Oh, dear—dear, I   ling at all."

"Oh, but there are some who do," continued the tailor.

"Very likely."

"My father," said the tailor's daughter, gravely indignant at his harping upon the subject of Don Cæsar's debt, "my father has had the honour of making some garments for one of the nobility, who has met with some sad misfortunes."

"Oh, dear! misfortunes indeed! haven't I had enough of misfortunes? and as for the honour, why, bless me, I look in my ledger, and I can't see that it at all helps me to balance it."

"Ah, father, father!" she said, reproachfully; "you will never forget that little debt that Don Cæsar owes."

"No, my dear, I never shall. I shall never get it paid, and yet I shall be told I ought to forget it, eh?"

"Certainly. I am sure Don Cæsar will one day repay you."

"I wish I may get it."

"You don't deserve it. I dare say this gentleman does not care about hearing this kind of conversation. Hold your tongue, husband—say no more about it. You know the delicacy of my nerves, and yet you will worry me about such a paltry affair."

The tailor slunk away, and cowed before the eye of his wife.

"Do you know anything of this Don Cæsar?" inquired the wife, helping the marquis to more wine.

"I know there is such a man—the title, I mean."

"Exactly."

"But he was a very rude, uncouth, and troublesome fellow."

"Indeed! I never saw so sweet a gentleman. Indeed, I would have done anything for so accomplished a gentleman, and one, too, so full of courage and wit."

"But he was executed," said the tailor. "He was shot, by order of the king."

"Indeed! then who the deuce was it I saw?" said the marquis.

"His ghost," said the tailor.

"His ghost?"

"Yes, honoured sir."

"Pshaw!"

"I saw it myself."

"My good man, you must be dreaming."

"I know very well I saw him; and, moreover, he came to me and obtained a discharge of the debt."

"Then he owes you nothing."

The tailor cast a rueful look at his wife, but made no answer.

"Was this Don Cæsar married?" inquired the

daughter, in a serious tone of voice, and with an evident interest in the answer, that she could not conceal.

"I really don't know—I am bothered and bewildered. Jose sometimes said one thing, and then another."

"Indeed!"

"Yes, he said my wife was the Countess de Bazan, and then ——"

"What then?"

"Oh, I don't know," said the marquis, suddenly recollecting he might be saying more than Jose would approve of, and then he might lose some good thing or other if he offended.

"But you have a Countess de Bazan in your mansion, my lord?"

"I had."

"Was she beautiful?"

"Yes, yes; she was very beautiful, and young, too."

The daughter sighed, and her cheeks paled, as she listened to the answer, and then she inquired,—

"Where is the Countess de Bazan?"

"I don't know."

"Nor Don Cæsar?"

"No, I do not, indeed."

"Was he not known as a nobleman? was he not universally known among the people, as brave and generous?"

"So he might be," interrupted the tailor, when it cost him nothing to be so."

"All I know is," said the marquis, "that there was such a person, but he has run through a princely fortune, and is now, if living, a beggar. He couldn't pay his way, because he is of an honourable house of first rank."

The daughter sighed again, and the mother said,—

"It is a mysterious affair altogether. Some say he is dead, but some say not, while others say that they have seen and spoken to a ghost."

"Just see," said the marquis, "if the streets are clear of people."

The little tailor did so, and reported they were.

"Well," said the marquis, "give me another cloak. I will not venture out in that any more; they take me for some one else I do not wish to be taken for."

The marquis was accommodated, and the tailor was delighted at the handsome price the marquis gave him for it, and then De Rotondo entered the street to seek his way home, devoutly hoping that he would meet with no more adventures of a like character.

Indeed he thought few could recognize him, wrapped up as he was in the cloak he had bought of the tailor.

"But," thought the marquis, "great men cannot hide, even under the cover of a questionable cloak, their greatness; there is an air, a something that at once tells the passenger—there is a great man, he is a don, a grandee of the first class. Yes, there's no denying the truth, I may yet have to run much danger and much trouble, on account of my order. Yes, I may be a martyr, after all, and future ages will speak of me as—as ——"

Before, however, the marquis could find a similitude wherewith to liken himself, he received a sudden check, and he paused in his haste to get home, for he saw before him a host of individuals, who were gesticulating vehemently, and looking suspiciously around them.

Notwithstanding the lofty considerations he was indulging in regarding posthumous fame, he hesitated to advance, because this was not the moment he would have chosen, for a variety of considerations—it was not *the* moment, and that was the fact.

He was not afraid; no, he was valorous, and brave, and incapable of fear; but then great men had great destinies to fulfil, and it would have been against nature to have fallen beneath the violence of a mob composed of obscure men—mean, frantic, plebeians; there was nothing in that for posterity to care about, and it was beneath the dignity of a marquis to die in such an obscure way.

As we said, he paused and looked a variety of ways, but saw none by which he could escape; he would have waited, in vain attempts to admire the shutters of the shops, since they were all closed in consequence of the disturbance, but there was another mob of people coming in at the other end.

In this dilemma the marquis saw that nothing but violent measures would do, and he accordingly determined to attempt to pass the first knot of individuals, who had disturbed the equanimity of his thoughts upon martyrdom.

He approached them, and grasped his sword in his left hand, and boldly advanced towards them. They moved not, shrunk not from him; indeed, they took no notice of him as he passed by them.

"I think they'll hang all the aristocracy from their own windows," said one speaker.

"And a very good job too," remarked another, with much complacency.

"Then all the grandees, and marquises, and counts, will be hanged," said another; "what a glorious prospect."

"Yes, it will be a glorious prospect—when do you think they will do it?"

"Very shortly, I should say; there has been some of them already done for, and more will follow."

"Huzza! glorious! we shall have something for our share, and their ducats will be much better used than if they had the use of them themselves; what a glorious spectacle it will be to see them hanging from their own windows."

"Horrible, horrible!" thought the marquis, as soon as he got out of hearing, for he could not even think but that he should be detected while near them. Dreadful! who would think that there were such people in Madrid? Well, I do not wonder at there being troops when there are such people as these to govern; they ought to be shot by way of example."

While the marquis was thus engaged in getting home, there was another scene being enacted elsewhere.

There was an inmate of his house, and an attendant upon his lady, the marchioness, a young and beautiful lady, the daughter of an officer who fell in battle, much respected, of some rank, and a distant relation of the marquis.

She had been taken by the marchioness out of pity to her forlorn situation, and she was much embarrassed, being an orphan, without countenance, protection, or means of support. She had been several years with the marchioness, and had little to complain of, save the inordinate vanity and conceit of her mistress; this, of course, she could not do otherwise than acquiesce in, as others did.

There were many individuals who visited the marquis, who though, as was usual, they ministered to the marchioness's vanity and the luxurious folly of her husband, really admired the great beauty and innocence of Isabella.

Her virtue was unquestioned; she had been sought by several whose rank and birth, and natural, as well as adventitious advantages, might have turned a wiser head, and better directed understanding than hers. To their shame be it said, they had endeavoured to seduce her by every art of which they were severally masters, but they found their efforts fruitless, and innocence triumphed.

Nevertheless, there was one whose admiration and love for the unfortunate Isabella was sincere, and was not tinctured by any unworthy object or aim. This individual was the son of a nobleman of some wealth and importance, but who at that moment, for family considerations, could not make such proposals as would end in an immediate union, until he was placed in such a position that he could afford to lose the protection of his own family.

In the meantime, he did all he could to keep the affections of Isabella unchanged, and to shew how sincere and lasting was his own love, he was with her as often as he could be so, and often he would linger beneath her window, and serenade in the moonlight summer evenings.

This evening, the lover of Isabella had determined to serenade the object of his heart's best affections, and for that purpose he hired a select band of musicians, and, entering the garden behind the house, he approached the windows of the room in which she slept.

It so happened that the marchioness's apartment lay close by hers, and the music intended for one might readily be taken for the other. This, however, had not been thought of by the lover, who was well known to the marquis and marchioness; indeed, had he believed that any misapprehension could have been made with regard to the object, he would have forgone all rather than incur any reputation for gallantry with the Marchioness de Rotondo.

It would have brought down unsparing ridicule from his own friends, who would never have let him live in peace afterwards. Indeed, he could not think of such a thing; it was absurd.

The party arranged themselves beneath a large mulberry tree, and began to tune their instruments, and afterwards to play and sing some of the finest airs that were known.

As soon as the marchioness heard the tuning of the instruments, she affected to be distressed; she had a sinking at her heart, and yet really could not tell why.

"Ah, Isabella," she exclaimed, "how distressing; what shall I do? oh, dear!"

"Are you ill?" inquired Isabella, respectfully; "command me in anything."

"Oh, no, but I am distressed, terribly distressed; I am, indeed."

"On what account, my lady? On account of these serious riots of late?"

"Oh, no. Dear me, child, how inapprehensive you are. Don't you know," added the marchioness, "there are ailments of the heart as well as of the body?"

"Yes, my lady."

"Then that is my situation; I am distressed, delicately distressed."

"Indeed, my lady."

"Yes; have you never felt the conflicting emotions one must feel when favours are sought that one cannot grant?"

"No, my lady; duty would swallow up every feeling save that of indignation," replied Isabella.

"Oh! oh, dear! how my heart beats! That music! those strains! Oh, I declare it magnetises me!"

"Indeed, my lady; shall I order the servants to drive them hence?"

"By no means," said the marchioness, somewhat hastily; "don't you see they can't help their feelings, and are thus compelled to give vent to them in music. Oh, how beautiful!"

"It is, indeed, beautiful," replied Isabella, almost unconsciously, for she was thinking the strains were intended for her amusement; and, should the marchioness's folly go any further, her lover would, in all probability, be placed in some awkward dilemma, for their love was, as yet, a secret.

"Oh, my Isabella, you know not the feelings that arise in my gentle bosom; indeed, you cannot——"

"No, my lady."

"Then listen to me; but bring me the otto of roses, and sprinkle some; and, and—the other bottle of—you see."

"Yes, my lady," said Isabella who handed her a bottle containing some eau de vie, without troubling herself about the otto of roses.

The marchioness took an invigorating pull, and then disposed of some sweetmeats that were calculated to restore the breath to its pristine state, or to disguise what had just been disposed of medicinally—purely medicinally, for the purpose of restoring the tone of the mind.

"You see," she continued, "I am much admired—you may have noticed that?"

"Oh, yes, my lady, I have."

"Well, that is not my fault. I was born so, therefore could not help it."

"You were, my lady; there is no denying the truth of that."

"Exactly. Well, then, knowing all this as well as I do—for I am not without those who tell me of it —"

"Yes, my lady."

"I pity those who are so unfortunate as to conceive any tender feeling on my account; for the impossibility of their doing more than sigh in vain, certainly strikes me with remorse and pity."

"How good of you to feel such compassion for them," replied Isabella.

"Yes, yes—I couldn't do otherwise; it is their misfortune to feel, and mine to cause these unhappy failings, and I, therefore, blame myself for it, and yet cannot help it."

"No, no—you cannot help it."

"I would tear my eyes out rather than give a bit of uneasiness."

"Oh, don't think of it."

"And, then, you see, my dear Isabella, what can I do?"

"Dismiss these people that cause you so much annoyance."

"Annoyance—dear me, annoyance?"

"Yes, annoyance, my lady."

"I didn't say or mean quite that."

"My lady ——"

"I don't mean to say they annoy me, but I am distressed, delicately distressed to think such a thing should happen. I hope the marquis won't come in; he is so terribly jealous—dreadfully jealous."

"But he knows your virtue."

"Yes, yes, he knows that, and has every reliance upon it; but men are suspicious, naturally."

"But the marquis loves to hear you praised and admired."

"Yes, he does; but then, you see, this is in the cool evening hour, when we are alone and he out."

"You are not alone, my lady."

"No, that is very true; but when we feel we have excited the love of some unhappy fellow-creature by our own charms, then I cannot help feeling great regret and distress."

Isabella was quite unequal to the task of advising the marchioness in her wanderings and delicate distress. She smiled in her own heart to think of the unnecessary compunction she felt in this case, for the young gentleman would have as soon thought of serenading the moon as the Marchioness de Rotondo.

The marchioness drew near the balcony, and peeped gently through the blinds to ascertain who it was.

"Now Heaven forfend that Arguelles should see her," muttered Isabella. "He will come up, and then the marchioness's delicacy will indeed be put to a fine test."

She could not forbear laughing in her own heart at the oddness of the occurrence, if it were to take place.

"Arguelles will be no less annoyed than her ladyship, and much less pleased. He will have much to do to carry out the deception; and yet he will attempt it, or how else will he account for his being there?"

The countess again peeped through the blinds at the musicians.

"I pray Heaven the marquis may not come home, else something unpleasant may occur between them."

"Oh!" exclaimed the marchioness, "I do pity these unfortunate men; but then I have been so universally admired, that I am not at all surprised. Who can it be? I dare say some one of consequence. Who do you think it is, Isabella?"

"I haven't any notion, madam; there are so many who admire your ladyship."

"Ah, that's true. Oh, dear!"

"You sigh."

"Yes, I am sad."

"Sad and sighing."

"Yes; you cannot think the pang it causes a sensitive heart, like mine, to be the cause of so much unhappiness; it makes me sad—it makes me sigh. Heigho! heigho! heigho!"

"The music is very beautiful," remarked Isabella; "and that song ——"

"I wonder who it is?" said the marchioness. "Can it be Don Jose?"

"Don Jose?"

"Ay, he is always talking of my great beauty and charms. I shouldn't wonder if it were; he is a very gallant man. Don't you think, Isabella, I had better tell them to go away? If the marquis should come home, he would not be pleased."

"Shall I go, my lady?"

"No, I will ——"

"Send one of the servants?"

"No, no."

"My lady!"

"I will just beckon one of them in, and tell them myself."

"My lady!"

"Certainly I shall. What are you staring at, Isabella? Hadn't I better put an end to this scene at once, else I may be considered to acquiesce in their entertainment and its object?"

Isabella was silent, and saw that it would be useless to remonstrate with the countess, whose curiosity and vanity were too great to resist an opportunity of gratifying either.

The marchioness was somewhat doubtful as to the mode of calling them to her, but she at length dropped her embroidered handkerchief over the balcony, and then she retired back a few paces on one side, awaiting the result of her experiment. Isabella awaited too with some impatience and fear for the result. She had hardly expected to have seen the marchioness adopt so bold a plan.

In a moment after they could hear the light step upon the stones beneath, and then the form of Arguelles was seen clambering up the balcony, and he entered the apartment. For more than a minute he stood perfectly petrified at beholding two females instead of one. He was the picture of uncertainty and doubt; he looked at one and then at the other; he held the handkerchief still in his hand, and then he looked at that with an air of vexation, as if it were the cause of his unpleasant and perplexing dilemma. Isabella was much vexed also, but she could scarce help smiling at her lover's situation; he was so truly annoyed, and yet she felt pity for him.

The marchioness saw at once that it was not Don Jose—she, however, knew whom it was that had thus serenaded her, and she felt for a moment disappointed; but then the handsome form of the young officer pleased her vanity to think that one so young and so handsome should look up to her with admiration.

"I have to thank you," sighed the marchioness, "for your music, and—and—must beg you to desist."

"My lady!"

"I am sorry to appear ungrateful."

"My lady—it is impossible ——"

"I own it; but there are considerations which compel me to inform you, that I cannot listen with pleasure to such sounds, and allow you to continue blindly the pursuit of an object that can never be attained."

Arguelles bowed, and looked at Isabella, who had withdrawn behind the marchioness, and at the same time putting her finger to her lips with an arch smile, she pointed to her, at the same time she shrugged her shoulders.

Her lover appeared to comprehend the nature of the hint, but still was silent, merely placing the handkerchief against his heart in such an affecting manner that Isabella could scarce keep herself from laughing outright, and the marchioness became melted and in a tender mood.

"I thank you," she continued, "but must beg you will retire."

"And must I mourn in secret, and weep for the one bright luminary that cheers me on my lonely path?"

"Indeed I cannot listen to you," said the marchioness, sympathizingly.

"Not listen—not listen! Oh, what will become of me? I am a benighted mortal—an undone Spaniard!"

"Nay, there are others who are as beautiful as I am—more deserving, and who have no ties to render them incapable of reciprocal affection."

"As beautiful as you!"

"Yes."

"More deserving!"

"Yes."

"No ties!"

"Yes."

"Impossible—quite impossible, divine and lovely one; but mine is a hard lot—I am warmed to life by the vivifying rays of the sun, and yet I am suddenly deprived of his light, and I am thrown into worse than Egyptian darkness."

"Heigho! heigho! this is very dreadful, Isabella, very dreadful, indeed. What can I say? What shall I do?"

"Do, beautiful creature—do give me hope—give me life!"

"Alas! alas! this is very distressing; you pain me very much."

"Heavens! I cause pain—a moment's pain to you, heavenly creature?"

"Yes, great pain."

"I would ex—patriate—I would ex—ex—ex—anything to save you a single pang—a moment's uneasiness."

"Then leave me—leave me," sighed the marchioness, with great feeling; "I cannot tell you to remain; it would be improper—and yet I would not be cruel—but every consideration on earth compels me to do so—seek in others the happiness you desire."

"Happiness! Good Heavens! and where is that to be found, save here? I am doomed to eternal despair; I cannot live; I shall die, and become defunct."

"Oh! Heaven, what a trying scene is this! I would never have permitted you to come in here had I thought things would have come to this length."

"Indeed, lovely lady, you know not what awful havoc your great beauty causes; but vouchsafe to grant me one request,—only one request!"

"I fear I cannot."

"Do not say so; you will deprive me even of the power to quit your presence; I shall die at your feet."

"Ah! dear, don't do that; it will be dreadful."

"Promise, beautiful being."

"I fear I cannot."

"You may safely."

"Indeed, I cannot; I fear you would request something, to grant which would lead to misconstruction, and to future misfortunes; I cannot."

"Nay, do not say that—do not say that; it will not cause you any unhappiness or unpleasantness, but would, nevertheless, be a boon to me, one that would be some balm to my sufferings."

"Name it," sighed the marchioness.

"To allow me to do all I can to give you pleasure —to do all that will give you delight."

The marchioness shook her head, and Arguelles continued in his mock strain of gallantry,—

"I would beg of you to allow me the delight of beholding the mansion you dwell in, and the felicity of offering these entertainments for your pleasure, and happy shall I be if they please you."

"Indeed, I fear to do so; you will require more,— you will wish to see me, I am sure of it."

"I cannot deny my wishes; but, if you will consent to permit me, I will promise never to request it."

"Will you?"

"As great as the pain may be, I will promise that I will require but one thing more, and then I will remain content, though my heart yearns for more."

"What say you, Isabella? You are young, but you may be able, by chance, to give good advice."

"I, my lady?"

"Yes, you, Isabella."

"Then I should like to know what the gentleman's other request is before I give my opinion upon it."

"What is it, sir?" inquired the marchioness, a little coquettishly.

"That I may be permitted to see that young gentlewoman there, and learn from her all that I would know concerning your welfare and happiness. I would not be obtrusive on one so kind and gentle as yourself."

"I think we may grant these requests, Isabella," said the marchioness.

"As your ladyship pleases."

"Adorable marchioness."

"Hold, sir! If I grant your request, you must not attempt to encroach; if you do, you will be forbidden the place. Adieu! I can hear no more."

"And quite enough, too," exclaimed the marquis, who himself entered the apartment after he had reached his home in a fume, for he had been used with some indignity on his way home, and had again to trust to his own personal speed for safety. "And quite enough, too, Signior Arguelles. I did not think this of you. Pho—pho! it is quite hot. Had I not mislaid my sword—pho! pho!—I'd have taught you a lesson; but you wear a sword—pho! pho!"

"Indeed, marquis, I do; it is not a hot one, however, but it is ready when you desire it. Farewell!"

So saying, Signior Arguelles quitted the apartment as he entered it, leaving the marquis blowing, and threatening dark deeds of vengeance against everybody.

The marchioness shrieked and fainted, and the marquis ran to support her, his indignation being speedily changed to sorrow and tribulation, lest his adorable marchioness should die; he called himself all the names he could think of, and accused himself of wickedness and murder, at which period the lady showed symptoms of coming to.

CHAPTER LXI.

THE PANIC AMONG THE ATTENDANTS AT THE CHATEAU. — THE MYSTERIOUS VOICE IN THE GARDEN.

St. Paul accused the Athenians of superstition, and, if St. Paul were now in existence, he would find abundant material for continuing the accusation, go where he would; and possibly, in the course of his travels, that gentleman might make the valuable discovery that superstition was not a resident of any particular clime or place, but was incidental to the whole human race, and has gone hand-in-hand with religion since the beginning of the world.

If, however, there be among various forms of faith one or two more than others calculated to foster superstitious feelings, perhaps those are Presbyterianism and Catholicism—not but what we have *quantum suff.* of superstition among ourselves. Spain, however, has ever been the stronghold of such feelings, and its inhabitants (poor priest-ridden bigots!) have never had a very clear notion of which was the best policy—to propitiate the devil or laud the Almighty.

No wonder, then, that the sudden appearance of Don Cæsar, looking just as if nothing had happened to him, on the terrace, after half a dozen arquebuses had been discharged to all appearances clearly at him, should produce an amount of consternation as ludicrous as it was extensive.

So profound a mystery did his escape from absolute death appear, that no human solution could be formed of the circumstance; and consequently, as it must be accounted for somehow, those who saw him on the terrace, looking so cool and so composed, when he ought to all intents and purposes to be dead, could come to no other conclusion than that there was some dreadful necromancy in the business, and he was proof against all mortal means of doing him an injury.

Now there are a great many elastic, easy-going, pleasant consciences, which can get over a crime when no consequences of a disagreeable nature are likely to result from its commission. To shoot a man, provided he is hit and becomes uncommonly dead, is all very well; but to miss him, or to find that to hit him is to do him no harm, of course may well be supposed to produce some acrimony of feeling on his part, and so to render the position of those who have tried to do him an injury critical in the extreme.

This was precisely the view which Don Jose's rascally servants took regarding Don Cæsar. They had no particular objections to shoot him. The fact of having killed him would not have disturbed their repose, but to fail in it, and so convert him into an active enemy of unknown powers of mischief, made them turn pale, and filled them with a thousand fears.

Helter-skelter—pell-mell—one over the other, some shouting, some praying, and some nearly dead from fear, they bundled into the chateau in a confused mass, the moment they got over the first paralysing effect of finding that the supposed murdered man was really and seriously quite alive.

Arquebuses were thrown on one side, hats were lost, shoes escaped in the scuffle, and, after impeding each other to a great extent, they all reached the hall, or common waiting-room, where they were in the habit of sitting; and, closing and fastening the door on the inside, they looked at each other's pale faces with expressions of the most ludicrous alarm and consternation.

All this was the work of not more than a couple of minutes after they had first caught sight of Don Cæsar; and now arose the anxious question of "What shall we do?"

None spoke till a few moments after they all convinced themselves they were in safety, but terror was so legibly painted on every countenance that it could not be mistaken ; and one of the six scoundrels, who had a strong bias to corpulency, and consequently had lost breath considerably during the proceedings, sank into a chair with a gasp like the pant of a steam-engine when first starting, exclaiming,—

"We are lost—we are all lost ! What will become of us ? He must be the devil himself."

A general groan of horror burst from the whole lot as this most sagacious opinion was propounded, and mentally each one gave himself up as a doomed man.

"What will become of us all ?" moaned one. "I placed no less than two bullets this morning in my arquebus—that I could swear to."

"Then you will be twice as much served out as I shall," said another, "for I had only one in mine."

"But you levelled at him ?"

"Yes—I—I certainly did."

"And I," almost cried another,—"I made sure of hitting him, and I'm sure I did too ; but if people won't be shot, what are other people to do, you know ? We are all aware how very dead he ought to be. It's too bad, it is indeed. We are ill-used men, all of us, my friends."

"Oh, too bad—too bad !" said every one. "We are ill-used."

"But what's to be done ?" suggested the one who had the inclination to be corpulent. "What's to be done ? That's the question, comrades—What are we all to do ?"

"It's all very well for you, you fat fool," cried one, who was of an irascible temperament, "to go on asking what are we to do. How can we tell what we are to do ? If you cannot think of anything reasonable to do yourself, just hold your tongue, will you ?"

"You are a nice article," replied the corpulent man, "to put yourself out of temper when you ought to be confessing your sins."

"I—confessing ! Why should I be confessing more than any one else, eh ?—why should I be confessing ?"

"Because you took a pleasure in shooting at the—the—I don't know what to call him."

"I—a pleasure ?"

"Yes ; you grinned—I saw you grin. Now don't deny it ; you know you grinned."

"Now, by the mass ——"

"Hold him, comrades—hold him ; he's dangerous ; hold him ! When once Giachomo gets out of temper, he always wants to snap off some one's head. Hold him, good friends, hold him."

How far the quarrel might have proceeded it is hard to say, for the disputants were all ready, and were never more disposed to disputation ; but a sudden stop was put to it by a perceptible effort being made by some one to open the door of the apartment, which now they silently blessed their stars they had had the presence and forethought to lock.

It never occurred to them for a moment that the person who sought admission to the apartment might not be the daring intruder of the garden, who bore such a charmed life that a shower of bullets would not harm him. No ; he was uppermost in their thoughts,—and that he would be likely to pursue them, in order to achieve some revenge, was a harrowing consideration, that prevented them from taking an accurate view of anything.

The moment, therefore, they heard and saw the handle of the lock turning, such a pause came over 'them that any ore who could have seen those men, without knowing the cause of the great disturbance of their nerves, would have thought them, by their breathing, a set of people afflicted with ague. Not a word dared they speak for some seconds, but in mute terror they watched the door, to see if it gave way before what they considered the supernatural touch of the dread being who would not be shot by six arquebuses.

The lock resisted, and they breathed a little more freely. Then their hearts flew to their mouths again, when the person who sought admission gave a kick to the door, which threatened the demolition of one of its panels. A few more such hearty manifestations of a desire to get in, they felt assured would accomplish the result, and then what was to become of them. The inquiry was a fearful one.

After this salute to the panel of the door, the person outside, with a religious intensity that was dreadfully alarming, gave utterance to about four most swinging oaths all in a breath. No wonder that the hair nearly stood on end on the heads of the terrified rascals who had failed to accomplish a bad deed, and were consequently in such a state of abject terror.

A sudden idea now struck one of them, which no sooner found a place in his censorium, than he hastened to bestow upon it the meed of practical approbation. It was to hide, and a hiding-place suggested itself to him of a capital description.

There were three deeply set windows in the room, with permanent seats under them, the said seats forming large chests at the same time, and being accessible by lifting up the hinged top. It was in one of these places that the most ingenious of the party, fearing that the door would be burst open, prepared to ensconce himself.

Creeping towards it on tip-toes, and followed by the eyes of his comrades, who wondered what on earth he was about to do, and yet dared not ask him, for fear their voices should " prate their whereabouts," he lifted the lid of the seat, and in another moment had crept in, and was perfectly hidden by pulling the lid down again. There was plenty of room, and not a little did this ingenious person congratulate himself upon his presumed security.

The idea was felicitous, so thought his companions, and before any man of moderate powers of animation could have counted ten, the other two window-seats were similarly occupied, and then, by that means, out of the six persons who had attempted the life of Don Cæsar, three were completely put out of sight.

But if the situation of six men had been critical, although it was but one of whom they stood in such fear, how much more so was the situation of three, who, if terror would have allowed them to make any resistance at all, had, of course, but half the power to back them. Truly, those three felt desperate, like men who had been left upon a wreck, and saw no mode of escape.

Then there came another knock, and then a volley more oaths—and yet another, and yet more oaths. What was to be done ? The chimney—yes, the chimney—one thought of that, and he was up it, only leaving one leg visible, in a moment.

Another tried the same means of concealment. The chimney would hold two, and that was all. These two were a mutual support, but the third found it impossible to wedge himself in, and was not he, then, a desperate man ?

He felt like some forlorn wretch, abandoned by the whole human race—left alone to perish on some arid waste. Bang went the kicks upon the door. The lock was giving way—use had impaired its powers—it was certainly giving way. Desperate emergencies require desperate remedies. There was no hiding-place—no mode of escape, for he would have broken his neck had he tried to leave the room by one of the windows. Timid animals will turn and face the hunter, when too hotly pursued, and so with a desperate resolution this man waited until the door should be burst open, resolved to make a grand rush when it was so, and to escape if it were possible so to do.

He could fancy now the man who was on the other side, getting up his energies to make the assault which should force the door almost from its hinges. As plainly and clearly as if he had heard him announce such an intention, he knew he was about it by the ominous silence that prevailed.

The perspiration stood upon his brow. Like Bob Acres, he trembled with excess of valour, and could he have made the bargain at all available, he would at that moment have sold his life for a very small sum indeed.

He heard a scuffling noise—he held his breath—bang came the man outside against the door, and open it flew.

At the instant, he who had endured such terrors within, made his grand rush, and, as might naturally be expected, he met the other in mid career, and over they both rolled, nearly stunned by the force of the concussion.

Neither looked to see who or what was his opponent, but both fought with a desperation easier to be conceived than described. Kicking, striking, plunging, swearing. Such a tremendous riot as those two men made, until one got the other by the throat, and they looked in each others faces, seemed hardly credible. Then they found out, to their mutual surprise, that they were fellow-servants.

Relaxing their hold of each other, they glared in mutual surprise for some moments.

" Lopez," then gasped one.

" Carlos," groaned the other. " What in the name of all the saints, did you mean by pitching your head into my stomach in this extraordinary way?"

" What—what made you burst open the door?"

"Because I found it fast, and nobody said anything."

" Yes, but ——"

" But what—are you mad?"

" Nearly. I thought you were the man who wouldn't be shot in the garden. We all thought so."

" All?"

" Yes—hush. There are five hidden here—one in each of the window-seats, and two up the chimney."

" Indeed! say you so—hush! we may have some sport with their fears."

Those who were hidden had endured a world of agony during the bursting open of the door, and the subsequent conflict that had ensued. From their places of concealment, they heard but indistinctly what was going on, and the sudden cessation of the sounds of strife, and the low murmur of voices, filled them with a thousand imaginary fears.

Perhaps had they been more master of themselves, and less thoroughly unnerved by fear, they might have recognised the voice of one whom they well knew; but as it was, they did not, and to add to their terrors, he who had burst the door open, now with malice afore-thought, and a wonderful appreciation of the ludicrous, which was much enjoyed and silently encouraged by him, who had been, by the superior activity of his comrades, deprived of a hiding-place, took up an unloaded arquebus, and with the heavy butt-end of it, dealt such a blow upon each of the window-seats, that their occupants thought the end of the world was surely come, and were nearly distilled to jelly with fright; then, highly enjoying the joke, he poked the arquebus up the chimney, and made with it such an assault upon the legs of those who were there, that human endurance reached its limit, and down they came in no very enviable condition, into the room, bawling for mercy, and jumbling up prayers, oaths, and entreaties, in the strangest possible manner.

Of course an eclaircissement could not now be far off, and Lopez, fearing that the riot should reach the ears of Don Jose, hastened to enlighten those who were so terrified as to who he was. Then the window seats were relieved of their occupants, and a sufficiently strange and odd looking group they all appeared when collected. Scarcely, however, had they time to interchange a word when an eighth person was added to the group, in the shape of the woman who had been commissioned to act the double part of gaoler and attendant to poor persecuted Maritana.

Her looks sufficiently proclaimed that she had some fearful tidings to impart. Her eyes were preternaturally wide open—her face was pale, and she was evidently suffering from fear of no ordinary character.

" Gracious! what's the matter?" exclaimed every-body in a breath. " Holy saints deliver us!"

The woman sank into a chair, and said, " Oh—oh—oh—oh !" varying the interjection until it sunk into a whine like that of an expiring puppy dog.

This increased the consternation, and such a volley of questioning ensued that it was enough to deafen anybody.

" What is it? what's the matter? what have you seen? where is it? speak—tell us?"

" A ghost !" gasped the woman.

" We know it," said all the six, who had been at the attempted shooting of Don Cæsar—" we know it."

" A dreadful ghost !"

" Yes—yes—yes! St. Peter look down upon us! Where did you see him—where—where?"

" I—I didn't see him, I only heard him. Oh, it's awful ! In the garden ! Such a groaning under ground, and then a solemn voice all of a sudden says,— ' The saints have mercy upon me!' "

" A voice?"

" Yes, a solemn voice !"

" And under ground, too—did you say under ground?"

" Yes, a long way under ground. The place is haunted—I shall leave it. I wouldn't, and couldn't, and daren't sleep another night here for a thousand crowns."

" It is haunted," exclaimed one; " the six of us shot six arquebuses, some of them having two bullets each in them, at a man, and there he stood afterwards as well as ever. Ghosts have taken possession of the chateau, and I won't stay in it for one."

" Nor I,—nor I," said several. " Let us leave, and make the best of our way to Madrid, or some terrible calamity will befall us here, you may depend."

" But what will our master, Don Jose, say?"

" Never mind what he says. If he finds us, well and good. I'll give him leave to say what he likes if ever he claps eyes upon me again, I can tell you. I'm not going to remain here to become a prey of all sorts of supernatural things; who knows what may happen to us? It's really dreadful to think of it. I'm off for one—who'll go?"

" I'll go," said the woman. " I don't object to trifles, but when a voice comes from under ground, it's too much for my nerves."

After some further consultation, it was agreed by all those present that they would, in a body, leave the chateau at once, rather than encounter the supernatural beings who they now fairly believed had taken up their abode in it. Such a movement, to be sure, would leave Don Jose with only three attendants; but little they cared for that, nor would they have cared had they known what we and our readers happen to know already, that of those three attendants, one was tied to a tree outside the walls of the building, and another was at the bottom of a well within the walls.

Virtually, therefore, Don Jose was about to be left in the chateau with only one person devoted to his service, for we cannot, of course, reckon Lazarillo, who was eager to do him as much disservice as possible for his persecution of Don Cæsar, than whom, to the romantic-minded boy, there was not a more chivalrous, great, and perfect a character in all the world.

The domestics then having decided upon leaving the chateau, crept from what might be called their council chamber, and made their way into the now much dreaded garden, through the mazes of which Don Cæsar, had he known as much, might have chased them all with the greatest ease, and filled them, at the same time, with the most unbounded terror. As it

was, he was getting rid, when he least expected it, of a host of enemies, and the chateau was being left wonderfully clear for any operations he might choose to undertake, with a view to the release of his beautiful and much loved, much persecuted countess.

In traversing the garden the domestics had to pass near to the well where their comrade, who had in so dastardly a manner attempted to assassinate Don Cæsar, was confined, and he hearing, it is to be presumed, the sound of footsteps near his very uncomfortable and peculiar prison, set up a sudden shout that to them sounded as if it came from the very bowels of the earth, and filled them with such alarm that one and all took to their heels, and ran as if a hundred devils were after them.

They were clear of the garden in a few moments, and leaving the gate at which they emerged wide open, they scampered off through the little wood in the immediate vicinity, and which led to the high road to Madrid, with great precipitation.

It so happened that these people were doomed to experience a great number of false alarms, for once they passed near the tree to which the gentleman was tied, who thought to have got so easily the better of

Don Cæsar, although, from the luxuriant foliage around, they did not see him.

He then, hearing footsteps, and fancying, like his companion in the well, that there was a chance of escape, unconsciously added to the terror of the already sufficiently alarmed servants by calling loudly for help. Anger, or fear, or despair, might have, to a certain extent, changed his voice, but from whatever cause, certain it is that he was not recognised, and the only effect his shout for assistance had, was to induce one of the remaining lot to exclaim,—

"There he is—there he is! Run—run. Let us all run. He is after us now."

The hint was immediately taken, and what before was a tolerably quick progress, now became an absolute race, until the chateau, and all that it contained, was left far behind, and the city of Madrid was beginning to be visible in the distance.

Thus had superstition done what honour and honesty could not; namely, stripped Don Jose of his rascally dependants, and left him in a state of desolation, which he could never have anticipated for a moment, and which, if he had been at once aware of, would have filled him with the most lively sensations of alarm for his own personal safety, as well as for the success of the guilty projects he had in hand ; but he, of course, had no suspicion of what was going on ; and, indeed, the whole of the proceedings which we have been compelled to relate at some length, as occurring after the firing at Don Cæsar on the terrace, had occupied but a very short period of time in transacting, inasmuch as fright had tended most materially to accelerate the movements of the otherwise idle Spanish domestics.

In the meantime, however, affairs at Madrid were assuming a portentous aspect, and some of the characters of our tale were becoming involved in circumstances with which it is necessary we should make our readers acquainted.

CHAPTER LXII.

THE AGED PRISONER.—A GENEROUS ACT ILL REQUITED.—THE YELLOW DOMINO.

THE mob reigned triumphant for a short period in Madrid, and did what mobs usually do during their temporary supremacy—let the denizens of the gaols free ; setting at liberty those who were considered too profligate, and had offended against the good of society so deeply, that they were believed to be incapable of being good citizens, or of enjoying their liberty, save to the prejudice of all honest and good men. The prisons of Madrid were, as we have already related, on the first outbreak of the disturbance, all broken open and the prisoners set free. Among them were many whose liberty was an injury to the state, let who would be master—king, aristocrat, or democrat,—for the end of government, be the name under which it is carried on what it may, is, and must be, for the good of the community ; and, therefore, to let loose a number of criminals of the worst description upon the city, assisted only in making confusion worse confounded, and rendering even the questionable result of extracting good out of evil improbable.

But among the troop of crime-stained human beings thus returned to the population, there were a few who never deserved the state they were reduced to ; men who were thrown into dungeons, and there kept at the arbitrary will and pleasure of some one individual, and were, after a lapse of time, forgotten by those who had been the only cause of their lengthened incarceration : and young men sometimes grow old and grey-bearded ere they escape, finding when they come out all whom they once knew were either dead, or so far removed from their sphere, that it was impossible to recognize any one—they were lone men, who prayed that death might close their eyes, and thus permit them to escape inhabiting a dreary void.

Political offences, the most venial perhaps of any, are usually punished with more severity than any other, and the unrelenting hate and vengeance of the oppressor always followed the victim that was once in his power.

Madrid formed no exception to this, and its prisons had more than one victim of political oppression. How could it be otherwise—a state governed almost solely by the will of its prince.

In one of the prisons were a set of dungeons, denominated state dungeons, and these were little known to the inhabitants ; it was surmised by a few, but from the little mention of them being made, the fact was never contested.

However, here they were, and it was not until the gaolers, who had been driven from their office, made it known to the multitude, from compassion, or fear of the consequences, that they knew, or at all suspected, anything of the kind being in existence. He feared that the unfortunate men there confined would be starved to death, and if it afterwards became generally known, it would be the cause, perhaps, of dire vengeance being exacted from them.

Among these unfortunate prisoners was one whose fate was hard, and whose deserts were anything but such as he received from the hands of power—but we will give his own words.

———

I was born in Valentia, of noble parents, and a decent patrimony would descend to me on the decease of my father, who was an old man, and I was an only child.

At eighteen years of age I came to Madrid, for the purpose of finishing my education, under the care of an old friend of my father's, by becoming acquainted with all the politeness of this great city, and, if possible, to push my way into public business, honour and promotion.

There appeared a very good prospect of both, for my father's friend was well connected, and I was soon intrusted with several private commissions, which I had the good fortune in executing so as to obtain his favour and approbation. I was even invited to one of the numerous and splendid parties he was in the habit of giving to the nobility, and among them I saw the elite of Spanish nobility and wealth.

This was a scene fit to turn the head of any young fellow, and though it altered not my steadiness of purpose and sobriety of demeanour, yet it gave me greater hopes than I ought to have had.

Among those who visited the minister was the celebrated Don Sebastian, whose power and influence was so great that he could at any time procure the downfall of any man who displeased him, or gave him any cause for offence. He was a great commander, and, at the same time, he belonged to a very rich and powerful family.

I saw this nobleman at the minister's fete, and I saw also his daughter Christina ; she was the most beautiful being I had ever seen ; I was perfectly enraptured when I beheld her, and leaning myself against one of the marble pillars, I gazed upon her.

Christina was scarce sixteen years of age, but she was more perfectly lovely than anything I had ever beheld ; every lineament of her noble countenance bespoke more than mere beauty of form—she had a heart and mind within that graced the beautiful casket that held them ; her form was more perfect than the Venus di Medicis. I saw and loved, and my eyes feasted upon a form that I could not have believed it possible to exist.

" My friend," said a voice behind me, " beware how you gaze upon that animated piece of loveliness."

I turned, and saw my friend.

" Do you not think she is perfect ?" he inquired, with a smile.

" I do."

" And yet she is not more beautiful than she is good and accomplished."

" That enhances her beauty," I replied.

" It does."

" Who is she ?"

" The only child of Don Sebastian di Segoria, a nobleman of great power and wealth," was the reply.

" Can you present me to the daughter ?" I inquired.

" I can."

" Do so, and you will oblige me."

" I would rather not."

" Indeed ! and why ?"

" Because the consequences would be most fearful to yourself."

" I do not understand you," I replied, " nor can I see any consequences that I would have any fear about."

"You will fall in love with her I am sure," he answered.

"I am not sure; but what of that? if I were, there is no treason."

"But there is unhappiness."

"What, in loving a beautiful woman? my friend, I cannot agree with you."

"There is always unhappiness in unrequited love."

"Do you know it will be unrequited?" I inquired.

"No; but in either case, loved, or not loved in return, your case is equally desperate and equally hopeless."

"How?"

"Because Don Sebastian is too rich, too powerful, to look upon your union with a child, an only child of his, as the very extremity of audacity and presumption."

"Well?"

"Then he would immediately have you punished by some means or another; there would be no escape—he has more power than any man in Madrid, or even in Spain."

"He cannot harm me otherwise than by hiring assassins to poniard me."

"There is no knowing what a fierce, proud man will do when he considers himself injured or insulted."

"Well, well, I wish merely to be introduced to Donna Christina from motives of curiosity, to see if all that is said of her corresponds with the fact, and to ascertain if she be as well taught as she is beautiful, as amiable as lovely."

"Of that you will be too fatally convinced, I know full well; but since you urge me to do so, I cannot refuse you; do not blame me for my compliance with your wishes afterwards."

"Far from it—if any misfortune arises, I am to blame, and not you; do, therefore, my friend, introduce me."

Thus urged, my friend led me to the part of the saloon where this beautiful being sat surrounded by several of the very *elite* of the nobility, and who looked upon me with revengeful eyes, as I was presented to her in due form and ceremony.

I saw a slight blush mantle her cheek, but it quickly subsided, as did the smile of satisfaction that lit up her countenance.

I was fortunate enough to make myself agreeable, and was permitted to dance with her, as might have been expected. This produced me plenty of enemies; but I made good use of my time, and when it was necessary we should part, I had the satisfaction of perceiving that she regretted my quitting her.

The next day, when I was quietly thinking over the occurrences of the previous day, I was surprised at the entrance of a tall Spanish officer.

"Signior," said I, "what may be the cause of this visit?"

"A somewhat delicate affair," he said.

"Proceed, signior, I am all attention."

"My friend Captain Xavier Xantippe Alfonso Manfred de Castile, instructs me to call upon you to resign your pretensions to a certain lady with whom you danced last night, to his exclusion. He feels himself aggrieved, and demands that you renounce her."

"It is the first time I ever saw her, and therefore I do not feel myself at all called upon to act in the manner he demands."

"He will consider that a subterfuge, and will not take it as an answer."

"Indeed!"

"No."

"Then I am afraid he will get no other from me," I replied, angry at the absurdity of a mere captain seeking such an acknowledgment from me.

"You know the alternative?" replied the captain, gravely.

"An appeal to arms?"

"Exactly."

"There's the length of my sword," said I, unsheathing my weapon, and tendering him the same to measure.

The officer very coolly measured the blade, and, returning it to me with a bow, said,—

"At what hour shall we say, that will be convenient to you?"

"To-morrow morning, at day-break, if you please; near the ramparts." •

"I will be there with my principal."

With that he left my lodgings, and I saw no more of him.

The next morning I took a friend with me, and at daybreak proceeded towards the ramparts, and there I saw Captain Xavier Xantippe and his tall friend. I now recognised the captain to be one of those whose envious and revengeful looks I had incurred when I was first introduced to Christina by my friend.

"I am to understand," he said, "that you refuse to give over any pretensions you may have to the young lady my friend has mentioned to you?"

"I gave your friend my answer at the time. That was not deemed satisfactory, and you have the measure of my sword. I do not come here for nothing."

"Certainly not; but young gentleman, recollect, this is an important affair."

"It may be."

"It is. Are there no means of coming to an accommodation? You ought to understand that it is impossible you can succeed with the young lady."

"That impossibility ought to satisfy you, then," I replied.

"It does not."

"I cannot help it."

"Think again."

"Are you waiting for an interruption?" I inquired.

He darted a look of fury at me, and then turned to his second, and having exchanged a few words, we were placed, and our conflict began.

It was not of very long duration, and ended with my disarming my antagonist, and giving him a very slight wound. He was at my mercy, but I gave him his life.

"Are you satisfied?" I inquired.

He merely bowed.

"If there is aught more required of me, say so before I quit the ground; for, as far as I know, this is all I came for—to give you satisfaction."

"We are satisfied," replied the second of my adversary. "You have acted with great generosity."

We bowed to each other, and mutually parted. I made no stipulation, because I would not precipitate matters with Donna Christina, and I would not hurry things forward, or attract any observation with respect to her, lest her father should be the man he was described, and then my love might be nipped ere it had time to blossom.

It was some days ere I had the opportunity of again beholding Christina, and when I did I had the satisfaction of perceiving that her eyes brightened as I approached her, while she gazed about her as if she feared I might be the sufferer for her partiality.

I hastened to greet her, and in doing so my eyes encountered the form of the captain with whom I had fought. He did not seem much at home, but rather uneasy; however, as he did not condescend to notice me, I overlooked his presence, and sought only to render myself agreeable in the eyes of Christina, with whom I was madly in love.

This passion, however, I was careful to conceal from

every eye; but I believed, and wished that it did not escape that of the object beloved. Whether it was seen or not I cannot tell, or whether it was merely the feeling of pleasure she felt at my approach, I know not; but her eyes expressed more than mere courtesy. What could I attribute it to save love? You will say the time was too short. Not at all; her love might have been as sudden as my own, and, moreover, I do not think it was so, for the time was indeed too short for any serious feeling of friendship to arise.

Love may be the growth of a single interview, not so friendship, which requires time to detect virtues, and points of similarity of taste and thoughts. These are the springs of friendship, and they are known and palpable, whereas those of love are hidden and concealed, and often are never found out. Thus it was; I was in love, and I knew not the cause farther than the model of excellence and female beauty that I had met with.

I met Christina on several occasions at these parties, and yet we never had any opportunity to communicate our thoughts to each other; and, indeed, we might not have done so, had we the opportunity afforded us, for it was but recently that we became at all acquainted. However, we had a conversation, which did lead to something that was to me important. We were talking together about the various amusements given in Madrid, when she said, suddenly.—

"Do you go to the masquerade?"

"What masquerade?" I inquired.

"That given by the Marquis de Rosignal, at his palace."

"I had not heard of it."

"There will be a bull-fight of the most magnificent description."

"I have heard of it, and think I shall be there."

"You will, doubtless, be of the party to the masquerade."

"I have no doubt of it; but wherefore do you ask? Are you to be there, and grace the saloons with your presence?"

"I shall be there."

"In a mask, of course."

"Yes—yes; I shall be in a disguise. I mean to have a mask."

"May I ask what will be your disguise?" I inquired.

"And wherefore?"

"Because I would know my friends, those whom I most desire to see. If I were to see you, and have a delightful hour's conversation, uninterrupted by any human being, oh! that would be happiness."

"Indeed!"

"It would, I assure you. Will you forgive me for making the request?"

"Oh, yes."

"And grant it?"

"I will."

"Thanks, my best angel—my fondest hopes of happiness will be realised."

"I shall be there in a yellow domino."

"A yellow domino?"

"Yes."

"Very well, I shall be there in a black one, and shall soon know you. I will speak first to you."

"Very well."

This subject was then dropped, and we conversed upon other topics, and stopped as long as we dared with each other, and then separated.

I had noticed my vanquished rival; his dark eyes followed me everywhere, and I thought I beheld a flash of fire when he saw me gently press the hand of the beautiful Christina.

The day at length came on which the bull-fight was to take place. It was a grand spectacle; the noble and infuriated animal bellowed and pawed the earth, and galloped furiously around the arena, and more than one of his tormentors got badly gored, and were carried out.

At length a well-known matador stepped up, and, as the infuriated animal rushed in full charge against him, he passed the knife into his neck, and the animal fell at full length upon the earth. At the conclusion of the sight I went to the masquerade, and wore a black domino; and, after walking about some time, I met with the yellow domino, as I anticipated. I watched it for some time, and, being convinced it was the beautiful Christina, I addressed her, and found that I was quite satisfied of my hopes.

"Dear Christina," I said, "this is a greater happiness than I had dared to expect."

"Dare!" she replied; "if the young dare not, who dare? And wherefore did you not dare?"

"Because your beauty, goodness, wealth, and rank, were such that would almost cause me to be condemned for conceit, and perhaps worse motives than those I am actuated by."

"And what are your motives?" said my beautiful companion.

"Love! I love one of the fairest and most beautiful beings I ever thought of, even in moments when the imagination runs most wild, untrammelled by reality."

"You are enthusiastic; but I have heard that you are not without the due share of excellencies one would attribute to you."

"Indeed! and what are they?—for I must confess I am not without curiosity. I have not been so long in Madrid but I am anxious to know what the world says of me, if, indeed, it say anything."

"Yes, it says you have honour and generosity."

"That it may attribute the first to me, I can very well conceive; but, that it should the latter, I cannot understand."

"I have heard of a passage in the life of Captain Xavier Xantippe."

"Oh, have you heard of him?"

"Yes."

"Who is he?"

"He is nothing more than a spy that my father is pleased to place about me to step in and deter any one from approaching me."

"He is no suitor, then?"

"No, none; but he is a soldier, and of ancient family, and having fought several duels, in which he has taken life, he is very respectfully treated, and he saves my father much trouble. You have, however, incurred his displeasure, and I now warn you to be most cautious."

"Let us fly!" I exclaimed, suddenly. "Danger may surround us. What you have said is enough to cause me to fear the worst—we may be separated for ever."

"We may; but I cannot do so now—at another and more fitting opportunity."

"Ha!" exclaimed I, "there is another yellow domino!"

"Truly; but what a gigantic person. I will change mine."

She went into a passage, and turning her domino, she altered it to a black one.

The gigantic yellow domino stalked about, and then retired to a side table, at which he partook of refreshments on a scale that astonished every one.

"He has done that," whispered one person to another, "to my knowledge, six or eight times. Who can he be?"

"I don't know, but should say he must be the fiend, for he carries the bottomless pit in his stomach, or he could never eat so much, and drink. Good

Heavens! he has taken more than a dozen bottles of wine!"

The yellow domino arose, and walked about, and was received with great respect, for every one got out of his way. At length he went out for a short time, and then returned; the same operation was performed six or eight times more, to the utter horror of the whole assembly, who were nearly fainting with fear and disgust.

At length, some gentlemen drew their swords, and advanced to ascertain who it was, but had like to have paid for their temerity, for several got thrown over; but the yellow domino was torn off, and it was discovered it was one of the royal guard, who, having obtained a ticket of admission, passed it from one to the other, until the whole company were gratified and satisfied.

The company were amused at the oddness of the incident, and I quitted the masquerade, having made an assignation for the following evening with Christina. But I was never to keep that assignation, for when I quitted the mansion I was seized and bound, carried blindfolded, and thrust into prison, and here I have been years—Heaven knows how many. I am an old man now, and Christina must be an old woman, if living. I desire not to live; my love has outlived my hopes and my love of life. The enemy whose life I spared has been the cause of my imprisonment; I saw his dark visage, despite the muffled cloak. But have passed through a long life of imprisonment, and care not for liberty.

———

Thus ended the prisoner's tale, and he had scarce finished it when he became a corpse. The mob gazed for a few moments in pity, and then pursued their way, shouting "Liberty for ever!"

CHAPTER LXIII.
DON JOSE'S FRIGHT, AND THE PROGRESS OF EVENTS FOR AN HOUR.

DON JOSE took things coolly, and although, when first he heard the outcries and confusion created by the servants while he was in conversation with the king, he had started with alarm, the sudden cessation of the tumult, in consequence, as we happen to know, of those who had made it shutting themselves up in the common room appropriated to the use of the domestics, re-assured him.

He thought that it must be one of those idle clamours which will occur in all households, based upon nothing, and ending in nothing;—one of those foolish alarms to which the credulous and ignorant are subject, and which are scarcely, if at all, worth the trouble of inquiring into.

Hence, when all was quiet, he had continued, as we have duly recorded, his conversation with the king, and brought it to as successful a climax as he could; after which had ensued the slight conversation he had held with our friend Lazarillo, who had now as strong an objection to leave the chateau for the queen's residence at Aranjues, as he had before been anxious to do so, when he thought that such a proceeding would lead to the release of Maritana, and the benefit and ultimate happiness of Don Cæsar.

The information which Jose fancied he had got from Lazarillo, as regarded an attack upon the privacy of the chateau by a priest, whom he firmly believed the boy had knocked on the head, upon reflection, gave him more uneasiness than he liked to confess, even to himself, and tended, along with other matters, to obliterate the alarm which so short a time before had come so suddenly to his ears.

"The rascals!" he muttered; "the rascally priests! Oh, that they had all one head, that I might strike it off! the insatiable wretches! Shall I hazard a prophecy concerning my own career? If I do, it is that my downfall will come from the machinations against me of the church."

Don Jose was decidedly wrong when he uttered this prediction; it would have been an unwelcome truth for any one to have whispered to him, and perhaps dangerous to the discerning individual who made the discovery; but, the fact was, that with his talents, and freedom from the superstitions of the age in which he lived, Don Jose might even have defied the priesthood, and nothing could have materially shaken his power but his own vices, and his own ungovernable ambition.

These were the rocks on which the gay bark of his fortune was sure to be wrecked, and which would, sooner or later, involve him in a ruin as complete as it would be desperate.

But what man, standing on the pinnacle of greatness, and grasping yet for more, ever paused in his career to say,—"My ambition is boundless, and will be the ruin of me?" Not one—not one. The mere fact of making such a remark, would at once carry with it its own refutation; and the individual with discretion enough to make such discovery, would likewise have discretion enough to curb the haughty overbearing spirit, and make it succumb a little to circumstances.

Jose crossed his arms upon his breast, after he had left Lazarillo, and stood in a small ante-chamber, adjoining to one of the principal reception rooms, in deep thought.

"To-night," he kept muttering; "to-night. Yes, to-night."

Then he paced to and fro, and smiled for a moment—one of those hideous, fretful smiles, without mirth, which occasionally flitted across his face when he contemplated any more than usually monstrous villany.

"To-night—to-night," he again muttered. "Philip is surely getting into dotage. Never did I see him in such a state of irresolution as he has shown during the short time he has been in this chateau. He seems to be the very abject slave of every little circumstance which creates the least alarm; he has no confidence in his own power—no confidence in his own safety, and the feelings of foolish superstition which I thought I had half bantered, half reasoned him out of long ago, have now again taken hold strongly of his mind, as if the very atmosphere of this place were favourable to such feelings."

There was much bitterness in Don Jose's tones, but any one who knew him well—any one who was sufficiently familiar with his various moods to detect by his voice what feelings were struggling for existence in his breast, might have concluded that he too, as well as Philip of Spain, found an undefinable something about the very atmosphere of that chateau which was eminently calculated to provoke the growth, as well as the existence, of superstitious ideas, and strange supernatural fancies.

He was evidently fighting against a sense of depression of spirits, which he found it difficult to subdue, but which his pride would not suffer him to confess even to himself. He was as a man fighting against his own strong convictions, and finding the issue of the combat very doubtful.

"Yes," he continued, "it would seem that Philip has become dreadfully nervous since his visit here; and it would almost appear that this intrigue had ceased to have any charms for him, he is so chary of what means he employs to bring it to a successful and satisfactory issue. He trembles now at the very name of this girl, concerning whom he has taken so much trouble, and concerning whom I likewise have involved myself in more inconvenience and personal danger than I could sum up as belonging to the last half dozen years of my career.

"He talks of never again visiting this place. Well, what care I? Let him never again visit it. Be it so. I, however, will not let all the pains I have taken to bring about this intrigue be scattered to the winds. The queen—aye, the queen. The beauteous majesty of Spain—she shall yet be my bright, my glorious reward. I love her because she is lovely; I will have her because she is the queen, and, by the strong party she has around her, is a second authority in the state. My influence over Philip is as unbounded now as it is undoubted. Let me but once induce the queen to take a false step, and I have her at my command for ever!

"To-night Philip shall, by fraud, by force, or by entreaty——" Don Jose paused; he thought he heard a slight noise outside the window of the apartment in which he was. He turned upon his heel to face it, but a blind covered it on the inside, and he could see nothing.

"There was surely something," he said, as he drew his breath with labour; "I—I thought I heard something. Psha! what desperate folly is this? Am I to become such a drivelling idiot as the king, because I am here? Confound the chateau, I never before while within its walls felt such sensations of alarm. What can be the matter with me? Jose, Jose, arouse yourself, man, and shake off these most unmanly terrors."

He stamped with his foot, as if it were a point gained to break the strange solemn stillness that reigned in the place, and then drawing himself up more boldly, he added,—

"Idle fears. Superstitious fancies, born of a bad digestion for an hour, vanish! I, Don Jose De Santerem, rise superior to you, and defy you!"

His eyes were fixed upon the window, and he saw, or fancied he saw, that the light which came through the window was partially obscured by some form on the other side.

He rapidly changed colour and stepped back a pace. All was silent as the grave.

"What—what is this?" he muttered. "Where does that window look to? Let me think. The terrace, yes—it surely looks to the terrace—it must—it does! Some prying domestic—the scoundrel. If I were sure—I am sure; but if I were very sure, I swear my sword should quickly put an end to him and his dangerous curiosity. Surely there is some one there!"

He half drew his sword from its scabbard, and then returned it with a trembling hand, as if he feared that such an act of apparent hostility might bring upon him some stronger danger than he had power to avert. He could not turn his eyes from that window for his life's sake.

But it was not likely that such a man as Don Jose should long remain in such a situation. For a time a sudden accession of fear might cloud his mind, but it would be only for a time, and soon he must waver from the feeling. Gradually even now he began to shake off his dreamy fancies. With an oath, he strode towards the window, the blind of which was still darkened by the shadow of some one, as he thought, standing without.

"What should I fear?" he muttered; "I am here surrounded by these most unscrupulous dependants, who, by this day's work, have sufficiently shown their readiness and willingness to do my bidding. What should I fear, since he whom I most feared is dead—Don Cæsar—yes, at last I am rid of him; what then have I to fear? Away with these coarse thoughts. If this person be another of those shaven-crowned hypocrites, one of whom my young friend, Lazarillo,

has so happily got me rid of, there shall be yet another vacancy in the church."

This was a remarkably pleasant reflection, and seemed to put Don Jose on better terms with himself than he had been. He approached the window with more caution, and determined upon catching the intruder, if possible, before he could have a chance of escape, and so pleased was he and tickled by the idea of getting rid of two priests at the chateau, himself killing one, and Lazarillo the other, that his countenance assumed quite a different aspect, and all his superstitious fears seemed indeed to have

"Vanished into thin air."

Now he had got sufficiently near to the window to be able to lay his hand upon the blind, which was one that drew aside wholly, not rolling up as our luxuries of that description do. He took a firm hold of it, so that he could withdraw it from the window by one motion of his hand.

"Now, Sir Priest, or domestic," he muttered, "be you which you may, or who you may, you shall pay dearly for your temerity in attempting to play the spy upon my privacy."

With a vigorous movement, he withdrew the blind completely and exposed the whole of the window; it reached from the floor to the ceiling, and opened directly on to the terrace, which we have had occasion to mention so frequently. Directly on the outside, with his arms folded across his breast, and a stern, motionless aspect, stood Don Cæsar.

So unexpected a sight—so fearfully unlooked-for an apparition was indeed enough to make the blood in Don Jose's veins pause in its healthful current. He looked aghast—his lips separated, and his face became of a hideous yellow colour. Could he doubt the evidence of his own senses? There was Don Cæsar—there he stood, even as he had stood in life; the man against whose breast he had seen six loaded arquebusses actually levelled, actually fired — the man whom he had ordered to be murdered, and whom he had seen murdered before his own eyes. There he was, looking as calm, as uninjured, and altogether so much the same as when in life, that what conclusion could Don Jose come to but that what he now looked upon was some apparition come from the world of spirits to thwart him, and render life hideous to him so long as it should last.

It was horrible—no amount of scepticism could stand against such positive ocular demonstration as that which was now presented to him.

He did not rush from the spot, but it was not courage that held him there. No; it was the positive paralysis of absolute, horrible, and unmitigated fear. He did not remove; but it was not that he did not feel inclined to do so. He tried, but his tongue clove to the roof of his mouth, and would not aid him in the utterance of any sound.

Such fear was horrible—killing—soul-absorbing! Had it lasted very long, he felt that he must have fallen down dead; for who could hope to bear it long and live?

The figure advanced about half a step, and that brought it so close to the window that it touched it. Don Jose saw it hold out its ghost-like hand to undo the fastening. In another moment he should be confronted with that dreadful apparition. By such an effort as nearly choked him in the making, he contrived to suddenly shout,—

"Help!—help!—help!"

The sound of his own voice awoke the spell which had held his faculties enchained. He staggered back a pace or two, keeping his distended eyes still fixed upon the, to him, hideous form; then, suddenly turning, he dashed out of the little room, as if he had been followed by a thousand devils in *propria personæ*.

He got some distance along the corridor before he was aware that Lazarillo, whose post he had passed, was gazing after him with the greatest astonishment. A sudden thought struck him, and he turned to the boy, crying,—

"Close you the door—close you the door !"

"The door of the room you came from, signior ?"

"Yes; quick—quick! close it—fasten it! On your life, Lazarillo, fasten it securely !"

The boy sprang forwar d ,and shut a couple of bolts into their sockets outsid e the door. Then Don Jose sank on to the window-seat by which the page was keeping watch and ward, and shuddering from head to foot, he said faintly, as his eye glared around him in all directions,—

"Stay with me, boy !—stay with me ! I have had a fright. By the great God, I have been mistaken, and there are things in this world, and yet not of it, I little dreamt of."

CHAPTER LXIV.

JOSE'S FEARS AND LAZARILLO'S JOY.—THE ALARMING STATE OF THE CHATEAU.

WELL might Lazarillo, as indeed he did, look amazed to see a man of such a temperament and mode of thinking as his vicious and unprincipled master, Don Jose, so completely overwhelmed with fear as he now appeared to be. Well might he almost allow his arquebus to fall from his hands, and open his large, handsome, intelligent eyes to an extraordinary width as he looked at the trembling, kneeling, ghastly man before him, and asked himself,—

"Can this really be Don Jose, my most unscrupulous, cold-hearted, rascally patron and employer ?"

However, as all remained quiet for some minutes, and no attempt was made by the apparition of Don Cæsar to open the door of the apartment, which the page had just bolted, Jose began to gather a little courage, and some slight remembrance of his former colour visited his cheeks as he said, in a low tone,—

"Boy, you are surprised, and well you may be, to see me in such a mood as this."

Lazarillo could not deny, nor did he wish to do so, that he was very much surprised indeed, so he said,—

"I cannot guess, signior, what has so much disturbed your usual serenity of mind."

"No; nor would any one else guess," said Jose. "Lazarillo, do you believe in ghosts ?"

"Ghosts, signior ?"

"Ay; do you believe that the dead, in the likeness they bear while living, can come to this world again, to horrify us by looking with eyes that have no human interests in their gaze, into the faces of living, breathing men ?"

"No, signior."

"You do not believe it."

"Most certainly I do not."

"Nor did I—nor did I! But, Lazarillo, seeing is believing; no one could be a more stanch opponent, to a belief in such matters than I am myself, or, I should rather say, than I was; but now I cannot withhold my evidence to that which I have seen."

"Indeed, signior !"

"Yes—yes, boy, I have been just now so terrified at the sudden apparition of one whom I know to be dead, that it is a relief to me to talk to you, whom I know to be as I myself am, human, and of this world."

"You much surprise me, signior. But, perhaps, you only believed the person to be dead."

"I know him to be dead, I tell you—I know him to be dead—I saw him kill——I swear I saw him die. There can be no possible mistake now."

"It was a man, then ?"

"Yes."

"Indeed. May I presume, noble sir, to ask a question which occurs to me on this subject ?"

"Yes—yes. What is it, boy ?"

"I wish to know, signor, if the ghost you saw was provided with the ghost of a jerkin, a doublet, hose, a hat, boots, and general clothing, because, if so, that, to my mind, would be the most marvellous part of the affair, signior."

"The figure was clothed."

"Then if it be no offence to his ghostship, I will take leave to doubt its supernatural origin."

"You know not what you say, Lazarillo. There could be no possible mistake, I tell you. Listen to me. During the time you have been here, holding your watch at this chateau, have you heard no noises ?"

"I have, signior. I heard a discharge of fire-arms ?"

"Well, that discharge of fire-arms was the death of the individual whose apparition I have seen. Some of the attendants of the chateau were in the garden, and they saw a stranger. Heedlessly, I grant, and contrary to my orders, they levelled six loaded arquebuses at him, and he was, of course, killed."

"You saw him fall ?"

"I did."

"And yet he lives ?"

"No, Lazarillo. He visits the earth in the form he had while living, but he is among the dead."

"Oh, signior, tell me," cried the boy, with sudden energy of manner,—"my heart misgives me but the person who has come by this most sad misadventure is one whom I have cause to love. Don Jose, I implore you to tell me if it was Don Cæsar de Bazan. Oh, tell me truly, signior, was it, indeed, he, or some one with whom I am only called upon to take the common sympathy of humanity ?"

Don Jose was silent for a moment. He was debating in his own mind upon the prudence of trusting Lazarillo with the fact that it was his friend, Don Cæsar, because he feared that from the servants of the chateau he might learn the precise manner of his death, which would be strikingly at variance with the lying account that he, Don Jose, had just given him.

"I can interpret your silence," said the boy. "You need not tell me. It was—it must have been Don Cæsar."

"Nay, you have no grounds whatever for drawing such an inference, Lazarillo."

"I can guess it."

"That is absurd."

"Then tell me, sir, and end my doubts."

"I can caution the domestics," thought Jose ; "and it is better for me to tell him than for him to get at the fact accidentally from some other quarter, which he may."

"Well, Lazarillo, you are aware that Don Cæsar and I were very good friends, and hence it is with grief that I confess to you he really was the man."

"My heart told me so. And he is dead ?"

"He is."

"Alas—alas—poor Cæsar !"

"I lament his death as much as you can, and now that he is really no more, you can have no divided duty, but can devote your services entirely to me. Be assured that your reward shall be amply commensurate to all you do to give me satisfaction. I have said that I will make your fortune, and I will most surely keep my word."

"Alas—poor—poor—Cæsar !"

"Nay, do not grieve. I cannot, for the life of me, make out why his ghost should trouble me."

" Nor anybody else."

" Or why he should come here even in life, really, to me, is a great mystery. I am quite confounded at the whole transaction, to tell the truth, Lazarillo."

" And so am I."

" Now attend to me, boy. As I have told you, I have not only actually seen Don Cæsar killed, but I have seen his ghost, I am compelled to confess."

" Was it no delusion, signor ?"

" None whatever. On that point I am quite positive, and I now speak to you concerning it, that you may know what to do, should it appear to you."

" Yes—yes."

" Conjure it to rest in peace, Lazarillo, I charge you. One's life would indeed become insupportable, if one were haunted by such an appearance at any time."

" Your bidding shall be done, signior."

" See to it—see to it, boy. It will be, believe me, very much to your advantage, if you can lay this troublesome spirit. Can you for a moment believe it possible any man could escape from the bullets of six arquebuses, discharged so close to him, that the merest child could not miss the mark ?"

" Quite impossible."

" Even should he escape death, some serious wounds would of course ensue, Lazarillo."

" Of that there can be no doubt, signior."

" Then, of course," added Jose, as he rose with a shiver, " it was the apparition of Don Cæsar that I have seen ; and I, Don Jose de Santarem, at this time of day, am compelled to become a convert to a belief in ghosts. Oh, sad consummation !"

He walked slowly down the corridor, and as he went, the boy, who watched him narrowly, could see that he looked warily around him—that he started at the sound of his own footsteps, and was painfully alive to every little circumstance, which under any other circumstances would have escaped his notice entirely, or if they had obtruded themselves upon his attention, would have had no effect upon his mind or his imagination.

" The villain !" said Lazarillo, as he saw him disappear through a doorway at the end of the corridor. " The villain ! Little does he suspect that from every arquebus but the one I have here in my own possession, I have extracted the bullets, as I did from those at the prison. Live, Cæsar ! My heart told me you would be here. Thank Heaven that I have saved you once again. This is, indeed, joyful news, that Jose's fears have made him give me. Cæsar is here, and surely now all will be well, and his dear countess shall yet be saved. My heart told me he would be here—I knew it. Surely I knew it from some inspiration. Twice, Cæsar, have I, poor, weak, friendless, uninfluential Lazarillo, the armourer's boy, saved you from death. The hand of a good Providence is in this, or I could not have so well succeeded."

He drew from his pocket the instrument with which he had twice thus relieved the arquebuses of their bullets, and regarding the various pieces which, when screwed together, accomplished the purpose, with a glance of affection, he said,—

" How happy am I, that my old master, the armourer, forced me to acquire so well the use of this. He compelled me always to carry about with me the means of uncharging guns, in order that he might be spared the trouble. How I thought myself ill-used, to be given that department of the business ; but now how thankful am I, that I know it so well."

He carefully replaced the various unscrewed pieces in his pocket, and added, with a smile,—

" I shall preserve you as a sacred relic,—more sacred to me by far, than the toe-nail of St. Anthony, or a couple of bristles from the beard of Solomon.

Surely Maritana must now be saved. The good queen knows of her condition, and in so knowing it, must be well aware of the necessity for instant action, to save her from a fate which surely her woman's heart will revolt from. I much wonder that she is not here."

Lazarillo was silent now for some moments, after which he looked anxiously from the window, as he said,—

" How uncommonly silent the chateau is. I never knew it to be so still and quiet before. Everybody really seems to have gone to sleep, and yet it is not siesta time, I am positive. Really, now, I could almost fancy I was in some deserted house altogether. I hear no footsteps in the passage, no sound of voices such as sometimes have come to my ears. What can be the matter ?"

Well might the chateau be amazingly quiet, for, as we are aware, it was stripped of its domestics—all had now left it, save Lazarillo and one other. He was a deaf old man, who never heard anything, and consequently never put himself out of the way about anything. He had a wonderful facility in giving random answers to whoever talked to him, for with the obstinacy of age, and the peculiar idiosyncracy of many deaf people, he was so far from believing in, or confessing his own infirmity, that he considered it the greatest insult in the world for any one to look as if they imagined he was at all hard of hearing.

None of the other domestics had thought it worth while to explain to this old man that there was any real or fancied necessity for leaving the haunted chateau, so he was left alone in his glory, or at all events to whatever amount of glory he could possibly extract from the circumstance of being left alone.

He, Lazarillo, however, was the only one now actually within the building, if we except the deaf old man, who was entirely free from terrors of a superstitious nature. The king was most decidedly and deeply infected with such feelings ; and, indeed, so strangely had they taken possession of him, that had he been able to form any tolerable excuse to Don Jose, whose sneers he dreaded, he would now have been glad to get back to Madrid, and to give up altogether the nefarious scheme into which he had been dragged, not, however, unwillingly, by that most unscrupulous minister.

A strange compound character as was Philip, he was ever ready to find reasons connected with the most superstitious feelings and fancies for almost anything—a scoffer at religion, yet a weak-minded fanatic in all else. He seemed to have discarded all theological opinions which, whether wrong or not, in fact, were calculated to be productive of good in their results, but to have carefully retained every contemptible and unworthy superstition that from the commencement of the world had woven itself up with a belief in man's immortality.

And Don Jose too. He had received a shock which he found it impossible to get over. He felt that he could not disbelieve his own eyes. He was not so philosophical as we are now, when the appearance of a ghost would be resolved into a partial congestion of the minute ramifications of the blood-vessels of the cornea—seeing to him was believing. Don Cæsar was shot, killed ; could he doubt it ? and after that he had seen him to all appearance quite unhurt. Was it a ghost, or was Don Cæsar a necromancer,—one of those beings with a charmed life ? Truly, the ghost theory was by far the most rational of the two, and to it Don Jose was compelled to succumb, despite all the attendant reasons against any such absurdity which his better reason supplied.

With Dr. Johnson he could have said,—

" The belief in apparitions is one, which having existed in all ages, endows it with a certain importance

difficult to cast aside. Thousands of persons who can even deny it with their tongues, hesitate not to confess it with their fears."

At least he might have so quoted the learned but somewhat bombastic lexicographer; but as a popular ballad remarks, with reference to another gentleman in a different walk of life,—

> "One little thing prevented him,—
> He was not born till *arter* that."

And so Don Jose was left to his own fears and his own reflections, unaided by any ponderous aphorisms of the worthy doctor.

CHAPTER LXV.

THE DISAGREEABLE DISCOVERY MADE BY DON JOSE TO THE KING.—THE TRAVELLING FRIAR.—CÆSAR'S NEW RETAINER.

IF the intense stillness of the chateau had become a subject of surprise and some uneasiness to Lazarillo, as being something concerning which he could raise no reasonable hypothesis, it was much more so to Don Jose, who being by his fears rather unmanned, thought that he would endeavour to recover his customary coolness and serenity by the aid of a goblet of some of the generous wines with which he knew the chateau was well stocked, before he again sought an interview with the king.

He went into a small chamber, adjoining to which there ought to have been an attendant always in wait-

ing, and taking from the table a hand-bell, he produced the light, tinkling sound, which hitherto had always been followed by the prompt appearance of one of his own immediate personal attendants.

But this time the conjuration was in vain. He might ring as long as he pleased, but no one paid the least attention, for the best of all possible reasons, namely, that no one heard him.

Again and again he rang, and anger began to take the place of surprise. Like Glendower, he might

> " Call spirits from the vasty deep;
> But would they come when he did call?"

Or, like the famous trumpeter of some battle, who, when all his friends were killed, blew his trumpet loudly, when he might as well have blown his nose, for all the effects that ensued. He kept on ringing, until anger, which for a time had superseded fear, was again superseded by the original feeling, and Jose placed the bell upon a side table and turned a shade paler—perhaps yellower would be the more correct term, with regard to his peculiar complexion—than before.

" What can be the meaning of this?" he muttered. " No one here—no one within call. The chateau so silent, too! Where are the servants? are they dead? What can have happened? Have they seen the terrible apparition with which my eyes have been blasted? and are they afraid to answer my call? The knaves! the rascals! I must, perforce, seek them for once. I, powerful as I am, have no power, unless I am surrounded by those who choose to obey me."

This was a truth which such men as Don Jose very seldom give utterance to, but it is, nevertheless, a most important one. Slaves make tyrants, and then, like the savage inhabitants of the Caribees, who bow down before the ugly, carved idol they have just turned out of hand, they tremble before the object of their own creation.

Jose, with a slow step, left the apartment. The stillness of the place weighed most heavily upon his spirits. His own footsteps, light as they were—for he had not the courage to walk boldly—alarmed him, and it was a great relief to his mind when he came within sight again of the corridor where Lazarillo was posted, and saw the boy still on guard, leaning on his arquebus.

Don Jose approached him with a quickened step, and when he reached him, he said,—

" Lazarillo, have you seen any of the attendants lately ?"

" I have not, signior."

" Nor heard them ?"

" Nor heard them, signior. An unusual stillness has now for some time reigned throughout the chateau."

" You have remarked it ?"

" I have."

" And I too—and I too."

" I have been lost in wonder at it, signior, for some time. I could almost fancy you and I to be the only living beings within these dismal, dreary walls."

Jose started, as he exclaimed,—

" Indeed! say you so? Oh, but you are wrong there, Lazarillo. You know there are others here, boy. But, as you say, there is a strange silence about the place, which I know not what to think of. Be you true and faithful, and your reward shall be the greater, that you perchance may be the only one. I shall feel myself called upon to reward you for those qualities."

Lazarillo bowed.

" Remain here. I will search for the attendants, who, perhaps, have seen something which has paralysed them with fear."

" The ghost of Don Cæsar de Bazan, most probably, noble sir, which may be prowling about the chateau."

Don Jose stepped back a pace, as he said, in a whisper,—

" You—you have seen nothing, boy ?"

" Nothing; all is still. As we were friends when he lived, I wonder he does not show himself to me."

" You would be terrified."

" No, signior—no."

" You would. Your young blood would freeze in your veins at such a sight. I have no reason, nor has any mortal man, to shrink from the sight of the super-natural ; for what power has that which is immaterial to harm that which is material ? But it is no matter of reason. The imagination, filled with an unknown dread, shrinks appalled from a contact with the beings of another world, and the dread appearance has come and gone ere we can summon reason to aid us to strip it of all its adventitious terrors."

" Most honourable signior, if I were to see a ghost now ——"

" Well, well, what would you do ?"

" I should say, boldly,—' What harm have I ever done you while living, that you should torment me when dead ?' "

" Tush! tush! that is no argument. You know not what you talk of, boy. Keep a good watch."

Don Jose turned away, and walked slowly down the corridor, till he came to the staircase which led to the lower part of the building, down which he stepped noiselessly and cautiously.

Lazarillo followed him with his eyes, till he was no longer visible, and then he smiled, as he said,—

" The villain! I touched him there. Well may he tremble at the supposed apparition of the man he would have murdered. Well may his guilty heart feel the flutter of alarm, since he has it not in his power to make the speech I uttered even now. Oh, Cæsar! where are you ? I would that I dared leave this spot to search for you. Oh, that I could see you, to have but five minutes' converse with you in order to possess you with the truth regarding the state of affairs here. Something surely could be done. And where, too, is the queen ? The distance is short from Aran-jues to here, and yet she does not come. 'Tis very, very strange she does not come. This state of suspense in which I am left is very painful, and hard to bear. What shall I do—what shall I do to put an end to it ?"

While Lazarillo is attempting to answer this ques-tion to his satisfaction, we will follow Don Jose in his

endeavours to find the attendants of the chateau, who were in reality, as we are aware, so far advanced on their route to Madrid, feeling more comfortable as they placed each moment a greater distance between them and the chateau.

He entered the lower part of the building, and then he paused to listen, but no sound whatever met his ears. He walked into an apartment on the ground floor, but it was vacant. He summoned courage to stamp with his foot—a dismal echo was the only re-sponse, and Don Jose's alarm became each moment greater.

" What on earth can all this mean?" he said, " Am I left here alone ? What can have happened ? It must be all a dream. Am I awake? Am I Don Jose de Santarem ?"

After a few moments he left the room into which he had gone, and when he reached the landing with-out, he called out aloud,—

" Hilloa ! Hilloa !"

No response. All still as before. This was too much for human endurance. Jose never was treated half so badly, or he never could successfully have battled against the disagreeables that beset him. Jose drew his sword, and, with mingled feelings of anger and fear, he went from room to room, until he found the old deaf man, who was the only one left behind of all the attendants.

The moment Jose saw him he strode up to him, and rage predominating over every other feeling at the moment, now that he had some one to vent it on, he cried,—

" How now, rascal; why did you not answer my call ? You infernal old villain. You wear my livery, and yet sit as composedly, while I am summoning as-sistance, as if you knew me not. You villain, old as you are, I will make you know better manners. Speak, rascal, speak !"

The old deaf domestic, although he was as innocent as possible of knowing what Jose said to him, was not blind as well as deaf, and he knew his master well enough by sight. Rising from his seat, he made a very low bow, and remarked,—

" Very well, indeed, my good lord; and many thanks to you, always considering my age."

" Eh ? what ?"

" Very fine, indeed, my lord ; very fine."

" Are you mad ?"

" At your lordship's service ever, as I have always been proud to be."

" Or drunk, are you ?"

" Too much honour, my good lord. Too much honour for an old man. Such kind inquiries sensibly affect me. I shall never forget them—never while I live, which won't be long now."

" Why, what—what the devil do you mean ?"

" God bless you, noble signior. God bless you. It's my only ambition now to die in your service."

" Will you, or will you not, answer me a plain question ?"

" Oh, very—very. Especially at the change of seasons. Then I feel it in my back."

Jose drew himself up, and crossed his arms over his breast, as he said, half aloud, and looked sternly in the old man's face the while,—

" Now, is this a piece of acting or not ?—I should very much like to know."

" Remarkably so, my lord. Most remarkably."

" Are you deaf ?"

" Thanks, noble signior ; many thanks."

" The old fool !" exclaimed Jose, as he turned away. " He is in his dotage. The old idiot ! what can be the use of such a man to me ? He is as deaf as a post, too."

Striding from room to room, Don Jose now very soon

discovered, to his great dismay, that he was, indeed, comparatively alone in the chateau, for the servants were nowhere to be found. Then the noise he had heard while talking to the king came to his mind, and he paused in his fruitless search, as he said,—

"It must be so—it must be so. They have seen the apparition of Don Cæsar, and the sudden alarm that came upon my ears was a consequence of that occurrence. It has had a powerful effect upon their minds, and they have left the chateau in a body. I do not wonder at it, while I curse them for deserting me. Not a man of them but shall suffer for this most intensely. But what is to be done? Am I to suffer all my schemes to perish because I am abandoned by a parcel of rascally lacqueys?—Never. And that apparition, too. It seems to have disappeared. I have been now through the better part of the chateau and met it not. If there be such appearances,—and that there are I now dare not doubt,—who knows what strange and mysterious laws may affect them. Possibly they may not be able to appear more than once to the same person, and if that be the case I am free. I will believe it is so until my eyes are again blasted by the terrible sight."

He replaced his sword in its sheath, and stood for some moments motionless, in deep thought.

"This is very awkward, though. How are we to get attendance?—how food? By the mass, I know not where to help myself, if I could bring my mind to stoop to do so, and I suppose I must. At all events, I shall have to wait upon the king, for yon old deaf fool cannot. And yet a thought strikes me. I will write down what I want, and give the list to him. Then, surely, he can find the things. And if Philip to-night will not adopt measures such as I shall advise to silence all opposition to his wishes, on the part of Maritana, I shall advise him to relinquish the intrigue altogether, and return to Madrid, if possible, by the dawn."

"Peace be to all here!" said a voice suddenly from the outside of the room in which Don Jose was. "Peace be to all here! Peace and good-will, and the protection of all the saints!"

"Who can that be?" thought Jose. "The voice is quite strange to me, and it sounds like a cursed priestly salutation. Let him beware, if it be any one come to look after him who has had all his earthly cares, I hope, settled by Lazarillo's carbine; let him beware, I say, for I will send him to the other world to keep his comrade company, even were he ten times a priest."

"Peace!" cried the voice again, still louder. "Peace be to all here!" as if he who uttered the words was getting rather impatient that no one appeared to take notice of his pious greeting.

Don Jose again drew his sword, and opening the door of the room, he bounced out so quickly, that he who had been bestowing such benedictions upon the house and its inhabitants was seized with an instant panic, and ran up the staircase, which was close at hand, as quickly as possible.

Don Jose pursued him, and, being fleeter of foot, he caught him before he had got two-thirds of the flight up, upon which the stranger flung himself upon his knees, crying,—

"Mercy! signior, mercy! What have I done to anger you? Have mercy upon me. You see I am a man of peace by my garb. Spare my life."

The stranger was a man past the middle age. He was attired in the coarse grey serge frock of a travelling friar, and there was nothing whatever in his appearance to induce a belief that he was other than what he seemed by his dress to be.

His apparel was travel-worn, and his shoes shewed that even that day he must have come a considerable distance. The only marvel to Don Jose was, how he came there.

"Who are you?" he cried. "Answer me truly, or you shall surely die."

"My good signior, I have no motive whatever to answer you otherwise than truly. I am a wandering friar, living upon the alms of the charitable."

"But how the devil came you here?"

"Alas! my son, you speak dreadfully profanely—but, finding an open gate as I passed by this chateau, and knowing that many charitably disposed persons do leave an outer gate open, in case some poor pilgrim should pass, I walked in."

"An open gate in the garden wall!"

"Even so, good signior."

"Confusion!" muttered Jose. "Those abominable rascals of domestics must have left it so when they eloped. You may rise, sir pilgrim; I will do you no harm, for I believe your tale."

"Many thanks, noble sir. I perceive you are chafed—can I offer you any consolation?"

"Not by priestly cant."

"Oh, the saints!—have mercy upon us!"

"None of that nonsense here. I tell you I have no faith in any of you friars. Do you know me?"

"Alas! no, signior; but it is a dreadful grief to me to find you so irreligiously inclined—a very dreadful grief. To-night, I shall say forty aves, two and twenty misieres, thirty-six ——"

"Psha! I am Don Jose de Santerem."

"Don Jose de Santerem?"

"The same."

"Minister of Spain?"

"I am he."

"Pardon, noble sir, my boldness then in speaking to you as I have done. Being well aware from common report, which I believe for once is true, that you have no religion at all, and being quite sure that you have plenty of money, and being suspicious just now that you have no objection to a new adherent—I'm your man. Like you, I have no religion—unlike you, I have no money. I am active, smart, younger than I look, unscrupulous, can lie as fast as a mule can gallop—faithful to those who pay me, and have a profound admiration for your genius. Will you employ me?"

"Yes."

"It's a bargain, signior. I am henceforward your most humble servant in all things."

"Have you courage?"

"Yes—when I think I am the stronger."

"Are you superstitious?"

"Not at all."

"This place is haunted by an apparition of one who has been killed here."

"Indeed."

"You take it coolly."

"I always do anything."

"Then you have no fear of a ghost?"

"Not the least. They may come in legions if they like. The whole supernatural world may come before me, without exciting a terror. I assure you I have no fears of the sort. I like good eating, and good drinking; but am aways sober—oh, most religiously sober! I don't mind what I do to procure the good things of this life, I assure you, signior. You will find me the most unscrupulous scoundrel you have ever had in your employment; and, if report speaks truly of your establishment, that is saying a very great deal of my own merits."

"You are strange fellow."

"No, signior, no—I wish I was. Then I should make more money by it; but, unfortunately, there are too many of my sort. There's a world of competition now among rogues. You may have them for almost anything ; and, indeed, if you won't pay them for it, they will be rogues, in spite of any disadvantage, for absolutely nothing."

Don Jose coughed, as he said,—

" Well, well—the state of affairs here is simply this : I have a friend in this house who has ran off with a young lady, whom he loves, but who somehow does not precisely return his passion."

" Dear me ! Is he rich ?"

" Very !"

" Oh, the frailty of woman !"

" She resists him, and, in the midst of the trouble consequent thereupon, all the servants have run away, because of some ghost they say they have seen."

" Oh, the stupidity of man !"

" You may well say so. They have not received their wages."

" Humph !—indeed ! Perhaps, though, they have helped themselves to the plate, and other little portable valuables of the house."

" The devil !"

" Exactly. I only throw it out as a hint. I have some little knowledge of human nature, and I should not be at all surprised to find they had done so, signior."

" Now you mention it, I have no doubt upon the subject whatever. But now, what I require of you is, to be within call of me, so that, if I want any assistance, you are at hand to render it. You will likewise, down stairs, find a deaf old man ; no doubt he knows where to find things in the chateau, so that when I and my friend require anything, which we do now, you must discover from him where to get it, you understand."

" Perfectly, signior ; what do you require ?"

" Some wine to be placed in the room below, from where you saw me come."

" It shall be done, if wine there be in the house there to place."

"And close the garden-gate through which you came."

" I did so, signior. I thought one wandering friar was enough at a time, in the house, so I closed it and fastened it, in case any one else should come this way."

" You were right—I compliment you on your foresight."

" May you live a thousand years, signior."

So saying, the wandering friar went on his errand, and Don Jose, not a little pleased at the fortunate accident which had enabled him to retain so valuable an adherent, under the peculiar circumstances in which he was placed, ascended the remainder of the staircase, and hastened to the king, from whose august presence he had been absent much longer than he had intended, or than was at all agreeable, no doubt, to that illustrious personage ; whose state of mind was not such as to make him at all enamoured of his own reflections, or of the sublimity and beauty of solitude in that chateau of Don Jose's.

Lazarillo, posted as he was in the recess of the window, not far from the head of the staircase on which the brief conversation between Jose and the travelling friar had taken place, could not be off hearing the rush of feet, and the scuffle which had preceded that most edifying and satisfactory discourse.

Fearful that some harm was befalling his friend, Don Cæsar, the boy had, on the instant, rushed to the stair-head ; but then, hearing a strange voice sueing for mercy from Don Jose, he luckily paused, and, without his contiguity being at all thought of by Jose, he overheard that passed, and so became aware of some most important facts for the guidance of his conduct in the chateau while he should there remain.

He learnt from Jose's own lips a confirmation of his surmise that Cæsar had been attempted to be murdered in the garden of the chateau, and had not, as the minister had endeavoured to make him believe, been shot at promiscuously by the servants, as they would have fired upon any other stranger. He learnt, likewise, what he had no means before of learning the least clue to a knowledge of, that the chateau was deserted by its servants, and here he accounted for the stillness that had for some time pervaded the whole house.

" Now," he said to himself, " now we are safe. I know the whole of the disposable force here ; and, could I but meet with Cæsar, he and I would vanquish everybody, and rescue the countess by ourselves alone. What a glorious thing that would be ! As for that rascally travelling friar, I have somehow a strong notion that he will end his career in this house. My arquebus is loaded, and I don't know that it can possibly perform a better service to society at large, than in ridding it of such an uncompromising rascal as he avows himself to be. We will see, master travelling friar ; perhaps I may catch a glance at you from the window, in which case, why, I think I will hazard a long shot with this arquebus that has been idle so long."

Lazarillo looked earnestly from the window, and as Don Jose, when he crossed the corridor, saw him in that attitude, he had no suspicion whatever that he had been privy to his conversation and agreement with the rascally itinerant friar, but passed on to the king's chamber in a much pleasanter frame of mind than he had been able to congratulate himself upon for the last hour or two. In the bold defiance of all supernatural terrors uttered by the friar, he found some relief for his own mind, and a considerable decrease of his own fears.

" If he," he thought, " can hold the supernatural world in so much contempt, why may not I ? I feel convinced that the only way to meet such a subject effectually is to throw overboard completely the question of the existence, or the non existence of such things as apparitions, and to say at once, ' I care not if they be. Let them come, and I laugh their terrors to scorn. Let them come ! Ha, ha ! Let them come !' "

Don Jose was indeed now in a valorous frame of mind. Like the travelling friar, he felt as if he could look on unmoved, while the whole supernatural world filed before him, and it was in such a mood that he sought the king.

A hasty determination, which he formed, as he crossed the corridor, prevented him from communicating to Philip the disaffection and flight of the servants, for he knew that the knowledge of such a circumstance would terrify the majesty of Spain, and induce him, probably, to mount his horse, and be off in a moment for Madrid.

" I must not allow that," was Jose's reflection. " The intrigue must and shall be carried out with this Maritana, so that I can assure the queen, without a chance of being contradicted, of her dishonour ; and, then, at the moment of her anger, surely—surely, she will embrace some opportunity of having vengeance against her faithless and most profligate husband."

It was strange how pertinaciously Jose clung to this idea, notwithstanding his repeated rebuffs from the queen ; but it was one so much in accordance with his own nature that he could think of nothing else, and went on committing the fatal mistake into which all such men fall ; namely, in imagining that the motives which would act upon themselves, would be sufficient to produce similar actions in others.

He found the king pacing the room to and fro, with a disturbed and anxious manner. The moment Jose made his appearance, Philip turned upon him, exclaiming,—

" Where on earth have you been, Jose ? Is this the proper attention I should receive here ?"

"I beg your majesty to pardon me. I have been making some highly-important arrangements. Let me implore your majesty to bring this intrigue to a prompt conclusion."

"How, Jose, how?"

"To-night. Infuse a sleeping draught into the drink of this girl, and then, when sleep overpowers her senses, steal into her chamber."

"It shall be so, Jose; I charge you, give her the opiate."

"I will, your majesty; and, to-morrow morning, let us take her to Madrid. Your majesty can place her where you please, then. She will be more complying."

"No doubt, Jose; no doubt. Take the entire management now of all. I am sickened of these great delays. I am sickened of them. What if our queen should, from some officious person at Madrid, receive intelligence of our absence?"

"Ah, what, indeed?"

"She would set some spy upon us."

"No doubt, your majesty; no doubt."

"Which would be insufferable; besides being, under our present circumstances, as regards the church, highly inconvenient."

"Most inconvenient. I grieve to think that the church party are much against your majesty."

"It is disgraceful, Jose; but true, nevertheless."

"Most true; while, without exception, your majesty is really the most unprejudiced monarch that ever sat upon the throne of Spain."

"I believe I am."

"I am sure of it."

"You rightly estimate my character, Jose. I will, this evening, visit the lovely Countess de Bazan. She is, indeed, most beautiful; and this great opposition she gives to me augments her worth, Jose; she is not one of those yielding fair ones with whom one soon gets cloyed. Far from it; I think I will keep her long in splendour. How foolish, though, of her to carry her opposition to such unreasonable lengths."

"Very, your majesty, very. But then, how very few people in this world know their own interests."

This was true again. Don Jose was famous for uttering great truths; but how unfortunate it was that he never could apply them to his own condition and circumstances. Was he acting in a manner as if he knew his own interests? Verily, the great moralist who has described honesty as a piece of policy, might have addressed Don Jose to some effect, and possibly have convinced him that such was really the case.

CHAPTER LXVI.

MARITANA ALONE. — THE COMING NIGHT. — THE DREAD OF MADNESS. — THE PRAYER, AND THE MIND'S RESOURCE.

ALAS! poor, beautiful, much-injured Maritana! We feel that far too long have we neglected you in your dreary prison-house—dreary, though magnificent—for what beauty in your eyes had the costly furnishing, and the luxurious trappings of those apartments in which you were a prisoner?

Alas! not all the wealth, not all the art which can be brought to bear on so sad a subject can ever reconcile the bird, which has been wont to fly free as air, and convey its strains of melody to Heaven's gate, to its cage.

Maritana had no eyes for the gilding, the statues, the pictures, the rich hangings, and the general costliness of the apartment in which she was a prisoner.

After her last stormy interview with those who had already done her so much wrong, and caused her heart so many pangs, she had almost given herself up to despair.

"No hope!—no hope!" she cried. "Oh, Heaven, what will now become of me? For my wild, mad ambition, how fearfully am I punished! Not content with the humble, yet the free station in which fortune had placed me, I must e'en be sighing for more, and fate now has made me what I am—the saddest creature, surely, in all this sunny land!"

These were, indeed, dismal reflections, and not such as should have sprung from so young a heart as Maritana's; and if it be true that, in the progress of life, each human being is doomed to suffer much sorrow, surely her's was now at its climax, and she had some right to hope to be free for the remainder of her life. Who can tell what intense agony was her's—what pen can adequately describe the fears that each moment grew terribly stronger?

"Hope!—hope!" she exclaimed, "has passed from me; no succour comes! I hear no friendly voice—I see no friendly form! All is sadness—all is despair! What will become of me? I have already wearied Heaven with bootless prayers. I am lost—I am deserted! There is no hope for me. The night of despair has come!"

If, figuratively, she found that the night of despair was creeping over, she soon became aware, by the increasing glare of the apartment, that the actual night, which enveloped all nature in its sable arms, was rapidly approaching. She could not see—she could not dwell in thought upon the beauty of such a night as that which was closing around the chateau.

Towards sunset, the feathered inhabitants of the forests and glades are seen flitting about silent and with apparent haste, as though they feared darkness would surprise them before they found their shelter for the night. The sinking of the sun in the west was a signal to them which they obeyed in silence, and each grove or tree had its inhabitant who roosted without fear.

The sun had declined much, but there was not a cloud that would reflect back his radiant beams; he shone of pure golden light, without a spot to impede a single ray.

The shadows in the forest were falling thick, while the tops of the tall trees on the sides towards the sun shone with his effulgent light, and the rich glades on their upland surface were flooded, presenting a bright and beautiful contrast to the deep woodland shades that surrounded them on almost every side.

The venerable chesnut trees, by which the chateau was surrounded, cast their deep shadows upon the walls, and, over the grounds within, and, indeed, caused the little spot of earth to have a deep, sombre, and gloomy appearance to any one who might view it from the outside.

From the interior, indeed, it presented quite another aspect, and from those windows where a view of the surrounding country could be obtained, it amply repaid the beholder by the splendid and unique view that was obtained.

For miles, hill and dale were presented to the eye under the varying aspects of woodland and dale; the splendid foliage of the trees, varying in hue and colour, tinged by the sun's rays; the bright spots and the deep shade; the deep gloom of the woods, and the green of the undulating sward, presented contrasts of such a nature, that it filled the beholder with pleasure and delight.

Added to this, the deep silence that pervaded the entire space, the absence of everything that denoted life or habitation, called up the idea of what must have been the feelings of the first man when he gazed upon the world yet untrodden by his kind.

The solitariness gave a grandeur to the scene, and

a feeling of awe would steal across the mind, employed in contemplating the landscape.

The sun had now sunk beneath the horizon, and the changeful hue of the country was gone. There were dying and glorious tints to be seen; all was dark, deep, and sombre, and objects, at no very great distance, appeared almost undistinguishable, and those further off entirely so.

The sky, however, exhibited faint traces of the quarter where the sun had sunk, though, around the chateau, gloom and darkness prevailed.

Alas! alas! that man should mar all this beauty and delight by his own mad wickedness! Such a heart as Maritana's should be attuned to gaze on all such changes of nature with delight, instead of being, as hers really was, in a profound abyss of despair, destitute of one creation of joy.

Sad—sad, indeed, is it to dwell on the despair which had now found a home in that beautiful form; but painful as the picture is to contemplate, it is before us, and we must bend our gaze upon it, even in all its wretchedness, as it is.

She had now been a considerable time without any one visiting her, a circumstance which, at first, was rather a relief than otherwise; but in the end became a source of new alarm.

She had, of course, heard the loud report arising from the discharge of the arquebuses at Don Cæsar, and at the time she had been much startled at the sound; but it had not made the fearful impression on her mind which after a time it grew into.

Her fancy towards sunset became overwrought completely, and as she sat by the window of the apartment—that window which was so high that she felt convinced an attempt to leave the room by it would be equivalent to suicide—her thoughts assumed their darkest and dreariest complexion.

Now and then she pressed her hands upon her head, as if to still the wild throbbing of her brain, and occasionally she spoke with an incoherence which sufficiently proclaimed how fearful a result would follow a much longer continuance of such severe mental suffering.

Her tone of voice, too, was strangely altered, and occasionally she would glance around her, as if she expected to find herself not alone, but in the presence of some one more than mortal.

The night was deepening, and when about half-an-hour had passed away, there suddenly arose from behind the trees, as if by magic, a full and glorious moon.

Oh, how it shone, with all the magic of its silvery splendour, upon the fruits, the flowers, and the trees of that sweet garden. Its beams, too, fell upon the face of the beautiful Maritana, sadly but sweetly imparting to her an expression not earthly, and painfully, now and then, as sadder thoughts would come across her, showing the despair that there was mirrored.

Now for many minutes she sat in silence. Heaven could only know what fearful imaginings passed through the heart of that lovely girl during that awful time. But now she speaks. Low and plaintive as the soft breathing of a flute—she speaks; yes, she speaks.

"Unhappy—unhappy me. Alas! what have I done to so much provoke the vengeance of a Providence which surely is never unjust towards the very meanest of its creatures. I might have been forgiven for my presumption, even in wishing to be great. Heaven might well afford to smile at the weak aspirations of one of its creatures. That Heaven, which knows the futility and madness of all human desires, might have pardoned me my sin of ambition."

She covered her beautiful face with her hands, as if sweet moonlight was painful to her, and sobbed aloud. After a few moments, then a change came over her mind, and she looked around her with a strange and much altered expression—she spoke again, but it was in a voice very different from that in which she had breathed that lament, that had in it so much sad accusation against a Providence whose mysterious ways she did not appreciate, as, no doubt, she ought to have done.

"Is it real?" she said. "Is it real? That is a question. Am I mad? Has reason wholly deserted me? And are all these circumstances with which I seem to be surrounded but the brain-sick fancies of a disordered intellect? Can it be possible that I have gone distracted? A something seems to tell me it is so, and that this is some prison-house, perchance, to which, in absolute pity, I have been conveyed. Oh, horrible thought! More horrible than any which has yet found a home in my distracted breast. I must be mad. Yes, yes, I must be mad."

This was a horrible thought, and no wonder, that now it had suggested itself, it clung to her mind with a dreadful and an enduring tenacity, which was almost sufficient actually to bring about the very consummation she dreaded had really come to pass.

With a shudder she rose from the window at which she had been sitting, and turned her back upon the moonlight. The beautiful beams had become hateful to her. There seemed a sort of mockery in the cold white serenity of their smile—a mockery which she could endure no longer, and now she paced the apartment with agitated strides.

"All a dream. All a mad wild dream!" she muttered, "from the first to the last. I marvel much I never thought of that before. It must be all a dream of insanity. From the time that I was so happy in the streets of Madrid, singing and dancing the joyous hours away at the gay carnival, till now, too many circumstances of strange import have happened to me to be within even the ample bounds of probability. I am mad, and that accounts for all. The gay apparel, —the homage of such crowds as I have fancied I saw around me,—the new name given to me,—the marriage in the prison to one whom my young heart yearned to love,—yes, all convinces me that I am really mad."

She paused a moment, and passed her hand across her brow, as if striving, by a great effort, to collect her scattered thoughts, and then, with a shudder, she said, half aloud,—

"And there is one circumstance more convincing of my state of mind than all the rest. I know now that I am mad. When I fancied myself married, and in the prison at Madrid, I heard a sudden discharge of firearms. I have heard them again while here. That sound is not real, but a symptom of my insanity. I feel convinced of that, or I should not have heard it twice. Again and again, in all human probability, shall I hear that sound. Although but an imaginary one, it will continue, doubtless, to strike terror into my heart. Alas—alas! what will become of me? Poor—poor, mad Maritana!"

She sat down, and gave way to intense grief. Had Maritana been in a calmer frame of mind, the very fact of her being able thus to reason upon insanity would have convinced her that she, at least, was not a victim to that dreadful malady. There was far too much method in the argumentation by which she strove to induce herself to believe that she was surrounded by the unreal, for such to be really the fact. But, in her excited frame of mind, she was not able to deduce such a conclusion.

How long it would have taken, under such circumstances, really to topple reason from its throne, we cannot say, but certainly she was placed in the precise circumstances to produce such a result, were the persecutions by which she was surrounded to continue for a much longer period of time.

Happily, however, there had been placed by that Providence which had thought fit to visit her with such grievous trials, a limit to her sufferings, and now that limit was near at hand—much nearer at hand than she could have imagined, even had she been as full of hope as she was then of despair.

As she sat so still, so silent, so dreadfully dejected, in the mood which had now come over her, she heard, or fancied she heard, a low, rushing noise beneath the window of the garden. She looked up, and a change came over her countenance. She listened eagerly, and, for the moment, every other feeling seemed to be suspended in the intense desire to make out what sound it was that thus disturbed the death-like repose of that place.

Again she heard the noise. It seemed as if some one were continually treading beneath the window.

"This cannot be fancy," she gasped, eagerly. "This is surely real. There is no fancy here. This is real—real ——"

Suddenly, then, something was thrown through the open window. It fell upon the floor close to her feet, and before she could move to see what it was, she heard some one rapidly retreating from the spot immediately below the casement, as if, whoever it was, having completed his errand, he now made all the exertions in the world to get away with as much celerity as possible

The moonbeams passed into the apartment now with so much brilliancy, that every object was as plainly visible as it could have been at noonday. She cast her eyes down to the object which lay at her feet. It was a small pebble from one of the garden paths, apparently, screwed up in a piece of paper. To open it was the work of a moment. A few words were written on it, but they were full of joy. Oh, with what eager delight her eye perused them!

They were these,—

"Hope, Maritana! Don Cæsar is near. You have nothing to fear. Be patient, and hope the best."

"I will—I will—I will!" she cried, as she again and again read the few words of comfort. "I will. I am not mad—I am not mad!"

A gush of tears came to her relief, and when for a time they had flowed freely, a far better feeling was in her heart! She felt as if some dreadful load of care was removed from her. A sense of calmness and security was now hers, and she no longer regarded her situation with such gloomy mental eyes, but determined to look forward courageously and happily, whatever might occur, and not again to allow herself to become so deeply depressed as she had been.

"This scrap of paper," she said, "has restored me to myself. It comes from a friendly hand, and all is well. Some one is watching over me, and now I will not despair."

She looked with eyes of pleasure upon the beautiful moonlight. She now could appreciate its sublimity, and yet she feared that loneliness might again give birth to those sad feelings which had so lately appeared, when she turned from the window, saying,—

"I must have occupation. I must not leave myself to be so devoured by thought as I have been, or I may again fall into the deep despair from which I have been so recently rescued. I must have occupation."

From a side-table in the room she took a book of ballads and short sketches, and then by the sweet moonlight, that made the page look like a sheet of hammered silver, she found relief from the absorbing violence of her cares, in the offspring of another's imagination. Thus she read,—

In the southern parts of Spain the Moors long held possession of the country, ruled it for many generations, and when at length they were compelled to quit the country they had so long made their own, and held, by force of arms, they left imperishable monuments of their rule and existence behind them.

Their castles, cities, palaces, and forts, are, many of them, living monuments of their former greatness; besides which, they are no mean ornaments of the country, many of the best families in the south boasting of their Moorish blood, and glorying in the exploits of their ancestors against their Christian neighbours.

During the last war between the Spaniards and the Moors, when the latter, pressed by the Christians here, and by other enemies at home, were unable to draw over new levies, and though disputing the ground inch by inch, they were at last compelled to give way; then were many great and noble actions performed on either side.

During these last days of heroic struggle—of chivalry—when deeds of arms were, to the world, what the gilding rays of the departing sun are to the south—a halo of glory, there lived a Spanish cavalier named Don Gusman de Segovia, whose actions in several desperate engagements received great commendation and praise from many commanders.

Don Gusman had a large body of Spanish cavalry under his orders, and upon one occasion he signalized himself by charging a body of Moorish horsemen, the very elite of the enemy, and succeeded not only in dispersing them, but in vanquishing their commander, and taking him prisoner. This was a great feat, and when it came to the ears of the Spanish monarch, a new title was conferred upon Don Gusman, and he was admitted to the order of San Jago, a great and envied honour.

The Moorish captive was well treated by Don Gusman, and was detained in honourable bondage at the castle of his captor in Segovia, at that time free from the Moorish terrors, where he remained sighing for his native hills, and the companions of his arms.

It was in vain Don Gusman endeavoured to cheer the heart of the melancholy captive; he used all that art could devise—all that generosity could dictate, to give him a more cheerful and happy appearance; but no, the heart of the Moor was sad, and his eyes seldom shot forth a ray of pleasure.

At length there was great rejoicing in the castle of Don Gusman; he was about to wed the daughter of a Spanish grandee of the first class, one who could boast of royal blood, and her beauty was not less than her descent was ancient.

The whole castle was a scene of joy and happiness; there was but one person in that mighty pile that wore sadness next his heart, and that was the Moor.

Gusman was grieved to see his noble captive thus grieving beneath the weight of affliction, and could not reconcile, in his own mind the idea that extreme sorrow in a cavalier could exist from such a cause; for all who engaged in the cause of arms were subject to reverses, and a brave man should bear such reverses with fortitude commensurate with his bravery in action.

However, a few weeks passed over, and then Don Gusman determined to speak to his captive, and require if there was aught that he could do to assuage his grief, or make his situation as a prisoner in the castle less irksome than it was.

Youssouff was standing on the battlements, gazing earnestly on the south. The sun was sinking behind the mountains on the west; the tears coursed each other down the cheeks of the Moor; his lips moved as though he spoke, but no sound issued from them. He extended his arms as though he would embrace some distant object. The sun's rays were no longer visible, and Youssouff turned from the spot to return.

"Noble Youssouff," said the Spaniard, as he advanced to the Moor, "there have been rejoicings in my abode, and not a heart, save yours, felt melancholy or sorrow. Tell me, can I do aught that can render captivity less irksome to your soul?"

Youssouff shook his head sadly.

"The chances of war expose all men to the disasters it entails. You cannot grieve for what might have been my fate, had fortune been less partial. The cavalier, when he commits himself to the care of the god of arms, knows that reverses may occur, and the same spirit and courage that urge men on to feats of daring and arms, are required to bear them through the captivity and wounds which they may receive."

"It it true what you say. Oh, Spaniard, had I fallen on my shield, I would not have grudged leaving the world; and had I not loved, I would not have grudged you the praise you deserve, or the glory you have received by your strength and courage."

"Loved, say you?"

"Yes," replied Youssouff, sadly; "but that is a theme ill-fitting a warrior's mouth, and you may smile to think the captive Moor loved."

"Smile, Youssouff. Oh, no, believe me, the wisest and bravest men love the deepest and tenderest—'tis they who can most delight in love."

"You say rightly, Spaniard. My religion teaches me that, for we are taught by our Great Prophet, that love shall be our reward hereafter; but you Spaniards, I thought, were differently taught, and disregarded such happiness as merely of earth."

"Love," replied Gusman, "is great and ennobling, and we attach great happiness to it; but I would I could at once free you from the bonds that bind you, and were my will alone wanting, you should be free to seek her you love."

"Spaniard, when I took arms, I knew all, and I am prepared for even this; but tell me what cavalier, what brave man, ever enters the service of his prince, and has his thoughts fixed on defeat? He believes that he can always conquer; the ardour of arms carries away all fear of defeat or captivity."

"It does so. You are right, Youssouff—you are right. I feel it."

"Guess what would have been your own feelings, if on the eve of battle you left your intended bride, with promises to return and wed her. What promised happiness have I thus lost! Think, Spaniard, that had it been your fate, would you not have grieved, not that you were a brave foe's captive, but you would lamented that you left an expectant bride to mourn your absence?"

"Ah, my friend, I see now how it is. Your bravery in battle was too great to let you grieve, because fortune made me the victor."

"No, no."

" was then my happiness that made sp a contrast with your present station?"

"It was."

"How can I serve you? I would do aught that lay in my power for so brave a foe."

"Spaniard, Youssouff thanks you, but you can do him no more favours. When he regains his liberty, then indeed he may be happy, should his bride still be left him."

"Shall I have a horseman despatched with any message or token to the bride you love so well? It shall be done, if you desire it."

"Nay, Spaniard, nay—it would never reach her; none but myself could do so, and that is impossible. They would not receive the message, for sure I am he could not find the abode of her I love."

"Indeed!" replied the Spaniard, "I would I could have served you."

"Thou hast my thanks, Spaniard. I would I could show you the maid I love so well; you would acknow-

ledge that my love was not misplaced, and that she was well worthy a warrior's love."

"I would you could, and yet it might be done."

"Might be done?"

"Yes; you are a warrior, and a brave man; you have also power with your own people."

"I have."

"Then, I will ride with you, as a brother, to your own abode, so that you might visit the object of your love, and make her happy by your presence; but, Youssouff, you must pledge me your word, as a warrior, that you will return with me in captivity."

"Thanks, generous Christian, your offer is a noble one; I do promise, and may my prophet reject me if I break faith with thee. On my faith, as a Mussulman, my honour as a soldier, I swear to be unto you as a brother, and will return with you to captivity. No harm shall happen to thee from my people."

"Then by to-morrow, at sunrise, we will depart together, with but my page for an attendant, and two mounted men to take charge of our horses."

With mutual good wishes Don Gusman and the Moor parted for the night, and Youssouff spent the time more happily than any he had yet passed since he had been Don Gusman's captive.

The morning came, and Youssouff sprang to the saddle with a joy he could not conceal. His whole appearance was changed; he was the same proud, haughty man that thundered in the van of his men; his eye was piercing, and his whole demeanour changed from the spirit-broken captive.

Don Gusman, followed by his page, attended by two troopers, and accompanied by the Moor, quitted the fortress, and proceeded towards the place where the Moorish city lay.

They were admitted within the gates, and Youssouff was hailed with joy by his countrymen, who, when they knew he was a captive, would have fallen upon the Spaniards, but for Youssouff, who declared, if they offered any violence, he should be dishonoured, and would return to captivity nevertheless.

The Moor led them to a magnificent palace, where they were well entertained with everything that was to be had—delicious fruits and wines. Youssouff then quitted them, to have an interview with his bride; it would be needless to recount the interview—it was affecting to a degree, and their mutual joy scarcely exceeded the mutual grief each felt when it was known that they must part.

Youssouff led his intended bride to the place where Don Gusman was waiting for him, and there to thank him for all the kindness he had shown Youssouff. Don Gusman could but acknowledge the extreme beauty of the Moorish maiden.   *   *   *

They were returning towards the fortress, when Don Gusman gave his page some secret orders, and then he, with the two troopers, quitted him.

Since Don Gusman had seen the Moorish maiden he had become taciturn and silent; he spoke but little, and the captive did not notice it, as he was filled with contemplations of his future happiness, and present captivity.

When they arrived at the castle, the Moor was allowed to take his range over the building, as before; but Don Gusman was altered; he was cautious and hospitable, but he was reserved, and his bride trembled at the thought that something had changed the heart of her lord.

A few nights afterwards a party entered the castle; they were secret in their movements, and some person was placed in a distant part of the castle, that was scarcely inhabited by any one. Don Gusman was the only one who went there, and would stay there some time, to the amazement of his lady, who could not understand what could call him there.

One day Youssouff heard a Moorish melody, sung in a sweet, plaintive voice; he thought he knew it, and his heart trembled; he endeavoured to ascertain from whom it came, and, after much trouble and difficulty, he contrived to get to the apartments, when what a sight met his eyes! It was his own intended bride, the Moorish maid; they were instantly locked in each other's arms, and then came the explanation.

It would seem that Don Gusman had conceived a violent and uncontrollable passion for the Moorish maiden, and gave orders to his page to capture her, and bring her safe to the castle, where he intended she should remain until she consented to his wishes.

The indignant Moor would have accused Don Gusman of his treachery; however, by the advice of her he loved best, they determined to attempt an escape, which they effected, leaving Don Gusman to console himself as he might.

Some months after war was again carried on, and though in this case, as in some others, the Spaniards prevailed, yet Youssouff and Don Gusman met in battle. With a shout of fierce triumph the Moor spurred his horse against his enemy; the encounter was terrific, and Don Gusman was left for dead upon the field; the Moors were driven away, and the body of Gusman was recovered; he lived for years, but he was a cripple for life after, so well had Youssouff done his work of revenge.

——————

The tale was over, and Maritana closed the volume with a sigh, as she said,—

"Am I the only one of God's creatures who has ever known persecution and grief? Am I the only one who has suffered deeply, and yet innocently? Oh, no; and yet I was so full of mad, wild complaints. Just Heaven forgive me!"

She knelt by the window, and uttered a fervent prayer, one of those prayers that spring from the heart without an effort—one of those simple, eloquent appeals to Heaven which we cannot but believe are surely more acceptable than the carefully got-up printed appeals to the divinity, which people speak by rote in our own country.

Prayers now, forsooth, must have sentences nicely turned. Heaven would be offended at a solecism; and, as for a grammatical error, it would, of course, be enough to doom anybody, and serve him right too. Heaven must be addressed in polished language, although brevity likewise appears to be of no little consequence, for we have observed in the *Times* newspaper, lately, that special organ of all prejudice, bigotry, and intolerance, an advertisement concerning a book of family sermons, the great recommendation of which is, that "each only occupies six minutes in delivery."

Really the family that uses such a book must be economical of its time, that it can only spare six minutes of its time, even to Heaven!

But Maritana's prayer was one fresh, eloquent, and gushing from the heart—the prayer of a guileless mind—for blessing, and for peace—asked of that Heaven which is full of such high qualities, and which we may well suppose received the petition so breathed to it.

She rose from her knees—she felt composed—she felt almost happy—she could have smiled in her newly-recovered strength and consciousness of protection from above.

"I shall yet be happy," she said. "Surely I shall yet be happy; I am most innocent of evil intention, as I am of evil deeds. True, I have sinned, by being discontented at the station God had placed me in; but I have suffered, and have repented. I shall be forgiven.

"Yes, Maritana, a brighter day is dawning for you than ever yet shone upon your existence. The black night of your sufferings is passing away, and you will indeed know a joy greater than ever yet held a home in your young heart."

Suddenly the silence of the night was broken by the loud report of an arquebus ; the colour fled from Maritana's cheeks, as she exclaimed,—

"Heaven help me ! What was that ?"

CHAPTER LXVII.

DON CÆSAR AND THE TRAVELLING FRIAR.—THE UN-FORTUNATE DISGUISE. — THE ARQUEBUS. — THE JOYFUL MEETING.

LOTH as we are so to do, and ungallant as it may appear, we are compelled to leave Maritana to a consideration of the new alarm which had come over her in consequence of the sudden discharge of the arquebus that had met her ears while she was congratulating herself upon better hopes and prospects for the future, while we conduct the reader to another part of the chateau, in order to account for the report, and detail circumstances internally connected therewith.

We feel that for too long a period of time have we suffered our friend Don Cæsar to play the ghost—a character no doubt to the full as irksome to him to support, as it was terrifying and annoying to Don Jose de Santerem to see him do it.

When, then, Cæsar found, to his own vast astonishment, that he was quite unhurt, notwithstanding the fire of six arquebuses, which had been so very suddenly and so very unexpectedly opened upon him, he had scrambled to his feet again, for by the sudden shock of the surprise, he had stumbled and fallen on to the terrace, and not over it, as had appeared to the eyes of those who had in so dastardly a manner endeavoured to assassinate him at the command of Jose. Hence, when the smoke cleared away, and they saw him standing on the identical spot where he had been before, no wonder that a panic seized them, and the affair assumed an aspect of a serious character to their active imaginations.

Cæsar heard the cry "A ghost! a ghost!" as the attendants rushed with such mad precipitancy into the chateau, and that enabled him at once to understand the character he had to play, and a few moments' reflection opened his eyes to the great advantages such a new position in the grounds of Don Jose's chateau was calculated to give him.

"A ghost!" he said; "by Heavens, the rascals have done their best to make a ghost of me! I wonder I am not. Am I invulnerable? Six arquebuses, or more, for all I know, but certainly six, discharged at me, and I unhurt! Well, my little friend Lazarillo cannot surely this time have extracted the bullets. And yet who knows? Well, well, they think me a ghost; let them do so, until some favourable opportunity presents itself to me of proving to the rascals by hard blows directly the contrary. Let me come across any of them, and they shall find their reception will be anything but of a ghostly character. It shall be most strikingly natural."

He walked down the steps of the terrace, turning over in his mind what would be his next most prudent step to take, and he at length, after much consideration, decided upon endeavouring at once to make his way into the chateau.

"I will get in if it be possible," he remarked, "and go from room to room until I find her whom I seek. I have two chances of success now, where before I had but one. Those whom I meet as enemies, who have not sufficient prudence to be frightened at me as a supposed ghost, shall find that they had better have adopted that course, and got out of my way. I am not a man to stand upon trifles now ; I am on my guard, and if my object were even—as it is quite—not a sufficient justification of me to use my sword, I should find an ample one in the dastardly and cowardly attempt which has been made against my life by Don Jose's varlets.

While the servants were locked in the room they usually occupied, and were engaged in that panic-stricken discussion which ultimately ended in their hiding themselves in so many odd and out-of-the-way places, Don Cæsar walked entirely round the chateau, with the hope of finding some mode of ingress.

In this, however, he was disappointed, for the place had been built with an eye to security in every repect. There were very few doors, indeed, on the basement story, and those were all well secured. Windows, to be sure, there were, but all well-secured by iron bars, so that it was a matter of impossibility for Don Cæsar, or any one else, without fitting tools and much labour, to have made a successful entrance into the place by such means.

Having thus far satisfied himself that from the level of the garden he could not get into the chateau, Don Cæsar, without hesitation, once more ascended to the terrace, and by so doing he crossed the domestics in their flight, who by that time had made up their minds to leave the place in a body, and had just sallied out to carry such a resolve into execution, while Cæsar was equally hidden from their view, as they were from his, by one of the angles of the house, which was provided with heavy, jutting-out balconies.

There were many windows opening from the terrace into the interior of the house, but the frame-works of all of them were of iron, and of considerable thickness, while the panes of glass were so small that even were he to displace one of them, it could have afforded him no means of entrance.

"Confound this place," said Cæsar; "it is more impregnable than a fortress, especially when one don't want to make a noise in effecting an entrance into it."

In vain he went from window to window—all were fast ; and, although both outside and in, for some reason, were means of fastening the window, he invariably found that the inside was well and sufficiently secured.

Through many of these windows, which were not covered in the inside with display, he could obtain views of the interior of the house ; but, whenever that was the case, he was sure to find an empty apartment submitted to his gaze.

He had now traversed the terrace twice, in the vain hope of achieving something, and he paused, with a look of puzzled bewilderment, to ask himself what he should do next.

"This won't do," he remarked; " I must and will find my way into the chateau somehow, if I have to break through the very walls of it. The windows and doors are all fast. Humph ! and I with no stronger a weapon than my rapier, which is ill-fitted for the work of breaking down defences, and I might break it, too, by some unlucky blow, and then I should be unarmed, and comparatively at the mercy of every scoundrel who might chance to meet me and presume upon that circumstance."

After a few moments' more thought, he added,—

"I will make a vigorous and continued effort at one of the windows, and, at all events, I can undo the fastening outside, and, perhaps, some violence may succeed in forcing those on the inner."

With this intent he walked up to the window which was nearest to him, and, when he got within two paces of it, he heard a voice from within, either of some one conversing, or muttering to himself on some subject.

The latter was really the case, for it was the room in which was Don Jose, who, at that moment, caught sight of the shadow of the human face, which he was far from imagining to be that of Don Cæsar through the blind.

Not caring who it was, and rendered desperately impatient by the long delay to which he had been subjected, Don Cæsar stepped close to the window, just as Jose had mustered courage sufficient to take aside the curtain, and thus, as we have already described, had they met face to face with only the window-frame and its glass between them, an obstacle which looked nothing, although it was, in reality, amply sufficient to protect Jose, had he been in a frame of mind which would have enabled him to give to the subject more rational and collected consideration than his fears allowed him.

The precipitate retreat, coupled with the looks of consternation of Don Jose, at once convinced Don Cæsar that he too believed in his ghostly appearance; and, vexed and anxious as he was at the failure of his plans to get into the chateau, he could scarcely refrain from a laugh at the ludicrous terror of such a man as Jose, who had always made such a boast of his being superior to all fears of a supernatural description.

"The villain!" cried Cæsar; "what a fright he is in to be sure. How I should like to get him into some corner where he could not escape, and give him as much terror as would last him to think about as long as he lived—not that that will be long, I am thinking, when Jose and I meet, for he shall fight me, whether he will or no, or he shall die the death of a cur."

Vigorous were the attempts which Cæsar made at the window; but, although he broke some of the glass, he found that he could not open it, so artfully planned were the fastenings within.

"Foiled again," he said; "foiled again. I will search the garden for some weapon of strength and might, and we will see what a strong man can do against one of these windows yet."

He rapidly left the terrace, and descended to the garden, where he looked about him in vain. Not a weapon of any kind could he find, and he was on the point of giving that mode of operation up in despair, when suddenly he saw the door, which was near to the steps of the terrace, open, and a friar emerge from it.

This was Don Jose's new ally. In his hand he carried a jug, and was going to the well for some cold water, in which to cool the wine which he was about to place on the table before his new master, whom he had picked up so oddly.

Cæsar stepped aside, and allowed him to pass, and he heard him muttering to himself as he did so,—

"I wonder where this well is that the old deaf idiot told me was in the garden? Ah, well, I must look I suppose, till I find it."

He walked on, as his good fortune would have it, in the proper direction, and Don Cæsar much wondering who he could be, followed him.

"Oh," said the friar, as he came within sight of the well. "There it is, but I don't see the cord."

"No, nor you won't," thought Cæsar. "I wonder how my friend, who is at the bottom of the well, gets on?"

Perhaps the travelling friar, who had turned out

such a travelling rogue, might have heard the footsteps of Don Cæsar behind him, for the latter was not very cautious, had not his attention been suddenly attracted by a deep groan, in two senses of the word, from the bottom of the well, which caused him no little surprise.

He paused on the instant, and in a voice which went far to disprove his assertion to Don Jose, of how little he feared the supernatural, he suddenly cried,

"Hilloa—what was that?"

Another groan came from the well.

"God bless me," said the travelling friar, "where can that be from, eh? I don't see anybody!"

"Help, help," said the man in the well, and his voice from the depths of the uncomfortable place, had a very odd and disagreeable sound with it as it echoed up.

"I—I—have a good mind to go back," said the travelling friar. "I don't like this at all."

"Is there any Christian near?" groaned the man who had been so justly punished, and now had the impudence to talk of Christianity. "Is there any good Christian near?"

"No—no," said the travelling friar; "no. Whoever you are, and wherever you are, take your answer and begone."

"I'm in the well I'm in the well."

"The well?"

"Oh, yes—save me—save me!"

"If I do, may I be—a-hem! My friend, I have one maxim in life which I cannot but apply in your case."

"What is it?" groaned the fellow.

"I always let well alone."

"Oh, how cruel to joke with a man in my situation. My good Samaritan, whoever you are, get another rope and haul me up."

"How the deuce came you there?"

"Oh, a villain—a pickpocket—a robber—an assassin, put me down here, while he went to rob the chateau."

"Indeed."

"Oh, it's a fact—truth—truth!"

"Well, I've always heard that truth lies at the bottom of a well—so I think, my friend, you had better remain where you are."

"Whoever you are, you won't be so inhuman."

"Oh! dear, yes."

"Come, come now, you are joking."

"Am I—why don't you laugh then?"

"Laugh down here? Why, the water comes nearly up to my chin, and I must have been in a fortnight, at the very least."

"A fortnight? And this is human nature. A fortnight? Really now, that is too bad."

"You will help me?"

"Certainly not."

"Why, you said it was too bad."

"I meant, your lies. Now, I must inform you, my friend, that I pride myself upon being the greatest liar in all Spain, so I am not going to let you out to compete with me."

"Oh, this is cruel!"

"Gruel, did you say?"

"No—no—cruel."

"Oh, but it's well meant you know, if it is not well said, my facetious friend. Good day—good day! It's getting towards evening, and will soon be dark. If you are tired of your situation, I will give you a word of advice how to alter it."

"How—how?"

"Lie down."

So saying, the travelling friar, with a good chuckle at his own wit, turned to go away towards the chateau again, and now stood face to face with Don Cæsar, who, during this dialogue, with which he had been much amused, had walked close up to him, and stood with his arms folded, waiting until the very interesting conversation should be completely over before he declared himself.

The astonishment of the friar was sufficiently depicted in his countenance, which presented a singular admixture of cowardice, cunning, audacity, and fear. He dropped the pitcher which he had come to fill with water, and gazed at Don Cæsar in silence, as if he would endeavour to read his very soul.

CHAPTER LXVIII.

THE DISGUISE OF CÆSAR.—HIS NARROW ESCAPE.— THE ROBBERY, AND THE FLIGHT OF THE TRA- VELLING FRIAR FROM THE CHATEAU.

CÆSAR was very much amused at the look of curious dismay and doubt with which the man regarded him, into whose character he had now a very fair insight, from the conversation he had heard between him and the man who was repeating some of his sins at the bottom of the well.

Spain abounded, and still abounds, with these mendicant friars, who lead a vagabond life, and presume on their professional sanctity to claim the best of everything wherever they go. This Don Cæsar knew, and he saw at once that he had encountered some such scoundrel, although how he came to make one of Don Jose's household, he was at a loss to conjecture.

Touching the hilt of his sword slightly, Cæsar said,—

"If you make any attempt to escape me, I will follow you and run you through. I am fleet of foot, and am acquainted with the intricacies of this place."

"Signior, I—I—who may you be?"

"It matters not to you. Answer my questions, but ask none, and be sure you answer me truly."

"I don't know you, signior; but Heaven forbid that I should take upon me to deceive you."

"Take care you do not. Who are you?"

"A travelling friar."

"What do you here?"

"I am in the service of Don Jose, the most noble minister of state, and at the same time ——"

"The greatest scoundrel unhung."

"It would be the height of ill-manners in me to contradict you, signior."

"Who is here likewise?"

"A friend of his, whom I have not seen, and a lady, whom likewise I have not seen; and when, signior, you come to consider that my time of service does not at present reach half a day, you will not wonder at my ignorance."

"Not half a day?"

"No, signior. I came here by accident, and Don Jose finding me just such a vagabond as he wanted, at once engaged me."

"You are candid."

"It's almost my only fault, signior. I own to being candid. It was born with me, and I'm afraid it has kept me poor, for it will stick to me while I live."

"Hark ye, sir wandering friar," said Cæsar, after a pause, "I want to get into the chateau, and I will carry my point. What means have you of entering?"

"Signior, there is an old fool, as deaf as an adder, waiting with his ear at the other side of the door, in case I give a loud kick, and then he will admit me."

"He knows you?"

"He will recognize my garb."

"Ah! is it so? Then I will borrow it of you, wandering friar. Just be so good as to lend me your friar's gown, until I have secured a footing within the chateau."

"If I refuse?"

"I will force you."

"Very good. Then I yield at once, as a matter of course. Very good. I always bow to circumstances."

He took off his grey cassock, and handed it to Don Cæsar, who quickly put it on, after which he said,—

"Now, my friend, let me warn you of the conse- quences of betraying me. My sincere advice to you is, to leave the chateau at once; but if you persist in staying, remember, it is at your own peril. Mention one word of this adventure to Don Jose, or any inmate of the chateau, and depend upon it I will find you out, and make some half-a-yard of my Toledo acquainted with your internal anatomy. You understand me, friend?"

"Quite, quite. I am not at all slow of comprehen- sion, noble signior, under such circumstances. You may rely upon my utmost discretion. Allow me to show you the door."

"Mercy! Have mercy upon me, somebody!" said the man in the well. "Don't go away. Save me from this dreadful place! Have you no humanity?"

"Now really that is too bad," remarked the tra- velling friar. "You growling rascal, what do you mean by making such remarks?"

"Save me—save me!"

"Save you, indeed! You are not worth the saving. Sit down and be quiet. You are, without excep- tion, one of the most discontented, troublesome per- sons I ever encountered. Nothing seems to satisfy you. You are not content with *well* doing, but you want to give trouble to other people. Curb your de- sires, as the holy psalmist remarks, or they will eat you up completely. This way, signior, if you please. Allow me to show you to the door. This way, noble signior. That is a most unreasonable fellow down yonder in the well. He seems lost to all reflection."

"A truce with your buffooning," said Don Cæsar, and yet he could not help laughing as he spoke.

"Exactly, signior; as you please. I wish to do you good service, and why? Simply because I am afraid of you. I am a man of peace, and never resist anybody who I perceive is stronger than myself; so that a big fellow, like your noble self, signior, with a rapier that, no doubt, your noble self knows well how to use, finds me always his very humble and most obedient servant to command."

Don Cæsar made no further answer, for he found that every word he spoke was but a provocative to fresh loquacity on the part of the travelling friar, whose tongue it seemed as impossible to stop as any of the ordinary phenomena of nature.

They had now reached the door, on the inner side of which, as the friar had truly enough said, was the old deaf domestic, waiting to let him in when he should give a sufficiently hard kick at it to make his presence known.

"Allow me to kick," said the friar. "I wish to do you all the service I can. Allow me to kick, signior."

"As you please."

"He is dreadfully deaf. It's a great trial to have anything to explain to him, noble sir."

He raised his foot, and dealt against the door a heavy kick, which even then the old deaf man would not have heard, had not his ear been placed against it on the other side. The concussion aroused him to the fact that the friar had returned, and he opened the door a short distance.

"Merciful Providence!" said the friar, casting his eyes up the building; "she will be killed."

"She?" cried Cæsar. "Good God! Who—who?"

He stepped back a pace, and glanced up. In a mo- ment the friar slipped into the chateau, and barred and bolted the door on the inside, leaving Don Cæsar with only the poor satisfaction of having got possession of an old grey cassock.

In a moment more he was aware of the trick which had been played him, and he gave the door a most tremendous push; but he might as well have pushed against the stone walls of the villa itself, for it resisted his efforts completely.

"I deserve this," he said, "for trusting for a moment such a knave. I do deserve this trick for my folly. Let me catch you again, sir travelling friar, and if we don't be even for this, never trust Don Cæsar de Bazan again as long as you live. The infernal scoundrel, to play me such a trick. And I to be so simple, too—such an idiot as to be taken in by such a child's device. It is too bad—it is too bad."

The night was coming fast. Rapidly the sun's last rays were now leaving the earth, and Don Cæsar could feel the cool refreshing breeze of evening, as it swept over the flowers and fruits in the beautiful garden of the chateau.

He became almost maddened by a sense of his repeated disappointments in getting into the chateau. Hours had he been trying to accomplish such a result unsuccessfully—and yet then he was no forwarder than when he began—ending, too, by being foiled at the very moment of anticipated success.

No wonder that Don Cæsar got savage and angry. A flush of heightened colour came across his face, as he sprang once more upon the terrace, and getting as far out as he possibly could from the house, he cast a curious glance over that side of it, in the hope of seeing some mode of entrance, however desperate, troublesome, or dangerous.

Above him, out of reach, was a balcony, and he saw that a window which opened on to it was open.

"If I could reach that balcony," he thought, "all were well. Might I by a desperate effort climb up to it. Oh, for a rope! oh, for some means—any means of reaching it."

He walked completely under it, and he saw that the window which was on the level of where he stood, reached nearly to it.

"By breaking the squares of glass," he said, "and making footholds for my feet against the frame-work, I might get up and lay hold of the side of the balcony, and so reach it. It shall be done—it shall be done. I will break my neck, or do it. By Heavens, anything is better than remaining here in idleness and inactivity. It can but be tried. Good saints assist. Here goes for love, for honour, and for justice, against a villain. I will rescue you, my beautiful countess, or perish in the attempt so to do. Courage—courage. Why did I not think of this before? Courage, courage, courage!"   *   *   *   *

Lazarillo was wearied by his lonely watch. Small consideration had Don Jose for those who were doing him service. The boy might want much sleep, but what cared he? He might want food, but to that Jose would be equally indifferent; and to tell the truth, poor Lazarillo wanted both, and it was only his great energy and the natural buoyancy of his disposition, that at all supported him.

Now he leant heavily upon his arquebus, thinking of the various occurrences that had already chequered his young existence. He thought of those who had loved him in early life, now passed away into the tomb. He thought of a mother's smile, a father's kiss, a sweet sister's fond caress, but all were gone. He thought of the harshness and selfish cruelty of the old armourer, who had no consideration for the little escapades of the boy, but was perpetually seeking to crush the free happy spirit which he fancied he held in his keeping.

And last, but, oh, not least, did Lazarillo think of Cæsar, the noble, the reckless, the chivalrous, and the indiscreet.

"If he would but come," mused the boy—"if I could but see him for a moment now, just to tell him that his countess was here—that he was safe—that I, of all the rascally Jose's domestics, had remained, if we except the friar, and that I was ready to die to do him service—how happy I should be."

Lazarillo's head drooped more and more over the window-sill, and he was upon the point of dropping off asleep, when he suddenly gave himself a shake, exclaiming,—

"This must not be. Arouse yourself, Lazarillo—arouse yourself. This must not be. Here you talk of wishing to see Don Cæsar, and yet are on the point of going to sleep. Awake—awake."

He drew himself up, and after a few hearty shakes, he got rid, for the time, of the drowsiness that had began to fasten on him, as he there kept his lonely watch.

"The night is coming," he said, in a low tone, "the night is coming. Alas! poor Countess de Bazan! I wonder now if, by any possibility, I could carry to her a word of comfort? If I could but let her know that Don Cæsar was near at hand, and safe, she might find the hours pass far more lightly and pleasantly over her head than, I dare say, is the case at present."

This idea, once started, did not readily leave the mind of the page, and as he now paced slowly to and fro by the window, he revolved it in his mind in all its various phases, probabilities, and possibilities of action.

"I know well the window," he remarked, "of the room where she is placed. I know that a particular tree in the garden, which I could again recognise, is opposite to it, and so I could not fail to find it. There are writing materials in the rooms below. Now, if I dared count upon the absence of Don Jose for a quarter of an hour, all would be well, and I would contrive to give this lady some comfort in her deep affliction."

He placed his arquebus against the side of the window, and thought for a few moments silently.

"And if," he said—"if Don Jose should come and find me a few moments from my post, what then—what then? Let him say what he will—let him do what he will, Heaven knows I care not much for words from Don Jose. I will go—I will do it."

To once determine upon anything, with Lazarillo, was to put it into immediate practice; and now, with a noiseless step, he took his way down the great staircase, and finding in one of the lower rooms writing materials, he produced the short but expressive note which we are aware that Maritana received by the window of her apartment.

Lazarillo found no difficulty in leaving the chateau for a few moments, and running round the house until he reached the particular tree which he knew was opposite to the window of the room occupied by the Countess de Bazan, he wrapped his note round a pebble he picked from the grotto, and threw it in at the open casement.

Of its reception by Maritana, and the new hopes and better feelings it awakened in her bosom, we are well aware. By this little kindly manœuvre, Lazarillo had accomplished more than he had ever pictured to himself to do, for he saved the beautiful prisoner from such agonised reflections as the reader is aware of, although he, the page, was not.

To return to the corridor where he had been keeping guard, and to resume his arquebus, was to the nimble-footed boy the work of a very few moments. With a smile he said,—

"All's right—all's right; no one has been here."

Even at the moment he heard a strange noise at the window, and rising up, as if by magic, from the outside of the balcony he saw, as he imagined, the hateful figure of the rascally friar. He knew him by the grey cassock, although he had upon his head a cap and feathers. In an instant Lazarillo seized his arquebus, and exclaiming,—

"For once I cheerfully obey the orders of Don Jose," he discharged it at the figure.

CHAPTER LXIX.

THE QUEEN'S ILLNESS.—HER SOLITARY JOURNEY TO THE CHATEAU.—A WIFE'S DEVOTION.—THE MAN UNBOUND FROM THE TREE, AND THE MODE OF ADMITTANCE TO THE GARDEN.

THE non-arrival of the queen at the chateau, according to the promise she had made to the page, Lazarillo, was not from any want of energy or moral courage on her part to perform a promise of doing that which was hazardous and unpleasant, but it arose solely from sheer inability, in the shape of a severe illness, which she felt hourly making progress in her system, and which her attendants had foreseen.

The scenes she had gone through the last few days, the affair of the forest, and the exposure she suffered, all contributed to bring on a severe nervous affliction, accompanied by fever, and ere she had returned many hours to the Castle of Aranjues, she was compelled to summon her physician and ask his aid, previous to which, however, she became so helpless that she was carried to her bed exhausted, and unable to walk. A flood of tears came to her relief as she thought with sorrow of the fate of the unfortunate Countess de Bazan, who was thus left without aid or protection. This hastened on her disorder, and before many hours she was almost incapable of speech, and her physician ordered that she should be kept perfectly quiet.

The Lady Inez, the queen's favourite attendant, would not quit the chamber of her royal mistress, save once to consult the medical attendant. She was much grieved at the indisposition of the queen, and taking the physician, Signior Jerome Bino, aside, she said,—

"Tell me truly, good signior, the nature of our royal lady's disease?"

"I can scarcely call it a disease," said the doctor, "any more than I can call fatigue a disease. You see ——"

"Well, Signior Jerome?"

"You see the queen's disorder partakes much in character of the nature of fatigue."

"And she will get over it?"

"Undoubtedly she will," replied Signior Jerome Bino. "You see there is much of fatigue in the cause, good Lady Inez, and ——"

"And what, good signior? You alarm me. Tell me, I beseech you, is there any danger?"

"That you see is as may be."

"Goodness ——"

"Do not be impatient. I am endeavouring to explain and render things quite clear to you; but you must not be so impatient."

"I impatient?"

"Yes, good lady. I was speaking to you about fatigue, you see ——"

"The queen's illness ——"

"Exactly, proceeds from fatigue, both mentally and bodily, and somewhat from fright. The causes combined have deranged the system, and shaken the nerves; you see this, good Lady Inez?"

"I do."

"Well, then, you will understand that repose and some little medicine will do her, probably, so much good that she will soon recover."

"But she is speechless."

"Great prostration of powers," remarked the physician. "This will do wonders."

"She was unable to walk."

"Time and attention will restore to her the powers of locomotion."

"And her grief is great."

"Time will assuage her sorrow," remarked the physician, very coolly.

"Tut—tut! good doctor, you mock me."

"Not I, good Lady Inez. What would you have me do?"

"Pursue some more active line of conduct, and relieve her highness earlier."

"My good lady, I am answerable for my treatment, and, moreover, it is not in the power of a physician to hurry on a cure. You might as well endeavour to hurry a human being to sleep quicker than nature will allow. The means defeat the object. You must let many of these things subside of themselves. I can do a little towards effecting that object by soporifics and a few other matters."

"And you will do that?"

"I have ordered them, and they will be ready before the queen will be fit to take them. If she sleep of herself, the first medicine I propose to give her will be unnecessary."

"She does sleep."

"Then one less strong will answer the purpose; for so long as the medicine effects the desired object, it is better the weaker it should be, provided it hang not in the system, then, indeed, a stronger dose is necessary."

"I must return."

"Stay awhile, and I shall soon have done my explanation, which will serve to render you more easy; and—let me see—ah, in some cases, as I was saying, a stronger dose may be necessary; but when not, a milder dose injures the system less, and does not tear and rack it about so badly."

"Tear and rack the queen!" exclaimed Inez, lifting up her hands and eyes in great astonishment; "you wouldn't surely give her gracious majesty drugs that would in any way inconvenience her?"

"I cannot really help it," replied the physician— "physic is physic, all the world over, and I can't alter it, and if I did, I should see all its poison changed too, and then the physician would be useless, as he would have to study anew."

"Very well, my good signior," said the Lady Inez, very much puzzled; "what if the queen's mind should be affected?"

"Why, time only, combined with care and attention, will recover it. You see ——"

"Good bye, Signior Jerome, I must return to the bedside of my royal mistress; she may even now require my attendance."

The Lady Inez, dreading another dissertation upon disorders and medicine, and not being able to understand them, immediately re-entered the royal apartment, leaving the physician to his own meditations.

The queen's disorder did give way to the judicious and careful treatment of her physician, and when her mind was more at ease, and herself relieved from fatigue and fear, she began to think once more of performing the promise she had made to Lazarillo respecting her journey to Don Jose's villa.

It was not immediately determined upon; indeed the disaster had much shaken her courage, and caused her to think upon the possibility of her reaching them at all, as somewhat problematical and uncertain.

But as her strength came round, her courage grew greater, and she again canvassed the matter in her own mind, and determined upon again making the attempt.

"Inez," she said, as she was gazing upon the crucifix, that yet stood near the window.

"Yes, gracious lady," said Inez. "I am here at your majesty's command."

"I think I am sufficiently recovered now," said the queen, hesitating, " to—to——"

"What, gracious lady?"

"To make another attempt to reach that chateau we were unable to get to a short time back, Inez."

"Surely your majesty never can, never will,—no, you cannot mean Don Jose's?"

"I do."

"Let me beseech ——"

"Nay, Inez, you know the duty that devolves on me, and I may not shrink."

"I be-eech your majesty to pause before you attempt so dangerous a purpose which has ended once so fatally, so disastrously. Do let me implore your majesty to give over this intention — it is entirely hopeless."

"I think not, Inez."

"But your majesty will be liable to meet with the same accident on the road that you met before, and even should you be able to force your way through these men, then you have a further, and, perhaps, a more dreadful one to encounter at hand."

"How?"

"You may probably not get in at all, and should you do so, then what certainty have you of getting out again?"

"They dare not injure me, Inez."

"But they may seize and confine your majesty until all you would have prevented has been effected; and what would be your own feelings and position under such circumstances?"

"The worst."

"Exactly, they would. Then be persuaded, noble lady, and remain with us here. Where you go, there we go, even to death; but do not unnecessarily run into danger."

My mind is made up, Inez."

"My ——"

"Nay, I say my mind is made up—to you I commit the charge of having everything in readiness for my departure."

"It shall be done, your majesty; but I would rather it had been some other resolve, so sure am I of some disaster following."

The Lady Inez quitted the room, and had scarcely reached the hall before she informed the household of the resolve of the queen. There was a gloom upon every one's countenance, and at length it was agreed that they should go in a body to the queen, and represent to her the extreme danger of the attempt.

The Lady Inez was glad of this, and encouraged them to proceed to the royal apartments, and there to beseech her not to go.

She accordingly returned to the queen, saying,—

"Will your majesty permit your household to enter this apartment?"

"And why, Inez?" inquired the queen, surprised.

"They have a boon to ask," replied Inez.

"Indeed!"

"Yes, your majesty."

"Then admit them. I cannot, however, conceive what it is that they can require. Least of all, should it be thus urged."

The household were now admitted, and they urged her majesty not to quit Aranjues. They feared that some dreadful calamity must be in reserve for her, if she went on so dangerous an errand. They begged and implored her majesty to pause.

"Will you grant the prayer of your faithful and attached servants?" inquired Inez.

"I countermand my orders, Inez," said the queen, with tears in her eyes.

The joyful intimation was received with murmurs of applause, and they quitted the apartment with every demonstration of pleasure.

"Now, Inez," said the queen, after she had passed a few moments in silent meditation. "Leave, I would be alone."

Inez withdrew, leaving the queen alone in the apartment, meditating upon what course she should adopt; she did not like to do what they so earnestly besought her not to do; on the contrary, she felt much disinclination to disregard so much good will, though shown to her by inferiors. And yet she could not resolve to give up her intention.

"I must," she murmured, "go incognito, and see what my presence will produce,—what effect it will have; indeed, it is only by my presence that I have any hope of being useful, for most certainly my servants would do nothing by force, far from it. I should suffer if it were resorted to. What, then, need I care about attendants and parade? I will go, attended by one servant. I shall be the more likely to gain admittance than I should be if I even were to go in pomp and state. Moreover, I shall incur less danger, because resistance would be offered to violence, and therefore it will the less likely be offered."

Calling the Lady Inez, therefore, she determined to effect her purpose, at the same time she would conceal it from all.

"Inez."

"Your majesty."

"Tell Osmanlis, my Moorish groom, I desire to speak to him. I will send him, I think, as a messenger to the chateau, or Madrid."

"I think your majesty has acted wisely," replied Inez, as she left the apartment to obey the orders of the queen.

The Moor was not long in making his appearance before the queen, and in silence waited to receive her orders.

The queen gave Inez some trifling order while she spoke to Osmanlis, and when alone, she said,—

"Osmanlis, can you be discreet, and faithful?"

"I can, and will, your majesty."

"That is well; but have you courage to undertake a difficult, and perhaps a dangerous mission?" inquired the queen.

"I never wanted in courage, your majesty, and I am willing to risk life and limb in your service."

"You know, I dare say, the chateau of Don Jose, whither I was going?"

"I have seen it."

"That is enough—I intend to go there, and desire you to attend me. There may be danger."

"I care not for that, so it be such that will not light upon your majesty."

"I must trust to your arm for defence."

"Your majesty shall not trust in vain; but, bethink you, royal lady, is it danger that one man can guard against? Not that I care for defeat or death; but when I am laid low, there will be no further barrier between you and your enemies," said Osmanlis.

"I have thought of all that; therefore numbers will have no avail. You will be my escort, but be sure take two of your best mules, and remain beneath the cork-trees in the park, but in such a position that you cannot be seen from the windows of the palace."

"I will, your majesty."

"Be cautious and wary. You are, you understand, a messenger to the chateau of Don Jose."

Osmanlis bowed, and retired to carry his orders out, and execute them.

The queen herself having now fully made up her mind, sought means to account for her absence from her attendant, and after Inez had returned, she gave her a commission to execute, at the same time inform-ing her that she would not be disturbed for some time, that she should either be in the royal chapel, or her own apartment.

Thus quieting her attendants, the queen left the palace secretly, and habited merely as a Spanish lady; and, ere long, she came to the spot where Osmanlis was in waiting, with a mule of great value and speed for herself, and a strong horse for himself. Having armed himself carefully, at the same time, he wore a cloak over his livery.

"It is as I would have it," said the queen, as she looked upon him, and the way he had prepared for herself.

The day was getting far advanced; and, as the queen did not desire to be in the forest at night, she told Osmanlis that, as he knew the distance, he had better make such speed as he thought would enable them to reach in daylight the place of their destina-tion.

On their journey the queen ruminated on the past, and began to think upon the best course she could adopt in the present and future exigencies.

She could not conceal from herself that the conduct of the king was both immoral and dishonourable in the extreme, and such that, did she live with him, she must herself share the obloquy of, as she would seem to sanction it.

"I will endeavour to rescue the poor girl; I will endeavour to restore her to liberty; and then, as my husband no longer loves me, no longer cares for my society, but looks upon my very life as a cause of anger, I will leave him—I will leave the country, and he shall have no cause to say that I wished to embitter his life by my presence, which must put a check upon his actions. I would that he could be brought to a better state of mind, for his own sake, for mine has now no more to do with him; we have nothing in common, but I shall relieve him of a sore grievance, and leave Spain. Little did I think the fate that awaited me when I first received the proud title of Queen of Spain. Times are altered—sadly altered; I would that had never happened, and then I could not have complained; but now, the higher I am raised, the more I am seen, and what a sight for all Spain to see! A weeping queen!—royalty divested of power—the insignia without the office! Ah, well, I will not, even to myself, complain; he has more power than any one else—is flattered and ill-advised, and hence, his follies and crimes spring, not so much from himself as from others; and yet he must be prone, else he had not so cruelly erred against me."

The sun was now fast sinking, and the hour of even-ing was close at hand; the tops of the tall forest-trees were yet gilded by the sun's rays, as he was sinking behind the western mountains, but unseen by the tra-vellers, who were wrapped in the shade of the tall forest trees, as they were proceeding, at a rapid pace, through the forest towards the chateau.

"Have we far to journey, Osmanlis?" inquired the queen; "shall we reach it before nightfall?"

"We shall be there, your majesty, in less than half an hour."

"I hope no later, good Osmanlis."

"No later, your majesty."

"But what is that yonder?"

"That—what, your majesty? I see no one."

"But that by yon tree."

"Oh, it looks very like a water-bottle."

"But how came it there?"

"That is more than I can tell, your majesty; but I'll ride on and ascertain what it is."

"Do so," replied the queen, and immediately Osmanlis rode forward, and was followed closely by the queen, who began to be somewhat impatient of delay, and she feared her attendant might delay longer than she chose.

When they came up to the tree, there, true enough, lay a large water-jug.

"It is as I said," replied Osmanlis.

A groan at this moment attracted their attention, and, to the terror of the queen, and the amazement of Osmanlis, they saw a man buckled to a tree.

This was the very fellow who had fought Don Cæsar in the morning. .

"Hilloa!" said Osmanlis, riding up.

"Hilloa!" replied the fellow, kicking his heels on the earth.

"Who are you?" inquired the attendant.

"Who am I?"

"Yes."

"Why, I can hardly tell you. I don't know, and I don't think it hardly safe if I did. Curse me, but I'm tied up like a bag of rotten oranges."

"You must have done something very wrong to be tied up thus?"

"I did."

"What was it?"

"Let other men get the better of me when I couldn't help it."

"Explain this mystery, good fellow," said the queen, riding up.

"Ah, good lady, that is more than I am able to do," replied the man.

"What do you want?"

"I want to get up."

"Do you know which is Don Jose's chateau?" in-quired the queen.

"I did this morning."

"Come," said Osmanlis, dismounting, "speak more reverently, and more to the purpose, or the point of my sword is just of a temper to do you some hard favour."

"I would you kept your own sword's point for your own occasions; mine they don't suit. Why don't you release me, and then I can answer your questions; but here I am hungry, thirsty, and in some incon-venience."

"There is truth in what he says. Osmanlis unbind him, and he will be our guide."

"That I will be right willingly," replied the fellow, quickly.

Osmanlis undid the buckles, and relieved him from his awkward situation, and the fellow arose, stretch-ing his huge frame, and shaking himself like a wolf-hound.

"Now, my friend," said the queen, "tell me, will you bring me to the place where Don Jose lives, and where he has a villa?"

"I will, indeed; I belong to the place."

"You belong to Don Jose?"

"To the villa."

"Oh, well," said the queen, "that's the same."

"I'm not quite so sure of that, because—no matter —I do, or did belong to it."

"Can you get in?"

"I can."

"And let us in too?"

"Yes, I can do that; and you may do some service if you will enter the place with me," said the fellow to Osmanlis.

"I'll go with you; but how came you bound to the tree?"

"Why, I was attacked by some six or seven men, and, after as stout a resistance as one man may give against such odds, I was fairly taken and strapped here, and then they asked many questions concerning the chateau."

"Aye?"

"Yes, and I expect they have gone there, and

but I haven't heard any of them. However, I shall soon learn; but I shall take care this time, for I have had fighting enough for one day."

He then re-bolted the door and made all secure, and then left them, saying he would come again to them in a short time.

Thus were the queen and her attendant admitted into the chateau, or the gardens belonging to the chateau of Don Jose, kept for such a disreputable purpose.

The queen looked around her, and now that she had accomplished all—now she had got there, and there was no longer any excitement incident to over-coming opposition to urge her on, she could not forbear a shudder.

CHAPTER LXX.

LAZARILLO'S MISTAKE.—THE SHOT IN DON CÆSAR'S
HAT.—THE JOYFUL MEETING.

"TAKE that," said Lazarillo, as the loud report of his arquebus awakened a hundred echoes in the corridor. "Be you priest or layman, you will repent coming here, you scoundrel. Don Jose may employ what vagabonds he pleases to watch those whom I am anxious to protect, but he should recollect that I have an arquebus, and that I know how to use it."

As for any compunctions at shooting the travelling friar, Lazarillo had none in the world; and that he had lodged a bullet in his head he now firmly believed. Oh, how little he dreamed that his dearest, best friend on earth had been the object of his mistaken attack.

There was a silence for about a minute, for so sudden and unexpected to Don Cæsar had been the discharge of the arquebus at him, that he very nearly let go his hold, and fell on to the terrace.

Quickly, however, recovering, and feeling quite conscious that he was unhurt, the propriety of expediting his movements came strongly upon him.

"That rascal, whoever he is, is loading again," he thought, and then, by a vigorous effort, he raised himself up, and bounded at one spring into the balcony before the astonished eyes of Lazarillo.

The page had no more ammunition, or, doubtless, he would have been actively employed in reloading the arquebus; but when he saw, as he supposed, the travelling friar quite unhurt, still persevering in making an entrance by the window, he reversed his arquebus,

taken possession of the place by force, to pillage it, or something or other."

"Then we can't get in, or ascertain whether we can or not."

"Yes, yes; you follow me. I know how to get into the chateau, and can let you in below, by a door that I know of."

"That will do—that will do very well," said the queen. "Move on—we waste time."

"Follow me," said the fellow, walking from the spot, as though he had no objection to quit the place whatever. He strode forward at a rapid pace, until they came to a high wall, surrounded by trees, chiefly chesnut.

The man paused a moment, as if he scarce knew what to do; but then led them through the trees, until he came to a particular spot, saying,—

"Here you must dismount, and tie your horse and mule. I will get over and open this small door beneath."

They did as they were desired by the man, who gave a spring, and seizing some projection in the wall, he drew himself up, and, by some exertion he got over, and disappeared from their sight. After some few minutes spent in searching about, the door he had spoken of was undone, and the queen, followed by Osmanlis, entered the garden of the chateau.

"All is quiet, as yet," said the man.

"All what?"

"The people or the robbers, I don't know yet which;

and with the heavy stock of it he aimed a blow at the intruder which was more likely to be mischievous than the bullet.

Cæsar caught the descending weapon in his hands, and at the same moment he said,—

"Lazarillo!"

The page knew that voice in a moment. Its every accent was strongly impressed on his memory. A cry of joyful surprise burst from his lips. He dropped the arquebus, and exclaiming,—

"Cæsar—dear Cæsar!" sprang into the arms of his friend.

"And is it you, Lazarillo," said Don Cæsar as he lifted the slight form of the page into the room—"is it you who gave me so warm and startling a reception just now?"

"Oh, Cæsar, Cæsar, it was indeed. Can you ever forgive me?"

"Easily."

"But are you hurt? Oh, that I should be so mad as to fire an arquebus at you. If I had killed you, what would have become of me. I am horrified."

The page burst into a frantic passion of weeping, for all the horrors that might have arisen from his mistake, came with such a gush of terror across his mind, that he lost all strength and all confidence—but for Don Cœsar he must have fallen to the floor.

"Come, come, Lazarillo," said Cœsar, in a kindly voice of encouragement. "Be not discomfited at this little accident: it might have happened to the best of us. And, moreover, as I am unhurt, you see it is no accident at all."

"I cannot but shudder to think what it might have done."

"It was a good shot, Lazarillo."

"Oh! heavens."

"Nay, now, think no more of it. I would at any moment have gone through as much danger at the hands of any one else to get an interview with you— so think no more of it."

The boy clung to him convulsively.

"Who did you take me for?" asked Cæsar. "Surely I heard you congratulating yourself upon having shot some one."

"For a scoundrel in Jose's service, Cæsar—a travelling friar."

"Ah, that accounts for it. I have been foolish enough to retain this confounded hood and cassock belonging to him, and it has nearly cost me my life. Hence, foul disguise, go!"

He threw the friar's garment from him, and at the same moment he took off his hat, when something fell from it on the floor of the apartment.

"What's that?" said Cæsar.

"A bullet," replied Lazarillo, as he picked one from the floor.

"Then it must be from your arquebus, Lazarillo. I felt a twist of the hat at the moment you fired. You took a very fair aim."

"I will keep this," said Lazarillo, as he looked at the bullet, and a tear fell upon it, "as a memorial of my rashness."

"Nay, now, let me keep it," said Cæsar, as he pulled out several others from his pocket; "I have still here those you extracted from the arquebuses of the guard at the prison."

"Indeed!"

"Yes. And this one can go among the others. It is the most friendly bullet, I feel assured, that ever was discharged."

"The most mistaken one, Cæsar."

"A miss, Lazarillo, with a bullet, if it be but an inch, is as good as a league; so let me see you smile again, and say no more about it, my boy."

"But only to think now, Cæsar, that I should go through this villanous place to extract the bullets from every arquebus I could lay hold of, for fear we should be fired at, and then myself to discharge at you the only one which retained its power of mischief."

"Then I owe to you my exceedingly miraculous preservation from the volley that was fired at me on the terrace."

"Was that at you, Cæsar?"

"Indeed it was, Lazarillo."

"Then thank God I have twice saved you. Oh, what a happiness it is that I have been blessed with opportunites of showing to you how grateful I wish to be."

"You have amply, indeed, Lazarillo, repaid me for any little service I tried to do you. You have prevented others from shooting me, and, to crown the obligation, you have missed me yourself."

"Oh, if I had not!"

"Why, then you should have set it down as one of the accidents of life, Lazarillo, and not fretted about it. But since a kind fortune has now brought us together, and we are both in whole skins, tell me what is going on here, my young friend, and what I had best do to recover possession of her who is now more dear to me than ever?"

"I have much to tell you, Cæsar."

"Then quickly let me know it, boy. This place seems wonderfully poorly guarded."

"It is not now guarded at all. From what, by a rare chance, I have overheard Don Jose say, the place is nearly deserted, and that was one reason why I was very anxious to shoot the man whom I took you to be."

"Indeed!"

"Yes, Cæsar. It is a scoundrel whom Don Jose has employed, because the attendants have left the house."

"And who is here, then?"

"I think no one to molest us. No one in Don Jose's service but one old man, that friar I have mentioned to you and myself."

"And he is here?"

"He is. Relying principally upon me, no doubt."

"Then discharge yourself now from his service, and enter mine."

"Gladly."

"So you will break no faith, Lazarillo; and if we two are not a match for all here now, it will be odd to me. But now speak to me of my countess. Is she really here, Lazarillo, or have I been deceived by false reports and information?"

"Listen," said Lazarillo, "and you shall know all. Nothing can now prevent you taking possession of your countess."

"I thank Heaven."

"But before you attempt anything, you should know what it is you have to oppose."

"Ah!"

"Yes, Cæsar, and what is of more importance still, it is necessary you should know who your countess was before she became yours."

"Tell me that first."

"I will. Do you remember in the streets of Madrid, a young girl by name of Maritana?"

"Maritana? She who danced with so much grace —she whose beauty always attracted so many admirers?"

"The same."

"By Heavens, I know her well. Well, indeed, might the remembrance of her face, when I caught a glimpse of her at the Marquis de Rotondo's, come over me like the dim memory of a dream. Can it, indeed, be she? Are you sure, Lazarillo?"

"Quite sure; and although she is not noble, yet she has all capacity for nobleness. I think her as innocent as she is beautiful."

" Her beauty, Lazarillo," said Cæsar, "is an uncontested point. By accident, some time since, I heard a little of her history—she is not of the lowly station she seems. As for her innocence—that shall be tested. Again, boy, let me ask you, are you certain that my countess and this Maritana are one ?"

" Quite certain. But what know you of her, Cæsar, further than as the dancing girl of the streets ?"

" I have been told, Lazarillo, that she is the last of a noble family, who were exterminated in consequence of a political plot some twenty years ago. Every particle of their property was sacrificed, so that it would have been no boon to tell the fair dancing girl what she might have been."

" From whom had you this information, Cæsar ?"

" From a dying man, to whom I did a kindness—one of the Zingaro tribe, who knew her well. With his dying breath he said—

" ' Don Cæsar, there is one whom I know loves you well. It is Maritana, the dancing girl. Seek her out and protect her ; she is not what she seems.' And when I questioned him more closely, he told me all that I have told to you."

" When was this, Cæsar ?"

" On the day before I fought with the captain of the guard who held you in custody."

" Thank Heaven, then, you heard so much of her. That she is innocent, I believe, Cæsar."

" I will be assured," said Cæsar, as he slightly touched the hilt of his sword. " I will be assured, and woe be to those who have persecuted her if she be innocent, or tempted her to err if she be guilty. She bears my name, and my honour shall be satisfied."

A sudden peal of thunder at this moment filled the air with its loud reverberations.

" I am well housed," said Cæsar.

" Hark !" said the page, " some one comes."

He had heard a door creak on its hinges, and he laid his hand upon the arm of Don Cæsar, saying,—

" Step into the recess of the window. It is not that there can be any one to fear ; but hear all you can, and then make your appearance when you will."

" I would hide from one when I would not from a host," said Cæsar. " I will take your advice, Lazarillo. Perhaps it is Jose, and truly I should enjoy the giving him a more sudden fright than the seeing me here as he came would give him."

Cæsar stepped into the deep recess of the window, where he was completely concealed from any casual observation by the massive drapery that hung from it.

A storm of no common magnitude seemed now beginning, for another peal of thunder of greater intensity than the former one shook the chateau to its foundations.

Such storms are of frequent occurrence at all seasons of the year in Spain. They come on with amazing rapidity, and frequently spread great devastation over some miles of the country.

The rapidity with which the storm appeared to cross the country was very great ; so much so, that to any secluded person, who had not the prospect of many miles beyond where he was, it would seem instantaneous, in all places alike.

The thunder peals of great intensity were followed by no less intense and vivid flashes of lightning ; indeed, the whole heavens appeared to be on fire, and for many miles could be seen the flashes of light that darted hither and thither, as though the whole universe was about to burst, and be consumed.

The roar of the elements was speedily at its height ; indeed, after the first crashing peal of thunder it might be said to be so. So loud and incessant were the reports that it would have been difficult to have heard any one speak, so close and crashing were the rapid discharges of the aerial artillery. The rain, too, came down heavily in such deluges that none can tell but such as have seen them ; for the rain in temperate climates may be more frequent, but the storms are nothing in comparison to what they are in hotter countries.

The sound of the falling rain, which not only came down in such drenching quantities, as to obscure the prospect and narrow the range of vision very greatly, but it came with such violence that in the forest the noise was as loud to the senses as the thunder itself ; it was so close to the ears that it subdued all other sounds. The rattling on the boughs of the tall forest trees is indeed so common an occurrence there that those who live in the country pay but little attention to it ; but to any one else the noise and clamour appear insupportable. The appearance of the lightning is magnificent and sublime to those who can calmly look at it ; the vivid flashes, the sharp darting streaks of blue lightning, the broad sheets of fire that were emitted by opening clouds that appeared to set the heavens on fire, the lurid flashes that appeared to shoot and dart from cloud to cloud, from one point in space to another, all formed beautiful but terrific objects of observation ; they were awful and sublime. So quick were the flashes—so incessant was the rolling and reverberations of the thunder, that it would seem but the continuation of the same sound prolonged indefinitely. The streams became swollen torrents, and all the sloping parts were mere channels and watercourses, along which swept numerous currents of rain water. But this state of things did not last long ; the storm began to slacken and pass over.

Such was the kind of tempest that for a short time raged round that house of Don Jose's, and had more or less effect upon the minds of every one within its walls. The whole accession of the tempest, from its commencement to the last low, muttering thunder, did not last above ten minutes, and during that time neither Lazarillo nor Cæsar had spoken ; for if they had their voices would have been drowned completely in the noise of the rushing wind, and the numberless echoes which the thunder brought into existence.

Whoever it was, too, that the page had heard approaching when he advised Don Cæsar to secrete himself, seemed to have paused until the storm should have abated, for no one came into the corridor ; but, now, when comparative silence was restored, a hasty footstep was heard approaching, and Lazarillo firmly grasped his arquebus, which, although not loaded, at all events, presented a formidable appearance, and would be, no doubt, sufficient to deter any one from approaching too closely to his post, and discovering the presence of Don Cæsar.

When the person came within sight, Lazarillo was surprised to find that it was a stranger, who looked about him as he came, as if he were quite strange to the place, and knew not exactly which route to take.

" Who's that ?" whispered Cæsar to Lazarillo, from his place of concealment behind the curtain.

" I do not know," replied the page. " He is a stranger to me completely."

" Indeed !"

" Yes ; but he don't look like one of Don Jose's people."

At this moment the man caught sight of Lazarillo, and quickening his pace, which he had allowed to become very slow and lagging, he hastened up to him.

" Stand off !" said the page, levelling the arquebus.

" I am a friend," said the stranger.

" I don't know you though," said Lazarillo ; " whose friend are you ?"

" The Queen of Spain's."

" The queen !"

" Yes, young sir ; and if I mistake not, I have seen you at Aranjues in the train of Don Jose de Santarem ?"

"What then?"

"Why, simply then, I see no reason why you should point your arquebus at me so steadily."

"I have been taught suspicion," said Lazarillo, "since I have been in the train of Don Jose."

"Indeed!"

"Yes; and I advise you to keep off."

"Boy, you know not what you say. I wear a sword."

"And so do I."

"Pshaw! I cannot waste time by parleying with you. I have come here on a particular errand, and I am resolved to search this house until I have accomplished it."

"If you attempt to pass my post, I fire."

"Fire away."

"In the name of Heaven, man, whose friend are you? You call yourself a friend, whose friend do you mean? I don't suppose the Queen of Spain is in particular want of your friendship."

"If you must know, boy, I came here to rescue the Countess de Bazan from Don Jose."

"The devil you do?" said Cæsar, stepping out from his place of concealment. "And pray, sir, what put you upon so chivalrous an enterprise?"

The man stepped back a pace, and drew his sword, as he said,—

"My motives and intentions are no secrets; but I will not answer a question so put by any man."

"I don't blame you for that," said Cæsar, who always admired courage, be it exhibited in whom it might; "I don't blame you for that. But, in courtesy, I now ask you who you are?"

"I am an intruder here, and a question, so put, of course, requires a courteous answer. My name is Osmanlis."

"And mine, to return the compliment, is Don Cæsar de Bazan."

"Don Cæsar de Bazan!"

"The same. You look surprised."

"And well I may."

"On what grounds, boy?"

"Why, I always understood you were shot."

"Oh, think nothing of that. It's very difficult indeed to shoot me, is it not, Lazarillo?"

"Thank God, yes."

"I cannot doubt you, sir. And if you be as your frank bearing and this boy's testimony proclaim you, Don Cæsar de Bazan, I can have no sort of hesitation in entrusting you with the full particulars of my presence here in this house."

"You may trust my honour, sir."

"I am sure I may. The Queen of Spain being informed by, I believe, this honest lad, of the misfortunes and persecutions of the Countess de Bazan, determined to risk everything in an attempt to rescue her."

"Heaven reward her."

"She resolved to come here and demand the restoration of the Countess de Bazan to liberty."

"Yes—yes."

"Her attached attendants opposed the journey, for she was far from well; but, so strong a sense has she of right, that she would undertake it."

"And she will come?"

"She has come, Don Cæsar."

"Has come?"

"Yes. The Queen of Spain is now here, attended but by myself. I have left her in an arbour in the garden, where I persuaded her to stay until I entered the house, the doors of which were open, in search of some one who could tell me some news of the object of my noble mistress's compassion."

"The Queen of Spain so near at hand, and unattended?" said Cæsar, as he drew his sword.

"She is, indeed; and being much exhausted, she is resting."

"Lead me to her, friend. She shall not want such thanks and such honour as I can render to her. Now, indeed, Heaven smiles upon my cause. Lead me to her, and you and I, sir, will make around her a court more full of true loyalty and devotion than ever king or queen before possessed."

"Come on, then, sir, I will take you to her majesty."

"I follow. Lazarillo, why did you not tell me you had interested the queen in my favour?"

"I had not time, Cæsar. Shall I remain here?"

"Yes. Keep you your post as if nothing had occurred. Should you require me, a call from this window will, no doubt, reach my ears; for the garden is not extensive."

"Nor the queen far off," added Alvarez.

Don Cæsar followed him from the corridor, and, as they went, Cæsar remarked to him,—

"It was odd to find the door open."

"Such was the fact," he replied. "I was myself much surprised that such should be the case."

"It is surprising; for, although you found me in the chateau, I had to make an entrance in far from an easy manner, by one of the windows that open into the corridor, where yon brave and noble-hearted lad keeps guard."

"I saw the boy at Aranjues."

"He is worth his weight in gold. His life is more precious to me than my own."

"You speak warmly in his favour, sir."

"I do, but not a whit more warmly than I think. He has already saved my life twice."

"Indeed!"

"Yes; and, to-day, he fired an arquebus at me with so good an aim, that he actually lodged the bullet in my hat."

"Oh!"

"Indeed he did; another half inch, and it must have entered my brain, and killed me on the spot."

The queen's attendant looked at Cæsar, as if he thought him a little mad or so, as he said,—

"Was that one of the proofs of his great attachment and friendship for you, Don Cæsar?"

"It was."

"Humph! I would rather myself be without such very friendly demonstrations from any one."

"But he mistook me for some one else, who he knew to be an enemy."

"That alters the case."

"It does, and he was nearly dead with grief when he found how nearly he had destroyed the life of the person whom, above all others, he was most extremely anxious to preserve."

"It was an awkward mistake."

"Very. But still, as it turned out, it was a very satisfactory proof of great kindness and friendship."

The man laughed.

"You may laugh," said Cæsar, "but it is by such things we know our true friends."

"I would rather not come by the knowledge in so dangerous a way," said Alvarez; "although I am very far from wishing to detract from the merits of the boy of whom you speak."

"Do not; he is a right noble lad. Did you see no one below?"

"In truth, I did see one man."

"What manner of man?"

"He was either desperately deaf or desperately stupid, for when I asked him who was in the house, he said 'of course;' and when I said I was going to search, he said 'he was rather better than he had been.'"

"Let us seek him."

"This way, then."

They entered the room in which was the old deaf attendant, and where Don Cæsar was not without some expectation of finding the travelling friar; indeed, he rushed so suddenly into the room, that Osmanlis asked him the reason of it, saying,—

"Did you expect anybody here?"

"I did."

"There is no one but the old deaf man; and as you see, in consequence of his back being towards us, he is quite unconscious of our presence, not being able to hear us."

"I thought to have found a fellow who had on, when first I saw him, the garb of a travelling friar, but, from your account of the open doors, I much suspect he has taken himself off entirely, fearing that his situation here was a peculiar one. If I had found him now, I should certainly have made a vacancy in the holy brotherhood to which he might happen to belong."

"Do you wish to speak to the deaf man?"

"No, no; let us seek the queen."

"This way, then, signior, if you please; I can conduct you to the precise place where I left her, and from which I am sure she would not attempt to stray."

Cæsar followed him closely, and, during the progress of their route, they had to pass the well in which was still confined the man who had been placed there by Don Cæsar, and who, the moment he heard footsteps approaching, commenced wailing and groaning for help and assistance to extricate him from his perilous and really dreadful situation, where he had now been a number of hours.

"Help! help! help!" he cried. "Good Christians, help a miserable sinner. Kind, good Christians, save me!"

"God bless me!" said Alvarez, "who's that?"

"A gentleman in a well," replied Cæsar.

"In a well?"

"Yes, I put him there some time ago."

"You surprise me! What was it for that you condemned him to such an odd punishment?"

"He is an assassin."

"An assassin! then nothing is, or can be, too bad for him."

"You are right. I should have killed him, but I could not sully my sword with the blood of such a man; so, to keep him safe till I could turn over in my mind what to do with him, I popped him down the well."

"Has he been there long?"

"Oh, yes, a number of hours. I will speak with him."

Don Cæsar advanced to the well's brink, and, stooping down, he called out, in a loud voice,—

"Hilloa! hilloa!"

"Yes, gracious sir," said the trembling wretch.

"Are you afraid of being drowned?"

"Indeed I am, most noble and merciful individual."

"Then you may banish such a fear at once, for you are born to be hanged; and when some affairs of more importance are despatched, a long rope with a hook at the end of it will be sent down to fish you up."

"Have mercy upon me."

"You are an assassin. Were you any other species of rogue I could forgive you, but an assassin I can feel no compassion for; a more detestable crime there cannot be."

Cæsar walked away, and Alvarez, when they had got a little distance, said to him,—

"I rescued a fellow from a tree to which he was bound in this immediate neighbourhood."

"You did?"

"Yes, truly."

"I bound him there. Pray what became of him? He is one of Don Jose's hopeful set."

"Why, the fact is, it was by his means that we got into the garden here at all."

"Indeed!"

"Yes; so we felt ourselves a little obliged to him. I believe the queen gave him a jewel."

"And what became of him?"

"I know not. Suddenly he disappeared, and I am of opinion that he took himself off altogether, for he had muttered something about the chateau being too hot to hold him any more; therefore, I think he has taken to flight, thinking himself well off."

"A probable supposition enough."

"Don Jose appears to have had a desperate set of ruffians to attend upon him in this place."

"He had, and he is rightly served as regards them; for they have all deserted him, and he is left nearly alone—indeed, worse than alone, for the lad who keeps guard in the corridor has thrown off all respect for him and serves me."

"He is rightly served."

"He is a monstrous villain, and if I meet him he shall stand the issue of a contest, which I think will end in enforcing upon his majesty the absolute necessity of appointing a new minister forthwith. I have amply sufficient cause to quarrel now with Don Jose to justify me in drawing upon him and defying him to mortal combat."

"Which you intend doing?"

"Most certainly—let us meet when and where we will."

"Here is the arbour, where I left the queen."

"Hold!" said Don Cæsar, as he laid his hand upon the arm of the attendant; "I heard voices."

"Voices?"

"Yes. Listen!"

They did so, and it was evident that the sound of a man's voice came from the arbour. They moved onwards a pace or two, so that they could hear the sounds more distinctly, and, after a moment's pause, Cæsar inclined his mouth to the ear of Osmanlis, and said,—

"The time has come."

"The time—what time?"

"For justice! That is Don Jose's voice. He has found out the queen, and is now persecuting her with his audacious addresses."

CHAPTER LXXI.

THE QUEEN IN THE GARDEN.—THE ARBOUR.—THE APPEARANCE OF DON JOSE.—THE STORM, AND THE INSULTING PROPOSITION.

"I AM here at last," said the queen, as she felt herself compelled to lean upon the arm of her faithful attendant; "and now that I am here, I feel more than ever my own weakness."

"Take courage, your majesty—that will cause all terrors to fly your presence," said the attendant, encouragingly. "No harm can happen—none dare lift their hands against their queen;—they would not do it!"

"It is scarce personal fear, Osmanlis, that I feel, and yet I must not boast. I am weak, and fear evil, as though I had not been a queen."

"Will you walk a little, your majesty?—the air may do you good, and the exercise too."

"I know not, but I think yon mutterings portend a storm, and if it be so, they are not light or gentle."

"Shall we seek some place where your majesty can rest? There must be some such place hereabouts, or they never would have so large and carefully tended a place as this appears to be."

"Well, lead on, Osmanlis, lead on. To stay here will be no point gained, though I scarce have more inclination to move than stay. My heart misgives me, and I fear I have rashly undertaken more than I have strength to manage."

"Speak not despairingly, your majesty; and be assured that while Osmanlis has a life and a sword, they are both your majesty's service."

"My good Osmanlis, I hope there will be no need of your perilling the one or using the other."

"I would do so willingly."

"Your faithfulness shall not go unrewarded," said the queen.

"I want no reward," said Osmanlis. "My reward, your majesty, is the performance of my duty; that alone is a reward—for there are none about your majesty who would not willingly and with pleasure lose their lives in your majesty's service."

"It would grieve me to require it. I would not even have endangered you thus far, but the cause that brings me here is a good and holy one."

"Ay, your majesty would never engage in any other; and to know which side your majesty chose in a quarrel, would be to ascertain at once which was right—for none could doubt your majesty's kindness and justice."

"I have endeavoured to merit such approbation by acting conscientiously towards all. But is it not very strange we hear nothing?"

"Of the people in the chateau?"

"Yes, Osmanlis; I cannot hear, and I cannot see the slightest approach to a light."

"All is still, your majesty."

They walked some little way, the queen still leaning on her faithful attendant for support, until they came to a kind of arbour, partially formed by nature and partly by art. It was overtopped by some large tree, and the boughs had been brought down to support the roof, and shrubs and some trained branches supported the sides; and it was further secured and fastened by means of artificial roofing and sides; there was a seat, too, lying at the back, supported by blocks.

"This will, perhaps, serve as a concealment and a place of rest for your majesty," said the attendant, looking at the place.

"It will, Osmanlis—it will," said the queen; "and welcome it is to me just now."

The queen entered the arbour, and Osmanlis remained at the entrance, as guarding the place; in case any danger should occur, he would be the first to encounter it.

"Hear you nothing, Osmanlis?"

"Nothing, your majesty."

"I like not this silence," said the queen.

"Will your majesty allow me to search about and endeavour to discover who are here, and what danger may be apprehended?"

"I came here for a specific purpose, and it would be criminal to go back without effecting or attempting to effect it. But mind, Osmanlis, do not run into needless danger or bloodshed. You may go."

"Be assured your majesty's commands are law."

Osmanlis quitted the arbour, and by means of the moonlight soon found his way to the doors of the chateau. He advanced his sword so as to be within his grasp on the instant, and after listening a moment or two, and hearing nothing, he gently pushed the door and entered the chateau.

He paused a moment or two, and listened with the ears of one alive to danger, but willing to brave it in a good cause; but hearing no sound, he still advanced.

Thus it was that the queen's attendant, Osmanlis, came to enter the chateau, where for some time he found no one at all but the old deaf man, who, in addition to the mental confusion incidental to his malady, had been so much perplexed by the wars and tumults that had taken place around him, and the strange faces he had seen, that he was stupider than ever, and in answer to the inquiries of the attendant, had used the words which he, Osmanlis, had related to Don Cæsar.

Of the subsequent proceedings of Osmanlis we are aware. He ascended the great staircase, and then the storm had come on, during which he had thought it prudent to remain quiet; for, of course, he had ample opportunities of knowing how short in continuance as to time those tempests were in Spain.

Having then waited until the thunder, with its hundred reverberations, could no longer prevent him from being cognisant of any noises in the chateau, he had entered the corridor, as we have related, and held the brief but emphatic conversation recorded with the page, Lazarillo, and afterwards with Don Cæsar, who, upon mention of the name of his countess, had so speedily left his place of concealment behind the massive curtain in the recess of the window.

*　　　*　　　*　　　*　　　*

Let us now return to the garden where was left the queen, who sank upon a seat quite unnerved, notwithstanding to her faithful and attached servant she strove to put on an outward show of courage, which her heart was far, very far, from sanctioning.

After Alvarez had left her, she regretted that she had permitted him to do so, and a deep sense of the many dangers to which she might be exposed in that chateau of such an evil reputation came painfully and vividly across her mind.

All was very still, but she scarcely dared to breathe, for fear of attracting the attention of an enemy. And when the storm commenced, which we have described, she was wrought up to a pitch of painful excitement, which several times tempted her to leave the arbour and fly towards the house for refuge.

She, however, succeeded in restraining the impulse, and with a sensation of grateful feeling she heard it slowly subside, and felt then wonderfully relieved by the increased clearness and elasticity of the atmosphere, which had been deadened by the convulsion of the elements of nature.

"When will Osmanlis return?" she asked herself. "Each moment of painful expectation appears an hour of suffering."

It was not that the really high-minded, noble Queen of Spain regretted that she had taken an immediate and energetic step to rescue an unfortunate person from the clutches of the villain Jose; but real indisposition was assailing her, and the seeds of the insidious disease which, a very few years afterwards, hurried her to an early tomb, were already beginning to develope themselves.

The fatigue she had lately gone through; the terror she had experienced from the attack of the banditti in the forest; and, superadded to all, the deep anxiety she could not help incessantly labouring under with regard to her own sad position and prospects, had completely undermined her health, and the wonder was not that she was weak, and occasionally felt almost prostrated by the amount of suffering she endured, but that she was able at all to fight up against it, and did not sink entirely under it.

Besides, she was awkwardly situated as regarded this very expedition on which she had, with a ready generosity, come to Don Jose's chateau.

In the first place, she could not plead ignorance of the character of the place, nor could she be off from conceiving, if questioned, that she knew the king was there. Under such circumstances, then, had she alone consulted her dignity, and the feelings which found a home in her virtuous bosom; the chateau of Don Jose, the home of her husband's guilty intrigue, was the last place on earth in which she would willingly have shown herself.

If there was one house more than another in all Spain, from the threshold of which she would have shrunk, it was surely that.

Well she knew, too, what a mass of misrepresentation her conduct was likely to give rise to. Well she knew that Don Jose would have it in his power to insinuate to the king she had made up her mind to dog his footsteps, and to hunt him and persecute him with her presence wherever he might be.

No wonder that these thoughts, and feelings, and anticipations, gave such a person as the Queen of Spain the most exquisite uneasiness, and the most poignant distress.

It said worlds for her heart that, despite all personal, all private considerations to the contrary, and they were abundant enough, Heaven knows, she should still persevere in an attempt to rescue Maritana from the hands of her enemies.

She felt all the evil she might bring upon herself, and yet she shrunk not from her task—she felt the danger of her position, but she did not attempt to recede from it—she wept, but persevered, and even while alone in the arbour of the chateau garden, and while the storm was raging around her, it might fill her with new fears, but it could not check one generous impulse of that noble heart, which was all generosity.

The storm had passed away, and still Osmanlis came not. She recalled to mind the many anecdotes which had been related to her of the implacable animosity of Don Jose against those who stood in his way, and much she now feared that the life of that faithful attendant whom she had brought with her would fall a sacrifice to the same reckless, wicked, and sanguinary feeling that had induced the murder of him whom she had some time before sent to the palace of Madrid with a letter, and whose cruel and barbarous assassination must be still fresh in the minds of our readers.

When once this thought found a home in her breast, she much blamed herself for separating from Osmanlis, for she felt a confidence in her power to protect him, not from strength, but that she doubted even if Don Jose would dare to perpetrate a murder in her actual presence.

"Alas! alas!" she said, "I may have sacrificed him, as I fear all will be sacrificed who show to the unhappy Queen of Spain any attachment. When I have concluded this adventure—when I have rescued, as surely I shall be able to do, this Countess de Bazan, from the hands of Don Jose and the king, I will carry out my some time cherished intention, and taking with me the few faithful adherents who have clung to my falling fortunes, endeavour to find an asylum for them and for myself in some other land."

Such were the sad reflections of the queen, and such the afflicted state of mind in which she awaited the return of her faithful servant, who had gone to the chateau to ascertain there for her the actual state of affairs, and to discover, if possible, what was the most eligible mode of proceeding she could adopt for the furtherance of her high-minded, most generous, and virtuous purpose.

Move from the arbour she dared not, for she feared if she did so to miss Osmanlis should he return, and yet there now arose the anxious question of how long she should wait for him.

"Ah! what period of time," she asked herself, "shall I cease to expect him? When shall I give up his return as hopeless, and tell myself, almost for certain, that he has fallen a victim to Don Jose?"

This was, indeed, an anxious question—one which was as afflicting to decide upon as it was troublesome. Yet it was one each moment growing into greater importance—an importance borrowed from the progress of time—an importance growing each moment into a perfect horror, and she was, at length, upon the actual point of leaving the arbour, and herself proceeding towards the house in order to proclaim to the first person whom she might meet who and what she was, and to insist upon the accomplishment of the object for which she had come to that, to her, abode of terror and apprehensions, when she heard a footstep in the garden, and, with a gush of pleasure, she said to herself,—

"He comes—he comes. Osmanlis comes. He is not murdered. Surely that must be Osmanlis."

She listened with an intense eagerness to the footstep which absorbed every other faculty. At one moment it seemed retreating, then again advancing, until a world of apprehensions filled her breast, and she dreaded that it was some emissary of Don Jose's seeking her, after having, perhaps, taken the life of poor Osmanlis.

"And yet," said she, "I cannot say that it is so. The paths of this garden may be devious and wandering, and the sound of the footsteps even, as I hear them, now retreating, now advancing, may be occasioned by the windings of the walks. It may yet be Osmanlis; and, besides, this is his first visit here, and, of course, he is not familiar with the place. He may be most anxiously seeking me."

She waited now for some moments longer, and the sounds of the approaching footsteps came more clearly to her ears—she trembled with expectation that he was coming. She now fancied that she recognised the tread as that of her faithful and attached attendant, and then, suddenly, as if some malignant being was intent upon mocking her anxieties, all at once the sounds began to decrease, as if, whoever it was had suddenly turned off in completely another direction.

"Why does he not come?" she exclaimed. "Osmanlis, why keep me in this state of dreadful suspense?"

She walked to the entrance of the arbour and gazed wistfully into the garden, but she could see no one. She could hear nothing but the occasional low pattering of the heavy rain drops, as they fell from leaf to leaf of the fruit trees, and finally reached the ground, where they were immediately swallowed up in its recesses.

"Shall I call to him?" she said. "Dare I trust my voice in this place?"

Again the footsteps approached, or seemed to approach, and the queen, perplexed now beyond all measure, determined to risk the calling out the name of her attendant.

Advancing some few paces from the arbour, she raised her voice, and called as loudly as she could—

"Osmanlis—Osmanlis."

Immediately she heard an exclamation of surprise from some one, and then succeeded the crashing of boughs and plants—in another instant a man burst through the fringe of fruit and flowers that bordered the path every way. For a moment she felt sealed to the spot with alarm, and then she cast one glance upon his face.

The nights in Spain are never very dark, and there was ample light for her to see the features—that one glance was sufficient. It was Don Jose!

CHAPTER LXXII.

THE ALARMING INTERVIEW.—JOSE'S MISTAKE.—THE CRY FOR HELP, AND THE UNEXPECTED INTERRUPTION.

AT the first glance of recognition the queen cast upon the countenance of Don Jose, she felt almost paralyzed with apprehension, and he, indeed, was scarcely less surprised than she, and was silent likewise; but his surprise at so very unexpected a meeting was of a pleasurable nature, while the unhappy queen partook in no degree of such a feeling.

On the contrary, there could not possibly be, to her eyes, a more unwelcome object than the detestable Don Jose, who she well knew to be the main cause of much of the trouble she endured, by alienating from her the affections of the weak-minded king, in order to favour the advancement of his own inordinate and insatiable ambition.

Jose was the first to speak, and it was in a tone of voice, the surprise and intense excitation of which he did not attempt to conceal, that he at once exclaimed—

" The queen!"

The sound of his hateful voice broke the spell which seemed to have come over her faculties, and she was able to move. By an impulse rather than from reflection, she made a movement to fly towards the house, but Don Jose dashed towards her, as if he would detain her, at the same moment crying—

" Hold!"

Alarmed at his gesture, and fearful of being contaminated even by a touch of his hand, she stepped back into the arbour again, and then he immediately stationed himself at its entrance, saying—

" Your majesty sees before you the humblest of your servants."

The queen trembled so excessively that she could not speak, and Don Jose, with his usual audacity, translating her manner favourable to himself, took off his plumed hat, and in what he considered a bland and seductive tone of voice, said—

" Oh, beauteous majesty of Spain, to see you honouring this abode with your presence, may well, for a moment, intoxicate with joy the most fervent of your worshippers. Let me translate that amiable and sweet confession."

" Peace, Don Jose," said the queen, but although she strove to be firm, her trembling voice sufficiently proclaimed her agitation. " Peace, I say, and allow me to pass."

" To pass, your majesty? Heaven forbid that I should seek to detain you for an instant ——"

" Then stand aside."

" Longer, I would add, than absolutely necessary."

" Jose, you forget to whom you speak."

" Ah, no—forget you! Forget those eyes, which like load-stars have ever attracted my too sensitive heart."

The queen clasped her hands in despair.

" Don Jose," she said, " if I am subjected to another minute of this torture I will call for help."

" Ah, lady, there is no one here to respond to such a call. Since you have honoured this abode with your presence, I beseech you, honour me, its poor owner, with some portion of your regard. Do not now hesitate after coming here, but carry out the just intention which I know animates you."

" Which you know?"

" Yes, gracious madam. You come here to denounce the king even in the midst of his guilt. You come to satisfy yourself with your own eyes that you are dishonoured—that your marriage vows have been turned to mockery."

" No, no, as Heaven is my judge."

" Nay, say not so, my gracious queen. The king is here. Your husband. He who swore to love you with all manly and kingly affection—he is here, and you know it."

" I do know it."

" And you know why he is here. Alas, he would not be persuaded by me to be virtuous. If he had listened to my advice, what a happy man he might have been with so much loveliness as of right belonged to him in thee, and not have sought by low intrigue to render both you and himself miserable.

The king is here, your majesty, and now have you an opportunity which you may well embrace at once. Not that such, alas, will not occur again frequently, of satisfying yourself beyond the shadow of a doubt of his infidelity."

" And dare you imagine," said the queen, " that so infamous a motive brought me here?"

" Why, why, your gracious majesty must be aware surely, that from me you received information of the king's presence here, as well as of the object of his presence."

" From thee?"

" Aye, madam, from me, and you have come. Alas, I grieve to say it, but you have come at a moment when your worst fears may be at once confirmed."

" Worst fears?"

" Aye, madam. What a grievous task is mine, to have to tell to such chaste ears the tale that hangs upon my lips, but I reflect that it is my duty, and then I dare not hesitate."

" Arch hypocrite," cried the queen.

" Nay, call me what you will—my actions will speak for me. If I at present live under the heavy cloud of your majesty's displeasure, the bright sun of truth will pierce through the mist, and I shall seem the brighter for the contrast. You think me a hypocrite?"

" I know you are."

" Ah, that is harsh. From early life my soul was attuned to virtue, and I cultivated, perhaps, too conceitedly, virtue and goodness. That was my fault. Alas, how much I have lost by the blundering sincerity that has induced me to tell the king of his faults, when a base courtier, and one who was more a selfish man of the world, would have tried his best to distort those very errors into virtues."

" This is sickening," said the queen. " I command you to stand aside, and to hinder me not."

" Commands seem like gentle, winning requests," said Jose, " when coming from the lips we ardently love."

" Insolence!"

" Nay, nay, gracious lady—hear me out. I have fought for you—I have reasoned with the king, but stimulated by a passion for one who is so low in state, that the disgrace becomes doubled, his Majesty has forced me to give him up for a time this house, which was the abode of innocence and virtue, to carry on a low intrigue."

The queen waved her hand deprecatingly.

" An intrigue with a dancing girl—one of the very scum of society—taken from the very kennels of Madrid. Are you not moved to great and virtuous indignation?"

" I am."

" One who should never have had kingly eyes cast upon her—one so despicable, that to name her to your majesty at all, is to do her too much honour. And yet it is she who has usurped your proper empire in your husband's heart, and now, aye, even now, in this very house, resides with him as his mistress. Alas, it is too dark for you to see the crimson flush of indignation on my face."

" Have you done?" said the queen, calmly.

" Is not that enough?"

" More than enough, Don Jose."

" You are not a stick—a stone. You cannot be totally insensible to such an amount of most grievous insult. Think of it, and let the honest indignation of a wife burn in your bosom."

" It does burn there. Oh, that Osmanlis would come."

" Whom would you?"

" One who will rescue me from this unmanly persecution. Don Jose, I know you. Your hypocrisy is in vain. I know that the Countess de Bazan is here as well as you can tell me."

"The Countess de Bazan? Do not fancy her so high. Some vile trickery has made her assume that name."

"The trickery was yours."

"Mine, gracious madam?"

"Aye, yours; I am better informed than you imagine. I know all. My errand here to-night is one which will confound you."

"Indeed," said Jose, incredulously.

"Aye, indeed."

"Oh, I understand you. Some signal mark of your royal affection will be afforded me; but I am always confounded when I gaze on so much beauty."

The cool insolence of Don Jose was indeed astonishing, and the queen felt it as difficult to reply to him as to prevent herself from so doing. Osmanlis did not come, and her trouble and perplexity was each moment on the increase; she knew not what to do or what to think."

"Don Jose," she exclaimed, "you talk in vain.

You cannot hope to eradicate from my mind an impression of your villany. I have become acquainted with too many circumstances of your conduct to be able to find for you an excuse."

"But, hear me."

"I have heard you too long. No words can undo the deep iniquity of your acts; cease to attempt the hopeless task. I came here to rescue the Countess de Bazan, and, by heavens, I will do so."

"To rescue her?"

"Yes. She is kept here by force."

"Oh, how much misinformed is your majesty. Whoever had told you so artful a tale, has much abused your royal ears. Kept here by force? Alas! I wish it was so, for then I should myself have rescued her. She is here of her own free will. She glories in the magnificence which she has attained as the price of virtue and innocence."

"It is false."

"I dare not contradict your majesty."

"You know that what you say is false, Don Jose, and you do but add to your own iniquities by such protestations. You cannot move me from my purpose by calumnies."

"Calumnies?"

"Yes, Don Jose, calumnies, which, coming from your mouth, carry with them, as a natural consequence, their own refutation. Your praise is suspicious; your blame can never be a censure."

"Your majesty thinks by far too hardly of me."

"Not more hardly than your deserts, Don Jose. I tell you I am assured of the innocence of the Countess de Bazan."

"The page has played me false," thought Jose. "He shall die within this hour; it is his last on earth."

"Oh, madam, how much you wrong me."

"You have pursued that theme far enough already, Jose."

" Then what does your gracious beauty mean to do ?"

" I command you to move aside, and allow me to pass from this place at your peril."

" Spoken like a queen."

" Is the command obeyed like a subject ?"

" Yes ; a subject to such charms as surely never before adorned woman. I love you."

" This is past all endurance.'

" I love you—I have long loved you. While your husband was concerned in low intrigues, and seeking pleasure among the vilest of your sex, I alone saw the bright diamond he had thrown aside in all its radiant lustre to please himself with mock gems. I loved you—I pitied you. It is a love which time nor circumstance can change. I adore you, and bow at your feet. I offer you the homage of a heart which has long been all your own—which has never had a thought of affection but what applied to you. Now you know explicitly the long-cherished secret of my heart—now you know who it is that will shield you from all harm, and recompense you with a boundless affection for the injustice shown to you by your husband the king."

Jose spoke these words with sufficient fervour. To tell the truth, he was a little sincere ; for the queen was beautiful, and, moreover, the accomplishment of his purpose was one which had long been a cherished thought, as being the way to the utmost height of his ambition. No wonder, then, that Don Jose threw into the speech he had made a considerable share of real as well as assumed enthusiasm, and made it sound extremely like the genuine outpourings of a heart full of affection towards the object whom he addressed.

The queen felt, and, indeed, looked almost stunned with surprise at the great audacity of this speech. Indeed, she was so much astonished at the tremendous height to which Don Jose's presumption had reached, that she wanted power to interrupt him, and so heard him to the end without doing so ; a circumstance which gave him some guilty hopes that she was listening not altogether unfavourably to him.

Like some desperate gamester, he had now thrown all upon one cast, and he awaited her reply with trembling eagerness.

There was a dead silence for some moments, and then the queen spoke in a firm, though a low voice,—

" Your head, Don Jose de Santarem—your head," she said, " will pay the penalty for this."

" You reject my suit ?"

" Help—help ! what, ho ! help !"

" Hold !" cried Jose. " Before you utter another cry, hear what I have to threaten, as well as to promise."

" Threaten !" she exclaimed.

" Yes, threaten."

" Your threats I despise, as deeply as I do yourself. Oh, where can be Osmanlis ? why comes he not ?"

" Hear, madam, the threat you talk of despising before you carry your feelings towards it so far. If you again cry for help, I will join in the cry. There is but one person to answer it. That person is the king !"

" The king !"

" Yes, the king ; and I will tell him that I called to him because—because ——"

" What, villain ?"

" Ha, ha ! Because I surprised the beauteous majesty of Spain in this snug retreat with a paramour. Ha, ha, ha ! Philip is already jealous. He is not the strongest-minded man in the world. I have great influence over him. He will believe it."

" Now, Heaven protect me against such villany as this."

" Oh, it won't. It won't, you may depend upon it, madam ; Heaven will not interfere in the business "

" God help me !"

" No, no ; but I will. I can save you. Be mine. As well be a little uneasy, and escape, aye, far better than imminently suffer. On my soul, I think the king will take your life here upon the spot in his mad passion."

" Perish the devilish argument !" exclaimed the queen. " I am prepared to die."

" To die !"

" Yes, Don Jose. Death is only terrible to such men as thou art. It is but a change from suffering to joy to me. I have hopes above that I would not exchange for the earth's sovereignty, or an unlimited existence to enjoy the rule."

" Can you be so mad ?"

" I am not so mad as you would make me."

" Have you no woman's heart—no resentment—no jealousy ? Have you no passions ?"

" I have innocence."

" Psha ! a word merely. Love yourself, and be mine. Revenge yourself, and be mine. Enjoy existence, and be mine.'"

" Fiend !"

" Call me what you will ; but tell me you repent your rash determination. Your treatment by the king most abundantly justifies you in what I propose to you. Were you cherished by him the case would be widely different. But you are scorned, neglected, trampled on. You are disgraced. You are made the victim of a mad sensualist."

" I am firm."

" Firm in folly."

" Firm in innocence."

" Firm in madness. By Heaven and hell ! you know not what you say. Come with me, and I will show you, even now, the very chamber where the king, your husband, is dallying with his ignoble mistress. You shall hear his vows of love to another. Those vows which should be breathed to none but you."

" I will not."

" You shall hear her say she loves him. You shall hear him press kisses on her wanton lips."

" Hold, sir," cried the queen, loudly. " Hold, sir ; nor insult my ears so grossly. Don Jose, recollect to whom you speak."

" Then perish in your damnable obstinacy. I will not call it virtue, for never yet had woman any. Ha, ha ! a delusion ! a dream ! I go to call the king. You may stay, or follow me, which you will. He will in his rage most surely take your life. I go to call the king. Ha, ha, ha ! The king with whom you would threaten me. The ——"

" Before you do so," said Don Cæsar, stepping forward, " allow me to have a few words with you, Don Jose de Santarem."

CHAPTER LXXIII.

THE COMBAT IN THE GARDEN.—THE DEATH OF DON JOSE, AND RESCUE OF THE QUEEN.—THE KING AND THE COUNTESS DE BAZAN.

It would probably be far beyond the power of all language to depict the astonishment, rage, and fear which assailed the breast of the villain Jose at this most sudden and unexpected appearance of Don Cæsar. The manner, too, of his coming forward, and the words he used, were amply sufficient to convince Jose that he had been overheard in his infamous attempt to terrify the queen, and with that conviction he felt that he was a doomed man, and that his game of life was played. He absolutely staggered back as if he had been suddenly struck, so great was the mental shock he had received.

The queen clasped his hands in an ecstacy of delight, and sinking on her knees, she exclaimed,—

"I am saved—I am saved! Heaven has not deserted me. I am saved from worse than death."

Osmanlis drew his sword and stood upon the defensive, for he saw Don Jose glancing round him like a maniac.

"Be on your guard, Don Cæsar," he cried. "Yon scoundrel is, I am sure, even now meditating mischief."

"Let him meditate it," said Cæsar, as he glanced his eye along the shining blade of his trusty toledo. "Let him meditate it. His hours of meditation in this world are numbered."

Jose made a movement as if to fly from the place, but Osmanlis placed himself in an attitude that detained him, while Don Cæsar said, with a loud voice to the discomfited villain,—

"Don Jose, the opportunity I have wished for, and determined to embrace when it did come, is here at last."

"What opportunity?" said Jose, making a desperate effort to summon as much composure and effrontery as possible.

"The opportunity of measuring swords with you."

"You wish to murder me."

"No, cowardly scoundrel; but I will fight with you. What you do not deserve I will give you—a chance for your life. You shall have a fair fight for it, and no favour. Draw, Don Jose, and defend yourself; for on this spot one or both of us shall breathe his last."

Don Jose's lips turned of an ashy paleness, as, in a voice trembling with fear, he said,—

"Don Cæsar de Bazan, I will not fight with you."

"You shall, or die the death of a dog. In the cause of the Queen of Spain, forgetting in that more absorbing and more ennobling quarrel all my own wrongs, I challenge you, Don Jose, to mortal combat."

"And I'll not fight," said Jose.

"Coward, you wear a sword."

"I—I am ill, and cannot. If you have aught to urge against me, urge it lawfully. I will not fight."

"Spare him," said the queen. "Contempt is his portion; spare him, noble signor. He is not worthy of your sword."

"My gracious queen," said Cæsar, "contempt to such men is no punishment. What an unheard of amount of wickedness we should have perpetrated by many who now by fear are kept within the bounds of prudence, were contempt to be the only punishment inflicted upon evil doers."

"This gentleman speaks truly, gracious madam," said Osmanlis. "But if you will not allow him to fight with yon trembling wretch, allow me to draw a sword in your defence."

"I will not fight," said Jose. "I will not fight."

The queen retired to the further end of the arbour, and engaged herself in prayer; she seemed to consider the death of Jose as inevitable, and now that the trembling ruffian saw himself deserted by her, and that she used no arguments in his behalf, he called aloud, saying,—

"Madam—madam, will you see blood shed in your very presence? Save my life—save my life. I will not fight with this man, Don Cæsar. I cannot, I dare not. He is my evil genius."

"Your own bad conduct is your evil genius," said Cæsar.

"Let me go, or—or take me a prisoner; who can be forced to fight if he will not? Don Cæsar, you have been the bane of my life; and I do believe you bear a charmed life."

"And yet you shall fight me, dastardly coward. By any excuse, you would, I know, evade this conflict; but as there is a God in Heaven, you shall not."

"Mercy!" said Jose.

"Osmanlis," cried Don Cæsar, "place yourself so as to prevent his flight. He shall fight, or die the death of a dastardly coward, who had a sword, but would not draw it in his own defence."

Osmanlis placed himself with his sword drawn in such a situation that Don Jose saw escape was out of the question. He knew that his loudest outcries could bring no one to his rescue, for he doubted if the king would come at all, and even if he did, Don Cæsar had time to run him through a dozen times over before he could arrive. Hope abandoned him, and he very nearly fainted from very terror.

Don Cæsar advanced towards him, and struck him with the flat of his sword across his face, saying,—

"Coward, draw and defend yourself. At least, die with your sword in your hand."

The blow laid open the skin, and Jose's face was suffused with blood. In an instant a species of madness seemed to take possession of him. With a wild cry like that of some hunted wild animal, which, in the agony of death and despair turns to face its pursuers, and deal what destruction it can among them, he tore his sword from its scabbard, and commenced an attack so furious and so perfectly demoniac in its violence upon Don Cæsar, that had not the latter been the accomplished swordsman he was he must have sunk under the savage assault. As it was, he saw the state in which his adversary was in a moment, and he fought warily and calmly, making no attempt at an assault himself, but being satisfied to parry the ferocious lunges of Don Jose.

The swords rung together with a sharp sound. Jose tore up the ground with his feet as he made unavailing efforts to advance upon Cæsar, who kept him at bay without giving him an inch of ground.

Such a combat could not last very long. Exhaustion must speedily depress the energies of Jose, and then his wary and collected adversary would have him at his mercy.

Now he began to flag a little. He gave way. He fought with less fearful desperation, but yet he fought well. He fought for life. All was at stake—it was life or death.

Back, back he stepped, closely followed up by Cæsar, who moved his sword as if practising in the fencing school. The issue of the combat was not doubtful now. It was virtually over. Suddenly Don Cæsar altered his tactics, and without any of the fury which Jose had exhibited, he commenced an attack of so rapid a character that Jose's nerveless arm could not stand against it.

Suddenly there was a short, sharp cry of pain, and the hilt of Don Cæsar's rapier struck heavily against the breast of the discomfited villain. He was run through, but for a moment he did not fall, although Don Cæsar immediately withdrew his sword.

He reeled round like a drunken man, and fought the air wildly with his arms. Then, with a heavy plunge, he fell head foremost to the ground, and the earthly career of Don Jose was over. He was a bleeding corpse.

"So perishes," said Cæsar, as he returned his sword to its sheath, "as great a scoundrel as Spain can produce, and that, I believe, Osmanlis, is saying a great deal."

"He fought well."

"He did; and by all the saints in the calendar, I'm glad of it. I could not have killed him, had he persevered in not drawing his sword. As it was, 'tis well, and Spain is now rid of a man who has been her curse since he obtained office in the administration of her affairs."

"The queen has fainted," exclaimed Osmanlis, as he hastened into the arbour, and raised her inanimate form from the earth.

"Let us carry her majesty into the chateau," said

Cæsar. "There she will be safe, for I believe, Osmanlis, we are masters of this place."

Don Cæsar being much stronger and taller than Osmanlis, lifted the queen in his arms, and with long strides made his way towards the chateau with her, her light weight scarcely impeding him at all. He passed on till he came to a room in which there was a couch, on which he tenderly laid his insensible burthen, and then, turning to Osmanlis, he said,—

"My friend, I will leave you to attend to your royal mistress for a short time, while I search the chateau for one dear and near to me. She will soon recover—alarm at the clash of swords, no doubt, has caused this temporary swoon."

Don Cæsar then bounded up the great staircase, and hastily made his way towards the window, at which, with no small degree of impatience, the young page was waiting.

"Lazarillo," cried Cæsar.

"Here, here," said the boy.

"Where is the king?"

"In yonder chamber. I heard the clash of swords, Cæsar. What has happened? Oh tell me what has happened?"

"Jose has gone to his account."

"Dead?"

"Yes, boy. The office of prime minister of Spain is just vacant, and open to all aspirants."

"Whither go you, Cæsar?"

"To the king, to claim my countess."

"God speed you. That door conducts to a room from whence opens another. The countess, the king, or both of them for all I know, are there. Heaven speed you, Cæsar, but do nothing rash, for depend upon it that the villain Jose was the active agent and instigator of all."

"I do believe it. You see, boy, that I am cool and calm."

"You are—you are."

Don Cæsar walked towards the door indicated by the page. He turned the handle of it, but found it locked. Without any passion, he placed his shoulder against it, and with one desperate blow he forced the lock—a short faint scream met his ears, and by the light of a profusion of wax candles, he saw the terrified figure of his long sought countess, with her hands clasped, and a face as pale as marble from apprehension.

*   *   *   *   *

The king had been waiting for the appearance of Don Jose, to tell him that the sleeping draught had been given to Maritana. Fevered with impatience, and angry with himself, and all the world beside, he had sought the chamber in which his lovely captive was confined alone, determined to make her such offers as would present him with a fair chance of success, if they did not say much for the morality of his majesty.

At the very time that the queen and Osmanlis were separating, she to remain in the arbour, where she was found by Don Jose, and her faithful attendant to explore the chateau, the king, who had the key of the door which had been afterwards so unceremoniously broken open by Don Cæsar, crept along the corridor upon his infamous errand.

He found Maritana seeking a second time in prayer that relief which it had ever before afforded her, but his presence soon put an end to her orisons, and called her thoughts from Heaven to earth again.

"Maritana—countess—most beautiful of women," he said, "believe me that I am much struck with your constancy and virtue."

Wondering very much what such an exordium would lead to, Maritana looked indignantly upon him, but she spoke not.

"I come," continued the king, "to tell you that I repent me much that I have endeavoured to wean you from the virtuous feelings which so much adorn you."

"Indeed," said Maritana.

"You speak doubtingly, and yet why should you? You have not yet heard all I wished to say."

"I guessed I had not," said Maritana.

"Then, fair guesser, knowing who I am ——"

"I would some one," said Maritana, interrupting, "would convince me you were not what you have avowed yourself."

"Indeed."

"Yes, indeed, I am assured you are the king of Spain."

"And so I am."

"I grieve to hear it."

"Nay, girl, you should rather hear it with pride, on account of the conquest you have made, being that of the heart of a monarch."

"No," said Maritana, "I have no pride on such a subject. Time was, that in my simple judgment, when I heard the name of the king mentioned, I invested it with noble attributes, and fancied that feeling his position as a king, he would be, and must be, what he should be."

"What he should be?"

"Aye, sire, what he should be."

"And am not I?"

"Alas, no. Do you protect innocence and virtue? Do you throw the shield of your powerful protection over the oppressed? Do you cry hold to those who would oppress and drive one to despair such as I am? Are you that fountain of all honour and nobleness which a king should be?"

"You know not what you say."

"Alas, I know too well. The king of my imagination is but a creature of romance. I tremble and sicken at the reality which you present."

Philip bit his lips, and in a tone which showed that royalty, although it graciously condescends to do most unworthy things, by no means relishes being told of them, he said,—

"But you mistake my motives."

"Can I do so?"

"You do, on our honour. You are the widow of a noble."

"Alas, alas!"

"Had you yielded to our solicitations, and become our mistress, we should of course have not had the exalted opinion of you we now have."

Maritana looked surprised, and the king continued,—

"An exalted opinion which places you more on a level with ourselves. You must be aware by common report that our queen is alienated from us. You have heard so much?"

"I have heard so much. God bless her."

"The Church of Rome has divorced us from our queen. The marriage is declared null and void, we are free. To whom, then, beautiful Countess de Bazan, can we more becomingly offer a portion of our throne, our state and dignity, than yourself."

"To me?"

"Aye, be our queen."

"Your majesty is jesting."

"By Heavens, no. You shall be our queen. We admire, respect, and love you, countess, and know none in all our court more fitting to become the sharer of our crown."

"I decline the honour," cried Maritana, coldly.

"Decline?"

"I have said so, sire."

"Decline a crown—a kingdom? Decline, in lawful marriage, the hand of a king? Oh, 'tis you who jest."

"I never jest, sire."

"But you speak not your mind, lovely countess.

Consider for a moment the value of that which you reject."

" It has, in my eyes, none.".

" None ?"

" None, sire; I have loved — I shall never love again."

" This is madness."

" And yet a fixed feeling. I reject the offer; your majesty will find many to whom, no doubt, so dazzling a destiny will be most acceptable."

" And yet they told me, Maritana, that you were ambitious."

" I was."

" You were ?"

" I am not now. Oh, I have lived to see the sin, as well as the folly, of that wild ambition. I have but one boon new to ask of you, sire. Let me pass out from this place free and unmolested."

" My dear countess, you will accept my offer. Some delightful weeks we will pass together at my summer-palace, after which our nuptials shall be performed with all befitting honour."

" I understand you, sire. The device was a shallow one from the first."

" You—you doubt our royal word ?"

" Most grievously do I."

" By Heavens, girl, you must be mad. I swear to you."

" Nay, make no oaths, sire, your royal word carries with it quite sufficient weight. I have passed my word, which I mean to keep, that by death alone shall you conquer me. I will take my own life rather than yield to you, and pray to Heaven to pardon the self-murder."

" Was ever woman so desperately foolish !"

" Was ever woman, sire, so desperately injured ?"

" You will think better of this. Hark ye, girl; you may rest here to-night in security; refreshments shall be sent to you, and to-morrow morning you can again give me an answer, which, if unfavourable, shall procure your instant release."

" I cannot trust the king's word," said Maritana, with a shudder of apprehension.

" I cannot deceive you in this offer."

" I know not; it may hide some craft."

" You are far more suspicious," said the king, angrily, " than one who would be thought so very virtuous can possibly be."

" And who has taught me suspicion ?"

" I have not."

" You and your emissary, Jose. Oh, sire, get rid of that fiend, who is continually at your elbow prompting you to do wrong. Banish from your sight and councils the insidious demon, who would drag you down to any depth of sinfulness, so that, upon the ruin of your kingly state, he reared the foul structure of his own wild insatiable ambition."

Philip seemed for a moment struck with the home truth contained in these words, and he said,—

" Girl, what warrants you in speaking thus ?"

" My own observation."

" But no facts."

" Can you not furnish thousands ?"

" Psha! you talk of that you do not comprehend. To-night you are at peace—be assured of that."

He turned from her, and left the chamber, muttering as he went,—

" I cannot cope with her in speech; my conscious guilt peeps out from every feature of my face. Would to God now that I had never engaged in this mad adventure; but Jose deceived me. He prepared me to find a yielding beauty, and I find myself confronted with one who would suffer death, I feel convinced, rather than dishonour."

He took his way to the apartment in which he usually met Jose, and then he waited for that most exemplary minister, till the royal patience began to get considerably the worse for wear, and a vast amount of aggravation was accumulating in the royal bosom.

" Confound him !" muttered Philip, " where can he be ? I cannot go through the house searching for him, and he comes not."

The king little suspected it, but he had seen the last of his minister, and never in this world was he doomed to look upon Don Jose's face again.

He paced the room with a chafed expression. He rang a hand-bell which he had repeatedly; but he might as well have left it alone, for there was no one to attend to it.

True Lazarillo heard it, and guessed from whence it proceeded; but he was not inclined to answer it, and so the majesty of Spain was left alone in its glory, a striking example of the fact that, when a king forgets his own dignity, and elevated position, which should lift him above common vices, his dignity is apt to be forgot by any one else.

There he remained, fretting and fuming, and invoking maledictions upon the head of Don Jose—that head which he little supposed would so soon be laid so very low, never to rise again.

" Confound him !" he muttered; " why comes he not with the narcotic potion to give the girl ? It shall be given to her; I do regret much the foolish scruples that prevented me at first from adopting such a course, for it is one which would have saved me a world of uneasiness. But it is not too late—it is not, even now, too late, and shall be done."

Again he rang the bell, and with a similar result. No one answered him, and, moreover, darkness was coming on with rapid strides, and his gracious majesty would soon be quite alone, and incapable of seeing where he was.

Truly that was a very uncomfortable position for a king to be placed in. He got nearly desperate—he stepped to the door, and, holding it a little way open, he listened attentively to hear what was going on: but if what was going on was to be defined by what he heard of it, nothing was going on at all, for the whole seemed as still as the grave.

" Strange !" said the king; " this is very strange; I hear no one stirring—all is still—am I deserted here? Oh, no, that is impossible; something has occurred to keep Jose from me. I heard the report of an arquebus, too. What can have happened ? No danger surely to our royal schemes, or it would have made itself more apparent before this."

He fancied now that he heard a footstep on the staircase; but, although he listened with all the intensity he was capable of throwing into the act, he heard it not again, and he came to the conclusion that some other accidental noise had sounded like it, or that he altogether (considering the state of excitement he was in) had been deceived by fancy.

" I will wait some time longer," he said; " and then, if he does not come, I must prepare to descend to the lower part of this most accursed and unlucky building, to see the state of affairs."

Having formed this resolution, his gracious majesty sat down in the dark, and strove as well as he could (although that was very indifferently) to think on agreeable subjects, in order to chase from his royal mind the number of thick-coming superstitious fancies that began, under the influence of the hour and the circumstances, to beset it.

But, although Philip had made up his mind yet to wait a while, and then proceed to the lower part of the chateau in search of his rascally minister, he had not fixed any precise period to the duration of that waiting, and his courage was not of that order which increases as alarms thicken.

Therefore was it that, although Jose came not, he went not, and the royal wrath at one moment would prevail, while the royal fears at another would hold sovereign sway.

He heard now (for fear and general uneasiness make the senses more than naturally acute) the distant sounds which arose necessarily from some of the events we have recorded.

He heard footsteps in the house—he heard footsteps in the garden; and, as those sounds were taken up by various echoing responses, he was more puzzled, and to the full as much alarmed, as the queen had been while waiting for Alvarez, and listening to the tread of Don Jose de Santarem, or his poor persecuted victim, Maritana, as she held her lonely and dreadful watch in her chamber.

That something of a strange and a serious character must have occurred, he could not but imagine : and, finally, he heard the loud clash of swords, the sharp ringing sound of which made itself heard more plainly and distinctly than the distance would seem to warrant

"What can that mean !" he exclaimed, as he started to his feet ; "what can that mean ?"

Still the sound continued ; and, in all the variety of conjectures which came across his mind, little did he dream of suspecting that a mortal combat was at that moment proceeding between Don Cæsar, the man whom he had so much injured, and Don Jose, the minister of his pleasures.

He thought at one moment that the chateau was attacked by robbers ; he thought at another moment that some quarrels among the attendants was causing the confusion. Then he feared that some political enemies had found him out, and were intent upon his assassination. He drew his sword, and stood upon his guard, and then suddenly the sounds of strife ceased entirely, and all was as remarkably still as any one could suppose a place totally deserted could possibly be.

Don Jose was dead ; but not in that way did Philip of Spain account for the stillness ; he thought that some attack had been repelled, and now, each lagging minute he fully expected to hear the sound of his minister's footsteps hurrying towards him to apologise for delays, and do him what service could yet be done as regarded Maritana.

CHAPTER LXXIV.

THE MEETING BETWEEN DON CÆSAR AND MARI-
TANA.—THE REJECTION.—THE OATH.—THE RE-
CONCILIATION.

WHEN Don Cæsar de Bazan, feeling that the errand which brought him to Don Jose's chateau invested him with sufficient authority to go where he pleased, so unceremoniously broke in the door of the outer apartment of the two which were devoted to the use of the beautiful Maritana, he did not expect to find himself so immediately in her presence.

And, as for her, not even the most distant hope that it was Don Cæsar who was apparently committing such an outrage crossed her mind. No wonder, then, that for one brief moment they should both stand as it were transfixed with sudden emotion, neither of them uttering a word, but gazing into each other's faces with expressions of joy, astonishment, and perplexity.

Maritana, despite the remarkable change which had taken place in his general appearance, knew him well. She had by far too powerful a recollection of those features, which she had looked upon so often amid the bustling streets of Madrid, ever to forget them with any lapse of time or change of circumstances.

And he, too, now that he had been told by the page Lazarillo who the countess had been, wondered how for one moment, notwithstanding the very transient glance he had had of her at the Marquis de Rotondo's, he could have failed to recognise her.

Now, however, although she was much paler, and much less like her former self than she had been on that occasion, he knew her at once, and thus was there an immediate mutual recognition between those two persons, who had suffered so much in being separated, who had so longed to meet, and whose destinies, in consequence of the deep and intricate designing of Don Jose, had become so inextricably woven together.

"Cæsar !" exclaimed Maritana, and, almost at the same moment, he pronounced the name of—

"Maritana !"

Here she would have flown to his arms, but he drew himself proudly off, and checked her advance. She stood with clasped hands, regarding him with looks of devotion and grief; for she knew not why he should discard her.

But, although Don Cæsar had reason, from all he had heard, and by various ways had become acquainted, to acquire a well-grounded belief in the entire innocence of the beautiful girl, yet he felt that the subject was one which his honour made it necessary he should proceed in with the utmost caution.

He scarcely might be said to doubt, and yet he felt that, on such a subject, he ought to be more than sure that he was not made the victim of the ambitious intrigues of a woman, and hence he had made up his mind, that whenever he should see his countess, that not even all her exquisite loveliness, not all the seeming suffering she had gone through, and not all his own conviction of her truth and innocence, should induce him to take her to his arms, but that he would yet further judge for himself by a conversation with her what she really was.

Hence then was it that, at the moment when she would have thrown herself upon his breast, he repelled her advances, and cast upon her a glance stern and serious, which at once dispelled her first burst of joy.

"What—what is this ?" she gasped ; "Don Cæsar—my lord—my husband—what have I done to merit this ?"

"Maritana," he said, "I come not here as an accuser ; but I do come as a judge to you."

"Oh, then, judge me, as I am innocent."

"As it shall appear. To yourself I leave the task of explanation."

"And you—you are really Don Cæsar de Bazan—the being of my fondest dreams ! You are no impostor ! You live—you are my husband."

"Impostor !"

"Don Jose told me that the Don Cæsar whom I had seen so often was but an adventurer in the streets of Madrid."

"Indeed."

"He told me that the real Don Cæsar was a Spanish noble, with the best blood of Castile flowing in his veins ; that he mingled with none but the highest and the noblest."

"And well he might," said Cæsar, sorrowfully.

"He added that the Don Cæsar of the streets and the wine shops was dead ; but that the Don Cæsar of the court and of noble ancestry lived."

"He was right."

"Right—right, and yet I see you ! Can I be mistaken ?"

"No, Maritana, you are not mistaken, and yet was Don Jose, even in all his desperate wickedness, correct so far."

"Indeed. Oh, explain this seeming mystery ?"

"The Don Cæsar of the carnival and the wine

shops *is* no more. The Don Cæsar of noble ancestry and high descent lives, and is now before you. I am not what I was; I am a wiser, let me also hope a better, man, but I am Don Cæsar still."

"I understand," said Maritana, as tears of grateful feeling gushed from her eyes, "I understand you now."

"'Tis well, and then it is fitting I should understand you. I married you, Maritana, I am assured."

"You did. Tell me the words you addressed to your veiled bride in the prison as you led her to the altar. Do you recollect them?"

"Well. There is no particular of that scene which is not fresh and vivid in my memory."

"And they were ——"

"These:—' Lady, to you I devote the remainder of my existence.' "

"They were—they were. You are my husband!"

"You were ambitious."

"Alas! for me, I was, and how bitterly have I suffered for that wild, untamed passion."

"You sought rank, luxury, wealth, honour?"

"I did—I did!"

"And how have you found them? You wedded me with a knowledge that I was about being hurried to execution."

"Execution!"

"Yes, Maritana. Ere yet the echo of your marriage vows could well have died upon your lips, you must have listened to the discharge of arquebuses, which made you a titled widow."

"Oh, heavens! Cæsar—Cæsar ——"

"Nay, lady, hear me out."

She stood with her whole soul absorbed in his words, and, listening to him with an interest that even he (stern and inflexible as was his purpose—for in it was concerned his choicest possession, honour) was pierced to the heart to see.

He resumed,—

"You became a titled widow, and fit companion for the guilty leisure of the King of Spain."

"No—no, by Heaven!"

"But I say yes, Maritana. By little short of a miracle, I have escaped the death that was prepared for me, and which was believed to be inflicted almost in your very presence. I am here to question you; I am here in the defence of my honour. I am here not to denounce you as an impostor—not to dispute your right to the name and the title you bear as Countess de Bazan—but to demand of you, as having that name, how you have preserved its honour."

"As unsullied as the sun's light. Cæsar—Cæsar, I am innocent!"

"This house is not the home of innocence."

"And yet one I ——"

"It is notorious that this chateau is the resort of Don Jose and the king—a house in which passion takes unbridled license, and where is carried on those intrigues which have been the bane of the domestic policy of this nation."

"I was forced here, Cæsar—I was brought here a prisoner. Oh, why torture me with these cruel suspicions?"

"Suspicion may well point its trembling finger at the young and the beautiful within these walls."

"And point it wrongfully, Don Cæsar."

"You were ambitious. You have had a king for your suitor."

"Had he been ten times a king he had not moved me."

"Wealth, dignity, and luxury have been promised to you."

"Baubles, Cæsar, baubles."

"You have been tempted ——"

"Tempted? No, by the great God of Heaven, no! Not for one fleeting moment have I been tempted, for such a word would imply a wavering of the spirit towards the wickedness which was presented to its acceptance, and I have never wavered. I have been persecuted, Don Cæsar, but never tempted."

Don Cæsar stepped forward a pace. He felt inclined to clasp her to his heart, but he restrained the impulse.

"Hear me now," said Maritana, dejectedly. "You have spoken and charged me most cruelly, Cæsar. Now hear me."

"You shall be heard," he replied, in as cold and distant a tone as he could possibly command.

"I was ambitious. This man, Jose, sought me out and told me that the queen would be my friend. He assured me I should be wedded to you; that you loved me, and that the queen was restoring you to your fortunes and your former proud position; but he said the queen was compelled for a time to do all secretly, as the king was set against you. My imagination was dazzled, Cæsar, and I looked not for inconsistencies, which now I see too well in all he told me. I consented, and was conducted to the prison where we were married. I heard the sound of arquebuses, but, as Heaven is my judge, I no more knew or thought that such a sound was one of danger to you than that they were pointed at my own heart."

She paused a moment to weep.

"Go on," said Cæsar—"go on."

"I will—I will. Since then I have lived in splendid misery. My life has been one series of dreadful persecutions. In vain I demanded to see my husband. I was put off from time to time, and at length I was promised I should see him. A stranger was introduced to me as Don Cæsar de Bazan."

"And you ——"

"Detected the impostor at once and spurned him. Oh, Cæsar, he was as unlike you ——"

"Go on—go on."

"Then I began to feel myself a prisoner indeed. Persecuted and threatened by this man, my life became a burthen to me."

"But how came you here?"

"I know not. I must have been brought hither while I slept; but I am innocent, Cæsar—I am innocent."

"And know you who was this man who personated me?"

"I did not, but now I do."

"His name?"

"He is the King of Spain."

"Indeed!"

"Yes, Cæsar; but still am I innocent; and, now that I have told you so, do not suppose that I mean or wish to dog your honourable path, or to distress you by companionship with me. I wish you to rescue me from the persecutions I here endure because I bear your name. Then, Don Cæsar, I will leave you, and in some quiet seclusion I will wear out the remainder of my days, never forgetting that I am the Countess de Bazan, and should hold dearly the honour of that name, and never, at the same time, forgetting that I am not worthy to mate with you."

Cæsar turned aside to hide his emotion, as he said,—

"It is an artful and well-contrived tale."

"Now God help me!" cried Maritana, "did those cruel words come from your heart?"

"No!" exclaimed Cæsar, in a voice that echoed through the apartment. "No, my wife—my countess—my love—my only love. Welcome, welcome—thrice welcome to a husband's arms. Now—now, my Maritana, who will tear you from me?"

With a shriek of joy she flew into his arms. She

hung round his neck, sobbing with ecstacy. She hid her sweet face in his bosom, and wept aloud.

"You believe me innocent?"

"I do, as Heaven is my judge."

"And you will love me, Cæsar—dear, dear Cæsar? I shall be with you? You will raise me to your own high estate? You can love the poor, lowly Maritana?"

"No longer Maritana, but my countess—my prison bride—my own dear, beautiful countess. You are mine—mine only, and no power on earth shall ever again separate us. No power in Heaven will, for it has brought us together."

"Oh, joy—joy—joy!"

"Be calm, my Maritana—my countess, be calm. We have yet to leave this place."

"Oh, the villain Jose. Beware of him, dear Cæsar, He is an assassin. He knows no sentiment of honour. Oh, be wary of him."

"I need not."

"Need not?"

"He is dead, Maritana. His race is run."

"Gracious Heavens! Has he then indeed gone to that judgment which for him must be a dreadful one?"

"He has; but he died a better death than he deserved. At some more fitting time and place I will relate to you the manner of his end. At present there are other and far more important topics pressing."

"Yes, Cæsar—yes. Let us leave here at once. All seems quiet."

"Where is the king?"

"I know not. I have been a prisoner in these rooms since my most painful sojourn here."

"True—true. There seems an inner chamber there."

"There is."

"Go to it, and there remain until I come to you, or send our good friend Lazarillo."

"The page?"

"Yes, Maritana. Make much of him, for twice he has saved my life. Both times, too, at no little risk."

"Blessings on him! He shall be to me as some dear brother."

"Give him such a place in your heart, Maritana. He will fill it well, for a truer, braver, nobler spirit never inhabited a human bosom."

"And—and—you will not be long from me, Cæsar?"

"Most certainly not, dear Maritana."

She yet clung to him, and looked up in his face with eyes of adoration.

"You will be careful, Cæsar. For my sake you will go into no dangers. You will think now that you have some one to love you, and you rather avoid danger than seek it?"

"I will, Maritana. Life to me now has become a possession worth the keeping, since I have your love to grace it. Time was I thought but lightly enough of it."

"Farewell for a time."

"A brief time only, dear one."

"Ah, yet I know not how to let you go."

"But think of our precarious position here, Maritana."

"I can think of nothing but of thee."

"Nay, dearest, let me leave you now. I must seek the king."

"I feel as one who has recovered some lost treasure, and would not willingly again trust it from his eyes. But, go, Cæsar, I will have faith in your promise to run into no danger."

"You may, indeed. I will be what my worst enemies never accused me of being before."

"What is that?"

"A very model of discretion."

"Ah, that old, dear smile, that I have seen so often."

He kissed her tenderly, and whispering still further words of affection to her, he conducted her to the door of the inner apartment, where he left her, adding, as he did so,—

"Be of good cheer, dearest. I will soon return; but, let you hear what you will, or imagine what you will, I implore you not to move from this apartment."

"I will obey you, Cæsar."

"Adieu."

He turned away from the door of the inner chamber, and then he stood for the space of about half a minute in deep thought. Then, suddenly striding towards the door of the room, he said,—

"Now for the king. The dissolute majesty of Spain shall have a lesson of a practical nature to-day which it will be well for him to remember. I will make him suffer some of the pangs he has inflicted upon me, and a more complete, a more honourable, a more glorious revenge will I have of him than if I sheathed my rapier in his heart. The tool he has been of Don Jose, and now that he is no more, better councillors may surround the king, who, when I first dawned upon the court at Madrid, was not the man he now is, but, although fond of pleasure, he still had a sense of the honour which should be the brightest, highest, and the best of all kingly attributes. That sense of honour may be but slumbering, not killed, and if I can awaken it, happy will it be for Spain, and happier far for his noble-minded queen, who lies in a species of exile from his home and heart, and who has been exposed to such danger as that from which it was my happy lot to rescue her."

Cæsar walked hastily across the corridor towards the window, where the page was stationed, and to whom he said,—

"Lazarillo, I have a new post for you. It is to mount guard over the countess."

"With joy," said Lazarillo. "You have seen her, Cæsar?"

"I have, boy."

"And you have found her ——"

"All that I could wish. I am happy, Lazarillo, in the dear consciousness of having found her in all respects all that my most sanguine heart could hope. I love her, Lazarillo, for her virtues, as much—ay, far more, boy—than for her beauty."

"I rejoice to hear you say so, Cæsar."

"You shall have, Lazarillo, ample cause to rejoice. Methinks a brighter, better day is dawning on me. The end of my vagrant career is now nearly over, and once again shall I be, I hope, enabled to resume the station among the grandees of Spain, to which my title and my rank entitle me."

"And no one, Cæsar, will more joyfully see you in such a position than myself. You will adorn it, if you please; and, from the strange life you have led in the streets of Madrid, you may have learnt much which will enable you to do good to those beneath you, in a manner most suited to their wants."

"I believe I shall, Lazarillo—I believe I shall."

"There cannot be a doubt. You have been among the people, Don Cæsar; you know them and their habits. You know what are their painful wants, and what they could well do without, if at all necessary to make a sacrifice. Now if you are restored, as no doubt you will be, to your rank and station, you will have an opportunity of doing a world of good with a little of the trouble that many a great man takes to do a world of mischief."

"Right, my boy, right."

"And you will be able, likewise, to—to ——"

"Why do you pause?"

" Well, Cæsar, it's no business of mine; but I was going to say, you will be able to pay your creditors."

" Oh, so I should."

" You know, you have told me you owe everybody something."

" And so I do, Lazarillo, with the exception of one class of men in Madrid. To them I owe nothing."

" Indeed, Cæsar !"

" Ay, indeed, Lazarillo."

" And who may they be, Cæsar ?"

" Those who declined trusting me; and quite right

who disputes with me the debt that is due to him. Nevertheless, you shall not be the last that is paid, and that in full too."

" Oh, Cæsar, you know that I was your debtor long before I had an opportunity of making you, to any extent, mine."

" I don't know any such thing."

" 'Tis true."

" Then the best way to settle our quarrel, if we may dignify it by that name, will be by a mutual interchange of good offices to strive through life, each in paying off to the other as much kindness as one can."

" I will be your faithful follower, Cæsar."

" Indeed you will not."

" I will not? You do not intend to make me leave you ?"

" Who said so, Lazarillo ?"

" Nay, I understood you ——"

" Psha ! You mean you misunderstood me. You

they were, too, for some unlucky brawl might have settled my worldly career for ever, and then they would have had nothing at all but the barren and unprofitable honour of my name in their books, which I really very much fear they would have been far from appreciating."

" No doubt," said Lazarillo, as he laughed—" no doubt, Cæsar."

" And, most of all, Lazarillo, do I owe you."

" No—no—no."

" You will say no; but you are my only creditor shall not be my follower, Lazarillo, and that is only because I will have you for my friend."

" Your friend ?"

" Yes, my best, dearest friend."

" I cannot aspire so high as to be the friend of a noble."

" If you reject my proffered friendship, Lazarillo, I cannot help it. I have offered you mine freely."

" Reject it ! Oh, no, I do not say reject."

" Then say no more about it; but, as my dearest and best friend, go now and keep guard over the safety and the honour of my countess. I cannot ask of you to perform for me a dearer, higher trust."

" I go, Cæsar—and you ——"

" Go to seek the king. He must be in the chateau somewhere, and I will make him feel, were he ten times a king, that he cannot perpetrate a deadly wrong with impunity."

" Hush !" said the page, and he placed his hand on Don Cæsar's arm. " Look there, towards the door from whence you came."

Cæsar did so, and he saw the king, with his hands clasped behind him, in apparently pensive thought, proceeding towards the apartment contiguous to the one in which was Maritana. He looked around at the broken door, and then passed into the room with a quickened step.

CHAPTER LXXV.

THE AGITATING INTERVIEW BETWEEN THE KING AND DON CÆSAR.—THE KING'S RAGE, AND DON CÆSAR'S NOBLE CARRIAGE.

WITH a slightly heightened colour, Don Cæsar strode after the king; but Lazarillo pursued him, and, laying his hand imploringly upon his breast, he said,—

" Cæsar, dear Cæsar, you know that your honour is dear and precious to me ; but let me implore you to do nothing rash."

" Be under no apprehension."

" You will be calm ?"

" I will. I never was more perfectly master of myself, Lazarillo. I contemplate no violence, no rashness. You may safely trust me, boy, and feel no pang of uneasiness about this business."

" I feel that I may now."

" You are right, for you may indeed."

" Bless and prosper you, Cæsar ! Shall I wait here now for you ?"

" Wait within call. Within hearing, if you will; and then you will be completely satisfied that I am doing nothing rash."

He passed on, and the page lingered at the door which had been broken.

When Cæsar entered the outer apartment, he found that the king had passed through it, and was in the inner one. He heard the sound of Maritana's voice, as she said,—

" Your honour, sir ! Your honour should have forbidden this intrusion."

Two strides brought him to the door, and in the next instant he was in the chamber, and in presence of the king.

Philip made sure it was Jose, when he heard a footstep approaching, but when he saw that it was a stranger, his alarm and confusion were increased almost to the ludicrous.

Maritana made a movement to fly into Don Cæsar's arms ; but he said to her, softly, so that she only heard,—

" Leave us—leave us."

And then she converted the movement she had made into an exit by the open door, and Don Cæsar was alone with the extremely nervous and alarmed majesty of Spain, by the grace of God.

Cæsar took good care to stand near to the door, so that the king could not give him the slip, which, otherwise, he might have felt marvellously inclined to do, and then the pair looked at each other for a few moments in silence.

The king at last found it necessary to say something, or he considered it prudent to do so ; at all events, he was the first to break the exceedingly awkward silence, by saying,—

" Sir, I don't know you."

" I did not expect you did," replied Cæsar.

" And, pray, how came you here ?"

" By one of the windows."

" One of the windows ?"

" Yes. I couldn't come through the wall, and I found none of the doors open, so how was I to come but through one of the windows."

" But—but by the mass, what business had you to come here at all, by door or window ?"

" Oh, what business had I ? Oh, that's quite another thing. You didn't ask me that before."

" Well, but ——"

" Now, you know you didn't. You asked me how I came here, not why I came here ; but, since you have put the latter question to me, I don't mind telling you that the reason was, and is, a woman."

" A woman ?"

" Yes, and a remarkably pretty one, too. I saw her face at a window, and, if there be one thing more than another which would induce me to get in at any window, however seemingly impracticable, it is certainly a pretty woman."

" Your impertinence is beyond anything I ever heard of."

" Yes, ain't it. I thought you'd say that. My impertinence is beyond anything, as you remark."

It was difficult to fight out against such consummate impertinence as this, and for a moment or two the king was absolutely confounded, and knew not what to say next. At length, stamping with passion, he exclaimed,—

" D——n, sir, will you withdraw before I call for assistance, in which case your life would pay the penalty for your rash intrusion ?"

" No."

" You will not ?"

" In plain language, I will not. I've seen a pretty woman here, and I've taken so much pains to get here, and been nearly shot beside, that as for going away again I couldn't think of it."

The king rung a bell violently.

" Ring away—ring away," said Cæsar. " I don't think anybody will come to you. You can't get rid of me so easily."

" D——n !"

" Swear away—swear away. Something, do you know, strikes me that I know the form of her who attracted me."

" You know her ?"

" Yes, if she be the same, I saw her at a fete given by the Marquis de Rotondo, and heard her name there."

" Her name ?"

" Yes ; they called her the Countess de Bazan."

" Indeed !"

" Yes, she's a charming creature, and as there's no Count de Bazan, for I heard, on the best authority, he was shot, she must be a widow, you know, and a very charming one, too."

" How know you that Don Cæsar de Bazan is dead ?"

" I heard he had been duly executed."

" Then, sir, you have heard wrong."

" Indeed !"

" Yes, indeed ; but now allow me to require you, as a gentleman, if you can lay claim to that title, to leave this house immediately."

" At once ?"

" At once, sir."

" What ! without seeing the charming creature ?"

" Confound such impertinence. Do you think the house of a gentleman is to be invaded in this manner ?"

" Yes. Oh, yes."

Philip rung the bell violently, but with no better a result, and, muttering curses between his clenched teeth, he paced to and fro distractedly. Don Cæsar, however, placed such a good guard upon the door that it was impossible for him to escape, and, suddenly turning to his tormentor, he cried, vehemently,—

" You did see her ; she left the room as you intruded yourself into it."

" Call you that seeing her ? Oh, I wish to converse with her. To hold her fair soft hand in mine, to look upon the changing expressions of her sweet face. To plant a thousand kisses upon her ambrosial lips."

" A madman !—a madman !" said the king, the idea for the first time coming across his mind that it was some lunatic who had made his way into the chateau.

" Will you," he said, in a soothing tone, " allow me to leave the room ?"

" No."

" But, wherefore ?"

" Because it is my will that you should remain."

" But what right have you here ?"

" If such a question comes, sir, upon the tapis, what right have you here ?" said Cæsar.

" What right have I ? The right that any man has to be in his own house."

" Oh, then, this is your house ?"

" Of course it is. Whose did you suppose it was but mine ?"

" I really made no supposition on the subject. Since you have so kindly, and so blandly explained your right to the house, perhaps you will be equally obliging as regards your right to the lady whom I so much admire."

" The right of a husband."

" A husband! Did you say husband ?"

" I did."

" Oh, bother a husband. I think nothing of a husband. If you had said a lover, now the case would have been different."

" Have you no morality ?"

" Not a bit—not a bit. Who the devil are you, since you claim the right of a husband ?"

" I am, sir, Don Cæsar de Bazan, count of Orfilla."

" The devil you are. Then you ain't shot ?"

" You see me here. And, since with more good temper than these circumstances at all warrant, I have explained to you who I am, perhaps you will be equally explicit, and will tell me who the devil you are."

" Oh, certainly—certainly."

" Well, sir. Well."

" I am, sir, his majesty, the king of Spain."

" The devil you are."

" You see me here. And, since I have, with far more temper than the circumstances at all warrant, allowed myself to be so deeply insulted by a subject, allow me to command you to leave this place."

" Was there ever such consummate impudence ?" said the king to himself. " Was there ever in this world a man like this ?"

" And now I think of it, by-the-bye," added Cæsar, " you say you are Don Cæsar de Bazan, we believe."

" I am."

" Then what right, allow me to ask, have you to be alive ?"

" What right ?"

" Yes, they condemned you to be shot by virtue of our royal decree, made during the carnival, that all duellists should be condemned to death. You fought with a captain of our royal guard, and killed him. Now let me ask you, if you be Don Cæsar, and not some impostor, who has assumed that name and title to further some dishonourable ends of his own, what right have you to be alive at all ?"

" Your gracious majesty forgets," said Philip, " your pardon was sent off to the prison."

" Ah !"

" Yes ; and, therefore, your majesty must hold me excused for being alive still, since I am free."

" True," said Cæsar,—" true ! We had forgotten. The royal memory is treacherous—royal memories very often are. We ourselves sometimes forget what we ought to remember, and, by some odd means or another, remember what we ought to forget."

' Curses on the fellow !' said the king, in an under tone,—" does he know me ?" Then he said, more aloud,—" Perhaps your majesty, having made a gracious explanation so far, will now leave the house."

" My majesty will do no such thing," said Cæsar. " We have weighty reasons for coming here."

" 'Weighty reasons for intruding into another person's house ?"

" Yes—beauty attracted us; and when we are attracted by beauty, we do not mind confessing to you, Don Cæsar, that we care for no consequences, but throw aside all sense of right and justice. We have, Don Cæsar, a lively recollection now of your name and titles. We remember you were extravagant, and ruined your fortune ; but, at the same time, we remember not one act of dishonour that can be laid to your charge—and therefore is it that we speak freely to you, when otherwise we should be most cautious."

The king moved uneasily, as he said,—

" Pray proceed."

" You see the majesty of Spain then," added Cæsar, " in an awkward situation, and most decidedly under a cloud. We are not, you will perceive, surrounded by those who know us and our officers of state, because the affair, in which we are at present engaged, happens to be one which will not bear investigation, or even observation. In fact, we are engaged in an intrigue."

" Indeed !"

" Yes. It is unhappily too true. But we rely upon your honour, Don Cæsar de Bazan."

The king bit his lips, and uttered an oath at Jose, whose continued absence was exposing him to so much that was unpalatable and disagreeable.

" Hark ye, sir !" he said. " Allow me to ask of you then, since you seem so well aware of your error, why you linger here ?"

" Waiving," replied Don Cæsar, " the disrespectful manner in which you address your king, allow me to say that I consider I have a right here."

" A right ?"

" Yes. The right which one full of power, and holding a high station, has, or at all events which answers the same purpose, assumes to have, to do what wrong he chooses."

This was a bitter sarcasm, and the king felt it as such. He glared at Don Cæsar, as if he would have eaten him up, and, in a voice of suppressed passion, he said,—

" If you be the king of Spain, you act not royally or generously. Leave my house, and I shall be more inclined to believe you own the title you assume."

" You doubt us ?"

" Indeed do I. How do I know you are the king of Spain—how can I know ?"

" How do I know that you are Don Cæsar de Bazan —how can I know ? And yet, in courtesy, I have not disputed your assumption of the title."

" Assumption ?"

" Yes. If you are Don Cæsar de Bazan, Count of Orfilla, then am I Philip the Second, king of all Spain. And I trust we have sufficiently explained to you, Don Cæsar, why we are so poorly attended as we are at present—indeed, we may say, we are not attended at all."

" If respect for my monarch keeps my sword in its scabbard," said the king, " it ought not to encourage him in acting unworthily. Will you go ? D——n! —what do you want here ?"

" The Countess de Bazan !"

" Was ever such unparalleled impudence heard of? I tell you she is my wife."

" Well, what's that to us ? If we admire her, what matter to us is it whose wife she is ? You keep arguing that topic as if we had any notion of governing ourselves by the petty laws of every-day morality !"

" This is going too far," said the king, as he laid his hand on the hilt of his sword, menacingly. " Will you leave ?"

" Ah !" said Cæsar, as he crossed his arms over his breast with provoking coolness, " would you be the traitor to draw your sword upon your king ? Were I the subject and you the monarch, however unworthy of his rank and greatness the king had acted, I would not draw my sword upon him. I would endeavour to awaken him by some means to a sense of the wrong he had done ; but I would not, for the world, be a traitor !"

The king had moved his sword a few inches from its scabbard, but now he dashed it back again with a clang, as he said,—

" Who or what you are, I know not. But as you are a gentleman, I request you will leave this house, into which your presence is the greatest of all intrusions ?"

" I ask you to leave it !"

" Madman, I tell you it is my house.*

" Madman to you; I tell you I am the king, and carrying on an intrigue,—therefore, I consider no man's house sacred."

" You force me to this!" said the king, as he tore his sword from its scabbard. " At my sword's point I must repel this insult. Now, sir, if you wish not for bloodshed, I again say, leave this house.''

Don Cæsar drew his sword likewise, but it was only to cast it to the further end of the room ; as he did so, he said,—

" I will not fight !"

" Not fight—not fight ! Are you a coward ?"

" Cowards do not usually place themselves in such circumstances of danger as I may be in at present, and then cast away the only weapon they possess which might save them. I have other reasons for not fighting with you. Put up your sword, Don Cæsar—put up your sword."

" I am known," thought the king. " His conduct convinces me now. What an adventure is this! I am known—I am known."

He sank into a chair as he spoke these words, in a tone not above his breath ; and Don Cæsar regarded him with fixed attention, still keeping his arms across his breast.

After a slight pause, Philip spoke to him, saying,—

" Without reference to who or to what you are, you should see that, as a gentleman, you ought not to remain here."

" Do not blame me for a mental blindness which is equally shared by yourself. You have no more right in this house than I."

" The Countess de Bazan is here."

" Aye,—but you are not the count."

" Not the count ?"

" No. From the first moment that you announced yourself to be Don Cæsar, I detected the imposture. I knew him well. I have been, from his boyhood, most familiar with every trick and turn of his fortune. I should know him among a thousand resemblances of himself. You are not Don Cæsar de Bazan. You have not the smallest pretence of probability for passing yourself off as that nobleman—I may add, that much-injured nobleman."

" You question my words boldly, sir."

" I do, because I question them truly."

" Then who do you suppose I am ?"

" You more resemble one whom I have not seen so often—but whom to see once is not very easy to forget."

" Ah !"

" Yes, your majesty—you are Philip of Spain."

Don Cæsar took off his hat as he spoke, and knelt.

The king looked confused for a moment, and then he said,—

" We admit it. You know us—and disguise is useless. Follow me from this room, and ——"

" Nay," said Cæsar, suddenly rising, " we have some business to settle, your majesty, before we leave here."

" What, sir ?"

Again the king half drew his sword, and he made a step towards the door as did so. Don Cæsar, however, interrupted him ; and, turning the key in the lock, he placed it in his pocket, saying,—

" I am resolved that your majesty leaves not this chamber until we have settled an affair which lies next to my heart."

" Ah, traitor, would you make us prisoner ?"

" For a time I would. Has it not struck your majesty that if the title I assumed belongs of right to

you, it is just possible that that in which you decked yourself in order to substantiate a right to be here with the Countess de Bazan may be mine ?"

The king absolutely recoiled a step or two as if he had been struck, as Don Cæsar pronounced these words, for now he could have no doubt but that he stood in the presence of the man whom he had endeavoured so much to injure, and towards whom he had acted so unworthy a part.

How, or by what means Don Cæsar had come at such information as had brought him there, and even having the information, how in safety, notwithstanding all the precautions of Don Jose, he had got into the chateau, were questions which not a little perplexed the royal mind ; but these soon gave way to considerations of a much more absorbing character.

" Do you mean to tell us you are Don Cæsar ?" said the king.

" I am Don Cæsar de Bazan."

Philip seemed to shrink into one half of his ordinary dimensions, and for a moment or two there was an ominous pause. The king made a desperate effort to excuse himself from the disagreeable feelings of personal danger that were crawling over him, and he said,—

" Well, sir, well, are we to be your prisoner ?"

" I must have revenge," said Cæsar.

" Re—revenge !"

" Yes, revenge! I am an injured man—injured in a manner which, surely, no gentleman can do otherwise than wish to avenge. I tell you I must and will have revenge !"

Philip trembled. He almost gave himself up for lost, and yet Cæsar had cast away his sword—what could he mean ?

" I find," added Cæsar, " my countess,—she who holds in keeping the honour of my ancient name, here with you."

" Your countess is innocent," said the king.

" Innocent !" said Cæsar ; " how came she here if innocent ?"

" She was brought here. Be not too curious; I abandon this intrigue. Be satisfied, Don Cæsar, that your countess is innocent."

" Have I your royal word for that ?"

" Yes, and my oath—I swear it to you, by Heaven ! You have nothing to avenge, for your countess, I swear to you, is innocent."

" I cannot disbelieve an oath so solemnly uttered; I believe that my countess is innocent. I wonder who and what I have to thank that she is so ?"

Philip was silent.

" And," continued Cæsar, " is her abduction nothing ? Her agony of soul, nay, deep anxiety—the intention to do me grievous wrong—are all these things nothing ?"

" By Heavens, Don Cæsar, I did not know or believe you were in existence ! I was assured that you were dead."

" And hoped that it was true. I will still pursue my revenge. Listen to me, sire,—I have that to tell to you which may inform you what description of pang must have met my heart when I found that the Countess de Bazan was here in this house with your majesty."

" To tell me ?"

" Yes ; I am the bearer of rare news. Will it please your majesty to hear my tidings ?"

" Concern they us ?"

" Most surely."

" Go on—go on ; we attend."

" Your majesty has repeatedly desired the attendance of Don Jose. Believe me, he was far better, far more pleasantly occupied than in waiting upon a king."

"How—how mean you?"

"I will tell your majesty—pray have patience. A dear friend of mine let me know what was going on here, and I came, not without danger, not without difficulty, I own. I made my way into the garden of this most hospitable mansion, and was strolling about, endeavouring to find some means of entrance, when near to me I heard a sound of voices."

"Well, sir?"

"They seemed to come from a rustic summer-house or arbour, in the immediate vicinity of where I was. They were those of love—love and adoration—uttered by a man's tongue to some tender-hearted, perhaps, confiding woman. He was pouring out in that strain of eloquence which characterises the libertine rather than the true-hearted honourable lover, his tale of affection and deep devouring all absorbing devotion."

"What is all this to me?" said the king, impatiently.

"Much—much."

"Go on—go on."

"I crept closer still. For once I played the eaves dropper, and besides I had come here upon an errand which authorised me so to do; I then crept closer. The moonlight streamed in wondrous power and beauty into the arbour, and I then saw who were the amorous pair. I saw them clearly. The man was kneeling at the feet of the lady, still breathing soft vows, and making honied speeches."

"And who were they?"

"Cannot your majesty have a guess?"

"How can I guess the names of the actors in every vulgar intrigue which may take place within these walls?"

"Oh, but this was and is no vulgar intrigue. For, far from that, it is as high, and as choice, and as pretty an intrigue as any one could wish to see."

"Who were they then?"

"Nay, curb your royal impatience. I was myself transfixed with astonishment at the recognition of the persons. It was but just now before I came to your majesty."

The king stamped with rage, and Cæsar still continued with the same imperturbable coolness—

"They are there still; I left them there. The man at the feet of the lady in the garden."

"Now, by all the saints!"

"Well, well, your majesty shall no longer be kept in a state of doubt and uncertainty. The man was Don Jose."

"Don Jose?"

"Aye—your minister; I know you will perceive I might well say he was better occupied than in attending on his king. Don Jose is an ambitious man, and no doubt he considered that he was materially advancing his views."

"Advancing his views by a low intrigue?"

"Nay—once again let me implore your majesty not to call it a low intrigue, for were I to tell you the name of the other party engaged in it, you will not, I am sure, so characterise it."

"Indeed!"

"No—by-the-bye, of course they are there still; I left them both there, and I have been here some time, as your majesty is aware. Yet, you see, Don Jose does not come, which shows still how agreeably he must be occupied, and how totally he must have forgotten your majesty."

"The villain!"

"Aye, the villain!"

The king paced to and fro in the room angrily, and Cæsar added,—

"Your majesty has forgotten to ask who was—who is the lady."

"Ah—who?"

"The Queen of Spain!"

Had a bomb-shell suddenly exploded at the feet of Philip, he could not have been more astounded. The intelligence seemed for a moment to take away his very breath, and his countenance assumed the nearly black tint which it always did when his passion was very materially excited. He glanced at Don Cæsar like a maniac, and the latter, in a loud voice, that reached to the very heart's core of the king, cried,—

"The Queen of Spain—the queen! Your queen, sir! It was her feet at which the ambitious, audacious Don Jose was pouring out the fond confession of his love."

"A lie—a lie!" shouted Phillip.

"'Tis true," cried Cæsar, "on my honour it is true. The Queen of Spain—the queen! was the lady."

"Death and fury!"

"Bravo—bravo!"

"Damnation—hell!"

"Bravo—bravo!"

"The key—the key of the door! Let me fly to my revenge—they shall die. Locked in blood they shall die. Open the door—the door, I say; queen or devil, be you which you may, open the door."

"Oh, dear, no," said Cæsar.

"Do you want to drive me mad? Release me. The key—the key of this door. Let me seek the guilty pair. Dishonour, disgrace, shame. Oh, death and hell—open the door!"

"Not at all; be patient."

"Patient—patient, when such a foul stain is upon my honour? Patient, when my queen has driven me mad? Patient, when betrayed by the man I trusted? They shall both die by my own hand. This rapier shall drink their blood. Patience, indeed! a thousand curses on the word."

"Nay, think again," said Cæsar, as he threw himself negligently into a chair; "think again; after all, 'tis but an every day affair."

"The key—the key!"

"Nay, nay, I shall not allow you majesty to go."

"Not go? not go to punish those who would cover me with disgrace? Not go to run my sword through the heart of the ingrate who—who—curses on them both, I shall go distracted. The key—the key!"

"Your majesty shall not leave this room yet awhile."

"Not leave! What motive can you have in staying me?"

"Revenge."

"Revenge? revenge?"

"Yes; you now feel some of the pangs which you may imagine must have tortured my breast when I found my countess here. You now know what it is to be an injured man in the nicest point connected with your honour. What you projected against my peace of mind, has come home to yourself. The dishonour you would have heaped upon me, has fallen on your own head. How do you feel, king, under the infliction? This is my revenge. Think you it sufficient? Think you it ample? Swear, stamp, bawl with rage, you shall not leave this room. Here you shall remain, with the bitter consciousness that Don Jose, your confidential servant, has made you his dupe, and that he and your queen are at this present moment in the garden of this house."

"The key. God of heaven! the key," said the king. "Let me go; you have had your revenge; let me go."

"Not yet, not yet; I must tell you all. Your majesty must hear the whole story quite perfect. There must be no hiatus in it, through which you could entertain a doubt of what I say."

The king shook like an aspen, and Cæsar added,—

"The whole aim and object of this intrigue, which was sought to be carried out at the expense of my life, and the honour of my name, was for Don Jose to be able to attack the queen's virtue by exciting her jealousy."

The king groaned.

"Aye, you may well groan. He sent for her here. He, Jose, sent for her, in order to convince her that you kept a mistress here. Then he thought to take her in that moment of her heart's anguish and bitterness, and make her his. You understand the plot, sir. No wonder you have summoned Don Jose to come to you in vain. You see, now, what a puppet he has made of you. A royal puppet, but still a puppet, for all that."

Fury once more took possession of the king.

"Your sword!" he cried; "take up your sword, and detain me at its point, for not otherwise will I be kept in this room."

"No, I will not take up my sword."

"The key, then, the key."

"Nor will I surrender the key of the door. I do not choose to have Don Jose interrupted. You would have done your utmost, by fair means or foul, to dishonour me, and now I repay the compliment. I told you I would have my revenge, and I am now exquisitely enjoying it."

"Fiend, you shall not long live to enjoy it."

Philip advanced with his drawn sword, but Don Cæsar regarded him with an unflinching eye, and said,—

"Truly, it will much better your majesty's case to take the life of an unarmed man; I have no weapon, you see."

"Then receive your sword."

"I dare not lift it against my king."

"This respect is a mockery. One moment you drive your king mad, and the next assume a deference you cannot feel. Let your revenge be satiated. You have had it; now let me seek mine."

"What would your majesty do?"

"Sacrifice Don Jose to my just resentment."

"And it is for that your majesty requires the key of the door?"

"Do not, do not play upon my heart thus. I implore you, Don Cæsar, to let me go, or be beside me with your sword, so that I can at least attempt to force my way."

"Sire, let me ask you one question before you go?"

"Quick, quick. This is no time for questioning.'"

"But it concerns the subject before us. Heard you ever one word against the courage of the Bazans?"

"No—no—no."

"Or their honour, until it was attempted to be assailed by the king?"

"Well—well—no!"

"Then what on earth could induce your majesty, for one moment, to imagine it was necessary for you to seek that information I have mentioned to you as concerning the queen and Don Jose?"

"I do not understand you."

"When did a Spanish nobleman, of unsullied reputation for courage and for honour, ever forget to avenge the quarrels of his king?"

"What—what mean you?"

"Don Jose is still in the garden, your majesty. He's still close to the arbour where I heard him breathing his audacious vows to your queen—but as a living man, you will never look upon his face again!"

"Dead—dead?"

"Aye, dead. The sword which your majesty would have had me lift against you, took his life. It was in fair fight. In the king's name,—in the name of the wounded honour of my sovereign I challenged him then and there to mortal combat, and Heaven, blessing the cause, made me triumphant. Don Jose is no more. He lies a bleeding corpse within a few paces of the spot which witnessed his deep villany."

"And my queen?"

"Repelled him."

"Repelled!"

"As became a queen!"

"Thank—thank God."

The king sunk back into a chair, and his sword dropped from his hands. A great revulsion of feeling seemed to come over him. His rage all deserted him completely, and he turned of a death-like paleness. Don Cæsar was a little alarmed. The king might be dying for all he knew, and he flew towards him as he said—

"Your majesty is ill?"

"No—no," gasped the king, "but—but I have had, you know, too much excitement. Oh! Don Cæsar, you have, indeed—indeed, had your revenge—a most complete and bitter revenge."

"And yet," said Cæsar, "let me hope that it is one which will bear good fruits to all of us. It may have been a complete revenge, but do not, my liege, call it a bitter one."

"Well—well—well."

"Are you better now?"

"Much better. And so you killed him, Cæsar? Thanks, thanks—oh! how blinded I have been by that man, Don Cæsar. How he has led me through the devious paths of vice until I lost my way, and was compelled to lean wholly upon him for guidance and support."

"He's no more."

"Thank Heaven! It seems as if some grievous weight was taken off my heart, now that you tell me he is no more. And—and, Don Cæsar, my queen?"

"Is in perfect safety."

"But—but, she did repel him? You say she did repel him, Don Cæsar, when you heard them in the arbour?"

"Sure, you gave me your word of honour for the innocence of my countess, and I believed you, even as the words passed your lips. Take my word of honour, as a man, and a nobleman, take my solemn oath as a Christian before the great God of Heaven, that your queen repelled Don Jose with all the horror of virtue, and with all the dignity of her station."

"I—I, breathe again," said Philip.

"Breathe freely, for all danger is past for ever. Your majesty will scarcely find another Jose were you to search your dominions for one. A man at once so heartless and unprincipled, and with so much real tact and ability, let us hope, lives not now in Spain."

"I hope not, indeed. Oh, what infatuation—what blindness. Don Cæsar, I assure you, I thought you were dead."

"Do not disturb yourself, sire, on that head. I had no intention of dying if I could at all help it, although I do give Jose credit for making some of the most ingenious attempts to convert your majesty's thoughts into realities, that could well, under any circumstances, be made at all."

"I—I think he did."

"Indeed he did."

"Don Cæsar, I am happier now than I have been for long. I feel easier in spirit, and better thoughts are coming over me."

"I rejoice to hear it."

"Yes. I think I shall be a different man now to what I have been. This treachery of Don Jose's has given me a severe shock, Cæsar. I shall never forget what a serpent I have nurtured in my bosom, and how

·it has tried to sting me. I shall never again fall into the toils of such a man as Don Jose de Santarem."

"My liege, it is good news for Spain that you should say so. Long may your majesty live to persevere in your new intentions."

CHAPTER LXXVI.

THE SEARCH FOR THE QUEEN BY HER ATTENDANTS.—DON CÆSAR IN AUTHORITY.

As Don Cæsar uttered those words to the king there came upon their ears the sound of horses' feet, which seemed to pause outside the gate of the chateau.

"Hark! hark!" said Philip. "I hear the sound of horses' feet, and who can that be? We are not known to be here, Don Cæsar, by any one now but by yourself and your countess; who can those persons be?"

"If your majesty will permit me, I will soon solve that doubt."

"Yes, Cæsar, yes. Go—go. But remember, although known to you, Don Cæsar, we do not wish to be known to any one else."

"Your majesty is already known to Don Jose's page, Lazarillo; so do not fancy I have committed a breach of faith if your majesty should discover that he is acquainted with your rank."

"Don Jose's page! Oh, a mere lad."

"Yes; but as noble and gallant an one as ever stepped. I owe to him my life."

"Indeed! then I owe him much, and he shall not go unrewarded. Cæsar, I must entrust you with the task of making our peace with your countess."

"Never disturb yourself on that head, your majesty. All will be well now. The one arch villain who produced all the mischief is no more; and the elements of passion and discord will now subside again to peace and harmony. Believe me, all will now be well."

Voices now came plainly upon the morning air, and it was evident that a number of persons had made their way into the gardens of the chateau.

"Hasten—hasten, Cæsar," said the king, "and see who those are who have come to the place. Remember my incognito. I give you full power and authority here. Own the place as yours, and act in all respects as the master of this house."

"I thank your majesty. Like every one else, I owe your majesty much."

"Not at all—not at all."

Don Cæsar left the room, and in the outer one he found Maritana trembling and alarmed at the high words she had heard ensuing between the king and Cæsar. Immediately that he made his appearance she flew towards him, and clasping her arms about him, she cried,—

"You are safe—you are safe."

"I am; and all is arranged."

"Thank Heaven!"

"Can you forgive the king? He desires me to endeavour to make his peace with you."

"Have you forgiven him?"

"I have."

"Then do I forgive him, Cæsar! for your honour is my honour; my honour is yours. I forgive him."

"I approve that you should, dear countess. He has been sadly misled by the villain Jose, and is now full of repentance for the unworthy part he has been induced to play by that worst of men."

"And you have effected this great change, my husband. Dear, dear Cæsar, your presence like magic, has brought about peace and concord here."

"Thank God that I have had the temper to do so much," said Cæsar. "One month ago, I should not; but lately I have got more prudence for fear of losing the happiness I shall have with you."

"And is it for my sake?"

"Wholly—wholly for your sake; but heard you no horsemen just now in the gardens of the chateau."

"I did; and my alarm was much increased?"

"Where is Lazarillo?"

"Here," cried the page, who was keeping guard at the door.

"Very good, Lazarillo; keep your post over my countess. There is nothing now to fear—nothing to conceal. The king knows that you are aware of who he is, and all is satisfactorily arranged. Remember that this house now belongs to me, Don Cæsar de Bazan, if any one should question you."

"I will—I will."

"And you have been so kind and good a friend to us," said Maritana, as she took the page's hand.

His eyes filled with tears of joy, as he said,—

"I have endeavoured to be grateful to dear Don Cæsar."

"You love him?"

"With all my heart, lady."

"Then with all my heart will I love you. You shall never leave us, Lazarillo. Never—never; and you shall share with us all that we possess. A brighter day is now dawning upon the fortunes of Don Cæsar. It shall, believe me, Lazarillo, shed abundance of its radiance upon you."

"To serve him," said the boy, "to be ever near him, to watch over his welfare, will be my greatest delight; but you don't know how nearly I shot him, do you?"

"You nearly shot him?"

"Yes, lady. Of course, if I had, I should have shot myself afterwards. I could not have lived after that."

"Tell me how it was."

While Lazarillo is relating to Maritana how it was that he mistook Don Cæsar for the rascally monk, and nearly shot him dead as he was endeavouring to make good an entrance to the chateau by the balcony, we can briefly state how it was that a strong body of horsemen found their way to Don Jose's villa, and got fairly into the gardens thereof.

It so happened that the authorities of Madrid, when they had to a certain extent succeeded in allaying the popular disturbances which had then arisen, began to be very much surprised and alarmed at the non appearance of Don Jose de Santarem, who they feared had fallen a sacrifice somehow to popular resentment, as he could not be found at his residence, or at the palace.

Inquiry begat inquiry, and it was soon ascertained that the king was likewise absent.

A general consultation was held about what was to be done in such an emergency. It was considered that if once the fact, that the king and his minister could not be found, transpired, there would be a vast accession of popular discontent, and that the enemies of the government would seize upon such a circumstance as a pretext for a renewal of the disturbances which at one time had reached so very alarming a height as to threaten a permanent civil outbreak in Spain.

The great danger to a government of these sort of disturbances is, that the mob leaders become so far committed that, with safety to themselves, they cannot retreat; and, therefore, feeling that it is quite impossible they can be looked over in awarding punishment, they become reckless, and push the affair far beyond what they themselves originally contemplated, or than can at all be justified.

It had, however, fortunately for the lovers of peace and order, so happened that the principal mob leaders had been killed, so that the government was not placed in the difficulty of condemning or pardoning them, and the only thing that alarmed the authorities was the continued absence of the head authorities of all at such an uncomfortable crisis.

There is no secret so well kept but that it is

known to, or guessed at, by somebody or another, and thus, after much trouble, they got from Don Jose's private secretary a hint, under promise of secresy, that he and the king were both at the chateau, on the road to Aranjues, engaged in some manner, which he said he had no doubt had some special reference to the welfare of the country.

Of course, everybody who heard this understood quite well what it meant, and they forbore to question the secretary any further; but, after some consultation, resolved upon getting up a strong body of horsemen to go for him.

It was considered, too, by some of the graver among the councillors and grandees, that it would be no bad opportunity for having a cut at Don Jose, to go and tell the king in what danger his very throne had been while he was taken away from the capital by so dangerous an intriguante as Don Jose.

Besides, it would be sure to have the effect of stopping Jose from ever again making the chateau useful in the way of intrigues, for when the king was found there they felt pretty well assured he would take good care he was never found there again by any one.

If a few only had gone the anger of Philip might have fallen heavily upon them; but they guarded against such a contingency, by thirty of them, all nobles, agreeing to go together, and they were too many for any monarch of Spain to quarrel with all at once.

The distance was short, and they, accordingly, mounted, and making a goodly cavalcade, set forward at a round trot, which was calculated, in a very short time, indeed, to bring them to that chateau of Don Jose's, they each were aware of the existence of, but which not one of them had ever yet been invited to enter by its rascally owner.

*   *   *   *   *

By a coincidence which, under the circumstances, was extremely likely to occur, it so happened that the queen's household became aware of her mysterious absence at the very time that the nobles of Madrid were thinking of going after the king to Don Jose's chateau.

The love and attachment which was borne towards her by every one, from the highest to the lowest of those, who considered it a far greater honour to attend upon her in her voluntary exile, than to be the denizens of a profligate court, caused this absence of hers from Aranjues to be regarded with feelings of the most lively alarm, which soon turned into positive consternation when no news whatever could be procured concerning her movements.

The major domo of the household then determined upon a wise and judicious step, under the circumstances, which was to assemble the whole of the queen's attendants in one of the saloons of the building, and make the general inquiry at once if any one of them could throw a light upon the mysterious disappearance of the queen.

This was no sooner imagined than it was carried into effect, and in the course of another few minutes all were assembled, with the exception, of course, of Osmanlis.

His absence was soon noted, and several cried out at once,—

"Osmanlis is missing—Osmanlis is missing."

"Then," said the major domo, "my mind is easier, for now I feel convinced that our gracious mistress has gone on some expedition of goodness, and taken him with her."

"No doubt," said another. "Osmanlis was always treated with the greatest confidence by her majesty."

"My friends," said the major domo, after a few moments' thought, "it is not our duty to seek to pry into at the queen does not desire us to know; but it is

our duty to be on the alert for the protection of her majesty. I have no doubt but that she has gone to Madrid."

"Or to the chateau of Don Jose," said another.

"No, I think her majesty gave up all idea of going there; but such a thing is possible. Suppose, then, my friends, we take the horse, and go towards the spot. We can reconnoitre the place, and be at hand to form an escort for our beloved mistress if it is required."

This idea was at once acceded to, and immediate preparations were made to carry it out. There were ten good steeds at the chateau; and, accordingly, that number of horsemen, well armed, started from Aranjues within half-an-hour after the arrangement had been hinted at.

If anything the chateau of Don Jose was rather nearer to Aranjues than it was to Madrid, and it so happened, as if it had been the especial will of providence that such a circumstance should occur, that the party of thirty nobles from Madrid just started sufficiently before the little host from Aranjues to gain sufficient ground on them, so that there should be scarcely the interval of a minute between the arrival of the one lot and of the other at the garden gate of that house, which was never more to be devoted to the base purposes which it had come to while in the hands of the profligate and rascally Don Jose de Santarem, who now lay a corpse in his own garden.

Each party of horsemen heard the tramp of the other's steeds before they came actually within sight, and various were the conjectures on both sides as to who and what those who were approaching could possibly be.

Those who came from Madrid could not come to any very accurate judgment with regard to the numbers of the advancing party, for the sounds of their own horses' feet confused them; and as they neared the others, they took a more compact order, and placed themselves in a better attitude and position for defensive operations, should such appear to be necessary.

The queen's attendants were astonished to hear a tramp of horses' feet, which would indicate the advance of a strong body of pursuers, and when they came very close up to the chateau, they halted, and after a brief consultation, one of the number was deputed to go forward, and ascertain who composed the party in advance of them, which likewise had paused.

It was the major domo who galloped on a little in advance, and when he got sufficiently near to make his voice heard, he said,—

"Be you whom you may, I approach you as a friend!"

"Stop, friend; we must know who you are who come forward so readily with open front," said an old noble, who had been in the wars.

He clapped spurs to his horse as he spoke, and curvetted forward till he came up to the major domo, who reigned in his steed to meet him.

"Well, friend, who are you?" said he.

"Major domo to the Queen of Spain. Who are you?"

"Don Alancanta de Segovia, general and commander-in-chief of the armies of Spain."

"I salute you, signior, with all duty. I and a few of the attached attendants of the queen have come from Aranjues in search of her majesty, who has left us with but one attendant at unawares."

"Indeed!"

"It would seem so, for we miss one of the household whom we know to be greatly trusted by her majesty."

"Well, my friend, it is an odd enough thing, but

I and some others have come from Madrid in search of the king."

" In search of the king?"

" Even so."

" And is not our queen at Madrid?"

" Most certainly not, nor our king either. However singular and rare the circumstance may be, I do sincerely hope we shall find them together."

" I hope so too," said the major domo, " but I hope against my belief."

" Oh, I've known so many wonderful things come to pass," added the general, " that I am surprised at nothing now."

" But where seek you the king, noble signior?"

" Even here."

" Here, at Don Jose's villa?"

" Just so. We are informed that it is probable we may find him here; and, since you may take my assurance that the queen is not at Madrid, I advise you to go no further, but to pause here, and see what news

we can give you. We may procure for you some intelligence which you would find great difficulty in getting for yourselves at all from any one."

" True, signior. We could not ask the questions which in you are nothing. We will await here your leisure, signior."

" I would advise you to such a course, my friend; and, believe me, I will make it my urgent business to get what news for you I can. Don Jose himself we believe to be here."

" No doubt, signior—no doubt he is."

" Alas! for Spain!" muttered the general, as he wheeled his horse round to return to his troop. " Alas! for poor Spain! that she should be governed through the agency of such men as Don Jose de Santerem."

He proceeded to his party, and communicated to them what he had heard, adding to it,—

" My own impression is, gentlemen, that the queen has at length carried into effect a resolution which I only wonder she did not long ago embrace, and that

is, to leave Spain altogether, where she held so high and yet so troublesome a position. She is a noble and a right-minded lady, gentleman, and has been hardly used."

" Restrain your honest indignation, Don Segovia," said another. " Were an enemy to hear you say as much, he might do you harm."

" Nay, I will say it to the face of Philip himself. I have fought for him and his, and surely I may, in all honesty of purpose, tell him of it when I think he is doing grievously wrong."

" It is dangerous."

" That I am used to."

" Oh, but not to the machinations of such a man as Don Jose, general. A brave man, like yourself, who has never taken a mean advantage of a foe, can have no notion of the wiles of such a man as Don Jose de Santerem, Philip's favourite."

" Let him beware. I have a sword that may some day find its way to the heart of even a king's favourite."

" This is strange!" suddenly exclaimed one.

" What—what?" cried several.

" The gate of the chateau is open. The place wears a completely deserted appearance. Any one may walk into this house without trouble."

" Indeed!"

" Even so. See, there is no guard left. There is no one to ask a question of any kind of any intruders. Surely neither the king nor Don Jose de Santerem can be here in this deserted, unguarded-looking place!"

" You are surely right; but still we will enter and explore the house. Some one may be here who can give us some intelligence."

The garden gate, which had been left open by the last man who had absconded from the chateau—and he was the travelling friar—was quite large enough to admit a horseman, if he would condescend to stoop as he rode in, and this the whole of the nobles who had come from Madrid did, and entered the garden, so that the noise of horses' feet upon the gravel walks inside it was that which had come so very plainly upon the ears of the king and Don Cæsar.

Still they saw no one; and not the least surprised persons in that place at hearing such a tramping, and being by that assured of such a numerous arrival, were the queen and Osmanlis, who were waiting in anxious expectation of some news from Don Cæsar.

"What can be the meaning of all that, Osmanlis?" said the queen.

"I cannot conjecture, gracious madam, and I dread to leave you one moment to make inquiry."

"Nay, but Osmanlis, surely we cannot expect to find them enemies. I have, surely, no enemies."

"You should have none but the warmest friends, madam. If you will allow me now, since Don Cæsar is so long in coming, to escort you to the house, you will be, to my mind, in greater safety."

"As you please, Osmanlis. I will yield to your discretion. The air is too cold here now, and I am much fatigued."

"This way, then, madam. I hope to find a small door still open, which I noticed on my former visit to the building. Be of good cheer, for he who was, I believe, your only enemy, as he was every one's else, is, as you know, now no more."

"Yes, Don Jose is dead, and my greatest fears are dead with him. I will accompany you, Osmanlis. Pray lead the way."

The queen got into the chateau comfortably enough, without being seen by the horsemen, who naturally made a slight halt, to consult upon what was next to be done, when they had thus made good an entrance to the gardens. It was during that slight halt that Osmanlis succeeded in conducting the queen into the house, and he was ascending the great staircase with her, when some one was heard coming rapidly down.

Osmanlis drew his sword, crying,—

"Hold! Friend or foe?"

"As it turns out," said Don Cæsar, for it was he, and his Toledo was from its sheath in an instant.

Osmanlis recognized Cæsar's voice, although the latter had not done his, and he at once said,—

"Don Cæsar! Thank God, we have met you! The queen is with me. The garden is full of armed and mounted men."

"I heard them, and was even now coming to ascertain their errand."

Osmanlis and the queen advanced to the corridor, and Cæsar added,—

"Your majesty will, I am sure, permit me to make you welcome here to what is now my house."

"Your house?"

"Yes, by gift of your royal husband, who is here, and will, I am sure, be happy to see you. I have explained all to him."

"To the king?"

"Yes, madam; and if the humblest and most devoted of your majesty's servants might presume to make a suggestion ——"

"Name it, Don Cæsar."

"It is, that you would bury the past in oblivion, and strive to cultivate the good feelings which have awakened in the king's mind."

"Oh, with what joy!" said the queen, as she clasped her hands.

"Here, this way, gracious lady. I have now a happier duty than to ascertain who those armed men are. Will you perform that office, good Osmanlis, while I conduct her majesty to the king? This way, madam —this way."

_____

CHAPTER LXXVII.
CONCLUSION.

OSMANLIS descended the staircase, while Don Cæsar handed the queen through the door he had himself broken from its hinges, and into the outer room, where was his countess.

The Queen of Spain had been in the habit of making too many public appearances in Madrid not to be well known to Maritana, who recognised her the moment she made her appearance, and, kneeling to her, she said,—

"It is the queen!"

"Will your majesty allow me," said Cæsar, "to have the honour of introducing my countess to your majesty's kind regard?"

"With pleasure," said the queen,—"with pleasure. Rise, Countess de Bazan; and if the remainder of your life be as happy as I wish it, you will indeed be most happy."

"Blessed by your majesty's approval," said Maritana, "I cannot be otherwise than happy."

She rose as she spoke, and then the queen, turning to Don Cæsar, said, in a voice of agitation,—

"Where is the king?"

"In the adjoining chamber, madam. Is it your pleasure that I inform his majesty that you are here?"

"Yes—yes. Yet, stay; I think I ought perhaps to go to him. No. Do you go, Don Cæsar, and announce me."

Cæsar bowed, and passed on into the inner chamber, where, as may be well supposed, Philip was passing some very uncomfortable moments indeed.

The moment that Don Cæsar appeared, he said, hastily,—

"Well, Cæsar, well? What news—what news?"

"I have some news which I hope will be welcome to your majesty."

"We have need of some welcome news, for to tell the honest truth, Bazan, we have had but small comforts lately."

"I have a hope that your majesty's comforts will be much on the increase in consequence of the intelligence I have the honour and the satisfaction of bringing to you at this moment."

"Indeed!"

"Yes, your majesty. The queen ——"

Philip started, as he said,—

"The queen—the queen! What of the queen?"

"She is aware of your majesty's presence here."

"Aware of our presence! Humph! I had hoped she looked upon that as a fable of Don Jose's."

"No, your majesty. It is far better as it is. Your queen wishes to see you, and is disposed to bury the past in oblivion, and to meet your majesty with all loving kindness as of old, before Don Jose de Santerem, by his vile arts, removed your majesty's affections from one who has always been faithful to you, and most mindful of your honour as a king."

"But I shall be involved in some awkward explanation, Cæsar."

"Not one, your majesty,--not one."

"Well, then, in that case, I—I ——"

"Your majesty will receive the queen, and proceed to your palace at Madrid with her?"

"We will—we will."

"Thank Heaven. May I have the honour of introducing her majesty to this chamber?"

"Yes—yes, Bazan, yes. By-the-bye, who are the horsemen who are without? Have you ascertained?"

"I have not, sire; but one upon whom I can depend has gone on that errand, while I returned to your majesty to announce your queen."

"Well, well; let us know as early as convenient, and make as immediate preparations as you can,

Cæsar, for leaving this place, which has now become so very odious to me."

"Your majesty's orders shall be obeyed."

Cæsar left the room, and closed the door after him. He immediately hastened up to the queen, to whom he said,—

"My gracious madam, the king is well pleased to see you here, and has conferred upon me the honour of a permission to conduct you to him. He is, however, fearful that your majesty, having just cause of complaint, may ask him questions he would find it painful to answer."

"Let him banish that fear," said the queen. "Gladly—most gladly would I forget all the past, if the future wore a different complexion."

"I think it will."

"I hope it will, Cæsar."

"It is a hope well grounded, your majesty. Don Jose is dead, and therefore is it a hope well grounded."

"True, Cæsar, true; there is much in that. As you say, Don Jose is dead. While he lived, there was no hope whatever."

"There could be none. He had acquired a fatal influence over the mind of the king—an influence which, I fear, nothing could have broken."

"Most true—most true. It is very sad to be forced to rejoice in the death of any one; but who can help feeling that, for Spain, the death of Don Jose is a blessing."

Don Cæsar took the hand of the queen, and led her into the adjoining apartment, in the centre of which the king was waiting, looking more fidgetty than ever he had looked in his life.

Notwithstanding Don Cæsar's assurance to the contrary, he could not believe it possible but that the queen would question him about what brought him there, and how he came to be in apartments of the Countess de Bazan; but the first words she uttered convinced him that his fears were groundless, and brought him so much relief, that he did what he very rarely ever did—that is, he actually allowed his face to relax into a smile.

"Philip," she said, "let us meet as if the past estrangement had been all a dream. Let us never revert to it or to any of its real or supposed causes. The future is our own, and in it we may be happy; the past we will completely forget."

"Isabella," said Philip, in a tone which shewed that he was affected, despite the smile that for an instant had played upon his features,—"Isabella, you are generous. I can never forget that this is a piece of unexampled generosity on your part."

"Nay, Philip, say not so."

"I must say it; and it induces me to say more. I have been very, very much to blame, Isabella."

"Enough—enough, dear Philip."

"But I have been misled by evil councillors. He who has dragged me through many scenes and into many vices, is now no more; and I have a conviction that from this time henceforward I shall be an altered man."

Tears of joy, which she could not restrain, burst from the queen's eyes, and she cast herself on the breast of the king.

Don Cæsar had, immediately upon introducing the queen into the apartment, left it; but neither of their majesties knew that that he had done so, until, after a few moments silence, the king sad,—

"We have to thank Don Cæsar de Bazan for this happy reconciliation, Isabella. To him is due much gratitude from both of us, and he shall not find that we have such a feeling towards any one without making him feel most munificently its existence."

"Yes; to Cæsar we owe these present feelings of satisfaction, which have for so long been strangers to my heart. Where is he?"

"He has left us."

"We will seek him now, and thank him. You will think, Philip, of some great honour you will bestow upon him."

"I will—I will. The ancient dignity of his house shall be restored, and there shall not be a noble in all Spain who can hold his head higher than Don Cæsar de Bazan."

"Oh, what joy it is to hear you say so. His countess shall be specially attached to us—we will invest her with much honour."

"Hark! some one comes in haste."

The sound of hasty footsteps was heard outside the room door, and in another moment a low respectful rap announced some one.

"Come in," said the king.

Don Cæsar opened the door, and appeared upon its threshold.

"What news, Cæsar?"

"Your majesty will, perhaps, be not displeased to hear that the horsemen have turned out to be a retinue of the nobles of Spain who have come in search of your majesty."

"In search of us?"

"Yes, sire."

"How knew they we were here?"

"That I cannot inform your majesty; but it appears that owing to the maladministration of Don Jose, Madrid has, since your majesty was last there, been the scene of the most serious riots and disturbances."

"Indeed!"

"But which are now happily suppressed."

"Happily, indeed."

The king remained musing for some few moments, and then he said, suddenly turning to Cæsar,—

"Don Cæsar, what would you advise us to do?"

"To receive the nobles graciously."

"But it is awkward. There will be surmises."

"There cannot be now, your majesty. Receive the nobles with your queen by your side, and so put an end at once to all surmising."

"True—true."

"Permit me to personate the master of this house still, and your majesty's host. Let them then think what they may, all will be hushed, and not a breath of scandal can assault your majesty."

"'Tis a good plan. Summon your countess, Cæsar."

Don Cæsar led in the Countess de Bazan, and then he said,—

"If your majesties will pardon my boldness, I would suggest, humbly, that your majesties should be seated, and that the Countess de Bazan and I should be in dutiful attendance upon you."

"Well said—well said."

"While the page, Lazarillo, shall introduce the nobles."

"Yes, yes; be it so. You would be puzzled, though, Cæsar, were we to extend our hospitality by inviting them to supper."

"I think I should, your majesty; for my household is at present in rather a damaged and unhinged state."

"We will not put you to that inconvenience, Cæsar. Let it all be as you have arranged."

"Then I may have them summoned?"

"You may, most certainly."

Don Cæsar at once went out to the page, to whom he said,—

"Lazarillo, in the garden are thirty of the nobles of Spain, who have come here to see the king. They expect, no doubt, to find the king very much confused at their coming, and engaged in some intrigue. Now, Lazarillo, the king and the queen are reconciled; you understand?"

"I am very glad to hear it."

"And so will be thousands more. Under these circumstances, you understand, then, everything must be done by us to disappoint these parties who expect to detect the king in indifferent company."

"I see—I see, Don Cæsar."

"The countess and I are to wait upon them. You must go down to these nobles, and, as if it were a mere matter of course, say you have the orders of the king to conduct them to his presence. Do not let them know that the queen is with him, and if any questions are asked, evade them."

"I will, Cæsar, I will."

"Then go at once, Lazarillo. I know I can safely trust to your address to manage this affair."

"I will do my best."

"And that is sure to do. Go—go."

The boy placed his arquebus on one side, and with an air of consequence proceeded down the grand staircase, and so on out into the garden; when the first person he met was the rather choleric Don Segovia, who had dismounted, and tied his horse to a tree, as, indeed, had most of the nobles.

"In the name of the king," said the page, darting out so suddenly that several of them gave a jump.

"And what in the name of the king?" said Don Segovia.

"His majesty graciously condescends to grant you an audience."

"Oh, indeed!"

"I am commissioned to conduct you to his presence."

"Pray, my lad, who are you?"

"The humble individual who bears to you the royal commands."

"Yes; but where is Don Jose?"

"It's difficult to say."

"But this is his house?"

"It's bad manners to argue with one's betters."

"Why, what ails you, lad? Is the king alone?"

"It is disloyal to prate about his majesty."

"Now, confound you! Cannot you answer a plain question?"

"No."

"No?"

"I never could, sir, from the earliest infancy; but I can tell you one thing."

"And what may that be?"

"That I am the humble individual who is commanded by the King of Spain to conduct you to his presence."

"Psha! you said that before."

"I did; but as you seemed to have forgotten it, I thought it had better be repeated."

"Segovia," said one, "you will get nothing by conversing with such a young jackanapes. We had better follow him."

"Much better," said Lazarillo.

The old nobleman muttered an oath, and then said,—

"Lead on, boy; lead on."

Lazarillo led them up the grand staircase, and into the anti-chamber. There, in a whisper, he desired them to wait, and he stepped into the adjoining room, where the king and queen were seated, and Don Cæsar behind the king's chair, while the Countess de Bazan occupied a similar place behind the queen.

"Please, your majesty, the nobles are here," said the page.

"Admit them," said the king.

Lazarillo threw open the door, and then, to the surprise of the noblemen who had come from Madrid, they saw the group within.

"Well, Segovia," said Philip, "to what are we indebted for this unexpected visit?"

"Sire?"

"I say, unexpected visit. Cannot we, with our queen, visit our old and esteemed friend, Don Cæsar, without being hunted up in such a manner?"

The grandees looked confused, and the king rose, saying,—

"Don Cæsar, we need not delay our departure. You will understand that, as a mark of our royal favour for your great hospitality, we depute you to the governorship of the whole of Arragon, now vacant."

Cæsar bowed low.

"My lords," added the king, turning to the astonished nobles, "we will accept your escort to Madrid."

* * * * *

Don Cæsar lived long and happily to enjoy the favour of his sovereign, who heaped wealth and honour upon him, while the queen was equally mindful of Maritana.

As for Lazarillo, he became a friend of Cæsar's in every acceptation of the word, and, finally, received a commission in the royal guards.

Don Cæsar paid all his debts. Yes, he did; and it was a satisfaction to him to the end of his days to know that he had been the happy means of restoring the king and queen to a good understanding, which was never again broken.

THE END.